FAITH OF THE FALLEN

*Also by Terry Goodkind in
Victor Gollancz/Millennium*

THE SWORD OF TRUTH

Wizard's First Rule
Stone of Tears
Blood of the Fold
Temple of the Winds
Soul of the Fire

FAITH OF THE FALLEN

Terry Goodkind

VICTOR GOLLANCZ

LONDON

The right of Terry Goodkind to be identified as
the author of this work has been asserted by him
in accordance with the Copyright, Designs and Patents Act 1988.

This edition first published in Great Britain in 2000 by
Victor Gollancz
An imprint of Orion Books Ltd
Orion House, 5 Upper St Martin's Lane,
London WC2H 9EA

Second impression 2000

To receive information on the Millennium list e-mail us at:
smy@orionbooks.co.uk

A CIP catalogue record for this book is available
from the British Library

ISBN 0575070811

Printed in Great Britain by
Clays Ltd, St Ives plc

To Russell Galen,
my first true fan,
for his steadfast faith in me

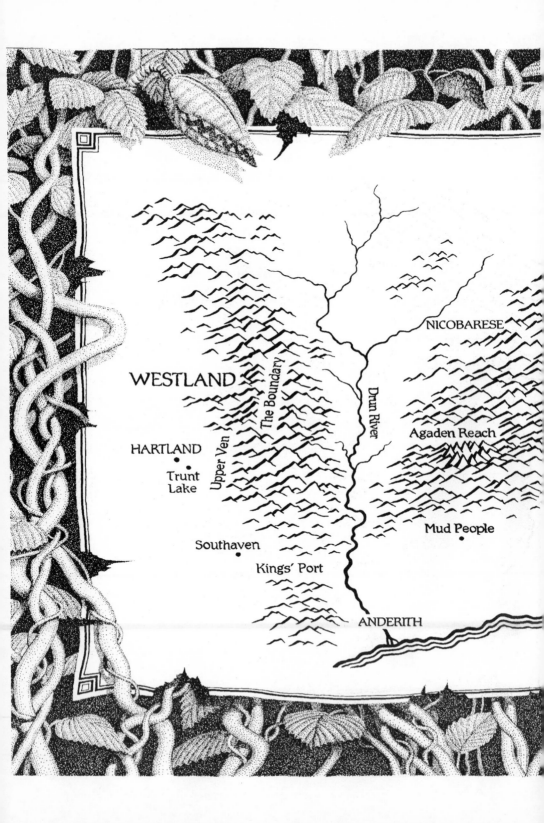

AYDINDRIL

Rang'Shada Mountains

D'HARA

THE
MIDLANDS

The Boundary

GALEA

PEOPLE'S
PALACE

KELTON

Azrith
Plains

• Tamarang

Kern River

THE WILDS

Renwold

THE
OLD WORLD

Callisidrin River

TANIMURA

Grafan Harbor

TERRY
GOODKIND

FAITH OF
THE FALLEN

She didn't remember dying.

With an obscure sense of apprehension, she wondered if the distant angry voices drifting in to her meant she was again about to experience that transcendent ending: death.

There was absolutely nothing she could do about it if she was.

While she didn't remember dying, she dimly recalled, at some later point, solemn whispers saying that she had, saying that death had taken her, but that he had pressed his mouth over hers and filled her stilled lungs with his breath, his life, and in so doing had rekindled hers. She had had no idea who it was that spoke of such an inconceivable feat, or who "he" was.

That first night, when she had perceived the distant, disembodied voices as little more than a vague notion, she had grasped that there were people around her who didn't believe, even though she was again living, that she would remain alive through the rest of the night. But now she knew she had; she had remained alive many more nights, perhaps in answer to desperate prayers and earnest oaths whispered over her that first night.

But if she didn't remember the dying, she remembered the pain before passing into that great oblivion. The pain, she never forgot. She remembered fighting alone and savagely against all those men, men baring their teeth like a pack of wild hounds with a hare. She remembered the rain of brutal blows driving her to the ground, heavy boots slamming into her once she was there, and the sharp snap of bones. She remembered the blood, so much blood, on their fists, on their boots. She remembered the searing terror of having no breath to gasp at the agony, no breath to cry out against the crushing weight of hurt.

Sometime after—whether hours or days, she didn't know—when she was lying under clean sheets in an unfamiliar bed and had looked up into his gray eyes, she knew that, for some, the world reserved pain worse than she had suffered.

She didn't know his name. The profound anguish so apparent in his eyes told her beyond doubt that she should have. More than her own name, more than life itself, she knew she should have known his name, but she didn't. Nothing had ever shamed her more.

Thereafter, whenever her own eyes were closed, she saw his, saw not only the helpless suffering in them but also the light of such fierce hope as could only be kindled by righteous love. Somewhere, even in the worst of the darkness blanketing her mind, she refused to let the light in his eyes be extinguished by her failure to will herself to live.

At some point, she remembered his name. Most of the time, she remembered it.

Sometimes, she didn't. Sometimes, when pain smothered her, she forgot even her own name.

Now, as Kahlan heard men growling his name, she knew it, she knew him. With tenacious resolution she clung to that name—Richard—and to her memory of him, of who he was, of everything he meant to her.

Even later, when people had feared she would yet die, she knew she would live. She had to, for Richard, her husband. For the child she carried in her womb. His child. Their child.

The sounds of angry men calling Richard by name at last tugged Kahlan's eyes open. She squinted against the agony that had been tempered, if not banished, while in the cocoon of sleep. She was greeted by a blush of amber light filling the small room around her. Since the light wasn't bright, she reasoned that there must be a covering over a window muting the sunlight, or maybe it was dusk. Whenever she woke, as now, she not only had no sense of time, but no sense of how long she had been asleep.

She worked her tongue against the pasty dryness in her mouth. Her body felt leaden with the thick, lingering slumber. She was as nauseated as the time when she was little and had eaten three candy green apples before a boat journey on a hot, windy day. It was hot like that now: summer hot. She struggled to rouse herself fully, but her awaking awareness seemed adrift, bobbing in a vast shadowy sea. Her stomach roiled. She suddenly had to put all her mental effort into not throwing up. She knew all too well that in her present condition, few things hurt more than vomiting. Her eyelids sagged closed again, and she foundered to a place darker yet.

She caught herself, forced her thoughts to the surface, and willed her eyes open again. She remembered: they gave her herbs to dull the pain and to help her sleep. Richard knew a good deal about herbs. At least the herbs helped her drift into stuporous sleep. The pain, if not as sharp, still found her there.

Slowly, carefully, so as not to twist what felt like double-edged daggers skewered here and there between her ribs, she drew a deeper breath. The fragrance of balsam and pine filled her lungs, helping to settle her stomach. It was not the aroma of trees among other smells in the forest, among damp dirt and toadstools and cinnamon ferns, but the redolence of trees freshly felled and limbed. She concentrated on focusing her sight and saw beyond the foot of the bed a wall of pale, newly peeled timber, here and there oozing sap from fresh axe cuts. The wood looked to have been split and hewn in haste, yet its tight fit betrayed a precision only knowledge and experience could bestow.

The room was tiny; in the Confessors' Palace, where she had grown up, a room this small would not have qualified as a closet for linens. Moreover, it would have been stone, if not marble. She liked the tiny wooden room; she expected that Richard had built it to protect her. It felt almost like his sheltering arms around her. Marble, with its aloof dignity, never comforted her in that way.

Beyond the foot of the bed, she spotted a carving of a bird in flight. It had been sculpted with a few sure strokes of a knife into a log of the wall on a flat spot only a little bigger than her hand. Richard had given her something to look at. On occasion, sitting around a campfire, she had watched him casually carve a face or an animal from a scrap of wood. The bird, soaring on wings spread wide as it watched over her, conveyed a sense of freedom.

Turning her eyes to the right, she saw a brown wool blanket hanging over the doorway. From beyond the doorway came fragments of angry, threatening voices.

14

"It's not by our choice, Richard. . . . We have our own families to think about . . . wives and children . . ."

Wanting to know what was going on, Kahlan tried to push herself up onto her left elbow. Somehow, her arm didn't work the way she had expected it to. Like a bolt of lightning, pain blasted up the marrow of her bone and exploded through her shoulder.

Gasping against the racking agony of attempted movement, she dropped back before she had managed to lift her shoulder an inch off the bed. Her panting twisted the daggers piercing her sides. She had to will herself to slow her breathing in order to get the stabbing pain under control. As the worst of the torment in her arm and the stitches in her ribs eased, she finally let out a soft moan.

With calculated calm, she gazed down the length of her left arm. The arm was splinted. As soon as she saw it, she remembered that of course it was. She reproached herself for not thinking of it before she had tried to put weight on it. The herbs, she knew, were making her thinking fuzzy. Fearing to make another careless movement, and since she couldn't sit up, she focused her effort on forcing clarity into her mind.

She cautiously reached up with her right hand and wiped her fingers across the bloom of sweat on her brow, sweat sown by the flash of pain. Her right shoulder socket hurt, but it worked well enough. She was pleased by that triumph, at least. She touched her puffy eyes, understanding then why it had hurt to look toward the door. Gingerly, her fingers explored a foreign landscape of swollen flesh. Her imagination colored it a ghastly black-and-blue. When her fingers brushed cuts on her cheek, hot embers seemed to sear raw, exposed nerves.

She needed no mirror to know she was a terrible sight. She knew, too, how bad it was whenever she looked up into Richard's eyes. She wished she could look good for him if for no other reason than to lift the suffering from his eyes. Reading her thoughts, he would say, "I'm fine. Stop worrying about me and put your mind to getting better."

With a bittersweet longing, Kahlan recalled lying with Richard, their limbs tangled in delicious exhaustion, his skin hot against hers, his big hand resting on her belly as they caught their breath. It was agony wanting to hold him in her arms again and being unable to do so. She reminded herself that it was only a matter of some time and some healing. They were together and that was what mattered. His mere presence was a restorative.

She heard Richard, beyond the blanket over the door, speaking in a tightly controlled voice, stressing his words as if each had cost him a fortune. "We just need some time . . ."

The men's voices were heated and insistent as they all began talking at once. "It's not because we want to—you should know that, Richard, you know us. . . . What if it brings trouble here? . . . We've heard about the fighting. You said yourself she's from the Midlands. We can't allow . . . we won't . . ."

Kahlan listened, expecting the sound of his sword being drawn. Richard had nearly infinite patience, but little tolerance. Cara, his bodyguard, their friend, was no doubt out there, too; Cara had neither patience nor tolerance.

Instead of drawing his sword, Richard said, "I'm not asking anyone to give me anything. I want only to be left alone in a peaceful place where I can care for her. I wanted to be close to Hartland in case she needed something." He paused. "Please . . . just until she has a chance to get better."

Kahlan wanted to scream at him: *No! Don't you dare beg them, Richard! They have no right to make you beg. They've no right! They could never understand the sacrifices you've made.*

But she could do little more than whisper his name in sorrow.

"Don't test us. . . . We'll burn you out if we have to! You can't fight us all—we have right on our side."

The men ranted and swore dark oaths. She expected, now, at last, to hear the sound of his sword being drawn. Instead, in a calm voice, Richard answered the men in words Kahlan couldn't quite make out. A dreadful quiet settled in.

"It's not because we like doing this, Richard," someone finally said in a sheepish voice. "We've no choice. We've got to consider our own families and everyone else."

Another man spoke out with righteous indignation. "Besides, you seem to have gotten all high-and-mighty of a sudden, with your fancy clothes and sword, not like you used to be, back when you were a woods guide."

"That's right," said another. "Just because you went off and saw some of the world, that don't mean you can come back here thinking you're better than us."

"I've overstepped what you have all decided is my proper place," Richard said. "Is this what you mean to say?"

"You turned your back on your community, on your roots, as I see it; you think our women aren't good enough for the great Richard Cypher. No, he had to marry some woman from away. Then you come back here and think to flaunt yourselves over us."

"How? By doing what? Marrying the woman I love? This, you see as vain? This nullifies my right to live in peace? And takes away her right to heal, to get well and live?"

These men knew him as Richard Cypher, a simple woods guide, not as the person he had discovered he was in truth, and who he had become. He was the same man as before, but in so many ways, they had never known him.

"You ought to be on your knees praying for the Creator to heal your wife," another man put in. "All of mankind is a wretched and undeserving lot. You ought to pray and ask the Creator's forgiveness for your evil deeds and sinfulness—that's what brought your troubles on you and your woman. Instead, you want to bring your troubles among honest working folks. You've no right to try to force your sinful troubles on us. That's not what the Creator wants. You should be thinking of us. The Creator wants you to be humble and to help others—that's why He struck her down: to teach you both a lesson."

"Did he tell you this, Albert?" Richard asked. "Does this Creator of yours come to talk with you about his intentions and confide in you his wishes?"

"He talks to anyone who has the proper modest attitude to listen to Him," Albert fumed.

"Besides," another man spoke up, "this Imperial Order you warn about has some good things to be said for it. If you weren't so bullheaded, Richard, you'd see that. There's nothing wrong with wanting to see everyone treated decent. It's only being fair minded. It's only right. Those are the Creator's wishes, you've got to admit, and that's what the Imperial Order teaches, too. If you can't see that much good in the Order—well then, you'd best be gone, and soon."

Kahlan held her breath.

In an ominous tone of voice, Richard said, "So be it."

16

These were men Richard knew; he had addressed them by name and reminded them of years and deeds shared. He had been patient with them. Patience finally exhausted, he had reached intolerance.

Horses snorted and stomped, their leather tack creaking, as the men mounted up. "In the morning we'll be back to burn this place down. We'd better not catch you or yours anywhere near here, or you'll burn with it." After a few last curses, the men raced away. The sound of departing hooves hammering the ground rumbled through Kahlan's back. Even that hurt.

She smiled a small smile for Richard, even if he couldn't see it. She wished only that he had not begged on her behalf; he would never, she knew, have begged for anything for himself.

Light splashed across the wall as the blanket over the doorway was thrown back. By the direction and quality of the light, Kahlan guessed it had to be somewhere in the middle of a thinly overcast day. Richard appeared beside her, his tall form towering over her, throwing a slash of shadow across her middle.

He wore a black, sleeveless undershirt, without his shirt or magnificent gold and black tunic, leaving his muscular arms bare. At his left hip, the side toward her, a flash of light glinted off the pommel of his singular sword. His broad shoulders made the room seem even smaller than it had been only a moment before. His clean-shaven face, his strong jaw, and the crisp line of his mouth perfectly complemented his powerful form. His hair, a color somewhere between blond and brown, brushed the nape of his neck. But it was the intelligence so clearly evident in those penetrating gray eyes of his that from the first had riveted her attention.

"Richard," Kahlan whispered, "I won't have you begging on my account."

The corners of his mouth tightened with the hint of a smile. "If I want to beg, I shall do so." He pulled her blanket up a little, making sure she was snugly covered, even though she was sweating. "I didn't know you were awake."

"How long have I been asleep?"

"A while."

She figured it must have been quite a while. She didn't remember arriving at this place, or him building the house that now stood around her.

Kahlan felt more like a person in her eighties than one in her twenties. She had never been hurt before, not grievously hurt, anyway, not to the point of being on the cusp of death and utterly helpless for so long. She hated it, and she hated that she couldn't do the simplest things for herself. Most of the time she detested that more than the pain.

She was stunned to understand so unexpectedly and so completely life's frailty, her own frailty, her own mortality. She had risked her life in the past and had been in danger many times, but looking back she didn't know if she had ever truly believed that something like this could happen to her. Confronting the reality of it was crushing.

Something inside seemed to have broken that night—some idea of herself, some confidence. She could so easily have died. Their baby could have died before it even had a chance to live.

"You're getting better," Richard said, as if in answer to her thoughts. "I'm not just saying that. I can see that you're healing."

She gazed into his eyes, summoning the courage to finally ask, "How do they know about the Order way up here?"

"People fleeing the fighting have been up this way. Men spreading the doctrine

17

of the Imperial Order have been even here, to where I grew up. Their words can sound good—almost make sense—if you don't think, if you just feel. Truth doesn't seem to count for much," He added in afterthought. He answered the unspoken question in her eyes. "The men from the Order are gone. The fools out there were just spouting things they've heard, that's all."

"But they intend us to leave. They sound like men who keep the oaths they've sworn."

He nodded, but then some of his smile returned. "Do you know that we're very close to where I first met you, last autumn? Do you remember?"

"How could I ever forget the day I met you?"

"Our lives were in jeopardy back then and we had to leave here. I've never regretted it. It was the start of my life with you. As long as we're together, nothing else really matters."

Cara swept in through the doorway and came to a halt beside Richard, adding her shadow to his across the blue cotton blanket that covered Kahlan to her armpits. Sheathed in skintight red leather, Cara's body had the sleek grace of a falcon: commanding, swift, and deadly. Mord-Sith always wore their red leather when they believed there was going to be trouble. Cara's long blond hair, swept back into a single thick braid, was another mark of her profession of Mord-Sith, member of an elite corps of guards to the Lord Rahl himself.

Richard had, after a fashion, inherited the Mord-Sith when he inherited the rule of D'Hara, a place he grew up never knowing. Command was not something he had sought; nonetheless it had fallen to him. Now a great many people depended on him. The entire New World—Westland, the Midlands, and D'Hara—depended on him.

"How do you feel?" Cara asked with sincere concern.

Kahlan was able to summon little more voice than a hoarse whisper. "I'm better."

"Well, if you feel better," Cara growled, "then tell Lord Rahl that he should allow me to do my job and put the proper respect into men like that." Her menacing blue eyes turned for a moment toward the spot where the men had been while delivering their threats. "The ones I leave alive, anyway."

"Cara, use your head," Richard said. "We can't turn this place into a fortress and protect ourselves every hour of every day. Those men are afraid. No matter how wrong they are, they view us as a danger to their lives and the lives of their families. We know better than to fight a senseless battle when we can avoid it."

"But Richard," Kahlan said, lifting her right hand in a weak gesture toward the wall before her, "you've built this—"

"Only this room. I wanted a shelter for you first. It didn't take that long—just some trees cut and split. We've not built the rest of it yet. It's not worth shedding blood over."

If Richard seemed calm, Cara looked ready to chew steel and spit nails. "Would you tell this obstinate husband of yours to let me kill someone before I go crazy? I can't just stand around and allow people to get away with threatening the two of you! I am Mord-Sith!"

Cara took her job of protecting Richard—the Lord Rahl of D'Hara—and Kahlan very seriously. Where Richard's life was concerned, Cara was perfectly willing to kill first and decide later if it had been necessary. That was one of the things for which Richard had no tolerance.

Kahlan's only answer was a smile.

"Mother Confessor, you can't allow Lord Rahl to bow to the will of foolish men like those. Tell him."

Kahlan could probably count on the fingers of one hand the people who, in her whole life, had ever addressed her by the name "Kahlan" without at minimum the appellation "Confessor" before it. She had heard her ultimate title—Mother Confessor—spoken countless times, in tones ranging from awed reverence to shuddering fear. Many people, as they knelt before her, were incapable of even whispering through trembling lips the two words of her title. Others, when alone, whispered them with lethal intent.

Kahlan had been named Mother Confessor while still in her early twenties—the youngest Confessor ever named to that powerful position. But that was several years past. Now, she was the only living Confessor left.

Kahlan had always endured the title, the bowing and kneeling, the reverence, the awe, the fear, and the murderous intentions, because she had no choice. But more than that, she *was* the Mother Confessor—by succession and selection, by right, by oath, and by duty.

Cara always addressed Kahlan as "Mother Confessor." But from Cara's lips the words were subtly different than from any others. It was almost a challenge, a defiance by scrupulous compliance, but with a hint of an affectionate smirk. Coming from Cara, Kahlan didn't hear "Mother Confessor" so much as she heard "Sister." Cara was from the distant land of D'Hara. No one, anywhere, outranked Cara, as far as Cara was concerned, except the Lord Rahl. The most she would allow was that Kahlan could be her equal in duty to Richard. Being considered an equal by Cara, though, was high praise indeed.

When Cara addressed Richard as Lord Rahl, however, she was not saying "Brother." She was saying precisely what she meant: Lord Rahl.

To the men with the angry voices, the Lord Rahl was as foreign a concept as was the distant land of D'Hara. Kahlan was from the Midlands that separated D'Hara from Westland. The people here in Westland knew nothing of the Midlands or the Mother Confessor. For decades, the three parts of the New World had been separated by impassable boundaries, leaving what was beyond those boundaries shrouded in mystery. The autumn before, those boundaries had fallen.

And then, in the winter, the common barrier to the south of the three lands that had for three thousand years sealed away the menace of the Old World had been breached, loosing the Imperial Order on them all. In the last year, the world had been thrown into turmoil; everything everyone had grown up knowing had changed.

"I'm not going to allow you to hurt people just because they refuse to help us," Richard said to Cara. "It would solve nothing and only end up causing us more trouble. What we started here only took a short time to build. I thought this place would be safe, but it's not. We'll simply move on."

He turned back to Kahlan. His voice lost its fire.

"I was hoping to bring you home, to some peace and quiet, but it looks like home doesn't want me, either. I'm sorry."

"Just those men, Richard." In the land of Anderith, just before Kahlan had been attacked and beaten, the people had rejected Richard's offer to join the emerging D'Haran Empire he led in the cause of freedom. Instead, the people of Anderith willingly chose to side with the Imperial Order. Richard had taken Kahlan and walked away from everything, it seemed. "What about your real friends here?"

"I haven't had time . . . I wanted to get a shelter up, first. There's no time now. Maybe later."

Kahlan reached for his hand, which hung at his side. His fingers were too far away. "But, Richard—"

"Look, it's not safe to stay here anymore. It's as simple as that. I brought you here because I thought it would be a safe place for you to recover and regain your strength. I was wrong. It's not. We can't stay here. Understand?"

"Yes, Richard."

"We have to move on."

"Yes, Richard."

There was something more to this, she knew—something of far greater importance than the more immediate ordeal it meant for her. There was a distant, troubled look in his eyes.

"But what of the war? Everyone is depending on us—on you. I can't be much help until I get better, but they need you right now. The D'Haran Empire needs you. You are the Lord Rahl. You lead them. What are we doing here? Richard . . ." She waited until his eyes turned to look at her. "Why are we running away when everyone is counting on us?"

"I'm doing as I must."

"As you must? What does that mean?"

Shadow shrouded his face as he looked away.

"I've . . . had a vision."

A vision?" Kahlan said in open astonishment.

Richard hated anything to do with prophecy. It had caused him no end of trouble.

Prophecy was always ambiguous and usually cryptic, no matter how clear it seemed on the surface. The untrained were easily misled by its superficially simplistic construction. Unthinking adherence to a literal interpretation of prophecy had in the past caused great turmoil, everything from murder to war. As a result, those involved with prophecy went to great lengths to keep it secret.

Prophecy, at least on the face of it, was predestination; Richard believed that man created his own destiny. He had once told her, "Prophecy can only say that tomorrow the sun will come up. It can't say what you are going to do with your day. The act of going about your day is not the fulfillment of prophecy, but the fulfillment of your own purpose."

Shota, the witch woman, had prophesied that Richard and Kahlan would conceive an infamous son. Richard had more than once proven Shota's view of the future to be, if not fatally flawed, at least vastly more complex than Shota would have it seem. Like Richard, Kahlan didn't accept Shota's prediction.

On any number of occasions, Richard's view of prophecy had been shown to be correct. Richard simply ignored what prophecy said and did as he believed he must. By his doing so, prophecy was in the end often fulfilled, but in ways that could not have been foretold. In this way, prophecy was at once proven and disproved, resolving nothing and only demonstrating what an eternal enigma it truly was.

Richard's grandfather, Zedd, who had helped raise him not far from where they were, had not only kept his own identity as a wizard secret. In order to protect Richard, he also hid the fact that Richard had been fathered by Darken Rahl and not George Cypher, the man who had loved and raised him. Darken Rahl, a wizard of great power, had been the dangerous, violent ruler of far-off D'Hara. Richard had inherited the gift of magic from two different bloodlines. After killing Darken Rahl, he had also inherited the rule of D'Hara, a land that was in many ways as much a mystery to him as was his power.

Kahlan, being from the Midlands, had grown up around wizards; Richard's ability was unlike that of any wizard she had ever known. He possessed not one aspect of the gift, but many, and not one side, but both: he was a war wizard. Some of his outfit came from the Wizard's Keep, and had not been worn in three thousand years—since the last war wizard lived.

With the gift dying out in mankind, wizards were uncommon; Kahlan had known fewer than a dozen. Among wizards, prophets were the most rare; she knew of the existence of only two. One of those was Richard's ancestor, which made visions all the more within the province of Richard's gift. Yet Richard had always treated prophecy as a viper in his bed.

Tenderly, as if there were no more precious thing in the whole world, Richard lifted her hand. "You know how I always talk about the beautiful places only I know way back in the mountains to the west of where I grew up? The special places I've always wanted to show you? I'm going to take you there, where we'll be safe."

"D'Harans are bonded to you, Lord Rahl," Cara reminded him, "and will be able to find you through that bond."

"Well, our enemies aren't bonded to me. They won't know where we are."

Cara seemed to find that thought agreeable. "If people don't go to this place, then there won't be any roads. How are we going to get the carriage there? The Mother Confessor can't walk."

"I'll make a litter. You and I will carry her in that."

Cara nodded thoughtfully. "We could do that. If there were no other people, then the two of you would be safe, at least."

"Safer than here. I had expected the people here to leave us to ourselves. I hadn't expected the Order to foment unrest this far away—at least not this quickly. Those men usually aren't a bad lot, but they're working themselves up into a dangerous mood."

"The cowards have gone back to their women's skirts. They won't be back until morning. We can let the Mother Confessor rest and then leave before dawn."

Richard cast Cara a telling look. "One of those men, Albert, has a son, Lester. Lester and his pal, Tommy Lancaster, once tried to put arrows into me for spoiling some fun Tommy was about to have hurting someone. Now Tommy and Lester are missing a good many teeth. Albert will tell Lester about us being here, and soon after, Tommy Lancaster will know, too.

"Now that the Imperial Order has filled their heads with talk of a noble war on behalf of good, those men will be fancying what it would be like to be war heroes. They aren't ordinarily violent, but today they were more unreasonable than I've ever seen them.

"They'll go drinking to fortify their courage. Tommy and Lester will be with them by then, and their tales of how I wronged them and how I'm a danger to decent folks will get everyone all worked up. Because they greatly outnumber us, they'll begin to see the merit in killing us—see it as protecting their families and doing the right thing for the community and their Creator. Full of liquor and glory, they won't want to wait until morning. They'll be back tonight. We have to leave now."

Cara seemed unconcerned. "I say we wait for them, and when they come back, we end the threat."

"Some of them will bring along other friends. There will be a lot of them by the time they get here. We have Kahlan to think about. I don't want to risk one of us being injured. There's nothing to be gained by fighting them."

Richard pulled the ancient, tooled-leather baldric, holding the gold-and-silver-wrought scabbard and sword, off over his head and hung it on the stump of a branch sticking out of a log. Looking unhappy, Cara folded her arms. She would rather not leave a threat alive. Richard picked his folded black shirt off the floor to the side, where Kahlan hadn't seen it. He poked an arm through a sleeve and drew it on.

"A vision?" Kahlan finally asked again. As much trouble as the men could be, they were not her biggest concern just then. "You've had a vision?"

"The sudden clarity of it felt like a vision, but it was really more of a revelation."

"Revelation." She wished she could manage more than a hoarse whisper. "And what form did this vision revelation thing take?"

"Understanding."

Kahlan stared up at him. "Understanding of what?"

He started buttoning his shirt. "Through this realization I've come to understand the larger picture. I've come to understand what it is I must do."

"Yes," Cara muttered, "and wait until you hear it. Go ahead, tell her."

Richard glared at Cara and she answered him in kind. His attention finally returned to Kahlan.

"If I lead us into this war, we will lose. A great many people will die for nothing. The result will be a world enslaved by the Imperial Order. If I don't lead our side in battle, the world will still fall under the shadow of the Order but far fewer people will die. Only in that way will we ever stand a chance."

"By losing? You want to lose first, and then fight? . . . How can we even consider abandoning the fight for freedom?"

"Anderith helped teach me a lesson," he said. His voice was restrained, as if he regretted what he was saying. "I can't press this war. Freedom requires effort if it is to be won and vigilance if it is to be maintained. People just don't value freedom until it's taken away."

"But many do," Kahlan objected.

"There are always some, but most don't even understand it, nor do they care to—the same as with magic. People mindlessly shrink from it, too, without seeing the truth. The Order offers them a world without magic and ready-made answers to everything. Servitude is simple. I thought that I could convince people of the value of their own lives, and of liberty. In Anderith they showed me just how foolish I had been."

"Anderith is just one place—"

"Anderith was not remarkable. Look at all the trouble we've had elsewhere. We're having trouble even here, where I grew up." Richard began tucking in his shirt. "Forcing people to fight for freedom is the worst kind of contradiction.

"Nothing I can say will inspire people to care—I've tried. Those who value liberty will have to run, to hide, to try to survive and endure what is sure to come. I can't prevent it. I can't help them. I know that now."

"But Richard, how can you even think of—"

"I must do what is best for us. I must be selfish; life is far too precious to be casually squandered on useless causes. There can be no greater evil than that. People can only be saved from the coming dark age of subjugation and servitude if they, too, come to understand and care about the value of their own lives, their freedom, and are willing to act in their own interest. We must try to stay alive in the hope that such a day will come."

"But we can prevail in this war. We must."

"Do you think that I can just go off and lead men into war, and because I wish it, we will win? We won't. It takes more than my wishing it. It will take vast numbers of people fully committed to the cause. We don't have that. If we throw our forces against the Order, we will be destroyed and any chance for winning freedom in the future will be forever lost." He raked his fingers back through his hair. "We must not lead our forces against the army of the Order."

He turned to pulling his black, open-sided tunic on over his head. Kahlan struggled to give force to her voice, to the magnitude of her concern.

"But what about all those who are prepared to fight—all the armies already in the field? There are good men, able men, ready to go against Jagang and stop his Imperial Order and drive them back to the Old World. Who will lead our men?"

"Lead them to what? Death? They can't win."

Kahlan was horrified. She reached up and snatched his shirtsleeve before he could lean down to retrieve his broad over-belt. "Richard, you're only saying this, walking away from the struggle, because of what happened to me."

"No. I had already decided it that same night, before you were attacked. When I went out alone for a walk, after the vote, I did a lot of thinking. I came to this realization and made up my mind. What happened to you made no difference except to prove the point that I'm right and should have figured it out sooner. If I had, you would never have been hurt."

"But if the Mother Confessor had not been hurt, you would have felt better by morning and changed your mind."

Light coming through the doorway behind him lit in a blaze of gold the ancient symbols coiled along the squared edges of his tunic. "Cara, what would happen if I'd been attacked with her, and we had both been killed? What would you all do then?"

"I don't know."

"That is why I withdraw. You are all following me, not participating in a struggle for your own future. Your answer should have been that you would all fight on for yourselves, for your freedom. I have come to understand the mistake I've made in this, and to see that we cannot win in this way. The Order is too large an opponent."

Kahlan's father, King Wyborn, had taught her about fighting against such odds, and she had practical experience at it. "Their army may outnumber ours, but that doesn't make it impossible. We just have to outthink them. I will be there to help you, Richard. We have seasoned officers. We can do it. We must."

"Look how the Order's cause spreads on words that sound good"—Richard swept out an arm—"even to distant places like this. We know beyond doubt the evil of the Order, yet people everywhere passionately side with them despite the ghastly truth of everything the Imperial Order stands for."

"Richard," Kahlan whispered, trying not to lose what was left of her voice, "I led those young Galean recruits against an army of experienced Order soldiers who greatly outnumbered us, and we prevailed."

"Exactly. They had just seen their home city after the Order had been there. Everyone they loved had been murdered, everything they knew had been destroyed. Those men fought with an understanding of what they were doing and why. They were going to throw themselves at the enemy with or without you commanding them. But they were the only ones, and even though they succeeded, most of them were killed in the struggle."

Kahlan was incredulous. "So you are going to let the Order do the same elsewhere so as to give people a reason to fight? You are going to stand aside and let the Order slaughter hundreds of thousands of innocent people?

"You want to quit because I was hurt. Dear spirits, I love you Richard, but don't do this to me. I'm the Mother Confessor; I'm responsible for the lives of the people of the Midlands. Don't do this because of what happened to me."

Richard snapped on his leather-padded silver wristbands. "I'm not doing this because of what happened to you. I'm helping save those lives in the only way that has a chance. I'm doing the only thing I can do."

"You are doing the easy thing," Cara said.

Richard met her challenge with quiet sincerity. "Cara, I'm doing the hardest thing I have ever had to do."

Kahlan was sure now that their rejection by the Anderith people had hit him harder than she had realized. She caught two of his fingers and squeezed sympathetically. He had put his heart into sparing those people from enslavement by the Order. He had tried to show them the value of freedom by allowing them the freedom to choose their own destiny. He had put his faith in their hands.

In a crushing defeat, an enormous majority had spurned all he had offered, and in so doing devastated that faith.

Kahlan thought that perhaps with some time to heal, the same as with her, the pain would fade for him, too. "You can't hold yourself to blame for the fall of Anderith, Richard. You did your best. It wasn't your fault."

He picked up his big leather over-belt with its gold-worked pouches and cinched it over the magnificent tunic.

"When you're the leader, everything is your fault."

Kahlan knew the truth of that. She thought to dissuade him by taking a different tack.

"What form did this vision assume?"

Richard's piercing gray eyes locked on her, almost in warning.

"Vision, revelation, realization, postulation, prophecy . . . understanding—call it what you will, for in this they are all in one the same, and unequivocal. I can't describe it but to say it seems as if I must have always known it. Maybe I have. It wasn't so much words as it was a complete concept, a conclusion, a truth that became absolutely clear to me."

She knew he expected her to leave it at that. "If it became so clear and is unambiguous," she pressed, "you must be able to express it in words."

Richard slipped the baldric over his head, laying it over his right shoulder. As he adjusted the sword against his left hip, light sparkled off the raised gold wire woven through the silver wire of the hilt to spell out the word TRUTH.

His brow was smooth and his face calm. She knew she had at last brought him to the heart of the matter. His certainty would afford him no reason to keep it from her if she chose to hear it, and she did. His words rolled forth with quiet power, like prophecy come to life.

"I have been a leader too soon. It is not I who must prove myself to the people, but the people who must now prove themselves to me. Until then, I must not lead them, or all hope is lost."

Standing there, erect, masculine, masterful in his black war wizard outfit, he looked as if he could be posing for a statue of who he was: the Seeker of Truth, rightfully named by Zeddicus Zu'l Zorander, the First Wizard himself—and Richard's grandfather. It had nearly broken Zedd's heart to do so, because Seekers so often died young and violently.

While he lived, a Seeker was a law unto himself. Backed by the awesome power of his sword, a Seeker could bring down kingdoms. That was one reason it was so important to name the right person—a moral person—to the post. Zedd claimed that the Seeker, in a way, named himself by the nature of his own mind and by his actions, and that the First Wizard's function was simply to act on his observations by officially naming him and giving him the weapon that was to be his lifelong companion.

ent qualities and responsibilities had converged in this man she
netimes wondered how he could reconcile them all.

you so sure?"

the importance of the post, Kahlan and then Zedd had sworn their
se of Richard as the newly named Seeker of Truth. That had been
Kahlan had met him. It was as Seeker that Richard had first come to
at had been thrust upon him, and to live up to the extraordinary trust
put in him.

His gray eyes fairly blazed with clarity of purpose as he answered her.

"The only sovereign I can allow to rule me is reason. The first law of reason is this: what exists, exists; what is, is. From this irreducible, bedrock principle, all knowledge is built. This is the foundation from which life is embraced.

"Reason is a choice. Wishes and whims are not facts, nor are they a means to discovering them. Reason is our only way of grasping reality—it's our basic tool of survival. We are free to evade the effort of thinking, to reject reason, but we are not free to avoid the penalty of the abyss we refuse to see.

"If I fail to use reason in this struggle, if I close my eyes to the reality of what is, in favor of what I would wish, then we will both die in this, and for nothing. We will be but two more among uncounted millions of nameless corpses beneath the gray, gloomy decay of mankind. In the darkness that will follow, our bones will be meaningless dust.

"Eventually, perhaps a thousand years from now, perhaps more, the light of liberty will again be raised up to shine over a free people, but between now and then, millions upon millions of people will be born into hopeless misery and have no choice but to bear the weight of the Order's yoke. We, by ignoring reason, will have purchased those mountains of broken bodies, the wreckage of lives endured but never lived."

Kahlan found herself unable to summon the courage to speak, much less argue; to do so right then would be to ask him to disregard his judgment at a cost he believed would be a sea of blood. But doing as he saw they must would cast her people helpless into the jaws of death.

Kahlan, her vision turning to a watery blur, looked away.

"Cara," Richard said, "get the horses hitched to the carriage. I'm going to scout a circle to make sure we don't have any surprises."

"I will scout while you hitch the horses. I am your guard."

"You're my friend, too. I know this land better than you. Hitch the horses and don't give me any trouble about it."

Cara rolled her eyes and huffed, but marched off to do his bidding.

The room rang with silence. Richard's shadow slipped off the blanket. When Kahlan whispered her love to him, he paused and looked back. His shoulders seemed to betray the weight he carried.

"I wish I could, but I can't make people understand freedom. I'm sorry."

From somewhere inside, Kahlan found a smile for him. "Maybe it isn't so hard." She gestured toward the bird he had carved in the wall. "Just show them that, and they will understand what freedom really means: to soar on your own wings."

Richard smiled, she thought gratefully, before he vanished through the doorway.

All the troubling thoughts tumbling through her mind kept Kahlan from falling back to sleep. She tried not to think about Richard's vision of the future. As exhausted as she was by pain, his words were too troubling to contemplate, and besides, there was nothing she could do about it right then. But she was determined to help him get over the loss of Anderith and focus on stopping the Imperial Order.

It was more difficult to shake her thoughts about the men who had been outside, men Richard had grown up with. The haunting memory of their angry threats echoed in her mind. She knew that ordinary men who had never before acted violently, could, in the right circumstances, be incited to great brutality. With the way they viewed mankind as sinful, wretched, and evil, it was only a small step more to actually doing evil. After all, any evil they might do, they had already rationalized as being predestined by what they viewed as man's inescapable nature.

It was unnerving to contemplate an attack by such men when she could do nothing but lie there waiting to be killed. Kahlan envisioned a grinning, toothless Tommy Lancaster leaning over her to cut her throat while all she could do was stare helplessly up at him. She had often been afraid in battle, but at least then she could fight with all her strength to survive. That helped counter the fear. It was different to be helpless and have no means to fight back; it was a different sort of fear.

If she had to, she could always resort to her Confessor's power, but in her condition that was a dubious proposition. She had never had to call upon her power when in anything like the condition in which she now found herself. She reminded herself that the three of them would be long gone before the men returned, and besides, Richard and Cara would never let them get near her.

Kahlan had a more immediate fear, though, and that one was all too real. But she wouldn't feel it for long; she would pass out, she knew. She hoped.

She tried not to think of it, and instead put her hand gently over her belly, over their child, as she listened to the nearby splashing and burbling of a stream. The sound of the water reminded her of how much she wished she could take a bath. The bandages over the oozing wound in her side stank and needed to be changed often. The sheets were soaked with sweat. Her scalp itched. The mat of grass that was the bedding under the sheet was hard and chafed her back. Richard had probably made the pallet quickly, planning to improve it later.

As hot as the day was, the stream's cold water would be welcome. She longed for a bath, to be clean, and to smell fresh. She longed to be better, to be able to do things for herself, to be healed. She could only hope that as time passed, Richard, too, would recover from his invisible, but real, wounds.

Cara finally returned, grumbling about the horses being stubborn today. She looked up to see the room was empty. "I had better go look for him and make sure he's safe."

"He's fine. He knows what he's doing. Just wait, Cara, or he will then have to go out and look for you."

Cara sighed and reluctantly agreed. Retrieving a cool, wet cloth, she set to mopping Kahlan's forehead and temples. Kahlan didn't like to complain when people were doing their best to care for her, so she didn't say anything about how much it hurt her torn neck muscles when her head was shifted in that way. Cara never complained about any of it. Cara only complained when she believed her charges were in needless danger—and when Richard wouldn't let her eliminate those she viewed as a danger.

Outside, a bird let out a high-pitched trill. The tedious repetition was becoming grating. In the distance, Kahlan could hear a squirrel chattering an objection to something, or perhaps arguing over his territory. He'd been doing it for what seemed an hour. The stream babbled on without letup.

This was Richard's idea of restful.

"I hate this," she muttered.

"You should be happy—lying about without anything to do."

"And I bet you would be happy to trade places?"

"I am Mord-Sith. For a Mord-Sith, nothing could be worse than to die in bed." Her blue eyes turned to Kahlan's. "Old and toothless," she added. "I didn't mean that you—"

"I know what you meant."

Cara looked relieved. "Anyway, you couldn't die—that would be too easy. You never do anything easy."

"I married Richard."

"See what I mean?"

Kahlan smiled.

Cara dunked the cloth in a pail on the floor and wrung it out as she stood. "It isn't too bad, is it? Just lying there?"

"How would you like to have to have someone push a wooden bowl under your bottom every time your bladder was full?"

Cara carefully blotted the damp cloth along Kahlan's neck. "I don't mind doing it for a sister of the Agiel."

The Agiel, the weapon a Mord-Sith always carried, looked like nothing more than a short, red leather rod hanging on a fine chain from her right wrist. A Mord-Sith's Agiel was never more than a flick away from her grip. It somehow functioned by means of the magic of a Mord-Sith's bond to the Lord Rahl.

Kahlan had once felt the partial touch of an Agiel. In a blinding instant, it could inflict the kind of pain that the entire gang of men had dealt Kahlan. The touch of a Mord-Sith's Agiel was easily capable of delivering bone-breaking torture, and just as easily, if she desired, death.

Richard had given Kahlan the Agiel that had belonged to Denna, the Mord-Sith who had captured him by order of Darken Rahl. Only Richard had ever come to understand and empathize with the pain an Agiel also gave the Mord-Sith who wielded it. Before he was forced to kill Denna in order to escape, she had given him her Agiel, asking to be remembered as simply Denna, the woman beyond the appellation of Mord-Sith, the woman no one but Richard had ever before seen or understood.

That Kahlan understood, and kept the Agiel as a symbol of that same respect for women whose young lives had been stolen and twisted to nightmare purposes and duties, was deeply meaningful to the other Mord-Sith. Because of that compassion—untainted by pity—and more, Cara had named Kahlan a sister of the Agiel. It was an informal but heartfelt accolade.

"Messengers have come to see Lord Rahl," Cara said. "You were sleeping, and Lord Rahl saw no reason to wake you," she added in answer to Kahlan's questioning look. The messengers were D'Haran, and able to find Richard by their bond to him as their Lord Rahl. Kahlan, not able to duplicate the feat, had always found it unsettling.

"What did they have to say?"

Cara shrugged. "Not a lot. Jagang's army of the Imperial Order remains in Anderith for the time being, with Reibisch's force staying safely to the north to watch and be ready should the Order decide to threaten the rest of the Midlands. We know little of the situation inside Anderith, under the Order's occupation. The rivers flow away from our men, toward the sea, so they have not seen bodies to indicate if there has been mass death, but there have been a few people who managed to escape. They report that there was some death due to the poison which was released, but they don't know how widespread it was. General Reibisch has sent scouts and spies in to learn what they will."

"What orders did Richard give them to take back?"

"None."

"None? He sent no orders?"

Cara shook her head and then leaned over to dunk the cloth again. "He wrote letters to the general, though."

She drew the blanket down, lifted the bandage at Kahlan's side, and inspected its weak red charge before tossing it on the floor. With a gentle touch, she cleaned the wound.

When Kahlan was able to get her breath, she asked, "Did you see the letters?"

"Yes. They say much the same as he has told you—that he has had a vision that has caused him to come to see the nature of what he must do. He explained to the general that he could not give orders for fear of causing the end of our chances."

"Did General Reibisch answer?"

"Lord Rahl has had a vision. D'Harans know the Lord Rahl must deal with the terrifying mysteries of magic. D'Harans do not expect to understand their Lord Rahl and would not question his behavior: he is the Lord Rahl. The general made no comment, but sent word that he would use his own judgment."

Richard had probably told them it was a vision, rather than say it was simply a realization, for that very reason. Kahlan considered that a moment, weighing the possibilities.

"We have that much luck, then. General Reibisch is a good man, and will know what to do. Before too long, I'll be up and about. By then, maybe Richard will be better, too."

Cara tossed the cloth into the pail. As she leaned closer, her brow creased with frustration and concern.

"Mother Confessor, Lord Rahl said he will not act to lead us until the people prove themselves to him."

"I'm getting better. I hope to help him get over what happened—help him to see that he must fight."

"But this involves magic." She picked at the frayed edge of the blue blanket. "Lord Rahl said it's a vision. If it is magic, then it's something he would know about and must handle in the way he sees it must be done."

"We need to be a little understanding of what he's been through—the loss we've all suffered to the Order—and remember, too, that Richard didn't grow up around magic, much less ruling armies."

Cara squatted and rinsed her cloth in the pail. After wringing it out, she went back to cleaning the wound in Kahlan's side. "He is the Lord Rahl, though. Hasn't he already proven himself to be a master of magic a number of times?"

Kahlan couldn't dispute that much of it, but he still didn't have much experience, and experience was valuable. Cara not only feared magic but was easily impressed by any act of wizardry. Like most people, she couldn't distinguish between a simple conjuring and the kind of magic that could alter the very nature of the world. Kahlan realized now that this1 wasn't a vision, as such, but a conclusion Richard had arrived at.

Much of what he'd said made sense, but Kahlan believed that emotion was clouding his thinking.

Cara looked up from her work. Her voice bore an undertone of uncertainty, if not despairing bewilderment. "Mother Confessor, how will the people ever be able to prove themselves to Lord Rahl?"

"I've no idea."

Cara set down the cloth and looked Kahlan in the eye. It was a long, uncomfortable moment before she finally decided to speak.

"Mother Confessor, I think maybe Lord Rahl has lost his mind."

Kahlan's immediate thought was to wonder if General Reibisch might believe the same thing.

"I thought D'Harans do not expect to understand their Lord Rahl and would not question his behavior."

"Lord Rahl also says he wants me to think for myself."

Kahlan put her hand over Cara's. "How many times have we doubted him before? Remember the chicken-that-wasn't-a-chicken? We both thought he was crazy. He wasn't."

"This is not some monster chasing us. This is something much bigger."

"Cara, do you always follow Richard's orders?"

"Of course not. He must be protected and I can't allow his foolishness to interfere with my duty. I only follow his orders if they do not endanger him, or if they tell me to do what I would have done anyway, or if it involves his male pride."

"Did you always follow Darken Rahl's orders?"

Cara stiffened at the unexpected encounter with the name, as if speaking it might summon him back from the world of the dead. "You followed Darken Rahl's orders, no matter how foolish they were, or you were tortured to death."

"Which Lord Rahl do you respect?"

"I would lay down my life for any Lord Rahl." Cara hesitated, and then touched her fingertips to the red leather over her heart. "But I could never feel this way for any other. I . . . love Lord Rahl. Not like you love him, not like a woman loves a man, but it is still love. Sometimes I have dreams of how proud I am to serve and defend him, and sometimes I have nightmares that I will fail him."

Cara's brow drew down with sudden dread. "You won't tell him that I said I love him, will you? He must not know."

Kahlan smiled. "Cara, I think he already knows, because he has similar feelings about you, but if you don't wish it, I won't say anything."

Cara let out a sigh of relief. "Good."

"And what made you come to feel that way about him?"

"Many things. . . . He wishes us to think for ourselves. He allows us to serve him by choice. No Lord Rahl has ever done that before. I know that if I said I wished to quit him, he would let me go. He would not have me tortured to death for it. He would wish me a good life."

"That, and more, is what you value about him: he never pretended any claim to your lives. He believes no such claim can ever rightfully exist. It's the first time since you were captured and trained to be Mord-Sith, that you have felt the reality of freedom.

"That, Cara, is what Richard wants for everyone."

She swished a hand, as if dismissing the seriousness of the whole thing. "He would be foolish to grant me my freedom if I asked for it. He needs me too much."

"You wouldn't need to ask for your freedom, Cara, and you know it. You already have your freedom, and because of him you know that, too. That's what makes him a leader you are honored to follow. That's why you feel the way you do about him. He has earned your loyalty."

Cara mulled it over.

"I still think he has lost his mind."

In the past, Richard had more than once expressed his faith that, given a chance, people would do the right thing. That was what he had done with the Mord-Sith. That was also what he had done with the people of Anderith. Now . . .

Kahlan swallowed back her emotion. "Not his mind, Cara, but maybe his heart."

Cara, seeing the look on Kahlan's face, dismissed the seriousness of the matter with a shrug and a smile. "I guess we will simply have to bring him around to the way things are going to be—talk some sense into him."

Cara dabbed away the remnant of a tear as it rolled down Kahlan's cheek.

"Before he comes back, how about getting that stupid wooden bowl for me?"

Cara nodded and bent to retrieve it. Kahlan was already fretting, knowing how much it was going to hurt, but there was no avoiding it.

Cara came up with the shallow bowl. "Before those men came, I was planning on making a fire and warming some water. I was going to give you a bed bath—you know, with a soapy cloth and a bucket of warm water. I guess I can do it when we get where we are going."

Kahlan half closed her eyes with the dreamy thought of being at least somewhat clean and fresh. She thought she needed a bath even more than she needed the wooden bowl to relieve herself.

"Cara, if you would do that for me, I would kiss your feet when I get better, and name you to the most important post I can think of."

"I am Mord-Sith." Cara looked nonplussed. She finally drew the blanket down. "That is the most important post there is—except perhaps wife to the Lord Rahl. Since he already has a wife, and I am already Mord-Sith, I will have to be content with having my feet kissed."

Kahlan chuckled, but a stab of pain through her abdomen and ribs brought it to an abrupt halt.

31

Richard was a long time in returning. Cara had made Kahlan drink two cups of cold tea heavily laced with herbs to dull the pain. It wouldn't be long before she was in a stupor, if not exactly asleep. Kahlan had been just about to yield to Cara's desire to go look for Richard, when he called from a distance to let them know it was him.

"Did you see any of the men?" Cara asked when he appeared in the doorway.

With a straight finger, Richard swiped glistening beads of sweat off his forehead. His damp hair was plastered to his neck. "No. They're no doubt off to Hartland to do some drinking and complaining. By the time they come back we'll be long gone."

"I still say we should lie in wait and end the threat," Cara muttered. Richard ignored her.

"I cut and stripped some stout saplings and used some canvas to make a litter." He came closer and with a knuckle nudged Kahlan's chin, as if to playfully buck up her courage. "From now on we'll just let you stay on the litter, and then we can move you in and out of the carriage without . . ." He had that look in his eyes—that look that hurt her to see. He showed her a smile. "It will make it easier on Cara and me."

Kahlan tried to face the thought with composure. "We're ready then?"

His gaze dropped as he nodded.

"Good," Kahlan said, cheerfully. "I'm in the mood for a nice ride. I'd like to see some of the countryside."

He smiled, more convincingly this time, she thought. "You shall have it. And we'll end up at a beautiful place. It's going to take a while to get there, traveling as slow as we must, but it will be worth the journey, you'll see."

Kahlan tried to keep her breathing even. She said his name over and over in her head, telling herself that she would not forget it this time, that she would not forget her own name. She hated forgetting things; it made her feel a fool to learn things she should have remembered but had forgotten. She was going to remember this time.

"Well, do I have to get up and walk? Or are you going to be a gentleman and carry me?"

He bent and kissed her forehead—the one part on her face that the soft touch of his lips would not hurt. He glanced at Cara and tilted his head to signal her to get Kahlan's legs.

"Will those men be drinking a long time?" Kahlan asked.

"It's still midday. Don't worry, we'll be long gone before they ever get back here."

"I'm sorry, Richard. I know you thought these people from your homeland—"

"They're people, just like everyone else."

She nodded as she fondly stroked the back of his big hand. "Cara gave me some of your herbs. I'll sleep for a long time, so don't go slow on my account—I won't feel it. I don't want you to have to fight all those men."

"I won't be doing any fighting—just traveling my forests."

"That's good." Kahlan felt daggers twist in her ribs as her breathing started getting too fast. "I love you, you know. In case I forgot to say it, I love you."

Despite the pain in his gray eyes, he smiled. "I love you, too. Just try to relax. Cara and I will be as gentle as we can. We'll go easy. There's no rush. Don't try to help us. Just relax. You're getting better, so it won't be so hard."

She had been hurt before and knew that it was always better to move yourself because you knew exactly how to do it. But she couldn't move herself this time.

32

She had come to know that the worst thing when you were hurt was to have someone else move you.

As he leaned over, she slipped her right arm around his neck while he carefully slid his left arm under her shoulders. Being lifted even that much ignited a shock of pain. Kahlan tried to ignore the burning stitch and attempted to relax as she said his name over and over in her mind.

She suddenly remembered something important. It was her last chance to remind him.

"Richard," she whispered urgently just before he pushed his right arm under her bottom to lift her. "Please . . . remember to be careful not to hurt the baby."

She was startled to see her words stagger him. It took a moment before his eyes turned up to look into hers. What she saw there nearly stopped her heart.

"Kahlan . . . you remember, don't you?"

"Remember?"

His eyes glistened. "That you lost the baby. When you were attacked."

The memory slammed into her like a fist, nearly taking her breath.

". . . Oh . . ."

"Are you all right?"

"Yes. I forgot for a moment. I just wasn't thinking. I remember, now. I remember you told me about it."

And she did. Their child, their child that had only begun to grow in her, was long since dead and gone. Those beasts who had attacked her had taken that from her, too.

The world seemed to turn gray and lifeless.

"I'm so sorry, Kahlan," he whispered.

She caressed his hair. "No, Richard. I should have remembered. I'm sorry I forgot. I didn't mean to . . ."

He nodded.

She felt a warm tear drop onto the hollow of her throat, close to her necklace. The necklace, with its small dark stone, had been a wedding gift from Shota, the witch woman. The gift was a proposal of truce. Shota said it would allow them to be together and share their love, as they had always wanted, without Kahlan getting pregnant. Richard and Kahlan had decided that, for the time being, they would reluctantly accept Shota's gift, her truce. They already had worries enough on their hands.

But for a time, when the chimes had been loose in the world, the magic of the necklace, unbeknownst to Richard and Kahlan, had failed. One small but miraculous balance to the horrors the chimes had brought had been that it had given their love the opportunity to bring a child to life.

Now that life was gone.

"Please, Richard, let's go."

He nodded again.

"Dear spirits," he whispered to himself so softly she could hardly hear him, "forgive me for what I am about to do."

She clutched his neck. She now longed for what was coming—she wanted to forget.

He lifted her as gently as he could. It felt like wild stallions tied to each limb all leaped into a gallop at the same instant. Pain ripped up from the core of her, the shock of it making her eyes go wide as she sucked in a breath. And then she screamed.

The blackness hit her like a dungeon door slamming shut.

A sound woke her as suddenly as a slap. Kahlan lay on her back, still as death, her eyes wide, listening. It wasn't so much that the sound had been loud, but that it had been something disturbingly familiar. Something dangerous.

Her whole body throbbed with pain, but she was more awake than she had been in what seemed like weeks. She didn't know how long she had been asleep, or perhaps unconscious. She was awake enough to remember that it would be a grave mistake to try to sit up, because just about the only part of her not injured was her right arm. One of the big chestnut geldings snorted nervously and stamped a hoof, jostling the carriage enough to remind Kahlan of her broken ribs.

The sticky air smelled of approaching rain, though fits of wind still bore dust to her nostrils. Dark masses of leaves overhead swung fretfully to and fro, their creaking branches giving voice to their torment. Deep purple and violet clouds scudded past in silence. Beyond the trees and clouds, the field of blue-black sky held a lone star, high over her forehead. She wasn't sure if it was dawn or dusk, but it felt like the death of day.

As the gusts beat strands of her filthy hair across her face, Kahlan listened as hard as she could for the sound that didn't belong, still hoping to fit it into a picture of something innocent. Since she'd heard it only from the deepness of sleep, its conscious identity remained frustratingly out of her reach.

She listened, too, for sounds of Richard and Cara, but heard nothing. Surely, they would be close. They would not leave her alone—not for any reason this side of death. She recoiled from the image. She ached to call out for Richard and prove the uninvited thought a foolish fear, but instinct screamed at her to stay silent. She needed no reminder not to move.

A metallic clang came from the distance, then a cry. Maybe it was an animal, she told herself. Ravens sometimes let out the most awful cries. Their shrill wails could sound so human it was eerie. But as far as she knew, ravens didn't make metallic sounds.

The carriage suddenly lurched to the right. Her breath caught as the unanticipated movement caused a stitch of pain in the back of her ribs. Someone had put weight on the step. By the careless disregard for the carriage's injured passenger, she knew it wasn't Richard or Cara. But if it wasn't Richard, then who? Gooseflesh tickled the nape of her neck. If it wasn't Richard, where was he?

Stubby fingers grasped the top of the corded chafing strip on the carriage's side rail. The blunt fingertips were rounded back over grubby, gnawed-down little half-button fingernails. Kahlan held her breath, hoping he didn't realize she was in the carriage.

A face popped up. Cunning dark eyes squinted at her. The man's four middle upper teeth were missing, leaving his eyeteeth looking like fangs when he grinned.

"Well, well. If it ain't the wife of the late Richard Cypher."

Kahlan lay frozen. This was just like her dreams. For an instant, she couldn't decide if it was only that, just a dream, or real.

His shirt bore a dark patina of dirt, as if it was never removed for anything. Sparse, wiry hairs on his fleshy cheeks and chin were like early weeds in the plowed field of his pockmarked face. His upper lip was wet from his runny nose. He had no lower teeth in front. The tip of his tongue rested partway out between the yawning gap of his smirk.

He brought up a knife for her to see. He turned it this way and that, almost as if he were showing off a prized possession to a shy girl he was courting. His eyes kept flicking back and forth between the knife and Kahlan. The slipshod job of sharpening appeared to have been done on rough granite, rather than on a proper whetstone. Dark blotches and rust stained the poorly kept cheap steel. But the scratched and chipped edge was no less deadly for any of it. His wicked, toothless grin widened with pleasure as her gaze followed the blade, watching it carve careful slices of the air between them.

She made herself look into his dark, sunken eyes, which peered out from puffy slits. "Where's Richard?" she demanded in a level voice.

"Dancing with the spirits in the underworld." He cocked his head to one side. "Where's the blond bitch? The one my friends said they saw before. The one with the smart mouth. The one what needs to have her tongue shortened before I gut her."

Kahlan glared at him so he would know she had no intention of answering. As the crude knife advanced toward her, his stench hit her.

"You would have to be Tommy Lancaster."

The knife paused. "How'd you know that?"

Anger welled up from deep inside her. "Richard told me about you."

The eyes glittered with menace. His grin widened. "Yeah? What did he tell you?"

"That you were an ugly toothless pig who wets his pants whenever he grins. Smells like he was right."

The smirking grin turned to a scowl. He raised up on the step and leaned in with the knife. That was what Kahlan wanted him to do—to get close enough so she could touch him.

With the discipline borne of a lifetime of experience, she mentally shed her anger and donned the calm of a Confessor committed to a course of action. Once a Confessor was resolved to releasing her power, the nature of time itself seemed to change.

She had but to touch him.

A Confessor's power was partly dependent on her strength. In her injured condition, she didn't know if she would be able to call forth the required force, and if she could, whether she would survive the unleashing of it, but she knew she had no choice. One of them was about to die. Maybe both.

He leaned his elbow on the side rail. His fist with the knife went for her exposed throat. Rather than watching the knife, Kahlan watched the little scars, like dusty white cobwebs caught on his knuckles. When the fist was close enough, she made her move to snatch his wrist.

Unexpectedly, she discovered she was snugly enfolded in the blue blanket. She hadn't realized Richard had placed her on the litter he'd made. The blanket was wrapped around her and tightly tucked under the stretcher poles in order to hold her as still as possible and prevent her from being hurt when the carriage was moving. Her arm was trapped inside what was about to become her death shroud.

Hot panic flared up as she struggled to free her right arm. She was in a desperate race with the blade coming for her throat. Pain knifed her injured ribs as she battled with the blanket. She had no time to cry out or to curse in frustration at being so unwittingly snared. Her fingers gathered a fold of material. She yanked at it, trying to pull some slack from under the litter she lay atop so she could free her arm.

Kahlan had merely to touch him, but she couldn't. His blade was going to be the only contact between them. Her only hope was that maybe his knuckles would brush her flesh, or maybe he just might be close enough as he started to slice her throat that she could press her chin against his hand. Then, she could release her power, if she was still alive—if he didn't cut too deep, first.

As she twisted and pulled at the blanket, it seemed to her an eternity as she watched the blade poised over her exposed neck, an eternity to wait before she had any hope of unleashing her power—an eternity to live. But she knew there was only an instant more before she would feel the ripping slash of that rough blade.

It didn't happen at all as she expected.

Tommy Lancaster wrenched backward with an earsplitting shriek. The world around Kahlan crashed back in a riot of sound and motion with the abrupt readjustment to the discontinuation of her intent. Kahlan saw Cara behind him, her teeth clenched in a grim commitment of her own. In her pristine red leather, she was a precious ruby behind a clod of dirt.

Bent into the Agiel pressed against his back, Tommy Lancaster had less hope of pulling away from Cara than if she had impaled him on a meat hook. His torment would not have been more brutal to witness, his shrieks more painful to hear.

Cara's Agiel dragged up and around the side of his ribs as he collapsed to his knees. Each rib the Agiel passed over broke with a sharp crack, like the sound of a tree limb snapping. Vivid red, the match of her leather, oozed over his knuckles and down his fingers. The knife clattered to the rocky ground. A dark stain of blood grew on the side of his shirt until it dripped off the untucked tails.

Cara stood over him, an austere executioner, watching him beg for mercy. Instead of granting it, she pressed her Agiel against his throat and followed him to the ground. His eyes were wide and white all around as he choked.

It was a slow, agonizing journey toward death. Tommy Lancaster's arms and legs writhed as he began to drown in his own blood. Cara could have ended it quickly, but it didn't appear she had any intention of doing so. This man had meant to kill Kahlan. Cara meant to extract a heavy price for the crime.

"Cara!" Kahlan was surprised that she could get so much power into the shout. Cara glanced back over her shoulder. Tommy Lancaster's hands went to his throat and he gasped for air when she rose up to stand over him. "Cara, stop it. Where's Richard? Richard may need your help."

Cara leaned down over Tommy Lancaster, pressed her Agiel to his chest, and gave it a twist. His left leg kicked out once, his arms flopped to the side, and he went still.

Before either Cara or Kahlan could say anything, Richard, his face set in cold ferocity, sprinted up toward the carriage. He had his sword to hand. The blade was dark and wet.

36

The instant Kahlan saw his sword, she comprehended what had awakened her. The sound had been the Sword of Truth announcing its arrival in the evening air. In her sleep, her subconscious recognized the unique ring of steel made by the Sword of Truth when it was drawn, and she instinctively grasped the danger that that sound represented.

On his way to Kahlan's side, Richard only glanced at the lifeless body at Cara's feet.

"Are you all right?"

Kahlan nodded. "Fine." Belatedly, yet feeling triumphant at the accomplishment, she pulled her arm free of the blanket.

Richard turned to Cara. "Anyone else come up the road?"

"No. Just this one." She gestured with her Agiel toward the knife on the ground. "He intended to cut the Mother Confessor's throat."

If Tommy Lancaster hadn't already been dead, Richard's glare would have finished him. "I hope you didn't make it easy on him."

"No, Lord Rahl. He regretted his last vile act—I made certain of it."

With his sword, Richard indicated the surrounding area. "Stay here and keep your eyes open. I'm sure we got them all, but I'm going to check just to be certain no one else was holding back and trying to surprise us from another direction."

"No one will get near the Mother Confessor, Lord Rahl."

Dust rose in the gloomy light when he gave a reassuring pat to the shoulder of one of the two horses standing in their harnesses. "Soon as I get back, I want to get going. We should have enough moon—for a few hours, anyway. I know a safe place to make camp about four hours up the road. That will get us a good distance away from all this."

He pointed with his sword. "Drag his body past the brush over there and roll him off the edge, down into the ravine. I'd just as soon the bodies weren't found until after we're long gone and far away. Probably only the animals will ever find them way out here, but I don't want to take any chances."

Cara snatched a fistful of Tommy Lancaster's hair. "With pleasure." He was stocky, but the weight gave her no difficulty.

Richard trotted soundlessly off into the gathering darkness. Kahlan listened to the sound of the body scraping across the ground. She heard small branches snapping as Cara pulled the dead weight through the brush, and then the muffled thuds and tumbling scree as Tommy Lancaster's body rolled and bounced down a steep slope. It was a long time before Kahlan heard the final thump at the bottom of the ravine.

Cara ambled back to the side of the carriage. "Everything all right with you?" She casually pulled off her armored gloves.

Kahlan blinked at the woman. "Cara, he nearly had me."

Cara flicked her long blond braid back over her shoulder as she scanned the surrounding area. "No he didn't. I was standing right there behind him the whole time. I was nearly breathing down his neck. I never took my eyes from his knife. He had no chance to harm you." She met Kahlan's gaze. "Surely, you must have seen me."

"No, I didn't."

"Oh. I thought you saw me." Looking a little sheepish, she tucked most of the cuffs of the gloves behind her belt and folded the rest down over the front. "I guess maybe you were too low in the carriage to see me there behind him. I had my attention on him. I didn't mean to let him frighten you."

"If you were there the whole time, why did you allow him to nearly kill me?"

"He did not nearly kill you." Cara smiled without humor. "But I wanted to let him believe it. It's more of a shock, more of a horror, if you let them think they've won. It crushes a man's spirit to take him then, when you've caught him dead to rights."

Kahlan's head was swimming in confusion and so she decided not to press the issue. "What's going on? What's happened? How long have I been asleep?"

"We have been traveling for two days. You have been in and out of sleep, but you didn't know anything the times you were awake. Lord Rahl was fretful about hurting you to get you into the carriage, and about having told you . . . what you forgot."

Kahlan knew what Cara meant: her dead baby. "And the men?"

"They came after us. This time, though, Lord Rahl didn't discuss it with them." She seemed especially pleased about that. "He knew in enough time that they were coming, so we weren't taken by surprise. When they came charging in, some with arrows nocked and some with their swords or axes out, he shouted at them—once— giving them a chance to change their minds."

"He tried to reason with them? Even then?"

"Well, not exactly. He told them to go home in peace, or they would all die."

"And then what?"

"And then they all laughed. It only seemed to embolden them. They charged, arrows flying, swords and axes raised. So Lord Rahl ran off into the woods."

"He did what?"

"Before they came, he had told me that he was going to make them all chase after him. As Lord Rahl ran, the one who thought he would cut your throat yelled at the others to 'get Richard, and finish him this time.' Lord Rahl had hoped he would draw them all away from you, but when that one went after you instead, Lord Rahl gave me a look and I knew what he wanted me to do."

Cara clasped her hands behind her back as she scrutinized the gathering darkness, keeping watch, should anyone try to surprise them. Kahlan's thoughts turned to Richard, and what it must have been like, all alone as they chased him.

"How many men?"

"I didn't count them." Cara shrugged. "Maybe two dozen."

"And you left Richard alone with two dozen men chasing after him? Two dozen men intent on killing him?"

Cara shot Kahlan an incredulous look. "And leave you unprotected? When I knew that toothless brute was going after you? Lord Rahl would have skinned me alive if I had left you."

Tall and lean, shoulders squared and chin raised, Cara looked as pleased as a cat licking mouse off its whiskers. Kahlan suddenly understood: Richard had entrusted Cara with Kahlan's life; the Mord-Sith had proven that faith justified.

Kahlan felt a smile stretch the partly healed cuts on her lips. "I just wish I'd known you were standing there the whole time. Now, thanks to you, I won't need the wooden bowl."

Cara didn't laugh. "Mother Confessor, you should know that I would never let anything happen to either of you."

Richard appeared out of the shadows as suddenly as he had vanished. He stroked the horses reassuringly. As he moved down beside them, he quickly checked the neck collars, the trace chains, and the breaching to make sure it was all secure.

"Anything?" he asked Cara.

"No, Lord Rahl. Quiet and clear."

He leaned in the carriage and smiled. "Well, as long as you're awake, how about I take you for a romantic moonlight ride?"

She rested her hand on his forearm. "Are you all right?"

"I'm fine. Not a scratch."

"That's not what I meant."

His smile vanished. "They tried to kill us. Westland has just suffered its first casualties because of the influence of the Imperial Order."

"But you knew them."

"That doesn't entitle them to misplaced sympathy. How many thousands have I seen killed since I left here? I couldn't even convince men I grew up with of the truth. I couldn't even get them to listen fairly. All the death and suffering I've seen is ultimately because of men like this—men who refuse to see.

"Their willful ignorance does not entitle them to my blood or life. They picked their own path. For once, they paid the price."

He didn't sound to her like a man who was quitting the fight. He still held the sword, was still in the grip of its rage. Kahlan caressed his arm, letting him know that she understood. It was clear to her that even though he'd been justly defending himself, and though he was still filled with the sword's rage, he keenly regretted what he'd had to do. The men, had they been able to kill Richard instead, would have regretted nothing. They would have celebrated his death as a great victory.

"That was still perilous—making them all chase after you."

"No, it wasn't. It drew them out of the open and into the trees. They had to dismount. It's rocky and the footing is poor, so they couldn't rush me together or with speed, like they could out here on the road.

"The light is failing; they thought that was to their advantage. It wasn't. In the trees it was even darker. I'm wearing mostly black. It's warm, so I'd left my gold cape behind, here in the carriage. The little bit of gold on the rest of the outfit only serves to break up the shape of a man's figure in the near-dark, so they had an even harder time seeing me.

"Once I took down Albert, they stopped thinking and fought with pure anger—until they started seeing blood and death. Those men are used to brawls, not battles. They had expected an easy time murdering us—they weren't mentally prepared to fight for their own lives. Once they saw the true nature of what was happening, they ran for their lives. The ones left, anyway. These are my woods. In their panic, they became confused and lost their way in the trees. I cut them off and ended it."

"Did you get them all?" Cara asked, worried about any who might escape and bring more men after them.

"Yes. I knew most of them, and besides, I had their number in my head. I counted the bodies to make sure I got them all."

"How many?" Cara asked.

Richard turned to take up the reins. "Not enough for their purpose." He clicked his tongue and started the horses moving.

Richard rose up and drew his sword. This time, when its distinctive sound rang out in the night, Kahlan was awake. Her first instinct was to sit up. Before she even had time to think better of it, Richard had crouched and gently restrained her with a reassuring hand. She lifted her head just enough to see that it was Cara, leading a man into the harsh, flickering light of the campfire. Richard sheathed his sword when he saw who Cara had with her: Captain Meiffert, the D'Haran officer who had been with them back in Anderith.

Before any other greeting, the man dropped to his knees and bent forward, touching his forehead to the soft ground strewn with pine needles.

"Master Rahl guide us. Master Rahl teach us. Master Rahl protect us," Captain Meiffert beseeched in sincere reverence. "In your light we thrive. In your mercy we are sheltered. In your wisdom we are humbled. We live only to serve. Our lives are yours."

When he had gone to his knees to recite the devotion, as it was called, Kahlan saw Cara almost reflexively go to her knees with him, so ingrained was the ritual. The supplication to their Lord Rahl was something all D'Harans did. In the field they commonly recited it once or, on occasion, three times. At the People's Palace in D'Hara, most people gathered twice a day to chant the devotion at length.

When he'd been a captive of Darken Rahl, Richard, often in much the same condition as Tommy Lancaster just before he died, had himself been forced to his knees by Mord-Sith and made to perform the devotion for hours at a time. Now, the Mord-Sith, like all D'Harans, paid that same homage to Richard. If the Mord-Sith saw such a turn of events as improbable, or even ironic, they never said as much. What many of them had found improbable was that Richard hadn't had them all executed when he became their Lord Rahl.

It was Richard, though, who had discovered that the devotion to their Lord Rahl was in fact a surviving vestige of a bond, an ancient magic invoked by one of his ancestors to protect the D'Haran people from the dream walkers. It had long been believed that the dream walkers—created by wizards to be weapons during that ancient and nearly forgotten great war—had vanished from the world. The conjuring of strange and varied abilities—of instilling unnatural attributes in people—willing or not, had once been a dark art, the results always being at the least unpredictable, often uncertain, and sometimes dangerously unstable. Somehow, some spark of that malignant manipulation had been passed down generation after generation, lurking unseen for three thousand years—until it rekindled in the person of Emperor Jagang.

Kahlan knew something about the alteration of living beings to suit a purpose—Confessors were such people, as had been the dream walkers. In Jagang, Kahlan saw a monster created by magic. She knew many people saw the same in her. Much as some people had blond hair or brown eyes, she had been born to grow tall, with warm brown hair, and green eyes—and the ability of a Confessor. She loved and laughed and longed for things just the same as those born with blond hair or brown eyes, and without a Confessor's special ability.

Kahlan used her power for valid, moral reasons. Jagang, no doubt, believed the same of himself, and even if he didn't, most of his followers certainly did.

Richard, too, had been born with latent power. The ancient, adjunct defense of the bond was passed down to any gifted Rahl. Without the protection of the bond to Richard—the Lord Rahl—whether formally spoken or a silent heartfelt affinity, anyone was vulnerable to Jagang's power as a dream walker.

Unlike most other permutations conjured by wizards in living people, the Confessor's ability had always remained vital; at least it had until all the other Confessors had been murdered by order of Darken Rahl. Now, without such wizards and their specialized conjuring, only if Kahlan had children would the magic of the Confessors live on.

Confessors usually bore girls, but not always. A Confessor's power had originally been created for, and had been intended to be used by, women. Like all other conjuring that introduced unnatural abilities in people, this, too, had had unforeseen consequences: a Confessor's male children, it turned out, also bore the power. After it had been learned how treacherous the power could be in men, all male children were scrupulously culled.

Kahlan bearing a male child was precisely what the witch woman, Shota, feared. Shota knew very well that Richard would never allow his and Kahlan's son to be slain for the past evils of male Confessors. Kahlan, too, could never allow Richard's son to be killed. In the past, a Confessor's inability to marry out of love was one of the reasons she could emotionally endure the practice of infanticide. Richard, in discovering the means by which he and Kahlan could be together, had altered that equation, too.

But Shota didn't simply fear Kahlan giving birth to a male Confessor; she feared something of potentially far greater magnitude—a male Confessor who possessed Richard's gift. Shota had foretold that Kahlan and Richard would conceive a male child. Shota viewed such a child as an evil monster, dangerous beyond comprehension, and so had vowed to kill their offspring. To prevent such a thing from being required, she had given them the necklace to keep Kahlan from becoming pregnant. They had taken it reluctantly. The alternative was war with the witch woman.

It was for reasons such as this that Richard abhorred prophecy.

Kahlan watched as Captain Meiffert spoke the devotion a third time, Cara's lips moving with his. The soft chant was making Kahlan sleepy.

It was a luxury for Kahlan to be able to be down with Richard and Cara in the sheltered camp, beside the warmth of the fire, rather than having to stay in the carriage, especially since the night had turned chilly and damp. With the litter they could move her more easily and without causing her much pain. Richard would have made the litter sooner, but he hadn't expected to have to abandon the house he had started to build.

They were far off the narrow, forsaken road, in a tiny clearing concealed in a cleft in a steep rock wall behind a dense expanse of pine and spruce. A small meadow close by provided a snug paddock for the horses. Richard and Cara had pulled the carriage off the road, behind a mass of deadfall, and hidden it with spruce and balsam boughs. No one but a D'Haran bonded to their Lord Rahl had much of a chance of ever finding them in the vast and trackless forest.

The secluded spot had a fire pit Richard had dug and ringed with rocks during a previous stay, nearly a year before. It hadn't been used since. A protruding shelf of rock about seven or eight feet above them prevented the light of the campfire from shining up the rock wall, helping keep the camp hidden. Its slope also kept them snug and dry in the drizzle that had begun to fall. With a fog closing in, too, it was as protected and secure a campsite as Kahlan had ever seen. Richard had been true to his word.

It had taken more like six hours than four to reach the campsite. Richard had proceeded slowly for Kahlan's sake. It was late and they were all tired from a long day of traveling, to say nothing of the attack. Richard had told her that it looked like it might rain for a day or two, and they would stay in the camp and rest up until the weather cleared. There was no urgency to get where they were going.

After the third devotion, Captain Meiffert came haltingly to his feet. He clapped his right fist to the leather over his heart in salute. Richard smiled and the two men clasped forearms in a less formal greeting.

"How are you doing, Captain?" Richard grasped the man's elbow. "What's the matter? Did you fall off your horse, or something?"

The captain glanced at Cara, to his side. "Ah, well, I'm fine, Lord Rahl. Really."

"You look hurt."

"I just had my ribs . . . tickled, by your Mord-Sith, that's all."

"I didn't do it hard enough to break them," Cara scoffed.

"I'm truly sorry, Captain. We had a bit of trouble earlier today. Cara was no doubt worried for our safety when she saw you approaching in the dark." Richard's eyes turned toward Cara. "But she still should have been more careful before risking injuring people. I'm sure she's sorry and will want to apologize."

Cara made a sour face. "It was dark. I'm not about to take any foolish chances with the life of our Lord Rahl just so—"

"I would hope not," Captain Meiffert put in before Richard could reprimand her. He smiled at Cara. "I was once kicked by a stalwart warhorse. You did a better job of putting me down, Mistress Cara. I'm gratified to find Lord Rahl's life is in capable hands. If sore ribs are the price, I willingly accept it."

Cara's face brightened. The captain's simple concession disarmed a potentially nettlesome situation.

"Well, if the ribs bother you, let me know," Cara said dryly, "and I'll kiss them and make them better." In the silence, as Richard glowered at her, she scratched her ear and finally added, "Anyway, sorry. But I didn't want to take any chances."

"As I said, a price I willingly pay. Thank you for your vigilance."

"What are you doing here, Captain?" Richard asked. "General Reibisch send you to see if the Lord Rahl is crazy?"

Although it was impossible to tell in the firelight, Kahlan was sure that the man's face turned scarlet. "No, of course not, Lord Rahl. It's just that the general wanted you to have a full report."

"I see." Richard glanced down at their dinner pot. "When's the last time you ate, Captain? You look a little drawn, besides having sore ribs."

"Well, ah, I've been riding hard, Lord Rahl. I guess yesterday I must have eaten something. I'm fine, though. I can have something after—"

"Sit down, then." Richard gestured. "Let me get you something hot to eat. It will do you good."

As the man reluctantly settled down on the mossy ground beside Kahlan and Cara, Richard scooped some rice and beans into a bowl. He cut a big piece of bannock from what he'd left to cool on the griddle off to the side of the fire. He held the bowl out to the man. Captain Meiffert saw no way to prevent it, and was now mortified to find himself being served by none other than the Lord Rahl himself.

Richard had to lift the food toward him a second time before he took it. "It's only some rice and beans, Captain. It's not like I'm giving you Cara's hand in marriage."

Cara guffawed. "Mord-Sith don't marry. They simply take a man for a mate if they wish him—he gets no say in it."

Richard glanced up at her. Kahlan knew by Richard's tone that he hadn't meant anything by the comment—but he didn't laugh with Cara. He knew all too well the truth of her words. Such an act was not an act of love, but altogether the opposite. In the uncomfortable silence, Cara realized what she'd said, and decided to break some branches down and feed them to the fire.

Kahlan knew that Denna, the Mord-Sith who had captured Richard, had taken him for her mate. Cara knew it, too. When Richard would sometimes wake with a start and cling to her, Kahlan wondered if his nightmares were of things imaginary or real. When she kissed his sweat-slicked brow and asked what he had dreamed, he never remembered. She was thankful for that much of it.

Richard retrieved a long stick that had been propped against one of the rocks ringing the fire. With his finger, he slid several sizzling pieces of bacon off the stick and into the captain's bowl, and then set the big piece of bannock on top. They had with them a variety of food. Kahlan shared the carriage with all the supplies Richard had picked up along their journey north to Hartland. They had enough staples to last for a good long time.

"Thank you," Captain Meiffert stammered. He brushed back his fall of blond hair. "It looks delicious."

"It is," Richard said. "You're lucky: I made dinner tonight, instead of Cara."

Cara, proud of being a poor cook, smiled as if it were an accomplishment of note.

Kahlan was sure it was a story that would be repeated to wide eyes and stunned disbelief: the Lord Rahl himself serving food to one of his men. By the way the captain ate, she guessed it had been longer than a day since he had eaten. As big as he was, she figured he had to need a lot of food.

He swallowed and looked up. "My horse." He began to stand. "When Mistress Cara . . . I forgot my horse. I need—"

"Eat your food." Richard stood and clapped Captain Meiffert's shoulder to keep him seated. "I was going to check on our horses anyway. I'll see to yours as well. I'm sure it would like some water and oats, too."

"But, Lord Rahl, I can't allow you to—"

"Eat. This will save time; when I get back, you'll be done and then you can give me your report." Richard's shape became indistinct as he dissolved into the shadows, leaving only a disembodied voice behind. "But I'm afraid I still won't have any orders for General Reibisch."

In the stillness, crickets once again took up their rhythmic chirping. Some distance away, Kahlan heard a night bird calling. Beyond the nearby trees, the horses whinnied contentedly, probably when Richard greeted them. Every once in a while a feather of mist strayed in under the overhang to dampen her cheek. She wished she could turn on her side and close her eyes. Richard had given her some herb tea and it was beginning to make her drowsy. At least it dulled the pain, too.

"How are you, Mother Confessor?" Captain Meiffert asked. "Everyone is terribly worried about you."

A Confessor wasn't often confronted with such honest and warm concern. The young man's simple question was so sincere it almost brought Kahlan to tears.

"I'm getting better, Captain. Tell everyone I'll be fine after I've had some time to heal. We're going someplace quiet where I can enjoy the fresh air of the arriving summer and get some rest. I'll be better before autumn, I'm sure. By then, I hope Richard will be . . . less worried about me, and be able to put his mind to the needs of the war."

The captain smiled. "Everyone will be relieved to know you're healing. I can't tell you how many people told me that when I return they want to hear how you're doing."

"Tell them I said I'll be fine and I asked for them not to worry anymore about me, but to take care of themselves."

He ate another spoonful. Kahlan saw in his eyes that there was more to the man's anxiety. It took him a moment before he addressed it.

"We are concerned, too, that you and Lord Rahl need protection."

Cara, already sitting straight, nevertheless managed to straighten more, at the same time making the subtle shift in her posture appear threatening. "Lord Rahl and the Mother Confessor are not without protection, Captain; they have me. Anything more than a Mord-Sith is just pretty brass buttons."

This time, he didn't back down. His voice rang with the clear tone of authority. "This is not a matter of disrespect, Mistress Cara, nor is presumption intended. Like you, I am sworn to their safety, and that is my proper concern. These brass buttons have met the enemy before in the defense of Lord Rahl, and I don't really believe a Mord-Sith would want to deter me from that duty for no more reason than petty pride."

"We're going to a remote and secluded place," Kahlan said, before Cara could answer. "I think our solitude, and Cara, will be ample protection. If Richard wishes it otherwise, he will say so."

With a reluctant nod, he accepted her answer. The last of it, anyway, settled the matter.

When Richard had taken Kahlan north, he had left their guard forces behind. She knew it was deliberate, probably part of his conviction about what he felt he had to do. Richard wasn't opposed to the concept of protection; in the past, he had accepted troops being with them. Cara, too, had been insistent on having the security of those troops along. It was different, though, for Cara to admit it directly to Captain Meiffert.

They had spent a good deal of time in Anderith with the captain and his elite forces. Kahlan knew him to be a superb officer. She thought he must be approaching his mid-twenties—probably a soldier for a decade already and the veteran of a number of campaigns, from minor rebellions to open warfare. The sharp wholesome lines of his face were just beginning to take on a mature set.

Over millennia, through war, migration, and occupation, other cultures had mixed

44

in with the D'Haran, leaving a blend of peoples. Tall and broad-shouldered, Captain Meiffert was marked as full-blooded D'Haran by blond hair and blue eyes, as was Cara. The bond was strongest in full-blooded D'Harans.

After he had finished about half his rice, he glanced over his shoulder, into the darkness where Richard had gone. His earnest blue eyes took in both Cara and Kahlan.

"I don't mean it to sound judgmental or personal, and I hope I'm not speaking out of turn, but may I ask you both a . . . a sensitive question?"

"You may, Captain," Kahlan said. "But I can't promise we will answer it."

The last part gave him pause for a moment, but then he went on. "General Reibisch and some of the other officers . . . well, there have been worried discussions about Lord Rahl. We trust in him, of course," he was quick to add. "We really do. It's just that . . ."

"So what are your concerns, then, Captain?" Cara put in, her brow drawing tight. "If you trust him so much."

He stirred his wooden spoon around the bowl. "I was there in Anderith through the whole thing. I know how hard he worked—and you, too, Mother Confessor. No Lord Rahl before him ever worried about what the people wanted. In the past, the only thing that mattered was what the Lord Rahl wanted. Then, after all that, the people rejected his offer—rejected him. He sent us back to the main force, and just left us"—he gestured around himself—"to come here. Out in the middle of nowhere. To be a recluse, or something." He paused while searching for the right words. "We don't . . . understand it, exactly."

He looked up from the fire, back into their eyes, as he went on. "We're worried that Lord Rahl has lost his will to fight—that he simply no longer cares. Or perhaps . . . he is afraid to fight?"

The look on his face told Kahlan that he feared reprisal for saying the things he said, and for asking such a question, but he needed the answer enough to risk it. This was probably why he had come to give a report, rather than send a simple messenger.

"About six hours before he cooked that nice dinner pot of rice and beans," Cara said in a casual manner, "he killed a couple dozen men. All by himself. Hacked them apart like I've never seen before. The violence of it shocked even me. He left only one man for me to dispatch. Quite unfair of him, I think."

Captain Meiffert looked positively relieved as he let out a long breath. He looked away from Cara's steady gaze and back into his bowl to stir his dinner.

"That news will be well received. Thank you for telling me, Mistress Cara."

"He can't issue orders," Kahlan said, "because he unequivocally believes that, for now, if he takes part in leading our forces against the Imperial Order, it would bring about our defeat. He believes that if he enters the battle too soon, we will then have no chance of ever winning. He believes he must wait for the right time, that's all. There's nothing more to it."

Kahlan felt a bit conflicted, helping to justify Richard's actions, when she wasn't entirely in favor of them. She felt it was necessary to check the advance of the Imperial Order's army now, and not give them a chance to freely pillage and murder the people of the New World.

The captain mulled this over as he ate some bannock. He frowned as he gestured with the piece he had left. "There is sound battle theory for such a strategy. If you have any choice in it, you only attack when it's on your terms, not the enemy's."

He became more spirited as he thought about it a moment. "It is better to hold an attack for the right moment, despite the damage an enemy can cause in the interim, than to go into a battle before the right time. Such would be an act of poor command."

"That's right." Kahlan laid her arm back and rested her right wrist on her brow. "Perhaps you could explain it to the other officers in those words—that it's premature to issue orders, and he's waiting for the proper time. I don't think that's really any different from the way Richard has explained it to us, but perhaps it would be better understood if put in such terms."

The captain ate the last bite of his bannock, seeming to think it over. "I trust Lord Rahl with my life. I know the others do, too, but I think they will be reassured by such an explanation as to why he is withholding his orders. I can see now why he had to leave us—it was to resist the temptation to throw himself into the fray before the time was right."

Kahlan wished she was as confident of the reasoning as the captain. She recalled Cara's question, wondering how the people could prove themselves to Richard. She knew he would not be inclined to try it through a vote again, but she didn't see how else the people could prove themselves to him.

"I'd not mention it to Richard," she said. "It's difficult for him—not being able to issue orders. He's trying to do what he believes is right, but it's a difficult course to hold to."

"I understand, Mother Confessor. 'In his wisdom we are humbled. We live only to serve. Our lives are his.' "

Kahlan studied the smooth lines and simple angles of his young face lit by the dancing firelight. In that face, she saw some of what Richard had been trying to say to her before. "Richard doesn't believe your lives are his, Captain, but that they are your own, and priceless. That is what he is fighting for."

He chose his words carefully; if he wasn't worried about her being the Mother Confessor, since he hadn't grown up fearing the power and the rule of such a woman, she was still the Lord Rahl's wife.

"Most of us see how different he is from the last Lord Rahl. I'm not claiming that any of us understands everything about him, but we know he fights to defend, rather than to conquer. As a soldier, I know the difference it makes to believe in what I'm fighting for, because . . ."

The captain looked away from her gaze. He lifted a short branch of firewood, tapping the end on the ground for a time. His voice took on a painful inflection. "Because it takes something precious out of you to kill people who never meant you any harm."

The fire crackled and hissed as he slowly stirred the glowing coals. Sparks swirled up to spill out from around the underside of the rock overhang.

Cara watched her Agiel as she rolled it in her fingers. "You . . . feel that way too?"

Captain Meiffert met Cara's gaze. "I never realized, before, what it was doing to me, inside. I didn't know. Lord Rahl makes me proud to be D'Haran. He makes it stand for something right. . . . It never did before. I thought that the way things were, was just the way things were, and they could never change."

Cara's gaze fell away as she privately nodded her agreement. Kahlan could only imagine what life was like living under that kind of rule, what it did to people.

"I'm glad you understand, Captain," Kahlan whispered. "That's one reason he worries so much about all of you. He wants you to live lives you can be proud of. Lives that are your own."

He dropped the stick into the fire. "And he wanted all the people of Anderith to care about themselves the way he wants us to value our lives. The vote wasn't really for him, but for themselves. That was why the vote meant so much to him?"

"That's why," Kahlan confirmed, afraid to test her own voice any further than that.

He stirred his spoon around to cool his dinner. It no longer needed cooling, she was sure. She supposed his thoughts were being stirred more than his dinner.

"You know," he said, "one of the things I heard people say, back in Anderith, was that since Darken Rahl was his father, Richard Rahl was evil, too. They said that since his father had done wrong, Richard Rahl might sometimes *do* good, but he could never *be* a good person."

"I heard that too," Cara said. "Not just in Anderith, but a lot of places."

"That's wrong. Why should people think that just because one of his parents was cruel, those crimes pass on to someone who never did them? And that he must spend his life making amends? I'd hate to think that if I'm ever lucky enough to have children, they, and then their children, and their children after that, would have to suffer forever for the things I've done serving under Darken Rahl." He looked over at Kahlan and Cara. "Such prejudice isn't right."

In the silence, Cara stared into the flames.

"I served under Darken Rahl. I know the difference in the two men." His voice lowered with simmering anger. "It's wrong of people to lay guilt for the crimes of Darken Rahl onto his son."

"You're right about that," Cara murmured. "The two may look a little alike, but anyone who has ever looked into the eyes of both men, as I have, could never begin to think they were the same kind of men."

47

Captain Meiffert ate the rest of his rice and beans in silence. Cara offered him her waterskin. He took it with a smile and his nod of thanks. She dished him out a second bowlful from the pot, and cut him another piece of bannock. He looked only slightly less mortified to be served by a Mord-Sith than by the Lord Rahl. Cara found his expression amusing. She called him "Brass Buttons" and told him to eat it all. He did so as they listened to the sounds of the fire snapping and water dripping from the pine needles onto the carpet of leaves and other debris of the forest floor.

Richard returned, loaded down with the captain's bedroll and saddlebags. He let them slip to the ground beside the officer and then shook water off himself before sitting down beside Kahlan. He offered her a drink from a full waterskin he'd brought back. She took only a sip. She was more interested in being able to rest her hand on his leg.

Richard yawned. "So, Captain Meiffert, you said the general wanted you to give a full report?"

"Yes, sir." The captain went into a long and detailed account on the state of the army to the south, how they were stationed out on the plains, what passes they guarded in the mountains, and how they planned on using the terrain, should the Imperial Order suddenly come up out of Anderith and move north into the Midlands. He reported on the health of the men and their supply situation—both good. The other half of General Reibisch's D'Haran force was back in Aydindril, protecting the city, and Kahlan was relieved to hear that everything there was in order.

Captain Meiffert relayed all the communications they'd received from around the Midlands, including from Kelton and Galea, two of the largest lands of the Midlands that were now allied with the new D'Haran Empire. The allied lands were helping to keep the army supplied, in addition to providing men for rotation of patrols, scouting land they knew better, and other work.

Kahlan's half brother, Harold, had brought word that Cyrilla, Kahlan's half sister, had taken a turn for the better. Cyrilla had been queen of Galea. After her brutal treatment in the hands of the enemy, she became emotionally unbalanced and was unable to serve as queen. In her rare conscious moments, worried for her people, she had begged Kahlan to be queen in her stead. Kahlan had reluctantly agreed, saying it was only until Cyrilla was well again. Few people thought she would ever have her mind back, but, apparently, it looked as if she might yet recover.

In order to soothe the ruffled feathers of Galea's neighboring land, Kelton, Richard had named Kahlan queen of Kelton. When Kahlan first heard what Richard had done, she had thought it was lunacy. Strange as the arrangement was, though, it suited both lands, and brought them not only peace with each other, but also into the fold of those lands fighting against the Imperial Order.

Cara was pleasantly surprised to hear that a number of Mord-Sith had arrived at the Confessors' Palace in Aydindril, in case Lord Rahl needed them. Berdine would no doubt be pleased to have some of her sister Mord-Sith with her in Aydindril.

Kahlan missed Aydindril. She guessed the place you grew up could never leave your heart. The thought gave her a pang of sorrow for Richard.

"That would be Rikka," Cara said with a smile. "Wait until she meets the new Lord Rahl," she added under her breath, finding that even more to smile about.

Kahlan's thoughts turned to the people they had left to the Imperial Order—or more accurately, to the people who had chosen the Imperial Order. "Have you received any reports from Anderith?"

"Yes, from a number of men we sent in there. I'm afraid we lost some, too. The ones who returned report that there were fewer enemy deaths from the poisoned waters than we had hoped. Once the Imperial Order discovered their soldiers dying, or sick, they tested everything on the local people, first. A number of them died or became sick, but it wasn't widespread. By using the people to test the food and water, they were able to isolate the tainted food and destroy it. The army has been been laying claim to everything—they use a lot of supplies."

The Imperial Order was said to be far larger than any army ever assembled. Kahlan knew that much of the reports to be accurate. The Order dwarfed the D'Haran and Midland troops arrayed against them perhaps ten or twenty to one— some reports claimed more than that. Some reports claimed the New World forces were outnumbered by a hundred to one, but Kahlan discounted that as outright panic. She didn't know how long the Order would feed off Anderith before they moved on, or if they were being resupplied from the Old World. They had to be, to some extent, anyway.

"How many scouts and spies did we lose?" Richard asked.

Captain Meiffert looked up. It was the first question Richard had asked. "Some may yet turn up, but it appears likely that we lost fifty to sixty men."

Richard sighed. "And General Reibisch thinks it was worth losing the lives of those men to discover this?"

Captain Meiffert cast about for an answer. "We didn't know what we would discover, Lord Rahl; that was why we sent them in. Do you wish me to tell the general not to send in any more men?"

Richard was carving a face in a piece of firewood, sporadically tossing shavings into the fire. He sighed.

"No, he must do as he sees fit. I've explained to him that I can't issue orders."

The captain, watching Richard pick small chips of wood from his lap and pitch them into the fire, tossed a small fan of pine needles into the flames, where it blazed in short-lived glory. Richard's carving was a remarkably good likeness of the captain.

Kahlan had, on occasion, seen Richard casually carve animals or people. She once had strongly suggested that his ability was guided by his gift. He scoffed at such a notion, saying that he had liked to carve ever since he was little. She reminded him that art was used to cast spells, and that once he had been captured with the aid of a drawn spell.

He insisted this was nothing like that. As a guide, he said he'd passed many an evening at camp, by himself, carving. Not wanting to carry the added weight, he would toss the finished piece into the fire. He said he enjoyed the act of carving, and could always carve another. Kahlan considered the carvings inspired and found it distressing to see them destroyed.

"What do you intend to do, Lord Rahl? If I may ask."

Richard took a smooth, steady slice that demarcated the line of an ear, bringing it to life along with the line of the jaw he had already cut. He looked up and stared off into the night.

"We're going to a place back in the mountains, where other people don't go, so we can be alone, and safe. The Mother Confessor will be able to get well there and gain back her strength. While we're there, I may even make Cara start wearing a dress."

Cara shot to her feet. "What!" When she saw Richard's smile, Cara realized he was only joking. She fumed, nonetheless.

"I'd not report that part of it to the general, were I you, Captain," Richard said.

Cara sank back down to the ground. "Not if Brass Buttons, here, values his ribs," she muttered.

Kahlan struggled not to chuckle, lest she twist the ever present knives in her ribs. Sometimes, she felt as if she knew how the chunk of wood Richard was carving felt. It was good to see Richard, for once, get the best of Cara. It was usually she who had him flustered.

"I can't help you, for now," Richard said, his serious tone returning. He went back to his work with his knife. "I hope you can all accept that."

"Of course, Lord Rahl. We know that you will lead us into battle when the time is right."

"I hope that day comes, Captain. I really do. Not because I want to fight, but because I hope there to be something to fight for." Richard stared into the fire, his countenance a chilling vision of despair. "Right now, there isn't."

"Yes, Lord Rahl," Captain Meiffert said, finally breaking the uncomfortable silence. "We will do as we think best until the Mother Confessor is better and you are then able to join us."

Richard didn't argue the time schedule, as the captain had described it. It was one Kahlan hoped for, too, but Richard had never said it would be that soon. He had, in fact, made it clear to them that the time might not ever come. He cradled the wood in his lap, studying what he had done.

He ran his thumb along the fresh-cut line of the nose as he asked, "Did the returning scouts say . . . how it faired for the people in Anderith . . . with the Imperial Order there?"

Kahlan knew he was only torturing himself by asking that question. She wished he hadn't asked; it could do him no good to hear the answer.

Captain Meiffert cleared his throat. "Well, yes, they did report on the conditions."

"And . . .?"

The young officer launched into a cold report of the facts they knew. "Jagang set up his troop headquarters in the capital, Fairfield. He took over the Minister of Culture's estate for himself. Their army is so huge that it swallowed the city and overflows far out onto the hills all around. The Anderith army put up little resistance. They were collected and all summarily put to death. The government of Anderith for the most part ceased to exist within the first few hours. There is no rule or law. The Order spent the first week in unchecked celebration.

"Most people in Fairfield were displaced and lost everything they owned. Many fled. The roads all around were packed solid with those trying to escape what was happening in the city. The people fleeing the city only ended up being the spoils for the soldiers in the hills all around who couldn't fit into the city. Only a trickle—mostly the very old and sickly—made it past that gauntlet."

His impersonal tone abandoned him. He had spent time with those people, too. "I'm afraid that, in all, it went badly for them, Lord Rahl. There was a horrendous amount of killing, of the men, anyway—in the tens of thousands. Likely more."

"They got what they asked for." Cara's voice was as cold as winter night. "They picked their own fate." Kahlan agreed, but didn't say so. She knew Richard agreed, too. None of them were pleased about it, though.

"And the countryside?" Richard asked. "Anything known about places outside Fairfield? Is it going better for them?"

"No better, Lord Rahl. The Imperial Order has been methodically going about a process of 'pacifying' the land, as they call it. Their soldiers are accompanied by the gifted.

"By far, the worst of the accounts were about one called 'Death's Mistress.' "

"Who?" Cara asked.

" 'Death's Mistress,' they call her."

"Her. Must be the Sisters," Richard said.

"Which ones do you think it would be?" Cara asked.

Richard, cutting the mouth into the firewood face, shrugged. "Jagang has both Sisters of the Light and Sisters of the Dark held captive. He's a dream walker; he forces both to do his bidding. It could be either; the woman is simply his tool."

"I don't know," Captain Meiffert said. "We've had plenty of reports about the Sisters, and how dangerous they are. But they're being used like you said, as tools of the army—weapons, basically—not as his agents. Jagang doesn't let them think for themselves or direct anything.

"This one, from the reports, anyway, behaves very differently from the others. She acts as Jagang's agent, but still, the word is she decides things for herself, and does as she pleases. The men who came back reported that she is more feared than Jagang himself.

"The people of one town, when they heard she was coming their way, all gathered together in the town square. They made the children drink poison first, then the adults took their dose. Every last person in the town was dead when the woman arrived—close to five hundred people."

Richard had stopped carving as he listened. Kahlan knew that unfounded rumors could also be so lurid as to turn alarm into deadly panic, to the point where people would rather die than face the object of their dread. Fear was a powerful tool of war.

Richard went back to the carving in his lap. He held the knife near the tip of the point, like a pen, and carefully cut character into the eyes. "They didn't get a name for her, did they? This Death's Mistress?"

"I'm sorry, no, Lord Rahl. They said she is simply called by everyone 'Death's Mistress.' "

"Sounds like an ugly witch," Cara said.

"Quite the contrary. She has blue eyes and long blond hair. She is said to be one of the most beautiful women you could ever lay eyes upon. They say she looks like a vision of a good spirit."

Kahlan couldn't help notice the captain's furtive glance at Cara, who had blue eyes and long blond hair, and was also one of the most beautiful women you could ever lay eyes upon. She, too, was deadly.

Richard was frowning. "Blond . . . blue eyes . . . there are several it could be. . . . Too bad they didn't catch her name."

"Sorry, but they gave no other name, Lord Rahl, only that description. . . . Oh yes, and that she always wears black."

"Dear spirits," Richard whispered as he rose to his full height, gripping his carving by its throat.

"From what I've been told, Lord Rahl, though she looks like a vision of one, the good spirts themselves would fear her."

"With good reason." Richard said, as he stared into the distance, as if looking beyond the black wall of mist to a place only he could see.

"You know her, then, Lord Rahl?"

Kahlan listened to the fire pop and crackle as she waited along with the other two for his answer. It almost seemed Richard was trying to find his voice as his gaze sank back down to meet the eyes of the carving in his hand.

"I know her," he said, at last. "I know her all too well. She was one of my teachers at the Palace of the Prophets."

Richard tossed his carving into the flames.

"Pray you never have to look into Nicci's eyes, Captain."

L ook into my eyes, child," Nicci said in her soft, silken voice as she cupped the girl's chin.

Nicci lifted the bony face. The eyes, dark and wide-set, blinked with dull bewilderment. There was nothing to be seen in them: the girl was simple.

Nicci straightened, feeling a hollow disappointment. She always did. She sometimes found herself looking into people's eyes, like this, and then wondering why. If she was searching for something, she didn't know what it was.

She resumed her leisurely walk down the line of the townspeople, all assembled along one side of the dusty market square. People in outlying farms and smaller communities no doubt came into the town several times a month, on market days, some staying overnight if they had come from far away. This wasn't a market day, but it would suit her purpose well enough.

A few of the crowded buildings had a second story, typically a room or two for a family over their small shop. Nicci saw a bakery, a cobbler's shop, a shop selling pottery, a blacksmith, an herbalist, a shop offering leatherwork—the usual places. One of these towns was much the same as the next. Many of the town's people worked the surrounding fields of wheat or sorghum, tended animals, and had extensive vegetable plots. Dung, straw, and clay being plentiful, they lived in homes of daub and wattle. A few of the shops with a second story boasted beam construction with clapboard siding.

Behind her, sullen soldiers bristling with weapons filled the majority of the square. They were tired from the hot ride, and worse, bored. Nicci knew they were a twitch away from a rampage. A town, even one with meager plunder, was an inviting diversion. It wasn't so much the taking as the breaking that they liked. Sometimes, though, it was the taking. The nervous women only rarely met the soldiers' bold stares.

As she strolled past the scruffy people, Nicci looked into the eyes watching her. Most were wide with terror and fixed not on the soldiers, but on the object of their dread: Nicci—or as people had taken to calling her, "Death's Mistress." The designation neither pleased nor displeased her; it was simply a fact she noted, a fact of no more significance to her than if someone had told her that they had mended a pair of her stockings.

Some, she knew, were staring at the gold ring through her lower lip. Gossip would have already informed them that a woman so marked was a personal slave to Emperor Jagang—something lower even than simple peasants such as themselves. That they stared at the gold ring, or what they thought of her for it, was of even less significance to her than being called "Death's Mistress."

Jagang only possessed her body in this world; the Keeper would have her soul for eternity in the next. Her body's existence in this world was torment; her spirit's existence in the next would be no less. Existence and torment were simply the two sides of the same coin—there could be no other.

Smoke, rolling up from the fire pit over her left shoulder, sailed away on a fitful wind to make a dark slash across the bright blue afternoon sky. Stacked stones to each side of the communal cooking pit supported a rod above the fire. Two or three pigs or sheep, skewered on the rod, could be roasted at once. Temporary sides were probably available to convert the fire pit into a smokehouse.

At other times, an outdoor fire pit was used, often in conjunction with butchering, for the making of soap, since making soap was not something typically done indoors. Nicci saw a wooden ash pit, used for making lye, standing to the side of the open area, along with a large iron kettle that could be used for rendering fat. Lye and fat were the primary ingredients of soap. Some women liked to add fragrance to their soap with herbs and such, like lavender or rosemary.

When Nicci was little, her mother made her go each autumn, when the butchering was being done, to help people make soap. Her mother said helping others built proper character. Nicci still had a few small dots of scars on the backs of her hands and forearms where she had been splashed and blistered by the hot fat. Nicci's mother always made her wear a fine dress—not to impress the other people who didn't have such clothes, but to make Nicci conspicuous and uncomfortable. The attention her pink dress attracted was not admiration. As she stood with the long wooden paddle, stirring the bubbling kettle while the lye was being poured in, some of the other children, trying to splash the dress and ruin it, burned Nicci, too. Nicci's mother had said the burns were the Creator's punishment.

As Nicci moved past, inspecting the assembled people, the only sounds were the horses off behind the buildings, the sporadic coughs of people, and the flags of flame in the fire pit snapping and flapping in the breeze. The soldiers had already helped themselves to the two pigs that had been roasting on the rod, so the aroma of cooking meat had mostly dissipated on the wind, leaving the sour smells of sweat and the stink of human habitation. Whether a belligerent army or a peaceful town, the filth of people smelled the same.

"You all know why I'm here," Nicci announced. "Why have you people made me go to the trouble of such a journey?" She gazed down the line of maybe two hundred people standing four and five deep. The soldiers, who had ordered them out of their homes and in from the fields, greatly outnumbered them. She stopped in front of a man she had noticed people glancing at.

"Well?"

The wind fluttered his thin gray hair across his balding, bowed head as he fixed his gaze on the ground at her feet. "We don't have anything to give, Mistress. We're a poor community. We have nothing."

"You are a liar. You had two pigs. You saw fit to have a gluttonous feast instead of helping those in need."

"But we have to eat." It was not an argument, so much as a plea.

"So do others, but they are not so fortunate as you. They know only the ache of hunger in their bellies every night. What an ugly tragedy, that every day thousands of children die from the simple want of food, and millions more know the gnawing pain of hunger—while people like you, in a land of plenty, offer nothing but selfish excuses. Having what they need to live is their right, and must be honored by those with the means to help.

54

"Our soldiers, too, need to eat. Do you think our struggle on the behalf of the people is easy? These men risk their lives daily so you may raise your children in a proper, civilized society. How can you look these men in the eye? How can we even feed our troops, if everyone doesn't help support the cause?"

The trembling man remained mute.

"What must I do to impress upon you people the seriousness of your obligation to the lives of others? Your contribution to those in need is a solemn moral duty—sharing in a greater good."

Nicci's vision suddenly went white. With a pain like scorching hot needles driven into her ears, Jagang's voice filled her mind.

Why must you play this game? Make examples of people! Teach them a lesson that I am not to be ignored!

Nicci swayed on her feet. She was completely blinded by the pain bursting inside her head. She let it wash through her, as if watching it happen to a stranger. Her abdominal muscles twitched and convulsed. A rusty, barbed lance driven up through her, ripping her insides, could not have hurt more. Her arms hung limp at her sides while she waited for Jagang's displeasure to end, or for death.

She was unable to tell how long the torture lasted. When he was doing it, she was never able to sense time—the pain was too all-consuming. She knew, from what others told her when they saw it done to her, and from seeing it done to others, that it sometimes lasted only an instant. Sometimes it lasted hours.

Making it last hours was a waste of Jagang's effort—she couldn't tell the difference. She had told him as much.

Suddenly, she was unable to draw a breath. It felt like a fist squeezed her heart to a stop. She thought her lungs might burst. Her knees were about to buckle.

Do not disobey me again!

With a gasp, air filled her lungs. Jagang's discipline ended, as it always did, with an impossibly tart, sour taste on her tongue, like an unexpected mouthful of fresh raw lemon juice, and pain searing the nerves at the back of her jaw under her earlobes. It left her head ringing and her teeth throbbing. As she opened her eyes, she was surprised, as she always was, not to see herself standing in a pool of blood. She touched the corner of her mouth, and then brushed her fingers to an ear. She found no blood.

She wondered in passing why Jagang had been able to come into her mind now. Sometimes, he couldn't. It didn't happen that way for any of the other Sisters—he always had access to their minds.

As her vision cleared, she saw people staring at her. They didn't know why she had paused. The young men—and a few of the older ones, too—were sneaking peeks at her body. They were used to seeing women in drab, shapeless dresses, women whose bodies exhibited the toll taken by endless hard work and almost constant pregnancy from the time they were old enough for the seed to catch. They had never before seen a woman like Nicci, standing straight and tall, looking them in the eye, wearing a fine black dress that hugged a nearly flawless shape marred by neither hard work or the labor of birth. The stark black material contrasted the pale curve of cleavage revealed by the cut of the laced bodice. Nicci was numb to such stares. Occasionally, they suited her purposes, but most of the time they didn't, and so she disregarded them.

She began walking down the line of people again, ignoring Emperor Jagang's orders. She rarely complied with his orders. She was, for the most part, indifferent to his punishment. If anything, she welcomed it.

Nicci, forgive me. You know I don't mean to hurt you.

She ignored his voice, too, as she studied the eyes peering up at her. Not everyone did. She liked to look into the eyes of those courageous enough to risk a glimpse of her. Most were filled with simple terror.

There would soon be abundant justification for such apprehension.

Nicci, you must do as I tell you, or you are only going to end up forcing me to do something terrible to you. Neither of us wants that. Someday, I am going to end up doing something from which you will be unable to recover.

If that is what you wish to do, then do it, she thought, in answer.

It was not a challenge; she simply didn't care.

You know I don't want to do that, Nicci.

Without the pain, his voice was little more than a fly annoying her. She paid it no heed. She addressed the crowd.

"Do you people have any concept of the effort being put into the fight for your future? Or is it that you expect to benefit without contributing? Many of our brave men have given their lives fighting the oppressors of the people, fighting for our new beginning. We struggle so that all people will be able to share equally in the coming prosperity. You must help us in our effort on your behalf. Just as helping those in need is the moral obligation of every person, so, too, is this."

Commander Kardeef, displaying a look of sour displeasure, planted himself in front of her. The sunlight slanting across his lined face cast his hooded eyes in deep shadows. She was not moved by his disfavor. He was never satisfied with anything. Well, she corrected herself, almost never.

"People can only achieve virtue through obedience and sacrifice. Your contribution to the Order is to implement their compliance. We are not here to hold civic lessons!"

Commander Kardeef was confident in his privileged mastery over her. He, too, had given her pain. She endured what Kadar Kardeef did to her with the same detachment with which she endured what Jagang did to her.

Only in the furthest depths of pain could she begin to feel anything. Even pain was preferable to the nothingness she usually felt.

Kadar Kardeef was probably unaware of the punishment Jagang had just completed, or his orders; His Excellency didn't use Commander Kardeef's mind. It was an arduous undertaking for Jagang to control those who didn't possess the gift—he could do it, but it was rarely worth his effort; he had the gifted to control people for him. A dream walker somehow used the gift in those who possessed it in order to help complete the connection to their minds. In a way, the gifted made it possible for Jagang to so easily control them.

Kadar Kardeef glowered down at her as she gazed up at his darkly tanned and creased face. He was an imposing figure, with the studded leather straps that crossed his massive chest, his armored leather shoulder and breast plates, his chain mail, his array of well-used weapons. Nicci had seen him crush men's throats in one of his big, powerful hands. As silent witness to his bravery in battle, he bore a number of scars. She had seen them all.

Few officers ranked higher or were more trusted than Kadar Kardeef. He had been with the Order since his youth, rising through the ranks to fight alongside Jagang as they expanded the empire of the Imperial Order out of their homeland of Altur'Rang to eventually subjugate the rest of the Old World. Kadar Kardeef was the hero of the Little Gap campaign, the man who almost single-handedly turned the course of the battle, breaking through enemy lines and personally slaying the three great kings who had joined forces to trap and crush the Imperial Order before it could seize the imaginations of the millions of people living in a patchwork of kingdoms, fiefdoms, clans, city-states, and vast regions controlled by alliances of warlords.

The Old World had been a tinderbox, waiting for the spark of revolution. The preachings of the Order were that spark. If the high priests were the Order's soul, Jagang was its bone and muscle. Few people understood Jagang's genius—they saw only a dream walker, or a ferocious warrior. He was far more.

It had taken Jagang decades to finally bring the rest of the Old World to heel—to put the Order on its final path to greater glory. During those years of struggle for the Order, while engaged in nearly constant war, Jagang toiled building the road system that allowed him to move men and supplies great distances with lightning speed. The more lands and peoples he annexed, the more laborers he put to the construction of yet more roads by which he could conquer yet more territory. He was thus able to maintain communications and to react to situations faster than anyone would have believed possible. Formerly isolated lands were suddenly connected to the rest of the Old World. Jagang had knitted them together with a net of roads. Along those roads, the people of the Old World had risen up to follow him as he forged the way for the Order.

Kadar Kardeef had been part of it all. More than once he had taken wounds to save Jagang's life. Jagang had once taken a bolt from a crossbow to save Kardeef. If Jagang could be said to have a friend, Kadar Kardeef was as close as any came to it.

Nicci first met Kardeef when he had come to the Palace of the Prophets in Tanimura to pray. Old King Gregory, who had ruled the land including Tanimura, had disappeared without a trace. Kadar Kardeef was a solemnly devout man; before battle he prayed to the Creator for the blood of the enemy, and after, for the souls of the men he had killed. That day he was said to have prayed for the soul of King Gregory. The Imperial Order was suddenly the new rule in Tanimura. The people celebrated in the streets for days.

Over the course of three thousand years, the Sisters, from their home at the Palace of the Prophets in Tanimura, had seen governments come and go. For the most part, the Sisters, led by their prelate, considered matters of rule a petty foolishness best ignored. They believed in a higher calling. The Sisters believed they would remain at the Palace of the Prophets, undisturbed in their work, long after the Order had vanished into the dust of history. Revolutions had many times come and gone. This one, though, caught them up.

Kadar Kardeef had been nearly twenty years younger, then—a handsome conqueror riding into the city. Many of the Sisters were fascinated by the man. Nicci never was. But he was fascinated by her.

Emperor Jagang, of course, did not send such invaluable men as Commander Kardeef out to pacify conquered lands. He had entrusted Kardeef with a much more important task: guarding his valuable property—Nicci.

Nicci turned her attention away from Kadar Kardeef and back to the people.

She settled her gaze on the man who had spoken before. "We cannot allow anyone to shirk their responsibility to others and to our new beginning."

"Please, Mistress . . . We have nothing—"

"Disregard of our cause is treasonous."

He thought better of disagreeing with that pronouncement.

"You don't seem to understand that this man behind me wants you to see that the Imperial Order is resolute in their devotion to their cause—if you don't do your duty. I know you have heard the stories, but this man wants you to experience the grim reality. Imagining it is never quite the same. Never quite as gruesome."

She stared at the man, waiting for his answer. He licked his weather-cracked lips.

"We just need some more time. . . . Our crops are doing well. When the harvest comes in . . . we could contribute our fair share toward the struggle for . . . for . . ."

"The new beginning."

"Yes, Mistress," he said, bobbing his head, "the new beginning." When his gaze returned to the dirt at his feet, she moved on down the line.

Her purpose was not really to collect, but to cow.

The time had come.

A girl gazing up at her snagged Nicci to a stop, distracting her from what she had intended. The girl's big, dark eyes sparkled with innocent wonder. Everything was new to her, and she was eager to see it all. In her dark eyes shone that rare, fragile, and most perishable of qualities: a guileless view of life that had yet to be touched by pain or loss or evil.

Nicci cupped the girl's chin, staring into the depths of those thirsting eyes.

One of Nicci's earliest memories was of her mother standing over her like this, holding her chin, looking down at her. Nicci's mother was gifted, too. She said that the gift was a curse, and a test. It was a curse because it gave her abilities others didn't have, and it was a test to see if she would wrongly exert that superiority. Nicci's mother almost never used her gift. Servants handled the work; she spent most of her time nested among her clutch of friends, devoting herself to higher pursuits.

"Dear Creator, but Nicci's father is a monster," she would complain as she wrung her hands. Some of her friends would murmur their sympathy. "Why must he burden me so! I fear his eternal soul is beyond hope or prayer." The other women would tsk in grim agreement.

Her mother's eyes were the same dull brown as a cockroach's back. To Nicci's mind, they were set too close together. Her mouth, too, was narrow, as if fixed in place by her perpetual disapproval. While Nicci never really thought of her mother as homely, neither did she consider her beautiful, although her friends regularly reassured her that she most surely was.

Nicci's mother said beauty was a curse to a caring woman and a blessing only to whores.

Puzzled by her mother's displeasure of her father, Nicci had finally asked what he had done.

"Nicci," her mother had said, cupping Nicci's small chin that day. Nicci eagerly awaited her mother's words. "You have beautiful eyes, but you do not yet see with them. All people are miserable wretches—that is the lot of man. Do you have any idea how it hurts those without all your advantages to see your beautiful face? That is all you bring to others: insufferable pain. The Creator brought you into the world for no reason but to ease the misery of others, and here you bring only hurt." Her mother's friends, sipping tea, nodded, whispering to one another their sorrowful but firm agreement.

That was when Nicci had first learned that she bore the indelible stain of some shadowy, nameless, unconfessed evil.

Nicci gazed into the rare face looking up at her. Today this girl's dark eyes would see things they could not yet imagine. Those big eyes eagerly watched without seeing. She could not possibly understand what was to come, or why.

What kind of life could she have?

It would be for the best, this way.

The time had come.

Before she could begin, Nicci saw something that ignited her indignation. She whirled to a nearby woman.

"Where is there a washtub?"

Surprised by the question, the woman pointed a trembling finger toward a two-story building not far off. "There, Mistress. In the yard behind the pottery shop are laundry tubs where we were washing clothes."

Nicci seized the woman by her throat. "Get me a pair of scissors. Bring them to me there." The woman stared in wide-eyed fright. Nicci shoved her. "Now! Or would you prefer to die on the spot?"

Nicci yanked free a well-worn, reserve studded strap bunched with several others and secured over Commander Kardeef's shoulder. He made no effort to stop her, but as she gathered up the strap, he seized her upper arm in his powerful grip.

"You had better be planning on drowning this little brat—or maybe cutting off hunks of her hide and then stabbing out her eyes." His breath smelled of onion and ale. He smirked. "In fact, you start in on her, and while she's screaming and begging for her life, I'll begin separating out some young men, or perhaps I'll select some women to be an example. Which would you prefer, this time?"

Nicci turned her glare down at his fingers on her arm. He removed them as he growled a warning. She turned to the girl and whipped the strap twice around her neck to serve as a collar, twisting it into a handle in the back so she could control the girl with it. The girl squeaked in choked surprise. She had probably never been handled so roughly in her entire life. Nicci forced her ahead, toward the building the woman had pointed out.

Seeing how angry Nicci had suddenly become, no one followed. A woman not far off, undoubtedly the girl's mother, began to cry out in protest, but then fell silent as Kardeef's men turned their attention on her. By then Nicci already had the perplexed girl around the corner.

Out back, drab laundry, deformed and crumpled from its ordeal on the washboard, and now stretched and pinned to lines, twisted in the wind as if struggling to escape. Smoke from the fire pit peeked over the top of the building. The nervous woman waited with a large pair of shears.

Nicci marched the girl up to a tub of water, drove her down on her knees, and shoved her head under the water. While the girl struggled, Nicci snatched the scissors from the woman. Her chore completed, the woman held her apron up over her mouth to muffle her wails as she ran off in tears, not wanting to watch a child being murdered.

Nicci pulled the girl's head up out of the water, and while she sputtered and gasped for air, began clipping her dark, soaking wet hair close to the scalp. When

Nicci had finished cutting it off in sodden clumps, she dunked the girl again while leaning over and scooping up a cake of pale yellow soap from the washboard on the ground beside the tub. Nicci hauled the girl's head up and then began scrubbing. The girl screeched, flailing her spindly arms and clawing at the strap around her neck by which Nicci controlled her. Nicci realized she was probably hurting her, but from within the grip of rage, it was only a dim realization.

"What's the matter with you!" Nicci shook the gasping girl. "Don't you know you're crawling with lice?"

"But, but—"

The soap was harsh and as rough as a rasp. The girl squealed as Nicci bent her over and put more muscle into the scouring.

"Do you like having a head full of lice?"

"No—"

"Well, you must! Why else would you have them?"

"Please! I'll try to do better. I'll wash. I promise!"

Nicci remembered how much she hated catching lice from the places her mother sent her. She remembered scrubbing herself, using the harshest soap she could find, only to again be sent off to another place, where she would get infested with the hated things all over again.

When Nicci had scrubbed and dunked a dozen times, she finally dragged the girl to a tub of clean water and swished her head about in it to rinse her off. The girl blinked furiously, trying to clear her eyes of the stinging, soapy water as it streamed down off her face.

Gripping the girl's chin, Nicci peered into her red eyes. "No doubt your clothes are lousy with nits. You're to scrub your clothes every day—underthings, especially—or the lice will just be right back." Nicci squeezed the girl's cheeks until her eyes watered. "You are better than to be filthy with lice! Don't you know that?"

The girl nodded, as best as she could with Nicci's strong fingers holding her face. The big, dark, intelligent eyes, although red from the water and wide with shock, were still filled with that rare sense of wonder. As painful and frightening as the experience was, this had not dispelled it.

"Burn your bedding. Get new." Given the way these people lived and worked, it seemed a hopeless challenge. "Your whole family must burn their bedding. Wash all their clothes."

The girl nodded her oath.

Task completed, Nicci marched the girl back toward the gathered crowd. Forcing her along by the studded strap used as a collar, Nicci was unexpectedly struck by a memory.

It was a memory of the first time she had seen Richard.

Nearly every Sister at the Palace of the Prophets had been gathered in the great hall to see the new boy Sister Verna had brought in. Nicci lingered at the mahogany rail, twining around her finger a lace dangling from her bodice, only to pull the lace straight and then to twine it again, when the pair of thick walnut doors opened. The rumbling drone of conversation, sprinkled with bright laughter, trailed to an expectant hush as the group, led by Sister Phoebe, marched into the chamber, past the white columns topped by gold capitals, and in under the huge vaulted dome.

The birth of gifted boys was rare, and a cause of expectant delight when they were discovered and finally brought to live at the palace. A grand banquet was planned for that evening. Most of the Sisters, dressed in their finery, stood on the floor below, eager to meet the new boy. Nicci remained near the center of the lower balcony. She didn't care whether she met him or not.

It came as something of a shock to see how Sister Verna had aged on her journey. Such journeys typically lasted at most a year; this one, beyond the great barrier to the New World, had taken nearly twenty. Events beyond the barrier being uncertain, Verna had apparently been sent off on her mission too far in advance.

Life at the Palace of the Prophets was as long as it was serene. No one at the Palace of the Prophets appeared to have aged at all in so trifling a span of time as two decades, but away from the spell that enveloped the palace, Verna had. Verna, probably close to one hundred and sixty years old, had to be at least twenty years younger than Nicci; yet she now looked twice Nicci's age. People outside the palace aged at the normal rate, of course, but to see it happen so rapidly to a Sister . . .

As the roaring applause thundered on in the huge room, many of the Sisters wept over the momentous occasion. Nicci yawned. Sister Phoebe held up her hand until the room fell silent.

"Sisters." Phoebe's voice trembled. "Please welcome Sister Verna home." She finally had to raise a hand to again bring the clamor of applause to a halt.

When the room had quieted, she said, "And may I present our newest student, our newest child of the Creator, our newest charge." She turned and held an arm out in introduction, wiggling her fingers, urging the apparently timid boy forward as she went on. "Please welcome Richard Cypher to the Palace of the Prophets."

Several of the women stepped back out of the way as he strode forward. Nicci's eyes widened; her back straightened. It was not a young boy. He was grown into a man.

The crowd, despite their shock, clapped and cheered with the warmth of their welcome. Nicci didn't hear it. Her attention was riveted by those gray eyes of his. He was introduced to some of the nearby Sisters. The novice assigned to him, Pasha, was brought before him and tried to speak to him.

Richard brushed Pasha aside, a stag dismissing a vole, and stepped out alone into the center of the room. His whole bearing conveyed the same quality Nicci beheld in his eyes.

"I have something to say."

The vast chamber fell to an astonished hush.

His gaze swept the room. Nicci's breath caught when, for an instant, their eyes met, as he probably met countless others.

Her trembling fingers clutched the rail for support.

Nicci swore at that moment to do whatever was necessary to be named as one of his teachers.

His fingers tapped the Rada'Han around his neck.

"As long as you keep this collar on me, you are my captors, and I am your prisoner."

Murmurs hummed in the air. A Rada'Han was put around a boy's neck not just to govern him, but to protect him as well. The boys were never thought of as prisoners, but wards who needed security, care, and training. Richard, though, did not see it that way.

"Since I have committed no aggression against you, that makes us enemies. We are at war."

Several older Sisters teetered on their heels, nearly fainting. The faces of half the women in the room went red. The rest went white. Nicci could not have imagined such an attitude. His demeanor kept her from blinking, lest she overlook something. She drew slow breaths, lest she miss a word. Her pounding heart, though, was beyond her ability to control.

"Sister Verna has made a pledge to me that I will be taught to control the gift, and when I have learned what is required, I will be set free. For now, as long as you keep that pledge, we have a truce. But there are conditions."

Richard lifted a red leather rod hanging on a fine gold chain around his neck. At the time, Nicci hadn't known it to be the weapon of a Mord-Sith.

"I have been collared before. The person who put that collar on me brought me pain, to punish me, to teach me, to subdue me."

Nicci knew that such could be the only fate of one like him.

"That is the sole purpose of a collar. You collar a beast. You collar your enemies.

"I made her much the same offer I am making you. I begged her to release me. She would not. I was forced to kill her.

"Not one of you could ever hope to be good enough to lick her boots. She did as she did because she was tortured and broken, made mad enough to use a collar to hurt people. She did it against her nature.

"You . . ." His gaze swept all the eyes watching him. "You do it because you think it is your right. You enslave in the name of your Creator. I don't know your Creator. The only one beyond this world who I know would do as you do is the Keeper." The crowd gasped. "As far as I'm concerned, you may as well be the Keeper's disciples."

Little did he know that some of them were.

"If you do as she, and use this collar to bring me pain, the truce will be ended. You may think you hold the leash to this collar, but I promise you, if the truce ends, you will find that what you hold is a bolt of lightning."

The room was as silent as a tomb.

He was alone, defiant, in the midst of hundreds of sorceresses who knew how to harness every nuance of the power with which they were born; he knew next to nothing of his ability, and was collared by a Rada'Han besides. In this, he may have been a stag, but a stag challenging a congregation of lions. Hungry lions.

Richard rolled up his left sleeve. He drew his sword—a sword!—in defiance of the prodigious power arrayed before him. The distinctive ring of steel filled the silence as the blade was brought free.

Nicci stood spellbound as he listed his conditions.

He finally pointed back with the sword. "Sister Verna captured me. I have fought her every step of this journey. She has done everything short of killing me and draping my body over a horse to get me here. Though she, too, is my captor and enemy, I owe her certain debts. If anyone lays a finger to her because of me, I will kill that person, and the truce will be ended."

Nicci couldn't fathom such a strange sense of honor, but somehow she knew it fit what she saw in his eyes.

The crowd gasped as Richard drew his sword across the inside of his arm. He turned it, wiping both sides in the blood, until it dripped from the tip. Nicci could plainly see, even if the others could not—much as she saw in his eyes a quality others did not see—that the sword united with, and completed, magic within him.

His knuckles white around the hilt, he thrust the glistening crimson blade into the air.

"I give you a blood oath!" he cried out. "Harm the Baka Ban Mana, harm Sister

Verna, or harm me, and the truce will be ended, and I promise you we will have war! If we have war, I will lay waste to the Palace of the Prophets!"

From the upper balcony, where Richard couldn't see him, Jedidiah's mocking voice drifted out over the crowd. "All by yourself?"

"Doubt me at your peril. I am a prisoner; I have nothing to live for. I am the flesh of prophecy. I am the bringer of death."

No answer came in the stupefied silence. Probably every woman in the room knew of the prophecy of the bringer of death, though none was certain of its intended meaning. The text of that prophecy, along with all the others, was kept in the vaults deep under the Palace of the Prophets. That Richard knew it, that he dared declare it aloud in such company, augured the worst possible interpretation. Every lioness in the room retracted her claws in caution. Richard drove his sword home into its scabbard as if to punctuate his threat.

Nicci knew that the profound importance of what she had seen in his eyes and in his presence would forever haunt her.

She knew, too, that she must destroy him.

Nicci had to surrender favors and commit to obligations she never imagined she would have willingly done, but in return, she became one of Richard's six teachers. The burdens she had taken on in return for that privilege were all worth it when she sat alone with him, across a small table in his room, lightly holding his hands—if one could be said to lightly grasp lightning—endeavoring to teach him to touch his Han, the essence of life and spirit within the gifted. Try as he might, he felt nothing. That, in itself, was peculiar. The inkling of what she felt within him, though, was often enough to leave her unable to bring forth more than a few sparse words. She had casually questioned the others, and knew they were blind to it.

Although Nicci could not comprehend what it was about his intellect that his eyes and his conduct revealed, she did know that it disturbed the numb safety of her indifference. She ached to grasp it before she had to destroy him, and at the same time ached to destroy him before she did.

Whenever she became confident that she was beginning to unravel the mystery of his singular character, and thought she could predict what he would do in a given situation, he would confound her by doing something completely unexpected, if not impossible. Time and again he reduced to ashes what she had thought was the foundation of her understanding of him. She spent hours sitting alone, in abysmal misery, because it seemed to be in plain sight, yet she couldn't define it. She knew only that it was some principle important beyond measure, and it remained beyond her grasp.

Richard, never happy about his situation, became increasingly distant as time passed. Forlorn of hope, Nicci decided that the time had come.

When she went to his room for what she meant to be his final lesson and his end, he surprised her by offering her a rare white rose. Worse, he offered it with a smile and no explanation. As he held it out, she was so petrified that she could only manage to say, "Why, thank you, Richard." The white roses were from only one kind of place: dangerous restricted areas no student should ever have been able to enter. That he apparently could, and that he would so boldly offer her the proof of his trespass, startled her. She held the white rose carefully between a finger and thumb, not knowing if he was warning her—by giving her a forbidden thing—that he was the bringer of death, and she was being marked, or if it was a gesture of simple, if strange, kindness. She erred on the side of caution. Once again, his nature had stayed her hand.

The other Sisters of the Dark had plans of their own. Richard's gift, as far as Nicci was concerned, was probably the least remarkable and by far the least important thing about him, yet Liliana, one of his other teachers, a woman of boundless greed and limited insight, thought to steal the innate ability of his Han for herself. It sparked a lethal confrontation which Liliana lost. The six of them—their leader, Ulicia, and Richard's five remaining teachers—having been discovered, escaped with their lives and little else, only to end up in Jagang's clutches.

In the end, Nicci understood that quality in his eyes no better than the first moment she had seen it.

It had all slipped through her fingers.

The girl ran for her mother when Nicci released her grip on the studded strap around her neck.

"Well?" Commander Kardeef shrieked. He planted his fists on his hips. "Are you through with your games? It's time these people learned the true meaning of ruthless!"

Nicci stared into the depths of his dark eyes. They were defiant, angry, and determined—yet they were nothing at all like Richard's eyes.

Nicci turned to the soldiers.

She gestured. "You two. Seize the commander."

The men blinked dumbly. Commander Kardeef's face went red with rage. "That's it! You've finally gone too far!" He wheeled to his men, a whole field of them—two thousand of them. He pointed a thumb back over his shoulder at Nicci. "Grab this lunatic witch!"

Half a dozen men nearest to her drew weapons as they rushed her. Like all Order field troops, they were big, strong, and quick. They were also experienced.

Nicci thrust a fist out in the direction of the closest as he lifted his whip to lash out and entangle her. With the speed of thought, both Additive Magic and Subtractive twined together in a lethal mix as she unleashed a focused bolt of power. It produced a burst of light so hot and so white that for an instant it made the sunlight seem dim and cold by comparison.

The blast blew a mellon-sized hole through the center of the soldier's chest. For an instant, before the internal pressure forced his organs to fill the sudden void, she could see men behind through the gaping hole in his chest.

The afterimage of the flare lingered in her mind's eye like lightning's arc. The acrid smell of scorched air stung her eyes. The clap of her power's thunder rumbled out across the surrounding green fields of wheat.

Before the soldier hit the ground, Nicci unleased her power on three more of the charging men, taking off one's entire shoulder, the wallop whirling him around like a ghastly fountain, the dangling limb flinging off into the crowd. A third man was cut almost in two. She felt the concussion of the following bolt deep in her chest and, amid a blinding flash, the fourth man's head came apart in a cloud of red mist and bony debris.

Her warning gaze met the eyes of two men with knives gripped in white-knuckled fists. They halted. Many more took a step back as the four reports, to her so separate yet so close atop one another that they almost merged into one ripping blast, still echoed off the buildings.

"Now," she said in a quiet, calm, composed voice that by its very gentleness betrayed how deadly earnest was the threat, "if you men do not follow my orders, and seize Commander Kardeef, I will seize him myself. But, of course, not until after I've killed every last one of you."

The only sound was the moan of wind between the buildings.

"Do as I say, or die. I will not wait."

The big men, knowing her, made their decision in the instant they knew was all she would grant them, and leaped to seize the commander. He managed to draw his sword. Kadar Kardeef was no stranger to pitched battle. He screamed orders as he fought them off. More than one man fell dead in the melee. Others cried out as they took wounds. From behind, men finally caught the deadly sword arm. Additional men piled on the commander until they had him disarmed, down on the ground, and finally under control.

"What do you think you're doing?" Kadar Kardeef roared at her as the men pulled him to his feet.

Nicci closed the distance between them. The soldiers held his arms twisted behind his back. She stared into his wild eyes.

"Why, Commander, I am merely following your orders."

"What are you talking about!"

She smiled without humor just because she knew it would further madden him.

One of the men glanced back over his shoulder. "What do you want done with him?"

"Don't hurt him—I want him fully conscious. Strip him and bind him to the pole."

"Pole? What pole?"

"The pole that held the pigs you men ate."

Nicci snapped her fingers, and they began pulling off their commander's clothes. She watched without emotion as he was finally stripped. His gear and prized weapons became plunder, quickly disappearing into the hands of men he had commanded. They grunted with effort as they fought to bind the struggling, naked, hairy commander to the pole at his back.

Nicci turned to the stunned crowd. "Commander Kardeef wishes you to know how ruthless we can be. I am going to carry out those orders, and demonstrate it for you." She turned back to the soldiers. "Put him over the fire to roast like a pig."

The soldiers bore the struggling, furious Kadar Kardeef, the hero of the Little Gap campaign, to the fire pit. They knew that Jagang watched them through her eyes. They had reason to be confident that the emperor would stop her if he wished to. After all, he was the dream walker, and they had seen him force her and the other Sisters to submit to his wishes countless times, no matter how degrading those wishes were.

They could not know that, for some reason, Jagang did not have access to her mind right then.

The wooden ends of the pole clattered into the sockets in the stone supports to each side of the fire pit. The pole sprang up and down with the weight of its load. The weight finally settled, leaving Kadar Kardeef to hang facedown. He had little choice but to watch the glowing coals beneath him.

Even though the fire had burned down, it wasn't long before the heat of the wavering, low flames began causing him distress. As people watched in silent dismay, the commander twisted as he shrieked orders, demanding that his men take him down, promising them punishment if they delayed. His diatribe trailed off as he began gasping for control of his growing dread.

Watching the eyes of the town's people, Nicci pointed behind her.

"This is how ruthless the Imperial Order is: they will slowly, painfully, burn to death a great commander, a war hero, a man known and revered far and wide, a man who has served them well, just to prove to you, the people of an insignificant little town, that they will not hesitate to kill anyone. Our goal is the good of all, and that goal is held more important than any mere man among us. This is the proof. Now, do you people, for any reason, still think that we would shrink from harming any or all of you if you don't contribute to the common good?"

Nearly everyone shook their heads as they all mumbled, "No, Mistress."

Behind her, Commander Kardeef writhed in pain. He again yelled at his men, commanding them to bring him down, and to kill "the crazy witch." None of the soldiers moved to comply with his orders. To look at them, they didn't even hear him. These men had no notion of compassion. There was only life, and death. They chose life; that choice required his death.

Nicci stood watching the eyes of the people as the minutes dragged on. The commander was up a good distance from the low flames, but there was a expansive bed of broiling hot coals. She knew that, from time to time, the gusty breeze diverted the fierce heat to give him a fleeting reprieve. It would only prolong his ordeal; the heat was inexorable. Still, it would take some time. She didn't ask for more firewood. She was in no hurry.

People's noses wrinkled; everyone could smell his body hair burning. No one dared speak. As the ordeal wore on, the skin across Kardeef's chest and stomach reddened, and then darkened. It was a good fifteen minutes before it finally began to crack and split open. He shrieked in pain nearly the entire time. The smell turned to a surprisingly pleasant aroma of cooking meat.

In the end, he gave in to wailing for mercy. He called her name, begging her to bring it to an end, to either free him or to finish him quickly. As she listened to him sob her name, she stroked the gold ring through her lower lip, his voice little more to her than the buzzing of a fly.

The thin layer of fat that lay over his powerful muscles began melting. He grew hoarse. Fueled by the fat, flames flared up, scorching his face.

"Nicci!" Kardeef knew his pleas for mercy were falling on indifferent ears. He betrayed his true feelings. "You vicious bitch! You deserved everything I did to you!"

She casually confronted his wild gaze. "Yes, I did. Give my regards to the Keeper, Kadar."

"Tell him yourself! When Jagang finds out about this, he'll tear you limb from limb! You'll soon be in the underworld, in the Keeper's hands!"

His words were once more but a trifling drone.

Sweat beaded on people's foreheads as the spectacle dragged on. They needed no spoken orders to know she expected them to remain and watch the whole thing. Their own imaginations, should they consider disobeying her unspoken orders, would dream up punishments she never could. Only the boys were fascinated by the remarkable exhibition. Knowing looks passed among them; torture such as this was a treat to the minds of young immortals. Someday, they might make good Order troops—if they didn't grow up.

Nicci met the glare of the girl. The hatred in those eyes was breathtaking. Even though the girl had been afraid of the dunking and scrubbing, her eyes, at the time, had shown that the world was still a wondrous place, and she was someone special. Now, her eyes betrayed her lost innocence.

The whole time, Nicci stood tall, with her back straight and shoulders square, to take the full blow of the girl's bright new hatred, feeling the rare sensation of experiencing something.

The girl had no idea that Commander Kardeef had taken her place in the flames.

When the commander finally went silent, Nicci turned her eyes from the girl and spoke to the town's people.

"The past is gone. You are part of the Imperial Order. If you people don't do the moral thing by contributing toward the well-being of your fellow citizens of the Order, I will return."

They did not doubt her. If there was one thing they obviously wanted, it was never to see her again.

One of the soldiers, his fists trembling at his sides, tramped forward in halting steps. His eyes were wide with bewildered pain. "I want you back, darlin'," he growled in a voice that didn't match the startled expression in his eyes. The voice turned deadly. "And I want you back right now."

There was no mistaking Jagang's voice, or the rage in it.

It was difficult for him to control the mind of one without the gift. He had the soldier in a tenacious grip. Jagang would not have used a soldier, thereby betraying his impotence, had he been able to reach in and control Nicci's mind.

She had absolutely no idea why he had suddenly lost the link to her. It had happened before. She knew he would eventually reestablish his ability to hurt her. She had merely to wait.

"You are angry with me, Excellency?"

"What do you think?"

She shrugged. "Since Kadar was your better in bed, I would think you would be pleased."

"Get yourself back here right now!" the soldier roared in Jagang's voice. "Do you understand? Right now!"

Nicci bowed. "But, of course, Excellency."

As she straightened, she yanked the soldier's long knife from the sheath at his belt and slammed it hilt-deep into his muscled gut. She gritted her teeth with the effort of pivoting the handle sideways, sweeping the blade in a lethal arc through his insides.

She doubted the man felt his messy death writhing at her feet while she waited for her carriage to make its way around the square. He died with Jagang's chuckle on his lips. Since a dream walker could only be in a living mind, for the time being, the afternoon returned to quiet.

After her carriage rocked to a dusty halt, a soldier reached up and opened the door. She leaned out from the step, turning back to the crowd, holding the outside handrail in order to stand straight so that they all might see her. Her blond hair fluttered in the sunny breeze.

"Do not forget this day, and how your lives were all spared by Jagang the Just! The commander would have murdered you; the emperor, through me, has instead shown his compassion. Spread the word of the mercy and wisdom of Jagang the Just, and I will have no need to return."

The crowd mumbled that they would.

"Do you want us to bring the commander with us," a soldier asked. The man, Kadar Kardeef's loyal second, now wore Kardeef's sword. Like vegetables, fidelity's fresh vitality was fleeting, its final fate stench and rot.

"Leave him to roast as a reminder. Everyone else will return with me to Fairfield."

"By your command," he said with a bow. He circled his arm and ordered the men to mount up and move out.

Nicci leaned out farther and looked up at the driver. "His Excellency wishes to see me. Although he has not said as much, I'm reasonably sure he would like you to hurry."

Nicci took her place on the hard leather cushion inside, her back straight against the upright seat, while the driver let out a shrill whistle and cracked his whip. The team leaped forward, jerking the carriage ahead. With a hand on the windowsill, she steadied herself as the ironbound wheels bounced over the hard, rough ground of the town square until they reached the road, where the carriage settled down into this familiar jolting ride. Sunlight slanted in the window, falling across the empty cushion opposite her. The bold bright patch glided off the seat as the carriage negotiated a curve in the road, finally slipping up to come to rest in her lap like a warm cat. Darkly clad riders to each side, ahead, and behind stretched forward over the withers of their galloping mounts. A rumbling roar along with billowing plumes of dust lifted into the air from the thundering hooves.

For the moment, Nicci was free of Jagang. She was surrounded by two thousand men, yet she felt totally alone. Before long, she would have pain to fill the terrible void.

She felt no joy, no fear. She sometimes wondered why she felt nothing but the need to hurt.

As the carriage raced toward Jagang, her thoughts were focused instead on another man, trying to recall every occasion that she had seen him. She went over every moment she had spent with Richard Cypher, or as he was now known—and as Jagang knew him—Richard Rahl.

She thought about his gray eyes.

Until the day she saw him, she had never believed such a person could exist.

When she thought about Richard, like now, only one haunting need burned in her: to destroy him.

Huge garish tents festooned the prominent hill outside the city of Fairfield, yet despite the festive colors erected amid the gloom, despite the laughing, the shouting, the coarse singing, and the riotous excess, this was no carnival come to town, but an occupying army. The emperor's tents, and those of his retinue, were styled in the fashion of the tents used by some of the nomadic people from Jagang's homeland of Altur'Rang, yet they were embellished far beyond any actual tradition. The emperor, a man vastly exceeding any nomadic tribal leader's ability to imagine, created his own cultural heritage as he saw fit.

Around the tents, covering the hills and valleys as far as Nicci could see, the soldiers had pitched their own small grimy tents. Some were oiled canvas, many more were made from animal skins. Beyond the shared basics of practicality, there was uniformity only in their lack of conformity to any one style.

Outside some of the shabby little tents, and almost as large, sat ornate uphol-stered chairs looted from the city. The juxtaposition almost looked as if it had been intentionally done for a comical effect, but Nicci knew the reality had no kinship to humor. When the army eventually moved on, such large, meticulously crafted items were too cumbersome to take and would be left to rot in the weather.

Horses were picketed haphazardly, with occasional paddocks holding small herds. Other enclosures held meat on the hoof. Individual wagons were scattered here and there, seemingly wherever they could find an empty spot, but in other places they had been set up side by side. Many were camp followers, others were army wagons with everything from basic supplies to blacksmith equipment. The army brought along minimal siege equipment; they had the gifted to use as weapons of that sort.

Brooding clouds scudded low over the scene. The humid air reeked of excrement from both animals and men. The green fields all around had been churned to a muddy morass. The two thousand men who had returned with Nicci had disappeared into the sprawling camp like a sprinkling of raindrops into a swamp.

An Imperial Order army encampment was a place of noise and seeming confu-sion, yet it was not as disorderly as it might appear. There was a hierarchy of author-ity, and duties and chores to attend. Scattered men worked in solitude on their gear, oiling weapons and leather or rolling their chain mail inside barrels with sand and vinegar to clean it of rust, while others cooked at fires. Farriers saw to the horses. Craftsmen saw to everything from repairing weapons to fashioning new boots to pulling teeth. Mystics of all sorts prowled the camp, tending impoverished souls or warding troublesome demons. Duties completed, raucous gangs gathered together for entertainment, usually gambling and drinking. Sometimes the diversions in-volved the camp followers, sometimes the captives.

Even surrounded by such vast numbers, Nicci felt alone. Jagang's absence from her mind left a feeling of staggering isolation—not a sense of being forsaken, but simply solitude by contrast. With the dream walker in her mind, not even the most intimate detail of life—no thought, no deed—could be held private. His presence lurked in the dark mental corners, and from there he could watch everything: every word you spoke; every thought you had; every bite you took; every time you cleared your throat; every time you coughed; every time you went to the privy. You were never alone. Never. The violation was debilitating, the trespass complete.

That was what broke most of the Sisters: the brutal totality of it, the awareness of his constant presence in your own mind, watching. Worse, almost, the dream walker's roots sunk down through you, but you never knew when his awareness was focused on you. You might call him a vile name, and, with his attention elsewhere, it would go unnoticed. Another time, you might have a brief, private, nasty thought about him, and he would know it the same instant you thought it.

Nicci had learned to feel those roots, as had many of the other Sisters. She had also learned to recognize when they were absent, as now. That never happened with the others; with them, those roots were permanent. Jagang always eventually returned, though, to once again sink his roots into her, but for now, she was alone. She just didn't know why.

The jumble of troops and campfires left no clear route for the team, so Nicci had left her carriage for the walk the rest of the way up the hill. It exposed her to the lecherous looks and lewd calls of the soldiers who crowded the slope. She supposed that before Jagang was finished with her, she might be exposed to far more from the men. Most of the Sisters were sent out to the tents from time to time to be used for the men's pleasure. It was done either to punish them or, sometimes, merely to let them know it could be ordered on a whim—to remind them that they were slaves, nothing more than property.

Nicci, though, was reserved for the exclusive amusement of the emperor and those he specifically selected—like Kadar Kardeef. Many of the Sisters envied her status, but despite what they believed, being a personal slave to Jagang was no grace. Women were sent to the tents for a period of time, maybe a week or two, but the rest of the time they had less demanding duties. They were valued, after all, for their abilities with their gift. There was no such time limit for Nicci. She had once spent a couple of months sequestered in Jagang's room, so as to be there for his amusement any time of day or night. The soldiers enjoyed the women's company, but had to mind certain restrictions in what they could do to them; Jagang and his friends imposed on themselves no such limits.

On occasion, for reason or not, Jagang would become furious at her and would heatedly order her to the tents for a month—to teach her a lesson, he would say. Nicci would obediently bow and pledge it would be as he wished. He knew she was not bluffing; it would have been a lesser torment. Before she could be out the door to the tents, he would turn moody, command her to return to face him, and then angrily retract the orders.

Since the beginning, Nicci had, measure by measure, inch by inch, acquired a certain status and freedom afforded none of the others. She hadn't specifically sought it; it just came about. Jagang had confided to her that he read the Sisters' thoughts, and that they privately referred to her as the Slave Queen. She supposed Jagang told her so as to honor her in his own way, but the title "Slave Queen" had meant no more to her than "Death's Mistress."

71

For now, she floated like a bright water-lily flower in the dark swamp of men. Other Sisters always made an attempt to look as drab as the men so as to go less noticed and be less desirable. They only deceived themselves. They lived in constant terror of what Jagang might do to them. What happened, happened. They had no choice or influence in it.

Nicci simply didn't care. She wore her fine black dresses and left her long blond hair uncovered for all to see. For the most part, she did as she wished. She didn't care what Jagang did to her, and he knew it. In much the way Richard was an enigma to her, she was an enigma to Jagang.

Too, Jagang was fascinated by her. Despite his cruelty toward her, there was a spark of caution mixed in. When he hurt her, she welcomed it; she merited the brutality. Pain could sometimes reach down into the dark emptiness. He would then recoil from hurting her. When he threatened to kill her, she waited patiently for it to be done; she knew she didn't deserve to live. He would then withdraw the sentence of death.

The fact that she was sincere was her safety—and her peril. She was a fawn among wolves, safe in her coat of indifference. The fawn was in danger only if it ran. She did not view her captivity as a conflict with her interests; she had no interests. Time and again she had the opportunity to run, but didn't. That, perhaps more than anything, captivated Jagang.

Sometimes, he seemed to pay court to her. She didn't know his real interest in her; she never tried to discover it. He occasionally professed concern for her, and a few times, something akin to affection. Other times, when she left on some duty, he seemed glad to be rid of her.

It had occurred to her, because of his behavior, that he might think he was in love with her. As preposterous as such a thought might be, it didn't matter one way or the other to her. She doubted he was capable of love. She seriously doubted that Jagang really knew what the word meant, much less the entire concept.

Nicci knew all too well what it meant.

A soldier near Jagang's tent stepped in front of her. He grinned moronically; it was meant to be an invitation by means of threat. She could have dissuaded him by mentioning that Jagang waited for her, or she could even have used her power to drop him where he stood, but instead she simply stared at him. It was not the reaction he wanted. Many of the men rose to the bait only if it squirmed. When she didn't, his expression turned sour. He grumbled a curse at her and moved off.

Nicci continued on toward the emperor's tent. Nomadic tents from Altur'Rang were actually quite small and practical, being made of bland, unadorned lambskin. Jagang had re-created them rather more grandly than the originals. His own was more oval than round. Three poles, rather than the customary one, held up the multi-peaked roof. The tent's exterior walls were decorated with brightly embroidered panels. Around the top edge of the sides, where the roof met the walls, hung fist-sized multicolored tassels and streamers that marked the traveling palace of the emperor. Banners and pennants of bright yellow and red atop the huge tent hung limp in the stale, late-afternoon air.

Outside, a woman beat small rugs hung over one of the tent's lines. Nicci lifted aside the heavy doorway curtain embellished with gold shields and hammered silver medallions depicting battle scenes. Inside, slaves were at work sweeping the expanse of carpets, dusting the delicate ceramic ware set about on the elaborate furnishings, and fussing at the hundreds of colorful pillows lining the edge of the floor. Hangings richly decorated with traditional Altur'Rang designs divided the space into several rooms. A few openings overhead covered with gauzy material let in a little light. All the thick materials created a quiet place amid the noise. Lamps and candles lent sleepy light to the soft room.

Nicci did not acknowledge the eyes of the guards flanking the inside of the doorway, or those of the other slaves going about their domestic duties. In the middle of the front room sat Jagang's ornate chair, draped with red silks. This was where he sometimes took audiences, but the chair was empty. She didn't falter, as did other women summoned by His Excellency, but strode resolutely toward his bedroom in the rear section.

One of the slaves, a nearly naked boy looking to be in his late teens, was down on his hands and knees with a small whiskbroom sweeping the carpet set before the entrance to the bedroom. Without meeting Nicci's gaze, he informed her that His Excellency was not occupying his tents. The young man, Irwin, was gifted. He had lived at the Palace of the Prophets, training to be a wizard. Now Irwin tended the fringe of carpets and emptied the chamber pots. Nicci's mother would have approved.

Jagang could be any number of places. He might be off gambling or drinking with his men. He could be inspecting his troops or the craftsmen who attended them. He might be looking over the new captives, selecting those he wanted for himself. He might be talking with Kadar Kardeef's second.

Nicci saw several Sisters cowering in a corner. Like her, they, too, were Jagang's slaves. As she strode up to the three women, she saw that they were busy sewing, mending some of the tent's gear.

"Sister Nicci!" Sister Georgia rushed to her feet as a look of relief washed across her face. "We didn't know if you were alive or dead. We haven't seen you for so long. We thought maybe you had vanished."

Being that Nicci was a Sister of the Dark, sworn to the Keeper of the underworld, she found the concern from three Sisters of the Light to be somewhat insincere. Nicci supposed that they considered their captivity a common bond, and their feelings about it paramount, overcoming their more basic rifts. Too, they knew Jagang treated her differently; they were probably eager to be seen as friendly.

"I've been away on business for His Excellency."

"Of course," Sister Georgia said, dry-washing her hands as she dipped her head.

The other two, Sisters Rochelle and Aubrey, set aside the bag of bone buttons and tent thread, untangled themselves from yards of canvas, and then stood beside Sister Georgia. They both bowed their heads slightly to Nicci. The three of them feared her inscrutable standing with Jagang.

"Sister Nicci . . . His Excellency is very angry," Sister Rochelle said.

"Furious," Sister Aubrey confirmed. "He . . . he railed at the walls, saying that you had gone too far this time."

Nicci only stared.

Sister Aubrey licked her lips. "We just thought you should know. So you can be careful."

Nicci thought this would be a poor time to suddenly begin being careful. She found the groveling of women hundreds of years her senior annoying. "Where's Jagang?"

"He has taken a grand building, not far outside the city, as his quarters," Sister Aubrey said.

"It used to be the Minister of Culture's estate," Sister Rochelle added.

Nicci frowned. "Why? He has his tents."

"Since you've been gone, he's decided that an emperor needs proper quarters," Sister Rochelle said.

"Proper? Proper for what?"

"To show the world his importance, I suppose."

Sister Aubrey nodded. "He's having a palace built. In Altur'Rang. It's his new vision." She arced an arm through the air, apparently indicating, with the slice of her hand, the grand scale of the place. "He's ordered a magnificent palace built."

"He was planning on using the Palace of the Prophets," Sister Rochelle said, "but since it was destroyed he's decided to build another, only better—the most opulent palace ever conceived."

Nicci frowned at the three women. "He wanted the Palace of the Prophets because it had a spell to slow aging. That was what interested him."

All three women shrugged.

Nicci began to get an inkling of what Jagang might have in mind. "So, this place he's at now? What is he doing? Learning to eat with something other than his fingers? Seeing how he likes living the fancy life under a roof?"

"He only told us he was staying there for now," Sister Georgia said. "He took most of the . . . younger women with him. He told us to stay here and see to things in case he wished to return to his tent."

It didn't sound like much had changed, except the setting.

Nicci sighed. Her carriage was gone. She would have to walk.

"All right. How do I find the place?"

After Sister Aubrey gave her detailed directions, Nicci thanked them and turned to go.

"Sister Alessandra has vanished," Sister Georgia said in a voice straining mightily to sound nonchalant.

Nicci stopped in her tracks.

She rounded on Sister Georgia. The woman was middle aged, and seemed to look worse every time Nicci saw her. Her clothes were little more than tattered rags she wore with the pride of a fine uniform. Her thin hair was more white than brown. It might once have looked distinguished, but it didn't appear to have seen a brush, much less soap, for weeks. She was probably infested with lice, too.

Some people looked forward to age as an excuse to become a frump, as if all along their greatest ambition in life had been to be drab and unattractive. Sister Georgia seemed to delight in dowdiness.

"What do you mean, Sister Alessandra has vanished?"

Nicci caught the slight twitch of satisfaction. Georgia spread her hands innocently. "We don't know what happened. She's just turned up missing."

Still, Nicci did not move. "I see."

Sister Georgia spread her hands again, feigning simplemindedness. "It was about the time the Prelate disappeared, too."

Nicci denied them the reward of astonishment.

"What was Verna doing here?"

"Not Verna," Sister Rochelle said. She leaned in. "Ann."

Sister Georgia scowled her displeasure at Rochelle for spoiling the surprise—and a surprise it was. The old Prelate had died—at least, that was what Nicci had been told. Since leaving the Place of the Prophets, Nicci had heard about all the other

Sisters, novices, and young men spending the night at the funeral pyre for Ann and the prophet, Nathan. Knowing Ann, there was obviously some sort of deception afoot, but even for her, such a thing would be extraordinary.

The three Sisters smiled like cats with a carp. They looked eager for a long game of truth-and-gossip.

"Give me the important details. I don't have time for the long version. His Excellency wishes to see me." Nicci took in the three wilting smiles. She kept her voice level. "Unless you want to risk him returning here, angry and impatient to see me."

Sisters Rochelle and Aubrey blanched.

Georgia abandoned the game and went back to dry washing her hands. "The Prelate came to the camp—when you were gone—and was captured."

"Why would she come into Jagang's midst?"

"To try to convince us to escape with her," Sister Rochelle blurted out. A shrill titter—jittery, rather than amused—burbled up. "She had some silly story about the chimes being loose and magic failing. Imagine that! Wild stories, they were. Expected us to believe—"

"So that was what happened . . ." Nicci whispered as she stared off in reflection. She realized instantly it was no wild story. Pieces began fitting together. Nicci used her gift, the others weren't allowed to, so they might not know if magic had failed for a time.

"That's what she claimed," Sister Georgia said.

"So, magic had failed," Nicci reasoned aloud, "and she thought that would prevent the dream walker from controlling your minds."

That might explain much of what Nicci didn't understand: why Jagang sometimes couldn't enter her mind.

"But if the chimes are loose—"

"Were," Sister Georgia said. "Even if it was true, for a time, they now have been banished. His Excellency has full access to us, I'm happy to say, and everything else concerning magic has returned to normal."

Nicci could almost see the three of them wondering if Jagang was listening to their words. But if magic was returned to normal, Jagang should be in Nicci's mind; he wasn't. She felt the spark of a possible understanding fizzle and die. "So, the Prelate made a blunder and Jagang caught her."

"Well . . . not exactly," Sister Rochelle said. "Sister Georgia went and got the guards. We turned her in, as was our duty."

Nicci burst out with a laugh. "Her own Sisters of the Light? How ironic! She risks her life, while the chimes have interrupted magic, to come and save your worthless hides, and instead of escaping with her, you turn her in. How fitting."

"We had to!" Sister Georgia protested. "His Excellency would have wished it. Our place is to serve. We know better than to try to escape. We know our place."

Nicci surveyed their tense faces, these women sworn to the Creator's light, these Sisters of the Light who had worked hundreds of years in His name. "Yes, you do."

"You'd have done the same," Sister Aubrey snapped. "We had to, or His Excellency would have taken it out on the others. It was our duty to the welfare of the others—and that includes you, I might add. We couldn't think only of ourselves, or Ann, but had to think of what was good for everyone."

Nicci felt the numb indifference smothering her. "Fine, so you betrayed the Prelate." Only a spark of curiosity remained. "But what made her think she could escape with you for good? Surely, she must have had some plan for the chimes.

What was she expecting to happen when Jagang once again had access to your minds?—and hers?"

"His Excellency is always with us," Sister Aubrey insisted. "Ann was just trying to fill our heads with her preposterous notions. We know better. The rest of it was just a trick, too. We were too smart for her."

"Rest of it? What was the rest of her plan?"

Sister Georgia huffed her indignation. "She tried to tell us some foolishness about a bond to Richard Rahl."

Nicci blinked. She concentrated on keeping her breathing even. "Bond? What nonsense are you talking about, now?"

Sister Georgia met Nicci's gaze squarely. "She insisted that if we swore allegiance to Richard, it would protect us. She claimed some magic of his would keep Jagang from our mind."

"How?"

Sister Georgia shrugged. "She claimed this bond business protected people's minds from dream walkers. But we aren't that gullible."

To still her fingers, Nicci pressed her hands to her thighs. "I don't understand. How would such a thing work?"

"She said something about it being inherited from his ancestor. She claimed that we had but to swear loyalty to him, loyalty in our hearts—or some such nonsense. To tell the truth, it was so preposterous I wasn't really paying that much attention. She claimed that was why Jagang couldn't enter her mind."

Nicci was staggered. Of course . . .

She had always wondered why Jagang didn't capture the rest of the Sisters. There were many more still free. They were protected by this bond to Richard. It had to be true. It made sense. Her own leader, sister Ulicia, and Richard's other teachers had escaped, too. But that didn't seem to make sense; they were Sisters of the Dark—like Nicci—they would have had to swear loyalty to Richard. Nicci couldn't imagine such a thing.

But then, Jagang was often unable to enter Nicci's mind.

"You said Sister Alessandra has vanished."

Sister Georgia fussed with the collar of her scruffy dress. "She and Ann both vanished."

"Jagang doesn't bother to inform you of his actions. Perhaps he simply had them put to death."

Georgia glanced at her companions. "Well . . . maybe. But Sister Alessandra was one of yours . . . a Sister of the Dark. She was caring for Ann—"

"Why weren't you caring for her? You are her Sisters."

Sister Georgia cleared her throat. "She threw such a fit about us that His Excellency assigned Sister Alessandra to look after her."

Nicci could only imagine that it must have been quite a fit. But after being betrayed by her own Sisters, it was understandable. Jagang would have thought the woman valuable enough that he wanted to keep her alive.

"As we marched into the city, the wagon with Ann's cage never showed up," Sister Georgia went on. "One of the drivers finally came around with a bloody head and reported that the last thing he saw before the world went dark was Sister Alessandra. Now the two of them are gone."

Nicci felt her fingernails digging into her palms. She made herself relax her fists. "So, Ann offered you all freedom, and you chose instead to continue to be slaves."

The three women lifted their noses. "We did what is best for everyone," Sister Georgia said. "We are Sisters of the Light. Our duty is not to ourselves, but to relieve the suffering of others—not cause it."

"Besides," Sister Aubrey added, "we don't see you leaving. Seems you've been free of His Excellency from time to time, and you don't go."

Nicci frowned. "How do you know that?"

"Well, I, I mean . . ." Sister Aubrey stammered.

Nicci seized the woman by the throat. "I asked you a question. Answer it."

Sister Aubrey's face reddened as Nicci added the force of her gift to the grip. The tendons in her wrist stood out with the strain. The woman's eyes showed white all around as Nicci's power began squeezing the life from her. Unlike Nicci, Jagang possessed their minds, and they were prohibited from using their power except at his direction.

Sister Georgia gently placed a hand on Nicci's forearm. "His Excellency questioned us about it, that's all, Sister. Let her go. Please?"

Nicci released the woman but turned her glare on Sister Georgia. "Questioned you? What do you mean? What did he say?"

"He simply wanted to know if we knew why he was from time to time blocked from your mind."

"He hurt us," Sister Rochelle said. "He hurt us with his questions, because we had no answer. We don't understand it."

For the first time, Nicci did.

Sister Aubrey comforted her throat. "What is it with you, Sister Nicci? Why is it His Excellency is so curious about you? Why is it you can resist him?"

Nicci turned and walked away. "Thank you for the help, Sisters."

"If you can be free of him, why do you not leave?" Sister Georgia called out.

Nicci turned back from the doorway. "I enjoy seeing Jagang torment you Witches of the Light. I stay around so that I might watch."

They were unmoved by her insolence—they were accustomed to it.

"Sister Nicci," Rochelle said, smoothing back her frizz of hair. "What did you do that made His Excellency so angry?"

"What? Oh, that. Nothing of importance. I just had the men tie Commander Kardeef to a pole and roast him over a fire."

The three of them gasped as they straightened as one. They reminded Nicci of three owls on a branch.

Sister Georgia fixed Nicci with a grim glare, a rare blaze of authority born of seniority.

"You deserve everything Jagang does to you, Sister—and what the Keeper will do to you, too."

Nicci smiled and said, "Yes, I do," before ducking through the tent opening.

The city of Fairfield had returned to a semblance of order. It was the order of a military post. Little of what could be said to make a city was left. Many of the buildings remained, but there were few of the people who had once lived and worked in them. Some of the buildings had been reduced to charred beams and blackened rubble, others were hulks with windows and doors broken out, yet most were much the same as they had been before, except, of course, that all had been emptied in the wanton looting. The buildings stood like husks, only a reminder of past life.

Here and there, a few toothless old people sat, legs splayed, leaning against a wall, watching with empty eyes the masses of armed men moving up and down their streets. Orphaned children wandered in a daze, or peered out from dark passageways. Nicci found it remarkable how quickly civilization could be stripped from a place.

As she walked through the streets, Nicci thought she understood how many of the buildings would feel if they could feel: empty, devoid of life, lacking purpose while they waited for someone to serve; their only true value being in service to the living.

The streets, populated as they were by grim-faced soldiers, gaunt beggars, the skeletal old and sick, wailing children, all amongst the rubble and filth, looked much like some of the streets Nicci remembered from when she was little. Her mother often sent her out to streets like this to minister to the destitute.

"It's the fault of men like your father," her mother had said. "He's just like my father was. He has no feelings, no concern for anyone but himself. He's heartless."

Nicci had stood, wearing a freshly washed, frilly blue dress, her hair brushed and pinned back, her hands hanging at her sides, listening as her mother lectured on good and evil, on the ways of sin and redemption. Nicci hadn't understood a lot of it, but in later years it would be repeated until she would come to know every word, every concept, every desolate truth by heart.

Nicci's father was wealthy. Worse, to Mother's way of thinking, he wasn't remorseful about it. Mother explained that self-interest and greed were like the two eyes of a monstrous evil, always looking for yet more power and gold to feed its insatiable hunger.

"You must learn, Nicci, that a person's moral course in this life is to help others, not yourself," Mother said. "Money can't buy the Creator's blessing."

"But how can we show the Creator we're good?" Nicci asked.

"Mankind is a wretched lot, unworthy, morbid, and foul. We must fight our depraved nature. Helping others is the only way to prove your soul's value. It's the only true good a person can do."

Nicci's father had been born a noble, but all his adult life he had worked as an armorer. Mother believed that he had been born with comfortable wealth, and instead of being satisfied with that, he sought to build his legacy into a shameless fortune. She said wealth could only be had by fleecing it from the poor in one fashion or another. Others of the nobility, like Mother and many of her friends, were content not to squeeze an undeserved share from the sweat of the poor.

Nicci felt great guilt for Father's wicked ways, for his ill-gotten wealth. Mother said she was doing her best to try to save his straying soul. Nicci never worried for her mother's soul, because people were always saying how caring, how kindhearted, how charitable Mother was, but Nicci would sometimes lie awake at night, unable to sleep with worry for Father, worry that the Creator might exact punishment before Father could be redeemed.

While Mother went to meetings with her important friends, the nanny, on the way to the market, often took Nicci to Father's business to ask his wishes for dinner. Nicci relished watching and learning things at Father's work. It was a fascinating place. When she was very young, she thought she might grow up to be an armorer, too. At home, she would sit on the floor and play at hammering on an item of clothing meant to be armor laid on an upturned shoe used as an anvil. That innocent time was her fondest memory of her childhood.

Nicci's father had a great many people working for him. Wagons brought four-square bars and other supplies from distant places. Heavy cast-metal sows came in on barges. Other wagons, with guards, took goods to far-off customers. There were men who forged metal, men who hammered it into shape, and yet other men who shaped glowing metal into weapons. Some of the blades were made from costly "poison steel," said to inflict mortal wounds, even in a small cut. There were other men who sharpened blades, men who polished armor, and men who did beautiful engraving and artwork on shields, armor, and blades. There were even women who worked for Nicci's father, helping to make chain mail. Nicci watched them, sitting on benches at long wooden tables, gossiping a bit among themselves, tittering at stories, as they worked with their pincers burring over tiny rivets in the flattened ends of all those thousands of little steel rings that together went into the making of a suit of chain-mail armor. Nicci thought it remarkable that man's inventiveness could turn something as hard as metal into a suit of clothes.

Men from all around, and from distant places, too, came to buy her father's armor. Father said it was the finest armor made. His eyes, the color of the blue sky on a perfect summer day, sparkled wonderfully when he spoke of his armor. Some was so beautiful that kings traveled from great distances to have armor ordered and fitted. Some was so elaborate that it took skilled men hunched at benches many months to make.

Blacksmiths, bellowsmen, hammermen, millmen, platers, armorers, polishers, leatherworkers, riveters, patternmakers, silversmiths, guilders, engraving artists, even seamstresses for the making of the quilted and padded linen, and, of course, apprentices, came from great distances, hoping to work for her father. Many of those with skills lugged along samples of their best work to show him. Father turned away far more than he hired.

Nicci's father was an impressive figure, upright, angular, and intense. At his work, his blue eyes always seemed to Nicci to see more than any other person saw, as if the metal spoke to him when his fingers glided over it. He seemed to move his limbs precisely as much as was needed, and no more. To Nicci, he was a vision of power, strength, and purpose.

Officers, officials, and nobility came round to talk to him, as did suppliers, and his workers. When Nicci went to her father's work, she was always astonished to see him engaged in so much conversation. Mother said it was because he was arrogant, and made his poor workers pay court to him.

Nicci liked to watch the intricate dance of people working. The workers would pause to smile at her, answer her questions, and sometimes let her hit the metal with a hammer. From the looks of it, Father enjoyed talking to all those people, too. At home, Mother talked, and Father said little, as his face took on the look of hammered steel.

When he did talk at home, he spoke almost exclusively about his work. Nicci listened to every word, wanting to learn all about him and his business. Mother confided that at his core his vile nature ate away at his invisible soul. Nicci always hoped to someday redeem his soul and make it as healthy as he outwardly appeared.

He adored Nicci, but seemed to think raising her was a task too sacred for his coarse hands, so he left it to Mother. Even when he disagreed with something, he would bow to Mother's wishes, saying she would know best about such a domestic duty.

His work kept him busy most of the time. Mother said it was a sign of his barren soul that he spent so much of his time at building his riches—taking from people, she often called it—rather than giving of himself to people, as the Creator meant all men to do. Many times, when Father came home for dinner, while servants scurried in and out with all the dishes they'd prepared, Mother would go on, in tortured tones, about how bad things were in the world. Nicci often heard people say that Mother was a noble woman because of how deeply she cared. After dinner Father would go back to work, often without a word. That would anger Mother, because she had more to tell him about his soul, but he was too busy to listen.

Nicci remembered occasions when Mother would stand at the window, looking out over the dark city, worrying, no doubt, about all the things that plagued her peace. On those quiet nights, Father sometimes glided up behind Mother, putting a hand tenderly to her back, as if she were something of great value. He seemed to be mellow and contented at those moments. He squeezed her bottom just a little as he whispered something in her ear.

She would look up hopefully and ask him to contribute to the efforts of her fellowship. He would ask how much. Peering up into his eyes as if searching for some shred of human decency, she would name a figure. He would sigh and agree. His hands would settle around her waist, and he would say that it was late, and that they should retire to bed.

Once, when he asked her how much she wished him to contribute, she shrugged and said, "I don't know. What does your conscience tell you, Howard? But, a man of true compassion would do better than you usually do, considering that you have more than your fair share of wealth, and the need is so great."

He sighed. "How much do you and your friends need?"

"It is not me and my friends who need it, Howard, but the masses of humanity crying out for help. Our fellowship simply struggles to meet the need."

"How much?" he repeated.

She said, "Five hundred gold crowns," as if the number were a club she had been hiding behind her back, and, seeing the opening she had been waiting for, she suddenly brandished it to bully him.

With a gasp, Father staggered back a step. "Do you have any idea of the work required to make a sum of that size?"

"You do no work, Howard—your slaves do it for you."

"Slaves! They are the finest craftsmen!"

"They should be. You steal the best workers from all over the land."

"I pay the best wages in the land! They are eager to work for me!"

"They are the poor victims of your tricks. You exploit them. You charge more than anyone else. You have connections and make deals to cut out other armorers. You steal the food from the mouths of working people, just to line your own pockets."

"I offer the finest work! People buy from me because they want the best. I charge a fair price for it."

"No one charges as much as you and that's the simple fact. You always want more. Gold is your only goal."

"People come to me willingly because I have the highest standards. That is my goal! The other shops produce haphazard work that doesn't proof out. My tempering is superior. My work is all proofed to a double-stamp standard. I won't sell inferior work. People trust me; they know I create the best pieces."

"Your workers do. You simply rake in the money."

"The profits go to wages and to the business—I just sank a fortune into the new battering-mill!"

"Business, business, business! When I ask you to give a little something back to the community, to those in need, you act as if I wanted you to gouge out your eyes. Would you really rather see people die than to give a pittance to save them? Does money really mean more to you, Howard, than people's lives? Are you that cruel and unfeeling a man?"

Father hung his head for a time, and at last quietly agreed to send his man around with the gold. His voice came gentle again. He said he didn't want people to die, and he hoped the money would help. He told her it was time for bed.

"You've put me off, Howard, with your arguing. You couldn't just give charitably of yourself; it always has to be dragged out of you—when it's the right thing to do in the first place. You only agree now because of your lecherous needs. Honestly, do you think I have no principles?"

Father simply turned and headed for the door. He paused as he suddenly saw Nicci sitting on the floor, watching. The look on his face frightened her, not because it was angry, or fierce, but because there seemed to be so much in his eyes, and the weight of never being able to express it was crushing him. Raising Nicci was Mother's work, and he had promised her he would not meddle.

He swept his blond hair back from his forehead, then turned and picked up his coat. In a level voice he said to Mother that he was going to go see to some things at work.

After he was gone, Mother, too, saw Nicci, forgotten on the floor, playing with beads on a board, pretending to make chain mail. Her arms folded, she stood over Nicci for a long moment.

"Your father goes to whores, you know. I'm sure that's where he's off to now: a whore. You may be too young to understand, but I want you to know, so that you don't ever put any faith in him. He's an evil man. I'll not be his whore.

"Now, put away your things and come with Mother. I'm going to see my friends.

It's time you came along and began learning about the needs of others, instead of just your own wants."

At her friend's house, there were a few men and several women sitting and talking in serious tones. When they politely inquired after Father, Nicci's mother reported that he was off, "working or whoring, I don't know which, and can control neither." Some of the women laid a hand on her her arm and comforted her. It was a terrible burden she bore, they said.

Across the room sat a silent man, who looked to Nicci as grim as death itself.

Mother quickly forgot about Father as she became engrossed in the discussion her friends were having about the terrible conditions of people in the city. People were suffering from hunger, injuries, sickness, disease, lack of skill, no work, too many children to feed, elderly to care for, no clothes, no roof over their heads, and every other kind of strife imaginable. It was all so frightening.

Nicci was always anxious when Mother talked about how things couldn't go on the way they were for much longer, and that something had to be done. Nicci wished someone would hurry up and do it.

Nicci listened as Mother's fellowship friends talked about all the intolerant people who harbored hate. Nicci feared ending up as one of those terrible people. She didn't want the Creator to punish her for having a cold heart.

Mother and her friends went on at great length about their deep feelings for all the problems around them. After each person said their piece, they would steal a glance over at the man sitting solemnly in a straight chair against the wall, watching with careful, dark eyes as they talked.

"The prices of things are just terrible," a man with droopy eyelids said. He was all crumpled down in his chair, like a pile of dirty clothes. "It isn't fair. People shouldn't be allowed to just raise their prices whenever they want. The duke should do something. He has the king's ear."

"The duke . . ." Mother said. She sipped her tea. "Yes, I've always found the duke to be a man sympathetic to good causes. I think he could be persuaded to introduce sensible laws." Mother glanced over the gold rim of her cup at the man in the straight chair.

One of the women said she would encourage her husband to back the duke. Another spoke up that they would write a letter of support for such an idea.

"People are starving," a wrinkled woman said into a lull in the conversation. People eagerly mumbled their acknowledgment, as if this were an umbrella to run in under to escape the drenching silence. "I see it every day. If we could just help some of those unfortunate people."

One of the other women puffed herself up like a chicken ready to lay an egg. "It's just terrible the way no one will give them a job, when there's plenty of work if it was just spread around."

"I know," Mother said with a tsk. "I've talked to Howard until I'm blue in the face. He just hires people who please him, rather than those needing the job the most. It's a disgrace."

The others sympathized with her burden.

"It isn't right that a few men should have so much more than they need, while so many people have so much less," the man with the droopy eyelids said. "It's immoral."

"Man has no right to exist for his own sake," Mother was quick to put in as she nibbled on a piece of dense cake while glancing again at the grimly silent man. "I tell Howard all the time that self-sacrifice in the service of others is man's highest moral duty and his only reason for being placed in this life.

"To that end," Mother announced, "I have decided to contribute five hundred gold crowns to our cause."

The other people gasped their delight, and congratulated Mother for her charitable nature. They agreed, as they sneaked peeks across the room, that the Creator would reward her in the next life, and talked about all they would be able to do to help those less fortunate souls.

Mother finally turned and regarded Nicci for a moment, and then said, "I believe my daughter is old enough to learn to help others."

Nicci sat forward on the edge of her chair, thrilled at the idea of at last putting her hand to what Mother and her friends said was noble work. It was as if the Creator Himself had offered her a path to salvation. "I would so like to do good, Mother."

Mother cast a questioning look at the man in the straight chair. "Brother Narev?"

The deep creases of his face pleated to each side as the thin line of his mouth stretched in a smile. There was no joy in it, or in his dark eyes hooded beneath a brow of tangled white and black hairs. He wore a creased cap and heavy robes as dark as dried blood. Wisps of his wiry hair above his ears curled up around the edge of the cap that came halfway down on his forehead.

He stroked his jaw with the side of a finger as he spoke in a voice that almost rattled the teacups. "So, child, you wish to be a little soldier?"

"Well . . . no, sir." Nicci didn't know what soldiering had to do with doing good. Mother always said that father pandered to men in an evil occupation—soldiers. She said soldiers only cared about killing. "I wish to help those in need."

"That is what we all try to do, child." His spooky smile remained fixed on his face as he spoke. "We here are all soldiers in the fellowship—the Fellowship of Order—as we call our little group. All soldiers fighting for justice."

Everyone seemed too timid to look directly at him. They glanced for a moment, looked away, then glanced back again, as if his face was not something to be taken in all at once, but sipped at, like a scalding-hot, foul-tasting remedy.

Mother's brown eyes darted around like a cockroach looking for a crack. "Why, of course, Brother Narev. That is the only moral sort of soldier—the charitable sort." She urged Nicci up and scooted her forward. "Nicci, Brother Narev, here, is a great man. Brother Narev is the high priest of the Fellowship of Order—an ancient sect devoted to doing the Creator's will in this world. Brother Narev is a sorcerer." She cast a smile up at him. "Brother Narev, this is my daughter, Nicci."

Her mother's hands pushed her at the man, as if she were an offering for the Creator. Unlike everyone else, Nicci couldn't take her gaze from his hooded eyes. She had never seen their like.

There was nothing in them but dark cold emptiness.

He held out a hand. "Pleased to meet you, Nicci."

"Curtsy and kiss his hand, dear," Mother prompted.

Nicci went to one knee. She kissed the knuckles so as not to have to put her lips on the spongy web of thick blue veins covering the back of his hairy hand floating before her face. The whitish knobs were cold, but not icy, as she had expected.

"We welcome you to our movement, Nicci," he said in that deep rattling voice of his. "With your mother's caring hand raising you up, I know you will do the Creator's work."

Nicci thought that the Creator Himself must be very much like this man.

From all the things her mother told her, Nicci feared the Creator's wrath. She was old enough to know that she had to start doing the good work her mother always talked about, if she was to have any chance at salvation. Everyone said Mother was a caring, moral person. Nicci wanted to be a good person, too.

But good work seemed so hard, so stern—not at all like her father's work, where people smiled and laughed and talked with their hands.

"Thank you, Brother Narev," Nicci said. "I will do my best to do good in the world."

"One day, with the help of fine young people like you, we will change the world. I don't delude myself; with so much callousness among men, it will take time to win true converts, but we here in this room, along with others of like mind throughout the land, are the foundation of hope."

"Is the fellowship a secret, then?" Nicci asked in a whisper.

Everyone chuckled. Brother Narev didn't laugh, but his mouth smiled again. "No, child. Quite the contrary. It is our most fervent wish and duty to spread the truth of mankind's corruption. The Creator is perfect; we mortals are but miserable wretches. We must recognize our wicked nature if we hope to avoid His righteous wrath and reap our deliverance in the next world.

"Self-sacrifice for the good of all is the only route to salvation. Our fellowship is open to all those willing to give of themselves and live ethical lives. Most people don't take us seriously. Someday they will."

Gleaming, mousy eyes around the room watched without blinking as his deep, powerful voice rose, like the Creator's own fury.

"A day will come when the hot flames of change will sweep across the land, burning away the old, the decaying, and the foul, to allow a new order to grow from the blackened remains of evil. After we burn clean the world, there will be no kings, yet the world will have order, championed by the hand of the common man, for the common man. Only then, will there be no hunger, no shivering in the cold, no suffering without help. The good of the people will be put above the selfish desires of the individual."

Nicci wanted to do good—she truly did. But his voice sounded to her like a rusty dungeon door grating shut on her.

All the eyes in the room watched her, to see if she was good, like her mother. "That sounds wonderful, Brother Narev."

He nodded. "It will be, child. You will help bring this to be. Let your feelings be your guide. You will be a soldier, marching toward a new world order. It will be a long and arduous task. You must keep the faith. The rest of us in this room will not likely live to see it flourish, but perhaps you will live long enough to one day see such a wondrous order come to pass."

Nicci swallowed. "I will pray for it, Brother Narev."

The next day, loaded with a big basket of bread, Nicci was let out of the carriage, along with a gaggle of other people from the fellowship, to fan out and distribute bread to the needy. Mother had attired her in a ruffled red dress for the special occasion. Her short white stockings had designs stitched in red thread. Filled with pride to at last be doing good, Nicci marched down the garbage strewn street, armed with her basket of bread, thinking about the day when the hope of a new order could be spread to all so that all could finally rise up out of destitution and despair.

Some people smiled and thanked her for the bread. Some took the bread without a word or a smile. Most, though, were surly about it, complaining that the bread was late and the loaves were too small, or the wrong kind. Nicci was not discouraged. She told them what Mother had said, that it was the baker's fault, because he baked bread for profit, first, and since he received a reduced rate for charity, baked that second. Nicci told them that she was sorry that wicked people treated them as second-rate, but that someday the Fellowship of Order would come to the land and see to it that everyone was treated the same.

As Nicci walked down the street, handing out the bread, a man snatched her arm and pulled her into the stench of a narrow dark alley. She offered him a loaf of bread. He swiped the basket out of her hands. He said he wanted silver or gold. Nicci told him she had no money. She gasped in panic as he yanked her close. His filthy probing fingers groped everywhere on her body, even violating her most private places, looking for a purse, but found none hidden on her. He pulled off her shoes and threw them away when he found they had no coins hidden in them.

His fist punched her twice in the stomach. Nicci crashed to the ground. He spat a curse at her as he stole away into the shadowed heaps of refuse.

Holding herself up on trembling arms, Nicci vomited into the oily water running from under the mounds of offal. People passing the alley looked in and saw her retching there on the ground, but turned their eyes back to the street and hurried on their way. A few quickly darted into the alley, bent, and scooped up bread from the overturned basket before rushing off. Nicci panted, tears stinging her eyes, trying to get her wind back. Her knees were bleeding. Her dress was splattered with scum.

When she returned home, in tears, Mother smiled at seeing her. "Their plight often brings tears to my eyes, too."

Nicci shook her head, her golden locks swinging side to side, and told Mother that a man had grabbed her and hit her, demanding money. Nicci reached for her mother as she wailed in misery that he was a wicked, wicked man.

Mother smacked her mouth. "Don't you dare judge people. You are just a child. How can you presume to judge others?"

Stopped cold, Nicci was bewildered by the slap, more startling than painful. The rebuke stung more. "But, Mother, he was cruel to me—he touched me everywhere and then he hit me."

Mother smacked her mouth again, harder the second time. "I'll not have you disgrace me before Brother Narev and my friends with such insensitive talk. Do you hear? You don't know what made him do it. Perhaps he has sick children at home, and he needs money to buy medicine. Here he sees some spoiled rich child, and he finally breaks, knowing his own child has been cheated in life by the likes of you and all your fine things.

"You don't know what burdens life has handed the man. Don't you dare to judge people for their actions just because you are too callous and insensitive to take the time to understand them."

"But I think—"

Mother smacked her across the mouth a third time, hard enough to stagger her. "You think? Thinking is a vile acid that corrodes faith! It is your duty to believe, not think. The mind of man is inferior to that of the Creator. Your thoughts—the thoughts of anyone—are worthless, as all mankind is worthless. You must have faith that the Creator has invested His goodness in those wretched souls.

"Feelings, not thinking, must be your guide. Faith, not thinking, must be your only path."

Nicci swallowed back her tears. "Then what should I do?"

"You should be ashamed that the world treats those poor souls so cruelly that they would so pitifully strike out in confusion. In the future, you should find a way to help people like that because you are able and they are not—that is your duty."

That night, when her father came home and tiptoed into her room to see if she was tucked in snugly, Nicci clutched two of his big fingers together and held them tight to her cheek. Even though her mother said he was a wicked man, it felt better than anything else in the world when he knelt beside the bed and silently stroked her brow.

In her work on the streets, Nicci came to understand the needs of many of the people there. Their problems seemed insurmountable. No matter what she did, it never seemed to resolve anything. Brother Narev said it was only a sign that she wasn't giving enough of herself. Each time she failed, at Brother Narev's or Mother's urging, Nicci redoubled her efforts.

One night at dinner, after being in the fellowship several years, she said, "Father, there is a man I've been trying to help. He has ten children and no job. Will you hire him, please?"

Father looked up from his soup. "Why?"

"I told you. He has ten children."

"But what sort of work can he do? Why would I want him?"

"Because he needs a job."

Father set down his spoon. "Nicci, dear, I employ skilled workers. That he has ten children is not going to shape steel, now is it? What can the man do? What skills has he?"

"If he had a skill, Father, he could get work. Is it fair that his children should starve because people won't give him a chance?"

Father looked at her as if inspecting a wagonload of some suspicious new metal. Mother's narrow mouth turned up in a little smile, but she said nothing.

"A chance? At what? He has no skill."

"With a business as big as yours, surely you can give him a job."

He tapped a finger on the stem of his spoon as he considered her determined expression. He cleared his throat. "Well, perhaps I could use a man to load wagons."

"He can't load wagons. He has a bad back. He hasn't been able to work for years because of his back troubling him so."

Father's brow drew down. "His back didn't prevent him from begetting ten children."

Nicci wanted to do good, and so she met his stare with a steady look of her own. "Must you be so intolerant, Father? You have jobs, and this man needs one. He has hungry children needing to be fed and clothed. Would you deny him a living just because he has never had a fair chance in life? Are you so rich that all your gold has blinded your eyes to the needs of humble people?"

"But I need—"

"Must you always frame everything in terms of what *you* need, instead of what others need? Must everything be for you?"

"It's a business—"

"And what is the purpose of a business? Isn't it to employ those who need work? Wouldn't it be better if the man had a job instead of having to humiliate himself begging? Is that what you want? For him to beg rather than work? Aren't you the one who always speaks so highly of hard work?"

Nicci was firing the questions like arrows, getting them off so fast he couldn't get a word through her barrage. Mother smiled as Nicci rolled out words she knew by heart.

"Why must you reserve your greatest cruelty for the least fortunate among us? Why can't you for once think of what you can do to help, instead of always thinking of money, money, money? Would it hurt you to hire a man who needs a job? Would it Father? Would it bring your business to an end? Would that ruin you?"

The room echoed her noble questions. He stared at her as if seeing her for the first time. He looked as if real arrows had struck him. His jaw worked, but no words came out. He didn't seem able to move; he could only gape at her.

Mother beamed.

"Well . . ." he finally said, "I guess . . ." He picked up his spoon and stared down into his soup. "Send him around, and I'll give him a job."

Nicci swelled with a new sense of pride—and power. She had never known it would be so easy to stagger her father. She had just bested his selfish nature with nothing more than goodness.

Father pushed back from the table. "I . . . I need to go back to the shop." His eyes searched the table, but he would not look at Nicci or Mother. "I just remembered . . . I have some work I must see to."

After he had gone, Mother said, "I'm glad to see that you have chosen the righteous path, Nicci, instead of following his evil ways. You will never regret letting your love of mankind guide your feelings. The Creator will smile upon you."

Nicci knew she had done the right thing, the moral thing, yet the thought that came to haunt her victory was the night her father had come into her room and silently stroked her brow as she had held two of his fingers to her cheek.

The man went to work for Father. Father never mentioned anything about it. His work kept him busy and away from home. Nicci's work took more and more of her time, as well. She missed seeing that look in his eyes. She guessed she was growing up.

The next spring, when Nicci was thirteen, she came home one day from her work at the fellowship to find a woman in the sitting room with Mother. Something about the woman's demeanor made the hair at the back of Nicci's neck stand on end. Both women rose as Nicci set aside her list of names of people needing things.

"Nicci, darling, this is Sister Alessandra. She's traveled here from the Palace of the Prophets, in Tanimura."

The woman was older than Mother. She had a long braid of fine brown hair looped around in a circle and pinned to the back of her skull like a loaf of braided bread. Her nose was a little too big for her face, and she was plain, but not at all ugly. Her eyes focused on Nicci with an unsettling intensity, and they didn't dart about, the way Mother's always did.

"Was it quite a journey, Sister Alessandra?" Nicci asked after she had curtsied. "All the way from Tanimura, I mean?"

"Three days is all," Sister Alessandra said. A smile grew on her face as she took in Nicci's bony frame. "My, my. So little, yet, for such grownup work." She held out a hand toward a chair. "Won't you sit with us, dear?"

"Are you a Sister with the fellowship?" Nicci asked, not really understanding who the woman was.

"The what?"

"Nicci," Mother said, "Sister Alessandra is a Sister of the Light."

Astonished, Nicci dropped into a chair. Sisters of the Light had the gift, just like her and Mother. Nicci didn't know very much about the Sisters, except that they served the Creator. That still didn't settle her stomach. To have such a woman right there in her house was intimidating—like when she stood before Brother Narev. She felt an inexplicable sense of doom.

Nicci was also impatient because she had duties waiting. There were donations to collect. She had older sponsors who accompanied her to some of the places. For other places, they said a young girl could get better results by herself, by shaming people who had more than they deserved. Those people, who had businesses, all knew who she was. They would always stammer and ask how her father was. As she had been instructed, Nicci told them how pleased her father would be to know they were thoughtful to the needy. In the end, most became civic-minded.

Then, there were remedies Nicci needed to take to women with sick children. There wasn't enough clothing for the children, either. Nicci was trying to get some people to give cloth and other people to sew clothes. Some people had no homes, others were crowded together in little rooms. She was trying to get some rich people to donate a building. Also, Nicci had been assigned the task of locating jugs for women to bring water from the well. She needed to pay a visit to the potter. Some of the older children had been caught stealing. Others had been fighting, and a few of them were beating younger children bloody. Nicci had been pleading on their behalf, trying to explain that they had no fair chance, and were only reacting to their cruel circumstance. She hoped to convince Father to take on at least a few so they might have work.

The problems just kept mounting, without any end in sight. It seemed like the more people the fellowship helped, the more people there were who needed help. Nicci had thought she was going to solve the problems of the world; she was beginning to feel hopelessly inadequate. It was her own failing, she knew. She needed to work harder.

"Do you read and write, dear?" the Sister asked.

"Not very much, Sister. Mostly just names. I've much too much to do for those less fortunate than myself. Their needs must come before any selfish desires of my own."

Mother smiled and nodded to herself.

"Practically a good spirit in the flesh." The Sister's eyes teared. "I've heard about your work."

"You have?" Nicci felt a flash of pride, but then she thought of how things never seemed to get better, despite all her efforts, and her sense of failure returned. Besides, Mother said pride was evil. "I don't see what's so special about what I do. The people in the streets are the ones who are special, because of their suffering in horrid conditions. They are the true inspiration."

Mother smiled contentedly. Sister Alessandra leaned forward, her tone serious. "Have you learned to use your gift, child?"

"Mother teaches me to do some small things, like how to heal little troubles, but I know it would be unfair to flaunt it over those less blessed than I, so I try my best not to use it."

The Sister folded her hands in her lap. "I've been talking to your mother, while we waited for you. She's done a fine job of getting you started on the right path. We feel, however, that you would have so much more to offer were you to serve a higher calling."

Nicci sighed. "Well, all right. Maybe I can get up a little earlier. But I already have my duties to the needy, and I will have to fit this other in as I can. I hope you understand, Sister. I'm not trying to get undeserved sympathy, honestly I'm not, but I hope you don't need this calling done too soon, as I'm already quite busy."

Sister Alessandra smiled in a long-suffering sort of way. "You don't understand, Nicci. We would like you to continue your work with us at the Palace of the Prophets. You would be a novice at first, of course, but one day, you will be a Sister of the Light, and as such, you will carry on with what you have started."

Panic welled up in Nicci like rising floodwaters. There were so many people who hung to life only by a thread she tended. She had friends at the fellowship whom she had come to love. She had so much to do. She didn't want to leave Mother, and even Father. He was evil, she knew, but he wasn't evil to her. He was selfish and greedy, she knew, but he still tucked her into bed, sometimes, and patted her shoulder. She was sure she would see something in his blue eyes again, if she just gave it time. She didn't want to leave him. For some reason, she desperately needed to again see that spark in his eyes. She was being selfish, she knew.

"I have needy people here, Sister Alessandra." Nicci blinked at her tears. "My responsibility is to them. I'm sorry but I can't abandon them."

At that moment, Father came in the door. He stopped in an awkward posture, his legs frozen in midstride, with his hand on the lever, staring at the Sister.

"What's this, then?"

Mother stood. "Howard, this is Alessandra. She is a Sister of the Light. She's come to—"

"No! I'll not have it, do you hear? She's our daughter, and the Sisters can't have her."

Sister Alessandra stood, giving Mother a sidelong glance. "Please ask your husband to leave. This is not his business."

"Not my business? She's my daughter! You'll not take her!"

He lunged forward to seize Nicci's outstretched hand. The Sister lifted a finger and, to Nicci's astonishment, he was thrown back in a sparkling flash of light.

Father's back slammed against the wall. He slid down, clutching his chest as he gasped for breath. Tears bursting forth, Nicci ran for him, but Sister Alessandra snatched her by the arm and held her back.

"Howard," Mother said through gritted teeth, "the child is my business to raise. I carry the Creator's gift. You gave your word when our union was arranged that if we had a girl and she had the gift I would have the exclusive authority to raise her as I saw fit. I believe this to be the right thing to do—what the Creator wants. With the Sisters she will have time to learn to read. She will have time to learn to use her gift to help people as only the Sisters can. You will keep your word. I will see to this. I'm sure you have work to which you must immediately return."

With the flat of his hand, he rubbed his chest. Finally, his arms dropped to his sides. Head down, he shuffled to the door. Before he pulled closed the door, his gaze met Nicci's. Through the tears, she saw the spark in his eyes, as if he had things to tell her, but then it was gone, and he pulled the door shut behind himself.

Sister Alessandra said it would be best if they left at once, and if Nicci didn't see him just now. She promised that if Nicci followed instructions, and after she was settled, and after she had learned to read, and after she had learned to use her gift, she would see him again.

Nicci learned to read and to use her gift and mastered everything else she was supposed to master. She fulfilled all the requirements. She did everything expected of her. Her life, as a novice to become a Sister of the Light, was numbingly selfless. Sister Alessandra forgot her promise. She was not pleased to be reminded of it, and found more work that Nicci needed to do.

Several years after she had been taken to the palace, Nicci again saw Brother Narev. She came across him quite by accident; he was working as a stablehand at the Palace of the Prophets. He smiled his slow smile with his eyes fixed on her. He told her that he had gotten the idea to go to the palace by her example. He said he wished to live long enough to see order come to the world.

She thought it an odd occupation for him. He said that he found working for the Sisters morally superior to contributing his labor to the evil of profit. He said it mattered not if she chose to tell anyone at the palace anything about him or his work for the fellowship, but he asked her not to tell the Sisters that he was gifted, since they would not allow him to continue to stay and work in the stables if they knew, and he would refuse to serve them should they discover his gift, because, he said, he wanted to serve the Creator in his own quiet way.

Nicci honored his secret, not so much out of any sense of loyalty, but mostly because she was kept far too busy with her studies and work to concern herself with Brother Narev and his fellowship. She rarely had occasion to see him, mucking out horse stalls, and as his importance in her childhood had faded into her past, she never really even gave him a second thought. The palace had work they wished her to put her attention to—much the same sort of work Brother Narev would have approved of. Only many years later did she come to discover his real reasons for having been at the Palace of the Prophets.

Sister Alessandra saw to it that Nicci was kept busy. She was allowed no time for such selfish indulgences as going home for a visit. Twenty-seven years after she had been taken away to become a Sister of the Light, still a novice, Nicci again saw her father. It was at his funeral.

Mother had sent word for Nicci to return home to see Father because he was in failing health. Nicci immediately rushed home, accompanied by Sister Alessandra. By the time Nicci arrived, Father was already dead.

Mother said that for several weeks he had been begging her to send for his daughter. She sighed and said she put it off, thinking he would get better. Besides, she said, she hadn't wanted to disturb Nicci's important work—not for such a trivial matter. She said it had been the only thing he asked for: to see Nicci. Mother thought that was silly, since he was a man who didn't care about people. Why should he need to see anyone? He died alone, while Mother was out helping the victims of an uncaring world.

By that time, Nicci was forty. Mother, though, still thinking of Nicci as a young woman because under the spell at the palace she had aged only enough to look to be maybe fifteen or sixteen, told her to wear a pretty, brightly colored dress, because it wasn't really a sad occasion, after all.

Nicci stood looking at the body for a long time. Her chance to see his blue eyes again was forever lost. For the first time in years, the pain made her feel something, down deep inside. It felt good to feel something again, even if it was pain.

As Nicci stood looking at her father's sunken face, Sister Alessandra told Nicci that she was sorry she had to take her away, but that in her whole life, she had not encountered a woman with the gift as powerful as it was in Nicci, and that such a thing as the Creator had given her was not to be wasted.

Nicci said she understood. Since she had ability, it was only right that she use it to help those in need.

At the Palace of the Prophets, Nicci was said to be the most selfless, caring novice they had under their roof. Everyone pointed to her, and told the younger novices to look to Nicci's example. Even the Prelate had commended her.

The praise was but a buzz in her ear. It was an injustice to be better than others. Try as she might, Nicci could not escape her father's legacy of excellence. His taint coursed through her veins, oozed from every pore, and infected everything she did. The more selfless she was the more it only confirmed her superiority, and thus her wickedness.

She knew that could mean only one thing: she was evil.

"Try not to remember him like this," Sister Alessandra said after a long silence as they stood before the body. "Try to remember what he was like when he was alive."

"I can't," Nicci said. "I never knew him when he was alive."

Mother and her friends at the fellowship ran the business. She wrote Nicci joyful letters, telling her how she had put many of the needy to work at the armorers. She said the business could afford it, with all the wealth it had accumulated. Mother was proud that that wealth could now be put to a moral use. She said Father's death had been a cloaked blessing, because it meant help at last for those who had always deserved it most. It was all part of the Creator's plan, she said.

Mother had to raise her prices in order to pay the wages of all the people she'd given work. A lot of the older workers left. Mother said she was glad they were gone because they had uncooperative attitudes.

Orders fell behind. Suppliers began demanding to be paid before delivering goods. Mother discontinued having the armor proofed because the new workers complained that it was an unfair standard to be held to. They said they were trying their best, and that was what counted. Mother sympathized.

The battering-mill had to be sold. Some of the customers stopped ordering armor and weapons. Mother said they would be better off without such intolerant people. She sought new laws from the duke to require work to be spread out equally, but the laws were slow in coming. The few remaining customers hadn't paid their account for quite a while, but promised to catch up. In the meantime, their goods were shipped, if late.

Within six months of Father dying, the business failed. The vast fortune he had built over a lifetime was gone.

Some of the skilled workers once hired by Father moved on, hoping to find work at armories in distant places. Most men who stayed could find only menial work; they were lucky to have that. Many of the new workers demanded Mother do something; she and the fellowship petitioned other businesses to take them on. Some business tried to help, but most were in no position to hire workers.

The armory had been the largest employer in the area, and drew many other people employed in other occupations. Other businesses, like traders, smaller suppliers, and cargo carriers, who had depended on the armory, failed for lack of work. Businesses in the city, everything from bakers to butchers, lost customers and were reluctantly forced to let men go.

Mother asked the duke to speak with the king. The duke said the king was considering the problem.

Like her father's armory, other buildings were abandoned as people left to find work in thriving cities elsewhere. Squatters, at the fellowship's urging, took over many of the abandoned buildings. The empty places became the sites of robberies and even murders. Many a woman who went near those places regretted it. Mother couldn't sell the weapons from her closed armory, so she gave them to the needy so they might protect themselves. Despite her efforts, crime only increased.

In honor of all her good work, and her father's service to the government, the king granted Mother a pension that allowed her to stay in the house, with a reduced staff. She continued her work with the fellowship, trying to right all the injustice that she believed was responsible for the failure of the business. She hoped one day to reopen the shop and employ people. For her righteous work, the king awarded her a silver medal. Mother wrote that the king proclaimed she was as close to a good spirit in the flesh as he had ever seen. Nicci regularly received word of awards Mother was given for her selfless work.

Eighteen years later, when Mother died, Nicci still looked like a young woman of perhaps seventeen. She wanted a fine black dress to wear to the funeral—the finest available. The palace said that it was unseemly for a novice to make such a selfish request, and it was out of the question. They said they would supply only simple humble clothes.

When Nicci arrived home, she went to the tailor to the king and told him that for her mother's funeral she needed the finest black dress he had ever made. He told her the price. She informed him she had no money, but said she needed the dress anyway.

The tailor, a man with three chins, waxy down growing from his ears, abnormally long yellowish fingernails, and an unfailing lecherous smirk, said there were things he needed, too. He leaned close, lightly holding her smooth arm in his knobby fingers, and intimated that if she would take care of his needs, he would take care of hers.

Nicci wore the finest black dress ever made to her mother's funeral.

Mother had been a woman who had devoted her entire life to the needs of others. Nicci could never again look forward to seeing her mother's cockroach-brown eyes. Unlike at her father's funeral, Nicci felt no pain reach down to touch that abysmal place inside her. Nicci knew she was a terrible person.

For the first time, she realized that for some reason she simply no longer cared.

From that day on, Nicci never wore any dress but black.

One hundred and twenty-three years later, standing at the railing overlooking the great hall, Nicci saw eyes that stunned her with their sense of an inner value held dear. But what had been an uncertain ember in her father's eyes was ablaze in Richard's. She still didn't know what it was.

She knew only that it was the difference between life and death, and that she had to destroy him.

Now, at long last, she knew how.

If only, when she had been little, someone had shown her father such mercy.

Trudging down the road between the edge of the city of Fairfield and the estate where the three Sisters had told her Emperor Jagang had set up his residence, Nicci scanned the surrounding jumble of the Imperial Order's encampment, looking for a specific station of tents. She knew they would be somewhere in the area; Jagang liked to have them close at hand. Regular sleeping tents, wagons, and men lay like a dark soot over the fields and hills as far as she could see. Sky and land alike seemed tinted by a dusky taint. Sprinkled through the dark fields, campfires twinkled, like a sky full of stars.

The day was becoming oppressively dim, not only with the approach of evening, but also from the dull overcast of churning gray clouds. The wind kicked up in little fits, setting tents and clothes flapping, fluttering the campfires' flames, and whipping smoke this way and that. The gusts helped coat the tongue with the fetid stench of human and animal waste, smothering any pleasant but weak cooking aroma that struggled to take to the air. The longer the army stayed in place, the worse it would get.

Up ahead, the elegant buildings of the estate rose above the dark grime at its feet. Jagang was there. Because he had access to Sisters Georgia, Rochelle, and Aubrey's minds, he would know Nicci was back. He would be waiting for her.

The emperor would have to wait; she had something else to do, first. Without Jagang able to enter her mind, she was free to pursue it.

Nicci saw what she was looking for, off in the distance. She could just make them out, standing above the smaller tents. She left the road and headed through the crowded snarl of troops. Even from the distance, she could distinguish the distinctive sounds coming from the group of special tents—hear it over the laughing and singing, the crackle of fires, the sizzle of meat in skillets, the scraping rasp of whetstones on metal, the ring of hammers on steel, and the rhythm of saws.

Boisterous men grabbed at her arms and legs or tried to snatch her dress as she marched along, picking her way through the disorder. The rowdy soldiers were but a minor consideration; she simply pulled away, ignoring their mocking calls of love, as she made her way through the throng. When a husky soldier seized her wrist in his powerful grip, yanking her around to a jerking halt, she paused only long enough to loose her power and burst his beating heart within his chest. Other men laughed when they saw him collapse to the ground with a thud, not yet realizing he was dead, but none tried to claim his intended prize. She heard the words "Death's Mistress" pass in whispers among the men.

She finally made her way through the gauntlet. Soldiers played dice, ate beans, or snored in their bedrolls beside the tents where captives screamed under the agony of torture. Two men lugged a corpse, dragging some of its innards, out of a big tent. They threw the flaccid form in a wagon with a tangle of others.

Nicci snapped her fingers at an unshaven soldier coming from the direction of another tent. "Let me see the list, Captain." She knew he was the officer in charge by the blue canvas cover of the register book he carried.

He scowled at her a moment, but when he glanced down at her black dress, a look of recognition came over his face. He passed her the grubby, rumpled book. It had a deep crease across the middle, as if someone had accidentally sat on it. The pages that had fallen out had been pushed back in, but they never fit right and their edges stuck out here and there to become frayed and filthy.

"Not much to report, Mistress, but please let His Excellency know that we've tried just about every skill known, and she isn't talking."

Nicci opened the book and began scanning the list of recent names and what was known about them.

"Her? Who are you talking about, Captain?" she mumbled as she read.

"Why, the Mord-Sith, of course."

Nicci turned her eyes up toward the man. "The Mord-Sith. Of course. Where is she?"

He pointed at a tent a ways off through the disarray. "I know His Excellency said he didn't expect a witch of her dark talents to give us any information about Lord Rahl, but I was hoping to surprise him with good news." He hooked his thumbs behind his belt as he let out a sigh of frustration. "No such luck."

Nicci eyed the tent for a moment. She heard no screams. She had never before seen one of those women, the Mord-Sith, but she knew a little about them. She knew that using magic against one was a deadly mistake.

She went back to reading the entries in the register. There was nothing of much interest to her. Most of the people were from around here. They were merely a sampling collected to check what they might know. They would not have the information she wanted.

Nicci tapped a line near the end of the writing in the book. It said "Messenger."

"Where is this one?"

The captain tilted his head, indicating a tent behind him. "I put one of my best questioners with him. Last I checked, there was nothing from him yet—but that was early this morning."

It had been all day since he had checked. All day could be an eternity under torture. Like all the rest of the tents used for questioning prisoners, the one with the messenger stood above the surrounding field tents, which were only large enough for soldiers to lie in. Nicci pushed the book at the officer's thick gut.

"Thank you. That will be all."

"You'll be giving His Excellency a report, then?" Nicci nodded absently at his question. Her mind was already elsewhere. "You'll tell him that there is little to be learned from this lot?"

No one was eager to stand before Jagang and admit they were unable to accomplish a task, even if there was nothing to accomplish. Jagang did not appreciate excuses. Nicci nodded as she strode away, heading for the tent holding the messenger. "I'll be seeing him shortly. I'll give him the report for you, Captain."

As soon as she threw back the flap and entered, she saw that she was too late. The messy remains of the messenger lay on a narrow wooden table affixed with glistening tools of the trade. The messenger's arms hung down off the sides, dripping warm blood.

Nicci saw that the questioner had a folded piece of paper. "What have you there?"

He held up the paper and flashed her a grin. "Something His Excellency will be very pleased to hear about. I've got a map."

"A map of what?"

"Where this fellow's been. I drew it all out from what he volunteered." He laughed at his own humor. She didn't.

"Really," Nicci said. The man's grin was what had her attention. A man like this only grinned when he had something he'd been seeking, something to bring him favor in the eyes of his superiors. "And where has the man been?"

"To see his leader."

He waved the paper like a treasure map. Tired of the game, Nicci snatched the booty from his hand. She unfolded the wrinkled yellow paper and saw that it was indeed a map, with rivers, the coastline, and mountains all meticulously drawn out. Even mountain passes were noted.

Nicci could tell that the map was authentic. When she had lived at the Palace of the Prophets, the New World was a far-off and mysterious place, rarely visited by anyone but a few Sisters. Any Sister who ventured there always kept exacting records that were added to maps at the palace. Along with many other esoteric items, all novices memorized those maps in the course of their studies. Even though, at the time, she had never expected to travel to the New World, she was thoroughly familiar with the lay of the land there. Nicci scrutinized the paper in her hands, carefully surveying the geography, overlaying everything on it that was new onto the memorized map in her mind.

The soldier pointed a thick finger at a single bloody fingerprint on the map. "That there is where Lord Rahl himself is hiding—on that dot, in those mountains."

Nicci's breath paused. She stared at the paper, burning the line of every stream and river, every mountain, every road, trail, and mountain pass, every village, town, and city into her memory.

"What did this man confess before he died?" She looked up. "His Excellency is waiting for my report. I was just on my way to see him." She snapped her fingers impatiently. "Let's have it all."

The man scratched his beard. His fingernails were crusted with dried blood. "You'll tell him, won't you? You'll tell His Excellency that Sergeant Wetzel was the one who got the information out of the messenger?"

"Of course," Nicci assured him. "You will receive full credit. I have no need of such recognition." She tapped the gold ring through her lower lip. "The Emperor is always—every moment of every day—in my mind. He no doubt this very moment sees through my eyes that you, not I, are the one who succeeded in getting the information. Now, what did this man confess?"

Sergeant Wetzel scratched his beard again, apparently trying to decide if he could trust her to credit him, or if he should be sure and take the information to Jagang. There was little trust among those in the Imperial Order, and good reason to distrust everyone. As he scratched his beard, flakes of dried blood stuck in its curly hair.

Nicci stared into his red-rimmed eyes. He smelled of liquor. "If you don't report everything to me, Sergeant Wetzel, and I mean right now, I will have you up on that table next, and I will have your report between your screams, and when I'm done with you, they will throw you in the wagon with the rest of the corpses."

He dipped his head twice in surrender. "Of course. I only wanted to be sure His Excellency knew of my success." When Nicci nodded, he went on. "He was just a messenger. We had a small unit of six men doing deep scouting patrol. They went on a circle far to the north, around any enemy forces. They had one of the gifted women with them to help them remain at a good distance, so they wouldn't be detected. They were somewhere northwest of the enemy force, when by chance they came across this man. They brought him back for me to question. I discovered he was one of a number of regular messengers sent back and forth to report to Lord Rahl."

Nicci waggled a finger at the paper. "But this, down here, looks like the enemy force. Are you saying Rich . . . Lord Rahl, isn't with his men? With his army?"

"That's right. The messenger didn't know why. His only duty was to carry troop positions and regular news of their condition to his master." He tapped the map in her hand. "But right here is where Lord Rahl is hiding, along with his wife."

Nicci looked up, her mouth falling open. "Wife."

Sergeant Wetzel nodded. "The man said Lord Rahl married some woman known as the Mother Confessor. She's hurt, and they're hiding way up there, in those mountains."

Nicci remembered Richard's feelings for her, and her name: Kahlan. Richard being married put everything in a new light. It had the potential to disrupt Nicci's plans. Or . . .

"Anything else, Sergeant?"

"The man said Lord Rahl and his wife have one of them women, them Mord-Sith, guarding them."

"Why are they up there? Why aren't Lord Rahl and the Mother Confessor with their army? Or back in Aydindril? Or in D'Hara, for that matter?"

He shook his head. "This messenger was just a low-ranking soldier who knew how to ride fast and read the lay of the land. That's all he knew: they're up there, and they're all alone."

Nicci was puzzled by such a development.

"Anything else? Anything at all?" He shook his head. She laid her hand on the man's back, between his shoulder blades. "Thank you, Sergeant Wetzel. You have been more help than you will ever know."

As he grinned, Nicci released a flow of power that shot up through his spine and instantly incinerated his brain inside his skull. He dropped with a crash to the hard ground, the air fleeing his lungs in a grunt.

Nicci held up the map she had committed to memory and with her gift set it aflame. The paper crackled and blackened as the fire advanced across the rivers and cities and mountains all carefully drawn out on it, until the hot glow surrounded the bloody fingerprint over a dot in the mountains. She let the paper rise from her fingers as it was consumed in a final puff of smoke. Ash, like black snow, drifted down onto the body at her feet.

Outside the tent where the Mord-Sith was held, Nicci cast a wary gaze across the surrounding camp to see if anyone was watching. No one was paying any attention to the business of the torture tents. She slipped in through the opening.

Nicci winced at the sight of the woman laid out on the wooden table. She finally made herself draw a breath.

A soldier, his hands red from his work, scowled at Nicci. She didn't wait for him to object, but simply commanded, "Report."

"Not a word from her," he growled.

Nicci nodded and placed her hand on the soldier's broad back. Wary of her hand, he began to step away from it, but he was too late. The man fell dead before he knew he was in trouble. Had she the time, she would have made him suffer first.

Nicci made herself step up to the table and look down into the blue eyes. The woman's head trembled slightly.

"Use your power . . . to hurt me, witch."

A small smile touched Nicci's lips. "To the bitter end, you would fight, wouldn't you?"

"Use your magic, witch."

"I think not. You see, I know a bit about you women."

Defiance blazed up from the blue eyes. "You know nothing."

"Oh, but I do. Richard told me. You would know him as your Lord Rahl, but he was for a time my student. I know that women like you have the ability to capture the power of the gifted, if that power is used against you. Then, you can turn it against us. So, you see, I know better than to use my power on you."

The woman looked away. "Then torture me if that is what you came to do. You will learn nothing."

"I'm not here to torture you," Nicci assured her.

"Then what do you want?"

"Let me introduce myself," Nicci said. "I am Death's Mistress."

The woman's blue eyes turned back, betraying for the first time a glint of hope. "Good. Kill me."

"I need you to tell me some things."

"I'll not . . . tell you . . . anything." It was a struggle for her to speak. "Not anything. Kill me."

Nicci picked up a bloody blade from the table and held it before the blue eyes. "I think you will."

The woman smiled. "Go ahead. It will only hasten my death. I know how much a person can take. I am not far from the spirit world. But no matter what you do, I'll not talk before I die."

"You misunderstand. I do not wish you to betray your Lord Rahl. Didn't you hear your questioner hit the ground? If you turn your head a little more, perhaps you can see that the man who did this to you is now dead. I don't wish you to tell me any secrets."

The woman glanced, as best she could, toward the body on the ground. Her brow twitched. "What do you mean?"

Nicci noticed that she didn't ask to be freed. She knew she was well past the point of hope to live. The only thing she could hope for, now, was for Nicci to end her agony.

"Richard was my student. He told me that he was once a captive of the Mord-Sith. Now, that's not a secret, is it?"

"No."

"That's what I want to know about. What is your name?"

The woman turned her face away.

Nicci put a finger to the woman's chin and turned her head back. "I have an offer to make you. I won't ask you anything secret that you aren't supposed to tell. I'll not ask you to betray your Lord Rahl—I wouldn't want you to. Those are not the things that are of interest to me. If you cooperate"—Nicci held up the blade again for the woman to see—"I will end it quickly for you. I promise. No more torture. No more pain. Just the final embrace of death."

The woman's lips began trembling. "Please," she whispered, the hope returning to her eyes. "Please . . . kill me?"

"What is your name?" Nicci asked.

Nicci, for the most part, was numb to sights of torture, but this she found disturbing. She avoided looking away from the woman's face, down at the naked body, so as not to have to consider what had been done to her. Nicci could not imagine how this woman could keep from screaming, or even how she was able to speak.

"Hania." The woman's hands and ankles were shackled to the table, so she was unable to move much other than her head. She stared up into Nicci's eyes. "Will you kill me? . . . Please?"

"I will, Hania, I promise. Quickly and efficiently—if you tell me what I want to know."

"I can't tell you anything." In despair, Hania seemed to sag against the table, knowing her ordeal was to go on. "I won't."

"I only want to know about when Richard was a captive. Did you know he was once a captive of the Mord-Sith?"

"Of course."

"I want to know about it."

"Why?"

"Because I want to understand him."

Hania's head rocked side to side. She actually smiled. "None of us understands Lord Rahl. He was tortured, but he never . . . took revenge. We don't understand him."

"I don't either, but I hope to. My name is Nicci. I want you to know that. I'm Nicci, and I'm going to deliver you from this, Hania. Tell me about it. Please? I need to know. Do you know the woman who captured him? Her name?"

The woman considered for a moment before she spoke, as if testing in her own mind whether or not the information was in any way secret, or could in any way harm him.

"Denna," Hania whispered at last.

"Denna. Richard killed her in order to escape—he already told me that much. Did you know Denna before she died?"

"Yes."

"I'm not asking anything of secret military importance, am I?"

Hania hesitated. She finally shook her head.

"So, you knew Denna. And did you know Richard at the time? When he was there, and she had him? Did you know he was her captive?"

"We all knew."

"Why is that?"

"Lord Rahl—the Lord Rahl at the time—"

"Richard's father."

"Yes. He wanted Denna to be the one to train Richard, to prepare him to answer without hesitation whatever questions Darken Rahl asked him. She was the best at what we do."

"Good. Now, tell me everything about it. Everything you know."

Hania drew a shaky breath. It took a moment before she spoke again. "I won't betray him. I am experienced at what is being done to me. You cannot trick me. I will not betray Lord Rahl just to spare myself this. I have not endured this much to betray him now."

"I promise not to ask anything about the present—about the war—anything that would betray him to Jagang."

"If I tell you only about when Denna had him, and not about now, about the war or where he is or anything else, do you give me your word that you will end it for me—that you will kill me?"

"I give you my word, Hania. I wouldn't ask you to betray your Lord Rahl—I know him and have too much respect for him to ask that of you. All I wish is to understand him for personal reasons. I was his teacher, last winter, instructing him in the use of his gift. I want to understand him better. I need to understand him. I believe I can help him, if I do."

"And then you will help me?" There was a shimmer of hope along with the tears. "You will kill me, then?"

This woman could aspire to nothing more, now. It was all that was left to her in this life: a quick death to finally end the pain.

"Just as soon as you're finished telling me all about it, I will end your suffering, Hania."

"Do you swear it by your hope to an eternity in the underworld in the warmth of the Creator's light?"

Nicci felt a sharp shiver of pain wail up from her very soul. She had started out near to one hundred and seventy years before wanting nothing but to help, and yet she could not escape the fate of her evil nature. She was Death's Mistress.

She was a fallen woman.

She ran the side of a finger down Hania's soft cheek. The two women shared a long and intimate look. "I promise," Nicci whispered. "Quick and efficient. It will be the end of your pain."

Tears overflowing her eyes, Hania gave a little nod.

The estate was a grand place, she supposed. Nicci had seen grandeur such as this before. She had also seen much greater majesty, to be sure. She had lived among such splendor for nearly one and three-quarters centuries, among the imposing columns and arches of immaculate rooms, the intricately carved stone vines and buttery smooth wood paneling, the feather beds and silk coverlets, the exquisite carpets and rich draperies, the silver and gold ornamentation, and the bright sparkle of windows made of colored glass composed into epic scenes. The Sisters there offered Nicci bright-eyed smiles and clever conversation.

The extravagance meant no more to her than the rubble of the streets, the cold wet blankets laid on rough ground, the beds made in the slime among greasy runnels in the muck of narrow alleys with nothing but the bitter sky overhead. The huddled people there never offered a smile, but gaped up at her with hollow eyes, like so many pigeons cooing for alms.

Some of her life was spent among splendor, some among garbage. Some people were fated to spend their lives in one place, some in the other, she in both.

Nicci reached for the silver handle on one of the ornate double doors flanked by two husky soldiers who had probably been raised in a sty with the hogs, and saw that her hand was covered in blood. She turned and casually wiped the hand on the filthy, bloodstained fleece vest worn by one of the men. The biceps of his folded arms were nearly as thick as her waist. Although he scowled as she cleaned her hand on him, he made no move to stop her. After all, it wasn't as if she were defiling him.

Hania had kept her part of the bargain. Nicci rarely resorted to using a weapon; she usually used her gift. But of course, in this case, that could have been a mistake. When she had held the knife over her throat, Hania had whispered her thanks for what Nicci was about to do. It was the first time anyone had ever thanked Nicci before she had killed them. Few people ever thanked Nicci for the help she provided. She was able, they were not; it was her duty to serve their needs.

When she had finished cleaning her hand on the mute guard, she flashed an empty smile at his dark glaring visage and then went on through the doors into a stately reception hall. A row of tall windows lining one wall of the room was trimmed with wheat-colored drapes. Near their tasseled edges, the curtains sparkled in the lamplight as if they might be embellished with gold thread. Late-summer rain spattered against tightly shut glass panes that revealed only darkness outside, but reflected the activity inside. The pale wool carpets, graced with flowers painstakingly sculpted in relief by means of different-length yarn, were tracked with mud.

Scouts came and went, along with messengers and soldiers giving their reports to some of the officers. Other officers barked orders. Soldiers carrying rolled maps followed a few of the higher-ranking men as they meandered around the stuffy room.

One of the maps lay unrolled across a narrow table. The table's silver candelabrum had been set aside on the floor behind the table. As Nicci passed the table, she glanced down and saw that it was missing many of the elements so carefully marked on the map drawn by the D'Haran messenger. On the map laid out over the narrow table, there was nothing but dark splotches from spilled ale in the area to the northwest; in the map etched in Nicci's mind, there were the mountains, rivers, high passes, and streams there, and a dot, marking the place where Richard was, along with his Mother Confessor bride, and the Mord-Sith.

Officers talked among themselves, some standing about, some half sitting on iron-legged, marble-topped tables, some lounging in padded leather chairs as they took delicacies from silver trays borne on the trembling hands of sweating servants. Others swilled ale from tall pewter mugs, and yet others drank wine from dainty glasses, all acting as if they were intimate with such splendor, and all of them looking as out of place as toads at tea.

An older woman, Sister Lidmila, apparently trying to be unobtrusive by cowering in the shadows beside the drapes, snapped upright when she saw Nicci marching across the room. Sister Lidmila stepped out of the shadows, briefly pausing to smooth her dingy skirts, an act that could not possibly produce any noticeable improvement; Sister Lidmila once had told Nicci that things learned in youth never left you, and were often much easier to recall than yesterday's dinner. Rumor had it that the old Sister, skilled in arcane spells known to only the most powerful sorceresses, had many interesting things from her youth to recall.

Sister Lidmila's leathery skin was stretched so tight over the bones of her skull that she reminded Nicci of nothing so much as an exhumed corpse. As cadaverous-looking as the aged Sister was, she advanced across the room in quick, sharp movements.

When she was only ten feet away, Sister Lidmila waved an arm, as if not sure Nicci would see her. "Sister Nicci. Sister Nicci, there you are." She seized Nicci's wrist. "Come along, dear. Come along. His Excellency is waiting for you. This way. Come along."

Nicci clasped the Sister's tugging hand. "Lead the way, Sister Lidmila. I'm right behind you."

The older woman smiled over her shoulder. It wasn't a pleasant or joyous smile, but one of relief. Jagang punished anyone who displeased him, regardless of their culpability.

"What took you so long, Sister Nicci? His Excellency is in quite a state, he is, because of you. Where have you been?"

"I had . . . business I had to attend to."

The woman had to take two or three steps for every one of Nicci's. "Business indeed! Were it up to me, I'd have you down in the kitchen scrubbing pots for being off on a lark when you are wanted."

Sister Lidmila was frail and forgetful, and she sometimes failed to realize she was no longer at the Palace of the Prophets. Jagang used her to fetch people, or to wait for them and show them the way—usually to his tents. Should she forget the way, he could always correct her route, if need be. It amused him to use a venerable Sister of the Light—a sorceress reputedly possessing knowledge of the most esoteric incantations—as nothing more than an errand girl. Away from the palace and its spell that slowed aging, Sister Lidmila was in a sudden headlong rush toward the grave. All the Sisters were.

The round-backed Sister, her dangling arm swinging, shuffled along in front of Nicci, pulling her by her hand, leading her through grand rooms, up stairways, and down hallways. At a doorway framed in gold-leafed moldings, she finally paused, touching her fingers to her lower lip as she caught her breath. Sober soldiers prowling the hall painted Nicci with glares as dark as her dress. She recognized the men as imperial guards.

"Here it is." Sister Lidmila peered up at Nicci. "His Excellency is in his rooms. Hurry, then. Go on. Go on, now." She swirled her hands as if she were trying to herd livestock. "In you go."

Before entering, Nicci took her hand from the lever and turned back to the old woman. "Sister Lidmila, you once told me that you thought I would be the one best suited for some of the knowledge you had to pass on."

Sister Lidmila's face brightened with a sly smile. "Ah, some of the more occult magic interests you, at long last, Sister Nicci?"

Nicci had never before been interested in what Sister Lidmila had occasionally pestered her to learn. Magic was a selfish pursuit. Nicci learned what she had to, but never went out of her way to go beyond, to the more unusual spells.

"Yes, as a matter of fact, I believe I am at last ready."

"I always told the Prelate that you were the only one at the palace with the power for the conjuring I know." The woman leaned close. "Dangerous conjuring, it is, too."

"It should be passed on, while you are able."

Sister Lidmila nodded with satisfaction. "I believe you are old enough. I could show you. When?"

"I will come see you . . . tomorrow." Nicci glanced toward the door. "I don't believe I will be able to take a lesson tonight."

"Tomorrow, then."

"If I . . . do come around to see you, I will be most eager to learn. I especially wish to know about the maternity spell."

From what Nicci knew of it, the oddly named maternity spell might be just what she needed. It had the further advantage that once invoked, it was inviolate.

Sister Lidmila straightened and again touched her fingers to her lower lip. A look of concern crossed her face.

"My, my. That one, is it? Well, yes, I could teach you. You have the ability—few do. I'd trust none but you to be able to bring such a thing to life; it requires tremendous power of the gift. You have that. As long as you understand and are willing to accept the cost involved, I can teach you."

Nicci nodded. "I will come when I can, then."

The old Sister ambled on down the hall, deep in thought, already thinking about the lesson. Nicci didn't know if she would live to take the lesson.

After she had watched the old Sister vanish around the corner, Nicci entered a quiet room lit by myriad candles and lamps. The high ceiling was edged with a painted leaf-and-acorn design. Plush couches and chairs upholstered in muted browns were set about on thick carpets of rich yellows, oranges, and reds, making them look like a forest floor in the autumn. Heavy drapes had been pulled closed across an expanse of windows. Two Sisters sitting on a couch leaped to their feet.

"Sister Nicci!" one virtually shouted in relief.

The other ran to the double doors at the other side of the room and opened one without knocking, apparently by instruction. She stuck her head into the room beyond to speak in a low voice Nicci couldn't hear.

The Sister leaped back when Jagang, in the inner room, roared, "Get out! All of you! Everyone else out!"

Two more young Sisters, no doubt personal attendants to the emperor, burst out of the room. Nicci had to step out of the way as all four gifted women made for the doorway leading out of the apartment. A young man Nicci hadn't noticed in the corner joined the women. None even glanced in Nicci's direction as they rushed to do as they were ordered. The first lesson you learned as a slave to Jagang was that when he told you to do something, he meant you to do it right now. Little provoked him more than delay.

At the door to the inner room, a woman Nicci didn't recognize ran out, following close on the heels of the others. She was young and beautiful, with dark hair and eyes, probably a captive picked up somewhere along the long march, and no doubt used for Jagang's amusement. Her eyes reflected a world gone mad for her.

Such were the unavoidable costs if the world was to be brought to a state of order. Great leaders, by their very nature, came with shortcomings in character, which they themselves viewed as mere peccadilloes. The far-ranging benefits Jagang would bring to the poor suffering masses of humanity far outweighed his crass acts of personal gratification and the relatively petty havoc he wrought. Nicci was often the object of his transgressions. It was a price worth paying for the help that would eventually accrue to the helpless; that was the only matter that could be considered.

The outer door closed and the apartment was finally empty of everyone but Nicci and the emperor. She stood erect, head held high, arms at her sides, relishing the quiet of the place. The splendor meant little to her, but quiet was a luxury she had come to appreciate, even if it was selfish. In the tents there was always the noise of the army pressed close around. Here, it was quiet. She glanced around the spacious and elaborately decorated outer room, contemplating the idea that Jagang would have acquired the taste for such places. Perhaps he, too, simply wanted quiet.

She turned back to the inner room. He was just inside, waiting, watching her, a muscled mass of fury coiled in rage.

She strode directly up to him. "You wished to see me, Excellency?"

Nicci felt a stunning pain as the back of his beefy hand whipped across her face. The blow spun her around. Her knees hit the floor. He yanked her to her feet by her hair. The second time, she clouted the wall before crashing to the floor again. Stupefying pain throbbed through her face. When she had her bearings, she got her legs under her and stood before him again. The third time, she took a freestanding candelabrum down with her. Candles tumbled and rolled across the floor. A long wisp of sheer curtain she had snatched as she grabbed for support ripped away and drifted down over her as she and an upturned table slammed to the floor. Glass shattered. Metal clattered as small items bounded away.

She was dizzy and stunned, her vision faltering. Her eyes felt as if they might have burst, her jaw as if it had been shattered, her neck as if the muscles had ripped. Nicci lay sprawled on the floor, savoring the strident waves of pain, wallowing in the rare sensation of feeling.

She saw blood splattered across the light fringe of the carpet beneath her and across the warm glow of wooden flooring. She heard Jagang yelling something at her, but she couldn't make out the words over the ringing in her ears. With a shaky arm, she pushed herself up onto her hip. Blood warmed her fingers when she touched them to her mouth. She relished the hurt. It had been so long since she had felt anything, except for that too brief moment with the Mord-Sith. This was a glorious wash of agony.

Jagang's brutality was able to reach down into the abyss, not only because of the cruelty itself, but because she knew she need not suffer it. He, too, knew that she was there by her choice, not his. That only intensified his anger, and thus, her sensations.

His rage seemed lethal. She merely noted the fact that she very probably wouldn't leave the room alive. She would probably not get to learn Sister Lidmila's spells. Nicci simply waited to discover what fate had already decided for her.

The room's spinning finally slowed enough for her to once more make it to her feet. She pulled herself up straight before the silent brawny form of Emperor Jagang. His shaved head reflected points of light from some of the lamps. His only facial hair was a two-inch braid of mustache growing above each corner of his mouth, and another in the center under his lower lip. The gold ring through his left nostril and its thin gold chain running to another ring in his left ear glimmered in the mellow lamplight. Except for a heavy ring on each finger, he was without the plundered assortment of royal chains and jewels he usually wore around his neck. The rings glistened with her blood.

He was bare-chested, but unlike his head, his chest was covered in coarse hair. His muscles bulged, their tendons standing out as he flexed his fists. He had the neck of a bull, and his temperament was worse.

Nicci, half a head shy of his height, stood before him, waiting, looking into the eyes she used to see in her nightmares. They were a murky gray, without whites, and clouded over with sullen, dusky shapes that stole across a surface of inky obscurity. Even though they had no evident iris and pupil—nothing but seeming dark voids where a normal person had eyes—she never had any doubt whatsoever as to when he was looking at her.

They were the eyes of a dream walker. A dream walker denied access to her mind. Now, she understood why.

"Well?" He growled. He threw up his hands. "Cry! Yell! Scream! Beg! Argue— make excuses! Don't just stand there!"

Nicci swallowed back the sharp taste of blood as she gazed placidly into his scarlet glare.

"Please be specific, Excellency, as to which one you would prefer, how long I should carry on, and if I should end it of my own accord, or wait for you to beat me into unconsciousness."

He lunged at her with a howl of fury. He seized her throat in his massive fist to hold her as he struck her. Her knees buckled, but he held her up until she was able to steady herself.

He released her throat with a shove. "I want to know why you did that to Kadar!"

She offered only a bloody smile to his anger.

He wrenched her arm behind her back and pulled her hard against him. "Why would you do such a thing! Why?"

The deadly dance with Jagang had begun. She dimly wondered again if this time she would lose her life.

Jagang had killed a number of the Sisters who had displeased him. Nicci's safety with him—such as it was—lay in her very indifference to her safety. Her utter disinterest in her own life fascinated Jagang because he knew it was sincere.

"Sometimes, you're a fool," she said with true contempt, "too arrogant to see what is in front of your nose."

He twisted her arm until she thought it surely would snap. His panting breath was warm on her throbbing cheek. "I've killed people for saying much less than that."

She mocked him through the pain. "Do you intend to bore me to death, then? If you want to kill me, seize me by the throat and strangle me, or slash me to a bloody mess so that I will bleed to death at your feet—don't think you can suffocate me with the sheer weight of your monotonous threats. If you wish to kill me, then be a man and do so! Or else shut your mouth."

The mistake most people made with Jagang was to believe, because of his capacity for such profound brutality, that he was an ignorant, dumb brute. He was not. He was one of the most intelligent men Nicci had ever met. Brutality was but his cloak. As an outgrowth of his access to the thoughts of so many different people's minds, he was directly exposed to their knowledge, wisdom, and ideas; such exposure augmented his intellect. He also knew what people most feared. If anything about him frightened her, it was not his brutality, but his intelligence, for she knew that intelligence could be a bottomless well of truly inventive cruelty.

"Why did you kill him, Nicci?" he asked again, his voice losing some of its fire.

In her mind, like a protective stone wall, was the thought of Richard. He had to see it in her eyes. Part of Jagang's rage, she knew, was at his own impotence at penetrating her mind, of possessing her as he could so many others. Her knowing smirk taunted him with what he could not have.

"It amused me to hear the great Kadar Kardeef cry for mercy, and then to deny it."

Jagang roared again, a beastly sound out of place for such a mannerly bedchamber. She saw the blur of his arm swinging for her. The room whirled violently around her. She expected to hit something with a bone-breaking impact. Instead, she upended and crashed onto unexpected softness: the bed, she realized. Somehow, she had missed the marble and mahogany posts at the corners—they surely would have killed her. Fate, it seemed, was trifling with her. Jagang landed atop her.

She thought he might beat her to death now. Instead, he studied her eyes from inches away. He sat up, straddling her hips. His meaty hands pulled at the laces on the bodice of her dress. With a quick yank of the material, he exposed her breasts. His fingers squeezed her bared flesh until her eyes watered.

Nicci didn't watch him, or resist, but instead went limp as he pushed her dress up around her waist. Her mind began its journey away, to where only she alone could go. He fell on her, driving the wind from her lungs in a helpless grunt.

Arms lying at her sides, her fingers open and slack, eyes unblinking, Nicci stared at the folds of the silk in the canopy of the bed, her mind unaffected in the distant quiet place. The pain seemed remote. Her struggle to breathe seemed trivial.

As he went about his coarse business, she focused her thoughts instead on what she was going to do. She had never believed possible what she now contemplated; now she knew it was. She had only to decide to do it.

Jagang slapped her, causing her to focus her mind back on him. "You're too stupid to even weep!"

She realized he had finished; he was not happy that she hadn't noticed. She had to make an effort not to comfort her jaw, stinging from what to him was a smack, but to the person receiving it was a blow nearly strong enough to cripple. Sweat dripped from his chin onto her face. His powerful body glistened from the exertion she had not perceived.

His chest heaved as he glared down at her. Anger, of course, powered the glare, but Nicci thought she saw a tinge of something else there, too: regret, or maybe anguish, or maybe even hurt.

"Is that what you wish me to do, then, Excellency? Weep?"

His voice turned bitter as he flopped onto his side beside her. "No. I wish you to react."

"But I am," she said as she stared up at the canopy. "It is simply not the reaction you wish."

He sat up. "What's the matter with you, woman?"

She gazed up at him a moment, and then turned her eyes away.

"I have no idea," she answered honestly. "But I think I must find out."

Jagang gestured. "Take off your clothes. You're spending the night. It's been too long." This time, it was he who stared off at the walls. "I've missed you in my bed, Nicci."

She didn't answer. She did not believe that in his bed he missed anything. She didn't believe she could conceive of him understanding what it was to miss a person. What he missed, she thought, was being able to miss someone.

Nicci sat up and threw her legs over the side of the bed as she untangled herself from the black dress. She pulled it off over her head and then laid it out across the back of a padded leather chair. She reclaimed her underthings from the tangles of the bed covering and tossed them on the chair before drawing off her stockings and placing them, too, on the seat of the chair. He watched her body the whole time, watched her as she tended to her dress, smoothing it to straighten what he had done to it, watched the mysterious allure of a woman acting a woman.

When she had finished she turned back to him. She stood proudly, to let him see that which he could have only by force, and never as a willing gift. She could detect the sense of privation in his expression. This, was the only victory she could have: the more he took her by force, the more he understood that that was the only way he could ever have her, and the more it maddened him. She would just as soon die as willingly give him the satisfaction of that gift, and he knew the brutal truth of that.

He finally forced himself away from his private, bitter longing and looked up into her eyes. "Why'd you kill Kadar?"

She sat on the edge of the bed opposite him, just out of his easy reach, but within range of his lunge, and shrugged her bare shoulders.

"You are not the Order. The Order is no single man, but an ideal of equity. As such, it will survive any one person. You serve that ideal and the Order, for now, in the capacity of but a brute. The Order could use any brute to serve its purpose. You, Kadar, or another. I simply eliminated someone who might one day have been a threat to you before you can rise above your present role."

He grinned. "You expect me to believe that you were doing me a kindness? Now you mock me."

"If it pleases you to think so, then do."

Her smooth white limbs were a vivid contrast to the heavy, dark, variegated verdant bedcover and sheets. He lay back atop them against several rumpled pillows, immodestly displayed before her. His eyes looked even darker than usual.

"What's all this talk I keep hearing about 'Jagang the Just'?"

"Your new title. It is the thing that will save you, the thing that will win for you, the thing that will bring you more glory than anything else. Yet, in return for eliminating a future threat to your standing, and for making you a hero to the people, you draw my blood."

He put an arm behind his head. "Sometimes you make me believe the stories that people tell, that you really are crazy."

"And if you kill everyone?"

"Then they will be dead."

"I have recently been through towns visited by your soldiers. It seems they didn't harm the people—at least, they didn't slaughter everyone in sight, as they did when they began their march into the New World."

He lunged and seized a fistful of her hair. With a snarl, he yanked her onto her back beside him. She caught her breath as he rose up on an elbow and directed his disturbing gaze down into her eyes.

"It is your job to make examples of people, to show them that they must contribute to our cause; to make them fear the Imperial Order's righteous wrath. That is the task I assigned you."

"Is that so? Then why did the soldiers not make examples, too? Why did they let those towns be? Why did they not contribute to striking fear into the hearts of the people? Why didn't they lay waste to every city and town in their path?"

"And then who would I rule but my soldiers? Who would do the work? Who would make things? Who would grow the food? Who would pay tribute? To whom will I bring the hope of the Order? Who will there be to glorify the great Emperor Jagang, if I kill them all?"

He flopped onto his back. "You may be called Death's Mistress, but we can't have it your way and kill everyone. In this world you are bound to the Order's purpose. If people feel the Order's arrival can mean nothing but their death, they will resist to the end. They must know that it is only their resistance which will bring a swift and sure death. If they realize our arrival offers them a moral life, a life which puts man under the Creator and the welfare of man above all else, they will embrace us."

"You dealt death to this city," she taunted, forcing him to unwittingly prove the validity of what she had done. "Even though they chose the Order."

"I've given orders that any people of the city still alive be allowed to go back to their homes. The rampage is ended. The people here betrayed their promises and thus invited brutality; they saw it, but now that is finished and a new day of order has come. The old ideas of separate lands are over, as it was ended in the Old World. All people will be governed together, and will enter a new age of prosperity together—under the Imperial Order. Only those who resist will be crushed—not because they resist, but because, ultimately, they are traitors to the well-being of their fellow man and must be eliminated.

"Here, in Anderith, was the turning point in our struggle. Richard Rahl was at last cast out by the people themselves, who came to see the virtue of what we offer. No longer can he claim to represent them."

"Yet you came in and slaughtered—"

"The leaders here betrayed certain promises to me—who knows how much of the general population may have collaborated in that—and so the people had to pay a price, but collectively they have also earned a place in the Order for their courage in emphatically rejecting Lord Rahl and the outdated, selfish, uninspired morals he offered them.

"The tide has turned. People no longer have faith in Lord Rahl, nor can he now have any faith in them. Richard Rahl is a fallen leader."

Nicci smiled inwardly, a sad smile. She was a fallen woman, and Richard was a fallen man. Their fate was sealed.

"Perhaps here, in this one small place," she said, "but he is far from defeated. He is still dangerous. After all, you failed to gain everything you sought here in Anderith because of Richard Rahl. He not only denied you a clear victory by destroying vast stores of supplies and leaving the systems and services of production in total disarray, but he also slipped right through your fingers when you should have captured him."

"I will have him!"

"Really? I wonder." She watched his fist, and waited until it relaxed before she continued. "When will you move our forces north, into the Midlands?"

Jagang stroked his hand down his woolly chest. "Soon. I want to give them time to become careless, first. When they grow complacent, I will strike north.

"A great leader must read the nature of the battle, to be able to adjust his tactics. We will be liberators, now, as we move north into the Midlands, bringing the Creator's glory to the people. We must win the hearts and minds of the unconverted."

"You have decided this change? On your own? You do not consider the will of the Creator in your campaign?"

He glared at her insolence, as if to tell her she knew better than to even ask such a question.

"I am the emperor; I need not consult our spiritual guides, but since their counsel is always welcome, I've already talked to the priests. They've spoken favorably about my plans. Brother Narev thinks it wise and has given his blessing. You had better keep to your job of extinguishing any ideas of opposition. If you don't follow my orders, well, no one will miss one Sister. I have others."

She was not moved by his threats, real as they were. By his suspicious look, he was beginning to understand her vision, too.

"What you are doing is fitting," she said, "but it must be cut up into little pieces the people can chew. They do not have the Order's wisdom in seeing what is best for them—the public rarely does. Even one as bullheaded as you must be able to see that I have anticipated your plans by helping those you can't afford to kill to understand that you are sparing them out of your sense of justice. Word of such deeds will win hearts."

He cast her a sidelong glance. "I am the Order's cleansing fire. The fire is a necessary conflagration, but not the important end—it is merely the means to the end. From the ashes I, Jagang, create, new order can sprout and grow. It is this end, this glorious new age of man, that warrants the means. In this, it is my responsibility— not yours—to decide justice, when and how I will dispense it, and who will receive it."

She grew impatient with his vanity. Scorn seeped into her voice. "I have simply put a name to it—Jagang the Just—and begun to spread your new title for you when the opportunity arose. I sacrificed Kadar to that end, for all the same reasons you've listed. It had to be done now in order for it to have the necessary time to spread and flourish, or the New World would soon harden irreversibly against the Order. I chose the time and place, and by using Kadar Kardeef's life—a war hero's life—proved your devotion to the cause of the Order above all else. You benefit.

"Any brute could ignite the conflagration; this new title shows your moral vision—another manifestation of worth over other men. I have planted the vital seed that will make you a hero to the common people and, even more important, to the priests. Are you going to pretend you think the title inadequate? Or that it will not serve you well?

"What I alone have done will help win what your powerful army cannot: willing allegiance without a battle, at a cost of nothing. With Kadar's life, I, Nicci, have made you more than you could make of yourself. I, Nicci, have given you the reputation of honor. I, Nicci, have made you into a leader people will trust because they believe you to be just."

He brooded for a time, turning his gaze from her hot glare. His arm finally fell open and his fingers tenderly trailed down her thigh. The touch was an admission for him—an admission that she was right, even if he would not say the words.

After a few moments he yawned, and then his eyes closed. His breathing evened, and he started to drift off into a nap, as was his way with her. He expected her to remain right where she was, so that when he awoke she would be available to him. She supposed she could leave. But it was not time. Not yet.

He finally awoke an hour later. Nicci was still staring up at the canopy, thinking about Richard. There seemed to be one piece missing in her plan, one more thing that she felt needed to fall into place.

In his sleep Jagang had rolled over on his side facing away from her. Now, he turned back. His dark eyes took her in with a look of lust rekindled. He drew her close. His body was as warm as a rock in the sun and only slightly softer.

"Pleasure me," he commanded in a husky growl that would have frightened any other woman into doing as ordered.

"Or what? You will kill me? If I feared that, I would not be here. This is by force, not consent. I will not willingly take part in it, nor will I allow you to deceive yourself into believing that I want you."

He backhanded her, knocking her across the bed. "You take part willingly!" He seized her by the wrist and dragged her back toward him. "Why else would you be here?"

"You ordered me here."

He smirked. "And you came when you could have fled."

She opened her mouth, but she had no answer she could put into words, no answer he would understand.

With a grin of victory, he fell on her and pressed his lips to hers. As much as it hurt her, for Jagang this was gentle behavior. He had told her several times that she was the only woman he ever cared to kiss. He seemed to believe that by expressing those emotions for her, she could have no alternative but to surrender feelings in kind, as if spoken feelings were currency with which he could purchase affection on demand.

It was only the beginning of a long night—a long ordeal—she knew. She would have to endure his forceful violation several more times before morning. His question haunted the distant place in her mind.

Morning came, accompanied by the dull throbbing of a headache from her succeeding beating, and the sharper aches from the places where he'd struck her when he came to find that what he thought was her willing submission was but a delusion that left him more angered than before. The pillows were stained with her blood. It had been a long night of rare sensations experienced.

She knew she was evil, and deserved to be violated in such a brutal fashion. She could offer no moral objection to it; even in the terrible things he did to her, Jagang was nowhere near as corrupt as she. Jagang erred in simple matters of the flesh, and that could only be expected—all people were corrupt in the flesh—but because of her indifference to the suffering around her, she failed in matters of the spirit. That, she knew, was pure evil. That was why she deserved to suffer whatever he did to her. For the moment, that deep dark place within came close to being sated.

Nicci touched her mouth and found the cuts painful, but closed. The healing of wounds, though, did not offer the warranted sensations of receiving them, so she resolved to have one of the other Sisters heal her, rather than give him the satisfaction of witnessing her suffering the inconvenience of the injures.

With that, her mind turned to thoughts of Sister Lidmila.

Nicci realized that Jagang wasn't in bed beside her. She sat up and saw him in a chair not far away, watching her.

She pulled the sheet up to cover her breasts, speckled with droplets of dried blood. "You are a pig."

"You can't get enough of me. Despite what you say, Nicci, you wish to be with me. If not, why would you stay?"

Those nightmare eyes of his watched her, trying to find a way into her mind. There was none. He could no longer be a nightmare for her. Richard guarded her mind.

"Not for the reasons you wish to believe. I stay because the ultimate cause of the Order is a moral one. I wish it to succeed. I wish the suffering of life's helpless victims to end. I wish everyone to finally be equal and to finally live with everything they need. I have worked nearly my entire life for those goals. The Order can see to it that such a fair world comes to be. If I must endure you—even aid you—for such an end, then it is but an insignificant gnat to swallow."

"You sound so very noble, but I think there is something more basic behind it. I think you would have left if you could, or"—he smiled—"if you could, you would have left if you really wanted to. Which is it, then, Nicci?"

She didn't want to contemplate the question. Her head hurt.

"What's all the talk about you building a palace?"

"So you heard, then." He took a deep breath and sighed wistfully. "It will be the grandest palace ever built. A fitting place for the Emperor of the Imperial Order, for the man who rules both the Old and the New Worlds."

"The man who *wants* to rule. Lord Rahl stands in your way. How many times has he bested you, now?"

Jagang's eyes flashed a rage she knew could turn violent. Richard had frustrated Jagang a number of times. Even if Richard hadn't been victorious over Jagang, he had stung him. Quite an accomplishment, really, for such a tiny force against the array of the Imperial Order. A man like Jagang hated the humiliation of a sting almost as much as he would hate to be gored.

"I will eliminate Richard Rahl, don't you worry," Jagang said in a low growl.

She changed the subject back to what she really wanted to know about. "Since when has the all-conquering Emperor Jagang turned soft and wanted to live in splendor?"

"Ah, but I am Jagang the Just, now. Remember?" He returned to the bed and flopped down beside her. "Nicci, I'm sorry I hurt you. I never want to hurt you, but you make me do it. You know I care about you."

"You care about me, yet you beat me? You care about me, yet you never bothered to tell me of such an enormous project as the building of a palace? I am insignificant to you."

"I told you, I'm sorry I hurt you—but that was your own fault and you know it." He spoke the words almost lovingly. With mention of the palace, his face had softened into a visionary look. "It's only proper and fitting that I at last have the prestige of such a monumental edifice."

"You, the man who was content in tents in the field, now wants to live in a resplendent building? Why?"

"Because once I bring the New World under the guidance of the Order, I will owe it to all the people, as their leader, to be seen in a majestic setting . . . but it will have more than simple splendor."

"But of course," she sniped.

He gathered up her hand. "Nicci, I will proudly wear the title Jagang the Just. You're right, the time has come for such a move. I was only angered because you wrongly made that move without first discussing it with me. But let us forget that, now."

She said nothing. He gripped her hand more tightly, to show his sincerity, she supposed.

"You're going to love the palace, when it's finished." He ran the back of the fingers of his other hand tenderly down her cheek. "We will all live there for a very long time."

The words struck a cord in her. "A very long time?"

For the first time she realized there was something more to this than simply his vanity of wanting a palace after Richard had denied him the Palace of the Prophets. He wanted what else Richard had denied him. Could it be . . .

She looked up into his face, searching for the answer. He simply smiled at the questions in her eyes.

"Construction has already begun," he said, turning his words away from those questions. "Architects and great builders from all over the Old World have gathered to work on it. Everyone wants to be part of such a grand project."

"And Brother Narev?" she probed. "What does he think of building such a frivolous monument to one man when there is important work to be done for so many needy people?"

"Brother Narev and his disciples greatly favor the project." Jagang flashed her a sly smile. "They will live there, too, of course."

Understanding washed over her.

"He's going to spell the new palace," she whispered in astonishment to herself.

Jagang only smiled as he watched her, clearly pleased with her reaction.

Brother Narev had been at the Palace of the Prophets almost as long as she, nearly one hundred and seventy years, but in all that time he seemed to have aged only ten or fifteen years—the same as she. No one but Nicci ever knew he was anything but a stablehand—they didn't know he was gifted.

In all that time, with her, along with everyone else, paying him little heed, he must have been studying the spell around the palace. From what she knew, most of Brother Narev's disciples had been young wizards from the Palace of the Prophets; they had access to the vaults. They, too, could have added information that helped him. But could he really do such a thing?

"Tell me about the palace," she said, preferring his voice to the silent scrutiny of his nightmare eyes.

He kissed her first, the way a man kisses a woman, not the way a brute kisses a victim. She endured it with no more favor than any of the rest of it. He seemed not to notice, this time, and by the smile of his face, appeared to have enjoyed it.

"It will be a walk of nearly fifteen miles to walk all the halls." He swept a hand out and began to give shape to the grand palace in the air before them. As he went on, he stared off at his imaginary outline, hanging there in space.

"The world has never seen anything to match it. While I carry on with our work of bringing the hope of the Order to the New World, of bringing the true word of the Creator to the wicked and the greedy, of banishing the selfish ideals of the ancient religion of magic, back in my homeland the work of building the palace will go on.

"Quarries will be busy for years extracting all the rock that will go into the construction. The variety of stone will leave no doubt about the glory of the place. The marble will be the finest. The woods will be only the best. Every material going into the palace will be exceptional. The best craftsmen will shape it all into a grand structure."

"Yes, but, despite the fact that others may live there," she mocked in cool disdain, "it will be but a pompous monument to only one man: the great and powerful Emperor Jagang."

"No, it will be devoted to the glory of the Creator."

"Oh? And will the Creator be taking up residence there, too, then?"

Jagang scowled at her blasphemy. "Brother Narev wishes the palace to be instructional to the people. He is contributing his spiritual guidance to the undertaking, and will personally oversee the construction while I cleanse the way for the Order."

That was what she wanted to know.

He stared off at the invisible shape still hanging in the air before them. His voice took on a reverent tone.

"Brother Narev shares my vision in this. He has always been like a father to me. He put the fire in my belly. His spiritual direction has been a lifelong inspiration. He allows me to stand at the fore, and take the glory of our victories, but I would be nothing without his moral teachings. What I win is only as the fist of the Order, and a fist is but one part of the whole, as we are all but insignificant fragments of society as a whole. You are right: many others could stand in my place for the Order. But it is my part to be the one to lead us. I would never do anything to betray the trust Brother Narev has placed in me—that would be like betraying the Creator Himself. He guides the way for all of us.

"I only thought to build a fitting palace for us all, a place from which to govern for the benefit of the people. It was Brother Narev who took up the dream and gave it moral meaning by envisioning everyone, when they see the vast structure, as seeing man's place in the new order—seeing that man can never live up to the glory of the Creator, and that, individually, he is but a meaningless member of the greater brotherhood of man and thus can have no greater part to play than to uplift all his brothers in need so all will thrive together. Yet, it will also be a place that will humble every man before it, by showing him his utter insignificance before the glory of his Creator, by showing man's depravity, his tortured, contorted, inferior nature, for all men in this world are such as this."

Nicci could almost see such a place when he spoke of it. It would indeed be a humbling inspiration to the people. He came near to inspiring her with such talk, as Brother Narev had at one time inspired her.

"This is why I have stayed," she whispered, "because the cause of the Order is righteous."

The piece that had been missing was now found.

In the quiet, Jagang kissed her again. She allowed him to finish it, and then pushed away from his embrace. With a distant smile, he watched as she rose and began dressing.

"You're going to love it there, Nicci. It will be a place befitting you."

"Oh? As the Slave Queen?"

"As a queen, if you wish it. I plan to give you the kind of authority you've never before had. We'll be happy there, you and I, truly happy. For a long, long time, we'll be happy there."

She drew a stocking up her leg. "When Sister Ulicia and the four with her found a way to leave you, I chose to ignore their discovery and stay, because I know the Order is the only moral course for mankind. But now I—"

"You stayed because you would be nothing without the Order."

She looked away from his eyes. She tugged her dress down over her head, poked her arms through the sleeves, and worked the skirt over her hips. "I am nothing without the Order, and I am nothing with it. No one is. We are all inadequate, miserable creatures; that is the nature of man; that is what the Creator teaches. But the Order shows man his duty to make a better life for the good of all."

"And I am the emperor of the Imperial Order!" His red face cooled more slowly than it had heated. He gestured vaguely in the hollow silence and he went on in a more mellow tone. "The world will be one under the Order. We'll be happy at the palace when it's finished, Nicci. You and I, under the spiritual guidance of our priests. You'll see. In time, when—"

"I'm leaving." She drew on a boot.

"I will not permit it."

Nicci paused at pulling on her other boot and glanced up into his dark eyes. She flicked a finger toward a stone vase on a table against the far wall. Light flashed. The vase exploded in a cloud of dust and chips with a sound that rocked the room. The draperies shuddered. The panes in the windows chattered.

When the dust had settled, she said, "*You* will not permit it?" She bent forward and began doing up the laces on her boots.

Jagang strolled over to the table and dragged his fingers through the dust that was all that remained of the stone vase. He turned back to her in all his naked, hairy, imperial glory.

"Are you threatening me? Do you actually think you could use your power against me?"

"I do not think it"—she yanked the laces tight—"I know it. The truth is I choose not to."

He struck a defiant pose. "And why is that?"

Nicci stood and faced him. "Because, as you said, the Order needs you, or rather, a brute like you. You serve the ends of the Order—you are their fist. You bring that cleansing fire. You perform that function very well. It could even be said that you perform that service with extraordinary talent.

"You are Jagang the Just. You see the wisdom in the title I have given you, and will use it to further the cause of the Order. That is why I choose not to use my power against you. It would be like using my power against the Order, against my own duty to the future of mankind."

"Then why do you want to leave?"

"Because I must." She gave him a look of icy determination, and deadly threat. "Before I go, I will be spending some time with Sister Lidmila. You are to immediately and completely withdraw from her mind and remain out of it the entire time I am with her. We will use your tents, since you are not using them. You will see to it that everyone leaves us entirely alone for however long it takes us. Anyone who enters, without my express permission, will die. That includes you. You have my oath, as a Sister of the Dark, on that. When I'm finished, and after I leave, you may do what you will with Sister Lidmila—kill her if that is your wish, although I don't see why you would want to bother, since she is going to be doing you a great service."

"I see." His huge chest rose. He let the deep breath out slowly. "And how long will you be gone, this time, Nicci?"

"This is not like the other times. This is different."

"How long?"

"Perhaps only a short time. Perhaps a very long time. I don't yet know. Leave me alone to do as I must, and, if I can, I will one day return to you."

He gazed into her eyes, but he could not look into her mind. Another man protected her mind, and kept her thoughts her own.

In all the time she had spent with Richard, Nicci had never learned that which she hungered most to know, but in one way, she had learned too much. Most of the time she was able to entomb that unwanted knowledge under the numb weight of indifference. Occasionally, though, it would, like now, unexpectedly rise up out of its tomb to seize her. When it did, she was helpless in its grip, and could do nothing but wait for the oblivion of numb detachment to bury it yet again.

Staring into the long dark night of Jagang's inhuman eyes, eyes that revealed nothing but the bleakness of his soul, Nicci touched her finger to the gold ring Jagang had ordered pierced through her lower lip to mark her as his personal slave. She released a thread-thin channel of Subtractive Magic, and the ring ceased to exist.

"And where are you going, Nicci?"

"I am going to destroy Richard Rahl for you."

Zeddicus Zu'l Zorander had been able to talk and smile his way past the other soldiers, but these were not moved by his explanation that he was Richard's grandfather. He supposed he should have entered the camp in the daylight—it would have avoided a lot of the suspicion—but he was tired and hadn't thought it would be that much trouble.

The soldiers were properly suspicious, which greatly pleased him, but he was weary and had more important things to do than answer questions: he wanted to ask them, instead.

"Why do you want to see him?" the bigger guard repeated.

"I told you, I'm Richard's grandfather."

"This is the Richard Cypher, you're talking about, who you now say—"

"Yes, yes, that was his name when he grew up and that's what I'm used to calling him, but I meant Richard Rahl, who he is now. You know, Lord Rahl, your leader? I would think being the grandfather of someone as important as your Lord Rahl would accord me some respect. Maybe even a hot meal."

"I could say I'm Lord Rahl's brother," the man said, keeping a tight grip on the bit in the mouth of Zedd's horse, "but that doesn't make it so."

Zedd sighed. "How very true."

As vexing as it was, Zedd, at some dim inward level, was pleased to see that the men weren't stupid, nor easily duped.

"But I'm also a wizard," Zedd added, drawing low his eyebrows for dramatic effect. "If I wasn't friendly, I could simply do you up crisp and be on my way past the both of you."

"And if I wasn't friendly," the man said, "I could give the signal—now that we've let you venture in this far so that you're completely surrounded—and the dozen archers hiding all around you in the dark would let fly the arrows that are at this moment trained on you, as they have been ever since you approached our encampment."

"Ah," Zedd said, holding up a finger in triumph, "all very well and good, but—"

"And even if I were to die in a final flame of service to the Lord Rahl, those arrows will let fly without me needing to give any signal."

Zedd harrumphed, lowering his finger, but inwardly he smiled. Here he was, First Wizard, and if he weren't entering a friendly camp, he would have been bested in this game of banter by a simple soldier.

Or maybe not.

"In the first place, Sergeant, I am, as I said, a wizard, and so I knew of the archers and have already dealt with the threat by spelling their arrows so they will fly no truer and with no more deadly effect than wet dishrags. I have nothing to fear from them. In the second place, even if I'm lying—which is precisely what you are considering at this very moment—you have made a mistake by telling me of the threat, which enables me, as a wizard of great repute, to now use my magic to nullify it."

A slow smile came to the man's face. "Why, that's remarkable." He scratched his head. He looked to his partner and then back to Zedd. "You're right, that was exactly what I was thinking: that you could be lying about knowing the archers were back there in the dark."

"You see there, young man? You're not so smart after all."

"You're right, sir, I'm not. Here I was, so busy talking to you and being so intimidated by your wizardly powers and all, that I plumb forgot to tell you about what else was out there in the dark, watching you . . ."—the soldier's brow lowered—"and it would be a mite more trouble than any simple arrows, I dare say."

Zedd scowled down at the man. "Now see here—"

"Why don't you do as I ask and come down here in the light, where I can see you better, and answer some of our questions?"

With a sigh of resignation, Zedd dismounted. He gave Spider a reassuring pat on her neck. Spider, a chestnut-colored mare, had a leggy black splotch on her creamy rump, from which she had acquired her name. Young, strong, and possessing an agreeably spirited nature, she made a pleasant traveling companion. The two of them had been through a great deal together.

Zedd stepped into the intimate circle of light from the watch fire. He turned his hand up and brought a white-hot flame to life just above the flesh of his palm. The two soldiers' eyes widened. Zedd scowled.

"But, I have my own fire, if you need to see better. Does this help you see things better, Sergeant?"

"Uh . . . why, yes it does, sir," the man stammered.

"Yes, it does indeed," a woman said as she stepped into the light. "Why didn't you simply use your Han and give a display of your craft in the first place?" She motioned into the darkness, as if signaling for others to stand down. She turned back with a smile that was no more than courteous. "Welcome, wizard."

Zedd bowed from the waist. "Zeddicus Zu'l Zorander, First Wizard, at your service . . . ?"

"Sister Philippa, Wizard Zorander. I am aid to the Prelate."

She gestured and the sergeant took the reins from Zedd's hand to lead the horse away. Zedd clapped the man on the back to let him know there were no hard feelings, and then gave a similar pat to Spider to let her know it was all right to go with the men.

"Treat her especially well, Sergeant. Spider is a friend."

The sergeant saluted by tapping his fist to his heart. "She'll be treated as a friend, sir."

After the soldiers had led Spider away, Zedd said, "The Prelate? Which one?"

The narrow-jawed Sister clasped her hands together. "Prelate Verna, of course."

"Oh, yes, of course. Prelate Verna."

The Sisters of the Light didn't know Ann was still alive. At least, she had been alive when Zedd last saw her, several months past. Ann had written in her journey book, telling Verna that she was alive, but also asking her to keep that information private for the time being. Zedd had been hoping that perhaps Ann had turned up at the D'Haran army camp, with her Sisters of the Light. He was sorry to learn she hadn't. It boded ill for her.

Zedd held no favor with the Sisters of the Light—a lifetime of disapproval was not easily forgotten—but he had come to respect Ann as a woman of self-discipline and resolve, even if he took a dim view of some of her convictions and past objectives. He knew that, at the least, he and Ann shared many important values. He didn't know about the rest of the Sisters, though.

Sister Philippa appeared middle-aged, but with Sisters that meant little. She might have lived at the Palace of the Prophets for only a year, or for centuries. With dark eyes and high cheekbones she was an exotic-looking woman. As in the Midlands, there were places in the Old World where the people had unique physical characteristics. Sister Philippa moved the way high-minded women tended to move, like a swan taken to human form.

"How may I be of service, Wizard Zorander?"

"Zedd will do. Is this Prelate of yours awake?"

"She is. This way, Zedd, if you please."

He fell in behind the woman as she glided off toward the dark shapes of tents. "Got anything to eat around here?"

She looked back over her shoulder. "This late?"

"Well, I've been traveling hard. . . . It's not really all that late, is it?"

In the dark, she assessed him briefly. "I don't believe it's ever too late, according to the teachings of the Creator. And you do look emaciated—from your travels, I'm sure." Her smile warmed a little. "Food is always at the ready; we have soldiers who are active through the night and need to be fed. I believe I could find something for you." She returned her gaze to the indiscernible path.

"That would be a kindness," Zedd said in a jovial voice as he scowled at her back. "And I'm not emaciated; I'm wiry. Most women find lean men appealing."

"Do they? I never knew that."

Sisters of the Light were a lofty lot, Zedd thought ruefully. For thousands of years it had been a death sentence for them to even set foot in the New World. Zedd had always been a little more lenient—but not by much. In the past, the Sisters only came into the New World to steal boys with the gift—they claimed to be saving them. It was a wizard's task to train wizards. If they came for the reason of taking a boy back beyond the great barrier to their palace, Zedd viewed it as the gravest of crimes.

They had come for that very reason only the winter before, and taken Richard. Sister Verna was the one who had captured him and taken him to the Old World. Under the spell of their palace, he could have ended up being there for centuries. Leave it to Richard to make friends with the Sisters of the Light, of all people.

Zedd guessed he and the Sisters were even—that they had good reason to view him in a harsh way. He had, after all, set the spell that Richard had used to destroy their palace. But Ann had helped, knowing it was the only way to prevent Jagang from capturing the palace and acquiring the prophecies therein for his own purposes.

All around, guards, big guards, prowled the encampment. In chain mail and leather armor, they were an imposing sight. They watched everything as they slipped through the darkness. The camp was relatively quiet, considering its size. Noise could give away a variety of information to an enemy. It was not easy to see to it that this many men kept quiet.

"I'm relieved that our first incursion by someone possessing the gift turned out to be a friend," the Sister said.

"And I'm glad to see that the gifted are helping to keep watch. But there are types of enemy forays that the regular sentries could not identify." Zedd wondered if they were really prepared for those kinds of troubles.

"If magic is involved, we will be there to detect it."

"I suppose you were watching me the whole time."

"I was," Sister Philippa said. "From the time you crossed the line of hills, back there."

Zedd scratched his jaw. "Really? That far away."

With a satisfied smirk she said, "That far."

He peered over his shoulder into the night. "Both of you. Very good."

She halted and turned to him. "Both? You knew there were two of us, watching?"

Zedd smiled innocently. "But, of course. You were just watching. She was farther away, following, conjuring some little nasty should I prove hostile."

Sister Philippa blinked in astonishment. "Remarkable. You could sense her touching her Han? From that distance?"

Zedd nodded with satisfaction. "They didn't make me First Wizard just because I was wiry."

Sister Philippa's smile finally looked sincere. "I am relieved you came as a friend, rather than one intent on harm."

There was more truth in that than the woman knew; Zedd had experience in the unpleasant, dirty business of magic in warfare. When he'd come near their camp, he saw the holes in their defense and the weaknesses in the way they used the gift for their purpose. They were not thinking as their enemy would think. Had he been intent on harm, the entire camp would be in an uproar by now, despite what they had done to prepare for one such as he.

Sister Philippa turned back to the night to lead him on. It was somewhat unsettling for Zedd to walk through a D'Haran camp—even though he knew they were now fighting on the same side. He had spent a good deal of his life dealing with D'Harans as the deadly enemy. Richard had changed all that. Zedd sighed. He sometimes thought that Richard might make friends with thunder and lightning and invite them both to dinner.

Dark shapes of tents and wagons loomed all around. Pole weapons were stacked upright in neat ranks, ready, should they be suddenly needed. Some soldiers snored, and some sat around in the dark, talking in low voices or laughing quietly, while others patrolled the inky shadows. Those passed close enough for Zedd to smell their breath, but in the darkness he could not make out their faces.

Well-hidden sentries were stationed at every possible approach route. There were very few fires in the camp, and those were mostly watch fires set away from the main force, leaving the mass of the camp a dark whole of night. Some armies carried on a considerable amount of work at night, performing repairs or making things they needed, and letting the men do as they would. These men remained quiet throughout the night so watching eyes and listening ears could gain little if any help for an invading force. These were well trained, disciplined, professional soldiers. From a distance it was difficult to tell the size of the camp. It was huge.

Sister Philippa brought Zedd to a sizable tent, one tall enough to stand in. Light from lamps hanging inside gave the canvas walls and roof a soft amber glow. She ducked beneath a tent line and poked her head in under the flap.

120

"I have a wizard out here who wishes to see the Prelate."

Zedd heard muffled, astonished acknowledgment from inside.

"Go on in." Sister Philippa smiled while giving his back a gentle push. "I'll see if I can find you some dinner."

"I would be not only grateful, but greatly in your debt," Zedd told her.

As he stepped inside the tent, the people were just coming to their feet to greet him.

"Zedd! You old fool! You be alive!"

Zedd grinned as Adie, the old sorceress known as the bone woman in their adopted homeland of Westland, rushed into his arms. He let out a grunt as she momentarily squeezed the wind from his lungs. He smoothed her square-cut, jaw-length black and gray hair as he held her head to his chest.

"I promised you'd see me again, now didn't I?"

"Yes, you did," she whispered into his heavy robes.

She pushed back, holding his arms, and looked him over. She reached up and smoothed down his unruly, wavy white hair.

"You look as lovely as ever," he told her.

She peered at him with her completely white eyes. Her sight had been taken from her when she was but a young woman. Adie now saw by means of her gift. In some ways, she saw better.

"Where be your hat?"

"Hat?"

"I bought you a fine hat and you lost it. I see you still have not replaced it. You told me you would get another. I believe you promised."

Zedd hated the hat with the long feather she'd bought for him when they'd acquired the rest of his clothes. He'd rather be wearing the simple robes befitting a wizard of his rank and authority, but Adie had "lost" them after he purchased the fancy maroon robes with black sleeves and cowled shoulders he now wore. Three rows of silver brocade circled the cuffs. Thicker gold brocade ran around the neck and down the front. A red satin belt set with a gold buckle gathered the outfit at his thin waist. Such clothes marked one with the gift as an initiate. For one without the gift, such clothes befitted nobility or in most places a wealthy merchant, so although Zedd disliked the ostentatious attire, it had at times been a valuable disguise. Besides, Adie liked him in the maroon robes. The hat, though, was too much for him. It had been "misplaced."

He noted that Adie had managed to keep her simple clothes along the way. Yellow and red beads around the neck of her robes, sewn in the shapes of the ancient symbols of her profession of sorceress, were the only ornamentation she wore.

"I've been busy," he said, flicking his hand, hoping to dismiss the matter, "or I would have replaced the hat."

"Bah," she scoffed. "You be up to mischief."

"Why, I've been—"

"Hush, now," Adie said. Holding his arm in a tight grip, she held out the long thin fingers of her other hand. "Zedd, this be Verna: Prelate of the Sisters of the Light."

The woman looked to be in her late thirties, perhaps early forties; Zedd knew her to be much older. Ann, Verna's predecessor, had told him Verna's age, and while he couldn't recall the exact number, it was somewhere close to one hundred and sixty years—young for a Sister of the Light. She had simple, attractive features and brown hair with just enough curl and body to add a hint of sophistication. Her intent, brown-eyed gaze looked as if it could scour lichen off granite. By the lines of a resolute expression enduringly fixed on her face, she appeared to be a woman with a shell as tight as a beetle's and just as hard.

Zedd bowed his head. "Prelate. First Wizard Zeddicus Zu'l Zorander, at your service." He let her know, by his tone, that it was merely a figure of speech.

This was the woman who had taken Richard away to the Old World. Even if she believed it was to save his life, Zedd, as First Wizard, viewed such an act as abhorrent. The Sisters—sorceresses all—believed they could train gifted young men to be wizards. They were wrong; such a task could only be adequately accomplished by another wizard.

She offered her hand with the sunburst-patterned gold ring of office. He bent forward and kissed it, out of what he thought must be their custom. She pulled his hand close when he had finished, and kissed it in return.

"I am humbled to meet the man who helped raise our Richard. You would have to be as rare a person as I found him to be when we helped begin his training." She forced a chuckle. "We found it a formidable labor, trying to teach that grandson of yours."

Zedd slightly altered his opinion of the woman, treating her with greater caution. The air in the tent was stuffy and uncomfortable.

"That is because you are all oxen trying to teach a horse to run. You Sisters should stick to work more befitting your nature."

"Yes, yes, you be a brilliant man, Zedd," Adie scoffed. "Simply brilliant. One of these days even I may come to believe you." She tugged his sleeve, turning him from Verna's scarlet face. "And this be Warren," Adie said.

Zedd inclined his head toward Warren, but the boy was already falling to his knees and bowing his blond head.

"Wizard Zorander! This is quite an honor." He popped back up and seized Zedd's hand in both of his, pumping it until Zedd thought his arm might come undone at the shoulder. "I'm so pleased to meet you. Richard told me all about you. I'm so pleased to meet a wizard of your standing and talent. I would be so happy to learn from you!"

The happier he looked, the more Verna scowled.

"Well, I'm pleased to meet you, too, my boy." Zedd didn't tell Warren that Richard had never mentioned him. But that was not out of disrespect or neglect; Richard had never had a chance to tell Zedd a great number of very important things. Zedd thought he could sense through Warren's grip that the young man was a wizard of unusual talents.

A bear of a man with a curly rust-colored beard, a white scar from his left temple to his jaw, and heavy eyebrows stepped forward. His grayish green eyes fixed on Zedd with fierce intensity, but he had a grin like a soldier on a long march who had spotted a lonely cask of ale.

"General Reibisch, commander of the D'Haran forces here in the south," the man said, taking Zedd's hand when Warren at last surrendered it and stepped back beside Verna. "Lord Rahl's grandfather! What good fortune to see you, sir." His grip was firm, but not painful. It got tighter. "What very good fortune."

"Yes, indeed," Zedd muttered. "Unfortunate as the circumstances are, General Reibisch."

"Unfortunate . . . ?"

"Well, never mind, for the moment," Zedd said, waving off the question. He asked another, instead. "Tell me, General, have you begun to dig all the mass graves, yet? Or do you intend the few who are left alive to simply abandon all the bodies."

"Bodies?"

"Why . . . yes, the bodies of all your troops who are going to die."

"I hope you like eggs," Sister Philippa sang out as she swept into the tent, holding out a steaming plate.

Zedd rubbed his hands together. "Delightful!"

Everyone else was still standing in stiff, stunned silence. Sister Philippa didn't seem to notice all the hanging jaws.

"I had the cook add some ham and a few other things he had about." She glanced down at Zedd's form. "I thought you could use some substance."

"Marvelous!" Zedd grinned as he relieved her of the plate mounded high with scrambled eggs and ham.

"Ah . . ." the general began, seemingly befuddled as to how to frame his question, "might you kindly explain . . . what you mean by that, Wizard Zorander?"

"Zedd will do." Zedd looked up from inhaling the intoxicating aroma of the dish. "Dead." He drew the fork across his throat. "You know, dead. Nearly all of them. Dead." He turned back to Sister Philippa. "This smells delightful." He again inhaled the steam lifting from the plate of eggs. "Simply delightful. You are a woman of a kind heart and a skillful mind, to think to have the cook add such a splendid complement of ingredients. Simply delightful."

The Sister beamed.

The general lifted a hand. "Wizard Zorander, if I may—"

Adie hushed the burly general. "You be poor competition to food. Be patient."

Zedd took a forkful, humming his pleasure at the flavor he encountered. As he took a second forkful, Adie guided him to a simple bench at the side of the tent. A table in the middle held a few mugs and a lamp that lent the cozy tent not only its light but its oily odor as well.

Despite Adie's advice to be patient, everyone began talking at once, asking questions and offering objections. Zedd ignored them as he shoveled in the scrambled eggs. The large chunks of ham were delicious. He waved a particular juicy piece of meat to the confounded spectators to indicate his pleasure with it. The spices, the onions, the peppers, and the warm lumps of cheese were delightful. He rolled his eyes and moaned in bliss.

It was the best food he'd had in days. His traveling rations were simple and had long ago become boring. He had often grumbled that Spider ate better than he did. Spider seemed smug about it, too, which he had always found annoying. It wasn't good for a horse to be smug with you.

"Philippa," Verna growled, "must you be so pleased about a plate of eggs?"

"Well the poor man is practically starving." Puzzled by Verna's scowl, she waggled her hand at Zedd. "Just look at him. I'm simply happy to see him enjoy his meal, and pleased I could help one of the Creator's gifted."

Zedd slowed when he all too soon approached the end of his meal, putting off the last few bites. He could have eaten another plate the same size. General Reibisch, sitting on a bench on the opposite side of the small tent, had been furiously twisting a strand of beard. Now, he leaned forward, his intent gaze fixed on Zedd.

"Wizard Zorander, I need—"

"Zedd. Remember?"

"Yes, Zedd. Zedd, the lives of these soldiers are my responsibility. Could you please tell me if you think they are in danger?"

Zedd spoke around a mouthful. "I already did."

"But . . . what is the nature of the danger?"

"The gifted. You know, magic."

The general straightened with a sober expression. His fingers dug into his muscular thighs. "The gifted?"

"Yes. The enemy has gifted among them. I thought you knew."

He blinked a few times as he seemed to run it through his mind again, trying to discover the nugget of invisible danger in Zedd's simple statement.

"Of course we know that."

"Ah. Then why haven't you dug some mass graves?"

Verna shot to her feet. "In the name of Creation! What do you think we are, serving wenches? Here to bring you dinner? We are gifted Sisters, here to defend the army from Jagang's captive Sisters!"

Adie stealthily signaled Verna to sit down and keep quiet. Her voice came out like gravel in honey. "Why don't you tell us what you have found, Zedd? I be sure the general and the Prelate would like to hear how to improve our defenses."

Zedd scraped the small yellow lumps across the plate, collecting them into a final, pitifully small forkful. "Prelate, I didn't mean to imply a deliberate inadequacy on your part."

"Well you certainly—"

"You are all too good, that's all."

"I beg your pardon?"

"Too good. You and your Sisters have spent your lives trying to help people."

"Well . . . I, we—why, of course we help people. That's our calling."

"Killing is not. Jagang will be intent on killing you all."

"We know that, Zedd." The general scratched his beard, his gaze darting back and forth between Verna and Zedd. "The Prelate and her Sisters have helped us with detecting a number of enemy scouts and such. Just the same as Sister Philippa, here, found you when you approached our camp, they've found others intent on harm. They've done their part, Zedd, and without complaint. Every soldier in this camp is glad to have them here."

"All well and good, but when the army of the Imperial Order attacks, it will be different. They will use the gifted to lay waste to your forces."

"They will try," Verna insisted, trying to be convincing without shouting, which she was clearly itching to do, "but we are prepared to prevent such a thing,"

"That's right," Warren said, nodding his confidence. "We have gifted at the ready at all times."

"That's good, that's good," Zedd drawled, as if he might be reconsidering. "Then you have dealt with the simple threats. The albino mosquitoes and such."

General Reibisch's bushy eyebrows wrinkled together. "The what?"

Zedd waved his fork. "So, tell me, then—just to satisfy my curiosity—what are the gifted planning to do when the enemy charges our forces? Say, with a line of cavalry?"

"Lay down a line of fire before their cavalry," Warren said without hesitation. "As they charge in, we'll incinerate them before they can so much as launch a spear."

"Ah," Zedd said. "Fire." He put the last forkful in his mouth. Everyone silently watched him chew. He paused in his chewing and looked up. "Big fire, I presume? Colossal gouts of flame, and all?"

"What mosquitoes is he talking about," General Reibisch muttered under his breath toward Verna and Warren beside him on his bench opposite Zedd and Adie.

"That's right," Verna said, ignoring the general. He sighed and folded his arms across his barrel chest. "A proper line of fire." Verna waited until Zedd swallowed. "Do you find something unsatisfactory about that, First Wizard?"

Zedd shrugged. "Well . . ." He paused, then frowned. He leaned toward the general, peering more closely. Zedd wagged a bony finger at the man's folded arms.

"There's one now. A mosquito is about to suck your blood, General."

"What? Oh." He swatted it. "They've been thick this summer. I think the season for them is drawing to an end, though. We'll be happy to be rid of the little pests, I can tell you."

Zedd waggled his finger again. "And were they all like that one?"

General Reibisch lifted his forearm and glanced down at the squashed bug. "Yes, the bloodthirsty little . . ." His voice trailed off. He peered more closely. With a finger and thumb he gingerly lifted the tiny insect by a wing, holding it up to have a better look.

"Well I'll be . . . this thing is"—his face lost a shade of color—"white." His grayish-green eyes turned up toward Zedd. "What was that you were saying about . . . ?"

"Albino mosquitoes," Zedd confirmed as he set his empty plate on the ground. He gestured with a sticklike finger at the general's flat assailant. "Have you ever seen the albino fever, General? Have any of you? Terrible thing, albino fever."

"What's albino fever?" Warren asked. "I never heard of it. I've never read anything about it, either, I'm sure."

"Really? Must be just a Midlands thing."

The general peered more closely at the tiny white insect he was holding up. "What does this albino fever do to a person?"

"Oh, your flesh turns the most ghastly white." Zedd waved his fork. "Do you know," he said, frowning in thought as if distracted by something as he looking up at the ceiling of the tent, "that I once saw a wizard lay down a simply prodigious font of flame before a line of charging cavalry?"

"Well, there you go," Verna said. "You know its value, then. You've seen it in action."

"Yes . . ." Zedd drawled. "Problem was, the enemy had been prepared for such a simpleminded trick."

"Simpleminded!" Verna shot to her feet. "I don't see how you could possibly consider—"

"The enemy had conjured curved shields just for such an eventuality."

"Curved shields?" Warren swiped back a curly lock of his blond hair. "I've never heard of such a thing. What are curved—"

"The wizard who laid down the fire had been expecting shields, of course, and

126

so he made his fire resistant to such an expected defense. These shields, though, weren't conjured to stop the fire"—Zedd's gaze shifted from Warren's wide eyes to Verna's scowl—"but to roll it."

"Albino fever?" The general waved his bug. "If you might, could you explain—"

"Roll the fire?" Warren asked as he leaned forward.

"Yes," Zedd said. "Roll the fire before the cavalry charge—so that instead of a simple cavalry assault, the defenders now had deadly fire rolling back at them."

"Dear Creator . . ." Warren whispered. "That's ingenious—but surely the shield would extinguish the fire."

Zedd twirled his fork as he spoke, as if to demonstrate the shield rolling the flames. "Conjured by their own wizard for the expected defense, the fire had been hardened against shields, so instead of fizzling, it stayed viable. That, of course, enabled the curved shield to roll the fire back without it extinguishing. And, of course, being hardened to shields, the wizard's own quickly thrown up defensive shields couldn't stop his own fire's return."

"But he could just cut it off!" Warren was becoming panicked, as if seeing his own wizard's fire coming back at him. "The wizard who created it could call it and cut it off."

"Could he?" Zedd smiled. "He thought so, too, but he hadn't been prepared for the peculiar nature of the enemy's shield. Don't you see? It not only rolled the fire back, but in so doing rolled around the fire as it went, protecting it from any alteration by magic."

"Of course . . ." Warren whispered to himself.

"The shield was also sprinkled with a provenance-seeking spell, so it rolled the fire back toward the wizard who conjured it. He died by his own fire—after it had seared through hundreds of his own men on its way to him."

Silence settled into the tent. Even the general, still holding out the albino mosquito, sat transfixed.

"You see," Zedd finally went on, tossing his fork down onto his plate, "using the gift in war is not simply an act of exercising your power, but an act of using your wits."

Zedd pointed. "For example, consider that albino mosquito General Reibisch is holding. Under cover of darkness, just like right now, tens of thousands of them, conjured by the enemy, could be sneaking into this camp to infect your men with fever, and no one would even realize they were under attack. Then, in the morning, the enemy strikes a camp of weak and sick soldiers and slaughters the lot of you."

Sister Philippa, over on the other side of Adie, swished her hand in alarm at a tiny buzzing mosquito. "But, the gifted we have could counter such a thing." It was more a plea than an argument.

"Really? It's difficult to detect such an infinitesimal bit of magic. None of you detected these minuscule invaders, did you?"

"Well, no, but . . ."

Zedd fixed a fierce glare on Sister Philippa. "It's night. In the night, they simply seem to be ordinary mosquitoes, pesky, but no different from any other. Why, the general here didn't notice them. Neither did any of you gifted people. You can't detect the fever they carry, either, because it, too, is such a tiny speck of magic you aren't watching for it—you're looking for something huge and powerful and fearsome.

"Most of the gifted Sisters will be bitten in their sleep, without ever knowing it happened, until they awake in the pitch blackness with the shivering chills of a frightful fever, only to discover the first truly debilitating symptom of this particular fever: blindness. You see, it isn't the blackness of night they awake to—dawn has already broken—but blindness. Then they find that their legs won't obey their wishes. Their ears are ringing with what sounds like an endless, tingling scream."

The general's gaze darted about, testing his eyesight as Zedd went on. He twisted a big finger in an ear as if to clean it out.

"By now, anyone bitten is too weak to stand. They lose control of their bodily functions and lie helpless in their own filth. They are within hours of death . . . but those last hours will seem like a year."

"How do we counter it?" On the edge of his seat, Warren licked his lips. "What's the cure?"

"Cure? There is no cure! Now a fog is beginning to creep toward the camp. This time, the few gifted left can sense that the wide mass of seething murk is foul with dark, suffocating magic. They warn everyone. Those too sick to stand wail in terror. They can't see, but they can hear the distant battle cries of the advancing enemy. In a panic not to be touched by the deadly fog, anyone able to rise from their bedrolls does so. Too delirious to stand, a few manage to crawl. The rest run for their lives before the advancing fog.

"It's the last mistake they ever make," Zedd whispered. He swept a hand out before their white faces. "They run headlong into the horror of a waiting death trap."

Everyone was wide-eyed and slack-jawed by now, sitting on the edge of their benches.

"So, General," Zedd said in a bright, cheery tone as he sat back, "what about those mass graves? Or are you planning on any of you left alive just abandoning the sick for dead and leaving the bodies to rot? Probably not a bad idea. There will be enough to worry about without the burdensome task of trying to care for the dying and burying all the dead—especially since the very act of touching their white flesh will contaminate the living with a completely unexpected sickness, and then—"

Verna shot to her feet. "But what can we do!" She could plainly see the potential for chaos all around her. "How can we counter such vile magic?" She threw open her arms. "What do we need to do?"

Zedd shrugged. "I thought you and your Sisters had it all figured out. I thought you knew what you were doing." He waggled his hand over his shoulder, gesturing off to the south, toward the enemy. "I thought you said you had the situation well in hand."

Verna silently sank back down to the bench beside Warren.

"Uh, Zedd . . ." General Reibisch swallowed in distress. He held out the mosquito. "Zedd, I think I'm starting to feel dizzy. Isn't there anything you can do?"

"About what?"

"The fever. I think my vision is getting dimmer. Can you do nothing?"

"No, nothing."

"Nothing."

"Nothing, because there's nothing wrong with you. I just conjured a few albino mosquitoes to make a point. The point is that what I saw when I came into this camp scared the wits out of me. If the gifted among the enemy are at all diabolical, and with Jagang we have ample reason to believe they are, then this army is ill prepared for the true nature of the threat."

Sister Philippa haltingly lifted a hand like a schoolgirl with a question. "But, with all the gifted among us, surely, we would . . . know . . . or something."

"That's what I'm trying to tell you: the way things are now, you won't know. It's the things you never heard of, haven't seen before, don't expect, and can't even imagine, that are going to be coming for you. The enemy will use conventional magic, to be sure, and that will be trouble enough, but it's the albino mosquitoes you must fear."

"As you said, though, you only conjured them to make a point," Warren said. "Maybe the enemy isn't as smart as you, and won't think of such things."

"The Order did not take over all of the Old World by being stupid but by being ruthless." Zedd's brow drew lower. He lifted a finger skyward to mark his words. "Besides, they have already thought of just such things. This past spring, one of the Sisters in the hands of the enemy used magic to unleash a deadly plague that could not be detected by anyone with the gift. Tens of thousands of people, from newborn infants to the old, suffered gruesome deaths."

Those Sisters, in the hands of the enemy, were a grave and ever-present danger. Ann had gone off alone on a mission to either rescue those Sisters or eliminate them. From what Zedd had seen when he had been down in Anderith, Ann had failed in her mission. He didn't know what had become of her, but he knew that Jagang still held Sisters captive.

"But we stopped the plague," Warren said.

"Richard stopped it, as only he could." Zedd held the gaze of the young wizard. "Did you know that in order to save us from that grim fate, he had to venture to the Temple of the Winds, hidden away beyond the veil of life in the underworld itself? Neither you nor I can imagine the toll such an experience must have taken on him. I saw a shadow of the specter in his eyes when he spoke of it.

"I can't even hazard a guess as to how trifling a chance at success he had when he started on so hopeless a journey. Had he not prevailed against all odds, we would all be dead by now from an unseen death brought on by magic we could not detect and could not counter. I'd not want to again count on such an auspicious deliverance."

No one could disagree with him; they nodded slightly, or looked away. The tent had become a gloomy place.

Verna rubbed her fingers across her brow. "Pride is of no use to the dead. I admit it: those gifted among us have little knowledge of what we're doing when it comes to using our gift in warfare. We know some things about fighting, perhaps even a great many things, but I admit we could be woefully lacking in the depth of knowledge needed.

"Think us fools if you will, but don't ever think us at odds with you, Zedd; we are all here on the same side." Her brown eyes betrayed nothing but simple sincerity. "We not only could use your help, we would gratefully welcome it."

"Of course he will help us," Adie scoffed while giving Zedd a scolding frown.

"Well, you have a good start. Admitting that you don't know something is the first step to learning." Zedd scratched his chin. "Every day, I amaze myself with all I don't know."

"That would be wonderful," Warren said. "If you would help us, I mean." He sounded hesitant, but forged ahead anyway. "I would really like to have the benefit of a real wizard's experience."

Despondent with the weight of his other troubles, Zedd shook his head. "I would like to—and to be sure I will give you all some advice in the task at hand. However, I've been on a long and frustrating journey, and I'm afraid I'm not yet finished with it. I can't stay. I must soon be off again."

Warren swiped back his curly blond hair. "What sort of journey have you been on, Zedd?"

Zedd pointed a bony finger. "You don't need to keep that flattened mosquito, General."

General Reibisch realized it was still between his finger and thumb. He tossed it away. Everyone awaited Zedd's words. He smoothed the heavy maroon robes over his twiglike thighs as his gaze absently studied the dirt floor.

He let out a crestfallen sigh. "I was recovering from my own auspicious deliverance from grappling with remarkable magic I'd never before encountered, and, as I regained my senses, spent months searching. I was down in Anderith, and saw some of what happened after the Order swept in there. It was a dark time for the people. Not only from the rampaging soldiers, but also from one of your Sisters, Verna. Death's Mistress they called her."

"Do you know which one it is?" Verna asked in a bitter voice at hearing of a Sister causing harm.

"No. I only saw her once, from a goodly distance. Had I been fully recovered, I might have tried to remedy the situation, but I wasn't myself yet and dared not confront her. She also had a few thousand soldiers with her. The sight of all the soldiers, led by a woman they had heard of and feared, had people in a panic. The Sister was young, with blond hair. She wore a black dress."

"Dear Creator," Verna whispered. "Not one of mine—one of the Keeper's. There are few women born with the strength of power such as she has. She also has power acquired by nefarious means; Nicci is a Sister of the Dark."

"I've gotten reports," General Reibisch said. By his grim tone, Zedd knew the reports must have had it right. "I've heard, too, that it's quieted considerably."

Zedd nodded. "The Order was at first brutal, but now 'Jagang the Just'—as they have taken to calling him—has spared them further harm. In most places, other than the capital of Fairfield where the most killing took place, people have turned to supporting him as a liberator come to deliver them into a better life. They're reporting neighbors, or travelers—whoever they suspect is not an adherent to the noble ideals of the Order.

"I was all through Anderith, and spent a good deal of time behind the enemy lines searching—without success. I then journeyed up into the wilds and north to a number of towns, and even a few cities, but I can find no sign of them. I guess my abilities were a long time in recovering; I only a short time ago discovered where you all were. I have to commend you, General, you've kept the presence of your forces well hidden—took me forever to find your army. The boy, though, seems to have vanished without a trace." Zedd's fists tightened in his lap. "I must find him."

"You mean Richard?" Adie asked. "You be searching for your grandson?"

"Yes. For Richard and Kahlan, both." Zedd lifted his hands in a helpless gesture. "However, without any success, I must admit. I've talked to no one who has seen even a sign of them. I've used every skill I possess, but to no avail. If I didn't know better, I'd say they no longer existed."

Looks passed among everyone else. Zedd peered from one surprised face to another. For the first time in months, Zedd's hopes rose. "What? What is it? You know something?"

Verna gestured under the bench. "Show him, General."

At her urging, the general lifted out a map roll. He pulled it wide in his callused hands and laid it on the ground at his feet. The map was turned around so Zedd could read it. General Reibisch tapped the mountains to the west of Hartland.

"Right here, Zedd."

"Right there . . . what?"

"Richard and Kahlan," Verna said.

Zedd gaped at her face and then down at the map. General Reibisch's finger hovered over a wild range of peaks. Zedd knew those mountains. They were an inhospitable place.

"There? Dear spirits, why would Richard and Kahlan be all the way up there in such a forbidding place? What are they doing there?"

"Kahlan be hurt," Adie said in a consoling tone.

"Hurt?"

"She was at the brink of passing into the spirit world. From what we be told, maybe she saw the world on the other side of the veil." Adie pointed to the map. "Richard took her there to recover."

"But . . . why would he do that?" With a hand, Zedd flattened his wavy white hair to the top of his head. His thoughts spun in a confusing jumble while he tried to take it all in at once. "She could be healed—"

"No. She be spelled. If magic be used to try to heal her, a vile hidden spell would be unleashed and she would die."

Understanding washed over him. "Dear spirits . . . I'm thankful the boy knew it in time." Before the horror of memories of the screams could come roaring to the fore of his thoughts, Zedd slammed a mental door on them. He swallowed with the pain of those that slipped through. "But still, why would he go there? He's needed here."

"He certainly is," Verna snapped. By her tone, it was a sore subject.

"He can't come here," Warren said. When Zedd only stared at him, he explained further. "We don't understand it all, but we believe Richard is following a prophecy of some sort."

"Prophecy!" Zedd dismissed it with a wave. "Richard doesn't take to riddles. He hates them and won't pay heed to them. There are times when I wish he would, but he won't."

"Well, this one he's paying heed to." Warren pressed his lips tight for a moment. "It's his own."

"His own . . . what?"

Warren cleared his throat. "Prophecy."

Zedd jumped to his feet. "What! Richard? Nonsense."

"He's a war wizard," Verna said with quiet authority.

Zedd passed a scowl among all the suddenly circumspect expressions. He made a sour face and, with a flourish of his robes, returned to his seat beside Adie.

"What is this prophecy?"

Warren twisted a little knot of his violet robes. "He didn't say, exactly."

"Here." General Reibisch pulled some folded papers from a pocket. "He wrote me letters. We've all read them."

Zedd stood and snatched the letters from the general's big fist. He went to the table and smoothed out the pages. As everyone else sat silently watching, Zedd leaned over the table and read Richard's words lying before him.

With great authority, Richard paradoxically turned away from authority. He said that after much reflection, he had come to an understanding that arrived with the power of a vision, and he knew then, beyond doubt, that his help would only bring about certain catastrophe.

In letters that followed, Richard said he and Kahlan were safe and she was slowly recovering. Cara was with them. In response to letters General Reibisch and others had written, Richard remained steadfast in his stand. He warned them that the cause of freedom would be forever lost if he failed to remain on his true path. He said that whatever decisions General Reibisch and the rest of them made, he would not contradict or criticize. He told them that his heart was with them, but they were on their own for the foreseeable future. He said possibly forever.

His letters basically gave no real information, other than alluding to his understanding or vision, and making it clear that they could expect no guidance from him. Nonetheless, Zedd could read some of what the words didn't say.

Zedd stared at the letters long after he had finished reading them. The flame of the lamp wavered slowly from side to side, occasionally fluttering and sending up a coiled thread of oily smoke. He could hear muffled voices outside the tent as soldiers on patrol quietly passed along information. Inside, everyone remained silent. They had all read the letters.

Verna's expression was tight with anxiety. She could hold her tongue no longer. "Will you go to see him, Zedd? Convince him to return to the struggle?"

Zedd lightly trailed his fingers over the words on paper. "I can't. This is one time I can be of no help to him."

"But he's our leader in this struggle." The soft lamplight illuminated the feminine grace of her slender fingers as she pressed them to her brow in vain solace. Her hand fell back to her lap. "Without him . . ."

Zedd didn't answer her. He could not imagine what Ann's reaction to such a development would be. For centuries she had combed through prophecies in anticipation of the war wizard who would be born to lead them in this battle for the very existence of magic. Richard was that war wizard, born to the battle he had suddenly abandoned.

"What do you think be the problem?" Adie asked in her quiet, raspy voice.

Zedd looked back to the letters one last time. He pulled his gaze from the words and straightened. All eyes around the dimly lit tent were on him as if hoping he could somehow rescue them from a fate they couldn't comprehend, but instinctively dreaded.

"This is a time of trial to the depth of Richard's soul." Zedd slipped his hands up opposite sleeves until the silver brocade at the cuffs met. "A passage, of sorts—thrust upon him because of his comprehension of something only he sees."

Warren cleared his throat. "What sort of trial, Zedd? Can you tell us?"

Zedd gestured vaguely as memories of terrible times flashed through his mind. "A struggle . . . a reconciliation . . ."

"What sort of reconciliation?" Warren pressed.

Zedd gazed into the young man's blue eyes, wishing he wouldn't ask so many questions. "What is the purpose of your gift?"

"Its purpose? Well, I . . . guess to . . . well, it just is. The gift is simply an ability."

"It is to help others," Verna stated flatly. She clutched her light blue cloak more tightly around her shoulders as if it were armor to defend her from whatever Zedd might throw at her in answer.

"Ah. Then what are you doing here?"

The question caught her by surprise. "Here?"

"Yes." Zedd waved his arm, indicating a vague, distant place. "If the gift is to help others, then why are you not out there doing it? There are sick needing to be healed, ignorant needing to be taught, and the hungry needing to be fed. Why are you just sitting there, healthy, smart, and well fed?"

Verna rearranged her cloak as she squared her shoulders into a posture of firm resolve. "In battle, if you abandon the gates to help a fallen comrade, you have given in to a weakness: your inability to steel yourself to an immediate suffering in order to prevent suffering on a much greater scale. If I run off to help the few people I could in that manner, I must leave my post here, with this army, as they try to keep the enemy from storming the gateway into the New World."

Zedd's estimation of the woman rose a little. She had come tantalizingly close to expressing the essence of a vital truth. He offered her a small smile of respect as he nodded. She looked more surprised by that than she had by his question.

"I can certainly see why the Sisters of the Light are widely regarded as proper servants of need." Zedd stroked his chin. "So then, it is your conviction that we with the ability—the gift—are born into the world to be slaves to those with needs?"

"Well, no . . . but if there is a great need—"

"Then we are more tightly bound in the chains of slavery to those with every greater need," Zedd finished for her. "Thus, anyone with a need, by right—to your mind—becomes our master? Indentured servant to one cause, or to any greater cause that might come along, but chattel all the same. Yes?"

This time, Verna chose not to dance with him over what she apparently regarded as a patch of quicksand. It didn't prevent her from glaring at him, though.

Zedd held that there could be only one philosophically valid answer to the question; if Verna knew it, she didn't offer it.

"Richard has apparently come to a place where he must critically examine his alternatives and determine the proper course of his life," Zedd explained. "Perhaps circumstances have caused him to question the proper use of his abilities, and, in view of his values, his true purpose."

Verna opened her hands in a helpless gesture. "I don't see how he could have any higher purpose than to be here, helping the army against the threat to the New World—the threat to the lives of free people."

Zedd sank back down onto the bench. "You do not see, and I do not see, but Richard sees something."

"That doesn't mean he's right," Warren said.

Zedd studied the young man's face for a moment. Warren had fresh features, but also a knowing look in his eyes that betrayed something beyond mere youth. Zedd wondered how old Warren was.

"No, it does not mean Richard is right. He may be making a heroic mistake that destroys our chance to survive."

"Kahlan thinks maybe it be a mistake," Adie finally put in, as if regretting having to tell him. "She wrote a note to me—I believe without Richard's knowledge, seeing as Cara wrote down Kahlan's words for her—and gave it to the messenger. Kahlan says that she fears Richard be doing this in part because of what happened to her. The Mother Confessor also confided that she be afraid Richard has lost his faith in people, and, because of his rejection by the people of Anderith, Richard may view himself as a fallen leader."

"Bah." Zedd waved his hand dismissively. "A leader cannot follow behind people, tail between his legs, sniffing for their momentary whims and wishes, whining to follow them this way and that as they ramble through life. Those kind of people are not looking for a leader—they are looking for a master, and one will find them.

"A true leader forges a clear path through a moral wilderness so that people might see the way. Richard was a woods guide because such is his nature. Perhaps he is lost in that dark wood. If he is, he must find his way out, and it must be a correctly reasoned course, if he is to be the true leader of a free people."

Everyone silently considered the implications. The general was a man who followed the Lord Rahl, and simply awaited his orders. The Sisters had their own ideas. Zedd and Adie knew the way ahead was not what it might seem to some.

"That's what Richard did for me," Warren said in a soft voice, staring off into memories of his own. "He showed me the way—made me want to follow him up out of the vaults. I had become comfortable down there, content with my books and my fate, but I was a prisoner of that darkness, living my life through the struggles and accomplishments of others. I never could understand precisely how he inspired me to want to follow him up and out." Warren looked up into Zedd's eyes. "Maybe he needs that same kind of help, himself. Can you help him, Zedd?"

"He has entered a dark time for any man, and especially for a wizard. He must come out the other side of this on his own. If I take him by the hand and lead him through, so to speak, I might take him a way he would not have selected on his own, and then he would forever be crippled by what I had chosen for him.

". . . But worse yet, what if he's right? If I unwittingly forced him to another course, it could doom us all and result in a world enslaved by the Imperial Order." Zedd shook his head. "No. This much I know: Richard must be left alone to do as he must. If he truly is the one to lead us in this battle for the future of magic and of mankind, then this can only be part of his journey as it must be traveled."

Almost everyone nodded, if reluctantly, at Zedd's words.

Warren didn't nod. He picked at the fabric of his violet robes. "There's one thing we haven't considered." As everyone waited, his blue eyes turned up to meet Zedd's gaze. In those eyes, Zedd saw an uncommon wisdom that told him that this was a young man who could gaze into the depths of things when most people saw only the sparkles on the surface.

"It could be," Warren said in a quiet but unflinching voice, "that Richard, being gifted, and being a war wizard, has been visited by a legitimate prophecy. War wizards are different from the rest of us. Their ability is not narrowly specific, but broad. Prophecy is, at least theoretically, within his purview. Moreover, Richard has Subtractive Magic as well as Additive. No wizard born in the last three thousand years has had both sides. While we can perhaps imagine, we could not possibly begin to understand his potential, though the prophecies have alluded to it.

"It could very well be that Richard has had a valid prophecy that he clearly understands. If so, then he may be doing precisely what must be done. It could even be that he clearly understands the prophecy and it is so gruesome he is doing us the only kindness he can—by not telling us."

Verna covered his hand with hers. "You don't really believe that, do you, Warren?" Zedd noticed that Verna put a lot of stock in what Warren said.

Ann had told Zedd that Warren was only beginning to exhibit his gift of prophecy. Such wizards—prophets—were so rare that they came along only once or twice a millennium. The potential importance of such a wizard was incalculable. Zedd didn't know how far along that path Warren really was, yet. Warren probably didn't, either.

"Prophecy can be a terrible burden." Warren smoothed his robes along his thigh. "Perhaps Richard's prophecy told him that if he is to ever have a chance to oversee victory, he must not die with the rest of us in our struggle against the army of the Imperial Order."

General Reibisch, silent about such wizardly doings, had nevertheless been listening and watching intently. Sister Philippa's thumb twiddled a button on her dress. Even with Verna's comforting hand on his, Warren, at that moment, looked nothing but forlorn.

"Warren"—Zedd waited until their eyes met—"we all at times envision the most fearful turn of events, simply because it's the most frightening thing we can imagine. Don't invest your thoughts primarily in that which is not the most likely reason for Richard's actions, simply because it is the reason you fear the most. I believe Richard is struggling to understand his place in all this. Remember, he grew up as a woods guide. He has to come to terms not only with his ability, but with the weight of rule."

"Yes, but—"

Zedd lifted a finger for emphasis. "The truth of a situation most often turns out to be that one with the simplest explanation."

The gloom on Warren's face finally melted away under the dawning radiance of a luminous smile. "I'd forgotten that ancient bit of wisdom. Thank you, Zedd."

General Reibisch, combing his curly beard with his fingers, pulled the hand free and made a fist. "Besides, D'Harans will not be so easily bested. We have more forces to call upon, and we have allies here in the Midlands who will come to aid in the fight. We have all heard the reports of the size of the Order, but they are just men, not evil spirits. They have gifted, but so do we. They have yet to come face-to-face with the might of D'Haran soldiers."

Warren picked up a small rock, not quite the size of his fist, and held it in his palm as he spoke. "I mean no disrespect, General, and I do not mean to dissuade you from our just cause, but the subject of the Order has been a pastime of mine. I've studied them for years. I'm also from the Old World."

"Fair enough. So what is it you have to tell us?"

"Well, say that the tabletop is the Old World—the area from which Jagang draws his troops. Now, there are places, to be sure, where there are few people spread over vast areas. But there are many places with great populations, too."

"It's much the same in the New World," the general said. "D'Hara has populous places, and desolate areas."

Warren shook his head. He passed his hand over the tabletop. "Say this is the Old World—the whole of this table." He held up the rock to show the general and then placed it on the edge of the tabletop. "This is the New World. This is its size—this rock—compared to the Old World."

"But, but, that doesn't include D'Hara," General Reibisch sputtered. "Surely . . . with D'Hara—"

"D'Hara is included in the rock."

"I'm afraid Warren is right," Verna said.

Sister Philippa, too, nodded grim acknowledgment. "Perhaps . . ." she said, looking down at her hands folded in her lap, "perhaps Warren is right, and Richard has seen a vision of our defeat, and knows he must remain out of it, or be lost with all the rest of us."

"I don't think that's it at all," Zedd offered in a gentle voice. "I know Richard. If Richard thought we would lose, he would say so in order to give people a chance to weigh that in their decisions."

The general cleared his throat. "Well, actually, one of the letters is missing from that stack. It was the first—where Lord Rahl told me about his vision. In it, Lord Rahl did say that we had no chance to win."

Zedd felt the blood drain down into his legs. He tried to keep his manner unconcerned. "Oh? Where is the letter?"

The general gave Verna a sidelong glance.

"Well, actually," Verna said, "when I read it, I was angered and . . ."

"And she balled it up and threw it in the fire," Warren finished for her.

Verna's face turned red, but she offered no defense. Zedd could understand the sentiment, but he would have liked to have read it with his own eyes. He forced a smile.

"Were those his actual words—that we had no chance to win?" Zedd asked, trying not to sound alarmed. He could feel sweat running down the back of his neck.

"No . . ." General Reibisch said as he shifted his shoulders inside his uniform while giving the question careful thought. "No, Lord Rahl's words were that we must not commit our forces to an attack directly against the army of the Imperial Order, or our side will be destroyed and any chance for winning in the future will be forever lost."

The feeling began to return to Zedd's fingers. He wiped a bead of sweat from the side of his forehead. He was able to draw an easier breath. "Well, that only makes sense. If they are as large a force as Warren says, then any direct attack would be foolhardy."

It did make sense. Zedd wondered, though, why Richard would make such a point of it to a man of General Reibisch's experience. Perhaps Richard was only being cautious. There was nothing wrong with being cautious.

Adie slipped her hand under Zedd's and cuddled her loose fist under his palm. "If you believe you must let Richard be in this, then you will stay? Help teach the gifted here what they must know?"

Every face was etched with concern as they watched him, hanging on what he might decide. The general idly stroked a finger down the white scar on the side of his face. Sister Philippa knitted her fingers together. Verna and Warren entwined theirs.

Zedd smiled and hugged Adie's shoulders. "Of course I'm not going to abandon you."

The three on the bench opposite him each let out a little sigh. Their posture relaxed as if ropes around their necks had been slackened.

Zedd passed a hard look among them all. "War is nasty business. It's about killing people before they can kill you. Magic in war is simply another weapon, if a frightening one. You must realize that it, too, in this, must be used for the end result of killing people."

"What do we need to do?" Verna asked, clearly relieved that he had agreed to stay, but not to the obvious extent of General Reibisch, Warren, or Sister Philippa.

Zedd pulled some of his robes from each side of his legs over into the middle, between them, as he gave the question some thought. It was not the sort of lesson he relished.

"Tomorrow morning, we will begin. There is much to learn about countering magic in warfare. I will teach all the gifted some things about the awful business of using what you always hoped to use for good, for harm, instead. The lessons are not pleasing to endure, but then, neither is the alternative."

The thought of such lessons, and worse, the use of such knowledge, could not be pleasant for any of them to contemplate. Adie, who knew a little bit about the horrific nature of such struggle, rubbed his back in sympathy. His heavy robes stuck to his skin. He wished he had his simple wizard's robes back.

"We will all do as we must to prevent our own people from falling to the monstrous magic of the Imperial Order," Verna said. "You have my word as Prelate."

Zedd nodded. "Tomorrow, then, we begin."

"I fear to think of magic added to warfare," General Reibisch said as he stood.

Zedd shrugged. "To tell the truth, the ultimate object of magic in warfare is to counter the enemy's magic. If we do our job properly, we will bring balance to this. That would mean that all magic would be nullified and the soldiers would then be able to fight without magic swaying the battle. You will be able to be the steel against steel, while we are the magic against magic."

"You mean, your magic won't be of direct help to us?"

Zedd shrugged. "We will try to use magic to visit harm on them in any way we can, but when we try to use magic as a weapon, the enemy will try to counter ours. Any attempt to use their power against us, we will try to counter. The result of magic in warfare, if properly and expertly done, is that it seems as if magic did not exist at all.

"If we fail to rise to the challenge, then the power they throw at us will be truly horrific to witness. If we can best them, then you will see such destruction of their forces as you can't imagine. But, in my experience, magic has a way of balancing, so that you rarely see such events."

"A deadlock, then, is our goal?" Sister Philippa asked.

Zedd turned his palms up, moving his hands up and down in opposition, as if they were scales holding great weight. "The gifted on both sides will be working harder than they have ever worked before. I can tell you that it's exhausting. The result, except with small shifts in the advantage, is that it will seem as if we are all doing nothing to earn our dinner."

Zedd let his hands drop. "It will be punctuated with brief moments of sheer horror and true panic when it seems beyond doubt that the world itself is about to end in one final fit of sheer madness."

General Reibisch grinned in an odd, gentle, knowing way. "Let me tell you, war, when you're holding a sword, looks about the same way." He held up a hand in

138

mock defense. "But I'd rather that, I guess, than have to swing my sword at every magic mosquito that came along. I'm a man of steel against steel. We have Lord Rahl to be the magic against the magic. I'm relieved we have Lord Rahl's grandfather, the First Wizard, to aid us, too. Thank you, Zedd. Anything you need is yours. Just ask."

Verna and Warren added silent nods as the general stepped to the entrance of the tent. When Zedd spoke, General Reibisch turned back, gripping the flap in one hand.

"You're still sending messengers to Richard?"

The general confirmed that they were. "Captain Meiffert was up there, too. He might be able tell you more about Lord Rahl."

"Have all of the messengers returned safely?"

"Most of them." He rubbed his bearded chin. "We've lost two, so far. One messenger was found by chance at the bottom of a rockslide. Another never returned, but his body wasn't found—which wouldn't be unusual. It's a long and difficult journey. There are any number of hazards on such a journey; we have to expect we might lose a few men."

"I'd like you to stop sending men up there to Richard."

"But Lord Rahl needs to be kept informed."

"What if the enemy should capture one of those messengers and find out where Richard is? If you have no scruples, most any man can eventually be made to talk. The risk is not worth it."

The general rubbed his palm on the hilt of his sword as he considered Zedd's words. "The Order is far to the south of us—way down in Anderith. We control all the land between here and the mountains where Lord Rahl is staying." He shook his head in resignation at Zedd's unflinching gaze. "But if you think it's a concern, I'll not send another. Won't Lord Rahl wonder, though, what's going on with us?"

"What's going on with us is not really relevant to him right now; he is doing as he must do, and he can't allow our situation to influence him. He has told you already that he won't be able to give you any orders, that he must stay out of it."

Zedd tugged his sleeves straight and sighed as he thought about it. "Perhaps when the summer is over, before the full grip of winter descends and they're snowed in way up there, I'll go and see how they fare."

General Reibisch gave a departing smile. "If you could talk to Lord Rahl, it would be a relief for us all, Zedd; he would trust your word. Good night, then."

The man had just betrayed his true feelings. No one in the tent really trusted what Richard was doing, except, perhaps, Zedd, and Zedd had his doubts, too. Kahlan had said that she believed Richard viewed himself as a fallen leader; these people who claimed not to understand how he could believe such a thing, at the same time didn't trust his actions.

Richard was all alone with only the strength of his beliefs to support him.

After the general had gone, Warren leaned forward eagerly. "Zedd, I could go with you to see Richard. We could get him to tell us everything, and we could then determine if it really is a prophecy, or as he says, just an understanding he's come to. If it's not really a prophecy, we might be able to make him see things differently.

"More important, we could begin teaching him—or you could, anyway—about his gift, about using magic. He needs to know how to use his ability."

As Zedd paced, Verna let out a little grunt to express her misgivings about Warren's suggestion. "I tried to teach Richard to touch his Han. A number of Sisters attempted it, too. No one was able to make any progress."

"But Zedd believes a wizard is the one to do it. Isn't that right, Zedd?"

Zedd halted his pacing and regarded them both a moment as he considered how to put his thoughts into words. "Well, as I said before, teaching a wizard is not really the work for sorceresses, but another wizard—"

"With Richard, I don't think you would have any better luck than we did," Verna railed.

Warren didn't give ground. "But Zedd believes—"

Zedd cleared his throat, bidding silence. "You're right, my boy; it is the job of a wizard to teach another wizard born with the gift." Verna rose an angry finger to object, but Zedd went right on. "In this case, however, I believe Verna is right."

"She is?" Warren asked.

"I am?" Verna asked.

Zedd waved in a mollifying gesture. "Yes, I believe so, Verna. I think the Sisters can do some teaching. After all, look at Warren, here. The Sisters have managed to teach him something about using his gift, even if it was at the cost of time. You've taught others—if in a limited way, to my view of it—but you couldn't manage to teach Richard the most simple of things. Is that correct?"

Verna's mouth twisted with displeasure. "None of us could teach him the simple task of sensing his own Han. I sat with him hours at a time and tried to guide him through it." She folded her arms and looked away from his intent gaze. "It just didn't work the way it should have."

Warren touched a finger to his chin while he frowned, as if recalling something. "You know, Nathan said something to me once. I told him that I wanted to learn from him—that I wanted him to teach me about being a prophet. Nathan said that a prophet could not be made, but that they were born. I realized, then, that everything I knew and understood about prophecy—really understood about it, in a whole new way—I had learned on my own, and not from anyone else. Could this, with Richard, be something like that? Is that your point, Zedd?"

"It is." Zedd sat down once more on the hard wooden bench beside Adie. "I would love, not only as his grandfather, but as First Wizard, to teach Richard what he needs to know about using his ability, but I'm coming to doubt that such a thing is possible. Richard is different from any other wizard in more ways than just his having the gift for Subtractive Magic in addition to the usual Additive."

"But still," Sister Philippa said, "you are First Wizard. Surely, you would be able to teach him a great deal."

Zedd pulled a fold of his heavy robes from between his bony bottom and the hard bench as he considered how to explain it.

"Richard has done things even I don't understand. Without my training, he has accomplished more than I can even fathom. On his own, Richard reached the Temple of the Winds in the underworld, accomplished the task of stopping a plague, and returned from beyond the veil to the world of life. Can any of you even grasp such a thing? Especially for an untrained wizard? He banished the chimes from the world of the living—how, I have no idea. He has worked magic I've never heard of, much less seen or understand.

"I'm afraid my knowledge could be more of an interference than an aid. Part of Richard's ability, and advantage, is the way he views the world—through not just fresh eyes, but the eyes of a Seeker of Truth. He doesn't know something is impossible, so he tries to accomplish it. I fear to tell him how to do things, how to use his magic, because such teaching also might suggest to him limits of his powers, thus creating them in reality. What could I teach a war wizard? I know nothing about the Subtractive side of magic, much less the gift of such power."

"Lacking another war wizard with Subtractive Magic, are you suggesting it would maybe take a Sister of the Dark to teach him?" Warren asked.

"Well," Zedd mused, "that might be a thought." He let out a tired sigh as he turned more serious. "I have come to realize that it would not only be useless to try to teach Richard to use his ability, but it may even be dangerous—to the world.

"I would like to go see him, and offer him my encouragement, experience, and understanding, but help?" Zedd shook his head. "I don't dare."

No one offered any objection. Verna, for one, had firsthand experience that very likely confirmed the truth of his words. The rest of them probably knew Richard well enough to understand much the same.

"May I help you find a spare tent, Zedd?" Verna finally asked. "You look like you could use some rest. In the morning, after you get a good night's rest, and we all think this over, we can talk more."

Warren, who had just been about to ask another question before Verna spoke first, looked disappointed, but nodded in agreement.

Zedd stretched his legs out straight as he yawned. "That would be best." The thought of the job ahead was daunting. He ached to see Richard, to help him, especially after searching for him for so long. Sometimes it was hard to leave people alone when that was what they most needed. "That would be best," he repeated, "I am tired."

"Summer be slipping away from us. The nights be turning chilly," Adie said as she pressed against Zedd's side. She looked up at him with her white eyes that in the lamplight had a soft amber cast. "Stay with me and warm my bones, old man?"

Zedd smiled as he embraced her. It was as much of a comfort to be with her again as he had expected. In fact, at that moment, if she had given him another hat with a feather, he would have donned it, and with a smile. Worry, though, ached through his bones like an approaching storm.

"Zedd," Verna said, seeming to notice in his eyes the weight of his thoughts, "Richard is a war wizard who, as you say, has in the past proven his remarkable ability. He's a very resourceful young man. Besides that, he is none other than the Seeker himself and has the Sword of Truth with him for protection—a sword that I can testify he knows how to use. Kahlan is a Confessor—the Mother Confessor—and is experienced in the use of her power. They have a Mord-Sith with them. Mord-Sith take no chances."

"I know," Zedd whispered, staring off into a nightmare swirl of thoughts. "But I still fear greatly for them."

"What is it that worries you so?" Warren asked.

"Albino mosquitoes."

Panting in exhaustion, Kahlan had to dance backward through the snarl of hobble-bush stitched through with thorny blackberry to dodge the swing of the sword. The tip whistled past, missing her ribs by an inch. In her mad dash to escape, she ignored the snag and tug of thorns on her pants. She could feel her heartbeat galloping at the base of her skull.

As he relentlessly pressed his attack, forcing her back over a low rise of ledge and through the swale beyond, mounds of fallen leaves kicked aloft by his boots boiled up into the late-afternoon air like colorful thunderheads. The bright yellow, lustrous orange, and vivid red leaves rained down over rocky outcrops swaddled in prickly whorls of juniper. It was like doing battle amid a fallen rainbow.

Richard lunged at her again. Kahlan gasped but blocked his sword. He pressed his grim attack with implacable determination. She gave ground, stepping high as she did so in order to avoid tripping over the snare of roots around a huge white spruce. Losing her footing would be fatal; if she fell, Richard would stab her in an instant.

She glanced left. There loomed a tall prominence of sheer rock draped with long trailers of woolly moss. To the other side, the brink of the ridge ran back to eventually meet that rock wall. Once the level ground tapered down to that dead end, the only option was going to be to climb straight up or straight down.

She deflected a quick thrust of his sword, and he warded hers. In a burst of fury, she pressed a fierce assault, forcing him back a dozen steps. He effortlessly parried her strikes, and then returned her attack in kind. What she had gained was quickly lost twice over. She was once again desperately defending herself and trading ground for her life.

On a low, dead branch of a balsam fir not ten feet away, a small red squirrel, with his winter ear tufts already grown in, plucked a leathery brown rosette of lichen growing on the bark. With his white belly gloriously displayed, he sat on his haunches at the end of the broken-off deadwood, his bushy tail raised up, holding the crinkled piece of lichen in his tiny paws, eating round and round the edges, like some spectator at a tournament eating a fried bread cake while he watched the combatants clash.

Kahlan gulped air as her eyes darted around, looking for clear footing among the imposing trunks of the highland wood while at the same time watching for an opportunity that might save her. If she could somehow get around Richard, around the menace of his sword, she might be able to gain a clear escape route. He would run her down, but it would buy her time. She dodged a quick thrust of his sword and ducked around a maple sapling into a bed of brown and yellow bracken ferns dappled by glowing sunlight.

Richard, driving forward in a sudden mad rush to end it, lifted his sword to hack her.

It was her opening—her only chance.

In a blink, Kahlan reversed her retreat and sprang ahead a step, ducking under his arm. She drove her sword straight into his soft middle.

Richard covered the wound with both hands. He teetered a moment, and then crumpled into the bed of ferns, sprawling flat on his back. Leaves lying lightly atop taller ferns were lifted by the disturbance. They somersaulted up into the air, finally drifting down to brightly decorate his body. The fierce red of the maple leaves was so vibrant it would have made blood look brown by comparison.

Kahlan stood over Richard, gasping to catch her breath. She was spent. She dropped to her knees and then threw herself across his supine body. All around them, fern fronds, the color of caramel candy, were curled into little fists as if in defiance of having to die with the season. The sprinkling of lighter, yellowish, hay-scented ferns lent a clean, sweet scent to the afternoon air. There were few things that could equal the fragrance of the woods in late autumn. In a spectacular bit of chance, a tall maple nearby, sheltered as it was by a protective corner in the rock wall, was not yet denuded, but displayed a wide spread of leaves so orange they looked tangy against the powder blue sky above.

"Cara!" Putting her left hand to Richard's chest, Kahlan pushed herself up on one arm to call out. "Cara! I killed Richard!"

Cara, not far off, laying on her belly at the edge of the ridge as she watched out beyond, said nothing.

"I killed him! Did you hear? Cara—did you see?"

"Yes," she muttered, "I heard. You killed Lord Rahl."

"No you didn't," Richard said, still catching his breath.

She whacked him across the shoulder with her willow-switch sword. "Yes I did. I killed you this time. Killed you dead."

"You only grazed me." He pressed the point of his willow switch to her side. "You've fallen into my trap. I have you at the point of my sword, now. Surrender, or die, woman."

"Never," she said, still gasping for breath as she laughed. "I'd rather die than be captured by the likes of you, you rogue."

She stabbed him repeatedly in his ribs with her willow practice sword as he giggled and rolled from side to side.

"Cara! Did you see? I killed him this time. I finally got him!"

"Yes, all right," Cara grouched as she intently watched out beyond the ridge. "You killed Lord Rahl. Good for you." She glanced back over her shoulder. "This one is mine, right, Lord Rahl? You promised this one was mine."

"Yes," Richard said, still catching his breath, "this one goes for yours, Cara."

"Good." Cara smiled in satisfaction. "It's a big one."

Richard smirked up at Kahlan. "I let you kill me, you know."

"No you didn't! I won. I got you this time." She whacked him again with her willow sword. She paused and frowned. "I thought you said you weren't dead. You said it was only a scratch. Ha! You admitted I got you this time."

Richard chuckled. "I let you—"

Kahlan kissed him to shut him up. Cara saw and rolled her eyes.

When Cara looked back over the ridge, she suddenly sprang up. "They just left! Come on, before something gets it!"

"Cara, nothing is going to get it," Richard said, "not this quickly."

"Come on! You promised this one was mine. I don't want to have gone through all this for nothing. Come on."

"All right, all right." Richard said as Kahlan climbed off him. "We're coming."

He held his hand out for Kahlan to help him up. She stabbed him in the ribs instead. "Got you again, Lord Rahl. You're getting sloppy."

Richard only smiled as Kahlan finally offered her hand. When he was up he hugged her in a quick gesture, and before turning to follow after Cara, said, "Good job, Mother Confessor, good job. You killed me dead. I'm proud of you."

Kahlan endeavored to show him a sedate smile, but she feared it came out as a giddy grin. Richard scooped up his pack and hefted it onto his back. Without delay, he started the descent down the steep, broken face of the mountain. Kahlan threw her long wolf's-fur mantle around her shoulders and followed him through the deep shade of sheltering spruce at the edge of the ridge, stepping on the exposed ledge rather than the low places.

"Be careful," Richard called out to Cara, already a good distance ahead of them. "With all the leaves covering the ground, you can't see holes or gaps in the rock."

"I know, I know," she grumbled. "How many times do you think I need to hear it?"

Richard constantly watched out for them both. He had taught them how to walk in such terrain and what to be careful of. From the beginning, marching through the forests and mountains, Kahlan noted that Richard moved with quiet fluidity, while Cara traipsed along, bounding up onto and off of rocks and ledges, almost like an exuberant youngster. Since Cara had spent most of her life indoors, she didn't know that it made a difference how you walked in such terrain.

Richard had patiently explained to her, "Pick where to put your feet in order to make your steps comparatively level. Don't step down to a lower spot if you don't need to, only to have to step up again as you continue your climb up the trail. Don't step up needlessly, only to have to step down again. If you must step up on something, you don't always need to lift your whole body—just flex your legs."

Cara complained that it was too hard to think about where to put her foot each time. He told her that by walking the way she did, she was actually climbing the mountain twice for each time he climbed it. He admonished her to think as she walked, and soon it would become instinctive and would require no conscious thought. When Cara found that her shin and thigh muscles didn't get as tired and sore when she followed his suggestions, she became a keen student. Now she asked questions instead of arguing. Most of the time.

Kahlan saw that as Cara descended the steep trail, she did as Richard had taught her and used a stick as an improvised staff to probe any suspicious low area where leaves collected before stepping there. This was no place to break an ankle. Richard said nothing, but sometimes he smiled when she found a hole with her stick rather than her foot, as she used to.

Forging a new trail on a steep slope like the one they were descending was dangerous work. Potential trails often withered into dead ends, requiring that you retrace your steps. On less severe slopes, hillsides, and flatter ground especially, animals often made good trails. In a valley, a suitable trail that shrank to nothing wasn't a big problem because there you could beat through the brush to more open ground. Making your own trail on a rocky precipice, a thousand feet up, was always arduous and often frustrating. In such conditions, particularly if the hour grew late, the desire not to have to backtrack a difficult climb tempted people into taking chances.

Richard said that it was hard work that demanded you put reason before your wish to get down, get home, or get to a place to camp. "Wishing gets people killed," he often said. "Using your head gets you home."

Cara poked her stick into a pile of leaves between bare granite rocks. "Don't step in the leaves here," she said over her shoulder as she hopped onto the far rock. "There's a hole."

"Why, thank you, Cara," Richard said in mock gratitude, as if he would have stepped there had she not warned him.

The cliff face they were on had a number of sizable ledges with rugged little trees and shrubs that provided good footing and the safety of a handhold. Below, the mountainside dropped away before them into a lush ravine. Beyond the defile, it rose up again in a steep slope covered with evergreens and the dull gray and brown skeletons of oaks, maples, and birches.

The raucous coats of autumn leaves had been resplendent while they lasted, but now they were but confetti on the ground, and there they faded fast. Usually, the oaks held on to their leaves until at least early winter, and some of them until spring, but up in the mountains icy winds and early storms had already stripped even the oaks bare of their tenacious brown leaves.

Cara stepped out onto a shelf of ledge jutting out over the chasm below. "There," she said as she pointed across the way. "Up there. Do you see?"

Richard shielded his eyes against the warm sunlight as he squinted higher up on the opposite slope. He made a sound deep in his throat to confirm that he saw it. "Nasty place to die."

Kahlan snugged the warm wolf fur up against her ears to protect them from the cold wind. "There's a good place?"

Richard let his hand drop from his brow. "I guess not."

Farther up the slope from where Cara had pointed, the forest ended in a place called the crooked wood. Above that, where no trees could grow, the mountain was naked rock ridges and scree. A little farther up, snow, white as sugar, sparkled in the slanting sunlight. Below the snow and bare rock, the crooked wood was exposed to harsh winds and bitter weather, causing the trees to grow in tortured shapes. The crooked wood was a line of demarcation between the desolation where little more than lichen could survive the forbidding weather, and the forest of trees huddled below.

Richard gestured off to their right. "Let's not waste any time, though. I don't want to be caught up here come dark."

Kahlan looked out to where the mountain opened onto a grand vista of snow-capped peaks, valleys, and the undulating green of seemingly endless, trackless forests. A roiling blanket of thick clouds had invaded those valleys, stealing in around the mountains, sneaking ever closer. In the distance, some of the snowcapped peaks stood isolated in a cottony gray sea. Lower down the mountains, below those dense, dark clouds, the weather would be miserable.

Both Richard and Cara awaited Kahlan's word. She didn't like the thought of being exposed in the crooked wood when the icy cold fog and drizzle arrived. "I'm fine, let's go and get it done. Then we can get down lower where we'll be able to find a wayward pine to stay dry tonight. I wouldn't mind sitting beside a hearty little fire sipping hot tea."

Cara blew warm breath into her cupped hands. "That sounds good to me."

It was on the first day Kahlan met Richard, more than a year before, that he had taken her to a wayward pine. Kahlan had never known about such trees in the deep woods of Westland. Wayward pines still held the same mystic quality for her as they did the first time she saw one silhouetted against a darkening sky, taller than all the trees around it. Such mature trees were a friend to travelers far from any conventional shelter.

A big wayward pine's boughs hung down to the ground all around. The needles grew mostly at the outer fringe, leaving the inner branches bare. Inside, under their dense green skirts, wayward pines provided excellent shelter from harsh weather. Something about the tree's sap made them resistant to fire, so if you were careful, you could have a cozy campfire inside while outside it rained and stormed.

Richard, Kahlan, and Cara often stayed in wayward pines when they were out in the mountains. Those nights getting warm around a small fire within the tree's confines brought them all closer, and gave them time to reflect, to talk, and to tell stories. Some of the stories made them laugh. Some brought a lump to their throats.

After Kahlan's assurance that she was up to it, Richard and Cara nodded and started down the cliff. She had recovered from her terrible wounds, but they still left it up to her to decide if she was prepared for the effort of such a descent and climb and then descent again before they found a sheltered campsite—hopefully in a wayward pine.

Kahlan had been a long time in healing. She had known, of course, that injuries such as she had suffered would take time to heal. Bedridden for so long, her muscles had become withered, weak, and nearly useless. For a long time, it had been hard for her to eat much. She became a skeleton. With the realization of just how weak and helpless she had become, even as she healed, she had inexorably spiraled down into a state of abject depression.

Kahlan had not comprehended completely the punishing effort that would be required if she was to be herself again. Richard and Cara tried to cheer her up, but their efforts seemed distant; they just didn't understand what it was like. Her legs wasted away until they were bony sticks with knobby knees. She felt not just helpless, but ugly. Richard carved animals for her: hawks, foxes, otters, ducks, and even chipmunks. They seemed only a curiosity to her. At the lowest point, Kahlan almost wished she had died along with their child.

Her life became a tasteless gruel. All she saw, day after day, week after week, were the four walls of her sickroom. The pain was exhausting and the monotony numbing. She came to hate the bitter yarrow tea they made her drink, and the smell of the poultice made of tall cinquefoil and yarrow. When after a time she resisted drinking yarrow, they would sometimes switch to linden, which wasn't so bitter but didn't work as well, yet it did help her sleep. Skullcap often helped when her head hurt, though it was so astringent it make her mouth pucker for a long time after. Sometimes, they switched to a tincture of feverfew to help ease her pain. Kahlan came to hate taking herbs and would often say she didn't hurt, when she did, just to avoid some horrid concoction.

Richard hadn't made the window in the bedroom very big; in the summer heat the room was often sweltering. Kahlan could see only a bit of the sky outside her window, the tops of some trees, and the jagged blue-gray shape of a mountain in the distance.

Richard wanted to take her outside, but Kahlan begged him not to try because

146

she didn't think it would be worth the pain. It didn't take much convincing for him to be talked out of hurting her. Every kind of day, from sunny and bright to gray and gloomy, came and went. Lying in her little room as time slipped away while she slowly healed, Kahlan thought of it as her "lost summer."

One day, she was parched, and Richard had forgotten to fill the cup and place it where she could reach it on the simple table beside the bed. When she asked for water, Richard came back with the cup and a full waterskin and set them both on the windowsill as he called to Cara, outside. He rushed out, telling Kahlan as he went that he and Cara had to go check the fishing lines and they would be back as soon as they could. Before Kahlan could ask him to put the water closer, he was gone.

Kahlan lay fuming in the silence, hardly able to believe that Richard had been so inconsiderate as to leave the water out of her reach. It was unusually warm for late summer. Her tongue felt swollen. She stared helplessly at the wooden cup setting in the windowsill.

On the verge of tears, she let out a moan of self-pity and smacked her fist against the bed. She rolled her head to the right, away from the window, and closed her eyes. She decided to take a nap in order not to think about her thirst. Richard and Cara would be back by the time she awoke, and they would get the water for her. And Richard would get a scolding.

Sweat trickled down her neck. Outside, a bird kept calling. Its repetitious song sounded like a little girl with a high pitched voice saying "who, me?" Once a "who, me?" bird started in, it was a long performance. Kahlan could think of little else besides how much she wanted a drink.

She couldn't make herself fall asleep. The annoying bird kept asking its question over and over again. More than once, she found herself whispering "yes, you," in answer. She growled a curse at Richard. She squeezed her eyes shut and tried to forget her thirst, the heat, and the bird and go to sleep. Her eyes kept popping open.

Kahlan lifted her sleeping gown away from her chest, ruffling it up and down to cool herself. She realized she was staring at the water in the window. It was out of her reach—clear over on the other side of the room. The room wasn't very big, but still, she couldn't walk. Richard knew better. She thought that maybe, if she could sit up and move to the bottom of the bed, she might be able to reach the cup.

With an ill-tempered huff, she threw the light cover off her bony legs. She hated seeing them. Why was Richard being so inconsiderate? What was the matter with him? She intended to give him a piece of her mind when he got back. She eased her legs over the side of the bed.

The mattress was a pliable woven mat stuffed with grasses and feathers and tow padding. It was quite comfortable, and Kahlan was pleased with her snug bed. With a great effort, she pushed herself up. For a long time, she sat on the edge of the bed holding her head in her hands as she caught her breath. Her whole body throbbed in pain.

It was the first time she had sat up all by herself.

She understood very well what Richard was doing. Still, she didn't appreciate his way of forcing her to get up. It was cruel. She wasn't ready. She was still badly hurt. She needed to rest in bed in order to recover. Her oozing wounds had finally closed up and healed over, but she was sure she was still too injured to be getting up. She feared to test broken bones.

Accompanied by a lot of groaning and grunting, she worked herself to the bottom of the bed. Sitting there, one hand holding the footboard to steady herself, she was still too far from the window to reach the water. She was going to have to stand.

She paused for a while to have dark thoughts about her husband.

After a day many weeks before, when she had called for a long time and Richard hadn't heard her weak voice, he had left a light pole beside her so she would be able to use it to reach out and knock on the wall or door if she was in urgent need of their help. Now, Kahlan worked her fingers around the pole lying alongside her bed and lifted it upright. She planted the thicker end on the ground and leaned on the pole for support as she carefully slid off the bed. Her feet touched the cool dirt floor. Putting weight on her legs made her gasp in pain.

She half stood, half leaned on the bed, prepared to cry out, but realized she was gasping more at the brutal pain she expected than from the actual pain. It did hurt, but she realized it wasn't too much to endure. She was a bit disgruntled to learn it wasn't nearly as bad as it had been; she had been planning on reducing Richard to tears with the torturous suffering he had so cavalierly forced upon her.

She put more weight on her feet and pulled herself up with the aid of the pole. Finally, she stood in wobbling triumph. She was actually on her feet, and she had done it by herself.

Kahlan couldn't seem to make her legs walk the way she wanted them to. In order to get to the water, she was going to have to make them do her bidding—at least until she reached the window. Then, she could collapse to the floor, where Richard would find her. She luxuriated in her mental picture of it. He wouldn't think his plan to get her out of bed so clever, then.

With the aid of the stout pole for support and her tongue poked out the corner of her mouth for balance, she slowly shuffled to the window. Kahlan told herself that if she fell, she was going to lie there in a heap on the floor, without any water, until Richard came back and found her moaning through cracked lips, dying of thirst. He would be sorry he had ever tried such a pitiless trick. He would feel guilty for the rest of his life for what he had done to her—she would see to it.

Almost wishing every difficult step of the way that she would fall, she finally made it to the window. Kahlan threw an arm over the sill for support and closed her eyes as she panted in little breaths so as not to hurt her ribs. When she had her wind back, she drew herself up to the window. She snatched the cup and gulped down the water.

Kahlan plunked the empty cup down on the sill and peered out as she caught her breath again.

Richard was sitting on the ground just outside, his arms hooked around his knees, his hands clasped.

"Hi there," he said with a smile.

Cara, sitting right beside him, gazed up without emotion. "I see you're up."

Kahlan wanted to yell at him, but instead she found herself trying with all her might not to laugh. She felt suddenly and overwhelmingly foolish for not trying sooner to get up on her own.

Tears stung her eyes as she looked out at the expanse of trees, the vibrant colors, the majestic mountains, and the huge sweep of blue sky dotted with fluffy white clouds marching off into the distance. The size of the mountains, their imposing slopes, their luscious color, was beyond anything she had ever encountered before. How could she possibly not have wanted more than anything to get up and see the world around her?

"You know, of course, that you've made a big mistake," Richard said.

"What do you mean?" Kahlan asked.

"Well, had you not gotten up, we'd have kept waiting on you—at least for a time. Now that you've shown us that you can get up and move on your own, we're only going to keep doing this—putting things out of your reach to make you start moving about and helping yourself."

While she silently thanked him, she was unwilling, just yet, to tell him out loud how right he had been. But inside, she loved him all the more for braving her anger to help her.

Cara turned to Richard. "Should we show her where she can find the table?"

Richard shrugged. "If she gets hungry, she'll come out of the bedroom and find it."

Kahlan threw the cup at him, hoping to wipe the smirk off his face. He caught the cup.

"Well, glad to see your arm works," he said. "You can cut your own bread." When she started to protest, he said, "It's only fair. Cara baked it. The least you can do is to cut it."

Kahlan's mouth fell open. "Cara baked bread?"

"Lord Rahl taught me," Cara said. "I wanted bread with my stew, real bread, and he told me that if I wanted bread, I would have to learn to make it. It was easy, really. A little like walking to the window. But I was much more good-natured about it, and didn't throw anything at him."

Kahlan could not help smiling, knowing it must have been harder for Cara to knead dough than for Kahlan to get up and walk. She somehow doubted that Cara had been "good-natured" about it. Kahlan would like to have seen that battle of wills.

"Give me back my cup. And then go catch some fish for dinner. I'm hungry. I want a trout. A big trout. Along with bread."

Richard smiled. "I can do that. If you can find the table."

Kahlan did find the table. She never ate in bed again.

At first, the pain of walking was sometimes more than she could tolerate, and she took refuge in her bed. Cara would come in and brush her hair, just so Kahlan wouldn't be alone. She had no power in her muscles, and could hardly move by herself. Brushing her own hair was a colossal task. Just getting to the table was exhausting, and all she could accomplish at first. Richard and Cara were sympathetic, and continually encouraged her, but they pushed her, too.

Kahlan was joyous to be out of the bed and that helped her to ignore the pain. The world was again a wondrous place. She was more than joyous to be able at last to go out to the privy. While she never said so, Kahlan was sure Cara was happy about that, too.

As much as she liked the snug home, going outside felt like finally being freed from a dungeon. Before, Richard had frequently offered to take her outside for the day, but she had never wanted to leave her bed, fearing the pain. She realized that because she was so sick, her thinking had slowly become dull and foggy. Along with her summer, she had for a time lost herself. Now, at long last, she felt clear-headed.

She discovered that the view outside her window was the least impressive of the surrounding sights. Snowcapped peaks towered around the small house Richard and Cara had built in the lap of breathtaking mountains. The simple house, with a bedroom at either end, one for Richard and Kahlan, and one for Cara, with a common room in the middle, sat at the edge of a meadow of velvety green grasses sprinkled with wildflowers. Even though it was late in the season when they had arrived, Richard managed to start a small garden in a sunny place outside Cara's window, growing fresh greens for the table and some herbs to add flavor to their cooking. Right behind the house, huge old white pines towered over them, sheltering them from the full force of the wind.

Richard had continued his carving, to pass the time as he sat by Kahlan's bed, talking and telling stories, but after she had at last gotten out of bed, his carvings changed. Instead of animals, Richard began sculpting people.

And then one day he surprised her with his most magnificent carving yet—in celebration, he said, of her getting well enough to finally come out into the world. Astonished by the utter realism and power of the small statue, she whispered that it could only be the gift that had guided his hand in carving it. Richard regarded such talk as nonsense.

"People without the gift carve beautiful statues all the time," he said. "There's no magic involved."

She knew, though, that some artists were gifted, and able to invoke magic through their art.

Richard occasionally spoke wistfully about the works of art he'd seen at the People's Palace, in D'Hara, where he had been held captive. Growing up in Hartland, he had never before seen statues carved in marble, and certainly none carved on such a grand scale, or by such talented hands. Those works had in some ways opened his eyes to the greater world around him and had made a lasting impression on him. Who else but Richard would remember fondly the beauty he saw while held captive and being tortured?

It was true that art could exist independent of magic, but Richard had been taken captive in the first place only with the aid of a spell brought to life through art. Art was a universal language, and thus an invaluable tool for implementing magic.

Kahlan finally stopped arguing with him about whether the gift helped him to carve. He simply didn't believe it. She felt, though, that, having no other outlet, his gift must be expressing itself in this way. Magic always seemed to find a way to seep out, and his carvings of people certainly did seem magical to her.

But the figure of the woman that he carved for her as a gift stirred profound emotion within her. He called it, an image nearly two feet tall carved from buttery smooth, rich, aromatic walnut, *Spirit*. The feminity of her body, its exquisite shape and curves, bones and muscle, were clearly evident beneath her flowing robes. She looked alive.

How Richard had accomplished such a feat, Kahlan couldn't even imagine. He had conveyed through the woman, her robes flowing in a wind as she stood with her head thrown back, her chest out, her hands fisted at her sides, her back arched and strong as if in opposition to an invisible power trying unsuccessfully to subdue her, a sense of . . . spirit.

The statue was obviously not intended to look like Kahlan, yet it evoked in her some visceral response, a tension that was startlingly familiar. Something about the woman in the carving, some quality it conveyed, made Kahlan hunger to be well, to be fully alive, to be strong and independent again.

If this wasn't magic, she didn't know what was.

Kahlan had been around grand palaces her whole life, exposed to any number of pieces of great art by renowned artists, but none had ever taken her breath with its thrust of inner vision, its sense of individual nobility, as did this proud, vibrant woman in flowing robes. The strength and vitality of it brought a lump to Kahlan's throat, and she could only throw her arms around Richard's neck in speechless emotion.

Now Kahlan went outside at every opportunity. She placed the carving of *Spirit* on the windowsill so she could see it not only from bed, but also when she was outdoors. She turned the statue so that it always faced outside. She felt it should always be facing the world.

The woods around the house were mysterious and alluring. Intriguing trails went off into the shadowy distance, and she could just detect light off at the end of the gently curving tunnel through the trees. She ached to explore those narrow tracks, animal trails enlarged by Richard and Cara on their short treks to tend fishing lines and forays in search of nuts and berries. Kahlan, with the aid of a staff, hobbled around the house and the meadow to strengthen her legs; she wanted to go with Richard on those treks, through the filtered sunlight and gentle breezes, over the open patches of ledge, and under the arched, enclosing limbs of huge oaks.

One of the first places Richard took her when she insisted she could walk for a short distance was through that tunnel in the thick, dark wood to the patch of light at the other end, where a brook descended a rocky gorge. The brook was sheltered on the hillside above them by a dense stand of trees. An enormous weight of water continuously plunged over that stepped tumble of rocks, surging around boulders and pouring in glassy sheets over ledges. Many of the bear-sized rocks sitting in the shady pools were flocked in a dark green velvet of moss and sprinkled with long tawny needles from the white pines that favored the rock slope. Flecks of sunlight winking through the dense canopy shimmered in the clear pools.

At the bottom of that gorge, in that sunny mountain glen off behind their house where the trail emerged from the woods, the brook broadened and slowed as it meandered through the expansive valley surrounded by the awesome jut of the mountains. Sometimes Kahlan would dangle her bony legs over a bank and let the cool water caress her feet. There, she could sit on the warm grass and soak up the sun while watching fish swim through the crystal-clear water flowing over gravel beds. Richard had been right when he told her that trout liked beautiful places.

She loved watching the fish, frogs, crayfish, and even the salamanders. Oftentimes, she would lie on her stomach on the low grassy bank, with her chin resting on the backs of her hands, and watch for hours as the fish came out from under sunken logs, from beneath rocks, or from the dark depths of the larger pools to snatch a bug from the surface of the water. Kahlan caught crickets, grasshoppers, and grubs and periodically tossed them in for the fish. Richard laughed when she talked to the fish, encouraging them to come up out of their dark holes for a tasty bug. Sometimes, a graceful gray heron would stand on its thin legs in the shallow marshes not far away and occasionally spear a fish or a frog with its daggerlike bill.

Kahlan could not recall, in the whole of her life, ever being in a place with such a vibrancy of life to it, surrounded by such majesty. Richard teased her, telling her she hadn't seen anything yet, making her curious and ever eager to get stronger so she could explore new sights. She felt like a little girl in a magical kingdom that was theirs and theirs alone. Having grown up a Confessor, Kahlan had never spent much time outdoors watching animals or water tumbling down over rocks or clouds or sunsets. She had seen a great many magnificent things, but they were in the context of travel, cities, buildings, and people. She had never lingered in one place in the countryside to really soak it all in.

Still, the thoughts in the back of her mind hounded her; she knew that she and Richard were needed elsewhere. They had responsibilities. Richard casually deflected the subject whenever she broached it; he had already explained his reasoning, and believed he was doing what was right.

They hadn't been visited by messengers for a very long time. That worry played on her mind, too, but Richard said that he couldn't allow himself to influence the army, so it was just as well that General Reibisch had stopped sending reports. Besides, he said, it only needlessly endangered the messengers who made the journey.

For the time being, Kahlan knew she needed to get better, and her isolated mountain life was making her stronger by the day, probably as nothing else could. Once they returned to the war—once she convinced him that they must return—this peaceful life would be but a cherished memory. She resolved to enjoy what she couldn't change, while it lasted.

Once when it had been raining for a few days and Kahlan was missing going out to the brook to watch the fish, Richard did the most unheard-of thing. He started bringing her fish in a jar. Live fish. Fish just for watching.

After he'd cleaned an empty lamp-oil jug and several widemouthed glass jars that had held preserves, herbs, and unguents for her injuries, along with other supplies he had purchased on their journey away from Anderith, he put some gravel in the bottom and filled them with water from the stream. He then caught some blacknose dace minnows and put them in the glass containers. They were yellowish olive on top speckled with black, with white bottoms, and a thick black line down each side. He even provided them with a bit of weed from the brook so they could have a place to hide and feel safe.

Kahlan was astonished when Richard brought home the first jar of live fish. She set the jars—eventually four jars and one jug in all—on the windowsill in the main room, beside several of Richard's smaller carvings. Richard, Kahlan, and Cara sat at the small wooden table when they ate and watched the marvel of fish living in a jar.

"Just don't name them," Richard said, "because eventually they're going to die."

What she had at first thought was an entirely daft idea became a center of fascination for her. Even Cara, who cited fish-in-a-jar as lunacy, took a liking to the little fish. It seemed that every day with Richard in the mountains held some new marvel to turn her mind away from her own pains and troubles.

After the fish became accustomed to people, they went about their little lives as if living in a jar were perfectly natural. From time to time, Richard would pour out part of their water, and add fresh water from the brook. Kahlan and Cara fed the little fish crumbs of bread or tiny scraps from dinner, along with small bugs. The fish ate eagerly, and spent most of their time pecking at the gravel on the bottom, or swimming about, looking out at the world. After a while, the fish learned when it was lunchtime. They would wiggle eagerly on the other side of the glass whenever anyone approached, like puppies happy to see their masters.

The main room had a small fireplace Richard had built with clay from stream banks he'd formed into bricks and dried in the sun, and then cooked in a fire. They had the table he'd made, and chairs constructed of branches intertwined and lashed together. He'd woven the chair bottoms and backs from leathery inner bark.

In the corner of the room was a wooden door over a deep root cellar. Against the back wall were simple shelves and a big cupboard full of supplies. They'd bought a lot of supplies along the way and carried them either in the carriage with Kahlan or strapped on the back and sides. For the last part of the journey Richard and Cara had lugged everything in, since the carriage couldn't make it over narrow mountain passes where there were no roads. Richard had blazed the trail in.

Cara had her own room opposite theirs. Once up and about, Kahlan was surprised to find that Cara had a collection of rocks. Cara bristled at the term "collection," and asserted that they were there as defensive weapons, should they be attacked and trapped in the house. Kahlan found the rocks—all different colors—suspiciously pretty. Cara insisted they were deadly.

While Kahlan had been bedridden, Richard had slept on a pallet in the main room, or sometimes outside under the stars. A number of times, at first, when she was in so much pain, Kahlan had awakened to see him sitting on the floor beside her bed, dozing as he leaned against the wall, always ready to jump up if she needed anything, or to offer her medicines and herb teas. He hadn't wanted to sleep in bed with her for fear of it hurting her. She almost would have been willing to endure it for the comfort of his presence beside her. Finally, though, after she was up and about, he was at last able to lie beside her. That first night with him in bed, she had held his big warm hand to her belly as she gazed at *Spirit* silhouetted in the moonlight, listening to the night calls of birds, bugs, and the songs of the wolves until her eyes closed and she drifted into a peaceful slumber.

It was on the next day that Richard first killed her.

They were at the stream, checking the fishing lines, when he cut two straight willow switches. He tossed one on the ground beside where she sat, and told her it was her sword.

He seemed in a playful mood, and told her to defend herself. Feeling playful herself, Kahlan took up the challenge by suddenly trying to stab him—just to put him in his place. He stabbed her first and declared her dead. She fought him again, more earnestly the second time, and he quickly dispatched her with a convincingly feigned beheading. By the third time she went after him, she was a little irked. She put all her effort into her assault, but he smoothly thwarted her attack and then pressed the tip of his willow-switch sword between her breasts. He announced her dead for a third time out of three.

Thereafter, it became a game Kahlan wanted to win. Richard never let her win, not even just to be nice when she was feeling low because of her slow progress at getting stronger. He repeatedly humbled her in front of Cara. Kahlan knew he was doing it to make her push herself to use her muscles, to forget her aches, to stretch and strengthen her body. Kahlan just wanted to win.

They each carried their willow-switch swords sheathed behind a belt, always at the ready. Every day, she would attack him, or he would attack her, and the fight was on. At first, she was no challenge to him, and he made it clear she was no challenge. That, of course, only made her determined to show him that she was no novice, that it was not so much a battle of strength, but of leverage, advantage, and swiftness. He encouraged her, but never gave her false praise. As the weeks passed, she slowly began making him work for his kills.

Kahlan had been taught to use a sword by her father, King Wyborn. At least, he had been king before Kahlan's mother took him for her mate. King was an insignificant title to a Confessor. King Wyborn of Galea had had two children with his queen and first wife, so Kahlan had both an older half sister and a half brother.

Kahlan wanted very much to make a good show of her training under her father. It was frustrating to know she was far better with a weapon than she was showing Richard. It wasn't so much that she didn't know what to do, but that she simply couldn't do it; her muscles were not yet strong enough, nor would they respond nearly quickly enough.

Something about it, though, was still unsettling: Richard fought in a way Kahlan had never encountered in her training, or in the real combat she had seen. She couldn't define or analyze the difference, but she could feel it, and she didn't know what to do to counter it.

In the beginning, Richard and Kahlan had most of their battles in the meadow outside their house, so that Kahlan wouldn't be as likely to trip over something, and if she did, not as likely to hit her head on anything granite. Cara was their ever-present audience. As time passed, the battles lasted longer, and grew more strenuous. They became furious and exhausting.

A couple of times Kahlan had been so upset by Richard's relentless attitude toward their sword fights that she didn't speak to him for hours afterward, lest she let slip words she didn't really mean and which she knew she would regret.

Richard would then sometimes tell her, "Save your anger for the enemy. Here it will do you no good; there, it can overcome fear. Use this time now to teach your sword what to do, so later it will do it without conscious thought."

Kahlan well knew that an enemy was never kind. If Richard gave in to kindness—awarded her false pride—it could only serve her ill. As aggravating as such lessons sometimes were, it was impossible to remain angry with Richard for very long, especially because she knew she was really only angry with herself.

Kahlan had been around weapons and men who used them all her life. A few of the better ones, in addition to her father, were on occasion her teachers. None of them had fought like Richard. Richard made fighting with a blade look like art. He gave beauty to the act of dealing death. There was something about it, though, tickling at her, something she knew she still wasn't grasping.

Richard had told her once, before she had been hurt, that he had come to believe that magic itself could be an art form. She had told him she thought that was crazy. Now, she didn't know. From the bits of the story she'd heard, she suspected that Richard had used magic in something of that way to defeat the chimes: he had created a solution where it had never before existed, or even been imagined.

One day, in one of their fierce sword fights, she had been positive she had him dead to rights and that she was delivering the stroke of victory. He effortlessly evaded what she had been sure was her killing strike and killed her instead. He made what had seemed impossible look natural.

It was in that instant that the whole concept came clear for her. She had been looking at it all wrong.

It wasn't that Richard could fight well with a sword, or that he could create beautiful statues with a knife and chisel, it was that Richard was one with the blade—the blade in any form: sword, knife, chisel, or willow switch. He was a master—not of sword fighting or carving as such, but, in the most fundamental way, of the blade itself.

Fighting was but one use of a blade. His balance for using his sword to destroy—magic always sought balance—was using a blade to carve things of beauty. She had been looking at the individual parts of what he did, trying to understand them separately; Richard saw only one unified whole.

Everything about him: the way he shot an arrow; the way he carved; the way he used a sword; even the way he walked with such fluid reasoned intent—they weren't separate things, separate abilities . . . they were all the same thing.

Richard paused. "What's the matter? Your face is turning white."

Kahlan stood with her willow sword lowered. "You're dancing with death. That's what you're doing with your sword."

Richard blinked at her as if she had just announced that rain was wet. "But, of course." Richard touched the amulet hanging at his chest. In the center, surrounded by a complex of gold and silver lines, was a teardrop-shaped ruby as big as her thumbnail. "I told you that a long time ago. Are you just now coming to believe me?"

She stood gaping. "Yes, I think I am."

Kahlan recalled all too clearly his chilling words to her when she had first seen the amulet around his neck, and she had asked him what it was:

"The ruby is meant to represent a drop of blood. It is the symbolic representation of the way of the primary edict.

"It means only one thing, and everything: cut. Once committed to fight, cut. Everything else is secondary. Cut. That is your duty, your purpose, your hunger. There is no rule more important, no commitment that overrides that one. Cut.

"The lines are a portrayal of the dance. Cut from the void, not from bewilderment. Cut the enemy as quickly and directly as possible. Cut with certainty. Cut decisively, resolutely. Cut into his strength. Flow through the gaps in his guard. Cut him. Cut him down utterly. Don't allow him a breath. Crush him. Cut him without mercy to the depths of his spirit.

"It is the balance to life: death. It is the dance with death.

"It is the law a war wizard lives by, or he dies."

The dance was art. It was no different, really, from carving. Art expressed through a blade. It was all one and the same to him. He saw no distinction, for within him, there was none.

They shared the meadow with a red fox who hunted it for rodents, mostly, but wasn't averse to chewing on whatever juicy bugs she could catch there. Their horses didn't mind the fox so much, but they didn't like the coyotes that sometimes visited. Kahlan rarely saw them, but she knew they were about when the horses snorted their displeasure. She often heard the coyotes barking at night, higher up in the surrounding slopes. They would let out long flat howls, followed by a series of yips. Some nights, the wolves sang, their long monotone howls, without the yapping of the coyotes, echoing through the mountains. Once Kahlan saw a black bear off in the trees, ambling along, giving them only a passing look, and once a bobcat passed near their house, sending the horses off in a panic. It took Richard the better part of a day to find the horses.

Chipmunks begged at their door, and regularly invited themselves into the house for a look around. Kahlan often caught herself talking to them and asking questions as if they could understand her every word. The way they paused and cocked their heads at her made her suspect they really could. In the early mornings, small herds of deer often visited the meadow, some leaving fresh, inverted heart-shaped tracks near the door as they passed. Lately, aggressive bucks in rut, bearing huge racks, had been showing up. One of the hides Kahlan wore was from a wolf injured by one of those bucks up in an oak grove not far away. Richard had spared the wounded animal a lingering, suffering death.

Beside the sword fights, they went on marches up into the mountains to help Kahlan strengthen her limbs. Those walks were taxing on her leg muscles, sometimes leaving her so sore she couldn't sleep. Richard would rub oil into her feet, calves, and thighs when they hurt too much for her to sleep. That usually worked, relaxing her and making her drowsy and able to fall asleep.

She distinctly remembered the rainy night after walking home in the wet and cold, when she lay on her back in bed, eyes shut, as Richard rubbed warm oil into her leg muscles. He whispered that her legs finally seemed to have gotten back all their tone and shape. Kahlan looked up and saw desire in his eyes. It was an almost forgotten thrill to know his hunger for her. She had been so startled that she felt tears trickle down her cheeks with the joy of suddenly feeling like a woman again—a desirable woman.

Richard raised her leg to his mouth and gently kissed her bare ankle. By the time his soft warm kisses reached her thighs, she was panting with suddenly and unexpectedly awakened desire. He laid open her nightshirt and rubbed the warm oil on her exposed belly. His big hands moved up her body to caress her breasts. He breathed through his mouth as he rolled her nipples until they were hard between his finger and thumb.

"Why, Lord Rahl," she said in a breathy whisper, "I do believe you are going to get carried away."

He paused, seeming to check himself and what he was doing, and then pulled back.

"I won't break, Richard," she said as she caught his hand and pulled it back. "I'm all right, now. I'd like it if you got carried away."

She clutched his hair in her fists as his kisses covered her breasts and then her shoulders and then worked up her neck. His panting warmed her ear. His exploring fingers made her frantic with need. His body against hers felt wildly erotic. She no longer felt weary. Finally, he tenderly kissed her lips. She let him know by the way she returned the kiss that he needn't be all that tender.

As the rain drummed on the roof, as lightning lit the lines and the clenched-fist strength of the statue in the window and thunder rumbled through the mountains, Kahlan, without fearing it, without worrying about it, without wondering if she would be able, held Richard tightly as they made quiet, gentle, fierce love. They had never needed each other as much as that night. All her fears and worries evaporated in the heat of overpowering need welling up through her. She wept with the strength of her pleasure and the release of her emotions.

When later Richard lay in her arms, she felt a tear roll off his face, and she asked him if something was wrong. He shook his head and said distantly that he had for so long feared losing her that sometimes he had believed he might go mad. It seemed as if he could finally allow himself release from his private terror. The pain Kahlan had first seen in his eyes when she couldn't remember his name was at last banished.

Their marches into the mountains ranged farther and farther. Sometimes they took packs and spent the night in the woods, often in a wayward pine, when they could find one. The rugged terrain offered a never-ending variety of vistas. In places, sheer rock cliffs towered over them. In other places, they stood at the brink of sheer drops and watched the sun turn the sky orange and purple as it went down while wispy clouds drifted through quiet green valleys below. They went to towering waterfalls with their own rainbows. There were clear, sunlit pools up in the mountains where they swam. They ate on rocks overlooking rugged sights no one but they ever saw. They followed animal trails through vast woods of gnarled trees, and others among the dark forest floor where grew trees with trunks like huge brown columns, so big twenty men couldn't have joined hands around them.

Richard had Kahlan practice with a bow to help strengthen her arms. They hunted small game for stews, or for roasting. Some they smoked and dried along with the fish they caught. Richard usually didn't eat meat, but occasionally he did. Not eating meat was part of the balance needed by his gift for when he was forced to kill. That need of balance was lessening because he wasn't killing. He was at peace. Perhaps the balance was now being served by his carving. As time passed, he was able to eat more meat. When they were out on journeys, they usually ate rice and beans along with bannock and any berries they collected along the way, in addition to game they caught.

Kahlan helped clean fish and salt them down and smoke yet others for their winter stores. It was a job that she had never before undertaken. They collected berries, nuts, and wild apples and put a lot of those away in the root cellar along with root crops he had purchased before coming up into the mountains. Richard dug up small apple trees, when he found any, and planted them in the meadow by the house so that, he said, someday they would have apples close at hand.

Kahlan wondered how long he intended to keep them away from where they were needed. The silent question always hung there, seen by all, but unspoken. Cara never asked him, but she sometimes made some small mention of it to Kahlan when they were alone. She was Lord Rahl's guard, and glad to be close at hand, so she generally offered no objection. He was, after all, Lord Rahl, and he was safe.

Kahlan had always felt the weight of their responsibilities. Like the towering mountains all around, looming over them, always shadowing them, that responsibility could never be completely forgotten. As much as she loved the house Richard had built on the edge of the meadow, and as much as she loved exploring the rugged, beautiful, imposing, and ever-changing mountains, with each passing day she more and more felt that weight and the anxious need to be back where they were needed most. She fretted at what could be going on that they weren't aware of. The Imperial Order was not going to stay put; an army that size liked to move. Soldiers, especially soldiers of that ilk, became restless in long encampments, and sooner or later started causing trouble. She worried about all the people who needed the reassurance of Richard's presence, his guidance—and hers. There were people who their whole lives had depended on the Mother Confessor always being there to stand up for them.

With winter coming on, Richard had made Kahlan a warm mantle, mostly out of wolf fur. The other two pelts were coyotes. Richard had found one of the coyotes with a broken leg, probably from a fall, and had put it out of its misery. The other had been a rogue chased off by the local pack. It had taken to raiding food from their little smokehouse. Richard had taken the sly looter with a single arrow.

They had collected most of the wolf pelts from injured or old animals. Richard, Kahlan, and Cara often tracked wolf packs as a way of helping to build Kahlan's strength. Kahlan came to recognize their tracks, and even learned to know at a glance, if the prints were in mud or soft dirt, their front paws from the rear. Richard showed her how the toes of the front spread out more, with a more well-defined heel pad than the rear paw. He had located several packs in the mountains, and the three of them often followed one group or family to see if they could do so without the wolves knowing. Richard said it was a kind of game guides used to play to keep in practice—to keep their senses sharp.

After Kahlan's mantle was completed, they had turned to collecting pelts for Cara's winter fur. Cara, who always wore the clothes of her profession, had liked the idea of Lord Rahl making something for her to wear—the same as he had made for Kahlan. While she had never said as much, Kahlan had always felt that Cara saw the mantle he was making for her as a mark of his feelings, his respect—proof that she was more than just his bodyguard.

This had been a journey to find pelts for Cara's mantle, and she had been eager. She had even cooked for them.

Now, coming down off the ridge where Kahlan had finally bested Richard in a sword fight, Kahlan was in a good mood. For the last two days they had been following the wolf pack up in the mountains to the west of their house. It was not simply a hunt, and not simply to get a pelt for Cara, but part of the never-ending pressure Richard put on Kahlan to keep up.

Almost every day for the last two months, Richard had her marching over the most difficult terrain, the kind of terrain that made her strain every muscle in her body. As Kahlan had gotten stronger, the marches had gotten longer. At first they were only across the house; now they were across mountains. On top of that, he frequently attacked her with his willow sword and poked fun at her if she didn't put in her absolute hardest fight.

In a way, finally beating Richard in one of their mock sword fights puzzled her. He might have been tired from carrying the heaviest pack and scouting some of the steeper trails by himself first and then coming back for them, but he hadn't slacked off, and she had still killed him. She couldn't help but be pleased with herself, even if she did question her victory. Out of the corner of her eye, she had caught him smiling as he looked at her. Kahlan knew Richard was proud of her for besting him. In a way, his losing was a victory for him.

Kahlan thought that she must be stronger, now, after all Richard had put her through, than at any time in her life. It had not been easy, but it had been worth at last feeling like the carving in the window of her bedroom.

Kahlan put a hand on Richard's shoulder as he followed Cara down broken granite blocks placed by chance like big, irregular steps. "Richard, how did I beat you?"

He saw in her eyes the seriousness of the question. "You killed me because I made a mistake."

"A mistake? You mean, perhaps you had gotten too confident? Perhaps you were just tired, or were thinking of something else."

"Doesn't really matter, does it? Whatever it was, it was a mistake that cost me my life in the game. In a real fight, I would have died. You've taught me a valuable lesson to redouble my resolve to always put in my absolute full effort. It just goes to remind me, though, that I could make a mistake at any time, and lose."

Kahlan couldn't help but to be struck by the obvious question: was he making a mistake in staying out of the effort to keep the Midlands free from the tyranny of the Imperial Order? She couldn't help feeling the pull to help her people, even though Richard still felt that if the people didn't want his leadership, his efforts could do no good. As Mother Confessor, Kahlan knew that while people didn't always understand that what a leader did was done in their best interest, that was no reason to abandon them.

With winter coming on, she hoped the Imperial Order would choose to stay put in Anderith. Kahlan needed to convince Richard to return to help the Midlands, but she was at a loss to know how. He was firm in his reasoning, and she could find no chink in the armor of his logic. Emotion did not sway him in this.

Cara led them down the craggy precipice, having to backtrack only twice. It was a difficult descent. Cara was pleased with herself, and that Richard had let her pick the route. It was her pelt they were going after, so he let her lead them across the tangle of undergrowth in the ravine at the bottom and then up the following lip of the notch where trees clung with roots like talons to the rocky rise.

The wind coming up the ravine had turned bitter. The clouds had thickened until they snuffed out the golden rays of sunlight. Their ascent took them up into a gloomy, dark wood of towering evergreens. Far over their heads, the treetops swayed in the wind, but down on the ground, it was still. Their footfalls were hushed by a thick spongy mat of brown needles.

The climb was steep, but not arduous. As they ascended, the big trees grew farther and farther apart. The boughs became scraggly, allowing more of the somber light to seep in. For the most part, the rocks higher up were bare of moss and leaves. In places they had to use handholds on the rock, or else roots, to help them climb. Kahlan pulled deep breaths of the cold air; it felt good to test her muscles.

They came out of the forest into the steel-gray light of late afternoon and the moaning voice of the wind. They were in the crooked wood.

The scree and rock were naked of the thick moss common lower down the mountain, but they bore yellow-green splotches of lichen outlined in black. Only a bit of scraggly brush clung to the low places here and there. But it was the trees that were the most odd, and gave the place at the top of the tree line its name. They were all stunted—few taller than Kahlan or Richard. Most of the branches grew to one side because of the prevailing winds, leaving the trees looking like grotesque, running skeletons frozen in torment.

Above the crooked wood, few things other than sedges and lichens grew. Above that, the snowcap held sway.

"Here it is," Cara said.

They found the wolf sprawled on the scree beside a low boulder with a dark stain of dried blood at the sharp edge. Up higher, the pack of gray wolves had been trying to take down a woodland caribou. The old bull had grazed the unlucky wolf with a kick. That in itself would likely not have been anything more than painful, but the wolf had slipped from the higher ledge and fallen to its death. Kahlan ran her fingers through the thick, yellow-gray coat tipped in black. It was in good condition, and would be a warm addition to Cara's winter mantle.

Richard and Cara started skinning the good-sized female animal as Kahlan went out to the edge of an overhang. She drew her own mantle up around her ears as she stood in the bitter wind surveying the approaching clouds. She was somewhat startled by what she saw.

"Richard, it's not drizzle coming our way," Kahlan said. "It's snow."

He looked up from his bloody work. "Do you see any wayward pines down in the valley?"

She squinted down to the valley floor spread out before her.

"Yes, I see a couple. The snow is still a ways off. If you're not long at that, we can probably make it down there and collect some wood before it gets wet."

"We're almost done," Cara said.

Richard stood to have a quick look for himself. With a bloody hand, he absently lifted his real sword a few inches and then let it drop back, a habit he had of checking to make sure the weapon was clear in its scabbard. It was an unsettling gesture. He had not drawn the weapon from its hilt since the day he had been forced to kill all those men who had attacked them back near Hartland.

"Is something wrong?"

"What?" Richard saw where her eyes were looking and glanced down at the sword on his hip. "Oh. No, nothing. Just habit, I guess."

Kahlan pointed. "There's a wayward pine, there. It's the closest, and good-sized, too."

Richard wiped the back of his wrist across his brow, swiping his hair away from his eyes. His fingers glistened with blood. "We'll be down there, sheltered by a wayward pine, sitting beside a cozy fire having tea before dark. I can stretch the hide on the branches inside and scrape it there. The snow will help insulate us inside the tree's boughs. We'll have a good rest before heading back in the morning. Down a little lower, it will only be rain."

Kahlan snuggled her cheek inside her wolf fur as a shiver tingled through her shoulders and up the back of her neck. Winter had snuck up on them.

When they arrived home two days later, the little fish in the jars were all dead.

They had used the same easier route over the pass that they had originally used to enter the valley when they had first come in with the horses, months before. Of course, Kahlan didn't recall that trip; she had been unconscious. It seemed a lifetime ago.

There was now a shorter trail to their home, one they had blazed down from the pass. They could have used that alternative route, but it was narrow and difficult and would have saved them only ten or fifteen minutes. They had been out for days, and as they had wearily stood in the windswept notch at the top of the pass looking down at their cozy home far below at the edge of the meadow, they had decided to take the easier passage, even though it took a little longer. It had been a relief to finally get inside the house, out of the wind, and drop all their gear.

As Richard brought in firewood and Cara fetched water, Kahlan pulled out a little square of cloth with some small bugs she'd caught earlier that day, intending to give her fish a treat, since they were sure to be hungry. She let out a little groan when she saw that they were dead.

"What's the matter?" Cara asked as she walked in lugging a full bucket. She came over to see the fish.

"Looks like they starved," Kahlan told her.

"Little fish like that don't often live long in a jar," Richard said as he knelt and started stacking birch logs atop kindling in the fireplace.

"But they did live a long time," Kahlan said, as if to prove him wrong and somehow talk him out of it.

"You didn't name them, did you? I told you not to name them because they would die after a time. I warned you not to let yourself get emotionally attached when it can only come to no good end."

"Cara named one."

"Did not," Cara protested. "I was just trying to show you which one I was talking about, that's all."

After the flames took from his flint, Richard looked up and smiled. "Well, I'll get you some more."

Kahlan yawned. "But these were the best ones. They needed me."

Richard snorted a laugh. "You've got quite the imagination. They only depended on us because we artificially altered their lives. Just like the chipmunks would stop hunting seeds for their winter stores if we gave them handouts all the time. Of course, the fish had no choice, because we kept them in jars. Left to their own initiative, the fish wouldn't need any help from us. After all, it took a net to catch them. I'll catch you some more, and they'll come to need you just as much."

Two days later, on a thinly overcast day, after they'd had a big lunch of thick rabbit stew with turnips and onions along with bread Cara had made, Richard went off to check the fishing lines and to catch some more of the blacknose dace minnows.

After he'd left, Cara picked up their spoons and put them in the bucket of wash water on the counter.

"You know," she said, looking back over her shoulder, "I like it here, I really do, but it's starting to make me jumpy."

Kahlan scraped the plates off into a wooden bowl with the cooking leavings for the midden heap. "Jumpy?" She brought the plates to the counter. "What do you mean?"

"Mother Confessor, this place is nice enough, but it's starting to make me go daft. I am Mord-Sith. Dear spirits, I'm starting to name fish in jars!" Cara turned back to the bucket and bent to cleaning the spoons with a washcloth. "Don't you think it's about time we convinced Lord Rahl that we need to get back?"

Kahlan sighed. She loved their home in the mountains, and she loved the quiet and solitude. Most of all, she treasured the time she and Richard were able to spend together without other people making demands of them. But she also missed the activity of Aydindril, the company of people, and the sights of cities and crowds. There was a lot not to like about being in places like that, but there was an excitement about it, too.

She'd had a lifetime to become used to the way people didn't always want or understand her help, and forging ahead anyway because she knew it was in their best interest. Richard never had to learn to face that cold indifference and go about his duty despite it.

"Of course I do, Cara." Kahlan placed the bowl of scraps on a shelf, reminding herself to empty it later. She wondered if she was to be a Mother Confessor who forever lived in the woods, away from her people, a people struggling for their liberty. "But you know how Richard feels. He thinks it would be wrong—more than that, he thinks it would be irresponsible to give in to such a wish when reason tells him he must not."

Cara's blue eyes flashed with determination. "You are the Mother Confessor. Break the spell of this place. Tell him that you are needed back there, and that you are going to return. What's he going to do? Tie you to a tree? If you leave, he will follow. He will have to return, then."

Kahlan shook her head emphatically. "No, I can't do that. Not after what he's told us. That's not the kind of thing you do to a person you respect. I may not exactly agree with him, but I understand his reasons and know him well enough to dread that he's right."

"But going back doesn't mean he would have to lead our side. You would only be making him follow you back, not making him return to leadership." Cara smirked. "But maybe when he sees how much he is needed, he will come to his senses."

"That's part of the reason he's brought us so far out in the mountains: he fears that if he's near the struggle, or if he goes back, he will see all that's happening and be drawn in. I can't use his feelings for me to force him into such a corner. Even if we did go back and he resisted the temptation to help people fighting for their lives and wasn't drawn into the struggle against the brutality of the Imperial Order, such an overt act of coercion on my part would create an enduring rift between us."

163

Kahlan shook her head again. "This is something he believes too strongly. I won't force him into returning."

Cara gestured with the dripping washcloth. "Maybe he doesn't really believe it, not really, not deep down inside. Maybe he doesn't want to go back because he doubts himself—over the Anderith thing—and so he thinks it's just easier for him to stay away."

"I don't believe Richard doubts himself in this. Not in this. Not for a second. Not one tiny little bit. I think that if he had any doubt whatsoever, he would return, because that is really the easier path. Staying away is harder—as you and I can attest.

"But you can leave at any time, Cara, if you feel so strongly about going back. He has no claim on your life. You don't have to stay here if you don't wish to."

"I am sworn to follow him no matter what foolish thing he does."

"Foolish? You follow him because you believe in him. So do I. That's why I could never walk away, forcing him to follow."

Cara pressed her lips tight. Her blue eyes lost their fire as she turned away and flopped the cloth back into the bucket of water. "Then we will be stuck here, condemned to live out our lives in paradise."

Kahlan smiled in understanding of Cara's frustration. While she wouldn't try to force Richard into something he was dead set against, that didn't preclude her from trying to change his mind. She drained her teacup and plunked it down on the counter. That would be different.

"Maybe not. You know, I've been thinking the same thing—that we need to go back, I mean."

Cara peered over with a suspicious sidelong glance. "So, what do you think we can do to convince him?"

"Richard is going to be gone for a while. Without him here to bother us, how about we have a bath?"

"A bath?"

"Yes, a bath. I've been thinking about how much I'd like to get cleaned up. I'm tired of looking like a backcountry traveler. I'd like to wash my hair and put on my white Mother Confessor's dress."

"Your white Mother Confessor's dress . . ." Cara smiled conspiratorially. "Ah. Now that will be the kind of battle a woman is better equipped to fight."

Out of the corner of her eye, Kahlan could see *Spirit* standing in the bedroom window, looking out at the world, her robes flowing in the wind, her head thrown back, her back arched, her fists at her sides in defiance of anything that would think to bridle her.

"Well, not exactly a battle the way you're thinking, but I believe I can state the case better if I'm dressed properly. That wouldn't be unfair. I will be putting the issue to him as the Mother Confessor. I believe that in some ways his judgment has been clouded; it's hard to think about anything else when you're worried sick about someone you love."

Kahlan's fists tightened at her sides as she thought about the danger hanging over the Midlands. "He's got to see that all of that is in the past, that I'm healthy, now, and that the time has come to return to our duties to our people."

Smirking, Cara swiped back a wisp of her blond hair. "He will see that, and more, if you were in that dress of yours, that's for sure."

"I want him to see the woman who was strong enough to win against him with a sword. I want him to see that Mother Confessor in the dress, too."

From the corner of her mouth, Cara puffed another strand of hair off her face. "To tell you the truth, I wouldn't mind a bath myself. You know, I think that if I stand beside you in a proper Mord-Sith outfit and my hair is washed and my braid is done up fresh and I'm looking properly Mord-Sith-like and I speak my agreement with what you say, Lord Rahl will be all the more convinced that we're right and inclined to see that the time has come for us to return."

Kahlan set the plates into the bucket of water. "It's settled, then. We've enough time before he comes back."

Richard had made them a small wooden tub, big enough to sit in and have a nice bath. It wasn't big enough to lie back and luxuriate in, but it was still quite the luxury for their mountain home.

Cara towed the tub from the corner, leaving drag marks across the dirt floor. "I'll put it in my room. You go first. That way, if he comes back sooner rather than later, you can keep your nosy husband busy and out of my hair while I wash it."

Together, Kahlan and Cara hauled in buckets of water from the nearby spring, heating some in a kettle over a roaring fire. When Kahlan finally sank into the steaming water, she let out a long sigh. The air was chilly, and the hot bath felt all the better for it. She would have liked to linger, but decided not to.

She smiled at recalling all the trouble Richard had had with women in bathwater. It was a good thing he wasn't there. Later, after they had their talk, she thought she would ask him to take a bath before bed. She liked the aroma of his sweat when it was clean sweat.

With the knowledge that she would face Richard with her hair washed and sparkling, and in her white dress, Kahlan felt more confident about the real possibility of their return than she had in a long time. She dried and brushed her hair by the heat of the fire as Cara boiled some more water. While Cara went in to take her bath, Kahlan went to her room to slip into her dress. Most people feared the dress because they feared the woman who wore it; Richard had always liked her in the dress.

As she tossed the towel on the bed, her eye was caught by the statue in the window. Kahlan fisted her hands at her sides and, standing naked, arched her back and threw her head back, mimicking *Spirit*, letting the feeling of it overcome her, letting herself be that strong spirit, letting it flow through her.

For that moment, she was the spirit of the statue.

This was a day of change. She could feel it.

It seemed a little odd, after being a woods woman for so long, to be back in her Mother Confessor's dress, to feel the satiny smooth material against her skin. Mostly, though, the feeling was the comfort of the familiar.

As Mother Confessor, Kahlan felt sure of herself. On a fundamental level, the dress was a form of battle armor. Wearing the dress, Kahlan also felt a sense of importance, in that she carried the weight of history, of exceptional women who had gone before her. The Mother Confessor bore a terrible responsibility, but also had the satisfaction of being able to make a real difference for the better in people's lives.

Those people depended on her. Kahlan had a job to do, and she had to convince Richard that she needed to do it. They needed him, too, but even if he would not issue orders, he needed to at least willingly return with her. Those fighting for their cause deserved to know the Mother Confessor was with them, and that she had not lost faith in them or their cause. She had to make Richard see that much of it.

Once she was back out in the main room, Kahlan could hear Cara splashing in the tub. "Need anything, Cara?" she called out.

"No, I'm fine," Cara called from her room. "This feels so good! I think there's enough dirt in this water to plant potatoes."

Kahlan laughed knowingly. She saw a chipmunk casting about outside the house. "I'm going to go feed Chippy some apple cores. If you need anything, call out."

Their universal name for all the chipmunks was "Chippy." They all answered to it; they knew the name augured well for a handout.

"All right," Cara said from her tub. "If Lord Rahl gets back, though, just kiss him or something to keep him busy but wait until I'm done before you talk to him. I want to be with you to help you convince him. I want to be sure we make him see the light."

Kahlan smiled. "I promise."

She plucked an apple core from the wooden bucket of little animal snacks they kept hanging on a piece of twine where the chipmunks couldn't get to them on their own. The squirrels loved apple cores, too. The horses preferred their apples whole.

"Here, Chippy," Kahlan called out through the door in the voice she always used with them. She raised the bucket back toward the ceiling and hooked the line to the peg on the wall. "Chip, Chip, you want an apple?"

Outside, Kahlan saw the chipmunk off to the side, foraging through the grass. The chill breeze caressed the long folds of her dress to her legs as she walked. It was almost cold enough to need the fur mantle. The bare branches of the oaks behind the house creaked and groaned as they rubbed together. The pines, reaching toward the sky where the wind was stronger, bowed deeply with some of the gusts. The sun had taken refuge behind a steel-gray overcast that made her white dress all the more striking in the gloom.

Near the window where *Spirit* stood watching out, Kahlan called the chipmunk again. The chipmunks were held spellbound by the soft voice Kahlan used when she talked to them. When he heard her, the furry little striped creature stood on his hind legs for a moment, stiff and still, checking that all was clear, and when he was sure it was safe, scurried to her. Kahlan squatted and rolled the apple core out of her hand onto the ground.

"Here you go, sweetheart," she cooed. "A nice apple for you."

Chippy wasted no time starting in on his treat. Kahlan's cheeks hurt from smiling at the way the chipmunk nibbled his way around the apple core as it rolled along the ground. She rose to her feet, brushing her hands clean as she watched, captivated by the little creature at his feverish work.

He suddenly flinched with a squeak and froze.

Kahlan looked up. She was staring right into a woman's blue eyes.

The woman stood not ten feet away in a pose of cool scrutiny. Kahlan's throat locked the gasp in her lungs. The woman had seemed to appear in the middle of nowhere, out of nowhere. Icy gooseflesh prickled up the backs of Kahlan's arms.

The woman's long blond hair cascaded over the shoulders of an exquisite black dress. She was of such shapely beauty, her face of such pure perfection, but especially her eyes were of such intelligent lucid witnesses to all around her, that she could only be a creature of profound integrity . . . or unspeakable evil.

166

Kahlan knew without doubt which it was.

This woman made Kahlan feel as ugly as a clod of dirt, and instinctively as helpless as a child. She wanted nothing so much as to shrink away. Instead, she stared into the woman's blue eyes for what couldn't have been more than a second or two, but in that span of time an eternity seemed to pass. In those knowing blue eyes flowed some formidable, frightful current of contemplation.

Kahlan remembered Captain Meiffert's description of this woman. For the life of her, though, Kahlan couldn't just then recall her name. It seemed trivial. What mattered was that this woman was a Sister of the Dark.

Without speaking a word, the woman lifted her hands out a little and turned her palms up, as if humbly offering something. Her hands were empty.

Kahlan committed to the vault through space necessary to close the distance. She committed to unleashing her power. With her resolution, the act had in a way already commenced. But she desperately needed to get closer if it was to be meaningful, or effective.

As she began to move, to make that reckless leap, the world went white in a bloom of pain.

Richard heard an odd sound that stopped him in his tracks. He felt a thump through the ground and deep in his chest. He thought he'd seen a flash in the treetops, but it had been so quick he wasn't sure.

It was the sound, though, as if some great hammer had struck off the top of a mountain, that made his blood go cold.

The house wasn't far off through the trees. He dropped the string of trout and the jar of minnows, and ran.

At the edge of the woods where it opened into the meadow, he skidded to a halt. His pounding heart felt as if it had risen up into his throat.

Richard saw the two women not far away, in front of the house, one dressed in white, and one in black. They were connected by a snaking, undulating, crackling line of milky white light. Nicci's arms were lifted slightly with her hands turned palms up and a little farther apart than the width of her hips.

The milky light went from Nicci's chest, across the space between the two women, and pierced Kahlan through the heart. The wavering aurora between the two turned blindingly bright, as if twisting in an agony it was unable to escape.

Seeing Kahlan trembling with the fury of that lance of light pinning her to the wall, Richard was paralyzed by fear for her, fear he knew all too well, from when she had been on the cusp of death. That bolt pierced Nicci's heart, too, connecting the two women. Richard didn't understand the magic Nicci was using, but he instinctively recognized it as profoundly dangerous, not only to Kahlan, but to Nicci as well, for she, too, was in pain. That Nicci would put herself at such risk gripped him with dread.

Richard knew he had to remain calm and keep his wits about himself if Kahlan was to have a chance. He viscerally wanted to do something to strike Nicci down, but he was certain that it wouldn't be as simple as that. Zedd's oft-repeated expression—nothing is ever easy—flashed into Richard's mind with sudden and tangible meaning.

In a desperate search for answers, everything Richard knew about magic cascaded in a torrent through his mind. None of it told him what to do, but it did tell him what he must not do. Kahlan's life hung in the balance.

Just then, Cara came flying out of the house. She was stark naked. It somehow didn't look all that odd. Richard was accustomed to the shape of her body in her skintight leather outfits. Other than the color, this didn't look all that different. She was dripping wet. Her hair was undone, which seemed more outlandishly indecent to him than her naked body. He was used to seeing her with a braid all the time.

Cara's fist clutched the red leather rod—her Agiel—as she crouched. The muscles of her legs, arms, and shoulders strained with tension demanding release.

"Cara! No!" Richard cried out.

He was already tearing across the meadow as Cara sprang and slammed her Agiel against the side of Nicci's neck.

Nicci shrieked in pain that dropped her to her knees. Kahlan cried out in equal pain and crumpled to her knees as well, her movement a close match to Nicci's.

Cara seized Nicci's hair in a fist and yanked her head back. "Time to die, witch!" Nicci was doing nothing to stop Cara as the Agiel hung only inches from her throat.

Richard dove toward the Mord-Sith, desperately hoping he wouldn't be too late. Cara's Agiel just grazed Nicci's throat as Richard tackled her around the middle, ramming her backward. The feel of her was briefly surprising—silky soft flesh over iron-hard muscle. The impact drove the wind from her when they hit the ground.

Cara was so enraged and in such a combative state that she lashed out with her Agiel at Richard, not really realizing it was him, knowing only that she was being prevented from protecting Kahlan.

The violent impact of the weapon to the side of Richard's face felt like a blow by an iron bar followed immediately by a lightning strike. The crack of pain through his skull was momentarily blinding. His ears rang. The jolt took his breath, staggering him, and brought back in a single instant an avalanche of macabre memories.

Cara was riveted on the kill and furious at any interference. Richard regained his senses just in time to seize her wrists and pin her to the ground before she could pounce on Nicci. A Mord-Sith was formidable, to be sure, but such a woman was instilled with the ability to counter magic, not muscle. That was why she had been trying to goad Nicci into using her power; only in that way could she capture the enemy's magic and so overpower her.

Cara's writhing naked body under him hardly registered in Richard's mind. He tasted blood in his mouth. His attention was focused on her Agiel and making sure she couldn't use it on him. His head throbbed with a painful ringing, and he had to fight not only Cara, but encroaching unconsciousness. It was all he could do to hold Cara down.

At that moment, the Mord-Sith was more of a threat to Kahlan's life than Nicci was. If Nicci intended to kill Kahlan, he was sure she could have already done so. Richard might not have understood specifically what Nicci was doing, but by what he had already seen, he grasped the general nature of it.

Blood dripped down onto Cara's bare chest, vivid red against the expanse of her white skin.

"Cara, stop!" His jaw worked, if painfully, so he reasoned it wasn't broken. "It's me. Stop. You'll kill Kahlan." Cara stilled under him, staring up in angry confusion. "What you do to Nicci happens to Kahlan, too."

"You had better listen to him," Nicci said from behind him in that velvety voice of hers.

Cara reached up when Richard released her wrists and touched the side of his mouth. "I'm sorry," she whispered, realizing what she had done. Her tone told him she meant it. Richard nodded and then stood, pulling her up by her hand before rounding on Nicci.

Nicci stood tall, in that proud and proper posture she had. Her attention and her magic was focused on Kahlan. The calm but violent power from within him had awakened, waiting to be commanded. Richard didn't know how to use it to stop Nicci. He held back, fearing that anything he did would only make Kahlan's peril worse.

Kahlan was on her feet, too, but once again pinned to the wall of the house by the milky rope of light. Her green eyes were wide with the trembling torment of whatever it was Nicci was doing.

Nicci's hands lifted. She laid her palms to her heart, over the light. Her back was to Richard, but he could see the light through her, like fire eating through the center of a piece of paper, the incandescent hole expanding outward, appearing to consume her. The twisting flare of light was doing the same thing to Kahlan, seeming to burn through her, yet Richard could see that she was not being killed by it. She was still breathing, still moving, still alive—not reacting at all the way a person would if they were really having holes burned through them. With magic, he knew better than to believe his eyes.

At the center of Nicci's chest, under her hands, she began to become solid again, re-forming where the light had spent itself in glowing rays working out toward the edges of her.

The light cut off. Kahlan, her own hands pressed to the wall behind her, sagged in relief as it extinguished, her eyes closing as if it was too much to endure looking at the woman standing before her.

Richard was restrained fury. His muscles screamed to be released. The magic within was a coiled viper waiting to strike. He wanted almost more than anything to cut down this woman. The only thing he wanted more was for Kahlan to be safe.

Nicci smiled pleasantly at Kahlan before turning to Richard. Her calm blue eyes momentarily took in his white-knuckled fist on the hilt of his sword.

"Richard. It's been a long time. You look well."

"What have you done?" He growled through gritted teeth.

She smiled. It was a smile a mother gave a child—a smile of indulgence. She took a breath, as if recovering from a difficult bit of labor, and lifted a hand to indicate Kahlan.

"I have spelled your wife, Richard."

Richard could hear Cara's breath close behind his left shoulder. She was staying out of the way of his sword arm.

"To what end?" he asked.

"Why, to capture you, of course."

"What's going to happen to her? What harm have you done?"

"Harm? Why, none. Any harm that comes to her will only be by your hand."

Richard frowned, understanding her, but wishing he were wrong. "You mean, if I hurt you, Kahlan will suffer it, too?"

Nicci smiled with the same discerning, disarming smile she used to have when she came to give him lessons. He could hardly believe that he used to imagine that she must look like nothing so much as a good spirit in the flesh.

Richard could sense the magic crackling around this woman. He had come to know in most cases, through his own gift, when a person had the gift. What others couldn't see, he saw. He could see it in their eyes, and sometimes sense the aura of it around them. He had rarely met gifted women who made the very air about them sizzle with their power. Worse, though, Nicci was a Sister of the Dark.

"Yes, and more. Much more. You see, we are now linked by a maternity spell. Odd name for a spell, yes? The name, in part, is derived from the spell's nurturing aspects. As in lifegiver—the way a mother nurtures her child and keeps it alive.

"That light you saw was an umbilical cord of sorts: an umbilical cord of magic. By bending the nature of this world, it links our lives, no matter the distance between us. Just as I am the daughter of my mother and nothing could ever change that, so neither can this magic be altered by anyone else."

She spoke as an instructor, as she had once spoken to him at the Palace of the Prophets when she had been one of his teachers. She always spoke with a quiet economy of words that he had once thought added an air of nobility to her bearing. Back then, Richard couldn't have imagined coarse words coming from Nicci's mouth, but the words she spoke now were vile.

She still moved with an unmatched, slow elegance. He had always thought her movements seductive. He now saw them as the sinuous movements of a snake.

The magic of his sword thundered through him, screaming to be loosed. The sword's magic had been created specifically to combat what the sword's wielder considered evil. At that moment, Nicci fit the requirement to such an extent that the magic of the sword was close to overpowering him, near to taking command in order to destroy this threat. With the pain from the Agiel still throbbing in his head, it was a struggle to maintain his control over the power of the sword. Richard could feel the raised gold letters of the word TRUTH on the hilt pressing into his palm.

This was a time, perhaps more than any other, that he knew had to be faced with truth, and not his raw wishes. Life and death hung in the balance.

"Richard," Kahlan said in a level voice. She waited until his eyes met hers. "Kill her." She spoke with a quiet authority that demanded obedience. In her white Mother Confessor's dress, her words carried the unequivocal weight of command. "Do it. Don't wait another moment. Kill her. Don't think about it, do it."

Nicci calmly watched to see what he might do. What he would finally decide seemed no more than a matter of curiosity to her. Richard had no need to think or to decide.

"I can't," he said to Kahlan. "That would kill you, too."

Nicci lifted one eyebrow. "Very good, Richard. Very good."

"Do it!" Kahlan shrieked. "Do it now, while you still have the chance!"

"Keep still," he said in a calm voice. He looked back at Nicci. "Let's hear it."

She clasped her hands in the way the Sisters of the Light were wont to do. Only she was not a Sister of the Light. There looked to be something deeply felt behind that blue-eyed gaze, but what those feelings could be, he didn't know and feared to imagine. It was one of those intense gazes that held a world of emotion, everything from longing to hatred. One thing he was sure he saw was a dead serious determination that was more important to her than life itself.

"It's like this, Richard. You are to come with me. As long as I live, Kahlan will live. If I die, she dies. It's as simple as that."

"What else?" he demanded.

"What else?" Nicci blinked. "Nothing else."

"What if I decide to kill you?"

"Then I will die. But Kahlan will die with me—our lives are now linked."

"That's not what I mean. I mean, you must have some purpose. What else will it mean if I decide to kill you."

Nicci shrugged. "Nothing. It's up to you to decide. Our lives are in your hands. Should you choose to preserve her life, you will have to come with me."

"And what do you intend to do with him?" Kahlan asked as she edged her way over to Richard's side. "Torture a sham confession out of him, so that Jagang can put him on some kind of show trial followed by a very public execution?"

If anything, Nicci looked surprised, as if such a thought had never occurred to

171

her, and she found it abhorrent. "No, none of that. I intend him no harm. For now, anyway. Eventually, of course, I will most likely have to kill him."

Richard glared. "Of course."

When Kahlan made a move forward, he caught her arm and restrained her. He knew what she intended. He didn't know exactly what would happen if Kahlan unleased her Confessor's power on Nicci while they were both linked by the spell, but he had no intention of finding out, since he was sure it could come to no good end. Kahlan was far too ready, as far as he was concerned, to forfeit her life to save his.

"Just hold on for now," he whispered to her.

Kahlan threw her arm out, pointing. "She just admitted she intends to kill you!"

Nicci smiled reassuringly. "Don't worry about that for now. If it comes to that, it will not likely be for a long time. Perhaps even a lifetime."

"And in the meantime?" Kahlan asked. "What plans do you have for him before you discard his life as if it were insignificant?"

"Insignificant . . . ?" Nicci opened her hands in an innocent gesture. "I have no plans. I expect only to take him away."

Richard had thought he understood what was going on, but he was less and less sure with everything Nicci said. "You mean, you want to take me away so that I can't fight against the Imperial Order?"

Her brow twitched. "If you wish to think of it in those terms, I admit it is true that your time as the leader of the D'Haran Empire is over. But that is not the point. The point is that everything about your life up until now"—Nicci glanced pointedly at Kahlan—"is over."

Her words seemed to chill the air. They surely chilled Richard.

"What's the rest of it?" He knew there had to be more, something that would make sense of it all. "What other terms are there if I want to keep Kahlan alive?"

"Well, no one is to follow us, of course."

"And if we do?" Kahlan snapped. "I might follow you and kill you myself, even if it means the end of my own life." Kahlan's green eyes shone with icy resolve as she cast a threatening glare on the woman.

Nicci lifted her brows deliberately as she leaned ever so slightly toward Kahlan, the way a mother would in cautioning a child. "Then that will be the end of it— unless Richard stops you from doing such a thing. That is all part of what he must decide to do. But you make a miscalculation if you think I care one way or the other. I don't, you see. Not at all."

"What is it you intend me to do?" Richard said, pulling Nicci's unsettlingly calm gaze from Kahlan. "What if I get where you're taking me, and I don't do as you wish?"

"You misunderstand, Richard, if you believe that I have some preconceived notion of what it is I wish you to do. I don't. You will do as you wish, I imagine."

"As I wish?"

"Well, naturally you won't be allowed to return to your people." She tossed her head, flicking back strands of her long blond hair that the wind had pulled across in front of her blue eyes. Her gaze never left his. "And I suppose if you were to be in some way impossibly and defiantly contrary, then in that case, such would obviously be an answer in and of itself. It would be a shame, of course, but I would then have no use for you. I would kill you."

"You would have no further use? You mean Jagang would have no further use."

172

"No." Once again, Nicci looked surprised. "I do not act on behalf of His Excellency." She tapped her lower lip. "You see? I removed the ring he put through my lip marking me as his slave. I do this on behalf of myself."

A yet more disturbing thought surfaced. "How is it that he can't enter your mind? That he can't control you?"

"You don't need me to answer that question, Richard Rahl."

It made no sense to him; the bond to the Lord Rahl worked for those loyal to him. He could see no way that this could be construed as an act of loyalty. This was unequivocally an act of aggression and against his will; the bond shouldn't work for her. He reasoned that perhaps Jagang was in her mind and she unaware of it. The thought occurred to him that maybe Jagang was in her mind, and it had driven her insane.

"Look," Richard said, feeling like they weren't even speaking the same language, "I don't know what you think—"

"Enough talk. We are leaving."

Her blue eyes watched him without anger. It almost seemed to Richard that for Nicci, Kahlan and Cara were not there.

"This doesn't make any sense. You want me to go with you, but you aren't acting on behalf of Jagang. If that's true, then—"

"I believe I've made it as clear as possible and quite simple, besides. If you wish to be free, you may kill me at any opportunity. If you do, Kahlan will also die. Those are your only two choices. Although I believe I know what you will do, I am in no way certain. Two paths now lie before you. You must take one."

Richard could hear Cara's angry breath behind him. She was a coiled spring ready to strike. Fearing she might do something of irredeemable harm, he lifted his hand just to be sure she knew he meant for her to stay behind him.

"Oh, and one additional matter, should you think to resort to some plot or treachery, or, for that matter, refuse to do the simple things I ask of you: through the spell that joins us, I can at any time end Kahlan's life. I have but to will it. It is not necessary for me to die. She lives every day from now on only by my grace, and thus yours.

"I wish her no harm, and have no feelings one way or the other about her life. In fact, if anything, I wish it to be long. She has brought you a measure of happiness, and in return for that, I hope she will not have to forfeit her life. But then, you have some influence over that by your behavior."

Nicci cast a deliberate glare over Richard's shoulder, to Cara. She then reached out and with her fingers gently wiped blood from his mouth. She finished cleaning his chin with her thumb. "Your Mord-Sith has hurt you. I can help you if you wish."

"No."

"Very well." She wiped her bloody fingers clean on the skirt of her black dress. "Unless you want to risk other people causing Kahlan's death without your intending it, I suggest you insure that others don't act without your consent. Mord-Sith are resourceful and determined women. I respect their devotion to duty. However, if your Mord-Sith follows us—and my magic will tell me if she does—Kahlan will die."

"And just how will I know Kahlan is all right? We could get a mile away from here, and you could use that magic link to kill her. I would never know."

Nicci's brow creased together. She looked genuinely puzzled.

"Why would I do that?"

A storm of rage and panic pushed his emotions first one way, and then the other. "Why are you doing any of this!"

She regarded him in silent curiosity for a moment. "I have my reasons. I'm sorry, Richard, that you must suffer in this. Making you suffer is not my purpose. I give you my word that I will not harm Kahlan without informing you."

"You expect me to believe your word?"

"I've told you the truth. I have no reason to lie to you. In time, you will come to understand everything better. Kahlan will come to no harm from me as long as I am safe, and you come with me."

For reasons he couldn't fathom, Richard found himself believing her. She seemed dead honest and completely sure of herself, as if she had reasoned it all out a thousand times.

He didn't believe that Nicci was telling him everything. She was making it simple so that he could grasp the important elements and have an easier time deciding what to do. Whatever the rest of it was, it couldn't be as devastating as this much of it. The thought of being taken from Kahlan was agony, but he would do almost anything to save her life. Nicci knew that.

The enigma resurfaced. It was somehow linked to this.

"The spell that protects a person's mind from the dream walker works only for those loyal to me. You can't expect to be safe from Jagang if you do this. It's an act of treachery."

"Jagang does not frighten me. Don't fear for my mind, Richard. I'm quite safe from His Excellency. In time, perhaps you will come to see how wrong you have been in so many things."

"You're deceiving yourself, Nicci."

"You only see part of it, Richard." She lifted an eyebrow in a cryptic manner. "At heart, your cause is the cause of the Order. You are too noble a person for it to be otherwise."

"I may die at your hands, but I will die hating everything you and the Order stand for." Richard's fists tightened. "You'll not get what you want, Nicci. Whatever it is, you'll not get it."

She regarded him with great compassion. "This is all for the best, Richard."

Nothing he said seemed to hold any sway with her, and he could make no sense of the things she said. The fury inside boiled up. The magic of the sword fought him for control. He could barely contain it. "Do you really expect me to ever come to believe that?"

Nicci's blue eyes seemed to be focused somewhere beyond him.

"Possibly not."

Her gaze fixed on him once more. She put two fingers between her lips as she turned and whistled. In the distance, a horse whinnied and trotted out of the woods.

"I have another horse for you, waiting up on the other side of the pass."

Terror clawed at his bones. Kahlan's fingers tightened on his arm. Cara's hand touched his back. Memories of being captured before and all it meant, all the things he had endured, made his pulse race and his breath come in rapid pulls. He felt trapped. Everything was slipping through his fingers and there didn't seem to be anything he could do about it.

He wanted more than anything to fight, but he couldn't figure how. He wished it were as simple as striking down his adversary. He reminded himself that reason, not wishing, was his only chance. He seized the calm center within, and used it to quell the rising storm of panic.

Nicci stood tall, her shoulders square, her chin up. She looked like someone facing an execution with courage. He realized then that she truly was prepared for whichever way it was to go.

"I have given you your choice, Richard. You have no other options. Choose."

"There is no choice to make. I'll not allow Kahlan to die."

"Of course not." Nicci's posture eased almost imperceptibly. A small smile of reassurance warmed her eyes. "She will be fine."

The horse slowed from its trot as it approached. When the handsome dappled mare halted beside her, Nicci took ahold of the reins near the bit. Its gray mane ruffled in the cold breeze. The mare snorted and tossed her head, uneasy before strangers, and eager to be away.

"But . . . but," Richard stammered as Nicci stepped up into the stirrup. "But, what am I allowed to take?"

Nicci swung her leg over the horse's rump and settled into the saddle. She squirmed herself into position and adjusted her shoulders, setting them back. Her black dress and blond hair stood out in stark relief against the iron sky.

"You may bring anything you like, as long as it isn't a person." She clicked her tongue, urging her horse around to face him. "I suggest you take clothes and such. Whatever you wish to have with you. Take all you can carry, if you want."

Her voice took on an edge. "Leave that sword of yours, though. You won't be needing it." She leaned down, her expression for the first time turning cold and threatening. "You are no longer the Seeker, or Lord Rahl, leader of the D'Haran empire, or for that matter, you are no longer the husband of the Mother Confessor. From now on, you are nobody but Richard."

Cara stepped out beside him, a thunderhead of dark fury. "I am Mord-Sith. If you think I'm going to allow you to take Lord Rahl, you're crazy. The Mother Confessor has already stated her wishes. My duty, above all else, is to kill you."

Nicci curled three fingers around the reins, her thumbs holding them tight. "Do as you must. You know the consequences."

Richard held out a restraining arm to prevent Cara from going up after Nicci and dragging her off the horse. "Take it easy," he whispered. "Time is on our side. As long as we're all still alive, we have the chance to think of something."

The strain of Cara's weight against his arm eased. She reluctantly backed a step.

"I have to get some things," Richard said to Nicci, trying to buy that time. "Wait, at least, until I can get my pack together."

Nicci laid the reins over and stepped her horse back toward him. She rested her left wrist across the saddle's pommel.

"I'm leaving." With a long graceful finger of her other hand, she pointed. "You see that pass up there? You be with me by the time I'm at the top, and Kahlan will live. If I cross over and you aren't with me, Kahlan will die. You have my word."

It was all happening too fast. He needed to think of a way to stall. "Then what good will any of this have done you?"

"It will have told me what means more to you." She sat back up in her saddle. "When you think about it, that is quite a profound question. It is yet to be answered. By the time I get to the top of the pass, I will have the answer."

Nicci rocked her hips in the saddle, urging the horse ahead into a walk. "Don't forget—top of the pass. You have until then to say your good-byes, pack what you wish to take, and then catch up with me if you wish Kahlan to live. Or, if you choose to stay, you have until then to say your good-byes before she dies. Understand, though, when making your choice, that the first will be as final as the second."

Kahlan struggled to run toward the horse, but Richard clutched her around her waist.

"Where are you taking him?" she demanded.

Nicci stopped her horse momentarily and gazed down at Kahlan with a look of frightening finality.

"Why, into oblivion."

As she watched Nicci turn her dappled mare toward the pass and the distant blue mountains beyond, Kahlan was still struggling to overcome her dizziness from what the woman had done to her. Off near the distant trees, a doe and her nearly grown fawn, two of the small herd of deer that frequented the meadow, stood at alert, their ears perked, watching Nicci, waiting to see if she might be a threat. Spooked by what they saw when Nicci turned their way, both deer flicked their tails straight up and bounded for the trees.

Kahlan refused to allow herself to give in to the disorientation. But for Richard's iron arms around her waist, she would have thrown herself at the Sister of the Dark. Kahlan had desperately wanted to unleash her Confessor's power. No one had ever deserved it more.

Had her senses not still been floundering in a daze, she might have been able to invoke her power through the Con Dar, the Blood Rage of an ancient ability she possessed. Such rare magic would have bridged the relatively small distance, but, reeling from the lingering force of Nicci's conjuring, the attempt had been futile. It was all Kahlan could do to keep her feet under her and her last meal in her stomach.

It was frustrating, infuriating, and humiliating, but Nicci had surprised her and with magic as swift as Kahlan's Confessor's power had taken her before she could react. Once Nicci's talons clutched her, Kahlan had been powerless.

She had grown up being trained not to be taken by surprise. Confessors were always targets; she knew better. Any number of times in similar situations she had prevailed. Lulled by months of tranquillity, Kahlan had lost her edge. She vowed never to let it happen again . . . but that would do her no good now.

She could still feel Nicci's vital magic sizzling through her, as if her soul itself had been scorched in the heat of the ordeal. Her insides roiled as waves of the onslaught had yet to settle down. The cold air rushing across the meadow, bending the brown grass, swept up to chill her burning face. The wind carried an unfamiliar scent into the valley, something that her jumbled senses perceived as vaguely portentous. The big pines behind the house bowed and twisted but stood tall as the wind broke against them with a sound not unlike waves rushing against stone cliffs.

Whatever sort of magic had been unleashed in her, Kahlan was convinced Nicci had told the truth about its consequence. Despite how much she hated the woman, because of the maternity spell Kahlan felt a connection to her, a connection that she could only interpret as . . . affection. It was a bewildering sensation. While positively disturbing, it was also, in a way, a comforting connection to the woman beyond her vile magic and twisted purpose. There seemed to be something deep within Nicci worth loving.

Regardless of Kahlan's far-fetched feelings, her perception and reasoning told her the truth of the matter: such impressions were illusion. If she got the opportunity, she would not again hesitate for an instant to kill Nicci.

"Cara," Richard said, glaring at Nicci's back as she walked her horse across the meadow, "I don't want you even thinking about trying to stop her."

"I'm not going to allow—"

"I mean it. I mean it more than any order I've ever given you. If you ever brought Kahlan to harm in such a way . . . well, I trust you'd never do such an evil thing to me. Why don't you go get dressed."

Cara growled a curse under her breath. Richard turned to Kahlan as the Mord-Sith marched off into the house. Kahlan only then really noticed that Cara was naked. She must have been interrupted in her bath. The magic Nicci used had fogged Kahlan's mind, blurring her memory of recent events.

Kahlan did recall quite clearly, though, the feel of the Agiel. The shattering torture of the Mord-Sith's weapon had spiked through Nicci's magic like a lance through straw. Even though Cara had used her Agiel on Nicci, Kahlan felt it as if it had been used directly against the side of her own neck.

Kahlan gently touched Richard's jaw in sympathy, then took hold of his upper arms instead when he gave her a look that suggested no need for sympathy. His big hands closed on her waist. She stepped into his embrace and rested her forehead against his cheek.

"This can't be," she whispered. "It just can't."

"But it is."

"I'm so sorry."

"Sorry?"

"That I let her take me by surprise." Kahlan trembled with anger at herself. "I should have been alert. If I'd done as I should have, and killed her first, it would never have come to this."

Richard ran a hand gently down the back of her head, holding her to his shoulder.

"Remember how you killed me in a sword fight the other day?" She nodded against him. "We all make mistakes, get caught off guard. Don't blame yourself. No one is perfect. It could even be that she cast a web of magic to dull your awareness so she could slip up to you like . . . like some silent unseen mosquito."

Kahlan had never considered that. Caught off guard or not, though, it made her furious with herself. If only she had not been paying attention to the stupid chipmunk. If only she had looked up sooner. If only she had acted without waiting a split second to analyze the true nature of the threat to decide if it warranted the unleashing of her devastating magic.

Almost from birth, Kahlan had been instructed in the use of her power, with the mandate of unleashing it only upon being certain of the need. Much like killing, a Confessor's power was the destruction of who a person was. Afterward, the person acted exclusively on behalf of the Confessor, and at the direction of the Confessor. It was as final as death.

Kahlan looked up into Richard's gray eyes. They looked all the more gray with the gray sky behind him.

"My life is a precious and sacred thing to me," she said. "Yours is no less to you. Don't throw yours away to be a slave to mine. I couldn't stand it."

"It's not come to that yet. I'll figure something out. But for now, I have to go with her."

"We'll follow, but stay well back." He was already shaking his head. "But, she won't even be aware—"

"No. For all we know, she could have others with her. They could be waiting to catch you if you follow. I couldn't bear the thought of knowing that at any moment she could use magic or somehow find out you were following. If that happened, you would die for nothing."

"You mean you think she could . . . hurt you to make you tell her I planned to follow."

"Let's not let our imaginations get the better of us."

"But I should be close, for when you make a move—for when you figure a way to stop her."

Richard cupped her face tenderly in his hands. He had a strange look in his eyes, a look she didn't like.

"Listen to me. I don't know what's going on, but you mustn't die just to free me."

Tears of desperation stung her eyes. She blinked them away. She fought to keep her voice from becoming a wail.

"Don't go, Richard. I don't care what it means for me, as long as you can be free. I would die happy if doing so would keep you from the enemy's cruel hands. I can't allow the Order to have you. I can't allow you to endure the slow grinding death of a slave in exchange for my life. I can't allow them to—"

She bit off the words of what she feared most; she couldn't bear the thought of him being tortured. It made her even more dizzy and sick to think of him being maimed and mutilated, of him suffering all alone and forgotten in some distant stinking dungeon with no hope of help.

But Nicci said they wouldn't. Kahlan told herself that, for her own sanity, she had to believe Nicci's word.

Kahlan realized Richard was smiling to himself, as if trying to commit to memory every detail of her face while at the same time running a thousand other things through his thoughts.

"There's no choice," he whispered. "I must do this."

She clutched his shirt in her fist. "You're doing just as Nicci wants—she knows you'll want to save me. I can't allow you to make that sacrifice!"

Richard looked up briefly, gazing out at the trees and mountains behind their house, taking it all in, like a condemned man savoring his last meal. His gaze, more earnest, settled once more on hers.

"Don't you see? I am making no sacrifice. I am making a fair trade. The reality that you exist is my basis for joy and happiness.

"I make no sacrifice," he repeated, stressing each word. "To be a slave, even if that is what happens to me, and yet know you're alive, is my choice over being free in a world in which you don't exist. I can live with the first. I can't, with the second. The first is painful, the second unbearable."

Kahlan beat a fist against his chest. "But you will be a slave or worse and I can't bear that!"

"Kahlan, listen to me. I will always have freedom in my heart because I understand what it is. Because I do, I can work toward it. I will find a way to be free.

"I cannot find a way to bring you back to life.

"The spirits know that in the past I've been willing to forfeit my life for a just

179

cause and if my life would truly make a difference. In the past, I have knowingly imperiled both our lives, been willing to sacrifice both our lives—but not in return for nothing. Don't you see? This would be a fool's bargain. I'll not do it."

Kahlan pulled her breaths in small gasps, trying to told back the tears as well as her rising sense of panic. "You're the Seeker. You must find a way to freedom. Of course you will. You will, I know." She forced a swallow past the constriction in her throat as she tried to reassure Richard, or perhaps herself. "You'll find a way. I know you will. You'll find a way and you'll come back. You did before. You will this time."

The shadows of Richard's features seemed dark and severe, cast as they were in a mask of resignation.

"Kahlan, you must be prepared to go on."

"What do you mean?"

"You must find joy in the fact that I, too, live. You must be prepared to go on with that knowledge and nothing else."

"What do you mean, nothing else?"

He had a terrible look in his eyes—some kind of sad, grim, tragic acceptance. She didn't want to look into his eyes, but, standing there with her hand against his chest, feeling the warmth of him, the life within him, she couldn't make herself look away as he spoke.

"I think it's different this time."

Kahlan pulled her hair back when the wind dragged it over her eyes. "Different?"

"There's something very different about the feel of this. It doesn't make sense in the way things in the past have made sense. There's something deadly serious about Nicci. Something singular. She's planned this out and she's prepared to die for it. I can't lie to you to deceive you. Something tells me that, this time, I may never be able to find a way to come back."

"Don't say that." In weak fingers trembling with dread, Kahlan gathered his dark shirt into a wrinkled knot. "Please don't say that, Richard. You must try. You must find a way to come back to me."

"Don't ever think I won't be doing my best." His voice was impassioned, almost to the point of sounding angry. "I swear to you, Kahlan, that as long as there is a breath in my lungs, I'll never give up; I'll always try to find a way. But we can't ignore the possibility just because it's painful to contemplate: I may never be back.

"You must face the fact that it looks like you must go on without me, but with the knowledge that I'm alive, just as I will have that awareness of you in my heart where no one can touch it. In our hearts, we have each other and always will. That was the oath we swore when we were married—to love and honor each other for all time. This can't change it. Distance can't change it. Time can't change it."

"Richard . . ." She choked back her wail, but she couldn't keep the tears from coursing down her face. "I can't stand the thought of you being a slave because of me. Don't you see that? Don't you see what that would do to me? I'll kill myself if I must so that she can't do this to you. I must."

He shook his head, the wind ruffling his hair. "Then I would have no reason to escape her. Nothing to escape for."

"You won't need to escape, that's just it—she won't be able to hold you."

"She's a Sister of the Dark." He threw open his hands. "She will simply use another means I won't know how to counter—and if you're dead, I won't care to."

"But—"

"Don't you see?" He seized her by her shoulders. "Kahlan, you must live to give me a reason to try to escape her."

"Your own life is your reason," she said. "To be free to help people will be your reason."

"The people be cursed." He released her and gestured angrily. "Even people where I grew up turned against us. They tried to murder us. Remember? The lands that have surrendered into the union with D'Hara will likely not remain loyal, either, when they see the reality of the Imperial Order's army moving up into the Midlands. Eventually, D'Hara will stand alone.

"People don't understand or value freedom. The way it now stands, they won't fight for it. They've proven it in Anderith, and in Hartland, where I grew up. What more clear evidence could be seen? I hold out no false hope. Most of the rest of the Midlands will quail when it comes time to fight against the Imperial Order. When they see the size of the Order's army and their brutality with those who resist, they will surrender their freedom."

He looked away from her, as if regretting his flash of anger in their last moments together. His tall form, so stalwart against the sweep of mountains and sky, sagged a little, seeming to huddle closer to her as if seeking comfort.

"The only thing I have to hope for is to get away so I can come back to you." His voice had lost all traces of heat as he spoke in a near whisper. "Kahlan, please don't take that hope from me—it's all I have."

In the distance she could see the fox trotting across the meadow. Its thick, white-tipped tail followed out straight behind as the fox made its inspection for any rodents that might be about. As Kahlan's gaze tracked its movement, from the corner of her eye she caught a glimpse of *Spirit* standing proud and free in the window. How could she lose the man who had carved that for her when she needed it most?

She could, she knew, because now he needed what only she could give him. Looking back up into his intense gray eyes, she realized she could not hope to deny him his earnest plea and only request, not at a time like this.

"All right, Richard. I won't do anything rash to free you. I'll wait for you. I'll endure it.

"I know you. I know you won't ever give up. You know I expect no less from you. When you get away—and you will—I'll be waiting for you, and then we'll be together again. We'll never be apart in our hearts. As you said, our oath of love is timeless."

Richard closed his eyes with relief. He tenderly kissed her brow. He lifted her hand from his chest and pressed soft kisses to her knuckles. She saw then how much her pledge meant to him.

Kahlan pulled her hand back and quickly removed her necklace, the one Shota had given her as a wedding gift. It was meant to prevent her from getting pregnant. She turned Richard's hand over and pushed the necklace into his palm. He frowned in confusion at the small, dark stone hanging from the gold chain draped over his fingers.

"What's this about?"

"I want you to take it." Kahlan cleared her throat to keep her voice. She could only manage a whisper. "I know what she wants of you—what she will make you do."

"No, that's not what . . ." He shook his head. He said, "I'm not taking this," as if turning it away would somehow deny the possibility.

Kahlan put her hand to the side of his face. His face wavered before her in a watery blur.

"Please, Richard. Please take it. For me. I couldn't bear the thought of another woman having your child." Or even the thought of the attempt at its creation—but she didn't say that part of it. "Especially not after mine . . ."

He looked away from her eyes. "Kahlan . . ." Words failed him.

"Just do it for me. Take it. Please, Richard. I'm doing as you ask and will endure your captivity; please honor my request in return. I couldn't stand the thought of that bewitching blond beast having your child—the child that should be mine. Don't you see? How could I ever love something I hated? And how could I ever hate something that was part of you? Please, Richard, don't let it come to that."

The cold wind lifted and twisted her hair. Her whole life, it seemed, was twisting out of her control. She could hardly believe that this place of such joy, peace, and redemption, a place where she had come to live again, could be a place where it would all be taken away.

Richard held the necklace out to her, as if it were a thing that might bite him. The dark stone swung under his fingers, gleaming in the gloom.

"Kahlan, I don't think that's what this is about. I really don't. But anyway, she could simply refuse to wear it and threaten your life if I didn't . . ."

Kahlan pulled the gold chain from his fingers and laid it all in a small neat mound in his palm. The dark stone glimmered from its imprisonment behind the veil of tiny gold links. She closed his fingers around the necklace and held his fist shut with both of her hands.

"You're the one who demands we not ignore those things that are painful to contemplate."

"But if she refuses . . ."

Kahlan gripped his fist tighter in her trembling fingers. "If it comes to a time when she makes that demand of you, you must convince her to wear the necklace. You must. For me. It's bad enough for me to think she might take my love, my husband, from me like that, but to also fear . . ."

His big hand felt so warm and familiar and comforting to her. Her words came choked with desperate tears. She could do no more than beg. "Please, Richard."

He pressed his lips tight, then nodded and stuffed the necklace in a pocket. "I don't believe those are her intentions, but if it should turn out to be so, you have my word: she will wear the necklace."

Kahlan sagged against him with a sob.

He took her by the arm. "Come on. Hurry. I have to get whatever I need to take. I've only got a few minutes, or all this will be for nothing. I can take the shorter trail and still catch up with her at the top of the pass, but I don't have much time."

Kahlan was aware of Cara, wearing her bloodred leather, standing in the door-way to their bedroom watching Richard cram his things into his pack. Kahlan nodded as she and Richard exchanged brief, stilted instructions. They had already come to terms with the life-and-death issues. It seemed they both feared to say anything of consequence for fear of disturbing the delicate, desperate, difficult agreements they had reached.

The meager light coming in the small window did little to brighten the gloom. Cara, over in the doorway, blocked some of the light. The room had the feel of a dungeon. Richard, dressed in dark clothes, looked like a shadow. So many times, as she lay in bed recovering, Kahlan had thought of it that way—as her dungeon. Now it had the palpable sense of a dungeon, but with the clean aroma of pine walls instead of the stench of a stone cell from where trembling, sweating prisoners were taken to their death.

Cara looked forlorn one moment and the next like lightning seeking ground. Kahlan knew that the Mord-Sith's emotions had to be as torn as her own, balancing on a knife's edge with despair and grief on one side and rage on the other. Mord-Sith were not used to being in such a position, but then, Cara was now more than simply Mord-Sith.

Kahlan watched Richard pack the black trousers, black undershirt, black and gold tunic, silver wristbands, over-belt with its pouches, and golden cloak into his pack, where they took up a good portion of the available space. He was wearing his dark forest garb; he didn't have time to change. Kahlan hoped a time would soon come when he would escape and again wear the clothes of a war wizard to lead them against the Order. They all needed him to lead the D'Haran Empire against the invading horde from the Old World.

For reasons that weren't always entirely clear, Richard had become the linchpin of their struggle. Kahlan knew his feelings about that—that people must be willing to fight for themselves and not only for him—were valid. If an idea was sound, it had to have a life beyond a leader, or the leader had failed.

As he threw other clothes and small items into his pack, Richard told Kahlan that maybe she could find Zedd, that he might have some ideas. She nodded and said she would, knowing Zedd wouldn't be able to do anything. This terrible triangle was not liable to be susceptible to influence by outsiders—Nicci had seen to that. It was just a hope Richard was giving her, the only bouquet he could offer in the desolate void of reality.

Kahlan didn't know what to do with her hands. She stood twining her fingers together as tears dripped off her chin. There must be something to say, something important, some last words while she had the chance, but she couldn't think of them.

She supposed he knew what she felt, what was in her heart, and words couldn't add anything to that. She pressed her fist against the aching knot of anxiety in the pit of her stomach.

A sense of doom crowded in the room like a fourth person, a grim guard waiting to take Richard away. This was the heart of terror, being controlled by what you couldn't see, couldn't reason with, couldn't persuade or battle. The doom waited, implacable, immune, indifferent.

As Cara vanished from the doorway, Richard pulled a fistful of gold and silver from an inside pocket in his leather pack. He hastily dropped roughly half back in the pack and then held out the rest.

"Take this. You might need it."

"I'm the Mother Confessor. I don't need gold."

He tossed it on the bed for her anyway, apparently not wanting to argue with her in their last moments together.

"Do you want any of the carvings?" she asked. It was a stupid question and she knew it, but she had to fill the awful silence and it was the only thing to come into her head, other than a hopeless plea.

"No. I've no need for them. When you look at them, think of me, and remember I love you." He rolled a blanket tight, wrapped it with a small patch of oiled canvas, and tied it with leather thongs to the bottom of his pack. "I guess if I were to want any, I could always carve some."

Kahlan handed him a cake of soap.

"I don't need your carving to remind me of your love. I'll remember. Carve something to make Nicci see that you should be free."

Richard glanced up with a grim smile. "I plan on seeing to it that she knows I won't ever give in to her and the Order. Carvings won't be necessary. She thinks she has this all planned out, but she's going to find out I'm bad company." Richard jammed a fist in his pack, making more room. "Very bad company."

Cara rushed back in, carrying small bundles with the corners tied in knots at the top. She plopped them down one at a time onto the bed.

"I put together some food for you, Lord Rahl. Things that will keep for traveling—dried meat and fish and such. Some rice and beans. I . . . I put a loaf of bread that I made on top, so eat it first, while it's still good."

He thanked her as he put the small bundles into his pack. He put the bread to his nose for a deep whiff before packing it away. He gave Cara a smile of appreciation.

Richard straightened. His smile evaporated in a way that for some reason made Kahlan's blood go cold. Looking like he was in the throes of committing himself to some last, grim deed, Richard pulled the baldric off over his head. He held the gold-and-silver wrought scabbard in his left hand and drew the Sword of Truth in his white-knuckled right fist.

The blade rang out with its unique metallic sound, announcing its freedom.

Richard drew his sleeve up his arm and wiped the sword across his forearm. Kahlan winced as she watched. She didn't know if he cut deeply accidentally, or on purpose. With an icy sensation she recalled that Richard cut very precisely with any sharp steel edge.

He turned the blade and wiped both sides in gouts of vivid red blood. He bathed the blade in it, giving it a voluptuous taste, wetting its appetite for more. Kahlan didn't know what he was doing or why he was doing it now, but it was a frightening ritual to witness. She wished he had drawn it before and cut down Nicci. Her blood, Kahlan would not fear seeing.

Richard picked up the scabbard and slammed the Sword of Truth home. Blood running over his hand left greasy red smears across the scabbard as he slid his hand down the length of it, to the tip, and then seized the sheathed weapon at its center point in his fist. His head bowed, his eyes on the dull silver and gold reflections lustrous even through his own blood, he loomed closer to her.

Richard looked up, and Kahlan saw the lethal rage of magic dancing in his eyes. He had invoked the sword's terrible wrath, called it forth, and then put it away. She'd never seen him do such a thing before.

He lifted the sword in its scabbard to her. The tendons in the back of his fist stood out in the strain. The white of his knuckles showed through the blood.

"Take it," he said in a hoarse voice that betrayed the struggle within.

Spellbound, Kahlan lifted the scabbard in her palms. For that instant, until he pulled away his bloody hand, she felt a jolting shock as if she were suddenly welded to the weapon by hot fury unlike anything she had ever experienced. She half expected to see a burst of sparks. She could feel such rage emanating from the cold steel that it nearly dropped her to her knees. She might have dropped the weapon itself in that first instant, had she been able to let go of it. She could not.

Once Richard removed his hand, the sheathed sword lost the passionate rage and felt no different from any other weapon.

Richard lifted a finger in caution. The dangerous magic still glazed his eyes. The muscles of his jaw tightened until she could see it standing out all the way up through his temples.

"Don't draw this sword," he warned in that awful hoarse whisper, "unless it's a matter of your life. You know the ghastly things this weapon can do to a person. Not only the one under the power of the blade, but the one under the power of the hilt."

Kahlan, arrested by the intensity of his gaze, could only nod. She clearly recalled the first time Richard had used the sword to kill a man. The first time he came to learn the horror of killing had been to protect her.

Using the weapon that first time, unleashing the magic the first time, had nearly killed Richard as well. It had been a struggle for him to learn how to control such a storm of magic as the Sword of Truth freed.

Without the rage of the sword's magic, Richard's eyes were capable of conveying menace. Kahlan could recall several times when his raptor's glare, by itself, had brought a roomful of people to silence. There were few things worse than the need to escape the look in those eyes. Now, those eyes hungered to deliver death.

"Be angry if you must use this," he growled. "Be very angry. That will be your only salvation."

Kahlan swallowed. "I understand." She nodded. "I remember."

Righteous rage was the only defense against the crippling pain the sword exacted as payment for its service.

"Life or death. No other reason. I don't know what will happen, and I'd just as soon you not find out. But I'd prefer that, to you being without this terrible defense if you need it. I've given it a taste of blood, it will come out voracious. When it comes out, it will be in a blood rage."

"I understand."

His eyes cooled at last. "I'm sorry to give you the terrible responsibility of this weapon, especially in this way, but it's the only protection I can offer."

With a hand on his arm to gently reassure him, Kahlan said, "I won't have to use it."

"Dear spirits, I hope not." He glanced over his shoulder, taking a last look at their room, and then at Cara. "I have to get going."

She ignored his words. "Give me your arm, first."

He saw she had bandages left over from when Kahlan was still recovering. Without objection, he held out his blood-soaked arm. Cara used a wet cloth to quickly swab his arm before she wound it in clean bandages.

Richard thanked her as she was finishing. Cara split the end, put the tails around his wrists, and tied a quick knot. "We will come part of the way with you."

"No. You will stay here." Richard pulled down his sleeve. "I don't want to risk it."

"But—"

"Cara, I want you to protect Kahlan. I'm leaving her in your hands. I know you won't let me down."

Cara's big beautiful blue eyes, glistening with tears, reflected the kind of pain Kahlan was sure Cara never allowed anyone to see.

"I swear to protect her as I would protect you, Lord Rahl, if you swear to get away and return."

Richard flashed her a brief smile, trying to ease her misery. "I'm Lord Rahl—I don't need to remind you that I've wiggled out of tighter spots than this." He kissed her cheek. "Cara, I swear I'll never give up trying to get away—you have my word."

Kahlan realized he hadn't really sworn to Cara's words. He wouldn't, she knew, want to make a promise he might not be able to keep.

Bending to the bed, he pulled his pack close. "I have to go." He held the strap in a stranglehold. "I can't be late."

Kahlan's fingers tightened on his arm, Cara laid a hand on his shoulder. Richard turned back and gripped Kahlan's shoulders.

"Listen to me, now. I wish you would stay here, in this house in these mountains where it's safe for you, but I don't think anything short of my dying request could convince you to do that. At least stay for four or five days, in case I'm able to figure out what's going on and can escape Nicci. She may be a Sister of the Dark, but I'm no longer exactly a stranger to magic. I've escaped powerful people before. I've sent Darken Rahl back to the underworld. I've gone to the Temple of the Winds in another world in order to stop the plague. I've escaped worse than this. Who knows—this might be simpler than it seems. If I do escape her, I'll come back here, so wait for a while, at least.

"If I can't get away from Nicci for now, try to find Zedd. He might have some idea of what to do. Ann was with him the last time we saw him. She's the Prelate of the Sisters of the Light and knew Nicci for a very long time. Perhaps she knows something that, along with what Zedd might be able to come up with, could help."

"Richard, don't worry about me. Just take care of yourself. I'll be waiting for you when you get away, so just be at ease about that much of it and put all your effort into escaping from her. We'll wait here for a while—I promise."

"I will watch over her, Lord Rahl. Don't worry about the Mother Confessor."

Richard nodded. He turned back to Kahlan. His fingers on her arms tightened. His brow drew down.

"I know you and I know the way you feel, but you have to listen to me. The time has not yet come. It may never come. You may think I'm wrong in this, but if you close your eyes to the reality of what is, in favor of what you would wish just because you're the Mother Confessor and feel responsible for the people of the Midlands, then there is no reason for us to bother hoping we'll be together again because we won't. We will be dead, and the cause of freedom will be dead."

His face loomed closer. "Above all else, our forces must not attack the heart of the Order's army. It's too soon. If they—if you—carry an assault directly into the heart of the Order thinking you can win, it will be the end of our forces, and the end of our chances. All hope for the cause of freedom, and all hope to defeat the Order, will be lost for generations to come.

"It's the same way we must use our heads with Nicci, and not fight her in a direct attack, or we will both die. You promised you would not kill yourself to free me. Don't throw that promise away by going against what I'm telling you now."

It all seemed so unimportant at the moment. The only thing that mattered was that she was losing him. She would have cast the rest of the world to the wolves if she could just keep him.

"All right, Richard."

"Promise me." His fingers were hurting her arms. He shook her. "I mean it. You could throw it all away if you don't heed my warning. You could destroy the hope of people for the next fifty generations. You could be the one who destroys freedom and brings a dark age upon the world. Promise me you won't."

A thousand thoughts swirled in chaotic turmoil through her mind. Kahlan stared up into his eyes. She heard herself say, "I promise, Richard. Until you say so, we'll make no direct attack."

He looked like a great weight had been lifted from his shoulders. A smile spread on his face as he pulled her into an embrace. His fingers combed into her hair and cradled her head as she rose to his kiss. Her hands slipped up the backs of his shoulders as she held him. It only lasted a moment, but in that moment of stolen bliss, they shared a world of emotions.

All too soon the kiss, the embrace, was over. His warm presence swirled away from her, allowing the awful weight of doom to settle firmly down atop her. Richard briefly hugged Cara before he hefted his pack onto a shoulder. He turned back at the bedroom doorway.

"I love you, Kahlan. Never anyone before you, nor ever after. Only you." His eyes said it even better.

"You're everything to me, Richard. You know that."

"I love you, too, Cara." He winked at her. "Take good care of the both of you until I'm back."

"I will, Lord Rahl. You have my word as Mord-Sith."

He gave her a crooked smile. "I have your word as Cara."

And then he was gone.

"I love you, too, Lord Rahl," Cara whispered to the empty doorway.

Kahlan and Cara ran into the main room and stood in the doorway watching him running across the meadow.

Cara cupped her hands around her mouth. "I love you too, Lord Rahl," she shouted.

Richard turned as he ran and acknowledged her words with a wave.

Together, they watched Richard's dark figure flying through the dead brown grass, his fluid gait swiftly carrying him away. Just before he disappeared into the trees, he stopped and turned. Kahlan shared a last look with him, a look that said everything. He turned and vanished into the woods, his clothes making him impossible to distinguish from the trees and undergrowth.

Kahlan collapsed to her knees, sitting back on her heels as she lost control of her emotions. She wept helplessly, her head in her hands, at what seemed the end of the world.

Cara squatted beside her to put an arm around her shoulders. Kahlan hated to have Cara see her cry that way, cry in such weakness. She felt a distant gratitude when Cara held her head to her shoulder and didn't say anything.

Kahlan didn't know how long she sat on the dirt floor in her white Confessor's dress, sobbing, but after a time, she was able to make herself stop. Her heart continued to spiral down into hopeless gloom. Each passing moment seemed unendurable. The bleak future stretched out before her, a wasteland of agony.

She finally looked up and gazed about at the house. Without Richard it was empty. He had given it life. Now it was a dead place.

"What do you wish to do, Mother Confessor?"

It was getting dark. Whether it was the sunset, or the clouds getting thicker, Kahlan didn't know. She wiped at her eyes.

"Let's begin to get our things together. We'll stay here a few days, like Richard asked. After that, anything the horses can't carry that will spoil, we'd better bury. We should board up the windows. We'll close up the house good and tight."

"For when we return to paradise, someday?"

Kahlan nodded as she looked about, trying desperately to focus her mind on a task and not on that which would crush her. The worst part, she knew, was going to be night. When she was alone in bed. When he wasn't with her.

Now, the valley seemed more like paradise lost. She had trouble believing that Richard was really gone. It seemed as if he were just off to catch some fish, or hunt berries, or scout the hills. It seemed as if, surely, he would be coming back soon.

"Yes, for when we return. Then it will be paradise again. I guess when Richard returns, wherever we are will be paradise."

Kahlan noticed that Cara didn't hear her answer. The Mord-Sith was staring out through the doorway.

"Cara, what is it?"

"Lord Rahl is gone."

Kahlan rested a comforting hand on Cara's shoulder. "I know it hurts, but we must put our minds to—"

"No." Cara turned back. Her blue eyes were strangely troubled. "No, that's not what I mean. I mean that I can't sense him. I can't feel the bond to Lord Rahl. I know where he is—he's going up the trail up to that pass—but I can't feel it." She looked panicked. "Dear spirits, it's like going blind. I don't know how to find him. I can't find Lord Rahl."

Kahlan's first flash of fear was that he fell and was killed, or that Nicci had executed him. She used reason to force the fear aside.

"Nicci knows about the bond. She probably used her magic to cloak it, or to sever it."

"Cloaked it, somehow." Cara rolled her Agiel in her fingers. "That's what it has to be. I can still feel my Agiel, so I know that Lord Rahl has to be alive. The bond is still there . . . but I cannot feel it to sense where he is."

Kahlan sighed with relief. "That has to be it, then. Nicci doesn't want to be followed, so she cloaked his bond with magic."

Kahlan realized that to be protected from the dream walker by the bond to Richard, people would now have to believe in him without the reassurance of feeling the bond. Their link would have to remain true in their hearts if they were to survive.

Could they do that? Could they believe in that way?

Cara stared out the doorway, across the meadow to the mountains where Richard had disappeared. The blue-violet sky behind the blue-gray mountains was slashed with blazing orange gashes. The snowcaps were lower than they had been. Winter was racing toward them. If Richard didn't soon escape and return, Kahlan and Cara would have to be gone before it arrived.

Bouts of dizzying grief threatened to drown her in a flood of tears. Needing to do something, she went to her room to take off her Confessor's dress. She would set to work with the task of closing up the house and preparing to leave.

As Kahlan pulled her dress off, Cara appeared in the doorway.

"Where are we going to go, Mother Confessor? You said we were going to leave, but you never said where we were going to go."

Kahlan saw *Spirit* standing in the window, fists at her sides as she looked out at the world. She lifted the carving off the sill and trailed her fingers over the flowing form.

Seeing the statue, touching it, feeling the power of it, made Kahlan want to reach deep inside for resolve. Once before, she had been hopeless, and Richard carved this for her. Her other hand fell to her side, and her fingers found Richard's sword lying across their bed. Kahlan focused her mind, ordering the turbulent swirl of despair thickening into wrath.

"To destroy the Order."

"Destroy the Order?"

"Those beasts took my unborn child, and now they've taken Richard. I will make them regret it a thousand times over and then another thousand. I once swore an oath of death without mercy to the Order. The time has come. If killing every last one of them is the only way to get Richard back, then that's what I will do."

"You swore an oath to Lord Rahl."

"Richard said nothing about not killing them, just about how. My oath was not to try to drive a sword through their heart. He said nothing about bleeding them to death with a thousand cuts. I won't break my oath, but I intend to kill every last one of them."

"Mother Confessor, you must not do that."

"Why?"

Cara's blue eyes gleamed with menace. "You must leave half for me."

CHAPTER 24

Richard had stopped to turn back and look at her only once as he ran, just before he went into the trees. She was standing in the doorway in her white Confessor's dress, her long thick hair tumbling down, her form the embodiment of feminine grace, looking as beautiful as the first time he saw her. They held each other's gaze for a brief moment. He was too far away to see the green of her eyes, a color he'd never beheld on anyone else, a color of such heart-piercing perfection that it sometimes would stop his breathing, and at other times quicken it.

But it was the mind of the woman behind those eyes that in reality captivated him. Richard had never met her equal.

He knew he was cutting the time close. As much as he hated the idea of turning his gaze away from Kahlan, her life hung in the balance. His purpose was clear. Richard had plunged into the woods.

He had traveled the trail often enough; he knew where he could run, and where he had to be careful. Now, with little time left, he couldn't afford to be too careful. He didn't try for a glimpse of the house.

He was alone in the woods as he ran, his thoughts but salt in a raw wound. For once he felt out of place in the woods—powerless, insignificant, hopeless. Bare branches clattered together in the wind, while others creaked and moaned, as if in mock sorrow to see him leaving. He tried not to think as he ran.

Fir and spruce trees took over as the ground rose out of the valley. His breath came in rapid pulls. In the cold shadows of the forest floor, the wind was a distant pursuer far overhead, chasing after him, shooing him along, hounding him away from the happiest place he had ever been. Spongy mounds of verdant moss lay dotting the forest floor in the low places where mostly cedars grew, looking like wedding cakes done up in an intense green, sprinkled over with tiny, chocolate brown, scale-like cedar needles.

Richard tiptoed on rocks sticking up above the water as he crossed a small stream. As the little brook tumbled down the slope, it went under rocks and boulders in places, making an echoing drumming sound, announcing him to the stalwart oaks along his march into imprisonment. In the flat gray light, he failed to see a reddish loop of cedar root. It caught his foot and sent him sprawling facedown in the trail, a final humiliation on his judgment and sentence of banishment.

As Richard lay in the cold, damp, discarded leaves, dead branches, and other refuse of the forest, he considered not getting up ever again. He could just lie there and let it all end, let the indifferent wind freeze his limbs stiff, let the sneaky spiders and snakes and wolves come to bite him and bleed him to death, and then finally the uncaring trees would cover him over, never to be missed except by a few, his vanishing a good riddance to most.

190

A messenger with a message no one wanted to heed.

A leader come too soon.

Why not just let it end, let silent death take them both to their peace and be done with it?

The scornful trees all watched to see what this unworthy man might do, to see if he had the courage to get to his feet and face what was ahead. He didn't know himself if he did.

Death was easier, and in that bottomless moment, less painful to consider.

Even Kahlan, as much as he loved her, wanted something from him he could not give her: a lie. She wanted him to tell her that something he knew to be so, was not. He would do anything for her, but he couldn't change what was. At least she had enough faith in him to let him lead her away from the shadows of tyranny darkening the world. Even if she didn't believe him, she was probably the only one willing, of her own free will, to follow him.

In truth, he lay on the ground for only seconds, regaining his senses from the fall and catching his breath as the thoughts flooded through his mind—brief seconds in which he allowed himself to be weak, in exchange for how hard he knew everything to come would be.

Weakness, to balance the strength he would need. Doubt, to balance his certainty of purpose. Fear, to balance the courage he would have to call upon.

Even as he wondered if he could get up, he knew he would. His convulsion of self-pity ended abruptly. He would do anything for her. Even this. A thousand times over, even this.

With renewed resolve, Richard forced his mind away from the dominion of dark thoughts. It wasn't so hopeless; he knew better. After all, he had faced trials much more difficult than this one Sister of the Dark. He had once gotten Kahlan out of the clutches of five Sisters of the Dark. This was but one. He would defeat her, too. Anger welled up at the thought of Nicci thinking she could make them dance at the end of her selfish strings.

Despair extinguished, rage flooded in.

And then he was running again, dodging trees as he cut corners off the trail. He hurdled fallen trees and leaped over gaps in the rock shelves, rather than taking the safe route down and up. Each shortcut or leap saved him a few precious seconds.

A broken tree limb snagged his pack, yanking it from his shoulder. He tried to hang on to it as he flew past, but it slipped from his grasp and spilled across the ground.

Richard exploded in fury, as if the tree had done it on purpose just to taunt him in his rush. He kicked the offending branch, snapping it out of its dry socket. He fell to his knees and scooped his things back into the pack, clawing up moss along with gold and silver coins, and a pine seedling along with the soap Kahlan had given him. He didn't have time to care as he shoved it all back in. This time, he put the pack onto his back, rather than letting it hang from one shoulder. He had been trying to save time before, and it had cost him instead.

The path, which in places was no more than sections of animal trails, began to rise sharply, occasionally requiring that he use both hands to hold on to rocks or roots as he climbed. He'd been up it enough times to know the sound handholds. As cold as the day was, Richard had to wipe sweat from his eyes. He skinned his knuckles on rough granite as he jammed his fingers into cracks for handholds.

In his mind's eye, Nicci was riding too swiftly, covering too much ground, getting too far ahead. He knew it had been foolhardy to take so much time before leaving, thinking he could make up for it on the trail. He wished he could have taken more time, though, to hold Kahlan.

His insides were in agony at the thought of how heartbroken Kahlan was. He felt, somehow, that it was worse for her. Even if she was free, and he was not, that made it worse for her because, in her freedom, she had to restrain herself when she wanted nothing more than to come after him. In bondage to a master, Richard had it easy; he had only to follow orders.

He burst out of the trees onto the wider trail at the top of the pass. Nicci was nowhere to be seen. He held his breath as he looked to the east, fearing to spot her going down the back side of the pass. Beyond the high place where he stood, he could see forests spread out before him with mountains to each side lifting the carpet of trees. In the distance, greater mountains yet soared to dizzying heights, their peaks and much of their slopes stark white against the gloom of heavy gray sky.

Richard didn't see any horse and rider, but since the trail twisted down into the trees not far beyond where he stood, that didn't really prove anything. The top of the pass was a bald bit of open ledge, with most of the rest of the horse trail winding through deep woods. He quickly inspected the ground, casting about for tracks, hoping she wouldn't be too far ahead of him and he could catch her before she did something terrible. His sense of doom eased when he found no tracks.

He peered out at the valley far below, across the straw-brown meadow, to their house. It was too far away to see anyone. He hoped Kahlan would stay there for a few days, as he had asked. He didn't want her going to the army, going to fight a losing war, endangering her life for nothing.

Richard understood Kahlan's desire to be with her people and to defend her homeland. She believed she could make a difference. She could not. Not yet. Maybe not ever. Richard's vision was really nothing more than the acceptance of that reality. Shaking your sword at the sky didn't keep the sun from setting.

Richard cast an appraising squint at the clouds. For the last two days, he had thought that the signs pointed to the first snow of the season soon rolling down onto their valley home. By the look of the sky and the scent in the wind, he judged he was right.

He knew he wasn't going to be able to escape Nicci so easily as to be able to get back to Kahlan within a few days. He had invented that story for another reason. Once the weather shifted and the snow arrived up in these mountain highlands, it tended to come in an onslaught. If the storm was as big as he estimated by the signs it could be, Kahlan and Cara would end up being stuck in their house until spring. With all the food they'd put up, as well as the supplies he'd brought in, they had plenty to last the two of them. The firewood he'd cut would keep them warm.

There, she would be safe. With the army, she would be in constant danger.

The dappled mare walked out of the trees, coming around a bend not far away. Nicci's blue eyes were on Richard from the first instant she appeared.

At the time the Sisters of the Light had taken him to the Palace of the Prophets in the Old World, Richard had mistakenly believed Kahlan wanted him taken away. He didn't know or understand she had sent him away to save his life. Richard thought she didn't ever want to see him again.

While in captivity at the palace, Richard thought Nicci was the personification of lust. He was hardly able to find his voice when around her. He had hardly been able to believe a creature of such physical perfection existed, other than in day-dreams.

Now, as he watched her swaying gently in her saddle as she walked her horse up the trail, her intense blue eyes locked on his, it seemed to him she wore her beauty with a kind of grim acceptance. She had so completely lost her stunning presence that he couldn't even envision any reason for his onetime sentiment about her.

Richard had since learned the true depths of what a real woman was, what real love was, and what real fulfillment was. In that light, Nicci paled into insignificance.

As he watched her coming closer, he was surprised to realize she looked sad. She seemed almost to be sorry to find him there, but more than that, there seemed to be a shadow of relief passing across her countenance.

"Richard, you lived up to my faith." Her voice suggested that it had been tenuous as best. "You're in a sweat; would you like to rest?"

Her feigned kindness drove hot blood all the way up to his scalp. He pulled his glare from her gentle smile and turned to the trail, walking ahead of her horse. He thought it best if he not say anything until he could get a grip on his rage.

Not far down the trail they came to a black stallion with a white blaze on its face. The big horse was picketed in a small grassy patch of open ground among towering pines.

"Your horse, as I promised," she said. "I hope you find him to your liking. I judged him to be big and strong enough to carry you comfortably."

Richard checked and found the smooth snaffle bit to his approval; she wasn't abusing the animals with cruel bits used to dominate, as he knew some of the Sisters did. The rest of the tack appeared sound. The horse looked healthy.

Richard took a few moments to introduce himself to the stallion. He reminded himself that the horse was not the cause of his problems, and he shouldn't let his attitude toward Nicci affect how he treated this handsome animal. He didn't ask the horse's name. He let it sniff his hand beneath its curled muzzle, then stroked the stallion's sleek black neck. He patted its shoulder, conveying a gentle introduction without words. The powerful black stallion stamped his front hooves. He was not yet all that pleased to meet Richard.

For the time being, there was no choice of routes; there was only the one trail and it ran from the direction of the house where Kahlan was back to the east. Richard took the lead so that he wouldn't have to look at Nicci.

He didn't want to jump right on the stallion at first sight and make a bad impression that would take a lot of work to overcome. Better to let the horse get to know him, first, if just for a mile or so. He held the reins slack under the stallion's jaw and walked in front of him, letting him get comfortable with following this strange new man. Putting his mind to the task of working with the horse helped divert him from thoughts that threatened to drag him under a sea of sorrow. After a time, the stallion seemed at ease with his new master and Richard mounted without any ado.

The narrow trail precluded Nicci walking her horse beside his. Her dappled mare snorted its displeasure at having to follow the stallion. Richard was pleased to know that he had already upset the order of things.

Nicci offered no conversation, sensing, he supposed, his mood. He was going with her, but there was no way she could hope to make him happy about it.

When it started getting dark, Richard simply dismounted beside a small brook where the horses could have a drink, and tossed his things on the ground. Nicci wordlessly accepted his choice of campsite, and unstrapped her bedroll from her saddle after she'd taken it down off her horse. She sat on her bedroll, looking a little downcast, more than anything else, and ate some sausage along with a hard biscuit washed down with water. After her first bite, she lifted the sausage to him, meeting his gaze in a questioning manner. He didn't acknowledge the offer. Nicci assumed he declined, and went back to eating.

When she was finished and had washed in the brook, she went behind the thick undergrowth for a time. When she came back, she crawled into her bedroll without a word, turned away from him, and went to sleep.

Richard sat on the mossy ground, arms folded, leaning the small of his back against his saddle. He didn't sleep the entire night. He sat watching Nicci sleep in the light of the overcast sky lit from the other side by a nearly full moon, watching her slow even breathing, her slightly parted lips, the slow pulse in the vein at the side of her throat, thinking the whole time how he might overcome what she had done to them. He thought about strangling her, but he knew better.

He had used magic before. He had in the past not only felt but unleashed incredible power through his gift. He had faced situations of enormous danger involving a wide variety of magic. Richard had called upon his gift to conjure such power as no one living had ever seen, and he had watched as it was brought to life at his conscious direction.

His gift was invoked mostly through anger and need. He had an abundant supply of both. He just didn't know how it could help him. He didn't understand well enough what Nicci had done to begin to think of what he might do to counter it. With Kahlan's life at the other end of Nicci's invisible cord of magic, he dared not do anything until he was sure of it. He would be, though; he just had to figure it out. Experience told him that it was a reasonable supposition. He told himself it was only a matter of time. If he wanted to keep his sanity, he knew he had to believe that.

The next morning, without speaking a word to Nicci, he saddled the horses. She sat watching him tighten the cinch straps, making sure they weren't pinching the horses, as she sipped from a waterskin. She took bread from her saddlebag lying beside her and asked if he would like a piece. Richard ignored her.

He would have been tired from not sleeping the whole cold night, but his anger kept him wide awake. Under a leaden sky, they rode at an easy but steady pace all that day through forests that seemed endless. It felt good to have a warm horse under him. Throughout the day, they continued their gradual descent from the higher country, where the house was, down into the lowlands.

Toward dark, the snow arrived.

At first, it was just a few furtive flakes swirling through the air. As it steadily increased, it seemed to leach the color from trees and ground alike, until the world turned white. Visibility steadily diminished as the snow thickened into a disorienting, drifting, solid wall. He had to keep blinking the fat flakes from his eyes.

For the first time since leaving with Nicci, Richard felt a sense of relief.

Kahlan and Cara, up higher in the mountains, would wake in the morning to several feet of snow. They would decide that it was foolish to try to leave when, they would believe, it was only an early snow that would melt down enough in a few days for them to have an easier time of traveling. Up in those mountains, that would be a mistake. It would stay cold. A storm would follow on the heels of this one, and they would soon have snow up to the shutters. They would be nervous about waiting, but would probably decide that it was now more important for them to delay until a break in the weather—after all, there was no urgency.

In all likelihood, they would end up safely stuck in the house for the winter. When he eventually escaped from Nicci's talons, Richard would find Kahlan snug in their home.

He decided that it would be foolish to let his anger dictate that they sleep on the open ground. They could freeze to death. He recalled all too well that if Nicci died, Kahlan died. When he spotted a big wayward pine, he walked his horse off the trail. Brushing against branches dumped wet snow on him. Richard flicked it off his shoulders and shook it from his hair.

Nicci glanced around, confused, but didn't object. She dismounted as she waited to see what he was doing. When he held a heavy bough to the side for her, she frowned at him before poking her head inside for a look. She straightened with an expression of childlike delight. Richard didn't return her wide grin.

Inside, under the thick boughs caked with snow, was a still, frigid world. With the snow crusting the tree, it was dark inside. In the dim light, Richard dug a small fire pit and soon caught fire to the deadwood he'd carefully stacked over shavings.

When the crackling flames built into a warm glow, Nicci gazed around in wonder at the inside of the wayward pine. The spoke-like branches over their heads were cast in a soft orange blush by the flickering light. The lower trunk was bare of limbs, leaving the inside of the tree a hollow cone with ample open space at the bottom for them.

Nicci quietly warmed her hands by the fire, looking contented—not like she was gloating that he'd given in and found shelter and built a fire, but contented. She looked as if she had been through a great ordeal, and now she could be at peace. She looked like a woman expecting nothing, but grateful for what she had.

Richard hadn't had breakfast with her, or anything the day before. His bitter resolve gave way to his hunger, so he boiled water from melted snow and cooked rice and beans. Starving wouldn't do him or Kahlan any good. Without words, he offered Nicci half the rice and beans poured into the crust of one end of his loaf of bread. She took the bread bowl and thanked him.

She offered him a sun-dried slice of meat. Richard stared at her thin, delicate fingers holding out the piece of meat. It reminded him of someone feeding a chipmunk. He snatched the meat from her hand and tore off a chunk with his teeth. To avoid her gaze, he watched the fire as he ate his rice and beans out of the heel of bread. Other than the crackle of the fire, the only sound was the thump of snow falling in clumps from limbs not stout enough to hold the load. Snowfalls often turned a forest to a place of eerie stillness.

Sitting by the low fire after he'd finished his meal, feeling the warmth of the flames on his face, the exhaustion from the long ride on top of his vigil the night before finally caught up with him. Richard stacked thicker wood on the dwindling fire and banked the coals around it. He unrolled his bedroll on the opposite side of the fire from Nicci as she silently watched him, climbed in, and, as he thought about Kahlan safe in their house, fell soundly asleep.

The next day they were up early. Nicci said nothing, but, once they were mounted, decisively cut her dappled mare in front of the black stallion and took the lead. The snow had changed to a cold drizzling mist. What snow was left on the

ground had melted down to gray slush. The lowlands were not quite ready to relinquish themselves to winter's grip. Up higher, where Kahlan was, it was colder and
would be snowing in earnest.

As they rode carefully along a narrow road at the side of a mountain, Richard
tried to watch the woods to keep his mind on other things, but he couldn't help
occasionally looking at Nicci riding right in front of him. It was cold and damp; she
wore a heavy black cloak over her black dress. With her back straight, her head held
high, and her blond hair fanned out over her cloak, she looked regal. He wore his
dark forest clothes and hadn't shaved.

Nicci's dappled mare was dark gray, almost black, with lighter gray rings over
its body. Its mane was dark gray, as were the lightly feathered legs, and the tail was
a milky white. It was one of the most handsome horses Richard had ever seen. He
hated it. It was hers.

By afternoon, they intersected a trail running to the south. Nicci, leading the way,
continued to the east. Before the day was out they would encounter a few more
paths, used mainly by an occasional hunter or trapper. The mountains were inhospitable. Even if you cleared the ground of trees, the soil was thin and rocky. In a few
places closer to Hartland or other population centers to the north or south, there
were grassy slopes that were able to support thin flocks of sheep or goats.

As he felt the stallion's muscles moving beneath him, Richard looked out at land
he knew and loved. He didn't know how long it would be until he was home
again—if ever. He hadn't asked where they were going, figuring Nicci wouldn't
likely tell him this soon. That they were headed east didn't mean much just yet
because their choice of routes was limited.

In the passive rhythm of the ride, Richard's mind kept returning to his sword,
and how he had given it to Kahlan. At the time it had seemed the only thing to do.
He hated that he had given it to her the way he had, yet he could think of no other
way to afford her any protection. He prayed she would never have to use the sword.
If she did, he'd given it a measure of his rage, too.

At his belt he wore a fine knife, but he felt naked without his sword. He hated
the ancient weapon, the way it pulled dark things from within him, and at the same
time he missed it. He often reminded himself of Zedd's words, that it was merely a
tool.

It was more, too. The sword was a mirror, albeit one bound in magic capable of
raining terrible destruction. The Sword of Truth would annihilate anything before
it—flesh or steel—as long as what stood before it was the enemy, yet it could not
harm a friend. Therein lay the paradox of its magic: evil was defined solely by the
perceptions of the person holding the sword, by what he *believed* to be true.

Richard was the true Seeker and heir to the power of the sword created by the
wizards in the great war. It should be with him. He should be protecting the sword.

A lot of things "should be," he told himself.

Late in the afternoon they left the eastern path they were on and took one tending
east and south. Richard knew the trail; it would pass through a village in another
day, and then become a narrow road. Since Nicci had deliberately taken the new
route, she must have known that, too.

Near dark they skirted the north shore of a good-sized lake. A small raft of
seagulls floated out near the middle of the rain-swept water. Seagulls weren't common in these parts, but they were not unheard of, either. He recalled all the seabirds
he had seen when he had been in the Old World. The sea had fascinated him.

In a cove on the far shore Richard could just make out two men fishing. On that side of the lake there was a trail worn to a deep rut over many generations by people coming up to fish from a hamlet to the south.

The two men, sitting on a broad flat rock jutting out into the lake, waved in greeting. It wasn't often one encountered riders out here. Richard and Nicci were too far away for the men to make them out. The men probably assumed they were trappers.

Nicci returned the wave in a casual manner, as if to say, "Good luck with the fishing. Wish we could join you."

They rounded a bend and finally disappeared from the men. Richard wiped his wet hair off his forehead as they rode along beside the lake, listening to the small waves lapping at the muddy shore. Leaving the lake behind, they cut into the forest as the trail rose on its way across a gentle slope. Nicci had put her hood up against the intermittent rain and drizzle purring through the trees. A darkening gloom descended on the woods.

Richard didn't want to do anything that would get Kahlan killed; the time had finally come when he had to speak.

"When we come upon someone, what am I to say? I don't suppose you want me telling people you're a Sister of the Dark out snatching victims. Or do you wish me to play the part of a mute?"

Nicci gave him a sidelong glance.

"You will be my husband, as far as everyone is concerned," she said without hesitation. "I expect you to adhere to that story under all circumstances. For all practical purposes, from now on, you are my husband. I am your wife."

Richard's fists tightened on the reins. "I have a wife. You are not she. I'm not going to pretend you are."

Swaying gently in her saddle, Nicci seemed indifferent to his words or the emotion behind them. She gazed skyward, taking in the darkening sky.

It was too warm down in the lowlands for snow. Through occasional breaks in the low clouds, though, Richard had caught glimpses of windswept mountain slopes behind them cloaked in thick white drifts. Kahlan was sure to be dry, warm, and stuck.

"Do you think you could find us another of those shelter trees?" Nicci asked. "Where it would be dry, like last night? I'd dearly love to get dry and warm."

Between sporadic gaps in the pine trees, and through the scramble of bare branches of the alder and ash, Richard surveyed the hillside descending before them.

"Yes."

"Good. We need to have a talk."

As Richard dismounted near one of his shelter trees at the edge of a small, slanted, open patch of grassy ground, Nicci took the reins of his horse. She could feel his smoldering glare on her back as she picketed the horses to the thick branches of an alder heavy with catkins. The horses were hungry, and promptly started cropping the wet grass. Without a word, Richard began casting about, collecting deadwood from under dense thickets of spruce trees, where, she supposed, it might be a little dryer.

She watched him, not openly, but casually, covertly, from the corner of her eye as he went about his chore. He was everything she remembered, and more. It was not so much that he was just big, physically, but he had a commanding presence that had matured since she had last seen him. Before, she had been tempted at times to think of him as little more than a boy. No more.

Now, he was a powerful wild stallion trapped in a pen of his own construction. She kept her distance, letting him kick at the walls of that pen. It would bring her no gain to taunt this wild beast. Taunting him, torturing him in his anguish, was the last thing in the world she wanted.

Nicci could understand his smoldering anger. It was to be expected. She could plainly see his feelings for the Mother Confessor, and hers for him. The integrity of the walls of his pen consisted of nothing more than the gossamer fence rails of his feelings for her. While Nicci sympathized with his pain, she knew that she, of all people, could do nothing to alleviate it. It would take time for his hurt to heal. Over time, the rails of his fence would be replaced by others.

Someday, he would come to terms with what had to be. Someday, he would come to understand the truth of the things she intended to show him. Someday, he would come to understand the necessity of what she was doing. It was for the best.

At the edge of the clearing, Nicci settled herself on a gray slab of granite that, by the unique angles of its broken face, had once belonged to the ledge poking out from under the deep green of balsam and spruce behind her, but over time had been moved away from it by the inexorable effort of nature, leaving a gap the shape of a jagged lightning bolt between their once-mated edges.

Nicci sat with her back straight, a habit instilled in her from a young age by her mother, and watched Richard going about unsaddling the horses. He let them both eat some oats from canvas nosebags while he collected rocks from the clearing. At first, she couldn't imagine what he was doing. When he took them, along with the wood he had collected, in under the boughs of the shelter tree, she realized he must be going to use the rocks to ring a fire pit. He was inside a long time, so she knew he must be working on building a fire out of the wet wood. She could have used her gift to help, had her gift enough power left to light wet wood. It didn't.

Richard seemed up to the task, though; she had watched him light a fire the night before, starting it in birch bark, shavings, and twigs. Nicci had never been one for such outdoor activities. She left him to it and set about the small chore of repairing her horse's cinch strap. The rain had let up for the time being, leaving behind the tingle of a fine mist against her cheeks.

As she worked at knotting the loose cords of the heavy twine strap back onto its buckle, she heard little crackling sounds coming from under the tree. The sputtering and popping told her that Richard had gotten the fire going. She heard the clang of a pot on rock, so she reasoned that we was leaving water to boil when the fire got hot enough.

Sitting on the slab of granite, Nicci quietly worked a tangle out of the cinch strap as he came back out to care for the horses. Free of the nosebags, the horses drank from a pool of water in a depression in the smooth tan ledge. Though Richard wore dark clothes appropriate for the woods, they could not diminish his bearing. His gray-eyed gaze swept over her, taking in what she was doing. He left her to her knot work as he went about his chore of currying the horses. His big hands worked smoothly, with a sure touch. She was certain the horses would appreciate having all the caked mud cleaned from their legs. She would, were she they.

"You said we needed to talk," Richard finally said to her as he stroked the curry comb over the mare's rump, whisking away a last spatter of mud. "I presume a talk consists of you dictating the terms of my imprisonment. I imagine you have rules for your captives."

By his icy inflection, it sounded as if he had decided to provoke her a little, to test her reaction. Nicci set the cinch strap aside. She met his challenging tone with one of genuine sympathy, instead.

"Just because something has happened to you before, Richard, don't assume that means it will again. Fate does not give birth to the same child over and over. Each is different. This is not like the two times before."

Her response, as well as the compassion in her eyes, appeared to have caught him off guard. He stared at her a moment before crouching to replace the curry comb in a pocket in the saddlebag and take out a pick.

"Two times before?" There was no way he could miss her meaning. His blank expression didn't betray what he might be thinking as he lifted the stallion's right forefoot to pick its hoof clean. "I don't know what you're talking about."

Just as he probed the hoof with his pick, she knew he was probing her as well, wanting to know just how much she knew of those two times, and what she thought was different, this time. He would surely want to know how she intended to avoid the mistakes of his past captors. Any warrior would.

He was not yet ready to accept how fundamentally different this was.

Richard worked his way around the big black horse, cleaning its hooves, until he ended at the left forefoot, close to her. As he finished and let the stallion's leg down, Nicci stood. When he turned around, she was close enough to feel his warm breath on her cheek. He fixed her with his glare, a look that was no longer as unsettling to her as it had been at first.

She found herself, instead of shrinking back, staring into that penetrating gaze of his, marveling that she had him. She finally had him. It could have been no more wondrous to her had she somehow managed to bottle the moon and stars.

"You are a prisoner," Nicci said. "Your anger and resentment are entirely understandable. I would never have expected you to be pleased about this, Richard. But it is not the same as those times before." She gently gripped his throat. He was surprised, but sensed he was in no immediate danger. "Before," she said in quiet solace, "you had a collar around your neck. Both times."

"You were at the Palace of the Prophets, where I was taken." She felt him swallow. "But the other . . ."

She released his throat. "I do not use a collar, as did the Sisters of the Light, to control you, to give you pain in order to make you obey, or to put you through their ridiculous tests. My purpose is nothing like that."

She pulled her cloak forward over her shoulders as she smiled distantly. "Remember when you first came to the Palace of the Prophets? Remember the speech you gave?"

Richard's words were brittle with caution. "Not . . . exactly."

She was still staring off into the memories. "I do. It was the first time I saw you. I remember every word."

Richard said nothing, but in his eyes she could see the shadows of his mind working.

"You were in a rage—not unlike now. You held out a red leather rod hanging around your neck. Remember, Richard?"

"I guess I did." His suspicious glare broke. "A lot has happened since then. I guess I'd put it out of my mind."

"You said that you had been collared before. You said that the person who had once put that collar around your neck had brought you pain to punish you, to teach you."

His posture shifted to stiff wariness. "What of it?"

She focused once more on his gray eyes, eyes that watched her every blink, her every breath, as he weighed her every word. It was all going into some inner calculation, she knew—some inner master analysis of how high was his fence, and if he could jump it. He could not.

"I always wondered about that," she said. "About what you had said about having been in a collar before. Some months back, we captured a woman in red leather. A Mord-Sith." His color paled just a little. "She said she was searching for Lord Rahl, to protect him. I persuaded her to tell me everything she knew about you."

"I'm not from D'Hara." His voice sounded confident, nevertheless, she sensed a subterranean torrent of dread. "A Mord-Sith would know next to nothing about me."

Nicci reached inside her cloak for the thing she had brought with her. She let the small red leather rod roll from her fingers to fall to the ground at his feet. He stiffened.

"Oh, but she did, Richard. She knew a great deal." She smiled a small smile, not pleasure, nor mockery, but in distant sadness at the memory of that brave woman. "She knew Denna. She had been at the People's Palace in D'Hara, where you were taken after Denna captured you. She knew all about it."

Richard's gaze fell away. On bended knee he reverently picked the red leather rod off the wet ground. He wiped the thing clean on his pant leg as if it were priceless.

"A Mord-Sith would not tell you anything." He stood and boldly met her gaze. "A Mord-Sith is a product of torture. She would say only enough to make you believe she was cooperating. She would feed you a clever lie to deceive you. She would die before speaking any words to harm her Lord Rahl."

With one long finger, Nicci pulled a sodden strand of blond hair off her cheek. "You underestimate me, Richard. That woman was very brave. I felt great sorrow for her, but there were things I wanted to know. She told it all. She told me everything I wanted to know."

Nicci could see the rage rising in him, bringing a flush to his cheeks. That was not what she had intended, or wanted. She was telling him the truth, but he rejected it, trying to overlay it instead with his own false assumptions.

A moment passed, and that truth finally found its way into his eyes. The rage departed reluctantly, replaced by the weight of sadness that made him swallow at his grief for this woman. Nicci had expected no less from him.

"Apparently," Nicci whispered, "Denna was very talented at torture—"

"I neither need nor want your sympathy."

"But I did feel sympathy, Richard, for what that woman put you through for no purpose but to give pain. That's the worst kind of pain, isn't it?—pain to no benefit, no confession? The pointlessness of it only adds to its torture. That was what you suffered."

Nicci gestured to the red leather weapon in his fist. "This woman did not suffer that kind of pain. I want you to know that."

He pressed his lips tight in mistrust as he looked away from her eyes, gazing out at the gathering darkness.

"You killed her, this Mord-Sith named Denna, but not before she did unspeakable things to you."

"So I did." Richard's expression hardened with the implied menace of his words.

"You threatened the Sisters of the Light because they, too, collared you. You told them they were not good enough to lick the boots of that woman, Denna, and so they were not. You told the Sisters that they thought they held the leash to your collar, but you promised them that they would find that what they held was a bolt of lightning. Don't think for one moment that I don't understand your feelings in this, or your resolve."

Nicci reached out and tapped the center of his chest.

"But this time, Richard, the collar is around your heart and it is Kahlan who will be forfeit, should you make a mistake."

His fists, at the ends of his rigid arms, tightened. "Kahlan would rather die than have me be a slave at her expense. She begged me to forfeit her life for my freedom. A day may dawn when it becomes necessary for me to honor her request."

Nicci felt a weary boredom at his threats. People so often resorted to threatening her.

"That is entirely up to you, Richard. But you make a great mistake if you think I care."

She couldn't begin to recall how many times Jagang had made solemn threats on her life, or how many of those times his hands had tightened around her throat choking the life out of her after he had beaten her senseless. Kadar Kardeef had at times been no less brutal. She'd lost count of the times she fully expected to die, starting with the time when she was little and the man pulled her into the alley to rob her.

But such men were not the only ones who promised her suffering.

"I cannot tell you the promises the Keeper of the underworld has made to me in my dreams, promises of unending suffering. That is my fate.

"So, please, Richard, do not think to frighten me with your petty threats. More savage men than you have made credible promises as to my doom. I long ago accepted my fate and ceased to care."

Her arms felt heavy at her sides. She felt empty of feeling. Thoughts of Jagang, of the Keeper, reminded her that her life was meaningless. Only what she had seen in Richard's eyes gave her a hint that there might be something more, something she had yet to discover or understand.

"What is it you want?" Richard demanded.

Nicci returned her mind to the here and now. "I told you. Your part in life now is as my husband. That is the way it is going to be—if you wish Kahlan to live. I've told you the truth about all of it. If you come with me and do the simple things I ask, such as assuming the role of my husband, then Kahlan will live a long life. I can't say it will be entirely happy, of course, for I know she loves you."

"How long do you think you can hold me, Nicci?" In frustration, Richard ran his fingers back through his wet hair. "It isn't going to work, whatever it is you want. How long until you tire of this absurd sham?"

Her eyes narrowed, studying his profound innocence, if not ignorance.

"My dear boy, I was born into this wretched world one hundred and eighty-one years past. You know that. Do you suppose I have not learned a great deal of patience, in all that time? Though our bodies may look about the same age, and in many ways I am no older than you, I have lived near to seven of your lifetimes. Do you honestly believe that you would have patience to exceed mine? Do you think me some young foolish girl for you to outwit or outwait?"

His demeanor cooled. "Nicci, I—"

"And don't think to make friends with me, or win me over. I am not Denna, or Verna, or Warren, or even Pasha, for that matter. I'm not interested in friends."

He turned a little and ran a hand over the stallion's shoulder when the horse snorted and stamped a hoof at the smell of the woodsmoke curling out from the upper limbs of the shelter tree.

"I want to know what vile thing you did to that poor woman to make her tell you about Denna."

"The Mord-Sith told me in return for a favor."

Frowning his incredulity, he turned to her once more. "What favor could you possibly do for a Mord-Sith?"

"I cut her throat."

Richard closed his eyes as his head sank with grief for this unknown woman who had died because of him. He clenched her weapon in his fist to his heart.

His voice lost its fire. "I don't suppose you know her name?"

It was this, his empathy for others, even others he didn't know, that not only made him the man he was, but shackled him. His concern for others would also be the thing that eventually brought him to understand the virtue in what she was doing. He, too, would then willingly work for the righteous cause of the Order.

"I do," Nicci said. "Hania."

"Hania." He looked heartsick. "I didn't even know her."

"Richard." With a finger under his chin, Nicci gently brought his face up. "I want you to know that I did not torture her. I found her being tortured. I was not happy about what I saw. I killed the man who did it. Hania was beyond any help. I offered her release from her pain, a quick end, if she would tell me about you. I never asked her to betray you in any way that the Order would want. I asked only about your past, about your first captivity. I wanted to understand what you said that first day at the Palace of the Prophets, that's all."

Richard didn't look relieved, as she had intended.

"You withheld that quick release, as you call it, until she had given you what you wanted. That makes you a party to her torture."

In the gloom, Nicci looked away in pain and anguish at the memory of that bloody deed. It had long since lost its ability to make her feel anything more than a ghost of emotions.

There were so many needing release from their suffering—so many old and sick, so many wailing children, so many destitute and hopeless and poor. This woman had merely been another of life's victims needing release. It was for the best.

Nicci had renounced the Creator in order to do His work, and sworn her soul to the Keeper of the underworld. She had to; only one as evil as she would fail to feel any fitting feelings, any proper compassion, for all the suffering and desperate need. It was grim irony—faithfully serving the needy in such a way.

"Perhaps you see it that way, Richard," Nicci said in a hoarse voice as she stared into the numb nightmare of memories. "I did not. Neither did Hania. Before I cut her throat for her, she thanked me for what I was about to do."

Richard's eyes offered no mercy. "And why did you make her tell you about me—about Denna?"

Nicci snugged her cloak tighter on her shoulders. "Isn't it obvious?"

"You couldn't possibly make the same mistake Denna made. You aren't the woman she was, Nicci."

She was tired. The first night, he had not slept, she knew. She had felt his eyes on her back. She knew how much he hurt. Turned away from him, she had wept silently at the hate his eyes held, at the burden of being the one to have to do what was best. The world was such an evil place.

"Perhaps, Richard," she said in a soft voice, "you will someday teach me the difference."

She was so very tired. The night before, when he had succumbed to his weariness, and turned away from her to sleep, Nicci had in turn stayed awake all night, watching him in his sound sleep as she felt the connection of magic to the Mother Confessor. The connection brought Nicci great empathy for her, as well.

It was all for the best.

"For now," Nicci said, "let's get inside out of this foul weather. I'm cold and I'm hungry. We need to get some rest, too. And as I've told you, we have things to discuss, first."

She couldn't lie to him, she knew. She couldn't tell him everything, of course, but she dared not lie to him in the things she did tell him.

The dance had begun.

Richard broke up the sausage Nicci gave him from her saddlebag and tossed it in the pot with the simmering rice. The things she had told him kept shouting in his mind as he tried to fit them into their proper order.

He didn't know how much of what she had said he dared to believe. He feared it was all true. Nicci just didn't seem to need to lie to him—at least not about what she had told him so far. She didn't seem as . . . hostile, as he thought she would have to be. If anything, she seemed melancholy, perhaps because of what she had done—although, he had trouble believing that a confessed Sister of the Dark would suffer a guilty conscience. It was probably just some bizarre part of her act, some artifice directed toward her ends.

He stirred the pot of rice with a stick he'd peeled the bark off of. "You said there were things to discuss." He rapped the stick clean on the edge of the pot. "I assume that means there are orders you wish to issue."

Nicci blinked, as if he'd caught her thinking about something else. She looked out of place, sitting prim and straight in a wayward pine, dressed as she was in her fine black dress. Richard would never before have ever thought of Nicci out-of-doors, much less sitting on the ground. The very idea had always seemed ludicrous to him. Her dress constantly made him think of Kahlan, not only because of it being so completely opposite that it evoked the comparison, but also because he so vividly recalled Nicci connected to Kahlan by that awful rope of magic.

That memory twisted him in agony.

"Orders?" Nicci folded her hands in her lap and met his gaze. "Oh, yes, I have a few requests I wish you to honor. First, you may not use your gift. Not at all. Not in any way. Is that clear? Since, as I recall, you have no love of the gift, this should be neither a burden nor a difficult request for you to follow, especially because there is something you do love which would not survive such a betrayal. Do you understand?"

Her cold blue eyes conveyed the threat perhaps even better than her words. Richard gave her a single nod, committing himself to what, exactly, he wasn't entirely sure at the moment.

He poured her steaming dinner in a shallow wooden bowl and handed it to her along with a spoon. Nicci smiled her thanks. He set the pot on the ground between his legs and took a spoonful of rice, blowing on it until it was cool enough to eat. He watched her from the corner of his eye as she took a dainty taste.

Beyond her physical perfection, Nicci had a singularly expressive face. She seemed to go cold and blank when she was unhappy, or when she meant to convey anger, threat, or displeasure. She didn't really scowl the way other people did when they felt those emotions; rather, a look of cool detachment descended on her. That look was, in its own way, far more disturbing. It was her impenetrable armor.

On the other hand, she was expressively animated when she was pleased or thankful. Even more than that, though, such pleasure or gratitude appeared genuine. He remembered her as aloof, and while she still possessed a noble bearing, to some extent her air of reticence had lifted to reveal an innocent delight in any kindness, or even simple courtesy.

Richard still had bread Cara had baked for him. He hated sharing that bread with this evil woman, but it now seemed a childish consideration. He tore off a piece and offered it to Nicci. She took it with the reverence due something greater than mere bread.

"I also expect you to keep no secrets from me," she said after another bite. "You would not like me to discover you were doing so. Husbands and wives have no need for secrets."

Richard supposed not, but they were hardly husband and wife. Rather than say so, he said instead, "You seem to know a lot about how husbands and wives behave."

Rather than rising to his bait, she gestured with her bread at her bowl. "This is very good, Richard. Very good indeed."

"What is it you want, Nicci? What is the purpose of this absurd pretense?"

The firelight played across her alabaster face, and lent her hair a torrid color it didn't in reality possess. "I took you because I need an answer which I believe you will provide."

Richard broke a stout branch in two across his knee. "You said husbands and wives have no need for secrets." He used half the branch to push the burning wood together before placing the branch atop the fire. "Then aren't wives, too, supposed to be honest?"

"Of course." Her hand with the bread lowered. She rested her wrist over her knee. "I will be honest with you, too, Richard."

"Then what's the question? You said you took me because you need an answer you think I can provide. What's the question?"

Nicci stared off again, once more looking anything but the grim captor. She looked as if memories, or perhaps fears, haunted her. It was somehow more unsettling than the sneer of an armed guard outside of the bars of his cage.

The rain outside had increased to a dull roar. They'd made camp just in time. Richard couldn't help but remember the cozy times he'd had in wayward pines huddled beside Kahlan. At the thought of Kahlan, his heart sank.

"I don't know," Nicci finally said. "I honestly don't, Richard. I seek something, but I will only know it when I find it. After nearly all my one hundred and eighty-one years without knowing it existed, I finally saw the first hint of it not long ago. . . ." She seemed to be looking through him again, to some point beyond. Her voice, too, seemed to be addressed to that distant place her vision beheld. "That was when you stood in a collar before all those Sisters, and defied them. Perhaps I will find the answer when I understand what it was I saw that day, in that room. It was not just you, but you were its center. . . ."

Her eyes focused once more on his face. She spoke with gentle assurance. "Until then, you will live. I have no intention of harming you. You need fear no torture from me. I'm not like them—that woman, Denna, or like the Sisters of the Light, using you for their games."

"Don't patronize me. You are using me for your own game, no less than they used me for theirs."

She shook her head. "I want you to know, Richard, that I have nothing but respect for you. I probably have more respect for you than any person you have ever met. That's why I took you. You are a rare person, Richard."

"I'm a war wizard. You've just never seen one of those before."

She spurned the notion with a dismissive flick of her hand. "Please don't try to impress me with your 'power.' I'm not in the mood for such silliness."

Richard knew it was no idle boast on her part. She was a sorceress of remarkable ability. He doubted he had any hope of outsmarting her knowledge of magic.

She was not acting the way he had expected a Sister of the Dark would act, though. Richard put his anger, hurt, and heartache aside for the moment, knowing he had to face what was, rather than putting his hope in wishes, and spoke to Nicci in the same gentle fashion she used with him.

"I don't understand what it is you want of me, Nicci."

She shrugged in an involuntary gesture of frustration. "Neither do I. Until I do, you will do as I ask and everything will be fine. I will not harm you."

"Considering the circumstances, do you really expect me to take your word?"

"I'm telling you the truth, Richard. If you were to twist your ankle, I would, like a good wife, put my shoulder under your arm and help you to walk. From now on, I am devoted to you, and you to me."

He could only blink at how crazy this was. He almost thought she might be mad. Almost. He knew that would be too easy an answer. As Zedd always said, nothing was ever easy.

"And if I choose not to go along with your wishes?"

Again, she shrugged. "Then Kahlan dies."

"I understand that, but if she dies, then you lose the collar around my heart."

She fixed him with cold blue eyes. "Your point?"

"Then you couldn't get what you wanted from me. You would have no leverage."

"I don't have what I want now, so I would be losing nothing. Besides, if you were to do that, then Emperor Jagang would welcome your head as a gift. I would no doubt be showered with gifts and riches."

Richard didn't think Nicci wanted gifts or riches showered on her. She was a Sister of the Dark, after all, and he supposed she could manage to be so showered if she really wished it.

Even so, he was sure his head would have a price, and she could salvage that much out of it if he proved ungovernable. She might not care for gifts and riches, but if there was one thing she did want, it had to be power. He was pretty sure she could gain a good measure of that, should she slay the enemy of the Imperial Order.

He bent over the pot between his legs and went back to his dinner, and his dark thoughts. Talking to her was useless. They just went around in circles.

"Richard," she said in a quiet tone, drawing his eyes to her gaze, "you think I'm doing this to hurt you, or to defeat you because you are the enemy of the Order. I am not. I told you my true reasons."

"So, when you finally find this answer you seek, in return for my 'help,' then you will let me go?" It was not really meant as a question, but as trenchant incrimination.

"Go?" She stared down into her bowl of rice and sausage, stirring it around as if it might reveal a secret. She looked up. "No, Richard, then I will kill you."

"I see." He hardly thought that was a way to encourage his cooperation in her search, but he didn't say so. "And Kahlan? After you kill me, I mean."

"You have my word that if I decide I must kill you, as long as I live, she will, too. I have no ill will toward her."

He tried to find solace in that much of it. For some reason, he believed Nicci. Knowing that Kahlan would be all right gave him courage. He could endure what was to happen to him, if only she would be all right. It was a price he was willing to pay.

"So, 'wife,' where are we going? Where is it you're taking me?"

Nicci didn't look at him but instead used her bread to sop up some of her dinner. She considered his question as she nibbled.

"Who are you fighting, Richard? Who is your enemy?" She took another small bite of her bread.

"Jagang. Jagang and his Imperial Order."

Like an instructor correcting him, Nicci slowly shook her head. "No. You are wrong. I think perhaps you are in need of answers, too."

Games. She was playing foolish games with him. Richard ground his teeth, but held his temper in check.

"Then who, Nicci? Who, or what, am I fighting if it is not Jagang."

"That is what I hope to show you." She watched his eyes in a way he found unsettling. "I am going to take you to the Old World, to the heart of the Order, to show you what you are fighting—the true nature of what you believe to be your enemy."

Richard frowned. "Why?"

Nicci smiled. "Let's just say it amuses me."

"You mean we're going back to Tanimura? Back to where you lived all that time as a Sister?"

"No. We are going to the heart and soul of the Old World: Altur'Rang. Jagang's homeland. The name means, roughly, 'the Creator's chosen.' "

Richard felt a chill run up his spine. "You expect to take me, Richard Rahl, there, into the heart of enemy territory? I hardly doubt we will be living as 'husband and wife' for long."

"Besides not using your magic, you will not use the name associated with that magic—Rahl—but instead the name you grew up with: Richard Cypher. Without your magic, or your name, no one will know you are anyone but a humble man with his wife. That is exactly what you shall be—what we both shall be."

Richard sighed. "Well, if the enemy should find I'm more, I guess a Sister of the Dark can . . . exert her influence."

"No, I can't."

Richard's eyes turned up. "What do you mean?"

"I can't use my power."

Gooseflesh prickled his arms. "What?"

"It's devoted to the link with Kahlan, to keeping her alive. That is how a maternity spell works. It requires a prodigious amount of power to even establish such a complex spell, much less maintain it. My power must be invested into the labor of preserving the living link. A maternity spell leaves nothing to spare; I doubt I could make a spark.

"If we have any trouble, you will have to handle it. Of course, I can at any time call upon my ability as a sorceress, but to do so I would have to draw the power from our link. If I do that without her near . . . Kahlan dies."

Alarm raced through him. "But what if you accidentally—"

"I won't. As long as you take good care of me, Kahlan will be safe enough. If, however, I should fall off my horse and break my neck, her neck snaps, too. As long as you take good care of me, you are taking good care of her. This is why it's important that we live as husband and wife—so that you can be close at hand, and so that I can guide and help you, too. It will be a difficult life with both of us living without our power, just as any other married couple, but I believe this to be necessary if I am to find what I seek from you. Do you understand?"

He wasn't sure he really did, but he said "Yes," anyway.

Numb dismay swamped him. He would never have believed this woman would have willingly given up her power for some unspecified knowledge. The very idea of it unleashed cold panic through his veins.

Richard couldn't make sense of it. With his mind groping blindly in a world gone insane, he spoke without even considering his words.

"I'm already married. I'll not sleep with you as your husband."

Nicci blinked in surprise, then let out a dainty titter, covering it with the back of her hand, not in shyness, but at his presumption. Richard felt his ears heating.

"That is not the way in which I want you, Richard."

Richard cleared his throat. "Good."

In the quiet of the wayward pine, with the rain outside falling in a gentle patter and the glowing checkered wood hissing softly, Nicci's focused, intense, resolute expression turned very cold and very still.

"But if I should decide I do, Richard, you will comply with that, too."

Nicci was a beautiful woman, the kind of woman most any man would eagerly accept. It was hardly that, though, that made him believe her. It was the look in her eyes. Never had the vague possibility of the act of sex seemed so vicious.

Her voice lost the conversational quality. It went on in a lifeless drone, a thing not human, pronouncing a sentence on his life. A sentence he himself would enforce, or Kahlan would die.

"You will act as my husband. You will provide for us as any husband would. You will care for me, and I for you, in the sense of worldly needs. I will mend your shirts and cook your meals and wash your clothes. You will provide us with a living."

Nicci's leaden words slammed into him with the deliberate methodical force of a beating delivered with an iron bar.

"You will never see Kahlan again—you must understand that—but as long as you do as I wish, you will know she lives. In that way you will be able to show your love for her. Every day she wakes, she will know you are keeping her alive. You have no other way to show her your love."

He felt sick to his stomach. He stared off into memories of another place and time.

"And if I choose to end it?" The weight of such madness was so crushing that he earnestly considered it. "Rather than be your slave?"

"Then perhaps that is the form the knowledge I seek will take. Maybe that senseless end will be what I must learn." She brought her first and second fingers together in a snipping motion, simulating the cutting of the umbilical cord of magic that sustained Kahlan's life. "One last evil convulsion to finally confirm the senselessness of existence."

It dawned on Richard that this woman could not be threatened, because she was a creature who, he was beginning to understand, welcomed any terrible outcome.

"Of all there is to me in this world," he whispered in dim agony, more to himself and to Kahlan than to his implacable captor, "there is only one thing that is irreplaceable: Kahlan. If I must be a slave in order for Kahlan to live, then I shall be a slave."

Richard realized Nicci was silently studying his face. He met her gaze briefly, then looked away, unable to bear the terrible scrutiny of her beautiful blue eyes while he held the image of Kahlan's love in his mind.

"Whatever you shared with her, whatever happiness, joy, or pleasure, will always be yours, Richard." Nicci seemed almost to be peering inside him, reading the pages of his past written in his mind. "Treasure those memories. They will have to sustain you. You will never see her again, nor she you. That chapter of your life is ended. You both have new lives, now. You may as well get used to it because that is the reality of the situation."

The reality of what was. Not the world as he would wish it. He himself had told Kahlan that they must act according to the reality of what was, and not waste their precious lives wishing for things that could not be.

Richard ran his fingertips across his forehead as he tried to hold his voice steady. "I hope you don't expect me to learn to be pleased with you."

"I am the one, Richard, who expects to learn."

Fists at his side, Richard shot to his feet. "And what is it you wish this knowledge for?" he demanded in unrestrained, violent bitterness. "Why is it so important to you!"

"As punishment."

Richard stared in stunned disbelief. "What?"

"I wish to hurt, Richard." She smiled distantly.

Richard sank back to the ground.

"Why?" he whispered.

Nicci folded her hands in her lap. "Pain, Richard, is all that can reach that cold dead thing within me that is my life. Pain is the only thing for which I live."

He stared numbly at her. He thought about his vision. There was nothing he could do to fight the advance of the Imperial Order. He could think of nothing he could do to fight his fate with this woman.

If not for Kahlan, he would, at that moment, have thrown himself into a battle with Nicci that would have decided it once and for all. He would have willingly gone to his death fighting this cruel insanity. Except his reason denied him that.

He had to live so that Kahlan would live. For that, and that alone, he had to put one foot in front of the other and march into oblivion.

Kahlan yawned as she rubbed her eyes. Squinting, she arched her back and stretched her sore muscles. The terrible desperate memories swooped in from the sleep-darkened corners of her mind, leaving little chance for any other thoughts to long survive.

She was beyond the realm of merciless anguish and crying; she had entered the sovereign dominion of unbridled anger.

Her fingers found the cold steel scabbard of his sword lying at her side. It felt alive with icy rage. That, the carving of *Spirit*, and her memories were about all she had of him.

There wasn't a lot of firewood, but since they wouldn't be needing much more anyway, Kahlan put another stick of what was left into the fire. She squatted, holding her hands close over the top of the feeble flames, hoping to bring feeling to her numb fingers. The wind shifted a little. Pungent smoke billowed up into her face, making her cough. The smoke rolled past her face and followed the rock overhang up and out from their shelter.

Cara was gone, so Kahlan pushed the little pot of water back onto the fire to warm it for tea for when the Mord-Sith returned. Cara was probably visiting their makeshift privy. Or maybe she was checking the traps they'd set the night before for rabbits. Kahlan didn't hold out any real hope that they would catch a rabbit for their breakfast. Not in this weather. They had brought enough provisions, in any event.

Through slits in the clouds, the crimson light of a cold crisp dawn penetrated gaps in the snow-crusted limbs of trees to slant in under the rock overhang, casting everything in their little campsite in a blush glow. The two of them had tried without avail to find a wayward pine. The screen of trees, along with a short wall of boughs she and Cara had cut and placed the night before to protect them from the wind, as Richard had taught them to do, shielded the secluded spot. With their improvements it had proven a fit shelter. They had been lucky to find it in the driving snow. Outside, the snow was fairly deep, but in the shelter they had had a relatively dry, if cold, night. Kahlan and Cara had huddled together under blankets and their thick wolf fur mantles to keep each other warm.

Kahlan wondered where Richard was, and if he was cold, too. She hoped not. Probably, since he had started out a few days sooner, he had been lucky and had made it down to the lowlands already, avoiding the snow.

Cara and Kahlan had stayed in their home, as he had asked, for three days. Snow had arrived the morning after he'd left. Kahlan had been tempted to wait for a break in the weather before they started out, but she had learned a bitter lesson from Sister

Nicci: don't wait, act. When Richard didn't return, Kahlan and Cara had immediately struck out.

It was hard going at first. They struggled through the drifts, leading the horses at times, riding them occasionally. They couldn't see very far, and most of the time had to keep the wind from the west at their right shoulder as their only clue as to which direction they faced. It was dangerous traveling over the passes in such conditions. For a time, they feared that they had made a terrible mistake leaving the safety of their house.

Through a break in the clouds just before dark the night before, as they were gathering boughs for their shelter, they'd caught a glimpse of the lower hills; they were green and brown, not white. They would be below the snow line before long. Kahlan was confident that they were through the worst of it.

As she stuffed an arm into a sleeve, pulling another shirt on over the top of the two she was wearing, Kahlan heard the crunch of snow underfoot. When she realized it was more than one pair of footsteps, she stood up in a rush.

Cara pushed her way through the boughs of the sheltering trees. "We have company," she announced in a grim voice. Kahlan saw that Cara's fist held her Agiel.

A bundled up squat woman came through the trees, following in Cara's footsteps. Under layers of cloaks, scarves, and other dangling corners of thick cloth, Kahlan was surprised to recognize Ann, the old Prelate of the Sisters of the Light.

Behind Ann came a taller woman, her scarves pushed back to reveal graying brown hair loose to her shoulders. She had an intense, steady, calculating gaze that had earned her an enduring network of fine wrinkles radiating out from the corners of her deep-set eyes. Her brow was less steady, twitching down several times toward her prominent nose. She looked like a woman who used a switch to teach children.

"Kahlan!" Ann rushed forward, seizing Kahlan's arms. "Oh, my dear, it's so good to see you!" She looked back when Kahlan glanced up behind her. "This is one of my Sisters, Alessandra. Alessandra, may I introduce the Mother Confessor—and Richard's wife."

The woman stepped forward and smiled. The pleasant grin completely altered her face, instantly erasing the severity of it with open good nature. It was a somewhat disorienting transformation, making her seem like two different people sharing one face. Or, Kahlan thought, perhaps one person with two faces.

"Mother Confessor, it's so good to meet you. Ann has told me all about you, and what a wonderful person you are." Her eyes took in the campsite with a quick glance. "I'm so happy for you and Richard."

Ann's eyes turned left and right, searching. Her gaze snagged on the sword.

"Where's Richard? Cara wouldn't say a word." She looked up into Kahlan's eyes. "Dear Creator," she whispered. "What's wrong? What's happened? Where's Richard?"

Kahlan finally managed to unclench her teeth. "One of your Sisters took him."

Ann pushed her scarves back off her gray hair and took ahold of Kahlan's arm again. The top of Ann's head came up only to Kahlan's chest, but she looked at least twice as wide.

"What are you talking about? What do you mean, a Sister took him? Which Sister?"

"Nicci," Kahlan growled.

Ann pulled back. "Nicci . . ."

Sister Alessandra gasped. "Sister Nicci?" She crossed both hands over her heart. "Sister Nicci isn't one of Ann's. Nicci is a Sister of the Dark."

"Oh, I'm well aware of that," Kahlan said.

"We have to go get him back," Ann said. "At once. He's not safe with her."

"There's no telling what Nicci might—" Sister Alessandra's mouth snapped shut.

The wind carried a sparkling gust into their faces, momentarily whiting out the red dawn. Kahlan blinked the snow away. Cara, in her red leather with both a cloak and her heavy fur mantle over top, ignored it. The other two women brushed their heavy woolen mittens across their eyes.

"Kahlan, everything will be all right," Ann said in a reassuring voice. "Tell us, now, what's happened? Tell us everything. Is he hurt?"

Kahlan swallowed against her rising rage. "Nicci used what she called a maternity spell on me."

Ann's mouth fell open. Sister Alessandra gasped again.

"Are you sure?" Ann asked in a careful tone. "Are you sure that was what it was? How do you know for sure?"

"She slammed some kind of magic into me. I've never heard of such a spell. All I know is that it was definitely powerful magic and she said it was called a maternity spell. She said that it connects us, somehow, through that magic."

Alessandra took a step forward. "That doesn't make it a maternity spell."

"When Cara used her Agiel on Nicci," Kahlan said, "it dropped me to my knees just the same as if Cara had used the Agiel on me."

Ann and Alessandra shared a silent look.

"But . . . but, if she were to . . ." Ann stammered.

Kahlan voiced what Ann was trying to say without saying it. "If she were to desire it, Nicci could snip that cord of magic, and I would die. That was the means by which she captured Richard. She promised I would live if Richard went with her. Richard surrendered himself into slavery to save my life."

"It can't be," Ann said, touching mitten-covered fingers to her chin. "Nicci wouldn't know how to use such an unusual spell—she's too young. Besides, such a rare spell requires great power. She must have done something else and just said that it was a maternity spell. Nicci couldn't do a maternity spell."

"Yes, she could," Sister Alessandra said in reluctant disagreement. "She has the power and ability. It would only have required someone with the specialized knowledge teaching her. Nicci doesn't have any great passion for magic, but she is as able as they come."

"Lidmila . . ." Ann whispered to Alessandra in sudden realization. "Jagang has Lidmila."

Kahlan turned a suspicious glare on Sister Alessandra. "And how do you know so much more about Nicci's ability than the Prelate herself?"

Sister Alessandra gathered her open cloak back together. Her face lost its warmth and reverted to a scowl—this time, though, with bitterness in the set of her mouth.

"I brought Nicci in to the Palace of the Prophets when she was but a child. I was responsible for her upbringing, and I guided her training in the use of her gift; I know her better than anyone. I know her darker powers because I, too, was a Sister of the Dark. I'm the one who brought her to the Keeper."

Kahlan could feel herself rocking with the force of her hammering heart. "So, you, too, are a Sister of the Dark."

"Was," Ann said, lifting a cautionary hand before Kahlan.

"The Prelate came into Jagang's camp and rescued me. Not just from Jagang, but from the Keeper, too. I once again serve the Light." The incandescent smile again transformed Alessandra's face. "Ann brought me back to the Creator."

As far as Kahlan was concerned, the claim was not worth the effort of confirmation. "How did you find us?"

Ann ignored the terse question. "We must hurry. We must get Richard away from Nicci before she delivers him to Jagang."

Kahlan kept her glare on Alessandra while she answered Ann. "She isn't taking him to Jagang. She said she isn't acting on behalf of His Excellency, but on behalf of herself. Those were her words. She said she had removed Jagang's ring from her lip and that she wasn't afraid of him."

"Did she say why, then, she was taking Richard?" Ann asked. "Or, at least, where?"

Kahlan moved her scrutiny back to Ann. "She said she was taking him into oblivion."

"Oblivion!" Ann gasped.

"I asked you a question," Kahlan said, anger seeping into her voice. "How did you find us?"

Ann tapped her waist. "I have a journey book. I used it to communicate with Verna, back with our forces. Verna told me about the messengers coming to see you. That's how I knew where to find you. Lucky I came as soon as I did; we nearly missed you. I can't tell you how happy I am to see you have recovered, Kahlan. We were so worried."

Kahlan saw that Cara, standing behind the two women, still had her Agiel clenched in her fist. Kahlan didn't need an Agiel; her Confessor's power boiled but an impulse away. She wouldn't again make an error for the sake of caution.

"The journey book. Of course. Then Verna would have told you about Richard's vision that he must not lead our troops against the Order."

Ann nodded reluctantly, apparently not eager to discuss such a vision. "Then, a few days ago, Verna sent a message when we were almost here, that the D'Harans are in quite a state because they suddenly lost their sense of direction to Richard. She said they are still protected from the dream walker by the bond to their Lord Rahl, but they suddenly lost their sense of where he is."

"Nicci cloaked his bond from us," Cara said in a growl.

"Well, we have to find him," Ann said. "We have to get him away from Nicci. He's our only chance. Whatever he's thinking, it's nonsense and we will have to set him straight, but first we must get him back. He has to lead our forces against the Imperial Order. He is the one named in prophecy."

"That's why you're here," Kahlan whispered to herself. "You heard from Verna about his declining to lead the army or even to give orders. You journeyed here in hopes of forcing him to fight."

"He must," Ann insisted.

"He must not," Kahlan said. "He has come to realize that if he leads us into battle, we will lose the cause of liberty for generations to come. He said he came to realize that people don't yet understand freedom and won't fight for it."

"He must simply prove himself to the people." Ann's scowl reddened. "He must prove himself their leader, which he has already begun to do, and they will follow him."

"Richard says that he has come to understand that it is not he who must prove himself to the people, but the people who must now prove themselves to him."

Ann blinked in astonishment. "Why, that's nonsense."

"Is it?"

"Of course it is. The boy was named in prophecy centuries ago. I've been waiting hundreds of years for him to be born in order for him to lead us in this struggle."

"Really. Then who are you to try to countermand Richard's decision—if you are so set on following him? He has come to his decision. If he is the leader you want, then you must abide by his lead, and therefore his decision."

"But this is not what prophecy demands!"

"Richard doesn't believe in prophecy. He believes we make our own destiny. I'm coming to see the grounds of his assertion that the belief in prophecy artificially alters events. It is the misplaced faith in prophecy itself—in some mystical outcome—that harms people's lives."

Ann's eyes grew round with dismay, and then narrowed. "Richard is the one named in prophecy to lead us against the Imperial Order. This is a struggle for the very existence of magic in this world—don't you understand that! Richard was born to fight this fight. We have to get him back!"

"This is all your fault," Kahlan whispered.

"What?" Ann's frown changed to a tolerant smile. "Kahlan, what are you talking about?" Her voice backslid to genial. "You know me, you know our struggle for the survival of freedom of magic. If Richard does not lead us, we have no chance."

Kahlan threw her arm out and seized a startled Sister Alessandra by the throat. The woman's eyes went wide.

"Don't move," Kahlan said through gritted teeth, "or I will unleash my Confessor's power."

Ann held her hands up, imploring. "Kahlan, have you lost your mind? Let her be. Calm down."

With her other hand, Kahlan pointed down at the fire. "The journey book. Throw it in the fire."

"What? I'm not going to do any such thing!"

"Now," Kahlan said through her clenched teeth. "Or Sister Alessandra will be mine. When I finish with her, Cara will see to it you throw that journey book in the fire, if you have to do so with broken fingers."

Ann glanced at the Mord-Sith towering over her shoulder.

"Kahlan, I know you're upset, and I completely understand, but we're on the same side in this. We love Richard, too. We, too, wish to stop the Imperial Order from taking the whole world. We—"

"We? If it wasn't for you and your Sisters, none of this would be happening. This is all your fault. Not Jagang's fault, not the Imperial Order's fault, but yours."

"Have you lost your—"

"You alone bear responsibility for what is befalling the world. Just as Jagang has his ring through the lip of his slaves, you've had yours through the nose of yours—Richard! You alone bear responsibility for the lives already lost, and those yet to be lost in bloody slaughters that will sweep across the land. You, not Jagang, are the one who has brought it!"

Despite the cold, beads of sweat dotted Ann's brow. "What in the name of Creation are you talking about? Kahlan, you know me. I was at your wedding. I have always been on your side. I have only followed the prophecies to help people."

"You create the prophecies! Without your help they would not have come to pass! They only come about because you have fulfilled them! You pull the ring through Richard's nose!"

Ann presented a face of calm to the storm of Kahlan's rage.

"Kahlan, I can only imagine how you must feel, but now you are truly losing all sense of reason."

"Am I? Am I, Prelate? Why does Sister Nicci have my husband? Answer me. Why!"

Ann's expression drew tight in a darkening glower. "Because she is evil."

"No." Kahlan's grip tightened on Alessandra's throat. "It's because of you. Had you not sent Verna into the New World in the first place, ordering her to take Richard back across the barrier into the Old World—"

"But the prophecies say the Order will rise up to take the world and extinguish magic if we fail to stop them! The prophecies say Richard is the only one to lead us! That Richard is the only one with a chance!"

"And you brought that dead prophecy to life. All by yourself. All because of your faith in bloodless words rather than your own reasoned choices. You're here today not to back the choices of your proclaimed leader, not to reason with him, but to enforce prophecy upon him—to give that ring a tug. Had you not sent Verna to recover Richard, what would have happened, Prelate?"

"Why, why, the Order—"

"The Order? The Order would still be trapped back in the Old World, behind the barrier. Wouldn't they! For three thousand years that wizard-created barrier has stood invincible against the pressure of the Order—or those like them—and their wish to swarm up here into the New World, bent on conquest.

"Because you had Richard captured, against his will, and ordered him brought back to the Old World, all in slavish homage to dead words in dusty old books, he was forced to destroy the barrier, and thus the Order now can flood into the New World, into the Midlands, my Midlands, slaughtering my people, taking my husband, all because of you and your meddling!

"Without you, none of this would be happening! No war, no mounds of butchered people in cities of the New World, no thousands of dead men, women, and children slaughtered at the hands of Imperial Order thugs—none of it!

"Because of you and your precious prophecies, the veil was breached and a plague was unleashed on the world. It would never have happened without your actions to 'save' us all from prophecy. I don't even dare to recall all the children I saw suffering and dying from the black death because of you. Children who looked up into my eyes and asked if they would be all right, and I had to say yes when I knew they would not survive the night.

"No one will ever know the tally of the dead. No one is left to remember all the small places wiped out of existence by that plague. Without your meddling, those children would be alive, their mothers would be smiling to themselves as they watched them play, their fathers would be teaching them the ways of the world—a world denied them by you for the sake of your faith in prophecy!

"You say this is a battle for the very existence of magic in this world—yet your work to fulfill prophecy may have already doomed magic. Without your intervention, the chimes would never have come to be loosed upon the world. Yes, Richard managed to banish them, but what irreversible harm was done? We may have our power back, but during the time the chimes withdrew magic from this world, crea-

215

tures of magic, things dependent on magic for their very existence, surely died out. Magic requires balance to exist. The balance of magic in this world was disturbed. The irrevocable destruction of magic may have already begun. All because of your slavish service to prophecy.

"If not for you, Prelate, Jagang, the Imperial Order's army, and all your Sisters would be back there, behind the barrier, and we would be here, safe and at peace. You cast blame everywhere but where it belongs. If freedom, if magic, if the world itself is destroyed, it will all be by your hand, Prelate."

The low moan of the wind was the only sound and made the sudden silence all that much more agonizing. Ann stared with tear-filled eyes up at Kahlan. Snow sparkled in the rays of a cold dawn.

"It isn't like that, Kahlan. It only seems that way to you in your pain."

"It is that way," Kahlan said with finality.

Ann's mouth worked, but this time no words came out.

Kahlan thrust out her hand, palm up.

"The journey book. If you think I would not destroy this woman's life, then you don't know the first thing about me. She's one of your Sisters, helping to destroy the world in the name of good, or else she is still one of the Keeper's Sisters, helping to destroy the world in the name of death. Either way, if you don't give me the journey book, and right now, her life is forfeit."

"What do you think this will accomplish?" Ann whispered in despair.

"It will be a start at halting your meddling in the lives of the people of the Midlands, and the rest of the New World—in my life, in Richard's life. It's the only beginning I can think to make, short of killing you both; you would not like to know how close I am to that alternative. Now, give me the journey book."

Ann stared down at Kahlan's hand open before her. She blinked at her tears. Finally, she pulled off a woolen mitten and worked the little book out from behind her belt. She paused a moment, reverently gazing at it, but in the end laid it on Kahlan's palm.

"Dear Creator," Ann whispered, "forgive this poor hurting child of yours for what she is about to do."

Kahlan tossed the book in the fire.

With ashen faces, Ann and Sister Alessandra stood staring at the book in the hissing flames.

Kahlan snatched up Richard's sword. "Cara, let's get going."

"The horses are ready. I was saddling them when these two showed up."

Kahlan dumped the hot water to the side while Cara started quickly collecting their belongings. They both stuffed items in the saddlebags. Other gear they slung over their shoulders and carried to the horses to be strapped back on the saddles.

Without looking back at Ann or Alessandra, Kahlan swung up into her cold saddle. With a grim Cara at her side, she turned her mount and cantered off into the swirling snow.

As soon as she saw Kahlan and Cara vanish like vengeful spirits into the whiteness, Ann fell to her knees and thrust her hands into the fire to snatch the burning journey book from its funeral pyre in the white-hot coals.

"Prelate!" Alessandra cried. "You'll burn yourself!"

Flinching back from the ferocity of the pain, Ann ignored the gagging stench of burning flesh and thrust her hands again into the wavering heat of the fire. She saw, rather than felt, that she had the priceless journey book in her fingers.

The entire rescue of the burning book took only a second, but, through the prism of pain, it seemed an eternity.

Biting down on her lower lip against the suffering, Ann rolled to the side. Alessandra came running back with her hands full of snow. She threw it on Ann's bloody blackened fingers and the journey book clenched in them.

She let out a low wail of agony when the wet snow contacted the burns. Alessandra fell to Ann's side, taking her hands by the wrists, gasping in tears of fright.

"Prelate! Oh, Prelate, you shouldn't have!"

Ann was in a state of shock from the pain. Alessandra's shrill voice seemed a distant drone.

"Oh, Ann! Why didn't you use magic, or even a stick!"

Ann was surprised by the question. In her panic over the priceless journey book burning there in the fire, her mind was filled only with the single thought to get it out before it was too late. Her reckless action, she knew, was precipitated by her bitter anguish over Kahlan's accusations.

"Hold still," Alessandra admonished through her own tears. "Hold still and let me see what I can do about healing you. It will be all right. Just hold still."

Ann sat on the snowy ground, dazed by the hurt, and by the words still hammering her from inside her head, as she let Alessandra work at healing her hands.

The Sister could not heal her heart.

"She was wrong," Alessandra said, as if reading Ann's thoughts. "She was wrong, Prelate."

"Was she?" Ann asked in a numb voice after the searing pain in her fingers finally began to ease, replaced by the achingly uncomfortable tingling of magic coursing into her flesh, doing its work. "Was she, Alessandra?"

"Yes. She doesn't know so much as she thinks. She's a child—she couldn't be a paltry three decades yet. People can't learn to wipe their own noses in that much time." Alessandra was prattling, Ann knew, prattling with her worry over the journey book, and with her worry over the anguish caused by Kahlan's words. "She's just a foolish child who doesn't know the first thing about anything. There's much more to it. Much more. It isn't so simple as she thinks. Not so simple at all."

Ann wasn't so sure anymore. Everything seemed dead to her. Five hundred years of work—had it all been a mad task, driven on by selfish desires and a fool's faith? Wouldn't she, in Kahlan's place, have seen it the same way?

Endless rows of corpses lay before her in the trial going on in her mind. What was there to say in her defense? She had a thousand answers for the Mother Confessor's charges, but at that moment, they all seemed empty. How could Ann possibly excuse herself to the dead?

"You're the Prelate of the Sisters of the Light," Alessandra rambled on during a pause in her work. "She should have been more considerate of who she was talking to. More respectful. She doesn't know everything involved. There's a great deal more to it. A great deal. After all, the Sisters of the Light don't casually choose their Prelate."

Nor did Confessors casually choose their Mother Confessor.

An hour passed, and then another, before Alessandra finally finished the difficult and tedious work of healing Ann's burns. Burns were difficult injuries to heal. It was a tiring experience, being helpless and cold while magic sizzled through her, while Kahlan's words sliced her very soul.

Ann flexed the aching fingers when Alessandra had finished. A shadow of the burning pain lingered, as she knew it would for a good long time. But they were healed, and she had her hands back.

When the matter was weighed, though, she feared she had lost a great deal more of herself than she had recovered.

Exhausted and cold, Ann, to Alessandra's worry, lay down beside the hissing remnants of the fire that had so hurt her. At that moment, she had no desire to ever rise again. Her years, nearly a thousand of them, seemed to have all caught up with her at once.

She missed Nathan terribly right then. The prophet doubtless would have had something wise, or foolish, to say. Either would have comforted her. Nathan always had something to say. She missed his boastful voice, his kind, childlike, knowing eyes. She missed the touch of his hand.

Weeping silently, Ann cried herself to sleep. Her dreams kept the sleep from being either restful, or deep. She awoke in late morning to the feel of Alessandra's comforting hand on her shoulder. The Sister had added more wood to the fire, so it offered warmth.

"Are you feeling better, Prelate?"

Ann nodded her lie. Her first thought was for the journey book. She gazed at it lying in the protection of Alessandra's lap. Ann sat up and carefully lifted the blackened book from the sling of Alessandra's dress.

"Prelate, I'm so worried for you."

With a sour wave of her hand, Ann dismissed the concern.

"While you slept, I've looked at the book."

Ann grunted. "Looks bad."

Alessandra nodded. "That's what I thought. I don't think it can be salvaged."

Ann used an easy, gentle flow of her Han to hold the pages—little more than ash—together as she carefully turned them.

"It has endured three thousand years. Were it ordinary paper, it would be beyond help—ended—but this is a thing of magic, Alessandra, forged in the fires of magic, by wizards of power not seen in all those three thousand years . . . until Richard."

"What can we do? Do you know a way to restore it?"

Ann shook her head as she inspected the curled, charred journey book. "I don't know if it can be restored. I'm just saying that it's a thing of magic. Where there is magic, there is hope."

Ann pulled a handkerchief from a pocket deep under the layers of her clothes. Laying the blackened book in the center of the handkerchief, she carefully folded the handkerchief up to hold it together. She wove a spell around it all to protect and preserve it for the time being.

"I will have to try to find a way to restore it—if I can. If it can even be restored."

Alessandra dry-washed her hands. "Until then, our eyes with the army are lost."

Ann nodded. "We won't know if the Imperial Order decides to finally leave their place in the south and move up into the Midlands. I can give no guidance to Verna."

"Prelate, what do you think will happen if the Order finally decides to attack— and Richard isn't there with them? What will they do? Without the Lord Rahl to lead them . . ."

Ann did her best to move the terrible weight of Kahlan's words to the side as she considered the immediate situation.

"Verna is the Prelate now—at least as far as the Sisters with the army are concerned. She will guide them wisely. And Zedd is with them, helping the Sisters prepare for battle, should it come. They could have no better counsel than to have a wizard of Zedd's experience with them. As First Wizard, he has been through great wars before.

"We will have to place our faith in the Creator that He will watch over them. I can't advise them unless I can restore the journey book. Unless I can do that, I won't even know their situation."

"You could go there, Prelate."

Ann brushed snow from the side of her shoulder, where she had been lying on the ground, as she considered that possibility.

"The Sisters of the Light think I'm dead. They've put their faith in Verna, now, as their Prelate. It would be a terrible thing to do to Verna—and to the rest of the Sisters—to come back to life in the middle of such trying circumstances. Certainly many would be relieved to have me back, but it also sows the seeds of confusion and doubt. Battle is a very bad time for such seeds to sprout."

"But they would all be encouraged by your—"

Ann shook her head. "Verna is their leader. Such a thing could forever undermine their trust in her authority. They must not lose their faith in her leadership. I must put the welfare of the Sisters of the Light above all else. I must keep their best interests at heart, now."

"But, Ann, you are the Prelate."

Ann stared off. "What good has that done anyone?"

Alessandra's eyes turned down. The wind moaned sorrowfully through the trees. Gusts kicked up blue-gray trailers of snow and whipped them along through the campsite. The sunlight had vanished behind somber clouds. Ann wiped her nose on the edge of her icy cloak.

Alessandra laid a compassionate hand on Ann's arm. "You brought me back from the Keeper, back into the Light of the Creator. I was in Jagang's hands, and treated you terribly when they captured you, yet you never gave up on me. Who else would have cared? Without you, my soul would be lost for all time. I doubt you could fathom my gratitude for what you did, Prelate."

Despite Alessandra's apparent return to the Creator's Light, Ann had been fooled by the woman before. Years before, Alessandra had turned to the Keeper, becoming a Sister of the Dark, and Ann had never known. How could one have faith in a person after such a betrayal?

Ann looked up into Alessandra's eyes. "I hope so, Sister. I pray such is really true."

"It is, Prelate."

Ann lifted a hand toward the shrouded sun. "And perhaps when I go to the Creator's Light in the next world, that one good act will erase the thousands of lives lost because of me?"

Alessandra looked away, rubbing her arms through the layers of clothes. She turned and put two sticks of wood on the fire.

"We should have a hot meal. That will make you feel better, Prelate. It will make us both feel better."

Ann sat on the ground watching Alessandra prepare her hearty camp soup. Ann doubted that even the pleasant aroma of soup would arouse her appetite.

"Why do you think Nicci took Richard?" Alessandra asked as she put dried mushrooms from a pouch into the soup.

Ann looked up at Alessandra's puzzled face. "I can't imagine, except to think that she may be lying, and she is taking him to Jagang."

Alessandra broke up dried meat and dropped it into the boiling pot of soup. "Why? If she had him, and he was forced to do as she asked—why lie? What would be the purpose?"

"She's a Sister devoted to the Keeper." Ann lifted her hands and let them flop back into her lap. "That's excuse enough to lie, isn't it? Lying is wrong. It's wicked. That's reason enough."

Alessandra shook her head in admonition. "Prelate, I was a Sister of the Dark. Remember? I know better. That isn't the way it is at all. Do you always tell the truth just because you are devoted to the Creator's Light? No; one lies for the Keeper just as you would lie for the Creator—to His ends, if lying is necessary. Why would Nicci lie about that? She was in control of the situation and had no need to lie."

"I can't imagine." Ann had difficulty caring enough to consider the question. Her mind was in a morass of hopeless thoughts. It was her fault Richard was in the hands of the enemy, not Nicci's.

"I think she did it for herself."

Ann looked up. "What do you mean?"

"I think Nicci is still looking for something."

"Looking for something? What ever do you mean?"

With a finger, Alessandra brushed a measure of spices into the pot from a waxed paper she'd unfolded. "Ever since the first day I took her from her home and brought her to the Palace of the Prophets, Nicci continually grew more . . . detached, somehow. She always did whatever she could to help people, but she was always a child who made me feel as if I was inadequate at fulfilling her needs."

"Such as?"

Alessandra shook her head. "I don't know. She always seemed to me to be looking for something. I thought she needed to find the Light of the Creator. I pushed her mercilessly, hoping it would open her eyes to His way and fill her inner need. I allowed her no room to think about anything else. I even kept her away from her family. Her father was a selfish lover of money and her mother . . . well, her mother was well intentioned, but always made me feel uncomfortable. I thought the Creator would fill that private void within Nicci." Alessandra hesitated. "And then I thought it was the Keeper she needed."

"So, you think she took Richard to fill some . . . inner need? How does that make sense?"

"I don't know." Alessandra breathed out heavily in frustration. She stirred the soup as she drizzled in a pinch of salt. "Prelate, I think I failed Nicci."

"In what way?"

"I don't know. Perhaps I failed to involve her adequately in the needs of others—gave her too much time to think of herself. She always seemed devoted to the welfare of her fellow man, but maybe I should have rubbed her nose in other people's troubles more, to teach her the Creator's way of virtue through caring more for her fellow man rather than her own selfish wants."

"Sister, I hardly think that could be it. Once she asked me for an extravagant black dress to wear to her mother's funeral, and of course I refused such a profligacy because it was unfitting for a novice needing to learn to put others first, but other than that one time, I never knew Nicci to once ask for anything for herself. You did an admirable job with her, Alessandra."

Ann recalled that, after that, Nicci started wearing black dresses.

"I remember that." Alessandra didn't look up. "When her father died, I went with her to his funeral. I always felt sorry for taking her away from her family, but I explained to her that she was so talented that she had great potential for helping others and must not waste it."

"It's always hard to bring young ones to the palace. It's difficult to part a child from loving parents. Some adapt better than others."

"She told me she understood. Nicci was always good that way. She never objected to anything, any duty. Perhaps I assumed too much because she always threw herself into helping others, never once complaining.

"At her father's funeral, I wanted to help her over her grief. Even though she had that same cool exterior she always had, I knew her, I knew she was hurting inside. I tried to comfort her by telling her not to remember her father like that, but to try to remember him as he was when he was alive."

"Those are kind words to one in such grief, Sister. You offered wise advise."

Alessandra glanced up. "She was not comforted, Prelate. She looked at me with those blue eyes of hers—you remember her blue eyes."

Ann nodded. "I remember."

"Well, she looked at me with those piercing blue eyes, like she wanted to hate me, but even that emotion was beyond her, and she said in that lifeless voice of hers that she couldn't remember him as he was when he was alive, because she had never known him when he was alive. Isn't that the strangest thing you've ever heard?"

Ann sighed. "It sounds like Nicci. She always was one to say the strangest things at the strangest times. I should have offered her more guidance in her life. I should have taken more interest in her . . . but there were so many matters needing my attention."

"No, Prelate, that was my job. I failed in it. Somehow, I failed Nicci."

Ann pulled her cloak tighter against a bitter gust of wind. She took the bowl of soup when Alessandra handed it to her.

"Worse, Prelate, I brought her to the shadow of the Keeper."

Ann looked over the rim of the bowl as she took a sip. She carefully set the steaming bowl in her lap.

"What's done is done, Alessandra."

While Alessandra sipped at her soup, Ann's mind wandered to Kahlan's words. They were words spoken in anger, and as such, were to be forgiven. Or were they to be considered in an honest light?

Ann feared to say Kahlan's words were wrong; she feared they were true. For centuries Ann had worked with Nathan and the prophecies, trying to avoid the disasters she saw, and the ones he pointed out to her. What if Nathan had been pointing out things that were only dead words, as Kahlan said? What if he only pointed them out so as to bring about his own escape?

After all, what Ann had set in motion with Richard had also resulted in the prophet's escape. What if she had been duped into being the one to bring about all those terrible results?

Could that be true? Grief threatened to overwhelm her.

She was beginning to greatly fear that she had been so absorbed in what she thought she knew that she had acted on false assumptions.

Kahlan could be right. The Prelate of the Sisters of the Light might be personally responsible for more suffering than any monster born into the world had ever brought about.

"Alessandra," Ann said in a soft voice after she finished her bowl of soup, "we must go and try to find Nathan. It's dangerous for the prophet to be out there, in the world that is defenseless against him."

"Where would we look?"

Ann shook her head in dismay at the enormity of the task. "A man like Nathan does not go unnoticed in the world. I must believe that if we set our minds to it, we could find him."

Alessandra watched Ann's face. "Well, as you say, it is dangerous for the prophet to be loose in the world."

"It is indeed. We must find him."

"It took Verna twenty years to find Richard."

"So it did. But part of that was by my design. I hid facts from Verna. Then again, Nathan is no doubt hiding facts from us. Nonetheless, we have a responsibility. Verna is with the Sisters, and with the army; they will do what they can in that capacity. We must go after Nathan. That part of it is up to us."

Alessandra set her bowl aside. "Prelate, I understand why you believe the prophet must be found, but just as you feel you must find him, I feel I must find Nicci. I'm responsible for bringing her to the Keeper of the underworld. I may be the only one who can bring her back to the Light. I have a unique understanding of that journey of the heart. I fear what will happen to Richard if I don't try to stop Nicci.

"Worse," Alessandra added, "I fear what will happen to the world if Richard dies. Kahlan is wrong. I believe in what you've worked for all these years. Kahlan is making a complex thing sound simple because her heart is broken, but without what you did, she would never even have met Richard."

Ann considered Alessandra's words. The seduction of acquittal was undeniable.

"But, Alessandra, we don't have the slightest idea where they went. Nicci is as smart as they come. If, as she says, she is acting on her own behalf, she will be clever about not being found. How would you even go about such a search?

"Nathan is a prophet loose in the world. You remember the trouble he's caused in the past. He could, by himself, bring about such calamity as the world has never seen. Nathan boasts when he's around people; he will surely leave such traces where he goes. With Nathan, I believe we at least have a chance of success. But hunting for Nicci . . ."

Alessandra met Ann's gaze with grim resolution. "Prelate, if Richard dies, what chance have the rest of us?"

Ann looked away. What if Alessandra was right? What if Kahlan was right? She had to catch Nathan; it was the only way to find out.

"Alessandra . . ."

"You don't completely trust me, do you, Prelate?"

Ann met the other woman's eyes, this time with authority. "No, Alessandra, I admit that I don't. How can I? You deceived me. You lied to me. You turned your back on the Creator and gave yourself to the Keeper of the underworld."

"But I've come back to the Light, Prelate."

"Have you? Would not one acting for the Keeper lie for him, as you yourself only moments ago suggested?"

Alessandra's eyes filled with tears. "That's why I must try to find Nicci, Prelate. I must prove that your faith in me was not misplaced. I need to do this to prove myself to you."

"Or, you need to help Nicci, and the Keeper?"

"I know I'm not worthy of trust. I know that. You said we must find Nathan—but we must also help Richard."

"Two tasks of the utmost importance," Ann said, "and no journey book to call for help."

Alessandra wiped at her eyes. "Please, Prelate, let me help. I'm responsible for Nicci going to the Keeper. Let me try to make amends. Let me try to bring her back. I know what the return journey is like. I can help her. Please, let me try to save her eternal soul?"

Ann's gaze sank to the ground. Who was she to question the value of another? What had her life been for? Had she herself been the Keeper's best ally?

Ann cleared her throat. "Sister Alessandra, you are to listen to me and you are to listen well. I am the Prelate of the Sisters of the Light and it is your duty to do as I command." Ann shook a finger at the woman. "I'll have no arguments, do you hear? I must go find the prophet before he does something beyond foolish.

"Richard is of utmost importance to our cause—you know that. I'm getting old and would only slow the search for him and his captor. I want you to go after him. No arguments, now. You are to find Richard Rahl, and put the fear of the Creator back into our wayward Sister Nicci."

Alessandra threw her arms around Ann, sobbing her thanks. Ann patted the Sister's back, feeling miserable about losing a companion, and afraid that she might have lost her faith in everything for which she stood.

Alessandra pushed away. "Prelate, will you be able to travel alone? Are you sure you're up to this?"

"Bah. I may be old, but I'm not useless. Who do you think came into the center of Jagang's army and rescued you, child?"

Alessandra smiled through her tears. "You did, Prelate, all by yourself. No one but you could have done such a thing. I hope I can do half as well for Nicci, when I find her."

"You will, Sister. You will. May the Creator cradle you in His palm as you go on your journey."

Ann knew that they were both going off on difficult journeys that could take years.

"Hard times lie ahead," Alessandra said. "But the Creator has two hands, does He not? One for me, and one for you, Prelate."

Ann couldn't help but smile at such a mental picture.

"Come in," Zedd grouched to the persistent throat-clearing outside his tent.

He poured water from the ewer into the dented metal pot that served as his wash-basin sitting atop a log round. When he splashed some of the water up onto his face, he gasped aloud. He was astonished that water that cold would still pour.

"Good morning, Zedd."

Still gasping, Zedd swiped the frigid water from his eyes. He squinted at Warren. "Good morning, my boy."

Warren blushed. Zedd reminded himself he probably shouldn't call someone twice his own age "boy." It was Warren's own fault; if the boy would just stop looking so young! Zedd sighed as he bent to forage for a towel among the litter of maps, dirty plates, rusty dividers, empty mugs, blankets, chicken bones, rope, an egg he'd lost in the middle of a lesson weeks back, and other paraphernalia that seemed to collect over time in the corner of his small field tent.

Warren was twisting his purple robes into a small wad at his hip. "I just came from Verna's tent."

Zedd halted his search and looked back over his shoulder.

"Any word?"

Warren shook his head of curly blond hair. "Sorry, Zedd."

"Well," Zedd scoffed, "that doesn't mean anything. That old woman has more lives than a cat I once had that was hit by lightning and fell down a well, both in the same day. Did I ever tell you about that cat, my boy?"

"Well, yes, you did, actually." Warren smiled. "But if you like, I wouldn't mind hearing it again."

Zedd dismissed the story with a feeble wave as he turned more serious. "I'm sure Ann is fine. Verna knows Ann better than I do, but I do know that that old woman is downright hard to harm."

"Verna said something like that." Warren smiled to himself. "Ann always could scowl a thunderstorm back over the horizon."

Zedd grunted his agreement as he went back to digging through his pile. "Tougher than bad meat, she is." He tossed two outdated maps over his shoulder.

Warren leaned down a little. "What is it you're looking for, if you don't mind my asking?"

"My towel. I know I had—"

"Right there," Warren said.

Zedd looked up. "What?"

"Your towel." Warren pointed again. "Right there on the back of the chair."

"Oh." Zedd snatched up the wandering towel and dried his dry face. He scowled at Warren. "You have the eyes of a burglar." He tossed the towel in the pile with everything else, where it belonged.

Warren's grin returned. "I'll take that as a compliment."

Zedd cocked his head. "Do you hear that?"

Warren's grin melted away as he joined Zedd in listening to the sounds outside. Horses clogged along the hard ground, men talked as they passed the tent, others called orders, fires crackled, wagons squeaked, and gear clanged and rattled.

"Hear what?"

Zedd's face twisted in vague unease. "I don't know. Like, maybe a whistle."

Warren lifted a thumb over his shoulder. "The men whistle now and again, to get the attention of their horses and such. Sometimes it's necessary."

They all did their best to keep the whistling and other noise down. Whistles, especially, carried in such open terrain. It was hard to miss something the size of the D'Harans' encampment, of course, so they moved camp from time to time to keep the enemy from getting too confident about their location. Sound could give away more than they would like.

Zedd shook his head. "Must have been that. Someone's long whistle."

"But still, Zedd," Warren went on, "it's long past time when Ann would have sent Verna a message."

"There were times when I was with Ann that she couldn't send messages." Zedd waved an arm expansively. "Bags, there was a time when I wouldn't let her use that confounded journey book. The thing gave me the shivers. I don't know why she couldn't just send letters, like normal people." His face, he knew, was betraying his concern. "Confounded journey books. Lazy way of doing things. I got to be First Wizard and I never needed a journey book."

"She could have lost it. That's what Verna suggested, anyway."

Zedd held up a finger. "That's right. She very well could have. It's small—it could have fallen from her belt and she didn't notice until she and Alessandra made camp. She'd never find the book in a circumstance like that." He shook the finger. "Makes my point, too. You shouldn't depend on little trick things of magic, like that. It just makes you lazy."

"That's what Verna thought, too. About it falling from her belt, I mean." Warren chuckled. "Or a cat could even have eaten it."

From beneath a furrowed brow, Zedd peered at Warren. "A cat? What cat?"

"Any cat." Warren cleared his throat. "I just meant . . . oh, never mind. I never was any good at jokes."

Zedd's knotted brow lifted. "Oh, I see. A cat could have eaten it. Yes, yes, I see." He didn't, but Zedd forced a chuckle for the boy's sake. "Very good, Warren."

"Anyway, she probably lost it. It's probably something as simple as that."

"If that's the case," Zedd reasoned, "she will likely end up coming here to let us know that she's all right, or at least she will send a letter, or messenger, or something. Ever more likely, though, she probably had nothing to tell us and simply saw no need to bother with sending a message in her journey book."

Warren made a skeptical face. "But we haven't had a message from her for nearly a month."

Zedd waved a hand dismissively. "Well, she was way north, up almost to where Richard and Kahlan are, last we heard. If she did lose the book and started right out to come here from there, she won't show up for yet another week or two. If she went on to see Richard first, then it will be longer, I imagine. Ann doesn't travel all that fast, you know."

"I know," Warren said. "She is getting up there in years. But that's just another reason why I'm so worried."

What really worried Zedd was the way the journey book went silent just as Ann was about to reach Richard and Kahlan. Zedd had been eagerly anticipating hearing that Richard and Kahlan were safe, that Kahlan was all healed. Maybe even that Richard was ready to return. Ann knew how eager they were for word and would certainly have had something to report. Zedd didn't like the coincidence that the journey book went silent right at that time. He didn't like it one bit.

The whole thing made him want to scratch as if he'd been bitten by a white mosquito.

"Now look here, Warren, a month isn't so long not to hear from her. In the past, it's sometimes been weeks and weeks between her messages. It's too early to start getting ourselves all worked up with worry. Besides, we have our own concerns which require our attention."

Zedd didn't know what they could do even if Ann were in trouble somewhere. They had no idea how to find her.

Warren flashed an apologetic smile. "You're right, Zedd."

Zedd moved a map and found a half loaf of bread left from the night before. He took a big bite, giving himself an excuse to chew instead of talk. When he talked, he feared he only let out the true level of his worry not just about Ann, but also about Richard and Kahlan.

Warren was an able wizard, and smarter than just about anyone Zedd had ever met. Zedd often had trouble finding something to talk about that Warren hadn't already heard of, or was intimately familiar with. There was something refreshing about sharing knowledge with someone who nodded knowingly at esoteric points of magic that no one else would fathom, someone who could fill in little gaps in the odd spell, or delighted at having his own little gaps filled in by what Zedd knew. Warren retained more about prophecy than Zedd thought anyone had a right to know in the first place.

Warren was a fascinating mix of obstinate old man and callow youth. He was at once set in his ways, and at the same time openly, infinitely, innocently, curious.

The one thing that made Warren fall silent, though, was when they discussed Richard's "vision." Warren's face would go blank and he would sit without comment while others argued over what Richard had said in his letters and if there was any validity to it. Whenever Zedd had Warren alone and asked him what he thought, Warren would say only "I follow Richard; he is my friend, and he is the Lord Rahl." Warren would not debate or discuss Richard's instructions to the army—or, more specifically, Richard's refusal to give instructions. Richard had given his orders, as far as Warren was concerned, and they were to be swallowed, not chewed.

Zedd noticed than Warren was twisting his robes again.

Zedd waved his bread. "You look like a wizard with his pants full of itching spells. Do you have something you need to let out, Warren?"

Warren grinned sheepishly. "Am I that obvious?"

Zedd patted the boy on the back. "No, Warren, I'm just that good."

Warren laughed at Zedd's joke. Zedd gestured with his bread toward the folding canvas chair. Warren looked behind himself at the chair, but shook his head. Zedd figured it must be important, if Warren felt he needed to stand to say it.

"Zedd, with winter upon us, do you believe the Imperial Order will attack, or wait until spring?"

"Well, now, that's always a worry. The not knowing leaves your stomach all in knots. But you've all worked hard. You've all trained and practiced. You'll do just fine, Warren. The Sisters, too."

Warren didn't seem to be interested in hearing what Zedd was saying. He was scratching his temple, waiting his turn to speak.

"Yes, well, thank you, Zedd. We have been working hard.

"Umm, General Leiden thinks winter is our best friend right now. He, his Keltish officers, and some of the D'Harans believe that Jagang would be foolhardy to start a campaign with winter just setting in. Kelton isn't all that far north of here, so General Leiden is familiar with the difficulty of winter warfare in the terrain we would fall back to. He's convinced the Order is waiting for spring."

"General Leiden in a good man, and may be second-in-command, after General Reibisch," Zedd said in an even voice as he watched Warren's blue eyes, "but, I don't agree with him."

Warren looked crestfallen. "Oh."

The general had brought his Keltish division down south a couple of months before to reinforce the D'Haran army, at General Reibisch's request. Regarding Kahlan as their queen, since Richard had named her so, the Keltish forces still had an independent streak, even if they were now part of the "D'Haran Empire," as everyone had taken to calling it.

Zedd didn't do anything to discourage such talk; it was better for everyone in the New World to be one mighty force than a collection of tribes. As far as Zedd was concerned, Richard had clearly had the right instincts in that. A war of this scale would have been ungovernable were the New World not one. Having everyone think of themselves as part of the D'Haran Empire first and foremost could only help make it so.

Zedd cleared his throat. "But that's just a guess, Warren. I could be wrong. General Leiden is an experienced man, and no fool. I could be wrong."

"But so could Leiden be wrong. I guess that puts you with General Reibisch. He's been pacing his tent every night for the last two months."

Zedd shrugged. "Is there something important to you, Warren, that hinges on what the Imperial Order does? Are you waiting for them to make up your mind for you about something?"

Warren held up his hands as if to ward the very notion. "No—no, of course not. It's just that . . . it's just that it would be a bad time to be thinking about such things, is all. . . . But if they were going to lie low for the winter . . ." Warren fussed with his sleeve. "That's all I meant. . . . If you thought they were going to wait until spring, or something . . ." His voice trailed off.

"And if they were, then—?"

Warren stared at the ground while he twisted his robes at his stomach into a purple knot. "If you think they might decide to move this winter, then it wouldn't be right for me—for us—to be thinking about such things."

Zedd scratched his chin and changed his approach. "Let's say I believe the Order is going to sit tight for the winter. Then what might you do, in that case?"

Warren threw his hands up. "Zedd will you marry Verna and me?"

Zedd's brow went up as he drew back his head. "Bags, my boy, that's a mouthful to swallow first thing in the morning."

Warren took two big strides closer. "Will you Zedd? I mean, only if you really think the Order is going to sit down there in Anderith for the winter. If they are, then, well, then it would be, I mean, we might as well—"

"Do you love Verna, Warren?"

"Of course I do!"

"And does Verna love you?"

"Well, of course she does."

Zedd shrugged. "Then I'll marry the both of you."

"You will? Oh, Zedd, that would be wonderful." Warren turned, reaching one hand toward the tent's opening, lifting his other back toward Zedd. "Wait. Wait there a moment."

"Well, I was about to flap my arms and fly to the moon, but if you want me to wait—"

Warren was already out the tent. Zedd heard muffled voices coming from outside. Warren came back in—right on Verna's heels.

Verna beamed from ear to ear, which Zedd found unsettling in its own way, being so unusual.

"Thank you for offering to marry us, Zedd. Thank you! Warren and I wanted you to do the ceremony. I told him you would do it, but Warren wanted to ask you and give you a chance to say no. I can't think of anything more meaningful than being wedded by the First Wizard."

Zedd thought she was a lovely woman. A little fussy about rules and such, at times, but well intentioned. She worked hard. She didn't shy from some of the things Zedd had asked of her. And, she obviously held Warren in warm regard, as well as respecting him.

"When?" Verna asked. "When do you think would be an appropriate time?"

Zedd screwed up his face. "Do you two think you can wait until I've had a proper breakfast?"

They both grinned.

"We were thinking more along the lines of an evening wedding," Verna said. "Maybe we could have a party, with music and dancing."

Warren gestured nonchalantly. "We were thinking something to make a pleasant break in all the training."

"A break? How much time do you two think you will be needing away from your duties—"

"Oh, no, Zedd!" Warren had gone as purple as his robes. "We didn't mean we would—I mean we would still be doing—we would only like—"

"We don't want any time away, Zedd," Verna put in, bringing Warren's bashful babbling to an end. "We just thought it would be a nice opportunity for everyone to have a well-earned party for an evening. We won't be leaving our posts."

Zedd put a bony arm around Verna's shoulders. "You two can have all the time away you want. We all understand. I'm happy for you both."

"That's great, Zedd," Warren said with a sigh. "We really—"

A red-faced officer burst into the tent without so much as announcing himself. "Wizard Zorander!"

Two Sisters charged in right behind him.

"Prelate!" Sister Philippa called.

"They're coming!" Sister Phoebe cried.

Both women were white-faced and looked to be on the verge of losing their breakfast. Sister Phoebe was trembling like a wet dog in winter. Zedd then saw that Sister Philippa's hair was singed on one side and the shoulder of her dress was blackened. She had been one of those on far watch for the enemy gifted.

Now Zedd knew what the whistling sound he thought he'd heard was. It was very distant screams.

Rolling up from the distance came the note of the secondary waypoint alarm horns. Zedd felt the faint tingle of magic woven through them, so he knew they were genuine. Outside the tent, the muted sounds of camp life rose into a din of activity. Weapons were being yanked from where they were stacked, fires hissed as they were dowsed, swords were being strapped on, others were being drawn, horses whinnied at the sudden racket.

Warren seized Sister Philippa's arm and started issuing orders. "Get the line coordinated. Don't let them be seen—keep behind the third ridge. Set the trips close—we need to give the enemy confidence. Cavalry?"

The woman nodded.

"Coming in two wings," the officer put in. "But they aren't charging yet—they don't want to get out too far ahead of their foot soldiers."

"Start the first fire behind them—once they're past the blast point—just like we've drilled," Warren told Sister Philippa as she nodded heedfully to his instructions. The intention was to trap any cavalry charge between walls of violent magic. It had to be focused properly to have any hope of piercing the enemy's shields.

"Prelate," Sister Phoebe said, still panting, "you can't imagine the numbers. Dear Creator, it looks like the ground is moving, like the hills are melting men toward us."

Verna put a comforting hand to the young Sister's shoulder. "I know, Phoebe. I know. But we all know what to do."

Verna was already ushering the two Sisters out and calling for her other aides, as yet more officers and returning scouts leaped from horses.

A big, bearded soldier, sweat running down his face, barged into the tent gasping for his breath.

"The whole blasted force. All of 'em."

"Cavalry with lances—enough to break their way and then some," another man shouted into the tent from atop a lathered horse, pausing only long enough to deliver the news to Zedd before charging off.

"Archers?" Zedd asked the two soldiers still in his tent.

The officer with the beard shook his head. "Too far to tell." He gulped air. "But I'd bet my life they're right behind the pikemen's shields."

"No doubt," Zedd said. "When they get close enough, they'll show themselves."

Warren grabbed the bearded officer's sleeve and pulled him along behind as he trotted out of the tent. "Don't worry, when they show themselves we'll have something to put out their eyes."

The other man ran on to his duties. In an instant, Zedd was standing alone in his tent, lit from the outside by early-morning winter sun. It was a cold dawn. It would be a bloody day.

Outside the tent, the racket exploded into the uproar of practiced pandemonium. Everyone had a job, and knew it well; these were mostly battle-tested D'Harans. Zedd had snuck close and had seen how fearsome the Imperial Order troops looked, but the D'Harans were their match in gristle. For generations, D'Harans prided themselves on being the fiercest fighters in existence. For a good part of his life, Zedd had battled D'Harans who had proven their boasts true.

Zedd could hear someone shouting, "Move, move, move." It sounded like General Reibisch. Zedd dashed to the tent's opening, pausing at the brink of a river of men flowing past in a great churning mass.

General Reibisch skidded to a halt just outside the tent.

"Zedd—we were right."

Zedd nodded his disappointment to have surmised the enemy's plans. This was one time he wished he'd been wrong.

"We're breaking camp," General Reibisch said. "We've not much time. I've already ordered the advance guard to shift their positions north to cover the supply wagons."

"Is it all of them—or just a jab to test us?"

"It's the whole bloody lot."

"Dear spirits," Zedd whispered. At least he had made what plans for this eventuality as could be made. He had trained the gifted to expect this so they wouldn't be thrown off balance. It would come just as Zedd told them it would; that would aid their confidence and give them courage. The day hinged on the gifted.

General Reibisch swiped his meaty hand across his mouth and jaw as he looked to the south, toward an enemy he couldn't yet see. The early sun made his rust-colored hair look red, and the scar that ran from his left temple to his jaw stand out like a streak of frozen white lightning.

"Our sentries pulled back along with the outer lines. No use in them standing ground, since it's the whole Imperial Order."

Zedd quickly nodded his agreement. "We'll be the magic against magic for you, General."

The man had a lusty glint in his grayish-green eye. "We're the steel for you, Zedd. We'll show them bastards a lot of both today."

"Just don't show them too much, too soon," Zedd warned.

"I'm not about to change our plans now," he said over the sound of the tumult.

"Good." Zedd snatched the arm of a soldier running past. "You. I need your help. Pack up my things in there for me, would you, lad? I need to get to the Sisters."

General Reibisch gestured the young soldier into Zedd's tent, and the young man leaped to the task.

"The scouts said they're all staying on this side of the Drun River, just as we hoped."

"Good. We won't have to worry about them flanking us, at least not from the west." Zedd swept his gaze over the dissolving camp as the men swiftly set about their jobs. He looked back to the general's weathered face. "Just get our men north into those valleys in time, General, so that we can't be surrounded. The gifted will cover your tails."

"We'll plug up the valleys, don't you worry."

"The river isn't frozen over, yet, is it?"

General Reibisch shook his head. "Maybe enough for a rat to skate on, but not the wolf that's after him."

"That should keep them from crossing." Zedd squinted off to the south. "I have to go check on Adie and her Sisters. May the good spirits be with you, General. They won't need to watch your back—we'll do that."

General Reibisch caught Zedd's arm. "There's more than we thought, Zedd. Twice the number at least. If my scouts weren't just stuttering, there may be three times the number. Think you can slow that many down while keeping them focused on trying to sink their teeth into my backside?"

The plan was to draw the enemy north while staying just out of their reach—close enough to make them salivate but not close enough to let them get a good bite. Crossing the river at this time of year would be impractical for an army that size. With the river on one side, and mountains on the other, a force the size of the Imperial Order couldn't so easily surround and overwhelm the "D'Haran Empire" troops, who were outnumbered ten or twenty to one.

The plan, too, was designed to keep in mind Richard's admonition about not attacking directly into the Order. Zedd wasn't sure about the validity of Richard's warning, but knew better than to so openly tempt ruin.

Hopefully, once they enticed the enemy into that tighter terrain, terrain more defensible, the Order would lose some of their advantage and their advance could be halted. Once the Imperial Order was stalled, the D'Harans could begin working the enemy down to size. The D'Harans thought nothing of being outnumbered; it just gave them a better opportunity to prove themselves.

Zedd stared off, imagining the hillsides darkened with the enemy pouring forth. He was already seeing the lethal powers he would unleash.

He knew, too, that in battle things rarely went as planned.

"Don't you worry, General, today the Imperial Order is going to begin paying a terrible price for its aggression."

The grinning general clapped Zedd on the side of the shoulder. "Good man."

General Reibisch charged off, calling for his aides and his horse, collecting a growing crowd of men around him as he went.

It had begun.

Arms resting on his thighs, Richard crouched in the belly of the beast.

"Well?" Nicci asked from atop her horse.

Richard stood beside a rib bone that towered to well over twice his height. He shielded his eyes against the golden sunlight as he briefly scanned the empty horizon behind himself. He looked back at Nicci, her hair honeyed by the low sun.

"I'd say it was a dragon."

When her mare began to dance sideways, trying to put distance between itself and the expanse of bones, Nicci took the slack out of the reins.

"Dragon," she repeated in a flat voice.

Here and there dried scraps of meat stuck to the bones. Richard swished a hand at the cloud of flies buzzing around him. The faint stench of decay hung over the site. As he stepped out of the cage of giant rib bones standing belly-up, he gestured toward the head, nestled in a bed of brown grass. There was enough room to walk between the ribs without them touching his shoulders.

"I recognize the teeth. I had a dragon's tooth, once."

Nicci looked skeptical. "Well, whatever it is, if you've seen enough, let's be on our way."

Richard brushed his hands clean. The stallion snorted and stepped away from him when he approached. The horse didn't like the smell of death, and didn't trust Richard after having been near it. Richard stroked the glossy black neck.

"Steady, Boy," he said in a comforting voice. "Easy now."

When she saw Richard finally mount up, Nicci turned her dappled mare and started off once more. The late-afternoon light cast long, clawed shadows of the rib bones toward him, as if reaching out, calling him back to the ghost of some terrible end. He glanced back over his shoulder at the length of the skeletal remains, stretched out in the middle of an empty, gently rolling grassland, before urging his stallion into a trot to catch up with Nicci. His horse needed little encouragement to be away from the dying place, and happily sprang into his easy loping gallop, instead.

In the month or so Richard had spent with the horse, the two of them had become used to each other. The horse was willing enough, but never really friendly. Richard wasn't interested enough to go to the effort of doing more; making friends with a horse was just about the last of his concerns. Nicci hadn't known if the horses had names, and didn't seem interested in naming animals, so Richard simply called the black stallion "Boy," and Nicci's dappled gray mare "Girl," and left it at that. Nicci seemed neither pleased or displeased about him naming the horses; she simply went along with his convention.

"Do you actually believe it's the remains of a dragon?" Nicci asked when he caught up with her.

The stallion slowed and, glad to be back in the herd, gave the mare's flanks a nuzzle. Girl merely turned her closest ear toward him in recognition.

"It's about the right size, as I remember."

Nicci tossed her head to flick her hair back over her shoulder. "You're serious, aren't you?"

Richard frowned his puzzlement. "You saw it. What else could it possibly be?"

She conceded with a sigh. "I just thought it was the bones of some long-extinct beast."

"With flies still buzzing around it? It still had a few bits of sinew dried to the bones. It's not some ancient thing. It couldn't be much older than six months—possibly much less."

She was watching him from the corner of her eye, again. "So, they really do have dragons in the New World?"

"In the Midlands, anyway. Where I grew up there were none. Dragons, as I understand it, have magic. There was no magic in Westland. When I came here I . . . saw a red dragon. From what I heard, they're very rare."

And now there was at least one less.

Nicci was little concerned about the remains of an animal, even if it was a dragon. Richard had long ago decided that, as much as he lusted to crush her skull, he would have a better chance of figuring a way out of his situation if he didn't antagonize her. Battling another person sapped your own strength, making it more difficult to reason your way out of the trouble. He kept his mind focused on what was most important to him.

He couldn't force himself to pretend to befriend Nicci, but he tried to give her no cause to become angry enough to hurt Kahlan. So far, it had been successful. Nicci didn't seem easily inclined to anger, anyway. When she became displeased, she submerged back into an indifference which seemed to smother her distant rancor.

They finally reached the road from where they had spotted the white speck that had turned out to be the remains of the dragon.

"What was it like growing up in a place with no magic?"

Richard shrugged. "I don't know. That's just the way it was. It was normal."

"And you were happy? Growing up without magic, I mean?"

"Yes. Very happy." The frown returned to his face. "Why?"

"And yet, you fight to keep magic in the world, so other children will have to grow up with it. Am I right?"

"Yes."

"The Order wishes to rid the world of magic, so that people can grow up happy, without the poisonous fog of magic always outside their door." She glanced over at him. "They want children to grow up much like you did. And yet you fight this."

It was not a question, so Richard chose not to turn it into one for her. What the Order chose to do was not his concern. He turned his thoughts to other things.

They were traveling east-southeast on a road traversed by the odd trader. They had smiled and nodded at two that day. The road, as it took the easiest route across the rolling hills, had that afternoon begun to turn more to the south. As they crested a rise, Richard spotted a flock of sheep in the far distance. Not far ahead, they had been told, was a town where they could pick up some needed provisions. The horses could use some grain, too.

Over his left shoulder, to the northeast, snowcapped mountains turning pink in the late sunlight rose up out of the foothills. To his right, the ground rolled off into the wilds. Beyond the town, it wouldn't be too far until they crossed the Kern River. They were not far at all from what used to be the wasteland where the great barrier had stood.

They were close to cutting south into the Old World.

Even though there was no longer a barrier to prevent his return once they crossed over, he felt downhearted about leaving the New World. It was like leaving Kahlan's world. Like leaving her by one more degree. As fiercely as he loved her, he could feel her slipping farther and farther into the distance.

Nicci's blond hair fluttered in the breeze as she turned toward him. "It's said they used to have dragons in the Old World, too."

Richard brought himself out of his brooding.

"But no more?" he asked. She shook her head. "How long ago was that?"

"Long ago. No one living has ever seen one—and that includes Sisters living at the palace."

He thought about it as he rode, listening to the rhythmic clop of hooves. Nicci had proven forthcoming, so he asked, "Do you know why not?"

"I can only tell you what was taught to me, if you would like to hear it." When Richard nodded, she went on. "During the great war, at the time when the barrier between the Old and New Worlds was raised, the wizards in the Old World worked toward revoking magic from the world. Dragons could not exist without magic, so they went extinct."

"But they still existed here."

"On the other side of the barrier. It may be that the old wizards' suppression of magic, on their side, had only a local, or even temporary, effect. After all, magic still exists, so obviously they failed to achieve their ends."

Richard was getting an uneasy feeling as he considered both Nicci's words and the bones he had seen.

"Nicci, may I ask you a question, a serious question, about magic?"

She gazed over at him as she slowed her horse to an easy walk. "What is it you wish to know?"

"How long do you think a dragon could exist without magic?"

Nicci considered his question for a moment, but in the end let out a sigh. "I only know about the history of the dragons in the Old World as it was taught. As you know, words written that long ago are not always dependable. It would only be an educated guess. I would say it could be mere moments, possibly days—or even longer, but not a great deal longer. It's a much simplified version of asking how long a fish could live out of water. Why do you ask?"

Richard raked his fingers back through his hair. "When the chimes were here, in this world, they drew away magic. All of the magic, or nearly all, anyway, was withdrawn from the world of life for a time."

She turned her eyes back to the road. "My estimation is that the withdrawal was total, for a time, at least."

That was what he had feared. Richard considered her words along with what he knew. "Not all creatures of magic depend on it. Us, for example; we are, in a way, creatures of magic, but we can live without it, too. I'm wondering if creatures that depended on magic for their very existence might not have made it through until the chimes were banished and magic was restored to the world of life."

"Magic was not restored."

Richard pulled his horse up short. "What?"

"Not in the way you are thinking about it." Nicci circled around to face him. "Richard, while I have no direct knowledge with precisely what happened, such an event could not be without consequence."

"Tell me what you know."

She frowned in curiosity. "Why do you look so concerned?"

"Nicci, please, just tell me what you know?"

She folded her wrists over the horn of her saddle.

"Richard, magic is a complex matter, so there can be no certainty." She held up a hand to forestall his cascade of questions. "This much, though, is certain. The world doesn't stay the same. It changes continuously.

"Magic is not merely part of this world. Magic is the conduit between worlds. Do you understand?"

He thought he might. "I accidentally used magic to call forth the spirit of my father from the underworld. I banished him back to the underworld with the use of magic. The Mud People, for example, use magic to communicate with their spirit ancestors beyond the veil in the underworld. I had to go to the Temple of the Winds, in another world, when Jagang sent a Sister there to start a plague which she brought back from that world."

"And what do all of those things have in common?"

"They used magic to bridge the gap between worlds."

"Yes. But there is more. Those worlds exist, but they are dependent on this one to define them, are they not?"

"You mean, like life is created into this world, and after death, souls are taken by the Keeper to the underworld?"

"Yes. But more, do you see the connection?"

Richard was getting lost. He hadn't grown up knowing anything about magic. "We're caught between the two realms?"

"No, not exactly." Her blue eyes flashed with intensity. She waited until his gaze steadied on hers, then she held up a finger to mark the importance of her words.

"Magic is a conduit between worlds. As magic diminishes, those other worlds are not just more distant to us, but the power of those worlds, in this world, diminishes. Do you see?"

Richard was getting goose bumps. "You mean, the other worlds have less influence, like . . . like a child who has grown and his parents have less influence over him."

"Yes." In the fading light her eyes seemed more blue than usual. "As the worlds grow more separate, it is something like a child growing and leaving home. But there is more to it, yet."

She leaned forward ever so slightly in her saddle. "You see, those other worlds can be said to exist only by their relationship to life—to this world." At that moment, she seemed like nothing to him so much as what she really was: a one-hundred-and-eighty-year-old sorceress. "It might even be said," she whispered in a voice that sounded like the shadows speaking, "that without magic to link those other worlds to this, those other worlds cease to exist."

Richard swallowed. "You mean, just as the child grows and leaves home, the parents become less important to his existence. When they eventually grow old and die, even though they were once vital and strongly linked to him, when they now cease to exist, he lives on without them."

"Exactly," she hissed.

"The world changes," he said almost to himself. "The world doesn't stay the same. That's what Jagang wants. He wants magic, and those other worlds, to cease to exist so that he will have this one all for himself."

"No," she said in a soft voice. "He wishes it not for himself, but for mankind." Richard started to argue, but she cut him off. "I know Jagang. I'm telling you what he believes. He may enjoy the spoils, but in his heart, he believes he is doing this for mankind, not himself."

Richard didn't really believe her, but he didn't see any point in quarreling with her. Either way, because of the changes taking place, such creatures as dragons might have already become extinct. Those white bones could very well have been the remains of the last red dragon.

"Because of events like the chimes, the world may already have irrevocably changed to a point where creatures of magic have died out," she said as she stared out over the empty twilight. "In an evolving world such as I describe, magic, even such as ours, would soon die out, too. Do you see, now? Without that conduit to other worlds, worlds that may no longer exist, magic would not come into existence when offspring of the gifted are born."

One thing was sure: when the time came, he was going to make Nicci extinct.

As they rode on, Richard gazed back over his shoulder at bones he could no longer see.

It was well after dark when they rode into the town. When Richard inquired of a passerby, he was told that the town, Ripply, was named after the rippling foothills. It was a quiet place, off in a nearly forgotten corner of the Midlands, its back to what used to be the wasteland from where no one ever returned. Many of the people grew wheat and raised sheep to provide themselves with trade goods, while keeping small animals and gardens for themselves.

There was a road coming in from the southwest, from Renwold, and other roads going off to the north. Ripply was a crossroads for trade between Renwold, the people of the wilds who traded at that outpost city, and villages to the north and east. Now, of course, Renwold was gone; the Imperial Order had sacked the city. Now, with only ghosts inhabiting the streets of Renwold, the people of the wilds who traded their goods there would suffer. The people from the towns and villages who came to Ripply would suffer, too; Ripply was falling on hard times.

Richard and Nicci created a small sensation. Strangers traveling through had become a sporadic event, what with Renwold gone. The two of them were tired, and there was an inn, but raucous drinking was going on there, and Richard didn't want to have to deal with that kind of trouble. There was a well-kept stable at the other end of town from the inn, and the man who owned it offered to let them stay in the hayloft for a silver penny each. The night was cold, and it would be warmer in the hayloft out of the wind, so Richard paid the man the penny each for themselves, and three more for the horses to be cared for and fed. The taciturn stable owner was so pleased with the extra penny for the horses that he told Richard he would tend their shoes while he had them.

When Richard thanked him and told him they were tired, the man smiled for the first time and said, "I'll be seeing to your horses, then. I hope you and your wife sleep well. Good night, then."

Richard followed Nicci up the rough wooden ladder at the back of the barn. They had a cold dinner sitting in the hay as they listened to the stable owner fetching grain and water for their horses. Richard and Nicci had only the bare bones of necessary conversation before they rolled themselves up in their cloaks and went to sleep. When they woke a little after dawn, they discovered a small gathering of skinny children and hollow-cheeked adults, come to see the "rich" folks traveling through. Apparently, their horses, better than any that had boarded at the stable in a long time, had been the source of gossip and speculation.

When Richard greeted the people, he got back only vacant looks. When he and Nicci walked to the supply store, not far away past a few drab buildings, the people all followed, as if it were a king and queen come to town, and they all wanted to see what such highborn people did with their day. Goats and chickens wandering Ripply's main street scattered before the procession. A milk cow cropping brown grass behind the leather shop paused for a look. A rooster atop a stump flapped his wings in annoyance.

When the bolder children asked who they were, Nicci told them that they were only travelers, husband and wife, looking for work. Such news was greeted with skeptical tittering. In her fine black dress, the people took Nicci for a queen looking for a kingdom. They thought only a little less of Richard.

When an older boy asked where they were going to look for work, as there was little to be found in Ripply, Nicci told them that they were going to the Old World. Some of the adults snatched up children and hurried away. Yet more remained close on Richard and Nicci's heels.

An older man who owned the supply store gently shooed the people away from his door when Richard went in. Once Richard had gone inside, he watched the people grow bolder and begin pawing at Nicci, begging for money, for medicine, for food. Nicci stayed outside with the people, asking them about their troubles and their needs. She moved through the crowd, inspecting the children. She had that blank look on her face that Richard didn't like.

"What can I get you," the proprietor asked.

"Ah, what about those people?" Richard asked instead.

He glanced out the sparkling-clean little window to see Nicci standing in the middle of the ragged group, talking about the Creator's love for them. They all listened as if she were a good spirit come to comfort them.

"Well, they're all sorts," the shop owner said. "Most wandered in from the Old World after the barrier came down. Some are just no-good locals—drunks and such—who'd just as soon beg or steal as work. When strangers from the Old World came in, some of the people here joined their ways. We get traders through here, and men like that, with goods to protect, find they have less trouble if they're generous with that sort. Some of them out there are folks who've had trouble—widows with children who can't find a husband; things like that. A few of them will work for me, when I have work, but most won't."

Richard was about to give the man a list of their needs, when Nicci glided in the door.

"Richard, I need some money."

Rather than argue with her, he passed her the saddlebag with the money. She reached in and pulled out a handful of gold and silver. The shop owner's eyes went wide when he saw how much she had in her fist. She paid him no heed. Richard stood slack-jawed as he watched Nicci, back out with the crowd, giving away all the money. Arms waved and reached for her. People cried out all the louder. A few ran off with what she had given them.

Richard pulled open the saddlebag, peering in to see how much they had left. It wasn't much. He could hardly believe what Nicci had just done. It made no sense.

"How about some barley flour, some oatmeal, some rice, some bacon, lentils, dried biscuits, and salt?" he asked the waiting proprietor.

"No oatmeal, but I've got the rest. How much do you want?"

Richard was running calculations through his head. They had a long journey, and Nicci had just given away most of their money. They'd used up the better portion of the supplies they had.

He laid six silver pennies on the counter. "Just what that will buy us." He pulled his pack off his back and set it on the counter beside the money.

The man scooped up the coins and sighed at the money he had almost made. He began pulling the items down from a shelf and placing them in the pack. As he worked, Richard requested a few other small things he remembered as the man was going about getting the order. He parted with another penny.

Richard had only a few silver pennies, two silver crowns, and no gold left. Nicci had handed out more money than most of those people had ever seen in their entire lifetimes. Worried about what they were going to do for supplies in the future, Richard slung his pack onto his back when the shop proprietor had finished, and rushed out to see if he couldn't slow Nicci down.

She was lecturing on the Creator's love of every man and asking the people to forgive the cruelty of heartless and uncaring people, as she handed the last gold coin to an unshaven man without teeth. He grinned his thanks and then licked his parched lips. Richard knew how he would wet them. There were yet more pleading hands thrusting toward her.

Worried, Richard seized Nicci's arm and pulled her back. She turned toward him.

"We have to get back to the stables," she said.

"That's what I'm thinking," Richard said, holding his anger in check. "Let's hope the stableman is done with them by now so we can get out of here."

"No," she said with a look of grim finality in her eye. "We need to sell the horses."

"What?" Richard blinked in angry astonishment. "May I at least ask why?"

"To share what we have with those who have nothing."

Richard was beyond words. He just stared at her. How were they going to travel? He considered the question briefly, and decided that he didn't really care how soon they got to wherever it was she was taking him. But they would have to carry everything. He was a woods guide, and used to walking with a pack, so he guessed he could walk. He let out his breath and turned toward the stables.

"We need to sell the horses," Richard told the stable owner.

The man frowned, looked at the horses standing in their stalls, and then back at Richard. He looked thunderstruck.

"Those are mighty fine horses, mister. We don't have horses like this around here."

"You do now," Nicci said.

He glanced uneasily at her. Most people were uneasy gazing at Nicci, either because of her startling beauty, or because of her cool, often denunciative, presence.

"I can't pay what horses like this are worth."

"We didn't ask you to," Nicci said in a dull voice. "We only asked to sell them to you. We need to sell them. We'll take what you can give us."

The man's eyes shifted from Richard's to Nicci's and back. Richard could tell the man was uneasy about cheating them in such a way, but he couldn't seem to figure out how to turn down such an offer.

"All I can pay is four silver marks for the both of them."

Richard knew they were worth ten times that much.

"And the tack," Nicci said.

The man scratched his cheek. "I guess I could throw in another silver, but that's all I got to my name. I'm sorry, I know they're worth more, but if you're bound and determined for me to buy them off you, that's all I got."

"Is there anyone else in town who might buy them for more?" Richard asked.

"I don't believe so, but to tell you the truth, son, it wouldn't be hurting my feelings if you were to go ask around. I don't like swindling folks, and I know you couldn't call five silver marks for the horses and tack anything else but a swindle."

The man kept glancing at Nicci, seeming to suspect that this transaction was beyond Richard's ability to control. Her steady blue eyes could make any man fidget.

"We accept your offer," Nicci said without any hesitation or uncertainty. "I'm sure it's quite fair."

The man sighed unhappily at his windfall. "I don't have that much money on me. I'll go in the house"—he lifted a thumb over his shoulder—"out back of the barn and get it, if you'd be so good as to wait a minute."

Nicci nodded and he hurried on his way, not so much eager to consummate the deal, Richard thought, as he was eager to be out from under Nicci's gaze.

Richard turned to her, feeling his face heating. "What's this all about?" He saw through the partly open stable doors that the crowd of people who had followed them were still out there.

She ignored his question. "Get your things—whatever you can carry. As soon as he comes back, it's time we were on our way."

Richard pulled his glare from her. He stalked over to his gear, sitting outside Boy's stall, and began stuffing everything he could into his pack. He strapped the waterskins around his waist and flipped the saddlebags over his shoulders. He was sure the stable owner wouldn't complain about not having the saddlebags with the rest of the tack. Richard thought that when they reached a more prosperous town, he could at least sell the saddlebags. While he worked, Nicci put her belongings into a pack she could carry.

When the man came back with the money, he offered it to Richard. Nicci held out her hand.

"I'll take it," she said.

He glanced to Richard's eyes once and then handed Nicci the money. "I threw in the silver pennies you paid me last night. That's all I have, I swear."

"Thank you," Nicci said. "That was very generous of you to share what you have. That is the Creator's way."

Without another word, Nicci turned and strode through the dimly lit stable and out the door.

"It's my way," the man muttered under his breath to her back. "Creator had no say in it."

Outside in the sunlight, Nicci began doling out the money she had just gotten for the horses. The people vied for her favor as she walked among them, speaking to them, asking questions, until she was out of sight, past the edge of the barn door.

Richard gave Boy a quick rub on the blaze of his forehead, hoisted his saddlebags onto his shoulder, and turned to the dumbfounded expression on the stable owner's face. He and Richard shared a helpless look.

"I hope she's a good wife to you," the man finally said.

Richard wanted to say that Nicci was a Sister of the Dark, and that he was her prisoner, but in the end he decided that it could serve no purpose. Nicci had made it clear to him that he was Richard Cypher, her husband, and she was Nicci Cypher, his wife. She had told him to stick to that story—for Kahlan's sake.

"She's just generous," Richard said. "That's why I married her. She's good to people."

Richard heard a woman's cry, and shouting. He bolted for the partly open door and ran out into the bright morning sunlight. He didn't see anyone. He raced around to the side of the barn, to where he heard scuffling.

A half dozen men had Nicci down on the ground, some swinging at her with their fists as she tried to fend them off with her bare hands. Others pawed at her, searching for a money pouch. They were fighting over the unearned before it was even out of her hands. A crowd of women, children, and other men stood around the scene in a circle, vultures waiting to pick the bones.

Richard crashed through the ring of people, seized the closest man by the back of his collar, and heaved him back. He was skinny, and flew through the air, crashing into the wall of the barn. The whole building shook. Richard kicked another in the ribs, tumbling him off Nicci and through the dirt. A third man spun and took a mighty swing at Richard. Richard caught the fist and bent it down until he felt a snap as the man cried out. At that, the men all scattered in every direction.

Richard started after one of them, but Nicci suddenly flew at him, restraining him.

"Richard! No!"

In his rage to get at the men, Richard nearly smashed her face, but, when he realized it was her, lowered his fists to his sides as he glared at the crowd.

"Please, my lord, please, my lady," one of the women wailed, "have mercy on us woeful folk. We's just the Creator's miserable wretches. Have mercy on us."

"You're a bunch of thieves!" Richard yelled. "Thieving from someone who was trying to help you!"

He made an effort to go after the lot of them, but Nicci held his wrists down. "Richard, no!"

The people vanished like mice before a hissing cat.

Nicci let Richard's fists drop. He saw then that she had blood on her mouth.

"What's the matter with you? Giving money to people who would rather rob you than wait for you to hand it to them willingly? Why would you give money to such vermin?"

"That's enough. I'll not stand here and listen to you insult the Creator's children. Who are you to judge? Who are you, with a full belly, to say what's right? You have no idea what those poor people have been through, and yet you are quick to judge."

Richard took a purging breath. He reminded himself yet again of what he had to keep uppermost in his mind. It was not really Nicci he had been protecting.

He pulled a shirtsleeve from the corner of his pack, wet it with water from a waterskin hanging around his waist, and carefully wiped her bloody mouth and chin. She winced as he worked but without protest let him inspect her injury.

"It's not bad," he told her. "Just a cut in the corner of your mouth. Hold still, now."

She stood quietly as he held her head in one hand while he cleaned the blood off the rest of her face with the other.

"Thank you, Richard." She hesitated. "I was sure one of them was going to cut my throat."

"Why didn't you use your Han to protect yourself?"

"Have you forgotten? To do that, I would have to take power from the link keeping Kahlan alive."

He looked into her blue eyes. "I guess I forgot. In that case, thank you for restraining yourself."

Nicci said nothing as they walked out of the town of Ripply, carrying everything they owned on their backs. As cold as the day was, it wasn't long before his brow was dotted with sweat.

Finally he could stand it no longer. "Do you mind telling me what that was all about?"

Her brow twitched. "Those people were needy."

Richard pinched the bridge of his nose, pausing in an effort to remain civil to her. "And so you gave them all our money?"

"Are you so selfish that you would not share what you have? Are you so selfish that you would ask the hungry to starve, the unclothed to freeze, the sick to die? Does money mean more to you than people's lives?"

Richard bit the inside of his cheek to check his temper. "And the horses? You virtually gave them away."

"It was all we could get. Those people were in need. Under the circumstances, it was the best we could do. We acted with the most noble of intentions. It was our duty to not be selfish and to joyfully give these people what they needed."

There was no road going their way as they walked on into what had not long ago been the wasteland from which no one returned.

"We needed what we had," he said.

Nicci glanced up into his eyes. "There are things you need to learn, Richard."

"Is that right."

"You have been lucky in life. You have had opportunities ordinary people never have. I want you to see how ordinary people must live, how they must struggle just to survive. When you live like them, you will understand why the Order is so necessary, why the Order is the only hope for mankind.

"When we get to where we're going, we will have nothing. We will be just like all the other miserable people of this wretched world—with little chance to make it on our own. You don't have any idea what that's like. I want you to learn how the compassion of the Order helps ordinary people live with the dignity they are entitled to."

Richard returned his gaze to the empty land stretching out before them. A Sister of the Dark who couldn't use her power, and a wizard who was forbidden from using his. He guessed they couldn't get any more ordinary than that.

"I thought it was you who wanted to learn," he said.

"I am also your teacher. Teachers sometimes learn more than their students."

Zedd lifted his head when he heard the distant horns. He struggled to regain his senses. He was well past dread, into a world of little more than numb awareness. The horns were those meant to signal the approach of friendly forces. Probably some of the scouting patrols, or perhaps yet more wounded being brought in.

Zedd realized he was slumped on the ground, his legs sprawled out to the side. He saw that he had been sleeping with his head on the burly chest of a cold corpse. In despair, he recalled that he had been trying everything he knew to heal the horribly wounded man. In mournful revulsion, he pushed away from the cold body and sat up.

He rubbed his eyes against the darkness from within, as well as the night. He was beyond aching. Acrid smoke hung thick as fog. The air reeked with the heavy, throat-clenching stink of blood. From various places around him, he could see the drifting haze illuminated around glowing orange fists of firelight. The moans of the wounded lifted from the blood-soaked ground to drift through the frigid night air. In the distance, men cried out in pain. When Zedd wiped a hand across his brow, he realized he wore gloves of crusted blood from those he had been trying to heal. It was an endless task.

Not far away, the ground was littered with shattered tree trunks, blasted asunder by the enemy gifted. Men lay sprawled, torn apart or impaled by huge splintered sections of those trees. It had been two of Jagang's Sisters who had done it, just before dark, as the D'Haran forces were all collecting into the valley, thinking the battle had ended. Zedd and Warren had ended it by taking those two Sisters down with wizard's fire.

By the dull ache in his head, Zedd knew he hadn't been asleep for more than a couple of hours, at most. It had to be the middle of the night. People passing by had let him sleep—or maybe they thought him one of the dead.

The first day had gone as well as could be expected. The battle had dragged on sporadically throughout the first night with relatively minor skirmishes, and then had erupted with full force at dawn of the second day. As night had fallen on the second day, the fighting had finally ended. Looking around, Zedd thought it seemed to be over—at least for the time being.

They had made the valley and succeeded in drawing the Order after them, away from other gateways up into the Midlands, but at a terrible price. They had little choice, if they were to engage the enemy with any chance of success, rather than allow them unhindered access into the Midlands. For the moment, anyway, the Order was stalled. Zedd didn't know how long that would last.

Unfortunately, the Order had gotten the better of the battle, by far.

Zedd peered about. It was not so much a camp as simply a place where everyone had dropped in exhaustion. Here and there, arrows and spears stuck up from the ground. They had fallen like rain as Zedd had worked throughout the night, the night before, trying to heal wounded soldiers. During the day, in the battles, he had unleashed everything he had. What had started out as skillful, calculated, focused use of his ability had in the end degenerated into the magic equivalent of a brawl.

Zedd staggered to his feet, worried about the distant thunder of horses. Horns closer into camp repeated the warning to hold arrows and spears, that it was friendly forces. It sounded like too many horses for any patrol they had out. In the back of his mind, Zedd tried to recall if he felt the twinge of magic that would tell him the horns were genuine. In the fog of fatigue, he had forgotten to pay attention. That was how people ended up dead, he knew—inattention to such details.

Men were rushing all about, carrying supplies, water, and linen for bandages, or messages and reports. Here and there Zedd saw a Sister working at healing. Other men struggled with repairs to wagons and gear in case they had to depart in a hurry. Some men sat staring at nothing. A few wandered as if in a daze.

It was difficult to see in the poor light, but Zedd was able to see well enough to tell that the ground was littered with the dead, the wounded, or the simply spent. Fires, both the common orange and yellow flames of burning wagons and the unnatural green blazes that were the remnants of magic, were left to burn out on their own. Horses as well as men lay everywhere, still and lifeless, torn open by ghastly wounds. The battlefields changed, but battle didn't. Now was a time of helpless shock. He remembered from his youth the stench of blood and death mingled with greasy smoke. It was still the same. He remembered in battles past thinking the world had gone mad. It still felt the same.

The rumble of horses was getting closer. He could hear quite a commotion, but he couldn't tell what sort of ruckus it was. Off to his right, he spotted a stooped woman shuffling toward him. He recognized Adie's familiar limp. A woman more distant, catching up to Adie from behind, was probably Verna. A little farther off, Zedd saw Captain Meiffert being lectured to by General Leiden. Both men turned to look toward the clatter of hooves.

Zedd squinted into the murk and saw in the distance soldiers scattering before a mass of approaching riders. Men waved their arms, as if in greeting. A few offered weak cheers. Many pointed in Zedd's direction, funneling the horsemen his way. As First Wizard, he had become a focal point for everyone. The D'Harans, in Richard's absence, relied on Zedd to be their magic against magic. The Sisters relied on his experience in the nasty art of magic in warfare.

In the wavering glow of fires still burning out of control, Zedd watched the column of horsemen coming relentlessly onward, points of light glinting off row upon row of armor and weapons, shimmering off chain mail and polished boots, as they each in turn passed the burning wagons and barricades. The thundering column slowed for nothing, expecting men to get out of its way. At their fore, long pennons flew atop perfectly upright lances. Standards and flags flapped in the cold night air. The ground thundered with thousands of horses charging over the blood-soaked ground. They rolled onward, like a ghost company riding out of the grave.

Orange and green smoke, lit from behind by the eerie light of fires, curled away to each side as the column of riders charged though the middle of the camp at an easy gallop.

Zedd saw, then, who was leading them.

"Dear spirits . . ." he whispered aloud.

Sitting tall atop a huge horse at the head of the column was a woman in leather armor with fur billowing out behind her like an angry pennant.

It was Kahlan.

Even at that distance, Zedd could see, sticking up behind her left shoulder, the gleam of light off the silver and gold hilt of the Sword of Truth.

His flesh went cold with tingling dread.

He felt a hand on his arm and turned to see Adie, her completely white eyes transfixed by the sight she beheld through her gift alone. Verna was still weaving her way through the wounded. Captain Meiffert and General Leiden rushed to follow in Verna's footsteps.

The column stretched out behind Kahlan as far as Zedd could see. They charged onward, collecting cheering men as they came. Zedd waved his arms as they all bore down on him, so that Kahlan would notice him, but it seemed as if she had had her eyes on him the whole time.

The horses skidded to a halt before him, snorting and stamping, tossing their armored heads. Plumes of steam rose from their nostrils when they blew great hot breaths in the icy air. Powerful muscles flexed beneath glossy hides as they pawed the ground. The eager beasts stood at the ready, their tails lashing side to side, slapping their flanks like whips.

Kahlan swept the scene with a careful gaze. Men were rushing up from all directions. Those gathering around stared in wonder. The horsemen were Galeans.

Kahlan had provisionally taken the place of her half sister, Cyrilla, as queen of Galea, until Cyrilla was well again—if that ever happened. Kahlan's half brother, Harold, was the commander of the Galean army, and didn't want the crown, feeling himself more fit to serve his land in the soldier's life. Kahlan had Galean blood in her veins, although, to a Confessor, matters of blood were irrelevant. They were not so irrelevant to Galeans.

Kahlan swung her right leg forward over the horse's neck and dropped to the ground. Her boots resounded like a hammer strike announcing the Mother Confessor's arrival. Cara, in her red leather, and similarly cloaked in a fur mantle, likewise jumped down off her horse.

Battle-weary men all around stood in rapt silence. This was not merely the Mother Confessor. This was Lord Rahl's wife.

For just an instant, as Zedd stared into her green eyes, he thought she might run into his arms and break down in helpless tears. He was wrong.

Kahlan pulled off her gloves. "Report."

She wore stealth-black light leather armor, a royal Galean sword at her left hip, and a long knife at her right. Her thick fall of hair cascaded boldly over the wolf's fur mantle topping a black wool cloak. In the Midlands, the length of a woman's hair denoted rank and social standing. No Midlands woman wore hair as long as Kahlan's. But it was the hilt of the sword sticking up behind her shoulder that held Zedd's gaze.

"Kahlan," he whispered as she stepped closer, "where's Richard?"

Whatever pain he had seen for that instant was gone. She swept a brief glare Verna's way, as the young Prelate still hurried toward them between the wounded, then met Zedd's gaze with eyes like green fire.

"The enemy has him. Report."

246

"The enemy? What enemy?"

Again her glare slid to Verna. Its power straightened Verna's back and slowed her approach.

Kahlan returned her attention to Zedd. Her eyes softened with a vestige of sympathy for the anguish she must have seen on his face. "A Sister of the Dark took him, Zedd." The respite of warmth in her voice and eyes faded as her countenance returned to the cold, empty mask of a Confessor. "I would like a report, please."

"Took him? But is he—is he all right? You mean she took him as a prisoner? Do they want ransom? He's still all right?"

She touched the side of her mouth and Zedd saw then that she had a swollen cut. "He's all right as far as I know."

"Well, what's going on?" Zedd threw up his skinny arms. "What's this about? What does she intend?"

Verna finally made it up to Zedd's left side. Captain Meiffert and General Leiden ran up to the other side of Adie, on his right.

"What Sister?" Verna asked, still getting her breath back. "You said a Sister took him. What Sister?"

"Nicci."

"Nicci . . ." Captain Meiffert gasped. "Death's Mistress?"

Kahlan met his gaze. "That's the one. Now, is someone going to give me a report?"

There was no mistaking the command, or the rage, in her voice. Captain Meiffert lifted an arm to the south.

"Mother Confessor, the Imperial Order forces, all of them, finally moved up from Anderith." He rubbed his brow as he tried to think. "Yesterday morning, I guess it was."

"We wanted to pull them up here, into the valley country," Zedd put in. "Our idea was to get them out of the grassland, where we couldn't contain them, up into country where we had a better chance to do so."

"We knew," Captain Meiffert went on, "that it would be a fatal mistake to let them get by us and stream into the Midlands unopposed. We had to draw them into action to prevent them from unleashing their might against the populace. We had to engage them and bog them down. The only way to do that was to taunt them into following us out of the open, where they had the advantage, into terrain that helped even the odds."

Kahlan nodded as she scanned the dismal scene. "How many men did we lose?"

"I'd guess maybe fifteen thousand," Captain Meiffert said. "But that's just a guess. It may be more."

"They flanked you, didn't they." It didn't sound like a question.

"That's right, Mother Confessor."

"What went wrong?"

The Galean troops behind her formed a grim wall of leather, chain mail, and steel. Officers with incisive eyes watched and listened.

"What didn't?" Zedd growled.

"Somehow," the captain explained, "they knew what we planned. Although, I guess it wouldn't be all that hard to figure out, since anyone would know it was our only chance against their numbers. They were confident they could defeat us, regardless, so they obliged our plan."

"Like I asked, what went wrong?"

"What went wrong!" General Leiden interrupted heatedly. "We were outnumbered beyond all hope! That's what went wrong!"

Kahlan settled her cool gaze on the man. He seemed to catch himself and fell to one knee.

"My queen," he added in formal address before falling silent.

Kahlan's gaze lost some of its edge as it moved back to Captain Meiffert.

Zedd noticed the captain's fists tightening as he went on with his report. "Somehow, Mother Confessor, near as we can tell they managed to get a division across the river. We're pretty sure they didn't use the open ground to the east—we had preparations should they try that, as we feared they might."

"So," Kahlan said, "they reasoned you would think it impossible, so they sent a division across the river—probably a great deal more, willing to bear their losses in the crossing—went north through the mountains, unsuspected, unseen, and undetected, and crossed back to this side of the river. When you got here, they were waiting for you, holding the ground you had planned to hold. With the Order hot on your heels, you had nowhere else to go. The Order intended to crush you between that division holding this defendable ground and their army on your tail."

"That's the gist of it," Captain Meiffert confirmed.

"What happened to the division waiting here?" she asked.

"We wiped them out," the captain said with a cool rage of his own. "Once we realized what had happened, we knew it was our only chance."

Kahlan gave him a nod. She knew full well what a mighty effort his simple words conveyed.

"They cut us to pieces from behind as we did so!" General Leiden's temper was getting frayed around the edges. "We had no chance."

"Apparently you did," she answered. "You gained the valley."

"What of it? We can't fight a force their size. It was insane to throw men into that meat grinder. What for? We gained this valley, but at a terrible price. We won't be able to hold a force that huge! They had their way with us from the first until the last. We didn't stop them, they just got tired of hacking us to pieces for the night!"

Some men looked away. Some stared at the ground. Only the crackle of fires and the moans of the wounded filled the frigid night air.

Kahlan glanced around again. "What are you doing sitting here, now?"

Zedd's brow went up, along with his own anger. "We've been at it for two days, Kahlan."

"Fine. But I don't allow the enemy to go to bed with victory. Is that clear?"

Captain Meiffert clapped a fist to his heart in salute. "Clear, Mother Confessor."

He glanced over his shoulders. Fists of attentive men near and far likewise went to their hearts.

"Mother Confessor," General Leiden said, dropping her title of queen, "the men have been up for two days, now."

"I understand," Kahlan said. "We have been riding without pause for three days, now. Neither changes what must be done."

In the harsh reflection of firelight, the creases in General Leiden's face looked like angry gashes. He pressed his lips together and bowed to his queen, but when he came up, he spoke again.

"My queen, Mother Confessor, you can't seriously be expecting us to carry out a night attack. There's no moon and clouds mostly hide the stars. In the dark such an attack would be a disaster. It's lunacy!"

248

Kahlan finally withdrew her cold glare from the Keltish general and passed a gaze among those assembled around her. "Where is General Reibisch?"

Zedd swallowed. "I'm afraid that's him."

She looked where Zedd pointed, at the corpse he had fallen asleep atop while trying to heal. The rust-colored beard was matted with dried blood. The grayish-green eyes stared without seeing, no longer showing pain. It had been a fool's task, Zedd knew, but he couldn't help trying to heal what could not be healed, giving it everything he had left. It hadn't been enough.

"Who is next in command," Kahlan asked.

"That would be me, my queen," General Leiden said as he took a stride forward. "But as the ranking officer, I can't allow my men to—"

Kahlan lifted a hand. "That will be all, Lieutenant Leiden."

He cleared his throat. "General Leiden, my queen."

She fixed him with an implacable stare. "To question me once is a simple mistake, Lieutenant. Twice is treason. We execute traitors."

Cara's Agiel spun up into her fist. "Step aside, Lieutenant."

Even in the haunting orange and green light of fires, Zedd could see the man's face pale. He took a step back and wisely, if belatedly, fell silent.

"Who is next in command?" the Mother Confessor asked again.

"Kahlan," Zedd said, "I'm afraid the Order used their gifted to single out men of rank. Despite our best efforts, I believe we lost all our senior officers. It cost them dearly, at least."

"Then who is next in command?"

Captain Meiffert looked around and finally lifted his hand.

"I'm not positive, Mother Confessor, but I believe that would be me."

"Very well, General Meiffert."

He inclined his head. "Mother Confessor," he said in a quiet, confidential voice, "that isn't necessary."

"No one said it was, General."

The new general softly struck a fist to his heart. Zedd saw Cara smile in grim approval. Of the thousands of faces watching, that was the only smile. It wasn't that the men disapproved, but rather that they were relieved to have someone so firmly in command. D'Harans respected iron authority. If they couldn't have Lord Rahl, they would take his wife, and an iron one at that. They might not have smiled, but Zedd knew they would be pleased.

"As I said, I don't allow the enemy to go to bed with victory." Kahlan scanned the faces watching her. "I want a cavalry raid ready to go within the hour."

"And who do you intend to send on such an attack, my queen?"

Everyone knew what the former General Leiden meant by the question. He was asking who she was sending to their death.

"There will be two wings. One to make their way unseen around the Order's camp so as to come in from their south, where they will least expect it, and another wing to hold back until the first is in place, and then come in from this side, from the north. I intend to have us spill some of their blood before bed."

She looked back to the new Lieutenant Leiden's eyes and answered his question. "I will be leading the southern wing."

Everyone, except the new general, began voicing objections. Leiden spoke up louder.

"My queen, why would you want us to get our men together for a calvary raid?"

He pointed to the wall of men, all on horses behind her: all Galeans—traditional adversaries of the Keltans, Leiden's homeland. "When we have these?"

"These men will be helping get this army back together, relieving those on duty to get needed rest, helping dig defensive ditches, and filling in wherever they are needed. The men who were bloodied are the ones who need to go to bed with the sweet taste of vengeance. I would not dare to deny D'Harans that to which they are so entitled."

A cheer went up.

Zedd thought that if war was madness, madness had just found its mistress.

General Meiffert took a step closer to her. "I'll have my best men ready within the hour, Mother Confessor. Everyone will want to go; I'll have to disappoint a lot of volunteers."

Kahlan's face softened when she nodded. "Pick your man for the northern wing, then, General."

"I will be leading the northern wing, Mother Confessor."

Kahlan smiled. "Very well."

She ordered the Galean troops off to their duties. With a sweep of her finger, she dismissed everyone but the immediate group and called that inner circle closer.

"What about Richard's admonition not to directly attack the Order?" Verna asked.

"I remember well what Richard said. I'm not going to directly attack their main force."

Zedd supposed she did remember it well. She had been there with Richard—they hadn't. Zedd brought up a touchy issue.

"The main force will be in the center, well protected. At their edges, where you attack, will be defenses, of course, but mostly the camp followers will be at the tail end of the Order's camp—the fringe to the south, mostly."

"I don't really care," she said with cold fury. "If they're with the Order, then they are the enemy. There will be no mercy." She was looking at her new general as she spoke her orders. "I don't care if we kill their whores or their generals. I want every baker and cook dead as much as I want every officer and archer dead. Every camp follower we kill will deprive them of the comforts they enjoy. I want to strip them of everything, including their lives. Is that understood?"

General Meiffert gave his nod. "No mercy. You'll get no argument from us, Mother Confessor; that is the D'Haran code of warfare."

Zedd knew that, in war, Kahlan's way was usually the only way to prevail. The enemy would grant no mercy, and would need none themselves had they not invaded. Every whore and hawker chose to be a part of that invasion, to make what they could off the blood and plunder spilled at the Order's feet.

Verna spoke up. "Mother Confessor, Ann was going to see you and Richard. We last heard from her over a month ago. Have you seen her?"

"Yes."

Verna licked her lips in caution at the steely look in Kahlan's eyes. "Was she all right?"

"The last I saw her, she was."

"Would you know why she hasn't sent any word to us?"

"I threw her journey book in the fire."

Verna stepped forward, making to snatch Kahlan by the shoulder. Cara's Agiel came up like lightning, barring her way.

"No one touches the Mother Confessor." Cara's cold blue eyes were as deadly as her words. "Is that clear? No one."

"You have one Mord-Sith and one Mother Confessor, here, both in very bad moods," Kahlan said in a level voice. "I would suggest you not give us an excuse to lose our temper, or we may never find it again in your lifetime."

Zedd's fingers found Verna's arm and gently urged her back.

"We're all tired," he said. "We have enough troubles with the Order." He shot Kahlan a scowl. "No matter how tired or distraught we are, though, let's remember we're all on the same side here."

Kahlan's eyes told him she challenged that statement, but she said nothing.

Verna changed the subject. "I will get together some of the gifted to escort you on the raid."

"Thank you, but we will be taking no gifted."

"But you will at least need them to help you find your way in the dark."

"We will have the enemy campfires to show us our way."

"Kahlan," Zedd said, hoping to interject some reason, "the Order will have gifted—including Sisters of the Dark. You will need protection from them."

"No. I don't want any gifted with us. They are expecting any attack to be accompanied by our gifted. Their gifted will be watching for shields of magic. Any riders they do see without detecting magic they will be more likely to discount. We'll be able to get in deeper and draw more blood without gifted along."

Verna sighed at such foolishness, but didn't argue. General Meiffert liked her plan. Zedd knew she was right about getting in deeper, but he knew, too, that getting back out would be more difficult, once the enemy was on to them.

"Zedd, I would like one bit of magic."

He scratched his brow in resignation. "What would you like me to do?"

Kahlan gestured at the ground. "Make that dust glow. I want it to show up in the dark, and I want it sticky."

"For how long?"

She shrugged. "The rest of the night would be enough."

After Zedd had spun a web over the dusty patch of ground, giving it a green glow, Kahlan bent and rubbed her hand in it. She walked around back of her horse and slapped the hand on each flank, leaving a glowing green handprint on each hindquarter.

"What are you doing?" Zedd asked.

"It's dark. I want them to be able to see me. They can't come after me if they can't find me in the dark."

Zedd sighed at the madness.

General Meiffert squatted and rubbed his hand in the glowing dust. "I'd also hate for them to miss me in the dark."

"Be sure to wash your hand clean before we go," she said.

After she had explained her plan to the new general, Kahlan, Cara, and General Meiffert started off to their tasks.

Before they could get far, Zedd halted Kahlan with a softly spoken question.

"Kahlan, do you have any idea how we can get Richard back?"

She gazed boldly into his eyes. "Yes. I have a plan."

"Would you mind sharing it with me?"

"It's simple. I plan on killing every Imperial Order man, woman, and child until I get to the very last one left alive, and then if she doesn't give him back, I'm going to kill her, too."

Kahlan focused past the black void to the glowing points of the fires as she leaned forward over the withers of her galloping horse, urging him onward, faster and faster. The muscles in her thighs strained as she pressed her weight against the stirrups and squeezed her legs against the feverish warmth of the massive body rhythmically, incessantly, frantically flexing and stretching, feeling its every pounding strike against the ground. Her ears were filled with the hammering of her own heart and the thunder of yet more hooves behind her. She was distantly aware of the weight of the Sword of Truth sheathed in its scabbard, an ever-present reminder of Richard.

She gripped the reins in one fist. With her other, she lifted her royal Galean sword high. The lights were coming. Unexpectedly, the first came out of nowhere and exploded into her vision.

Racing past what looked to be the light of a single candle, she was there, at last. Crying out with the sudden power of emotions that could no longer be stifled, she slammed her sword down against the dark shape of a man. The impact of the blade against bone jarred her wrist. The hilt stung against her palm.

On their way by, the men behind her unleashed their fury against the remaining sentries at the outpost. Kahlan held tight, knowing the greater unleashing of her need was yet to come. She would not be denied, now.

The fires of the outer fringes of the camp flew toward her. Her muscles were rigid with expectation. She felt at the brink of control. And then she was upon them. At last, she was there. She met them with all her strength. Her blade came down again and again, lashing against their bodies, slashing anyone within her reach. The outer fires shot past the sides of her horse with dizzying speed. She gasped for breath.

Laying the reins over, Kahlan pulled her big warhorse around in a tight circle. He was not as agile as she would have preferred, but he was well trained and for this job he would do. He bellowed with the excitement of battle begun.

Tents and wagons were scattered everywhere, with little apparent order. Kahlan could hear the merry laughter of those not yet aware of the enemy in their midst. She had brought a small attack force, keeping them tight and close on the way in so it wouldn't raise the kind of alarm a broad attack would. It had worked. She saw men around fires tipping up bottles, or eating meat off skewers. She saw men sleeping, with their feet sticking out of tents. She saw a man walking with his arm around the waist of a woman. In the dim light she saw men in tents between the legs of other women.

The couple, arm in arm—undoubtedly at a price—was close. The man was on the far side of the woman as Kahlan raced up behind them, so with a mighty swing she took off the woman's head, instead. The stupefied man clutched the headless body as it began to fall. The cavalry man right behind Kahlan took the startled man down.

Kahlan dug in her heels and charged her big warhorse over a haphazard row of tents with men and women inside. She could feel the huge hooves crushing bone. Screams rose around her and her mount.

A soldier with a pike stood with his legs spread in a stance of sudden alarm. On her way past, Kahlan snatched the pike from his grip, stabbed it into a small tent, twisting it, getting the canvas tangled up on its barbs, and then backed her horse, hauling the tent off a man and woman. Her men following behind stabbed the exposed couple as Kahlan pulled the remnants of the tent through a fire. As soon as it lit, she dragged the flaming canvas to a wagon, setting that wagon's tarp afire, and then threw the blazing remains in another wagon full of supplies.

With a backhanded swing of her sword, Kahlan smashed the face of a burly man who ran up to pull her off her horse. She had to yank the blade free of his skull. Before more men could snatch at her, she dug in her heels again and charged off toward another fire, where men were just jumping to their feet. The horse knocked down several, and her sword cut another. By now, the shrieks of women sent up an effective alarm, and men were rushing out of tents and wagons with weapons in their fists. The whole scene was one of erupting pandemonium.

Kahlan wheeled her mount, stabbing anyone within reach. Many were not soldiers. Her sword felled leatherworkers and wagon masters, whores and soldiers. High-stepping at her command, her horse trampled down a line of big tents where wounded were being cared for. Beside a lamp, Kahlan spotted a surgeon with needle and thread working on a man's leg. She drove her horse around to trample the surgeon and the man he was sewing up. The surgeon held his arms up before his face, but his arms were no good at warding the weight of a huge warhorse.

Kahlan signaled her men in. Army surgeons were valuable. The D'Harans killed every one they saw. She knew that killing each was as good as killing untold numbers of enemy soldiers. Kahlan and her men wreaked havoc through the whores' tents, toppled cook wagons, cut down soldiers and civilians alike. When her men saw lamps, they leaped off their horses and snatched them up to use to start fires. Kahlan hacked at an enraged cook who came at her with a butcher knife. It took three rapid cuts to dispatch him.

To her left, Cara's horse cut off a man about to throw a spear. Cara coolly went about killing him and anyone else within her reach. A twist of her Agiel usually seized up their hearts, and if not, Kahlan could at least hear bones snap. Their cries of death and pain seemed frightful enough to send a shiver up the spines of the dead, and did add to the general confusion and panic. It was glorious music to Kahlan's ears.

The Agiel would only function through the bond to the Lord Rahl. Because it worked, she and Cara knew Richard was alive. That alone gave Kahlan heart. It was almost as if he were there with her. His sword strapped to her back was like his hand touching her, encouraging her to throw herself into the fight, telling her to cut.

The indiscriminate nature of the killing in among the camp followers confused the enemy soldiers, and terrorized the people who commonly believed themselves impervious to the violence they ultimately fed off of. Now, rather than being the vultures picking at the carcasses, they were the hapless prey. Life in the Imperial Order's camp would never be the same—Kahlan would see to that. No more would the enemy soldiers enjoy the comforts provided by these people. They would now know they were no less targets than officers. They would know the price of their participation. The price was a merciless death and payment had come due.

Slashing her way through the running crowds of screaming people, Kahlan kept an eye on a large group of the Imperial Order's horses, stabled not far off, watching as soldiers threw saddles on their mounts. She drove her horse over men and tents, getting closer, until she was sure she was within earshot of those cavalry men saddling their horses.

Kahlan stood in her stirrups, waving her sword high in the air. Men paused to stare.

"I am the Mother Confessor! For the crime of invading the Midlands, I condemn you all to death! Every one of you!"

The hundred men with her sent up a cheer. Their voices joined in a chant.

"Death to the Order! Death to the Order! Death to the Order!"

Kahlan and her men charged their horses around in an ever-widening circle, trampling anyone they could, hacking anyone within reach, stabbing anyone who rushed them, setting fire to anything that would burn. These D'Haran soldiers were the best at what they did, and they did it with brilliant effectiveness. When they found a wagon with oil, they broke the barrels open and tossed on flaming logs they plucked up with lances from fires. Night whooshed into day. Everyone could plainly see Kahlan, now, as she charged through their midst, screaming her pronouncement of death.

Kahlan saw the Order's cavalry mounting up, pulling their lances from racks, drawing their swords. She reared her horse, holding her sword high.

"You are all cowards! You will never catch me or best me! You will all die like the cowards you are at the hands of the Mother Confessor!"

When her horse came down, she thumped its ribs with her boots. The horse charged off at a dead run, Cara right at her side, her hundred men at her heels, a few thousand infuriated Imperial Order cavalry right behind them, with more mounting up all the time.

Being at the edge of the Order's camp, they wouldn't have much ground to cover before they were out of the camp, again, and into the open countryside. As they raced away, Kahlan took the opportunity to kill anyone who presented themselves. It was too dark to tell if they were men or woman, and it didn't matter anyway. She wanted them all dead. Each time her sword made contact, slashing muscle or breaking bone, was a delicious release.

Running at full speed, past the last of the campfires, they plunged suddenly into the black void of night. Kahlan leaned forward over her horse's muscular neck, as they ran west, hoping there were no holes in the ground. If they hit one, it would be all over not just for her horse, but, most likely, for her as well.

She knew this land well enough, the gentle hills, the bluffs ahead. She knew where she was, even in the dark, and she knew where she was going. She was counting on the enemy not knowing. In the disorienting sweep of darkness, they would fixate on following the glowing handprints on her horse's rump, thinking one of their gifted had gotten close enough to mark her horse for them. They would be gleeful with the blinding anticipation of having her naked to their swords.

Kahlan used the flat of her own sword to smack her horse's flanks, urging him on, whipping him into a wild state. They were away from the excitement of battle, now, and out in the lonely openness of the countryside. Horses dreaded predators nipping at their flanks, especially in the dark. She encouraged him to think teeth were snapping at his hindquarters.

Her men were right behind her, but, as instructed, rode to each side so there was a gap, allowing the enemy to see the glowing marks on her horse. When Kahlan feared she was as close as they dared get, she signaled with a whistle. Over her shoulders, she watched her men, her protection, peeling away, off into the night. She would not see them again until she returned to the D'Haran camp.

With her advantage of the distant fires of the Order's camp in back of them, Kahlan was able to see the silhouette of the enemy cavalry close behind, coming at a full charge, their hungry gazes no doubt fixed on the glowing handprints on her horse's flanks, the only thing they could see out in the wide-open countryside on a moonless night.

"How far?" Cara called over from close beside her.

"Should be—"

Kahlan's words cut off when she suddenly spotted briefly what was right there before her.

"Now, Cara!"

Kahlan pulled her leg up just in time as Cara rammed her horse over. The two huge animals jostled dangerously. Kahlan threw her arm around Cara's shoulders. Cara's arm seized Kahlan's waist and yanked her over, off her horse. Kahlan gave her horse one last smack with the flat of her sword. The horse snorted in panic as it charged onward at full speed into the blackness.

Kahlan threw her leg over the rump of Cara's horse, sheathed her sword, and then held tight to Cara's waist as the Mord-Sith pulled her horse's head hard to the left, forcing it, at a full gallop, to turn away just in time.

For an instant, through a break in the clouds, Kahlan spied the dull slur of starlight reflecting off the churning, icy waters of the Drun River below.

She felt a pang of sorrow for her startled, bewildered, terrified horse as it sailed out over the bluff. It was giving its life to take many more with it. The beast would probably never know what had happened.

Neither would the Imperial Order cavalry as they followed the glowing handprints on into the dark. This was her Midlands; Kahlan knew what was there; they were invaders, and did not. Even if they did see it coming in the last twinkling of their lives, at a full charge into pitch blackness they would never have a chance to avert their doom.

She hoped, though, that those men did realize what was happening—just before they gasped in the frigid dark waters, or before their lungs burst with the need of air as the merciless river dragged them down into its inky embrace. She hoped every one of those men suffered a horrifying death in the dark depths of those treacherous currents.

Kahlan turned her thoughts away from the heat of battle. The forces of the D'Haran Empire could sleep, now, with a victory over their enemy and with the sweet taste of vengeance. Kahlan found that it did little, though, to quell the fires of her raging anger.

After a brief time, Cara's horse slowed to a canter, and then a walk. They heard no hoofbeats behind them, only winter's vast silence. After the crush of people, the noise, and the turbulence of the Imperial Order's camp, the isolation of the empty grasslands seemed somehow oppressive. Kahlan felt as if she were a speck of nothing in the middle of nowhere.

Cold and exhausted, Kahlan pulled her fur mantle around her shoulders. Her legs trembled from the effort finally finished. She felt as if everything had been washed out of her. Her head slumped forward to rest against Cara's back. Kahlan was aware of the weight of Richard's sword lying against her own back.

"Well," Cara said over her shoulder after they had ridden for a time through the hushed expanse of countryside, "we do this every night for a year or two, and that should just about wipe them all out."

For the first time in what seemed an eternity, Kahlan almost laughed. Almost.

By the time Kahlan and Cara rode in among the wounded, the exhausted, and the sleeping D'Haran troops, it was only a few hours from dawn. Kahlan had thought they might have to find a safe place out in the grasslands to sleep and wait for daylight in order to find their way back, but they had been fortunate; a break in the cloud cover had allowed the stars to show them the way. In the shimmering sweep of stars alone, they had been able to see the black drape of mountains at the horizon. With that visual guide, they were able to make their way far out into the empty country so that they could safely get around the Imperial Order, and then head back north to their own troops.

A reception party awaited them. Men rushed up to form cheering rows as they passed into camp. Kahlan felt a distant sense of pride that she had given these men what they needed most right then: a measure of retribution. From the back of Cara's horse, Kahlan lifted a hand to wave at the men she passed. She smiled for them alone.

Near the area where the horses were picketed, General Meiffert, having heard the cheering, was waiting impatiently. He trotted over to meet them. Beside the gate of the temporary corral, one of the soldiers took the reins to the horse as Kahlan and then Cara jumped down. Kahlan winced at the ache in her muscles from the recent days of hard riding, and the night of fighting. Her right arm socket throbbed from the blows she had landed. She mused to herself that her sword arm never hurt like that in her mock battles with Richard. For the benefit of anyone watching, she forced herself to walk as if she had just had a three-day rest.

General Meiffert, looking no worse for the battle he had seen that night, clapped a fist to his heart. "Mother Confessor, you can't imagine how relieved I am to see you."

"And I you, General."

He leaned forward. "Please, Mother Confessor, you aren't going to do anything that foolhardy again, are you?"

"It wasn't foolhardy," Cara said. "I was with her, watching out for her."

He frowned over at Cara, but didn't argue with her. Kahlan wondered how one could fight a war without doing anything foolhardy. The entire thing was foolhardy.

"How many men did we lose?" Kahlan asked instead.

General Meiffert's face split with a grin. "None, Mother Confessor. Can you believe it? With the Creator's help, they all came back."

"I don't recall the Creator wielding a sword with us," Cara said.

Kahlan was dumbfounded. "That's the best news I could have, General."

"Mother Confessor, I can't tell you what a boost that was to the men. But, please, you won't do anything like that again, will you?"

"I'm not here to smile and wave and look pretty for the men, General. I'm here to help them send those murderous bastards into the eternal arms of the Keeper."

He sighed in resignation. "We have a tent for you. I'm sure you're tired."

Kahlan nodded and let the general lead her and Cara through the now quiet camp. Men not sleeping stood and silently saluted with fists to their hearts. Kahlan tried to smile for them. She could see in their eyes how much they appreciated what she had done to turn the tide of the grim battle back a little in their favor. They probably thought she had done it for them. That was only partly true.

Arriving at a well-guarded group of a half-dozen tents, General Meiffert gestured to the one in the center.

"This was General Reibisch's tent, Mother Confessor. I had your things inside. I thought you should have the best tent. If it bothers you to sleep in his tent, though, I'll have your belongings moved to anywhere you wish."

"It will be fine, General." Kahlan took stock of the man's young face, seeing the shadow of sorrow. She reminded herself that he was about the same age as she. "We all miss him."

His expression showed only some of the pain she thought he must feel. "I can't replace a man like that, Mother Confessor. He was not just a great general, but a great man, too. He taught me a lot and honored me with his trust. He was the best man I ever served under. I don't want you to have any illusions about my replacing him. I know I can't."

"No one asked you to. Your best effort is all we expect and will serve us well, I'm sure."

He smiled at her generosity. "You'll have that, Mother Confessor. I promise you, you'll have that." He turned to Cara and changed the subject. "I had your things put in this tent, here, Mistress Cara." It was the one right beside Kahlan's tent.

Cara scanned the scene, taking note of the patrolling guards. When Kahlan told her that she was going to go right to bed, and that she should get some sleep, too, Cara agreed and bade the two of them a good night before disappearing into her tent.

"I appreciated your help, tonight, General. You should get some sleep, too."

He bowed his head, turned to leave, but then turned back.

"You know, I always hoped to someday become a general. Ever since I was a boy, I've dreamed of it. I imagined . . ." He looked away from Kahlan's eyes. "I guess I imagined it would make me proud and happy." He hooked his thumbs in his pockets and gazed out over the dark camp, perhaps seeing all those dreams from his past, or maybe seeing all his new duties.

"It didn't make me feel happy at all," he finally said.

"I know," she answered in sincere sympathy. "This wasn't the way any good man would want to gain rank, but sometimes challenges arise, and we must face them." She let out a silent sigh, and tried to envision how he must feel. "Someday, General, the pride and satisfaction will come. It comes from doing the job well and knowing that you are making a difference."

He nodded. "I know it felt pretty good, tonight, Mother Confessor, when I saw you on the back of Cara's horse, returning safely to camp. I look forward to the day when I see Lord Rahl ride into camp, too." He started away. "Sleep well. Dawn is in a couple of hours. Then we'll find out what the new day will bring. I'll have reports ready for you."

Inside her tent, Zedd was sitting alone, waiting. Kahlan groaned inwardly.

She was dead tired and didn't want to face the old wizard's questioning. Sometimes, especially if you were tired, his nettling questions could become irksome. She knew he meant well, but she was in no mood for it. She didn't think she could even be civil to him if he started down his road of a thousand questions. It was so late, and she was so tired, she simply wished he would let her be.

She stood just inside, saying nothing, watching him as he rose to his feet. His wavy white hair was more disorderly than usual. His heavy robes were filthy and spattered with blood. Around his knees the robes were dark with dried blood.

He gave her a long look, and then enclosed her in his skinny arms. She just wanted to sleep. He silently held her head to his shoulder. Maybe he thought she might be about to start crying, but there seemed no tears left. She felt numb. She supposed it was the constant rage, but she just couldn't cry anymore. She seemed only able to feel anger.

Zedd finally held her out at arm's length, squeezing her shoulders in his surprisingly strong fingers. "I just wanted to wait until you were back, and safe, before I went to bed. I wanted to let my eyes take you in." He smiled in a sad way. "I'm so very relieved you're safe. Sleep well, Kahlan."

Her bedroll, still tied up with its leather thongs, lay atop a pallet with a straw-filled mattress. Saddlebags were draped over her pack, sitting in the corner. Opposite the bed there was a small folding table and chair. Beside them, a basket with rolls of maps. Another little folding table held a ewer and basin. A clean towel was draped over the table legs' stretcher bar.

The tent was spacious, by army standards, but it was still cramped. The canvas looked heavy enough to keep out most any weather. Lamps, hanging at each end of the tent from a rod forming the peak of the roof, cast a warm glow inside the snug tent. Kahlan tried to imagine the burly General Reibisch pacing in such a small space, tugging his rust-colored beard, worrying over the problems of an army bigger than many cities.

Zedd looked exhausted. Creases etched an inner anguish on his bony face. She reminded herself that he had only just learned that his grandson, the only family he had left in the world, was in the cruel hands of the enemy.

Besides that, Zedd had been fighting for two days and healing soldiers at night. She had seen him, when she arrived, staggering to his feet beside the corpse of what turned out to be General Reibisch. She knew that if Zedd couldn't save the man, he was beyond saving.

With her fingers, Kahlan combed back her hair and then gestured to the chair.

"You could sit for a minute, Zedd. Couldn't you?"

He looked at the chair, then at her bedroll. "For a minute, I suppose, while you get your bed ready. You need some rest."

Kahlan couldn't argue with that. She realized her head was throbbing. The passions of battle masked little things, like a pounding headache. The straw-filled mattress looked as good as a feather bed to her right then. She tossed her wolf-fur mantle and her cloak on the bed. They would keep her warm.

Without comment, Zedd watched as she unstrapped the Sword of Truth and pulled it off her back. He had given the weapon to Richard. Kahlan had been there, and begged Zedd not to do it, but he said he had no choice, that Richard was the one. Zedd had been right. Richard was indeed the one.

She felt her face flush when, just before she laid the sword down, she kissed the top of the hilt, where Richard's hand had so often rested. Zedd, if he even noticed, said nothing, and she laid the gleaming scabbard and sword to rest beside her mattress.

In the awkward quiet, Kahlan took off the royal Galean sword. She saw then that there was blood running down the scabbard. She unstrapped and removed the layer of light leather armor and laid it beside her pack. When she leaned the royal sword and scabbard against the plates of leather armor, she saw then that they were splattered with blood.

She noticed, too, that the leather leg armor had bloody handprints here and there on it, and there were long gouges in the leather from mens' fingernails. She remembered men grabbing for her, trying to unhorse her, but she didn't recall their hands actually clawing at her. The images that started flooding back threatened to make her nauseated, so she directed her mind to other things.

"Cara and I crossed over the Rang'Shada mountains, north of Agaden Reach, and came down through Galea," she said into the uncomfortable silence.

"I gathered," he said.

She gestured vaguely to suggest the surrounding camp. "I thought I'd better bring some troops with me."

"We can use them."

Kahlan glanced up at his hazel eyes. "I brought all I could without waiting. I didn't want to wait."

Zedd nodded. "That was wise."

"Prince Harold wanted to come, but I asked him to gather together a larger force and then bring them down. If we're to defend the Midlands, we'll need more troops. He thought that was a good idea."

"Sounds so."

"Prince Harold will be here to help just as soon as he can gather his army from their defensive positions."

Zedd only nodded.

She cleared her throat. "I wish we could have gotten here sooner."

Zedd shrugged. "You came as fast as possible. You're here, now."

Kahlan turned away to the bedroll. She sank down to her knees and bent to the work of undoing the leather thongs holding the bedding all rolled up together. For some reason, the knots looked blurry—she guessed it was because she was so tired.

She glanced over her shoulder briefly in the dim lamplight and then went back to picking at the knot. "I suppose you'd like to know how that Sister of the Dark managed to capture Richard."

He was silent for a moment. His voice finally came, soft and gentle. "There's time enough for that later, Kahlan. There's no need tonight."

As she picked at the stubborn knot, her hair fell forward over her shoulder. She had to push it back in order to see what she was doing. The stupid leather thong was tightly knotted. She wanted to yell at the person who had tied it, but she had done it up herself and had no one else to blame.

"She used a maternity spell on me. It links us. She said she could—she could kill me if Richard didn't do as she said and go with her."

At the news, Zedd only let out a desolate sigh.

"Richard can't kill her, or I die, too."

She waited for his voice behind her. It finally came.

"I've only read about such spells, but from what I know, it sounds as if she told you the truth of it."

"I have a cut on my mouth. I didn't do it. It happened to me the other day—through that link. What happens to her happens to me. I hope Richard struck her. It was worth it."

"I don't think Richard would do that."

She knew he wouldn't. It was only a wish.

One of the little lamps was flickering, making shadows waver. The other was hissing softly. Kahlan wiped her nose on her sleeve.

"Richard gave up his freedom to keep me alive. I wish I could die, to free him, but he made me promise I wouldn't do that."

Kahlan felt a comforting hand on her shoulder. Zedd said nothing. It was the greatest kindness he could have given her at that moment—not burying her heart under an avalanche of questions.

Enjoying the calming effect of his hand, Kahlan finally managed to get the knot undone. Zedd sat back in his chair as she unfurled her bedding. The carving of *Spirit* was rolled up inside, for safekeeping. Its height was just right to fit crosswise in her bedroll. Kahlan lifted it out and held it to her heart a moment. She turned, then, and set *Spirit* on the little table.

Zedd slowly rose to his feet. He was a collection of bony angles under his maroon robes. With one arm crooked to point while he gaped at *Spirit* standing proudly atop the small table, his lanky body looked as stiff as a spindly tree in winter.

"Where else did you stop on your way here?" He cast a suspicious look in her direction. "Have you been looting treasures from palaces?"

She realized then that the look wasn't so much meant to be suspicious, as teasing. Kahlan ran a finger down *Spirit*'s flowing robes, letting her gaze follow the strength in the lines of the woman's strong pose. Something felt so right about the way her head was thrown back, with her fists at her sides, and her back arched, standing against the invisible power trying to subdue her.

"No." Kahlan swallowed. "Richard carved it for me."

Zedd's brow drew lower. He stared at the carving for a time before reaching out a sticklike finger to touch it, as if it were some priceless antiquity.

"Dear spirits . . ."

Kahlan pretended a smile. "Almost. It's called *Spirit*, he said. Richard carved it for me when I was feeling like I would never get better. It helped me . . ."

In the awful silence, Zedd finally turned from the woman with her fists at her sides and her head thrown back to peer into Kahlan's eyes. He frowned in the oddest way.

"It's you," he said half to himself. "Dear spirits . . . the boy carved a statue of your spirit. I recognize it. It's as plain as day."

Zedd was not only Richard's grandfather—he was now hers, too. He was not merely the First Wizard. He was also the man who had helped raise Richard. Zedd had no family left save Richard.

Other than a half sister and brother who were strangers but for blood, neither did she. She was as alone in the world as was Zedd.

Now, through Richard, Zedd was her family, but even if he wasn't, she realized he could mean no less to her.

"We'll get him back, dear one," he whispered in tender compassion. His sticklike hand reverently cupped her face. "We'll get him back."

Everything seemed to be swimming. Kahlan fell into his protective arms and dissolved into tears.

Warren carefully pulled the snow-laden pine bough aside for her. Kahlan peered through the gap.

"There," he said in a low voice. "You see?"

Kahlan nodded as she squinted off into the narrow valley far below. The scene was frosted white—white trees, white rocks, white meadows. Enemy troops moving up the distant valley floor looked like a dark line of ants marching across powdered sugar.

"I don't think you need to whisper, Warren," Cara said from behind Kahlan's other shoulder. "They can't hear you. Not from this far."

Warren's blue eyes turned to the Mord-Sith. Cara's red leather would have stood out like a beacon, were she not sheathed in wolf fur that made her melt into the background of snow-dusted brush. Kahlan's own fur mantle was soft and warm against the sides of her face. Sometimes, since Richard had made it for her, the feel against her skin was evocative of his gentle caress protecting her and keeping her warm.

"Oh, but their gifted can hear us, Cara, even from this distance, if we are too vociferous."

Cara's nose wrinkled. "What's that mean?"

"Loud," Kahlan whispered in a way as if to suggest Cara should use a little more caution and be more quiet.

Cara's face distorted with her displeasure at the thought of magic. She shifted her weight to her other foot, went back to watching the line of troops slowly flowing up the valley, and kept silent.

After she'd seen enough, Kahlan gestured, and the three of them started back through the ankle-deep snow. At their elevation in the mountains, they were right at the base of oppressive gray clouds, making it feel as if they were looking down from another world. She didn't like the world she had seen.

They trudged up the slope dense with pine and naked aspen, to the thickly wooded top of the ridge, where the backbone of rock broke through the snow here and there like half-buried bones. Their horses waited a good distance back down off the rocky slope. Farther back down the mountain, where Warren and Kahlan were sure they would not be detected by any gifted who might be protecting the Order troops, waited an escort of D'Haran guards General Meiffert had handpicked to protect Kahlan and the two with her, who were also protecting her.

"So you see?" Warren asked in little more than a whisper. "They're still at it—moving more and more men up this way, trying to get around us without us being aware of it."

Kahlan held up the fur to shelter her face as a light breeze dragged a curtain of snow past them. At least it wasn't snowing again, yet.

"I don't think so, Warren."

His questioning, handsome face turned her way. "Then what?"

"I think they want it to look like they're sending troops past us so we will send men way out here after them."

"A diversion?"

"I think so. It's just close enough to us to be likely we would discover them, yet far enough away and through difficult enough terrain that it would require us to split our forces in order to do anything about it. Besides, every one of our scouts came back."

"Isn't that good?"

"Sure it is. But what if they have gifted with them, as you believe? How is it that not one of our scouts failed to make it back to report these massive troop movements?"

Warren thought that over a moment as the three of them carefully made it over a high spot, sliding on their bottoms down the far side of the slippery sloping rock.

"I think they're fishing," Cara said as her boots thumped down on solid ground behind them. "Their gifted don't try to net the small fry, hoping to draw bigger fish close."

Kahlan brushed the snow from her backside. "Like us."

Warren looked skeptical. "You think this is all just some sort of elaborate trap to snare officers or gifted?"

"Well, no," Kahlan said. "That would only be a bonus for them. I think their main intent is to spur us into splitting our forces to deal with what they want us to believe is this threat."

Warren scratched his head of curly blond hair. His blue eyes twitched back in the direction the three of them had come down off the ridge, as if trying to look again at what he could not see.

"But if they're sending great numbers of troops north—even if it is to draw away some of our forces—shouldn't that concern us?"

"Of course it should," Kahlan said. "If it were true."

Warren glanced over at her as they struggled through deeper snow drifted under crags they passed beneath on their way up a steep little rise. Her legs were weary with the effort. Warren held out his hand to help her up a high step. He did the same for Cara. Cara gestured that she didn't need the hand, but she didn't level a scowl at him, either. Kahlan was always pleased to see evidence that Cara was learning that offers of modest aid were simply a courtesy and not necessarily accusations of weakness.

"Then I'm confused," Warren said as he panted.

Kahlan came to a halt to let them all catch their breath. She lifted an arm back toward the enemy troops off beyond the ridge.

"Yes, if it were true that great numbers of troops were going out around us and heading north, that would concern us. But I don't believe they are."

Warren swiped a blond lock off his forehead. "You don't think all those men are heading north? Where, then?"

"Nowhere," Kahlan said.

"That many men? You've got to be joking."

She smiled at the look on his face. "I believe it's a trick. I think it's only a small number of men."

"But the scouts have been reporting mass numbers of men moving north for three days now!"

"Hush," Cara warned, getting even with an air of mock scolding.

Warren covered his mouth with both hands when he realized he'd shouted.

They had their breath back, so Kahlan started out again, taking them over the top of the little rise onto flatter ground, following their footsteps back the way they had come.

"Remember what the scouts said yesterday?" she asked him. "They tried to go over to the mountains on the other side to have a look at the lay of the land beyond and the enemy troops moving north through it, but the passes were too heavily guarded?"

"I remember."

"I think I've just figured out why." She gestured by looping her hand around as she went on. "I think what we're seeing is a relatively small group of the same men just going around in a big circle. We're only seeing them at the point where they pass up this valley. We see troops marching by continuously for days and we assume they're moving a lot of men, but I think it's just a circle of the same ones going round and round."

Warren stopped to stare at her. His face turned grave at the implications. "So if we're tricked into thinking they're moving an army up this way, then we will split our army in response and send part of them out after this phantom force."

"We're already outnumbered," Cara said as she nodded to herself, "but we have the advantage of defending terrain that suits our purpose. However, if they could reduce our numbers substantially simply by getting us to send a large percentage off on some mission, first, their entire army might finally be able to overrun a smaller number of remaining defenders."

"Makes sense." Warren stroked his chin in thought, looking back at the ridge. "What if you're wrong?"

Kahlan turned to look back toward the ridge, too. "Well, if I'm wrong, then . . ."

Kahlan frowned at a fat old maple tree not ten feet away. She thought she saw the bark move. The dusting of snow on the scaly gray, furrowed bark began disappearing, melting away in an ever widening area. Like dross floating on the surface of a boiling cauldron, the bark moved.

Kahlan gasped as Warren seized her and Cara by the collar and flung them both down on their backs. The wind knocked from her lungs, Kahlan tried to sit up, but Warren dived to the ground between them, pinning them both down.

Before Kahlan had a chance to get her breath or ask what was wrong, blinding light flashed in the still woods. A deafening boom rent the air and jolted the ground beneath her. Splintered wood, from toothpick-size fragments to fence-post-size sections, howled past inches above her face. Huge sections of wood thunked as they rebounded off rocks. Others spun, caroming off tree trunks. Pieces tumbling along the ground kicking up snow peppered with frozen chunks of dirt. The air went white as the shock from the blast blew a wall of snow up into the air.

If any of them had been standing, they would have been torn to shreds.

As soon as the last pieces of timber, trailing smoke, thudded to ground, Warren rolled toward her. "Gifted," he whispered.

Kahlan frowned at him. "What?"

"Gifted," he whispered again. "They focused their power to boil the frozen tree inside and make it explode. That's how we lost so many men when we gathered back in that valley during the first battle, back just before you came to us. They surprised us."

Kahlan nodded. She peeked up, but saw no one. She glanced over to see if Cara was all right.

"Where's Cara," she asked in an urgent whisper.

Warren cautiously peered off, searching the empty scene. Kahlan lifted herself a little on an elbow and saw only the disturbed snow where Cara had been.

"Dear Creator," Warren said. "You don't suppose they've snatched her, do you?"

Kahlan saw tracks where there had been none before, leading off to the side. "I think—"

A scream that would have made a brave man blanch reverberated through the trees. It trailed off in an agonizing echo.

"Cara?" Warren asked.

"I don't think so."

Kahlan carefully sat up and saw that a hole had been torn open in the crowded growth of the forest crown, letting harsh light penetrate the shaded woodland sanctuary below. The ground all around was littered with splintered wood, broken branches, huge limbs fallen to ground, and boughs ripped from other trees. Gouges down through the white layer of snow into the dark forest floor radiated from a ragged bowl-shaped depression where the tree had been. Fragments of wood and root lay on the ground everywhere and were even caught up in the surrounding trees.

Warren put a hand to her shoulder, urging Kahlan to stay down as he rolled into a crouch. She flipped over onto her stomach and cautiously rose up onto her hands and knees.

Kahlan jumped up and pointed. "There."

Through the trees, she saw Cara returning. The Mord-Sith was herding a small man in obvious pain along before her. Each time he stumbled and fell, she kicked him in the ribs, rolling him through the snow before her. He cried out, his words coming as a whining cry that Kahlan couldn't make out because of the distance. The words weren't hard to imagine, though.

Cara had captured one of the gifted. It was for tasks such as this that Mord-Sith had been created. For someone with the gift, trying to use magic against a Mord-Sith was a mistake that cost them their control over their own ability.

Kahlan stood, brushing snow from herself. Warren, his violet robes crusted with snow, rose beside her, transfixed by the sight. This was one of the wizards responsible for killing so many men when the D'Harans had gathered in the valley after the Order began moving north. This was the vicious animal who did Jagang's bidding. He didn't seem like a vicious animal, now, as he wept and begged before the implacable captor driving him on before her.

He was a bundle of rags, flinging out around him as he rolled through the snow with a final mighty kick that deposited him at Kahlan and Warren's feet. He lay facedown, whimpering like a child.

Cara bent, seized him by his tangled mat of dark hair, and yanked him to his feet.

It was a child.

"Lyle?" Warren stared incredulously. "Lyle? It was you?"

Tears ran from wintery eyes. He wiped his nose on the back of a tattered sleeve as he glared at Warren. Young Lyle looked to be a boy of perhaps ten or twelve years, but since Warren knew him, Kahlan realized he was probably from the Palace of the Prophets, too. Lyle was a young wizard.

Warren reached out to cup the boy's bloody chin. Kahlan snatched Warren's wrist. The boy lunged to bite Warren's hand. Cara was quicker. She snatched him back by the hair as she rammed her Agiel into his back.

Shrieking in pain, he crumpled to the ground. She kicked the injured lad in the ribs.

Warren held his hands out, imploring. "Cara, don't—"

Her icy blue eyes turned up to challenge him. "He tried to kill us. He tried to kill the Mother Confessor."

She ground her teeth and, while looking Warren in the eye, kicked the whimpering boy again.

Warren licked his lips. "I know . . . but . . ."

"But what?"

"He's so young. It isn't right."

"And so it would be better if we just let him kill us? Would that make it right for you?"

Kahlan knew Cara was right. As difficult as it was to witness, Cara was right. If they died, how many men, women, and children would the Imperial Order go on to slaughter? Child though he was, he was a tool of the Order.

Nonetheless, Kahlan gestured Cara that that was enough. When Kahlan signaled, Cara again seized his tangled mat of dirty hair in her fist and hauled him to his feet. With Cara's thighs at his back, he stood shivering, blood running down his face, pulling short, ragged breaths.

As Kahlan stared down into terrified, tear-filled brown eyes, she put on her Confessor's face, the face her mother had taught her when she was but a little girl, the face that masked her inner tumult.

"I know you're, there, Jagang," she said in a quiet voice devoid of emotion.

The boy's bloody mouth turned up in a smile that was not his own.

"You made a mistake, Jagang. We'll have an army soon on its way to stop them."

The boy smiled a vacant bloody smile, but said nothing.

"Lyle," Warren said, his voice brittle with anguish, "you can be free of the dream walker. You must only swear loyalty to Richard and you will be free. Believe me, Lyle. Try. I know what it's like. Try, Lyle, and I swear I'll help you."

Kahlan thought that, with Warren there, a man he knew, he might throw himself toward the unexpected light coming from the open dungeon door. The boy behind the smile that was not his own watched Warren with longing that slowly curdled to loathing. This was a child who had seen the struggle for freedom bring horror and death and knew that servile obedience brought rewards and life. He was not old enough to understand what more there was to it.

With a gentle touch of her fingers, Kahlan urged Warren to back away. He reluctantly complied.

"This isn't the first of Jagang's wizards we've captured," she said, offhandedly, to Warren. Her words, though, were not meant for Warren.

Kahlan looked up into Cara's stern blue eyes and then glanced off to the side, hoping the Mord-Sith understood the instruction.

267

"Marlin Pickard," Kahlan said, as if recalling the name for Warren, but her words were still meant for Cara. "He was grown, and even with this pompous pretend emperor directing him, Marlin still wasn't able to give us much trouble."

Marlin had in fact given them a great deal of trouble. He had nearly killed Cara and Kahlan both. Kahlan hoped Cara remembered how tenuous was her control over someone possessed by the dream walker.

The mood in the quiet woods was still and tense as the boy glared up at Kahlan.

"We discovered your scheme in time, Jagang. You made a mistake thinking you could get by our scouts. I hope you're with those men, so that when we wipe them out we can cut your throat."

The bloody grin widened. "A woman like you is wasted on the side of the weak," the boy said in the menacing voice of a man. "You'd have a much better time serving strength, and the Order."

"I'm afraid my husband likes me right where I am."

"And where is your husband, darlin? I was hoping to say hello."

"He's around," Kahlan said in the same dispassionate voice.

She saw Warren, when she had spoken the words, move in a way that was a little too much like surprise.

"Is he, now?" The boy's eyes turned from Warren, back to Kahlan. "Why is it I don't believe you?"

She wanted to kick the boy's teeth in as she watched his cruel grin. Kahlan's mind raced, trying to figure out what Jagang could possibly know, and what he was trying to discover.

"You'll see him soon enough, when we get this poor child back to camp. I'm sure Richard Rahl will want to laugh in your cowardly face when I tell him how we discovered the great emperor's plan to sneak troops north. He'll want to personally tell you what a fool you are."

The boy tried to take a step toward her, but Cara's fist in his hair restrained him. He was a cougar on a leash, still testing its chains. The bloody smile remained, but it was not as self-satisfied as it had been. In the brown eyes, Kahlan thought she saw hesitation.

"Ah, but I don't believe you," he said, as if losing interest. "We both know he's not there at all. Don't we, darlin?"

Kahlan resolved to take a risk. "You'll see him for yourself, soon enough." She made to look as if she were going to turn away, but turned back to him instead.

Kahlan let a sarcastic smile taint her lips. "Oh—you must mean Nicci?"

The smile vanished from the boy's face. The brow drew down, but he managed to keep any anger out of his voice.

"Nicci? I don't know what you're talking about, darlin."

"Sister of the Dark? Shapely? Blond hair? Blue eyes? Black dress? Surely, you would remember a woman that hauntingly beautiful. Or, besides your other short-comings, are you also a eunuch?"

The eyes watched, and in them Kahlan could see careful calculations weighing her every word. But it was Nicci's words about Jagang that Kahlan was remembering.

"I know who Nicci is. I know every private inch of her. One day, I will come to know you as intimately as I know Nicci."

Such an obscene threat was somehow more chilling, coming as it did from the mouth of a boy. It made her sick to her stomach to hear a child express Jagang's vile thoughts.

The boy's arm gestured for his master. "One of my beauties, and quite the lethal lady, besides." Kahlan thought she detected in Jagang's gravelly growl a hint of the false bravado of a bluff. Almost in afterthought, he added, "You haven't really seen her."

Kahlan heard in the assertion the ghost of a question he dared not ask, and knew by it that there was something more to this. She wished she knew what.

She shrugged again. "Lethal? I wouldn't know."

He licked the blood from his lips. "That's what I thought."

"I wouldn't know because she didn't seem all that lethal. She didn't manage to harm any of us."

The grin returned. "You lie, darlin. If you really saw Nicci, she would have killed at least some of you, even if she didn't manage to kill you all. You couldn't best that one without her scratching someone's eyes out, first."

"Really? So sure, are we?"

The boy let out a belly laugh. "Darlin, I know Nicci. I'm sure."

Kahlan smiled her contempt into the boy's brown eyes. "You know I'm telling you the truth."

"Really?" he said, still chuckling. "How's that?"

"You know it's the truth because she's one of your slaves, so you should be able to enter her mind. You can't, though. I know why you can't. Even though you aren't too bright, I don't suppose you'll need to think too long to imagine why not."

Fierce rage fired the boy's eyes. "I don't believe you."

Kahlan shrugged. "Suit yourself."

"If you saw her, then where is she now?"

As she turned her back on him, Kahlan told him the brutal, bitter truth and let him interpret it his own way. "Last I saw her, she was on her way into oblivion."

Kahlan heard the bellow behind her. She spun back to see Cara trying to stop him with her Agiel. Kahlan heard the bone in his arm snap. It didn't even slow him. The boy, in a wild rage, his hands clawed, his teeth bared, lunged for Kahlan.

Half turned back to him, Kahlan lifted her hand against the full weight of the boy crashing toward her as he leaped for her throat. His small chest contacted her hand. His feet were clear of the ground. It felt not as if he were throwing himself at her, but no more than dandelion fluff, floating to her on a breath of air.

Time was hers.

It was not necessary for Kahlan to invoke her birthright, but merely to withdraw her restraint of it. Her feelings could provide her no safe haven; only the truth would serve her now.

This was not a small boy, hurt, alone, afraid.

This was the enemy.

The inner violence of her power's cold coiled force slipping its bounds was breathtaking. It surged up from that deep dark core within, obediently inundating every fiber of her being.

She could count each small rib under her fingers.

She contained no hate, no rage, no horror . . . no sorrow. In that infinitesimal spark of time, her mind was in a void where there was no emotion, only the all-consuming rush of time suspended.

He had no chance. He was hers.

Kahlan did not hesitate.

She unleashed her power.

From an ethereal state as part of her innermost essence, that power became all.

Thunder without sound jolted the air—exquisite, violent, and for that pristine instant, sovereign.

The boy's face was twisted by the hate of the man who had controlled him. In that singular moment, if she was the absence of emotion, then he was the embodiment of it. Kahlan stared back into that lost child's face, knowing that he saw only her merciless eyes.

His mind, who he was, who he had been, was already gone.

Trees all around shook from the force of the concussion. Snow dropped from branches and boughs. The terrible shock to the air lifted a ring of snow that grew around the two of them in an ever-expanding circle.

Kahlan had known that Jagang could slip into and out of a person's mind between thought, when time itself did not exist. She had no choice but to do as she had done. She could not afford to hesitate. With Jagang in a person's mind, even Cara could not control them.

Jagang had burned his bridges behind him as he fled the young mind.

The boy fell dead at Kahlan's feet.

Kahlan swayed on her feet as she stood over the crumbled body of the boy, feeling her emotions flood back in. As always happened, using her Confessor's power left her drained and exhausted. In the aftermath, the forest sat in silent judgment. Here and there, the virgin snow around the small body exhibited its red evidence.

Only then did Kahlan even pause to consider if she might have killed Cara, too.

A Mord-Sith would not live long after the touch of a Confessor. There had been no choice. She had done her best to warn Cara, to let her know to get clear, but in the end Kahlan couldn't allow her decision to be influenced by any consideration other than what had to be done. Hesitation could have meant disaster.

Now that it was over, though, dread roiled through.

Kahlan looked around, and to the right saw Cara sprawled in the snow. If she had been touching the boy when Kahlan unleashed her power . . .

Cara groaned. Kahlan staggered to her and dropped to a knee. She clutched the fur at Cara's shoulder and with a mighty effort pulled her over.

"Cara—are you all right?"

Cara squinted up with a look of disgust working its way to the surface of pain. "Well of course I'm all right. You didn't think I would be foolish enough to hang on to him, did you?"

Kahlan smiled in thankful relief. "No, of course not. I only thought you might have broken your neck jumping away."

Cara spat snow and dirt. "Nearly did."

Warren helped them both to their feet. Grimacing, he rubbed his shoulders and then his elbows. From what Kahlan had often been told, being too close to a Confessor unleashing her power was a painful experience, sending a shock of agony through every joint. Fortunately, it did no real damage and the suffering faded quickly.

As Warren glanced over at the dead boy, she knew that there was other pain that would not leave so quickly.

"Dear Creator," Warren whispered to himself. He looked back at Kahlan and Cara. "He was just a boy. Was it really necessary—"

"Yes," Kahlan said in a forceful voice. "I'm positive. Cara and I have encountered this situation before—with Marlin."

"But Marlin was grown. Lyle was so small . . . so young. What real harm—"

"Warren, don't start down the path of what-might-have-been. Jagang controlled his mind, just as he controlled Marlin's mind. We know about this. He was a deadly threat."

"If I couldn't hold him," Cara said, "nothing could."

Warren sighed in misery. He sank to his knees at the boy's side. Warren whispered a prayer as his fingers stroked the boy's temple.

"I guess the blame rightly lies at Jagang's feet." Warren stood and brushed the snow from his knees. "Ultimately, Jagang is the one who brought this about."

Kahlan could see the distant figures of their men, rushing up the hillside to rescue her. She started down toward them.

"If it pleases you to think so."

Cara stayed right with her. Warren struggled through the snow to catch up. He snatched Kahlan's arm and pulled her to a stop.

"You mean Ann, don't you?"

Kahlan schooled her anger as she studied Warren's blue eyes.

"Warren, you were a victim of that woman, too. You were taken to the Palace of the Prophets when you were young, weren't you?"

"I guess so, but—"

"But nothing. They came and took you. They came and took that poor dead child back there." Kahlan's fingernails dug into her palms. "They came and took Richard."

Warren pressed his hand gently to the side of Kahlan's arm. "I know how it seems. Prophecy is often—"

"There!" Kahlan angrily pointed back at the corpse. "There is prophecy! Death and misery—all in the sacred name of prophecy!"

Warren didn't try to answer her rage.

Kahlan forced control into her voice, if not the emotion behind it. "How many are going to die needlessly in a perverted devotion to seeing prophecy carried out? Had Ann not sent Verna here for Richard, none of this would be happening."

"How do you know that? Kahlan, I can understand how you feel, but how can you be sure?"

"The barrier stood for three thousand years. It could only be brought down by a wizard born with both sides of the gift. There has been none until Richard. Ann sent Verna to get him. Had she not, the barrier would still be there. Jagang and the Order would be on the other side. The Midlands would be safe. That boy would be playing ball somewhere."

"Kahlan, it's not so simple as you make it seem." Warren opened his hands in an expression of frustration. "I don't want to argue this with you, but I want you to understand that prophecy gets fulfilled in many ways. It often seeks its own solution. It could be that had Ann not sent for Richard, he would have, for some other reason, ventured down there and brought down the barrier. Who is to know the reason? Don't you see? It could be that it was bound to happen, and Ann was simply the means. If not her, then another."

Kahlan pulled angry breaths through gritted teeth. "How much blood, how many corpses, how much grief will it take before you see the harm prophecy has inflicted upon the world?"

Warren smiled sadly. "I am a prophet. I've always wanted to be a prophet in order to help people. I wouldn't put my faith in it if I truly thought it was the cause of harm." He smiled more brightly with a memory. "Don't forget, without prophecy, you would never have come to meet Richard. Aren't you better off having had him come into your life? I know I am."

Kahlan's look of cold fury took the warm smile from his face.

"I would rather have been condemned to a lonely life without love, than to know

272

that harm has come to him because he came into my life. I would rather never have met him, than to have come to know his value, and know that that value is being dashed on the rocks of this mad faith in prophecy."

Warren stuck his hands in the opposite sleeves of his purple robes as his gaze sank to the ground. "I understand how you can feel that way. Please, Kahlan, talk to Verna."

"Why? She's the one who carried out Ann's orders."

"Just talk to her. I almost lost Verna because she felt the same way as you do now."

"Verna?"

Warren nodded. "She came to believe she had been used maliciously by Ann. For twenty years she was on a fruitless search for Richard, when all the while Ann knew right where he was. Can you imagine how Verna felt when she discovered that? There were other things, too. Ann tricked us into believing she was dead. She maneuvered Verna into being Prelate." Warren pulled a hand from his sleeve and held his first finger and thumb an inch apart. "She was once this close to throwing her journey book into a fire."

"She should have."

Warren's sad smile returned. "I'm just saying it might make you feel better to talk to her. She will understand how you feel."

"What good is that going to do?"

Warren shrugged. "Even if you're right, so what? What's done is done. We can't undo it. Nicci has Richard. The Imperial Order is here in the New World. Whatever caused the events, they are upon us and we must now deal with that reality."

Kahlan appraised his sparkling blue eyes. "You learned this studying prophecy?"

His smile widened into a grin. "No. That was what Richard taught me. And, a pretty smart woman I know just told me not to start down the path of what-might-have-been."

As much as she was of a mind to hold on to it, Kahlan felt her anger slipping away. "I'm not so sure how smart she is."

Warren waved down at the troops charging up the hill with their swords drawn, signaling the all-clear. The men slowed to a fast walk, but didn't sheathe their weapons.

"Well," Warren said, "she was smart enough to figure out Jagang's plan, and in the middle of being attacked by his gifted minion to keep her wits about her and to trick him into thinking she had fallen for his scheme."

Kahlan drew her face into a peevish scowl. "How old are you, Warren?"

He looked surprised by the question. "I turned one hundred fifty-eight not long ago."

"That explains it," Cara griped, starting off down the hill. "Stop looking so young and innocent all the time, Warren. It's just plain irritating."

By the time Kahlan, Cara, Warren, and their escort of guard troops arrived back in camp several hours later, it was a scene of furious activity. Wagons were being loaded, horses hitched, and weapons readied. Tents were not yet being taken down, but soldiers in their leather and chain-mail armor, and still eating the remnants of their dinners, were gathered around officers, listening to instructions for when the order was given to send a force out to intercept the enemy moving north. Other officers in tents Kahlan passed were bent over maps.

The aroma of stew drifting through the afternoon air reminded her how hungry she was. Winter darkness came early, and the overcast made it feel like it was already evening. The endless cloudy days were getting to be depressing. There was little chance to see much of the sun; soon, heavier snow would make it down this far south.

Kahlan dismounted and let a young soldier take her horse. She no longer rode a big warhorse. She, and most of the cavalry, had switched to smaller, more agile mounts. For a clash between large units, big warhorses added weight to a charge, but since the D'Haran Empire forces were so outnumbered, they had decided it would be best to trade weight for speed and maneuverability.

By changing tactics in such a way, not just with the cavalry but with their entire army, Kahlan and General Meiffert had been able to keep the Order off balance for weeks. They let the enemy put a huge effort into a crushing attack, and then dodged it just enough to save themselves while letting the Order, being tantalizingly close, wear themselves out. When the Order tired from the effort of such massive attacks and paused to rest, General Meiffert sent in glancing attacks to step on their toes and make them dance. Once the Order dug in for the expected attack, Kahlan withdrew their forces to a more distant spot, rendering useless the Order's effort at building defenses.

If the Order tried the same thing again, the D'Harans continued to harry them day and night, buzzing around them like angry hornets, but staying out of reach of a heavy swat. If the Imperial Order tired of not being able to sink their teeth into their enemy, and turned their forces to go after population centers, then Kahlan had her men jump on their tails and put arrows in their backs as they struggled to get free. Eventually, they would have to forget their thoughts of plunder and turn back toward the threat.

The Imperial Order was maddened by the D'Harans' constant badgering tactics. Jagang's men were insulted by that kind of fighting; they believed real men met face-to-face in the field of battle, and exchanged blow for blow. Of course, it didn't trouble their dignity that they greatly outnumbered the D'Harans. Kahlan knew such a meeting would be bloody and only to the Order's advantage. She didn't care what they thought, only that they died.

The more angry and frustrating the Imperial Order became, the more recklessly they behaved, launching impetuous attacks into well-ordered defenses, or heedlessly pressing men into doomed attacks trying to take ground they couldn't possibly take in such a fashion. It sometimes stunned Kahlan to watch so many of the enemy march into range below their archers, fall dead, only to have yet more men march right in behind them, continuously adding corpses to a battlefield already choked with the dead and dying. It was insanity.

The D'Harans had suffered several thousand dead or seriously wounded. On the other hand, Kahlan and General Meiffert estimated that they had killed or wounded in excess of fifty thousand of the enemy. It was the equivalent of stepping on one ant as the colony poured out of its anthill. She could think of nothing else to do but to keep at it. They had no choice.

Kahlan, with Cara at her side, crossed a river of men to get to the command tents sporting blue cloth strips. Unless you knew the day's color code, finding the command tents would be nearly impossible. Because of the fear of an infiltrator or an enemy gifted finding and being able to kill a group of senior officers gathered to-gether, they met in nondescript tents. Colored cloth strips marked many of the tents—the men used them as as system of finding their units when they had to move on short notice and so often—so Kahlan got the idea of using the same system to identify the command tents. They changed the color code often so no one color would become known as the officers' colors.

Inside the cramped tent, General Meiffert looked up from where he bent over a table with a map unfurled at a cockeyed angle. Lieutenant Leiden, of Kelton, was there along with Captain Abernathy, the commander of the Galean forces Kahlan had brought down with her weeks before.

Adie was sitting quietly in the corner, as the representative of the gifted, watching the goings-on with her completely white eyes. Blinded as a young woman, Adie had learned to see using her gift. She was a remarkably talented sorceress. Adie was quite proficient at using that talent to do the enemy harm. Now she was there to help coordinate the Sister's abilities with the needs of the army.

When Kahlan inquired, Adie told her, "Zedd be down at the southern lines, checking on details."

Kahlan nodded her thanks. "Warren went down there to help, too."

Kahlan scrunched up her freezing toes in her boots, trying to bring feeling back to them. She blew warm air into her cupped hands and then turned her attention to the waiting general.

"We need to get together a good-sized force—maybe twenty thousand men."

General Meiffert sighed his frustration. "So they are moving an army up past us."

"No," she said. "It's a trick."

The three officers frowned their puzzlement as they waited for an explanation.

"I ran into Jagang—"

"You what!" General Meiffert shouted in unbridled panic.

Kahlan waved a hand, allaying his fears. "Not like you're thinking. It was through the body of one of his slaves." She stuck her hands under her arms to warm them. "The important thing is that I played along with Jagang's scheme so that he would think we were falling for his plan."

Kahlan explained how Jagang's ruse of troop movements was meant to work and how its true design was to draw away a good-sized force so as to leave those remain-ing behind weaker. The men listened as she laid it all out while pointing to the locations on the map.

"If we were to send that many men out," Lieutenant Leiden asked, "wouldn't that be just what Emperor Jagang wanted?"

"It would be," she told him, "but that's not what we're going to do. I want those men to ride out of camp, to make it look as if we were doing what he expected."

She leaned over the map, using a piece of charcoal to sketch in some of the nearby mountains she had just traveled through, and showed them a lowland pass around several.

Captain Abernathy spoke up. "We have my Galean troops—they're close to the number you need to serve as the decoy."

"That's what I was thinking," General Meiffert said.

"Done," Kahlan said. She pointed at the map again. "Circle around these moun-tains, here, Captain, so that when the Order attacks our camp, thinking to roll over us, your men can stick them in their soft side, right here, where they won't expect it."

Captain Abernathy, a trim man with a graying bushy mustache that matched his eyebrows, nodded as he watched Kahlan pointing out the route on the map. "Don't worry, Mother Confessor, the Order will believe we're gone, but we'll be standing ready to drive right into their ribs when they come for you."

Kahlan turned her attention back to the general. "We'll also need to secretly trickle another force out of camp to wait at the opposite side of the valley from Captain Abernathy, so that when the Order comes up the valley in the middle, we can drive into their ribs from both sides at once. They won't want to let us cut off and trap part of their force, so they'll turn tail. Then our main force can drive steel into their vulnerable backs."

The three officers considered her plan in silence, while outside the confusion of noise went on. Horses galloped past, wagons creaked and bounced along, snow underfoot crunched as soldiers shuffled past, and men called out orders.

Lieutenant Leiden's eyes turned up toward Kahlan. "Mother Confessor, my Keltans could be that other force. They've all served together a long time, and work well in our own units under my command. We could begin slipping out of camp at once and gather down there to wait for the attack. You could send a Sister with us to verify a prearranged signal, and then I could take my men in when Captain Abernathy attacks from the opposite side."

Kahlan knew the man wanted to redeem himself in her eyes. He was also looking to establish for Kelton a measure of autonomy within the D'Haran Empire.

"That will be a dangerous spot, Lieutenant. If anything goes wrong, we can't come to your aid."

He nodded. "But my men are familiar with the area and we're used to traversing mountainous country in the winter. The Imperial Order is from a warmer land. We have the advantage of weather and terrain. We can do the job, Mother Confessor."

Kahlan straightened, letting out a breath as she appraised the man. General Meiffert, she knew, would like the idea. Captain Abernathy would, too; Galea and Kelton were traditional rivals, so the two would just as soon fight their own way, and separately.

Richard had brought the lands together, so that they would all come to feel they were one, now. That was vital if they were to survive. She supposed that they were fighting for the same goal, so in that way they were working together—they would have to coordinate their attacks. Lieutenant Leiden did make sense, too; his troops were mountain fighters.

"All right, Lieutenant."

"Thank you, Mother Confessor."

Kahlan thought to add some insurance. "If you acquit yourself well in this, Lieutenant, it could move you up in command."

Lieutenant Leiden clapped a fist to his heart in salute. "My men will make their queen proud."

Kahlan acknowledged his pledge with the nod of the Mother Confessor. She addressed them all. "We had better get under way."

General Meiffert grunted his agreement. "This will be a good opportunity to knock down their numbers. If it goes even half right, this time we'll bleed them good." He turned to the other two officers. "Let's get started. We need to have your men moving at once to give them enough time to be in position by morning. There's no telling how long they might wait to attack, but if it comes as soon as dawn, I want you in position and ready."

"The Order favors attacking at dawn," Captain Abernathy said. "We can be on our way within the hour. We'll be in place and ready by dawn, should they come in early."

"As can we," Lieutenant Leiden agreed.

The two officers bowed and started to leave.

"Captain," Kahlan called. The men turned back.

"Mother Confessor?"

"Do you have any idea what could be keeping Prince Harold and the rest of your army? He should have been here long ago. We could really use the rest of your men."

Captain Abernathy's thumb twiddled a bone button on the front of his dark coat. "I'm sorry, Mother Confessor. I, too, thought they should have been here by now. I can't imagine what could be keeping the prince."

"He should have been here by now," she repeated under her breath to herself. She looked up at the captain. "Weather?"

"Perhaps, Mother Confessor. If there are storms, that could have delayed him. That is probably the reason, and in that case I don't imagine he should be much longer. Our men train in the mountains in such conditions."

Kahlan sighed. "Let's hope he's here soon, then."

Captain Abernathy confidently met her gaze. "I know for a fact that the prince was eager to collect his men and get down here to help. Galea spans the Callisidrin Valley. The prince personally told me that it was to our own best interest to halt the Imperial Order down here, rather than letting them advance further up into the Midlands, where our lands and our families would come under the terror of the enemy."

Kahlan could see in Lieutenant Leiden's eyes that he was thinking that if Prince Harold instead decided to make a stand in the Callisidrin Valley, in order to selfishly protect his homeland of Galea, such an obstacle very well could force the Order to instead bear toward the northeast in their advance, around the intervening mountains, and over into the Kern Plain—right toward Leiden's homeland of Kelton. If Lieutenant Leiden was imagining such treachery, he had the wisdom not to voice it.

"I know the weather was bad when I came down," Kahlan said. "It is winter, after all. I'm sure Prince Harold will soon be here to help his queen and the fellow people of the D'Haran Empire."

Kahlan offered them a smile to soften the subtle threat. "Thank you, gentlemen. You'd best get to your tasks. May the good spirits watch your backs."

After the men had saluted and hurried off to their work, Adie put her hands to her knees and levered herself to her feet.

"If you do not need me, I must see to informing the Sisters, Zedd, and Warren of our plans."

Kahlan nodded wearily. "Thank you, Adie."

Adie, her eyes completely white, saw with the aid of her gift. Kahlan could feel that gifted gaze on her.

"You have used your power," the old sorceress said. "I be able to see it in your face. You must rest."

"I know," Kahlan said. "But there are things needing to be done."

"They will not get done if you fall ill, or worse—which could happen." Adie's thin fingers gripped Cara's arm. "See to it that the Mother Confessor be left alone for a while, so she can at least rest her head on the table, if nothing else."

Cara swung the folding chair around and set it behind the table. She pointed at it while leveling a stern look at Kahlan.

"Sit. I will stand watch."

Kahlan was exhausted. Using her Confessor's ability sapped her strength. She needed time to recover. The hard ride back had only made matters worse. She went around the table and sat down heavily in the folding chair. She opened her fur mantle and set it back on her shoulders. Richard's sword was still strapped to her back, its hilt jutting up above her shoulder. She didn't bother to remove the sword.

Adie, at seeing Kahlan comply without complaint, smiled to herself and went on her way. Cara took up guard at the entrance as Kahlan's head sank down into her pillowed arms. Trying not to let the terrible events of the day overwhelm her, she instead thought of Richard, remembering his handsome smile, his penetrating gray eyes, his gentle touch. Her own eyes closed. In her weariness, the chair and table felt as if they were spinning her around. In moments, though, as she held her thoughts of Richard in her mind's eye, she felt herself sliding into sleep.

$\mathbf{M}$other Confessor?"

Kahlan squinted up at a dark shape above her. She blinked, clearing her vision, and saw that it was Verna. The gold sunburst ring of the Prelate of the Sisters of the Light reflected a glimmer of lamplight. Behind her, twilight tainted the tent canvas with a rusty glow.

Kahlan rubbed the sleep from her eyes. Verna wore a long, gray wool dress and a dark brown cloak. At her throat, the dress had a bit of white lace that softened the austerity of the outfit. Verna's brown hair had a carefree wave and spring to it, but her brown eyes held a troubled look.

"What is it, Verna?"

"If you have a moment, I would like to talk to you."

No doubt, Verna had been talking to Warren. Whenever Kahlan saw them together, the shared intimate glances, the chance furtive touch reminded her of the way she and Richard felt about each other. It softened Kahlan's feelings about Verna's stern exterior, to know she was in love—knowing, for that matter, that she was capable of tenderness. Kahlan knew that she, too, must be regarded with the same sort of curiosity, if not amazement, where tender feelings were concerned.

She sighed, wondering if this was going to be a "talk" about Ann and prophecy. Kahlan wasn't in the mood.

"Cara, how long have I been asleep?"

"A couple of hours. It will soon be dark."

As tight and sore as Kahlan's shoulders and neck were from sleeping with her head on the table, the lateness of the hour didn't come as a surprise. She stretched to the side and then saw the frail looking sorceress sitting on a short bench. She had a dark blanket over her lap.

"How do you feel?" Adie asked.

"I'm fine." Kahlan could see her breath in the frigid air. "The men we sent out?"

"Both groups be on their way, more than an hour ago," Adie said. "The first group, the Galeans, all left together in big columns. The Keltans dribbled out in small groups not as likely to be noticed by any spies watching."

Kahlan yawned. "Good."

She knew they had to fear an attack by the Imperial Order as soon as morning. At least that should give their men enough time to travel to their positions and be ready. Waiting for an attack made her stomach feel queasy. She knew the men, too, would be on edge and likely get little sleep.

Adie idly ran a thin finger back and forth along the red and yellow beads at the neckline of her modest robes. "I came back after the Galeans left, to help Cara keep people away so you would not be disturbed while you rested."

Kahlan nodded her thanks. Apparently, either Adie thought Kahlan had rested enough, or she thought Verna's visit was important.

"What is it, then, Verna?"

"We have . . . discovered something. Not so much discovered it, as had an idea."

"Who is 'we'?"

Verna cleared her throat. Under her breath she beseeched the Creator's forgiveness before she went on.

"Actually, Mother Confessor, I thought of it. Some of my Sisters helped me with it, but I'm the one who thought it up. The blame falls to me."

Kahlan thought that was an odd way of putting it. She didn't think Verna looked at all pleased by her own idea, whatever it was. Kahlan waited silently for her to go on.

"Well, you see, we have a problem getting things past the enemy's gifted. They have Sisters of the light, but also Dark, and we don't have their power. When we try to send things—"

"Send things?"

Verna pursed her lips. "Weapons."

When Kahlan's brow twitched with a questioning look, Verna bent and gathered something from the ground. She held out her open hand, showing Kahlan a collection of small pebbles.

"Zedd showed us how to turn simple things into devastating weapons. We can use our power to fling them or even with our breath blow on some small thing, like these pebbles, and use our magic to send them out faster than any arrow, even an arrow from a crossbow. The pebbles we flung out in this way cut down waves of advancing soldiers. The pebbles traveled so swiftly that sometimes each would pierce the bodies of half a dozen men."

"I remember those reports," Kahlan said. "But that stopped working because their gifted caught on to the artifice and now defend against such things."

Kahlan recognized the weary look of the weight of responsibility in Verna's brown eyes. "That's right. The Order learned how to look for things of magic, or even things propelled by magic. Most of our conjuring that is in any way similar has become useless."

"That's what Zedd told me—that in war magic is most often unseen, that each side manages only to balance the other."

Verna nodded. "It is so. We do the same against them. Things they used at first, we now know how to counter so we can protect our men. Our warning horns, for example. We learned that we must code them with a trace of magic to know they are genuine."

Kahlan drew her fur mantle up around her neck. She was chilled to the bone and couldn't seem to get warm. Not surprising, seeing as how she was spending all of her time outdoors. It was insanity to be carrying on a war in such conditions. She guessed that war in fine weather was no more sane. Still, she ached to be inside, beside a cozy fire.

"So what is this thing you thought up?"

As if reminded of the cold, Verna pulled her cloak tighter around her shoulders. "Well, I got the notion that if the enemy gifted are, in a sense, filtering for anything magic, or even anything being propelled by magic, then what we need is something not magic."

Kahlan gave Verna a grim smile. "We do. They're called soldiers."

Verna didn't smile. "No. I meant something the gifted could do to disable enemy troops without risk to our own men."

Adie shuffled forward to stand behind Kahlan's left shoulder as Verna reached into her cloak and pulled out a small leather pouch closed with a drawstring. She tossed it on the table before Kahlan, then set a piece of paper beside it.

"Pour a little on the paper, please." Verna was holding her stomach as if she were having indigestion. "But be careful not to touch it with your finger or get it on your skin—and whatever you do, don't blow on it. Be careful not to even breathe on it."

Adie leaned in to watch as Kahlan carefully poured a small quantity of a sparkling dust from the pouch onto the square of paper. She pushed at the little pile with the corner of the pouch. There were hints of pallid colors, but it was mostly a pale, glimmering, greenish-gray.

"What is it? Some kind of magic dust?"

"Glass."

Kahlan's eyes turned up. "Glass. You thought up glass?"

Verna let out a tsk at herself for how foolish she must have sounded. "No, Mother Confessor. I thought of breaking it. You see, this is just simple glass that has been broken and crushed into fine pieces—almost dust. But we used our Han to aid us when we crushed the glass with a mortar and pestle. By using our gift, we were able to break the glass into very tiny fragments, but in a special way."

Verna leaned over, her finger hovering above the little greenish-gray mound. Cara leaned in beside her in order to look down at the dangerous thing on the piece of paper.

"This glass—every piece—is sharp and jagged, even though each piece is very tiny. Each piece is hardly bigger than dust, so it weighs nothing, almost like dust."

"Dear spirits," Adie said before whispering a prayer in her own language.

Kahlan cleared her throat. "I don't understand."

"Mother Confessor, we can't get our magic past the defenses of the Order's gifted. They are prepared for magic, even if it's a simple pebble but uses magic to hurl it at their troops.

"This glass, however, even though we used magic to break it, has no magic properties—none at all. It's just inert material, the same as the dust kicked up by their feet. They can't detect it as magic, because it isn't magic. Through their gift, they will sense this as simple as dust, or mist, or possibly fog, depending on atmospheric conditions at the time."

"But we sent dust clouds at them before," Kahlan said. "Dust to make them sick and such. They mostly countered it."

Verna held up a finger to note her point as she smiled a grim smile. "But those were dust clouds containing magic. Mother Confessor, this does not. Don't you see? It's so light it floats in the air for a long time. We could use simple magic to cast it up into the air, and then withdraw the magic, or we could simply fling it up into the breeze, for that matter. Either way, we have only to let their troops run through it."

"All right." Kahlan scratched an eyebrow. "But what will it do to them?"

"It will get in their eyes," Adie said in her raspy voice from behind Kahlan's shoulder.

"That's right," Verna said. "It gets in their eyes, just as any dust would. At first, it will feel like dust in their eyes and they will try to blink it away. However, since the fragments are all still jagged and razor sharp, they will instead embed themselves in the body's tissue. It will stick in their eyes, and build up under their eyelids, where it will make thousands of tiny cuts across their eyes with each blink. The more they blink, the more it eats away at their delicate eyes." Verna straightened and pulled her cloak together. "It will blind them."

Kahlan sat in numb disbelief at the madness of it all.

"Are you sure?" Cara asked. "Might it just irritate them, like gritty dust?"

"We know for sure," Verna said. "We . . . had an accident, and know all too well what it does. It may do more damage when it gets in the throat, the lungs, and the gut—we don't know about that, yet—but we do know for sure that such special glass, if we grind it to just the right size particles, will float in the air and people passing through the cloud will be blinded in remarkably short order. As long as we can blind a man, he can't fight. It may not kill them, but as long as they are blind they can't kill us, or fight back as we kill them."

Cara, usually gleeful at the prospect of killing the enemy, did not seem so, now. "We would have but to line them up and butcher them."

Kahlan put her head in her hands, covering her eyes.

"You want me to approve its use, don't you? That's why you're here."

Verna said nothing. Kahlan looked up at last.

"That's what you want, isn't it?"

"Mother Confessor, I need not tell you that the Sisters of the Light abhor harming people. However, this is a war for our very existence, for the very existence of free people. We know it must be done. If Richard were here . . . I just thought that you would want to be made aware of this, and be the one to give such orders."

Kahlan stared at the woman, understanding then why she was holding her hand over a pain in her stomach.

"Do you know, Prelate," Kahlan said in a near whisper, "that I killed a child today? Not by accident, but on purpose. I would do it again without hesitation. But that won't make me sleep any better."

"A child? It was truly necessary to . . . kill a child?"

"His name was Lyle. I believe you know him. He was another one of the victims of Ann's Sisters of the Light."

Verna, her face gone ashen, closed her eyes against the news.

"I guess if I can kill a child," Kahlan said, "I can easily enough give the orders for you to use your special glass against the monsters who would use a child as a weapon. I have sworn no mercy, and I meant it."

Adie laid a gnarled hand on Kahlan's shoulder.

"Kahlan," Verna said in a gentle voice, "I can understand how you feel. Ann used me, too, and I didn't understand why. I thought she used everyone for her own selfish purposes. For a time, I thought her a despicable person. You have every reason to believe as you do."

"But I would be wrong, Verna? Is that what you were going to add? I'd not be so sure, were I you. You didn't have to kill a little boy today."

Verna nodded in sympathy but didn't argue.

"Adie," Kahlan asked, "do you think there would be anything you might be able to do for the woman who was accidentally blinded? Perhaps you could help her?"

Adie nodded. "That be a good idea. Verna, take me to her, and let me see what I can do."

Kahlan cocked her head as the two women moved toward the tent opening. "Did you hear that?"

"The horn?" Verna asked.

"Yes. It sounds like alarm horns."

Verna squinted in concentration. She turned her head to the side, listening attentively.

"Yes, it does sound like alarm horns," she finally declared, "but it doesn't have the right trace of magic through it. The enemy does that often—tries to get us to act based on false alarms. We've been having more and more lately."

Kahlan frowned. "We have? Why?"

"Why . . . what?"

Kahlan stood. "If we know they're false alarms, and they don't work, then why would the Order increase the attempts? That makes no sense."

Verna's gaze roved about as as if searching in vain for an answer. "Well, I don't know. I can't imagine. I'm no expert in the tactics of warfare."

Cara turned to go have a look. "Maybe it's just some scouts coming back in."

Kahlan turned her head, listening. She heard horses running, but that wasn't so rare. It could be, as Cara suggested, scouts returning with reports. But, by the sound of the hooves, the horses sounded big.

She heard men yelling. The clash of steel rang out—along with cries of pain.

Kahlan drew her Galean royal sword as she started around the table. Before any of them could get more than a step, the tent shuddered violently as something crashed against its walls. For an instant, the whole thing tipped at an impossible angle; then steel-tipped lances burst through the canvas. With a rush of wind the tent collapsed around them.

The heavy canvas drove Kahlan to the ground as it caved in. She couldn't get a grip on anything solid as the tent rolled her over and began dragging her along. Hooves thundered past, pounding the ground right beside her head.

She could smell lamp oil as it sloshed across the canvas. With a whoosh, the oil and the tent ignited. Kahlan coughed on the smoke. She could hear the crackle of flames. She could see nothing. She was trapped—rolled up in the bucking tent as it slid across the ground.

Tightly shrouded in stiff canvas, Kahlan couldn't see anything. She choked and gagged on the thick, acrid smoke burning her lungs. She pulled frantically at the canvas, trying to disentangle herself, but as she bounced and tumbled along the ground, she couldn't make any headway gaining her liberty. The heat of flames close to her face ignited in her a sense of panic. Her weariness forgotten, she kicked and struggled madly as she gasped for air.

"Where are you!"

It was Cara's voice. It sounded close, as if she, too, was being dragged along and strenuously engaged in her own fight for life. Cara was smart enough not to shout Kahlan's name or title when surrounded by the enemy; hopefully, Verna knew better, as well.

"Here!" Kahlan shouted in answer to Cara.

Kahlan's sword was trapped, pressed to her legs by the rolled canvas. She managed to wiggle her left hand up onto the knife at her belt. She yanked it free. She had to turn her face to try to keep away from the heat of the oily flames. The smothering smoky blindness was terrifying.

With angry resolve, Kahlan stabbed at the canvas, punching her knife through. Just then, the tent hit something and they were bounced into the air. The hard landing knocked the wind from her lungs. A gasp pulled in suffocating smoke. Again, Kahlan plunged her knife into the heavy canvas and slashed an opening as her entire shroud erupted into flame.

She yelled again to Cara. "I can't get—"

The tent hit something solid. Her shoulder whacked hard into what felt like a tree stump and she was flipped up and over the top of it. Had she not been wearing her stiff leather armor, the blow surely would have broken her shoulder. Crashing down on the other side, Kahlan tumbled free and across the snow. She spread her arms to stop herself from rolling.

Kahlan saw General Meiffert reach up, seize a fistful of chain mail, and unhorse the man who had been dragging her tent. The man's eyes gleamed from behind long, curly, greasy hair. His stout body was covered with hides and furs over chain mail and leather armor. He was missing his upper teeth. As he lunged at the general, he lost his head, too.

Yet more Order troops wheeled their big warhorses, striking down at the D'Harans scrambling both to escape the blows and to mount a defense. One of the warhorses charged Kahlan's way, its rider leaning out, swinging a flail. Kahlan sheathed both her knife and sword. She snatched up the lance of the man who had been dragging the tent. She brought the long weapon up and spun around just in time to plant the butt end in a frozen rut and let the charging warhorse take the steel-tipped point in his chest.

As the grinning Order soldier with the flail leaped from the staggering horse, he drew his sword with his free hand. Kahlan didn't wait; as he was still alighting on his feet, she spun while drawing her own sword and landed a solid backhanded blow across the left side of his face.

Without pause, she dove under the legs of another horse to dodge a blade when the horse's rider slashed down at her. She sprang up on the other side and hacked the rider's leg open to the bone twice before turning just in time to ram her sword up to its hilt into the chest of another horse sidling in, trying to crush her against the first. As the animal reared with a wild scream, Kahlan yanked her sword free and tumbled away just before the big horse crashed to the ground. The rider's leg was trapped, and he was at an awkward angle to defend himself. Kahlan made the best of the opportunity.

For the moment, the immediate area was clear, enabling her to scramble over to the tent where the general was on his knees, yanking at the snarled mess of canvas and rope. More Order cavalry were thundering past, threatening to trample Verna, Adie, and Cara still trapped in the tangle of tent. At least the burning section had pulled away.

Kahlan worked beside General Meiffert to tug and cut the canvas. At last they ripped open the heavy material, freeing Adie and Verna. The two women were rolled up together, nearly in each another's arms. Adie's head was bleeding, but she pushed away Kahlan's concerned hands. Verna emerged from the cocoon and stumbled to her feet, still dizzy from the wild ride.

Kahlan helped Adie up. The scrape on her brow didn't look too serious. General Meiffert pulled frantically at the canvas. Cara was still inside, somewhere, but they no longer heard her.

Kahlan seized Verna by the arm. "I thought they were false alarms!"

"They were!" Verna insisted. "Obviously, they tricked us."

All around, soldiers were engaged in pitched battle with Imperial Order cavalry. Men shouted in fury as they threw themselves into battle; some screamed as they were wounded or killed; others called out orders, commanding a defense, while the men on horseback ordered in their attack.

Some of the cavalry were setting fire to wagons, tents, and supplies. Others charged past, trampling men and tents. Pairs of riders teamed up to single out soldiers and take them down, then charged after another victim.

They were using the same tactics the D'Harans had used. They were doing what Kahlan had taught them to do.

When a soldier, draped in filthy fur and weapons, cried out in bravado as he rushed at her wielding a raised mace studded with glistening bloody spikes, Kahlan took his hand off with a lightning-swift blow. He staggered to a stop and stared a her in surprise. Without missing a beat, she drove her sword into his gut and gave it a wrenching twist before pulling it free. She turned her attention elsewhere as he crashed down atop a fire. His screams melted in with all the others.

Kahlan fell to her knees once more to help General Meiffert free Cara. He had found her amid the snare of rope and folds of canvas. From time to time one of them had to turn to fight off sporadic attackers. Kahlan could see Cara's red boots sticking out from under the canvas, but they were still.

Tent line was tangled around Cara's legs. With Kahlan and the general working together, they cut through the mire of rope and were finally able to unroll Cara. She held her head as she moaned. She wasn't unconscious, but she was groggy and unable to get her bearings. Kahlan found a lump in her hair, at the right side of her head, but it wasn't bleeding.

Cara tried to sit up. Kahlan pressed her down on her back.

"Stay there. You were hit on the head. I don't want you to get up just yet."

Kahlan looked over her shoulder and saw Verna, nearby, singling out Imperial Order troops, each twitch of her hands casting a fiery spell to blast them from their horses, or a focused edge of air as sharp as any blade, yet more swift and sure, to slice them down. Without the gift themselves, or one of the gifted to protect them, the enemy's simple armor was no defense.

Kahlan caught Verna's attention and motioned for her help. Seizing the woman's cloak at her shoulder, Kahlan pulled Verna close to speak into her ear so as to be heard above the noise of battle.

"See how she is, will you? Help her?"

Verna nodded and then huddled at Cara's side as Kahlan and the general turned to a fresh charge of cavalry. As one man galloped in close, wielding his lance around, General Meiffert dodged the strike and then leaped up onto the side of the horse, catching hold of the saddle's horn. With a grunt of angry effort, he drove his sword through the rider. The surprised man clawed at the blade in his soft middle. The general yanked his sword free, then grabbed the man by the hair and dragged him out of the saddle. As the dying man fell away, General Meiffert sprang up into the saddle, in his place. Kahlan snatched up the fallen cavalryman's lance.

The big D'Haran general wheeled the huge horse into the way of charging enemy cavalry, protecting Verna and Cara. Kahlan sheathed her sword and used the lance to good effect against the warhorses. Horses, even well-trained warhorses, didn't appreciate being stabbed in the chest. Many people considered them just dumb beasts, but horses were smart enough to understand that driving themselves onto a pointed lance was not what they wanted to do, and reacted accordingly.

As horses bucked and reared when Kahlan stabbed them with her lance, many of their riders fell. Some were injured from the fall onto scattered equipment or the frozen ground, but most came under the swarming attack of the D'Harans.

From atop his Imperial Order warhorse, General Meiffert commanded his men to form a defensive line. After directing them into place, he charged off, roaring a string of orders as he went. He didn't tell his men who to protect, so as not to betray Kahlan to the enemy, but they quickly saw what it was he intended them to do. D'Harans grabbed up the enemy lances, or came running with their own pikes, and soon there was a bristling line of steel-tipped pole weapons presenting a deadly obstacle to any approaching cavalry.

Kahlan called out orders to men on either side, and, as she joined the line, commanded them into position to block an Imperial Order cavalry unit of about two hundred who were trying to make good their escape. The enemy might have been emulating the raids the D'Haran cavalry had made on the Imperial Order's camp, but Kahlan wasn't about to allow them to succeed at it. She intended them to fail.

The enemy's horses balked when they encountered a solid line of advancing pikes brandished by men shouting battle cries. Soldiers coming from behind the Order cavalry rained down arrows. D'Harans dragged trapped riders from their saddles, down into the bloody hand-to-hand fighting on the ground.

"I don't want one of them escaping camp alive!" she yelled to her men. "No mercy!"

"No mercy!" every D'Haran within earshot called out in answer.

The enemy, so confident and arrogant as they had charged in, relishing the prospect of spilling D'Haran blood, were now nothing more than pathetic men in the ungainly grip of despair as the D'Harans hacked them to death.

Kahlan left the soldiers with the lances and pikes, now that a defensive line had been established and the enemy was trapped, and ran back through the fires and choking smoke to find Verna, Adie, and Cara. She had to dodge wounded soldiers of both armies on the ground. The fallen attackers who still had fight in them snatched at her ankles. She had to stab several who tried to rise up to grab her. Others afoot who suddenly appeared, she had to cut down.

The enemy knew who she was, or at least they were pretty sure. Jagang had seen her, and no doubt had described the Mother Confessor to his men. Kahlan was sure to have a heavy price on her head.

There seemed to be Imperial Order men scattered throughout the camp. She doubted there had been an attack by foot soldiers; they were probably cavalrymen who had lost their mounts. Horses were often easier moving targets to hit with arrows and spears than were men. In the gathering darkness it was hard to make out enemy soldiers. They were able to sneak through the camp undiscovered as they hunted targets of value, such as officers, or maybe even the Mother Confessor.

When the lurking enemy spotted Kahlan making her way through the chaos, they came out from their hiding places to go after her with wild abandon. Others, she came upon and surprised. Remembering not only her father's training, but Richard's admonition, Kahlan cut fiercely into the enemy soldiers. She gave them no opening; no chance; no mercy.

Her training under her father had been a good foundation for the esoteric tactical precepts that Richard had taught her when she was recovering from her wounds back in Hartland. Richard's way had seemed so strange, then; now, it seemed so natural. In much the same way a lighter horse could outmaneuver a big warhorse, her lighter weight became her edge. She didn't need the weight because she simply didn't clash with the enemy in the traditional manner, as they expected. She was a hummingbird, floating out of their reach, swooping in between their ponderous moves to efficiently deliver death.

Such moves were not at odds with the manner of fighting that her father had taught, but complemented it in a way that fit her. Richard had trained her not with a sword, but with a willow switch, a mischievous smile, and a dangerous glint in his eyes. Now, Richard's sword, strapped over the back of her shoulder, was an ever-present reminder of those playful lessons that had been not only unrelenting, but deadly serious.

She finally found Verna, bent over Cara, but didn't see the general anywhere. Kahlan snatched Verna's sleeve.

"How is she?"

"She threw up, but that seemed to have helped, once it passed. She will probably be woozy for a while, but I think she's otherwise all right."

"She has a thick skull," Adie said. "It not be cracked, but she should lie still for a time—at least until she recovers her balance."

Cara's hands groped as if having trouble finding the ground beneath her. Despite her obvious dizziness, she was cursing the Prelate and trying to sit up. Kahlan, squatting beside Cara, pressed her shoulder to the ground.

"Cara, I'm right here. I'm fine. Lie still for a few minutes."

"I want at them!"

"Later," Kahlan said. "Don't worry, you'll get your chance." She saw that the blood was cleaned from Adie's head. "Adie, how are you? How is your head?"

The old sorceress gestured dismissively. "Bah. I be fine. My head be thicker than Cara's."

Soldiers had gathered, forming a protective wall of steel. Verna, Adie, and Kahlan crouched over Cara, keeping an eye on the surrounding area, but the fighting immediately around them seemed to have ended. Even if pockets of battle remained, with the large number of D'Haran soldiers who had protectively closed ranks, the four women were safe for the time being.

General Meiffert finally returned, charging through the line of D'Haran defenders as they parted for him. He leaped from his enemy warhorse. The horse tossed his head at the indignity of being ridden by the enemy, and ran off. The young D'Haran general crouched down on the opposite side of Cara. Winded, he started talking anyway.

"I've been down checking with the front lines. This is a raid, much like what we've been doing to them. It looked bigger than it really was. When they spotted the Mother Confessor, they called their men into this area, so the damage was mostly focused in this section."

"Why didn't we know?" Kahlan asked. "What went wrong with the alarm?"

"Not sure." He was shaking his head, still getting his breath. "Zedd thinks that they learned our codes, and that when we blew the alarm, they must have used Subtractive Magic to alter the magic woven into the sound that tells our gifted that it's a real attack."

Kahlan let out an angry breath. It was all starting to make sense to her. "That's why there have been so many false alarms. They were numbing us to them so that when they attacked, we would be unconcerned, falsely believing our own alarms were just another enemy false alarm."

"I'm guessing you're right." He flexed his fist in frustration. He looked down then and noticed Cara scowling up at him. "Cara. Are you all right? I was so—I mean, we thought you might be badly hurt."

"No," she said, casting a cool glare at Verna and Kahlan, each of whom used a hand to hold her shoulders down. She casually crossed her ankles. "I just thought you could handle it, so I decided to take a nap."

General Meiffert gave her a quick smile and then turned a serious face to Kahlan.

"It gets worse. This cavalry attack was a diversion. They hoped it might get you, I'm sure, but it was meant to make us believe it was just a raid."

Kahlan felt her flesh go cold with dread. "They're coming, aren't they?"

He nodded. "The entire force. They're still a distance out, but you're right, they're coming. This was just to throw us into confusion and keep us distracted."

Kahlan stared, dumbfounded. The Order had never attacked at sunset before. The prospect of the onslaught of hundreds of thousands upon hundreds of thousands of Imperial Order troops storming in from the darkness was bloodcurdling.

"They've changed their tactics," Kahlan whispered to herself. "He's a quick study. I thought I'd tricked him, but I was the one who was taken in."

288

"What are you mumbling about?" Cara asked, her fingers locked together over her stomach.

"Jagang. He counted on me not being fooled by those troops going around in a circle. He wanted me to think I had outsmarted him. He played me for a fool."

Cara made a face. "What?"

Kahlan felt sick at the implications. She pressed a hand to her forehead as the awful truth inundated her.

"Jagang wanted me to think I had his scheme figured out, so we would pretend to play along and send out our troops. He probably figured they wouldn't be sent after his decoy, but would be used instead against his real plan of attack. He didn't care about that, though. All along, he was planning on changing his tactics. He was waiting only until those troops left so that he could attack before they were in place and while our numbers were reduced."

"You mean," Cara asked, "that whole time you were talking to him, pretending to believe he was moving troops north, he knew you were pretending?"

"I'm afraid so. He outsmarted me."

"Maybe, maybe not," General Meiffert said. "He hasn't succeeded, yet. We don't have to let him have it his way. We can move our forces before he can pounce."

"Can't we call back the men we sent out?" Verna asked. "Their numbers would help."

"They're hours away," General Meiffert said, "traveling through back country on the way to their assigned locations. They would never get back here in time to help us tonight."

Rather than dwell on how gullible she had been, Kahlan put her mind to the immediate problem. "We need to move fast."

The general nodded his agreement. "We could fall back on our other plans— about breaking up and scattering into the mountains."

He ran his fingers back through his blond hair. The gesture of frustration unexpectedly reminded Kahlan of Richard. "But if we do that, we would have to abandon most of our supplies. In winter, without supplies, a number of our men wouldn't last long. Either way, killed in battle or dying of hunger and cold—you're just as dead."

"Broken up like that, we would be easy pickings," Kahlan agreed. "That's a last resort. It may work later, but not now. For now, we need to keep the army together if we're to survive the winter—and if we're to keep the Order distracted from its designs at conquest."

"We dare not allow them to go uncontested into a city. It would not only be a bloodbath, but if they picked the right city, we would face a near impossible task of dislodging them." The general shook his head. "It could end up being the end of our hopes of driving them back to the Old World."

Kahlan gestured over her shoulder. "What about that valley we talked about, back there? The high pass is narrow—it can be defended on this side by two men and a dog, if need be."

"That's what I was thinking," he said. "It keeps the army together—and keeps the Order having to contend with us, rather than being able to turn their attention on any cities. If they try to move around us up into the Midlands, there are easy northern routes out of the valley from which we can strike. We have more men on the way, and we can send for others; we need to stay together and maintain our engagement with the Order's army until those forces arrive."

"Then what are we waiting for?" Verna asked. "Let's get moving."

He gave her a worried look. "The problem right now is that if we're to make it into that valley before the Order can pounce on us, we're going to need more time to do it. The pass is too narrow for wagons. The horses can make it, but not the wagons—they'll have to be dismantled. Most of our equipment is designed to be knocked down so the parts can be portaged, if need be. We'll have to leave a few that aren't. It won't take long to get started, but we're going to need time to funnel all the men and supplies over that narrow pass—especially in the dark."

"Torches will work well enough with a steady line of men," Adie said. "They must only follow the one in front, and even if the light be bad, they can do it."

Kahlan remembered the handprint made of glowing dust. "The gifted could lay down a glowing track to guide the men."

"That would help," the general said. "We're still left with our basic problem, though. While our men are trying to break down and move all our equipment and supplies, and waiting their turn to go over the pass, the Order will arrive. We'll find ourselves in a pitched battle trying to defend ourselves while withdrawing at the same time. A withdrawal requires the ability to move faster than the enemy, or at least keep him at bay while pulling back; the pass doesn't provide that."

"We've kept ahead of them before," Verna said. "This isn't the first attack."

"You're right." He pointed to his left. "We could try to withdraw up this valley, instead, but in the dark and with the Order attacking, I think that would be a mistake. Darkness is the problem, this time. They're going to keep coming. In daylight, we could establish defenses and hold them off—not at night."

"We already have defenses set up, here," Cara said. "We could stand where we are and fight them head-on."

General Meiffert chewed his lower lip. "That was my first thought, Cara, and still an option, but I don't like our chances in a head-on, direct confrontation like this, not at night when they can sneak great numbers of men in close. We couldn't use our archers to advantage in the dark. We can't see their numbers or movements accurately, so we wouldn't be able to position our men properly. It's a problem of numbers: theirs are almost unlimited, ours aren't.

"We don't have enough gifted to cover every possibility—and in war it's always what you don't cover that gets hit. The enemy could pour through a gap, get in behind us in the dark, without us even realizing it, and then we're finished."

Everyone was silent as the implications truly sank in.

"I agree," Kahlan said. "The pass is the only chance we have to keep from losing a major battle tonight—along with a huge number of our men. The risk without real benefit of standing and fighting is a poor choice."

The general appraised her eyes. "That still leaves us with the problem of how we're going to get over that pass before they annihilate us."

Kahlan turned to Verna. "We need you to slow the enemy down to give us the time we need to get our army over that pass."

"What do you wish me to do?"

"Use your special glass."

The general screwed up his face. "Her what?"

"A weapon of magic," Cara said. "To blind the enemy troops."

Verna looked thunderstruck. "But I'm not ready. We only made up a small batch. I'm not ready."

Kahlan turned back to the general. "What did the scouts say about how much time we have until the Order is upon us?"

"The Order could be here within an hour, at the soonest, two at the latest. If we don't slow them down, we'll never make it out of this valley with our men and supplies. If we can't find a way to delay them, we can only run for the hills, or stand and fight. Neither is a choice I would make except in desperation."

"If we just run for the hills," Adie said, "we be as good as dead. Together, we be alive and at least be a threat to the enemy. If we scatter, the Order will take the opportunity to attack and capture cities. If our only choice is to scatter, or stand our ground and fight, then we can only choose to stand and fight. Better to try, than to die one at a time out in the mountains."

Kahlan rubbed her fingers across her brow as she tried to think. Jagang had changed his tactics and decided to engage them in a night battle. He had never done that before because it would be so costly for him, but with his numbers, he apparently wasn't concerned about that. Jagang held life in little regard.

"If we have to fight him, in a full battle, here, now," Kahlan said in resignation, "we will probably lose the war by dawn."

"I agree," the general finally said. "As far as I see it, we have no choice. We have to act quickly and get as many of our men over the pass as we can. We'll lose all those who don't get over before the Order arrives, but we'll manage to preserve some."

The four of them were silent a moment, each considering the horror of that reality, of who would remain behind to die. Furious activity continued around them. Men were rushing around, putting out fires, collecting panicked horses, tending to wounded, and battling the few remaining invaders they had trapped. The Order soldiers were greatly outnumbered. Not for long, though.

Kahlan's mind raced. She couldn't help being furious with herself at being gulled. Richard's words echoed through her mind: think of the solution, not the problem. The solution was the only thing that mattered now.

Kahlan looked again to Verna. "We have an hour before they're upon us. You have to try, Verna. Do you think you have any chance at making your special glass and then deploying it before the enemy is upon us?"

"I will do my best—you have my word on that. I wish I could promise more." Verna scrambled to her feet. "I'll need the Sisters who are tending the wounded, of course. What about the ones working at the front lines? The ones countering enemy magic? Can I have any of them?"

"Take them all," Kahlan said. "If this doesn't work, nothing else is going to matter."

"I'll take them all, then. Every one," Verna said. "It's the only chance we have."

"You get started," Adie told Verna. "Go down near the front lines, on this side of the valley where you will be upwind from the attack. I will begin collecting the Sisters and get them down there to help you."

"We need glass," Verna said to the general. "Any kind. At least a few barrels full."

"I'll have men down there with the first barrel right away. Can we at least help to break it up for you?"

291

"No. It won't matter if what you throw in the barrels breaks, but beyond that, it must be done by the gifted. Just bring whatever glass you can collect, that will be all you can do."

The general promised her he would see to it. Holding her hem up out of her way, Verna ran off to the task. Adie was close on her heels.

"I'll get the men moving now," the general told Kahlan as he scrambled to his feet. "The scouts can mark the trail; then we can start moving the heavier supplies first."

If it worked, they would slip out of Jagang's grasp.

Kahlan knew that if Verna failed, they could all very well lose their lives, and the war, by morning. General Meiffert paused with one last hesitant look, one last chance for her to change her mind.

"Do it," she said to the general. "Cara—we have work."

K ahlan pulled her horse up short. She felt the heat of blood rushing to her face.

"What are you doing?" Cara asked as Kahlan threw her leg over the horse's neck and leaped to the ground.

The moon lit a layer of lacy clouds scudding past, giving a faint, serene illumination to the surrounding countryside. The thin layer of snow gathered the muted light of the moon to make it more luminous than it otherwise would be.

Kahlan pointed in the direction of the small figure she could just make out in the dim light. The skinny girl, surely not much past ten years, was standing at a barrel, ramming a metal rod down inside to smash the glass in the bottom. Kahlan handed the reins to Cara as soon as she had dismounted.

Kahlan stalked over to the Sisters working on the snowy ground. Running off in a haphazard line, to keep the wind at their backs, were over a hundred of the women, all focused intently on the work before them. Many had their cloaks tented around themselves and their work.

Not far down that line, Kahlan bent, put a hand under the Prelate's arm, and lifted her to her feet. Mindful of the serious nature of the work going on, Kahlan at least kept her voice quiet, since she wasn't able to make it congenial.

"Verna, what is Holly doing down here?"

Verna glanced over the heads of a dozen intervening Sisters kneeling before a long board, breeze at their backs, carefully griding glass chips with pestles in mortars. There being not nearly enough pestles and mortars, many of the women to the other side were using dished rocks and round stones to carefully crunch the glass chips. The concentration showed on each woman's face. The accident that had blinded a Sister had happened when the wind had changed, and a gust had blown her work back up in her face. The same thing could happen again at any time, although, as darkness had settled in, the wind had at least died down to a steady breeze.

Holly was bundled in an oversized cloak. She had a determined grimace as she lifted the rod and then let it drop down in the barrel set away from the Sisters' dangerous work. Kahlan saw that the rod had a faint greenish glow to it.

"She's helping, Mother Confessor."

"She's a child!"

Verna pointed off into the darkness, to what Kahlan hadn't seen. "So are Helen and Valery."

Kahlan pinched the bridge of her nose between her first finger and thumb and took a purging breath. "What madness would possess you to have children down here near the front helping to—to blind people?"

Verna glanced at the women working nearby. She took Kahlan's arm by the elbow and led her out of earshot of the others. Alone, where they were less likely to be heard, she folded her hands before herself as she assumed the stern visage that came so naturally to her.

"Kahlan, Holly may be a child, but she is a gifted child, and she is far from stupid besides. That goes for Helen and Valery as well. Holly has seen more in her young life than any child should see. She knows what's going on tonight, with that attack, and with the attack that's coming. She was terrified—all the children were."

"So you bring her to the front—to the greatest danger?"

"What would you have me do? Send her back somewhere to be watched over by soldiers? Do you wish me to force her to be alone at a time like this so she could only tremble in terror?"

"But this is—"

"She's gifted. Despite how horrific it seems, this is better for her, as it is for the others. She's with the Sisters, who understand her and her ability as other people can't. Don't you recall the comfort you derived from being with older Confessors who knew the way you felt about things?"

Kahlan did, but said nothing.

"The Sisters are the only family she and the other novices have, now. Holly is not alone and afraid. She may still be afraid, but she's doing something to help us, so that her fear is channeled into something that will assist in overcoming the cause of her fear."

Kahlan's brow was still set in a glare. "Verna, she's a child."

"And you had to kill a child today. I understand. But don't let that terrible event make it harder on Holly. Yes, this is an awful thing she is helping to do, but this is the reality of the way things are. She could die tonight, along with the rest of us. Can you even imagine what those brutes would do to her, first? At least that much is beyond the imagination of her young mind. What she can comprehend, though, is fear enough.

"If she wanted to hide somewhere, I would have let her, but she has a right—if she so chooses—to contribute to saving herself. She is gifted and can use her power to do the simple part of what needs doing. She begged me to give her the chance to help."

In anguish, Kahlan gathered her fur mantle at her throat as she glanced back over her shoulder at the little girl using both her spindly arms to lift the heavy steel rod and drop it again to break the glass in the bottom of the barrel. Holly's features were drawn tight as she concentrated on using her gift while at the same time lifting the weight of the rod.

"Dear spirits," Kahlan whispered to herself, "this is madness."

Cara impatiently shifted her weight to her other foot. It wasn't indifference to the situation, but a matter of priorities. Madness or not, there was little time left, and, as Verna said, they could all die before the night was finished. As cruel as it sounded, there were more important matters than the life of one child, or, for that matter, three.

"How is the work going? Are you going to be ready?"

Verna's bold expression finally faltered. "I don't know." She lifted a hand hesitantly, motioning out over the dark valley before them. "The wind is right, but the valley approach to our forces is quite broad. It's not that we won't have some, it's that we need to have enough so that when the enemy gets close, we can release the glass dust to float across the span of the entire field of battle."

"But you have some. Surely, what you have will do damage to the enemy."

"If there isn't enough, then they may skirt it, or it may not be concentrated enough to do the damage necessary to bring their forces to a halt. Their attack will not be turned back by a small number of casualties." Verna squeezed one fist in her other hand. "If the Creator will just slow the Imperial Order enough to grant us another hour, at the least, then I believe we may have enough."

Kahlan wiped a hand across her face. That was asking a lot, but with the darkness, she thought that it just might be possible that the Order would have to go slow enough to give Verna and her Sisters the time they needed.

"And you're sure we can't help? There is nothing any but the gifted can do to assist you?"

Verna's mask of authority again emerged in the moonlight.

"Well, yes, there is one thing."

"What is it, then?"

"You could leave me alone so I can work."

Kahlan sighed. "Just promise me one thing." Verna raised an eyebrow as if willing to listen prudently. "When the attack comes, and you have to use this special glass, get the children out of here first? Get them to the rear, where they can be taken over the pass to safety."

Verna smiled with relief. "We are of like minds in that, Mother Confessor."

As Verna hurried back to her work, Kahlan and Cara returned along the line of Sisters, past the end to where Holly was preparing glass to supply those gifted women. Kahlan couldn't help but to stop for a word.

"Holly, how are you getting along?"

When the girl rested the rod against the side of the barrel, Cara, absent any fondness for magic, aimed a suspicious frown at the faintly glowing metal. As Holly took her small hands from the metal, the greenish glow faded, as if a magical wick had been turned down.

"I'm fine, Mother Confessor. Except I'm cold. I'm getting terribly tired of being cold."

Kahlan smiled warmly as she ran a gentle hand down the back of Holly's fine hair. "As are we all." Kahlan crouched down beside the girl. "When we get over into another valley, you can get warm by a nice fire."

"That would be splendid." She cast a furtive glance at her steel rod. "I have to get back to work, Mother Confessor."

Kahlan couldn't resist pulling the girl close and kissing her frigid cheek. Hesitant at first, the thin little arms surrendered to desperately encircle Kahlan's neck.

"I'm so scared," Holly whispered.

"Me too," Kahlan whispered back as she squeezed the girl tight. "Me too."

Holly straightened. "Really? You get scared, too, that those awful men will murder us?"

Kahlan nodded. "I get frightened, but I know we have a lot of good people who will keep us safe. Like you, they work as hard as they can so that we can all someday be safe, and not have to be scared anymore."

The girl stuck her hands under her cloak to warm them. Her gaze sank to the ground at her feet. "I miss Ann, too." She looked up again. "Is Ann safe?"

Kahlan groped for words of comfort. "I saw Ann not long ago, and she was fine. I don't think you need worry for her."

"She saved me. I love her and miss her so. Will she be with us, soon?"

Kahlan cupped the girl's cheek. "I don't know, Holly. She had important business she was taking care of. I'm sure, though, that we'll see her again."

Pleased with that news and seemingly relieved to know that she was not alone in her fears, Holly turned back to her work with renewed determination.

As Kahlan and Cara collected their horses, they heard a horse approaching at a gallop. Before she recognized the rider, Kahlan saw and recognized the black splotch on its rump. When he saw her waving, Zedd trotted Spider around to her. He slid down off the animal's bare back.

"They're coming," the wizard announced without preamble.

Verna rushed up, having seen Zedd ride in. "It's too soon! They weren't supposed to be here this soon!"

He gaped at her in astonishment. "Bags, woman, shall I tell them that it would be rather inconvenient for them to attack right now and to please come back to kill us later?"

"You know what I mean," she snapped. "We don't have enough, yet."

"How long till they get here?" Kahlan asked.

"Ten minutes."

That thin sliver of time was the only bulwark between them and catastrophe. Kahlan felt as if her heart rose into her throat, recalling suddenly the forsaken feeling of being mobbed and beaten to death. Verna sputtered in wordless frustration, anger, and dread.

"Do you have any ready?" Zedd asked as calmly as if he were inquiring about dinner.

"Yes, of course," she said. "But if they will be here that soon, we've not enough. Dear Creator, we don't have nearly what we'll need in order to drift it out all across the front. Too little is as good as none."

"We've no choice, now." Zedd gazed off into the darkness, perhaps seeing what only a wizard could see. His jaw was set in bitter disappointment. He spoke in a disembodied voice, a man going through the motions when he knew he had come to the end of his options, perhaps even his faith. "Start releasing what you have. We'll just have to hope for the best. I have messengers with me; I'll send word of the situation back to General Meiffert. He will need to know."

To see Zedd seemly relinquish hope cast their fate in the most frightening light possible. Zedd was always the one who kept them focused and gave them courage, conviction, and confidence. He gathered up Spider's reins in one hand and gripped her mane with the other.

"Wait," Kahlan said.

He paused and looked back at her. His eyes were a window into an inner weariness. She couldn't imagine all the struggles he had faced in his life, or even in the last few weeks. Kahlan ran through seemingly a thousand thoughts as she searched frantically for some way of turning away their grim fate.

Kahlan couldn't let Zedd down. He had so often carried them; now he needed another shoulder to help endure the weight. She presented him a look of fierce determination before she turned to the Prelate.

"Verna, what if we didn't release it in the way we planned? What if we didn't simply let it drift out, hoping for the breeze to carry it where we need it?"

Verna opened her hands in a bewildered gesture. "What do you mean?"

"Won't it take more of the glass—the amount you say you need—simply so that there is enough to let it drift all the way across the valley, and yet have enough to hang in the air, too?"

"Well . . . yes, of course, but—"

"What if," Kahlan asked, "we released it in a line along the face of the front? Right where it was needed. Then it would take less, wouldn't it?"

"Well I suppose." Verna threw up her hands. "But I told you, we can't use magic to help us or they will detect our conjuring and then they will shield for the glass as fast as we release it. It will be useless. Better to release what we have and hope for the best."

Kahlan glanced out over the empty plain faintly lit by the placid clouds veiling the moon. There was nothing to be seen out in the valley. Soon, there would be. Soon, the virgin snow would be trampled by the boots of over a million men.

Only the sound of glass being crushed on stone and the thump of the steel rods in the barrels disturbed the quiet darkness. Soon, bloodcurdling battle cries would inundate the hush of the night.

Kahlan felt the suffocating dread she had felt when she first realized that all those men had caught her alone. She felt the anger, too.

"Collect what you've made so far," she said. "Let me have it."

They all stared at her.

Zedd's brow drew together in a wrinkled knot. "Just what are you thinking?"

Kahlan pulled her hair back from her face as she rapidly pieced together her plan, so that it was whole in her own mind, first.

"The enemy is attacking into the wind—not directly, but close enough for our purpose. I'm thinking that if I ride along the front of our line, right in front of the advancing enemy troops, and I release the glass dust, letting it dribble out as I go, then it will flow out in the wind behind me, right into the faces of the enemy. Delivering it right where it's needed, it won't take as much as it would were we to let it drift out from here hoping to spread it all across the valley." She looked from one startled face to another. "Do you see what I'm saying? Closer to the enemy, wouldn't it take much less to do the job?"

"Dear Creator," Verna protested, "do you have any idea how dangerous that would be?"

"Yes," Kahlan answered in grim resolve. "A lot less dangerous than facing a direct attack by their entire force. Now, would that work? Wouldn't it take considerably less if I were to ride along the front, trickling it out as I went, than letting it drift out to them from here? Well? We're running out of time."

"You're right—it wouldn't take nearly as much." Verna touched her lip as she stared off into the darkness while considering. "It's better than the way we were going to do it, that much is sure."

Kahlan started pushing her. "Get it together. Now. Hurry."

Verna abandoned her protests and ran off to collect what they had. Cara was about to unleash a tirade of objections when Zedd lifted a hand as if to ask she let him do the objecting, instead.

"Kahlan, it sounds like you might have something here, but someone else can do this. It's foolish to risk—"

"I'll be needing a diversion," she said, cutting him off. "Something to distract their attention. I'll be riding by in the dark, so they probably won't notice me, but it would be best if there were something to occupy their attention, just in case, something to make them look elsewhere—for the last time."

"As I was saying, someone else can—"

"No," she said in quiet finality. "I'll not ask someone else to do this. It was my idea. I'm doing it. I won't allow someone to take my place."

Kahlan deemed herself responsible for the peril they were in. It was she who had blundered and fallen for Jagang's trick. It was she who had come up with the plan and ordered the troops out. It was she who made Jagang's night attack possible.

Kahlan knew all too well the terror everyone felt, waiting for the attack. She felt it herself. She thought of Holly, fearful of being murdered by the marauding beasts coming out of the night for her. The fear was all too real.

It would be Kahlan who had lost the war for them, this very night, if they didn't get their army back across that pass to safety.

"I'm doing this myself," she repeated. "That's the way it's going to be. Standing here arguing about it can only cost us our chance. Now, I need a diversion, and I need one quickly."

Zedd let out an angry breath. The fire was back in his eyes. He flicked out his hand, pointing. "Warren is back there waiting for me. The two of us will move to separate locations and give you your diversion."

"What will you do?"

At last, Zedd surrendered to a grim, cunning grin. "Nothing fancy, this time. No clever devious tricks, like they no doubt expect. This time, we'll give them a good old-fashioned firefight."

Kahlan gave a sharp tug to the strap at her ribs holding her leather armor on her shoulders, chest, and back, cinching it down tight. She nodded once to seal the pact.

"Wizard's fire it is, then."

"Keep an eye to your right, to our side, as you ride. I don't want you to get in the way of what I mean for the enemy. You must also watch for what their gifted send back at me."

As she secured her cloak, she nodded assent to Zedd's brief instructions. She checked the straps on her leg armor, making sure they were tight, remembering how the enemy's strong fingers had clawed at her legs, trying to unhorse her.

Verna came rushing back, a big bucket at the end of each arm pulled down straight by the weight. Some of the Sisters were scurrying along beside her.

"All right," the winded Prelate said. "Let's go."

Kahlan reached for the buckets. "I'll take—"

Verna yanked them back. "How do you propose to ride and sprinkle this out? It's too much. Besides, you don't know its properties."

"Verna, I'm not letting you—"

"Stop acting like an obstinate child. Let's go."

Cara snatched one of the buckets. "Verna is right, Mother Confessor. You can't hold on to your horse, release the glass dust, and carry both buckets all at the same time. You two take that one, I'll take this one."

The willowy Sister Philippa rushed to Cara's side and lifted the bucket. "Mistress Cara is right, Prelate. You and the Mother Confessor can't do both buckets. You two take one; Mistress Cara and I will take the other."

There was no time to argue with the three determined women. Kahlan knew that no one would be able to talk her out of what she had to do, and they probably felt the same. Besides, they had a valid point.

"All right," Kahlan said as she pulled on her gloves.

She lashed tight the fur mantle she wore over the top of the wool cloak. She didn't want anything flapping in the wind. The hilt of her sword was covered, but she figured she wouldn't be needing it. The hilt of Richard's sword stuck up behind her shoulder, her ever-present reminder of him—as if she needed one. She quickly tied her hair back with a leather thong.

Verna tossed a handful of the fluffy snow, checking the wind. It had held its direction and was light, but steady. At least that much was in their favor.

"You two go first," Kahlan said to Cara. "Verna and I will wait maybe five minutes to let what you release drift in toward the enemy, so that we won't ride through it. Then, we'll follow you across the valley. That way we'll be sure to overlap what you release with ours so as not to have any gaps. We need to make sure there's no safe place for the Order to get through. We need the ruin and panic to be as uniform and widespread as possible."

Sister Philippa, noting what Kahlan had done, fastened her cloak securely at her neck and waist. "That makes sense."

"It would be more effective doubled like that," Verna agreed.

"I guess there's no time to argue this foolishness," Zedd grumbled as he seized Spider's mane and pulled himself up, laying across the horse's back on his belly. He swung a leg over Spider's rump and sat up. "Let me have a minute or two to get ahead of you and let Warren know, then we'll start showing the Imperial Order some real wizard work."

He pulled his horse around and smiled. It was heartening to see it again.

"After all this work, someone had better have some dinner waiting for me on the other side of that pass back there."

"If I have to cook it for you myself," Kahlan promised.

The wizard gave them a jaunty wave and galloped off into the darkness.

Kahlan stuffed a boot in the stirrup, grabbed the saddle horn, and sprang up into her seat. The cold leather creaked as she leaned over and held a hand down in order to help Verna up. Once the Prelate squirmed in close behind Kahlan, two Sisters carefully handed the heavy wooden bucket up to her. Cara and Sister Philippa were on their horse and ready, the Sister balancing her bucket on her thigh.

"Get the children back across the pass," Verna ordered.

Sister Dulcinia bobbed her head of gray hair. "I will see to it, Prelate."

"Whatever more of the glass you can have ready by the time the Mother Confessor and I ride out, you should release into the wind for good measure, then get yourselves spread out behind our lines to help if the Order breaks through. If we fail, the Sisters must do their best to hold the enemy off while as many as possible make it across the pass to safety."

Sister Dulcinia again promised to carry out the Prelate's orders.

They all waited a few minutes in silence while giving Zedd the head start he needed to reach Warren with instructions. There seemed nothing else to say. Kahlan concentrated on what she had to do, rather than worrying whether or not it would work. In the back of her mind, though, she was aware of how notoriously imperfect were such last-minute battle plans.

Judging that they had waited as long as they dared, Kahlan motioned with her arm, signaling Cara to start out. The two of them shared a last look. Cara offered a brief smile, *good luck*—then raced away, Sister Philippa holding tight to the Mord-Sith's waist with one arm and balancing the bucket on her thigh with the help of her other hand.

As the sound of hoofbeats from Cara's horse faded into the night, Kahlan for the first time realized that, in the distance, she could hear the collective yells of hundreds of thousands of Imperial Order troops. The countless voices fused into one continuous roar as their attack drew ever closer. It almost sounded like the moan of an ill wind through a canyon's rocky fangs. Her horse snorted and pawed the frozen ground. The awful drone made Kahlan's pulse race even faster. She wanted to race away, before the men got too close, but she had to wait, to give the glass dust Cara and Sister Philippa released time to drift out of the way.

"I wish we could use magic to protect ourselves," Verna said in a quiet voice, almost as if in answer to what Kahlan was thinking. "We can't, of course, or they would detect it."

Kahlan nodded, hardly hearing the woman. Verna was just saying anything that came to mind so as not to have to sit and listen to the enemy coming for them.

The bitter cold long forgotten, her heartbeat throbbing in her ears, Kahlan sat still as death, staring out into the empty night, trying to envision every aspect of the task at hand, trying to go through it all in her mind first, so she wouldn't be surprised by anything that might happen and then have to decide what to do. Better to anticipate, if you could, than to react.

As she quietly sat her horse, she let her anger build, too. Anger made a better warrior than fear.

Kahlan fed that anger with images of all the terrible things she had seen the Imperial Order do to the people of the Midlands. She let the memories of all the bodies she had seen pass through her mind, as if they came before the Mother Confessor to plead with stilled tongues for vengeance. She remembered the women she had seen wailing over murdered children, husbands, sisters, brothers, mothers and fathers. She remembered strong men in helpless anguish over the senseless slaughter of their friends and loved ones. In her mind's eye, she saw those men, women, and children suffering at the hands of a people to whom they had done no harm.

The Imperial Order was but a gang of killers without empathy. They merited no pity; they would get none.

She thought about Richard in the hands of that enemy. She savored her promise to kill every one of them if she had to until she got Richard back.

"It's time," Kahlan said through gritted teeth. Without looking back over her shoulder, she asked, "Are you ready?"

"Ready. Don't slow for anything, or we will end up its victims, too. Our only chance is to keep fresh air streaming over us to carry the glass dust all away from our bodies. When we get to the opposite side, after I've dumped it all, then we'll be safe. By that time, the Order should be in a state of mass confusion, if not complete panic."

Kahlan nodded. "Hold tight. Here we go."

The horse, already in an excited state, probably from the approaching cries, sprang away too fast, nearly dumping Verna off the back. Her arm jerked tight around Kahlan's middle. At the same time, Kahlan reached back and caught Verna's sleeve, holding her on. As they raced away and Verna fought to regain her balance, the bucket lurched, but Verna was able to steady it. Fortunately, it didn't spill.

Even as the muscular gelding was obeying her command and racing away, his ears were turned to the approaching clamor. He was skittish carrying the unfamiliar burden of two riders. He was well trained and had seen battle often enough, so he probably was also edgy because he knew what the war cries signified. Kahlan knew he was strong and quick. For what she had to do, speed was life.

Kahlan's heart galloped as fast as the horse as they thundered through the blackness of the valley. The enemy was much closer, now, than they had been when Cara passed through not long before. The horse's hoofbeats partly drowned out the battle cries of countless enemy soldiers to their left.

Terrifying bits of memories of fists and boots flashed unbidden into her mind as she heard men coming toward her in the dark, screaming for blood. She felt her vulnerability as never before. Kahlan turned those memories from fear to anger at the outrage of these brutes coming into her Midlands and murdering her people. She wanted every one of them to suffer, and every one of them dead.

There was no telling precisely how far the enemy had already advanced, or, with the moonlight behind her, even her own exact direction. Kahlan worried that she might have sliced it too close to the bone, and that they could unexpectedly encounter a wall of bloodthirsty men. She wanted to be close, though, to deliver the blinding dust right in their faces, to be sure it had the best chance to work, to turn back the attack. She resisted the urge to guide her horse to the right, away from the enemy.

The night suddenly ignited with harsh yellow light. The clouds went from gray to bright yellow-orange. White snow blazed with garish color. An awful droning sound vibrated deep under her ribs.

A hundred feet in front of her and maybe ten feet above the ground, tumbling liquid yellow and blue light roared headlong across her route, dripping honeyed fire, trailing billowing black smoke. The seething sphere of wizard's fire vividly illuminated the ground beneath it as it shot past. Even though not directed at her, the sound alone was enough to make Kahlan ache to cringe away in dread.

She knew enough about wizard's fire, how it clung tenaciously to the skin, to be more than wary of it. Once that living fire touched you, it couldn't be dislodged. Even a single droplet of wizard's fire would often eat through flesh down to bone. There was no one either brave or foolish enough not to fear it. Few people touched by such conjured flame lived to recount the horror of the experience. For those who did, revenge became a lifelong obsession.

Then, in the light of that bright flame streaking across the valley floor, Kahlan caught sight of the horde, all with swords, maces, flails, axes, pikes, and lances raised in the air as they yelled their battle cries. The men, grim, daunting, fierce, were all in the grip of a wild lust for the fight as they ran headlong out of the night.

In the moonlight, Kahlan could see for the first time since she had joined up with the army the full extent of the enemy forces. The reports had told the story, but could not fully convey the reality of the sight. The numbers were so far removed from her experience as to defy comprehension. Eyes wide, jaw hanging open, she gasped in awe.

Kahlan realized with alarm that the enemy was much closer than she had expected. Throughout the ocean of men, torches meant to be used to set fires sparkled like moonlight off the vast sea flooding into the valley. At the horizon, that moonlight gleaming off uncountable weapons blurred into a flat line over which she almost expected to see ships sailing.

The undulating leading edge, bristling shields and spears, threatened to close off her path. Kahlan used her right heel, back against her horse's flank, to guide him a little to the right so as to clear the wave of soldiers. After she had corrected his course, she thumped her heels against the animal's ribs, urging him on.

And then she realized, as arrows zipped past and spears plunged to the ground just in front of her, that in the light of the wizard's fire, the enemy could see her, too.

The ball of wizard's fire that had revealed her to the enemy wailed off into the darkness, leaving her in shadow and lighting tens of thousands of men at a time as it passed over their heads. Far in the distance, behind the advancing horde, the fire finally crashed to the ground, igniting a conflagration in the midst of the cavalry. Horsemen were often held back, ready to charge forth when their men encountered the D'Haran lines. The distant mortal screams of man and beast rose into the night.

An arrow skipped off her leather leg armor. More zipped past. One stuck in the saddle just below her stomach as she leaned forward over the galloping horse's withers. Apparently, in the moonlight they could still spot her and Verna racing past.

"Why aren't they blind?" Kahlan called over her shoulder.

She could see a cloud billowing out behind them. It looked little different than the dust the horse raised as it galloped, except Kahlan saw that it was coming from the bucket Verna rested against her thigh as she tipped it toward the enemy lines, a little more, a little less, controlling the amount that poured out, keeping it in a steady stream. Cara had already been past, yet the men showed no ill effect.

"It takes a little while to work," Verna said in Kahlan's ear. "They have to blink a bit."

Fire raced past right behind them. Fiery droplets splashed down onto the snow, splattering when they hit, hissing like rain on hot stones round a fire. The horse snorted as he raced onward in near panic. As she leaned over his withers, Kahlan stroked his neck reassuringly, reminding him that he wasn't alone.

Kahlan let her gaze sweep along the advancing enemy line as she raced before them. She saw that the men were doing little blinking. Their eyes were wide in their fervor for the coming battle.

The wizard's fire that had so spooked the horse from behind exploded through the enemy ranks. Liquid flames spilled across the mass of soldiers, touching off a shrill roar of ghastly cries. When burning men crashed into soldiers around them, fire splashed onto them, too, spreading the horror. Around the fire, the advancing line buckled. Yet other men running headlong through the night trampled those on the ground, only to lose their own footing and topple.

Another sphere of wizard's fire droned past to crash down, spilling its flame like water from a burst dam. So massive was the eruption that the surge swept men away, carrying them off in a flaming current.

A huge knot of fire erupted out of the enemy line not far in front of Kahlan, headed toward the D'Haran lines. Immediately, a small sphere of blue flame roared in from her right, meeting the ponderous globe of yellow flame in midair. The collision sent a shower of fire raining down around her as she rode past. Kahlan gasped and yanked the reins left as a fat gob of the plummeting fire crashed to the ground right before them, splattering flame everywhere.

They missed the fire by inches, but she now found herself closing with the enemy soldiers at an alarming rate. Kahlan could read some of the obscene oaths on their lips. She spurred the terrified horse to the right. He turned a little but not enough to divert them from angling in toward the enemy lines.

Glowing bits of fire rained down on the men as well as the open ground. The horse was running in a panic, too frightened to take direction from Kahlan. The stench of burning leather was adding fuel to the horse's fear. She glanced down and saw a bit of fire burning on the leather armor protecting her thigh. The small but fierce flame fluttered wildly in the wind. She dared not try to brush the glowing spot off lest it then stick to her hand. She feared to imagine what it would feel like when it finally burned through the leather. She would have to endure the pain when it did; she had no choice.

Verna didn't realize what was happening. She was twisted sideways, still releasing the glass dust. Kahlan could see the plume of it carried away behind them. The long trail curved, carried by the breeze, into the enemy, past the front lines, back through the ranks of soldiers, off into the blackness. Farther back in the Order's ranks, the torches lit the cloud as it mingled with the dust churned up from the frozen ground.

An arrow nicked the horse's shoulder and skipped up into the air. A surge of men, seeing her coming, ran with wild abandon in an effort to block her way. Kahlan yanked on the reins, trying to haul the powerful horse's head to the right. In the grip of terror, the horse galloped on. She felt helpless as she tried to get it to turn. It was doing no good. They were headed right toward a wall of men.

"We're getting too close!" Verna yelled in her ear.

Kahlan was too busy to answer. Her arm was shaking with the effort of pulling on the right rein, trying to turn the horse's head over and to the right, but the horse had the bit in his teeth and was stronger than she by far. Sweat trickled down her neck. She stretched her right leg back and dug her heel into the horse's right flank to turn him. The men before them brought their pikes and swords around to bear. Fighting was one thing, but not having any control and just watching her fate come at her was different.

"Kahlan! What are you doing!"

With the pressure of her heel in front of his right rear leg, she was finally forcing the horse to turn. It wasn't enough. She wasn't going to be able to divert the runaway horse. The enemy looked like a steel porcupine rushing at them.

Three strides away, the horse lowered his head.

"Good boy!" she cried.

Maybe he had a chance to clear the pikes. Kahlan took her weight off the saddle and angled forward, flattening her back. She bent her arms, giving the reins slack with her hands to either side of the horse's neck. She kept pressure on him with her lower legs, but let him have the freedom he needed.

She didn't know if it would work with the extra weight. If only the pikes were shorter. Kahlan screamed for Verna to hold on.

Wizard's fire suddenly streamed past in front of them, coming in low. The men who had rushed ahead in a line to block Kahlan's way dove to the ground. The entire line before them collapsed. The fire wailed past just over top of them, finally touching down off to Kahlan's left. The cries of a thousand men filled her ears.

The horse stretched his lowered head, getting his hocks underneath his body. At the last instant, his neck shortened and his head came up as he sprang upward, using his powerful hindquarters to launch himself. His back rounded as they sailed over the leading edge of men. Verna cried out, her arm like a hook around Kahlan's middle. They came down beyond the soldiers who had dropped flat. With her weight on the stirrups, Kahlan used her legs to absorb the shock—Verna couldn't. With the extra load, the horse nearly stumbled as it landed, but kept his balance and continued running. They were at last clear of the Order soldiers.

"What's the matter with you!" Verna yelled. "Don't do that or I won't be able to let it out evenly!"

"Sorry," Kahlan called over her shoulder.

Despite the cold wind in her face, sweat ran from her scalp. The Order soldiers seemed to fall away to their rear quarter. Giddy relief washed over her as she realized they had made it past the bulge in the Imperial Order's front lines.

In the distance behind them, a storm of fire lit the night. Zedd and Warren were showing them a good old-fashioned firefight, as Zedd had put it. It was a terrifying demonstration, if insufficient to stop an enemy as large as the Order. As the Order's gifted raced to the scene and threw up shields, it limited the death and devastation. The two wizards had bought Kahlan and Verna the time they had needed.

Kahlan heard Cara calling "Whoa!" as she galloped up close.

This time, with Cara's horse heading them off, the lathered mount rapidly came to a halt. The horse was exhausted, as was Kahlan. As they dismounted beside Cara and Sister Philippa, Verna tossed the empty bucket to the ground. Kahlan was glad it was dark, so that the others couldn't see her legs trembling. She was relieved to see that the spot of fire had expended itself before burning through.

The four of them watched as the night went mad with flame, most exploding against shields of magic, yet still doing damage to anyone too close. Zedd and Warren sent forth one tumbling sphere of fiery death after another. The cries of men could be heard all along the line. The fire was being returned, reaping death in the D'Haran lines, but the Sisters were throwing up their own shields.

Still the vast enemy army advanced. At most, the deadly flames only slowed them and disrupted their orderly attack.

As the gifted on both sides gained control, they managed to nullify each other's fiery attacks. Kahlan knew that the forward D'Haran lines had no hope of holding the onrushing flood of the Order. They had no hope of even slowing them. In the moonlight, she could see them beginning to abandon their positions.

"Why isn't it working?" Kahlan whispered, half to herself. She leaned toward Verna. "Are you sure it was made properly?"

Watching the enemy's headlong rush, and in the din of battle cries, Verna didn't seem to hear the question. Kahlan checked her sword. She realized how futile it would be to try to fight. She felt Richard's sword on her back, and considered drawing it, but decided that it would be better to run. She pushed Verna, urging her to their spent horse. Cara did the same with Sister Philippa.

Before she stepped into the stirrup, Kahlan noticed the Order slowing. She saw men stumbling. Some groped with outstretched arms. Others fell.

Verna pointed. "Look!"

An endless moan of frightened agony began rising up into the night, growing in intensity. Staggering men fell over one another. Some swung their swords at an invisible enemy, hacking instead their blinded fellow soldiers.

The progress of the men at the front slowed to a crawl. Soldiers kept coming, colliding with the stalled front line. Cavalry horses panicked, bucking off riders. Spooked horses ran off in every direction, oblivious of the men they trampled. Racing wagons overturned. Confusion swept the enemy's ranks.

The advance buckled. The Imperial Order ground to a halt.

Zedd and Warren rode up and dismounted, both sweating despite the frigid night air. Kahlan gave Zedd's bony hand a squeeze.

"You two saved our necks at the end, there."

Zedd gestured to Warren. "Him, not me."

Warren shrugged. "I saw your predicament."

They all stared in wonder, watching the army gone blind.

"You did it, Verna," Kahlan said. "You and your glass saved us."

At last, she and Verna threw their arms around each other, tears of relief coursing down their cheeks.

Kahlan was one of the last to cross over the pass. The valley beyond was well protected by towering rock walls around the southern half. It was a long and difficult route around those mountains if the Order had any thoughts of attacking them here. While the troops of the D'Haran Empire had no intention of letting themselves get trapped in that valley, for the time being it was a safe place.

Big old spruces filled the lap of the surrounding mountains, so they were somewhat protected from the wind, as well. Tents carpeted the forest floor. It was good to see all the campfires and smell the woodsmoke—a sign that they were safe enough for the men to have fires. The aroma of cooking filled the late-night air, too. It had been a lot of work moving the army and their equipment over the pass, and the men were hungry.

General Meiffert looked as pleased as any general would when the army he feared lost was at last safe—at least for the time being. He guided Kahlan and Cara through the darkness dotted by thousands of campfires to tents he had set up for them. Along the way, he filled them in on how everything with the army had gone, and ran through a list of what few things they had had to leave behind.

"It's going to be a cold night," General Meiffert said when they had reached the tents he had set aside for them between two towering spruce. "I had a sack of pebbles heated by a fire for you, Mother Confessor. You, too, Mistress Cara."

Kahlan thanked him before he left to see to his duties. Cara went off to go get something to eat. Kahlan told her to go ahead, that she just wanted to sleep.

Inside her tent, Kahlan found *Spirit* standing on a little table, the lamp hanging from the ridgepole lighting her proud pose. She paused to trace a finger down the flowing robes.

Kahlan, her teeth chattering, could hardly wait to crawl into bed and pull that sack of heated pebbles under the fur mantle with her. She thought about how cold she was, and then instead of climbing into her bed, went back outside and searched through the dark camp until she found a Sister. After following the Sister's directions, going between tents until she reached the area with the thick young trees, Kahlan found the small lean-to shelter set among the boughs for protection from the wind and weather.

She squatted down, peering inside at the bundle of blankets she could just make out in the light coming from nearby campfires.

"Holly? Are you in there?"

A little head poked out. "Mother Confessor?" The girl was shivering. "What is it? Do you need me?"

"Yes, as a matter of fact, I do. Come with me please."

Holly climbed out, swaddled in a blanket. Kahlan took her little hand and walked her back to her tent in silence. Holly's eyes grew big and round as Kahlan ushered in inside. Before the small table, the girl paused to stand still as a stump while she stared in wonder at *Spirit*.

"Like it?" Kahlan asked.

Trembling with the cold, Holly reverently ran her frail fingers down *Spirit*'s arm. "Where ever did you get something so beautiful?"

"Richard carved it for me."

Holly finally pulled her gaze from the statue and looked up at Kahlan. "I miss Richard." Kahlan could see Holly's breath in the motionless air of the tent. "He was always nice to me. A lot of people were mean, but Richard was always nice."

Kahlan felt an unexpected stab of anguish. She hadn't expected the subject to turn to Richard.

"What was it you needed, Mother Confessor?"

Kahlan turned her thoughts away from her sorrow and smiled. "I was proud of the work you did to help save us today. I promised you that you would be warm. Tonight, you will be."

The girl's teeth were chattering. "Really?"

Kahlan laid the Sword of Truth on the far side of the bed. She stripped off some of her heavier clothing, doused the lamp, and then sat down on the straw-filled pallet. Light from nearby campfires lent a soft glow to the tent's walls.

"Come. Climb into bed with me. It's going to be very cold tonight. I need you to keep me warm."

Holly only had to consider for a second.

As Kahlan lay down on her side, she pulled Holly's back against her stomach and then drew the sack of heated pebbles up against the girl's front. Holly hugged the sack and moaned with the thrill of warmth. The satisfied moan made Kahlan smile.

For a long time, she smiled, enjoying the simple pleasure of seeing Holly warm and safe. Having the girl there, holding her close, helped Kahlan to forget all the terrible things she had seen that day.

Far up in the mountains, a single wolf sang out in a long, lonely call. The cry echoed through the valley, trailing off, to be renewed again and again with forlorn persistence.

With his sword at her back, Kahlan's thoughts turned to Richard. Thinking about him, wondering where he was and if he was safe, she silently wept herself to sleep.

The next day, snow moved down from the higher mountains to rampage across the southern regions of the Midlands. The storms raged for two days. The second night of the blizzard, Kahlan shared her tent with Holly, Valery, and Helen. They sat under blankets, ate camp stew, sang songs, told stories of princes and princesses, and slept together to keep warm.

When the snowstorm finally ended in a bleak golden sunrise, most of the taller tents had snow drifted to their eaves on their downwind side. The smaller ones were completely covered over. The men dug themselves out, looking like so many woodchucks come up out of their burrows for a peek.

Over the next several weeks, the storms continued to roll past, dumping more snow. In such weather, fighting, or even moving an army very far, was difficult.

Scouts reported that the Imperial Order had withdrawn a week's march back to the south.

It would be a burden to care for blinded men. Within a days walk all around the place where the special glass had been released, the D'Haran scouts reported that they had seen well over sixty thousand frozen corpses, now drifted over with the snow—blind men unable to care for themselves in the harsh conditions. The Imperial Order had probably abandoned them to their fate. A few dozen of the blind had managed to make it over the pass, looking for help, begging for mercy. Kahlan had ordered them executed.

It was hard telling the exact number blinded by Verna's special glass; it could be that there were many who did in fact retreat with the Imperial Order, brought along to perform menial tasks. It was likely, though, that the corpses reported by the scouts were the bulk of those blinded. Kahlan could imagine that Jagang might not want them in his camp, using food and supplies, reminding his men of their stinging retreat.

She knew, though, that for Jagang retreat was but a momentary setback and not a reappraisal of his objectives. The Order had men enough to shrug off the loss of the hundred thousand killed since the fighting had started. For the time being, the weather prevented Jagang from striking back.

Kahlan didn't intend to sit and wait for him. A month later, when the representative from Herjborgue arrived, she met with him immediately in the small trappers' lodge they had found up in the trees to the west side of the valley. The lodge sat under the protection of towering, ancient pines, away from the open areas where the tents were congregated. The lodge had become Kahlan's frequent quarters, and often also served as their command center.

It greatly relieved General Meiffert when Kahlan would stay in the lodge, rather than a tent. It made him feel as if the army was doing something about providing better accommodations for the Mother Confessor—the wife of Lord Rahl. Kahlan and Cara did appreciate the nights they slept in the lodge, but Kahlan didn't want anyone to think she wasn't up to the conditions the rest of them had to endure. Sometimes, she would instead have the girls sleep in the lodge along with some of the Sisters, and sometimes she insisted Verna sleep there with Holly, Valery, and Helen. It didn't take a great deal of effort to persuade the Prelate.

Kahlan greeted Representative Theriault from the land of Herjborgue, inviting him into the cozy lodge. He was accompanied by a small guard unit, who waited outside. Herjborgue was a small country. Their contribution to the war effort was in the area of their only product: wool. Kahlan had need of the man.

After Representative Theriault knelt before the Mother Confessor, receiving the traditional greeting, he at last stood and pushed his heavy hood back on his shoulders. He broke into a broad grin.

"Mother Confessor, so good to see you well."

She returned a sincere smile. "And you, Representative Theriault. Here, come over by the fire and warm yourself."

By the stone fireplace, he pulled off his gloves and held his hands before the crackling flames. He glanced to the gleaming hilt of the sword sticking up behind her shoulder. His eye was caught by *Spirit* standing proudly on the mantel. He stared in wonder, as did everyone who saw the proud figure.

"We heard about Lord Rahl being captured," he finally said. "Has there been any word?"

Kahlan shook her head. "We know they haven't harmed him, but that's about all. I know my husband; he's resourceful. I expect he will find a way to get back to help us."

The man nodded, his brow furrowed as he listened earnestly.

Cara, standing beside the table, reminded of her Lord Rahl by Kahlan's words, idly rolled her Agiel in her fingers. Kahlan could tell by the look in Cara's blue eyes, and by the way she casually let the weapon dangle once more by the small gold chain around her wrist, that the Agiel, being linked to the living Lord Rahl, still possessed its power. As long as it worked, they knew Richard was alive. That was all they knew.

The man opened his heavy traveling cloak. "How goes the war? Everyone anxiously awaits word."

"As near as we can figure, we've managed to kill over a hundred thousand of their troops."

The man gasped. Such numbers were staggering to someone from a place as small as his homeland of Herjborgue.

"Then, they must be defeated. Have they run back to the Old World?"

Rather than meet his gaze, Kahlan stared at the logs checkering in the wavering glow of the flames. "I'm afraid that losing that many men is hardly crippling to the Imperial Order. We're taking their numbers down, but they have an army of well over ten times that many. They remain a threat, a week's march to the south of here."

Kahlan looked up to see him staring at her. She could tell by the look in his eyes that he was having difficulty trying to imagine that many people. His wind-reddened face had paled considerably.

"Dear spirits . . ." he whispered. "We've heard rumors, but to learn they are true . . ." With a despondent look, he shook his head. "How is it ever going to be possible to defeat a foe of that size?"

"Seems that I remember, a number of years back, you were in Aydindril to see the Council and you had a bit of trouble after a grand dinner. That big man from Kelton—I forget his name—was boasting and speaking ill of your small land. He called you some name. Do you remember that night?—what he called you?"

Representative Theriault's eyes sparkled as he smiled.

"Puny."

"Puny. That was it. I guess he felt that because he was twice your size, that made him your better. I recall men clearing off a table, and the two of you arm wrestling."

"Ah, well, I was younger back then, and I had a few glasses of wine with dinner, besides."

"You won."

He laughed softly. "Not by strength. He was cocky. I was clever, perhaps, and quick—that's all."

"You won; that was the result. Those hundred thousand Order troops aren't any less dead because they outnumbered us."

The smile left his lips. "Point taken. I guess the Imperial Order ought to quit now, while they have men left. I recall how those five thousand Galean recruits you led went after that force of fifty thousand, and eliminated them." He leaned an arm on the rough-hewn mantel. "Anyway, I see your point. When you are facing superior strength, you must use your wits."

"I need your help," Kahlan told the man.

His big brown eyes reflected the firelight as they turned toward her. "Anything, Mother Confessor. If it be in my power to do, anything."

Kahlan bent and shoved another log onto the fire. Sparks swirled around before ascending the chimney.

"We need wool cloaks—hooded cloaks—for the men."

He considered only briefly. "Just tell me the numbers, and I will see to it. I'm sure it can be arranged."

"I'll need at least a hundred thousand—our entire force down here at present. We're expecting more men any time, so if you could add half again that number, it would go a long way to helping destroy the Order."

As he went through mental calculations, Kahlan used the poker to set the new log to the back of the fire. "I know I'm not asking for something easy."

He scratched his scalp through his thick gray hair. "You've no need of hearing how difficult it will be, that won't help you win, so let me just say that you will have them."

Representative Theriault's word was a pledge as sound as gold, and as valuable. She stood and faced him.

"And I want them made from bleached wool."

He lifted an eyebrow in curiosity. "Bleached wool?"

"We need to be clever, as you can understand. The Imperial Order comes from far to the south. Richard was down there, once, and told me about how the weather is very different than it is up here, in the New World. Their winters are nothing like we have. If I don't miss my bet, the Order is not familiar with winter, nor is it used to surviving, much less fighting, in such weather. Winter conditions may be difficult, but this puts it to our advantage."

Kahlan made a fist before him. "I want to harry them mercilessly. I want to use the winter weather to make them suffer. I want to draw them out—make them have to fight—in conditions they don't understand as well as we do.

"I want the hooded cloaks to help disguise our men. I want to be able to use the conditions to get in close on raids, and then disappear right before their eyes."

"They don't have gifted?"

"Yes, but they're not going to have a sorceress telling every archer where to aim his arrow."

He stroked his chin. "Yes, I see your point." He slapped the mantel as if to seal his promise. "I'll have our people begin at once. Your men will need warm mittens, too."

Kahlan smiled appreciatively. "They will be grateful. Have your people start sending the cloaks down to us as soon as they have some made. Don't wait for them all. We can start our raids with any number and add to them as you deliver more."

Representative Theriault pulled his hood up and fastened his heavy wool cloak. "Winter has just set in. The more time you have to whittle them down while you have the advantage of weather, the better. I had best be on my way at once."

Kahlan clasped arms with the man—not something the Mother Confessor typically did, but something anyone else might do in sincere appreciation of aid.

As she and Cara stood outside the door, watching the representative and his guards trudging off through the snow, Kahlan hoped the supply of white cloaks would start arriving soon, and that they would be as effective as she hoped.

"Do you really think we can press the war effectively in winter?" Cara asked.

Kahlan turned back to the door. "We have to."

Before she went back inside, Kahlan caught sight of a procession coming up through the trees. When they were a little closer, she saw that it was General Meiffert, on foot, leading. She was able to pick out Adie, Verna, Warren, and Zedd, all walking along beside four riders. The midday sun sparkled off the hilt of the lead rider's sword.

Kahlan gasped when she saw who it was.

Without bothering to go back inside to get her cloak or fur mantle, she raced down through the snow to great him. Cara was right on Kahlan's heels.

"Harold!" she called out as she got closer. "Oh, Harold! Are we ever glad to see you!"

It was her half brother, come from Galea. Kahlan then saw some of the other men riding behind him, and gasped again in surprise. Captain Bradley Ryan, commander of the Galean recruits she had fought with was there, and his lieutenant, Flin Hobson. She thought she recognized Sergeant Frost, in the rear. Her face hurt from grinning as she ran up to them through the deep snow.

Kahlan wanted to pull her half brother off his horse and hug him. In a Galean field-officer uniform, far more muted than their dress uniform, he looked grand on his well-bred mount. She only now fully realized how worried she had been over his late arrival.

Carrying himself like the prince he was, Harold tipped his head to her as he bowed in his saddle. He offered only a small, private smile.

"Mother Confessor. I'm gratified to find you well."

Captain Ryan was grinning, even if Prince Harold wasn't. Kahlan had fond memories of Bradley and Flin, of their bravery, courage, and heart. The fighting had been horrifying, but the company of those fine soldiers, fine young men all, was a cherished memory. They had done the impossible before, and had come to help do it again.

Standing beside his horse, Kahlan reached up for Harold's hand. "Come inside. We've a good fire going." She motioned to the captain, the lieutenant, and the sergeant. "You, too. Come inside and get warm."

Kahlan turned to the others, who didn't look nearly as happy as Kahlan thought they should. "We'll all fit. Come inside."

Prince Harold stepped down out of the stirrup. "Mother Confessor, I—"

Kahlan couldn't resist. She threw her arms around her half brother. He was a big bear of a man, much like their father, King Wyborn. "Harold, I'm so relieved to see you. How's Cyrilla?"

Cyrilla, Harold's sister and Kahlan's half sister, was a dozen years older than Kahlan. Cyrilla had been ill for ages, it seemed. When she had been captured by the Order she had been thrown into the pit with a gang of murderers and rapists. Harold had rescued her, but the abuse she suffered had left her in an incoherent state, oblivious of those around her. She regained her senses only infrequently. When she came awake, she more often than not screamed and cried uncontrollably. One of the times when she was lucid, she had asked Kahlan to promise to be the queen of Galea and keep her people safe.

Harold, wishing to remain commander of the Galean army, refused the crown. Kahlan reluctantly had acceded to his wish.

Harold's eyes shifted to the others, briefly. "Mother Confessor, we need to have a talk."

At Prince Harold's instructions, Captain Ryan and his two men went to see to their troops and horses while the rest of them crowded into the small trapper's lodge. Zedd and Warren sat on a bench made of a board laid atop two log rounds. Verna and Adie sat against the opposite wall on another bench. Cara gazed out the small window. Standing near Cara, General Meiffert watched as the prince ran a finger back and forth along the front edge of the table. Kahlan folded her hands on the table before her.

"So," she began, fearing the worst, "how is Cyrilla?"

Harold smoothed the front of his coat. "The queen has . . . recovered."

"Queen . . . ?" Kahlan rose out of her chair. "Cyrilla has recovered? Harold, that's wonderful news. And she has at last taken her crown back? Even better!"

Kahlan was delighted to be relieved of the role of queen to Galea. As Mother Confessor, it was an awkward duty better served by Cyrilla. More than that, though, she was relieved to learn that her half sister had finally recovered. While the two of them were never close, they shared a mutual respect.

More than her cheer at Cyrilla's recovery, though, Kahlan felt a sense of deliverance that Harold had at last brought his troops down to join with them. She hoped he had been able to raise the hundred thousand they had previously discussed; it would be a good beginning for the army Kahlan needed to raise.

Harold licked his weather-cracked lips. By the slump in his shoulders, she was sure that the task of collecting his army had been trying, and the journey arduous. She had never seen his face looking so worn. He had a vague, empty look that reminded her of her father.

Kahlan smiled exuberantly, determined to show her appreciation. "How many troops did you bring? We could certainly use the whole hundred thousand. That would just about double what we have down here so far. The spirits know we need them."

No one was saying anything. As she looked from one person to the next, no one would meet her gaze.

Kahlan's sense of relief was sloughing away.

"Harold, how many troops did you bring?"

He ran his meaty fingers back through his long, thick, dark hair. "About a thousand."

She stared dumbly, sinking back into her chair. "A thousand?"

He nodded, still not meeting her eyes. "Captain Bradley and his men. The ones you led and fought beside, before."

Kahlan could feel her face heating. "We need all your troops. Harold, what's going on?"

He at last met her gaze.

"Queen Cyrilla refused my plan to take our troops south. Shortly after you were there and visited her, she came out of her illness. She was herself again—full of ambition and fire. You know what she was like. She was always tireless in her advocacy for Galea." His fingers idly tapped the table. "But I'm afraid she has been changed by her infirmity. She fears the Imperial Order."

"So do I," Kahlan said with quiet bottled rage. She could feel Richard's sword pressed against the back of her shoulder. She saw Harold's eyes take it in. "Everyone in the Midlands fears the Order. That is why we need those troops."

He was nodding as she spoke. "I told her all that. I did. She said that she is Queen of Galea, and as such, she must put our land first."

"Galea has joined the D'Haran Empire!"

He opened his hands in a helpless gesture. "When she was ill, she was . . . unaware of that event taking place. She said she only gave you the crown for the safekeeping of her people, not to surrender their sovereignty." His hands dropped to his sides. "She claims you never had any such authority and refuses to abide by the agreement."

Kahlan glanced at the others in the room, sitting mute, like a panel of grim judges.

"Harold, you and I have discussed all this in the past. The Midlands is under threat." She swept her arm out. "The entire New World is threatened! We must turn back that threat, not take to defending one land at a time—or have each land try to fend for itself. If we do that, we will all fall, one at a time. We must stand together."

"I agree with you, in principle, Mother Confessor. Queen Cyrilla does not."

"Then Cyrilla is not recovered, Harold. She is still sick."

"That may be, but it is not for me to say."

Elbow on the table, Kahlan rested her forehead against her fingertips. Thoughts were screaming around inside her head, demanding that this not be happening.

"What about Jebra?" Zedd asked from the side of the room. Kahlan was relieved to hear his voice, as if reason were returning to the lunacy of what she was hearing, as if the weight of another voice would set things straight. "We left the seer there to help care for Cyrilla and to advise you. Surely, Jebra must have advised Cyrilla against such actions."

Harold hung his head again. "I'm afraid that Queen Cyrilla ordered Jebra thrown into a dungeon. Moreover, the queen gave orders that if Jebra speaks one word of her blasphemy—as Queen Cyrilla calls it—she is to have her tongue cut out."

Kahlan had to tell herself to blink. It was no longer Cyrilla's behavior that so stunned her. Her words came sparse and brittle, the naked bones of dead respect.

"Harold, why would you follow the orders of a madwoman?"

His jaw took a set, as if injured by her tone. "Mother Confessor, she is not only my sister, but my queen. I am sworn to obey my queen in order to protect the Galean people. All those men of ours out there who have been fighting with your army are also sworn to protect the people of Galea above all else. I've already given them our queen's orders. We must all return to Galea at once. I'm sorry, but that is the way it must be."

Kahlan pounded her fist on the table and shot to her feet.

"Galea stands at the head of the Callisidrin Valley! It's a gateway right up the center of the Midlands! Don't you see what a tempting route it might be for the Imperial Order? Don't you see how they might want to split the Midlands?"

"Of course I do, Mother Confessor."

She aimed a stiff arm, pointing at the camp beyond the lodge.

"So you just expect all those men out there to put their lives between you and the Order? You and Queen Cyrilla callously expect all those men out there to die protecting you?—while you sit back in Galea?—hoping they prevent the Order from ever reaching you?"

"Of course not, Mother Confessor."

"What's the matter with you! Don't you see that if you fight with us to halt the Order, you are protecting the people of your homeland?"

Harold licked his lip. "Mother Confessor, all you say is probably true. It is also irrelevant. I am commander of the Galean army. My entire life has been devoted to serving the people of Galea and my sovereign—first my mother and father, and then my sister. From the time I was a boy at my father's knee, I was taught to protect Galea above all else."

Kahlan did her best to control her voice. "Harold, Cyrilla is obviously still sick. If you are honestly interested in protecting your people, you must see that what you're doing is not the way to accomplish it."

"Mother Confessor, I have been charged by my queen with protecting the people of Galea. I know my duty."

"Duty?" Kahlan wiped a hand across her face. "Harold, you can't blindly follow that woman's whim. The route to life and liberty exists only through reason. She may be queen, but reason can be your only true sovereign. To fail to use reason in this, to fail to think, is intellectual anarchy."

He looked at her as if she were some poor child who didn't understand the world of adult responsibility.

"She is my queen. The queen is devoted to the people."

Kahlan drummed her fingers on the table. "What Cyrilla is, is deluded by ghosts that still haunt her. She is going to bring harm to your people. You are going to aid her in delivering your people into ruin because you wish something to be true, even though it is not. You are seeing her as she once was, not as she is now."

He shrugged. "Mother Confessor, I can understand why you think what you think, but it can change nothing. I must do as my queen commands."

Elbows on the table, Kahlan held her face in her hands for a time, trembling with anger at the insanity of what she was hearing. She finally looked up, meeting her half brother's gaze.

"Harold, Galea is part of the D'Haran Empire. Galea has a queen only at the indulgence of the Empire. Queen though she may be, even if she does not recognize the rule of the D'Haran Empire, she is still, as she always has been, subordinate to the Mother Confessor of the Midlands. As Mother Confessor, as well as the leader of the D'Haran Empire in Lord Rahl's absence, I formally terminate that indulgence. Cyrilla is now without authority and is removed from office. She is no longer the queen of anything, much less Galea.

"You are ordered to return to Ebinissia, to put Cyrilla under arrest for her own protection, to release Jebra, and to return to this army with the seer and all Galean forces except a home guard for the crown city."

"Mother Confessor, I'm sorry, but my queen has ordered—"

Kahlan slammed the flat of her hand down on the table. "Enough!"

He fell silent as Kahlan rose. With her fingertips pressed to the table, she leaned closer to him.

"As Mother Confessor, I am commanding you to carry out my orders at once. That is final. I will hear no more."

The room seemed gripped by the grave consequence of what was happening. Each forbidding face watched, waiting to see how it was going to go.

Harold spoke in a voice that reminded Kahlan of her father's.

"I realize that it may make no sense to you, Mother Confessor, but I must choose my duty to my people above my duty to you. Cyrilla is my sister. King Wyborn always told me to run a good army. An officer must obey his queen. My men down here are ordered by their queen to return at once to protect Galea. I am a man bound by my honor to protect my people, as ordered by my queen."

"You pompous fool. How dare you speak to me of your honor? You are sacrificing the lives of innocent people to your delusions of honor. Honor is honesty to what is, not blind duty to what you wish to be. You have no honor, Harold."

Kahlan sank into her chair. She looked past him, to the side, staring into the hearth, into the flames.

"I have given you my orders. Do you refuse to obey them?"

"I must refuse, Mother Confessor. Let me say only that it is not out of malice."

"Harold," she said in a flat tone without looking at him, "you are committing treason."

"I realize that you may see it that way, Mother Confessor."

"Oh, I do. I do indeed. Treason to your people, treason to the Midlands, treason to our D'Haran union against the Imperial Order, and treason against the Mother Confessor. What do you suppose I ought to do about it?"

"I would expect that if you feel so strongly, you would have me put to death, Mother Confessor."

She looked up at him. "If you have enough sense to realize that, then what good will it do for you to stick to the orders of a madwoman? It will only bring your death, and then you will not be able to carry out your queen's orders. Staying to your course can only leave your people without your aid, which is what you claim to put above all else. Why not simply do the right thing and help us to help your people? Since you refuse, you have shown yourself, in truth, to be without common sense, much less honor."

His eyes turned to her, filled with smoldering anger. The knuckles of his fists went white.

"I will be heard, now, Mother Confessor. If I stand by my honor, even if it costs me my life, it will be honoring my family, my sister, my queen, and my homeland. A homeland forged by my father, King Wyborn, and my mother, Queen Bernadine. When I was young, my father, my sovereign king, was taken from my mother, my family, and my homeland of Galea, by the Confessors, taken by a Confessor's power for their selfish desire of a husband for your mother, for her selfish desire for a strong man to father her a child—you. Now, you, Mother Confessor—the daughter of that theft of that beloved man from us when I was but a boy—you would take me from my sister? Take her, too, from our land? Take me from my duty to serve my queen, my land, and above all my people? The last duty my father charged me with before your mother took him from us and destroyed him for no reason but that he was good and she wanted him, was that I should always honor my duty to my sister and my land. I will carry out my father's last charge to me, even if you think it madness."

Kahlan stared at him in cold shock.

"I'm sorry you feel that way, Harold."

His face had aged and hardened. "I know that you are not responsible for all that happened before you came to be, and I will always love that part of you that is my father, but I am still the one who must live with it all. Now I must be true to myself, to my own feelings."

"Your feelings," she repeated.

"Yes, Mother Confessor. Those are my feelings, and I must put my faith in them."

Kahlan swallowed past the painful constriction in her throat. Her fingers, lying limply on the table before her, tingled.

"Faith and feelings. Harold, you are as mad as your sister."

She drew herself up straight and folded her hands. She shared a last look with her half brother, a man she had never known, except in name, as she pronounced sentence on him.

"Beginning at sunrise tomorrow, the D'Haran Empire and Galea are at war. After sunrise tomorrow, if you are seen by me or any of our men, you will be put to death for the crime of treason.

"I will not allow those brave men out there to die for traitors. The Imperial Order will, in all likelihood, turn north up the Callisidrin Valley. You will be alone. They will butcher every man in your army, just as they butchered the people of Ebinissia. Jagang will give your sister to his men, as a whore.

"It will be by your doing, Harold, for refusing to use your ability to think, and instead following your feelings and faith in what does not exist."

Harold, hands clasped behind his back, chin held up, said nothing as Kahlan continued.

"Tell Cyrilla that she had better hope for the fate I have just described, because if the Order does not come through Galea, I will. I have promised no mercy to the Order. Galea's treason condemns her to the same fate as the Order. If the Order does not get Cyrilla, then I swear I will, and when I get her, I am going to take her back to Aydindril and I'm going to personally throw her back down into that pit from which you rescued her, and I am going to leave her down there with every criminal brute I can find for as long as she lives."

Harold's jaw dropped. "Mother Confessor . . . you wouldn't."

Kahlan's eyes told him otherwise. "You be sure to tell Cyrilla what's in store for her. Jebra probably tried to tell her, and was thrown in a dungeon for it. Cyrilla is refusing to see the open pit before her, and you are walking into it with her. Worse, you are taking your innocent people with you."

Kahlan drew her royal Galean sword. She grasped either end in a hand. Gritting her teeth, she pulled the flat of the blade against her knee. The steel bent, then finally snapped with a loud report. She tossed the broken blade on the floor at his feet.

"Now get out of my sight."

He turned to leave, but before he took a step, Zedd stood, holding out a hand as if to ask him to remain where he was.

"Mother Confessor," Zedd said, choosing his words carefully. "I believe you are letting your emotions get in the way."

Harold gestured to Kahlan, relieved to hear Zedd's intercession. "Tell her, Wizard Zorander. Tell her."

Kahlan couldn't believe her ears. She remained where she was, staring into

Zedd's hazel eyes. "Then would you mind explaining my error of emotion, First Wizard?"

Zedd glanced at Harold and then back to Kahlan. "Mother Confessor, Queen Cyrilla is obviously deranged. Prince Harold is not only doing her a disservice, but enabling her to bring only the specter of death to her people. If he chose the side of reason, he would be protecting his people, and honoring his sister's past admirable service when she was of sound mind.

"Instead, he has betrayed his duty to his people by embracing what he wishes to be true about her instead of facing what is true. In this way, he is embracing death, and in this case, embracing death for his people, too.

"Prince Harold has been justly found guilty of treason. Your emotions for him are interfering with your judgment. Obviously, he is now a danger to our cause, to the lives of our people, and to the lives of his own people. He cannot be allowed to leave."

Harold looked thunderstruck. "But Zedd . . ."

Zedd's hazel eyes, too, were a terrible pronouncement of guilt. He waited, as if challenging the man to further prove his treason. Harold's mouth moved, but he could offer no words.

"Does anyone disagree with me?" Zedd asked.

He looked at Adie. She shook her head. Verna likewise shook her head. Warren stared at Harold for a moment, then shook his head.

Harold's expression turned indignant. "I'm not going to stand for this. The Mother Confessor has given me until dawn to withdraw. You must honor her sentence."

He took two strides toward the door, but then paused, clutching his chest. Twisting slowly as he started to sink, his eyes rolling up in his head. His legs folded and he crashed to the floor.

Kahlan sat stunned. No one moved or said anything. General Meiffert went down on one knee beside the body, checking Prince Harold for breath or pulse. The general looked up at Kahlan and shook his head.

She passed her gaze from Zedd, to Adie, to Verna, to Warren. None revealed anything in their expression.

Kahlan stood and spoke softly. "I don't ever want to know which one of you did this. I'm not saying you were wrong . . . I just don't want to know."

The four gifted people nodded.

At the door, Kahlan stood in the bright sunlight a moment, feeling the cold air on her face, searching, until she saw Captain Ryan leaning against a stout young maple tree. He stood at attention as she strode out to him through the snow.

"Bradley, did Prince Harold tell you why he was coming here?"

Calling him by his given name, rather than his rank, changed the nature of the question. His rigid posture slackened.

"Yes, Mother Confessor. He said he had to tell you that he had been ordered back by his queen to defend Galea, and that he was further ordered to bring his men serving with you back to Galea with him."

"Then what are you doing here? Why did you and your men come along, if he was to take everyone back?"

He lifted his square jaw and looked at her with clear blue eyes. "Because we deserted, Mother Confessor."

"You what?"

"Prince Harold gave me his orders, as I just reported them. I told him that it was wrong, and could only harm our people. He said it was not for me to decide such things. He said it was not for me to think, but to follow orders.

"I've fought with you, Mother Confessor. I believe I know you better than Prince Harold does—I know you are devoted to protecting the lives of the people of the Midlands. I told him that what Cyrilla was doing was wrong. He was angry, and said it was my duty to follow my orders.

"I told him that, in that case, I was deserting the Galean army and was going to stand with you, instead. I thought he was going to have me put to death for disobeying him, but he would have had to put all thousand of us to death because all the men felt the same way. A good many came forward to tell him so. The fire seemed to go out of him, then, and he let us ride down here with him.

"I hope you aren't angry with us, Mother Confessor."

Kahlan couldn't force herself to be the Mother Confessor at that moment. She put her arms around him.

"Thank you, Bradley."

She gripped his shoulders and smiled at him through her watery vision. "You used your head. I couldn't be angry with that."

"You told us once we were a badger trying to swallow an ox whole. Looks to me you've taken to trying to do the same thing. If there ever was a badger who could swallow an ox whole, it would be you, Mother Confessor, but I guess we wouldn't want you to try it without us to help you do it."

They turned then and saw General Meiffert directing some of his men. They were carrying Prince Harold's limp body out of the lodge, holding him by the shoulders and feet. His hands dragged through the snow.

"I figured this wasn't going to come to any good end," the young captain said. "Ever since Cyrilla was hurt, Prince Harold just never seemed himself. I always loved the man. It hurt me to have to desert him. But he just wasn't making sense anymore."

Kahlan put a comforting hand on his shoulder as they watched the body being carried away.

"I'm sorry, Bradley. Like you, I always thought highly of him. I guess seeing his sister and his queen so long held in the grip of that kind of sickness just brought him to his wits' end. Try to keep your good memories of him."

"I will, Mother Confessor."

Kahlan changed the subject. "I'll need one of your men to take a message to Cyrilla. I was going to have Harold take it, but now we'll need a messenger."

"I will see to it, Mother Confessor."

She only then realized how cold it was outside, and that she didn't have a cloak. As the captain went to get his men quartered and to pick out a man to act as a messenger, Kahlan went back inside the lodge.

Cara was putting more wood on the hearth. Verna and Adie had gone. Warren was selecting a rolled map from the basket of maps and diagrams in the corner.

As he was leaving, Kahlan caught Warren's arm. She looked into the wizard's blue eyes, knowing they were much older than they appeared. Richard had always said that Warren was one of the smartest people he had ever met. Besides that, Warren's true talent was said to lie in the area of prophecy.

"Warren, are we all going to die in this mad war?"

His face softened with a shy but impish grin. "I thought you didn't believe in prophecy, Kahlan."

She released his arm. "I guess I don't. Never mind."

Cara, leaving to find some more firewood, followed Warren out. Kahlan warmed herself before the hearth as she stared at *Spirit* standing on the mantel. Zedd rested a comforting hand on her shoulder.

"What you had to say to Harold about using your mind, about reason, was very wise, Kahlan. You were right."

Her fingers touched the buttery smooth walnut robes of *Spirit*. "It was what Richard said, when he was telling me what he had finally come to understand about what he had to do. He said the only sovereign he could allow to rule him was reason."

"Richard said that? Those were his very words?"

Kahlan nodded as she gazed at *Spirit*. "He said the first law of reason is that what exists, exists; what is, is, and that from this irreducible, bedrock principle, all knowledge is built. He said that was the foundation from which life is embraced.

"He said thinking is a choice, and that wishes and whims are not facts, nor are they a means to discover them. I guess Harold proved the point. Richard said reason is our only way of grasping reality—that it's our basic tool of survival. We are free to evade the effort of thinking—to reject reason—but we are not free to avoid the penalty of the abyss we refuse to see."

She listened to the fire crackling at her feet as she let her gaze wander over the lines of the figure he had carved for her. When she heard nothing from Zedd, she looked over her shoulder. He was staring into the flames, a tear running down his cheek.

"Zedd, what's wrong?"

"The boy figured it out himself." The old wizard's voice was the uneasy sum of loneliness and quiet pride. "He understands it—he interpreted it perfectly. He even came to it on his own, by applying it."

"Came to what?"

"The most important rule there is, the Wizard's Sixth Rule: the only sovereign you can allow to rule you is reason."

Reflections of the firelight danced in his hazel eyes. "The Sixth Rule is the hub upon which all rules turn. It is not only the most important rule, but the simplest. Nonetheless, it is the one most often ignored and violated, and by far the most despised. It must be wielded in spite of the ceaseless, howling protests of the wicked.

"Misery, iniquity, and utter destruction lurk in the shadows outside its full light, where half-truths snare the faithful disciples, the deeply feeling believers, the selfless followers.

"Faith and feelings are the warm marrow of evil. Unlike reason, faith and feelings provide no boundary to limit any delusion, any whim. They are a virulent poison, giving the numbing illusion of moral sanction to every depravity ever hatched.

"Faith and feelings are the darkness to reason's light.

"Reason is the very substance of truth itself. The glory that is life is wholly embraced through reason, through this rule. In rejecting it, in rejecting reason, one embraces death."

319

By the next morning, about half of the Galean force had vanished, returning to their homeland and queen as ordered by Prince Harold before his death. The rest, like Captain Ryan and his young soldiers, remained loyal to the D'Haran Empire.

Lieutenant Leiden, the former general, and his entire force of Keltish troops had also departed by morning. He left Kahlan a letter, in it saying that with Galea choosing to break with the D'Haran Empire, he had to return to help protect Kelton, as surely the selfish actions of the Galeans meant the Order would be more likely to come up the Kern River Valley and threaten Kelton. He wrote that he hoped the Mother Confessor would realize how grave was the danger to Kelton, and understand that it was not his intention to desert her or the D'Haran Empire, but simply to help protect his people.

Kahlan knew of the men leaving; General Meiffert and Warren had come to tell her. She had expected it, and had been watching. She told General Meiffert to allow them to leave if they wished. War in their camp could come to no good end. The morale of the remaining men was boosted by a sense of being on the right side, and of doing the right thing.

That afternoon, as she was drafting an urgent letter to General Baldwin, commander of all Keltish forces, General Meiffert and Captain Ryan came to see her. After listening to their plan, she granted Captain Ryan permission to go with a like number of General Meiffert's handpicked D'Haran special forces to conduct raids on the Imperial Order force. Warren and six Sisters were sent to accompany them.

With the Imperial Order having moved so far back to the south, Kahlan needed information on what they were doing and what shape their force was in. More than that, though, with the foul weather in their favor, she wanted to keep pressure on the enemy. Captain Bradley Ryan and his band of nearly a thousand were experienced mountain fighters and had grown up in just such harsh conditions. Kahlan had fought beside the captain and his young Galean soldiers, and had helped train them in the ways of fighting a vastly superior force. If only the enemy force did not number over a million . . .

General Meiffert's special forces, which, until Kahlan had promoted him, he had ably commanded, were now led by Captain Zimmer, a young, square-jawed, bullnecked D'Haran with an infectious smile. They were everything Captain Ryan's young men were, tripled: experienced, businesslike under stress, tireless, fearless, and coolly efficient at killing. What made most soldiers blanch made them grin.

They preferred fighting just such as this, where they were free of massive battlefield tactics and could instead use their special skills. They treasured being let off the leash to do what they did best. Rather than check them, Kahlan gave them a free hand.

Each of those D'Harans collected enemy ears.

They felt a great fidelity to Kahlan, in part because she didn't try to rein them in and integrate them into the larger army, and, perhaps more so, because when they returned from missions, she always asked to see their strings of ears. They relished being appreciated.

Kahlan intended to later send them to collect Galean ears.

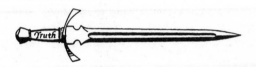

Kahlan glanced over her shoulder at the Prelate bent over the map basket in the corner. It had been almost a full phase of the moon since Warren had left on the mission with captains Ryan and Zimmer. Although it was difficult to judge accurately just how long such missions would last, they should have been back by now. Kahlan knew all too well the kind of worry that had to be churning beneath the woman's no-nonsense exterior.

"Verna," Kahlan asked as she rubbed her arms, "on your way past, could you throw some more wood on the fire, please?"

Cara hopped down off her stool, where she was perched, watching over Kahlan's shoulder. "I'll do it."

Verna pulled a map free and, on her way back to the table, thanked Cara. "Here it is, Zedd. I think this better shows the area you're talking about."

Zedd unfurled the new map over the top of the one already laid out on the table before Kahlan. It was a larger scale, giving a more detailed look at the southern regions of the Midlands.

"Yes," Zedd drawled as he peered at the new map. "See here?" He tapped the Drun River. "See how narrow the lowlands are down south, through here? That's what I was talking about. Rough country, with cliffs in places hemming the river. That's why I don't think they would try to go up the Drun Valley."

"I suppose you're right," Verna said.

"Besides"—Kahlan waggled a finger over the area to the north on the first map—"up this way is mostly only Nicobarese. They are rather isolated, and so a tempting target, but they aren't a wealthy land. The plunder and trade goods would be slim. The Order has much more opportunity for conquest if they stay over here. Besides, can you see how difficult it would be for them to get their army back over the Rang'Shada mountains, if they went up the Drun? Strategically, it wouldn't make as much sense for them to go up that way."

Verna idly twiddled with a button on her blue dress as she studied the map. "Yes . . . I see what you mean."

"But your point is well taken," Kahlan said. "It wouldn't be a bad idea if you sent a Sister or two to watch that area; just because it doesn't make as much logistic sense, that doesn't mean Jagang wouldn't try it. Come spring, he's bound to move on us. We wouldn't want to be surprised to find the Imperial Order storming in the back door to Aydindril."

Cara answered the knock at the door. It was a head scout named Hayes. Kahlan stood when she saw through the open door and nearby trees that Captain Ryan was also making his way toward the lodge.

Hayes saluted with a fist to his heart.

"Glad to see you back, Corporal Hayes," Kahlan said.

"Thank you, Mother Confessor. It's good to be back."

He looked like he could use a meal. After Captain Ryan rushed in through the door, Cara pushed it shut against the blowing snow. Hayes stepped to the side, out of the way of the captain.

Kahlan was relieved to see the young Galean officer. "How did everything go, Captain? How is everyone?"

He pulled off his scarf and wool hat as he caught his breath; Verna looked to be holding hers.

"Good," the captain said. "We did well. The Sisters were able to heal some of our wounded. Some needed to be transported for a ways before the Sisters could see to them. That slowed us. We had a few losses, but not as many as we feared. Warren was a great help."

"Where is Warren?" Zedd asked.

As if bidden by his name, Warren came in through the door, escorted by a swirling gust of snow. Kahlan squinted at the slash of bright light until the door was pushed shut once more. She caught the look on Verna's face, and recalled how lighthearted she always felt to see Richard back safely when they had been separated. Warren casually kissed Verna on the cheek with a quick peck. Kahlan noticed the look they shared, even if no one else did. She was happy for them, but still, the reminder was like a jab at the pain of her helpless heartache and worry over Richard.

"Did you tell them?" Warren asked, unbuttoning his cloak.

"No," Captain Ryan said. "We haven't had a chance yet."

Zedd's brow drew down. "Tell us what?"

Warren heaved a sigh. "Well, Verna's special glass worked better than we thought it had. We captured several men and questioned them at length. The ones we saw dead in the valley were only the ones who died at first."

Verna helped Warren shed his heavy, snow-crusted cloak. She put it on the floor by the fire, where Captain Ryan had laid his brown coat to dry.

"It seems," Warren went on, "that there were a great many—maybe another sixty, seventy thousand—who didn't go blind, but who lost the sight in one eye, or have impaired vision. The Order couldn't very well abandon them, because they can still see well enough to stay with the rest, but more important, it's hoped that maybe those men will heal, and regain full use of their sight—and their ability to fight."

"Not likely," Verna said.

"I don't think so, either," Warren said, "but that's what they are thinking, anyway. Another goodly number, maybe twenty five or thirty thousand, are sick—their eyes and noses red and horribly infected."

Verna nodded. "The glass will do that."

"Then some more, maybe half that number, are having breathing difficulty."

"So," Kahlan said, "with those killed and those injured enough to keep them from being effective fighters, that makes somewhere near one hundred fifty thousand put out of the way by the glass dust. Quite an accomplishment, Verna."

Verna looked as pleased as Kahlan. "It was worth that horse ride scaring the wits out of me. It wouldn't have worked had you not thought of doing it that way."

"What kind of success did you have, Captain?" Cara asked as she came to stand behind Kahlan.

"Captain Zimmer and I had the kind of success we hoped for. I'd guess we took out maybe ten thousand in the time we were down there."

Zedd let out a slow whistle. "Pretty heavy fighting."

"Not really. Not the way the Mother Confessor taught us to do it, and not the way Captain Zimmer works, either. Mostly we eliminate the enemy as efficiently as possible, and try to keep from having to fight at all. If you slit a man's throat in his sleep, you can accomplish a lot more, and you're less likely to get hurt yourself."

Kahlan smiled. "I'm glad you were such a good student."

Captain Ryan lifted a thumb. "Warren and the Sisters were a great help at getting us where we needed to be without being discovered. Any word about the white cloaks, yet? We could really use them. I can tell you for a fact that they would have enabled us to do more."

"We just got in our first load the day before yesterday," Kahlan told him. "More than enough for your men and Captain Zimmer's. We'll have more within a few days."

Captain Ryan rubbed his hands, warming his fingers. "Captain Zimmer will be pleased."

Zedd gestured to the south. "Did you find out why they withdrew so far back over ground they'd taken?"

Warren nodded. "From the men we questioned, we found out that they have fever going through their camp. Nothing we did, just your regular fever that happens in such crowded camp conditions in the field. But they've lost tens of thousands of men to the fever. They wanted to withdraw to put some distance between us, give themselves some breathing room. They aren't concerned about being able to push us out of their way when they wish."

That made sense. With their numbers, it was only natural for them to be confident, even cavalier, about dealing with any opposition. Kahlan couldn't understand why Warren and Captain Ryan looked so downhearted. She sensed that, despite their good news, there was something amiss.

"Dear spirits," Kahlan said, trying to give them some cheer. "Their numbers are dwindling away like snow beside the hearth. This is better than—"

Warren held up a hand. "I asked Hayes, here, to come and give you his report firsthand. I think you had better hear him out."

Kahlan motioned the man to come forward. He stepped smartly up to her table and snapped to attention.

"Let's hear what you have to report, Corporal Hayes."

His face looked chalky, and despite the cold, he was sweating.

"Mother Confessor, my scout team was down to the southeast, watching the routes in from the wilds, and watching, too in case the Order tried to swing wide around us. Well, I guess the short of it is, we spotted a column making its way west to resupply and reinforce the Order."

"They're a big army," Kahlan said. "They would have supplies sent from their homeland to augment what they can get as spoils. A supply column would have men guarding them."

"I followed them for a week, just to get an accurate count."

"How many," Kahlan asked.

"Well over a quarter million, Mother Confessor."

Kahlan's flesh tingled as if icy needles were dancing over it.

"How many?" Verna asked.

"At least two hundred and fifty thousand men at arms, plus drivers and civilians with the supplies."

Everything they had worked for, all the sacrifices, all the struggle to whittle down the Imperial Order, had just been nullified. Worse than nullified, their work had been erased, and nearly that many more had been added to the force the enemy had started with.

"Dear spirits," Kahlan whispered, "how many men does the Old World have to throw at us?"

When she met Warren's gaze, she knew that this number, even, was hardly surprising to him.

Warren gestured to the scout. "Hayes saw only the first group. The men we captured told us about the reinforcements. We weren't sure they were telling us the truth—we thought they might be trying to spook us—but then we met up with Corporal Hayes, on his way back. We did some further questioning and scouting—that's why we were delayed in returning."

"Another quarter million . . ." Kahlan's words trailed off. It all seemed so hopeless.

Warren cleared his throat. "That is just the first column of fresh troops. More are coming."

Kahlan went to the hearth and warmed her hands as she stared into the flames. She was standing beneath the statue Richard had carved for her, to make her feel better. Kahlan wished that at that moment she could recall the defiant feeling *Spirit* portrayed. It felt as if she could only contemplate death.

The news of the Imperial Order reinforcements, just as the news of departure of the Galeans and Keltans, spread through the camp faster than a storm wind. Kahlan, Zedd, Warren, Verna, Adie, General Meiffert, and all the rest of the officers held nothing back from the men. Those men were risking their lives daily and had a right to the truth. If Kahlan was passing through the camp, and a soldier was brave enough to ask her, she told him what she knew. She tried to give them confidence, too, but she didn't lie to them.

The men, having struggled for so long, were beyond fear. The bleak mood was a palpable pall smothering the spark of life out of them. They went about their tasks as if numb, accepting their fate, which now seemed sealed, resigned to the inevitable. The New World offered no shelter, no safe place, nowhere to hide from the boundless menace of the Imperial Order.

Kahlan showed the soldiers a determined face. She had no choice. Captain Ryan and his men, having been through such despair before, were less troubled by the news. They couldn't die; they were already dead. Along with Kahlan, the young Galeans had long ago taken an oath of the dead, and could only be returned to life when the Order was destroyed.

None of it mattered much to Captain Zimmer and his men. They knew what needed to be done, and they simply kept at it. Each of them now had multiple strings of ears. They began new strings at one hundred. It was a matter of honor to them that they kept only the right ear, so no two ears could be from the same man.

Representative Theriault of Herjborgue was as good as his word. The white wool cloaks, hats, and mittens arrived weekly, helping hide the men who regularly went on missions, while the weather was in their favor, to attack the Imperial Order. With the sickness in the Order's camp leaving so many of them weak, along with so many of the enemy having impaired vision, those missions were extraordinarily successful. Troops wearing the concealing cloaks were also sent to lie in wait and intercept any supply trains, hoping to neutralize the reinforcements before they could join with the enemy's main force.

Still, the attacks were little more than an annoyance to the Order.

Kahlan, after a meeting with a group just returned, found Zedd alone in the lodge, looking over the latest information that had been added to the maps.

"Good fortune," she said when he looked up, watching as she removed her fur mantle. "The men who just got in had few casualties, and they caught a large group out on patrol. They were able to cut them off and take them all out, including one of Jagang's Sisters."

"Then why the long face?"

She could only lift her hands in a forsaken gesture of futility.

"Try not to be so disheartened," Zedd told her. "Despair is often war's handmaiden. I can't tell you how many years it was, back when I was young, that everyone fighting for their lives in that war back then thought that it was only a matter of time until we were crushed. We went on to win."

"I know, Zedd. I know." Kahlan rubbed at the chill in her hands. She almost hated to say it, but she finally did. "Richard wouldn't come to lead the army because he said that the way things stand now, we can't win. He said whether or not we fight the Order, the world will fall under its shadow, and if we fight, it will only result in more death—that our side will be destroyed, the Order would still rule the world, and any chance for winning in the future would be lost."

Zedd peered at her with one eye. "Then what are you doing here?"

"Richard said we can't win, but, dear spirits, I can't let myself believe that. I would rather die fighting to be free, to help keep my people free, than to live the death of a slave. Yet, I know I'm violating Richard's wishes, his advice, and his orders. I gave him my word. . . . I feel as if I'm treading the quicksand of betrayal, and taking everyone with me."

She searched his face for some sign that Richard might have been wrong. "You said that he had figured out the Wizard's Sixth Rule on his own—that we must use our minds to see the reality of the way things are. I had hopes. I thought he had to be wrong about the futility of this war, but now . . ."

Zedd smiled to himself, as if finding fancy in something she saw as only horrifying.

"This is going to be a long war. It is far from beyond hope, much less decided. This is the agony of leadership in such a struggle—the doubts, the fears, the feelings of hopelessness. Those are feelings—not necessarily reality. Not yet. We have much yet to bring to bear.

"Richard said what he believed based on the way matters stood at the time he said them. Who is to say that the people are not now prepared to prove themselves to him? Prove themselves ready to reject the Order? Perhaps what Richard needed in order for him to commit to the battle, has already come about."

"But I know how strongly he warned me against joining this battle. He meant what he said. Still . . . I don't have Richard's strength, the strength to turn my back and let it happen." Kahlan gestured to her inkstand on the table. "I've sent letters asking that more troops be sent down here."

He smiled again, as if to say that proved it could be done.

"It will take continual effort to grind down the enemy's numbers. I think we have yet to deal the Order a truly serious blow, but we will. The Sisters and I will come up with something. You never know in matters of this kind. It could be that we will suddenly do something that will send them reeling."

Kahlan smiled and rubbed his shoulder. "Thanks, Zedd. I'm so thankful to have you with us." Her gaze wandered to *Spirit*, standing proudly above the hearth. She stepped over to the mantel, as if to an altar that held the sacred carving. "Dear spirits, I miss him."

It was a question without the words, hoping he would surprise her with something that he had thought of to help get Richard back.

"I know, dear one. I miss him, too. He's alive—that's the most important thing." Kahlan could only nod.

Zedd clapped his hands together, as if taken with a gleeful thought. "What we need, more than anything, is something to get everyone's mind off of the task at hand for a while. Something to give them a reason to cheer together for a while. It would do them more good than anything."

Kahlan frowned over her shoulder. "Like what? You mean some kind of game, or something?"

His face was all screwed up in musing. "I don't know. Something happy. Something to show them that the Order can't stop us from living our lives. Can't stop us from the enjoyment of life—of what life is really all about." He stroked a thumb along the sharp line of his jaw. "Any ideas?"

"Well, I can't really think of—"

Just then, Warren strode in. "Just got a report from over in the Drun Valley. Our lucky day—no activity, as we expected."

He stopped dead in his tracks, his hand still holding the door lever, looking from Kahlan to Zedd and back again.

"What's the matter? What's going on? Why are you two looking at me like that?"

Verna came up behind Warren and gave him a shove into the lodge. "Go on, go on, get in there. Close the door. What's the matter with you? It's freezing out there."

Verna huffed and shut the door herself. When she turned around and saw Zedd and Kahlan, she backed a step.

"Verna, Warren," Zedd said in a honeyed voice, "come on in, won't you?"

Verna scowled. "What are you two scheming and grinning at?"

"Well," Zedd drawled as he winked at Kahlan, "the Mother Confessor and I were just discussing the big event."

Verna's scowl darkened as she leaned in. "What big event? I've heard nothing about any big event."

Even Warren, rarely given to scowling, was scowling now. "That's right. What big event?"

"Your wedding," Zedd said.

Both Verna and Warren's scowls evaporated as they straightened. They were overcome with surprised, silly, radiant grins.

"Really?" Warren asked.

"Really?" Verna asked.

"Yes, really," Kahlan said.

It took more than two weeks to prepare for Verna and Warren's wedding. It wasn't that it couldn't have been done more quickly, but rather, as Zedd had explained to Kahlan, he wanted to "drag out the whole affair." He wanted to give everyone ample time to ponder it and to dream up lavish doings; time to organize, to make decorations, to cook special foods, to get the camp ready for a grand party; time to have a stretch where everyone could gossip about it as they eagerly looked forward to the big event.

The soldiers, at first merely pleased, soon got caught up in the spirit of the occasion. It became a grand diversion.

They all liked Warren. He was the sort of man that everyone felt a little sorry for, a bit protective of—the awkward shy type. Most didn't have the foggiest understanding of many of the things he babbled about. They thought that he just wasn't the type who would ever win a woman. That he had, to them seemingly against all odds, gave the men an inner pride that he was one of theirs, and he had done it: he'd won a woman's heart. It gave them hope that they might one day have a wedding, a wife, and a family, even if they were afraid that they, too, were often awkward and shy.

The men even openly expressed happiness for Verna. She was a woman they respected, but had never exactly felt warmly toward. Their bold well-wishes flummoxed her.

The entire camp was caught up in the spirit of the event even more than Kahlan had hoped. After a brief pause in the beginning, while it sank in, the men, so weary not only of fighting against such odds, the loss of friends, and being in the field away from their homes and loved ones for so long, but also the harsh, difficult, dreary weather, took to the diversion with gusto.

A large central area was cleared—tents moved, and the area cleaned of snow down to the bare ground. At the head of the cleared area, they built a platform—laid across anchored supply wagons—atop which the wedding was to take place. The platform was needed so that the men would have a better chance to see the ceremony. A dance area was set aside and those men with musical instruments, and not out on duty, spent night and day practicing. A choir was formed and went off to a secluded ravine to rehearse. Wherever Kahlan went, she could hear pipes and drums, or the piercing notes of a shawm, or the melodic chords of strings. Men came to fear playing off-key more than they feared the Imperial Order.

With over a hundred Sisters available, it was suggested that there could be dancing after the ceremony. The Sisters liked the idea, until they started doing the math and realized how many men there were to each woman, and how much dancing they would be doing. Still, they were titillated at the prospect of having attention lavished on them at a dance, and approved the idea. Women centuries old were blushing like girls again at all the requests from men in their teens and twenties for the promise of a turn with them at the wedding dance.

As the wedding approached the men made streets, of sorts, in a winding course through the camp, so that after the ceremony, the wedding party could pass in review through the entire camp. All the men wanted a chance to be a part in greeting the newly married couple and wishing them well.

Kahlan had the idea that, after the wedding, Warren and Verna should have the lodge. It was to be her wedding gift to them, so, for the most part, she kept it a secret. Kahlan had Cara direct the public pretense of having a tent set aside and reserved for the newly married couple. Cara moved Verna's things in the tent, and freshened it up with herbs and frozen sprigs with wild berries. The diversion worked; Verna believed the tent was to be hers and Warren's, and wouldn't let him into it until after they were married.

The day of the wedding dawned with sparkling blue skies, and wasn't so cold that people were likely to get frostbite. The fresh snow of the day before was quickly cleared out of the central area so that the festivities could take place without the Sisters getting snow down their boots as they danced. Some of the Sisters came out to inspect the dance floor, sauntering around, giving the men a look at who they might get to have a turn with—if they were lucky. It was all done with much humor and good cheer.

While Verna spent the early afternoon in her tent, submitting to having her hair fussed over, her face painted, and her wedding dress tended to by a gaggle of Sisters, Kahlan was finally able to have the secrecy she needed in order to decorate the lodge. Inside, she secured fragrant, feathery, balsam boughs to a cord and draped it in swags around the top of every wall. She tied red berries—as that was all she could come by—into the boughs to give them some color.

One of the Sisters had given Kahlan some plain weave fabric that Kahlan had made into a curtain for the window. She had worked on it when she retired to the lodge at night, stitching designs to give the simple material a lacy look. She kept it under her bed so that when they came in to go over battlefield strategy, Verna and Warren wouldn't know what she was doing. Kahlan was finally able to put the scented candles, donated by different Sisters as gifts, all around the room, and at last hang the curtain on a straight limb she stripped of bark.

The one thing Kahlan wouldn't leave to brighten the lodge for the newly wedded couple was *Spirit*. That, she would take to her new tent.

As Kahlan was making up the bed with fresh bedding, Cara came in with an armload of something blue.

Kahlan folded the blanket under the foot of the straw-filled mattress as she watched Cara shut the door.

"What have you got there?"

"You won't believe it," Cara said with a grin. "Wide blue silk ribbon. The Sisters have Verna tied to a chair while they're fussing over her, and Zedd has Warren off doing something, so I thought you and I could use the ribbon to decorate the place a little. Drape it around. Make it look pretty." She pointed. "Like up there—we could wind it around the balsam you hung to give it a fancy look."

Kahlan blinked in surprise. "What a good idea."

She didn't know what was more astonishing, actually seeing Cara with blue silk ribbon, or hearing her say "decorate" and "pretty" in the same breath. She smiled to herself, happy to have heard such a thing. Zedd was more of a wizard than he knew.

Kahlan and Cara each stood on a log round, working their way along the wall as they wove the ribbon through and around the swagged balsam boughs. It was so beautiful seeing the first wall completed that Kahlan couldn't stop gazing and grinning. They started in on the second wall, opposite the door, using extra ribbon for best effect when Verna and Warren first entered and saw their new place.

"Where did you ever get all this ribbon, away?" Kahlan asked around a mouthful of pins.

"Benjamin got it for me." Cara chuckled as she threaded the ribbon around the cord. "Can you believe it? He made me promise not to ask him where he got it from."

Kahlan took the pins from her mouth. "Who?"

"Who what?" Cara mumbled before she stuck her tongue out the corner of her mouth while wiggling a pin into a tight place.

"Who did you say got you the ribbon?"

Cara lifted another length of blue silk to the ceiling. "General Meiffert. I don't have a clue where he—"

"You said Benjamin."

Cara lowered the ribbon and stared at Kahlan. "No I didn't."

"Yes, you did. You said Benjamin."

"I said General Meiffert. You only thought—"

"I never knew that General Meiffert's first name was Benjamin."

"Well . . ."

"Is 'Benjamin' General Meiffert's first name?"

Had Cara been wearing her red leather, her face would have matched it. As it was, her dark scowl matched the brown leather she had on.

"You know it is."

A smile grew on Kahlan's lips. "I do now."

Kahlan wore her white Mother Confessor's dress. She was a bit surprised to notice that it fit a little loosely, but all things considered, she supposed it was to be expected. Because of the cold, she also wore the wolf fur mantle Richard had made for her, but draped it around her shoulders more like a stole. She stood with her back straight and chin held high, overseeing the ceremony and gazing out at the tens of thousands of quiet faces. Behind her was a rich verdant wall of woven boughs that enabled distant spectators to more easily pick out the six people up on the platform. An ethereal mist of silent breath lifted in the still, golden, late-afternoon air.

As he conducted the wedding ceremony, Zedd's back was to her. Kahlan was fascinated to see his wavy white hair, perpetually in disarray, now brushed and smoothed down. He wore his fine maroon robes with black sleeves and cowled shoulders. Silver brocade circled the cuffs, while gold brocade ran around the neck and down the front. A red satin belt set with a gold buckle gathered the outfit at his waist. Adie stood beside him, wearing her simple sorceress's robes with their yellow and red beads at the neckline. Somehow, the contrast looked as grand.

Verna wore a rich violet dress done up with gold stitching at the square neckline.

The intricate gold needlework ran down the tight sleeves showing under slashed sham sleeves tied at the elbow with gold ribbon. The delicate smocking over the midriff extending in a funnel shape down into a gored skirt flaring nearly to the floor. Verna's wavy brown hair was festooned with blue, gold, and crimson flowers the sisters had made from little pieces of silk. With her serene smile, she made a beautiful sorceress bride standing beside the handsome blond groom in his violet wizard's robes.

Everyone seemed to lean in a little as the ceremony reached the climax.

"Do you, Verna, take this wizard to be your husband for life," Zedd went on in a clear tone that carried out over the crowd, "mindful of his gift and duty to it, and swear to both love and honor him without pause for as long as you live?"

"I do," Verna said in a silken voice.

"Do you, Warren," Adie said, her voice all the more raspy in contrast to Verna's, "take this sorceress to be your wife for life, mindful of her gift and duty to it, and swear to both love and honor her without pause for as long as you live?

"I do," Warren said in a confident tone.

"Then, it being of your free will, I accept you, sorceress, as being agreeable and give my joyful blessing to this union." Zedd raised outstretched arms up into the air. "I ask the good spirits to smile on this woman's oath."

"Then, it being of your free will, I accept you, wizard, as being agreeable and give my joyful blessing to this union." Adie raised outstretched arms up into the air. "I ask the good spirits to smile on this man's oath."

The four of them crossed their arms and joined hands. With heads bowed, the air in the center of their circle glowed with a living light shining on the union. The brilliant flare sent a golden ray skyward, as if carrying the oath to the good spirits.

Together, Zedd and Adie said, "From this time forward, you are forever joined as husband and wife, both by oath, by love, and now by gift."

The magical light dissolved from the bottom up until it was but a solitary star directly above them in an empty, late-afternoon sky.

In the silent winter air tens of thousands of spellbound eyes watched a trembling Verna meet Warren's kiss to seal a wedding unlike any they were likely to ever see again: the marriage of a sorceress and a wizard, bound by more than any mere oath—bound also by a covenant of magic.

When Verna and Warren parted, both wearing broad smiles, the crowd went wild. Cheers, along with hats, rose into the air.

Both beaming, Verna and Warren joined hands after they turned to the soldiers. They waved with their free arms high in the air. Soldiers cheered, applauded, and whistled as if it were their own sister or best friend who was just married.

The voices of the choir then built in an extended note that reverberated through the trees all around. It made Kahlan's skin tingle with the quality of its haunting tone. The sound brought a reverent hush to the valley.

Cara leaned close to Kahlan and whispered in astonishment that the choir was singing an ancient D'Haran wedding ceremonial song, the origin of which went back thousands of years. Since the men had gone off to practice alone, Kahlan hadn't heard it before the wedding. It was so powerful it swept her emotions away with the rise and fall of the joined voices. Verna and Warren stood on the edge of the platform, likewise gripped by the achingly beautiful song to their union.

Flutes joined in, and then drums. The soldiers, mostly D'Haran, smiled as they listened to the music they knew well. It struck Kahlan then, since she had so long thought of D'Hara as an enemy land, that she had never really thought of D'Harans as having traditions that could be meaningful, or stirring, or beloved.

Kahlan glanced over at Cara, standing beside her, smiling distantly as she listened to the music. There was an entire land of D'Hara that was largely a mystery to Kahlan; she had only seen their soldiers. She knew nothing of their women—other than the Mord-Sith, and they were hardly typical—or their children, or their homes, or their customs. She had come to think of them as joined together at last, but she now realized that they were a people she didn't know, a people with their own heritage.

"It's beautiful," Kahlan whispered to Cara.

Cara nodded blissfully, carried away on the strains of music that was an old acquaintance to her, and a exotic wonder to Kahlan.

As the choir came to the end of their tribute to the newly wedded couple, Verna reached back and squeezed Kahlan's hand. It was an apology of sorts—an acknowledgment of how difficult this ceremony must be for Kahlan.

Refusing to let that hurt tarnish this joyous event, Kahlan beamed at Verna's quick glance. She came forward, standing behind Warren and Verna with an arm around each. The noise of the crowd trailed off so Kahlan could speak.

"These two people belong together. Perhaps they always have. Now they forever shall be. May the good spirits be with them always."

With one voice, the entire crowd repeated the prayer.

"I want to thank Verna and Warren from the bottom of my heart," Kahlan said as she gazed out at the tens of thousands of faces watching, "for reminding us what life is really about. There is no more eloquent demonstration of the simple yet deep meaning of our cause than this wedding today."

Heads as far as she could see bobbed in agreement.

"Now," Kahlan called out, "who wants to see these two have the first dance?"

The men cheered and hooted as they spread back to open up the central area. Musicians lined up along the benches at the sides.

As they waited for Verna and Warren to make their way down to the dance area, Kahlan draped an arm over Zedd's shoulder and kissed his cheek.

"This is the best idea you ever had, wizard."

He took her in with hazel eyes that seemed to see all the way to a person's soul.

"Are you all right, dear one? I know this has to be hard."

Kahlan nodded, holding her grin firmly in place. "I'm fine. It has to be hard on you, twice over."

A smile took him unexpectedly. "There you go again, Mother Confessor. Worrying about others."

Kahlan watched a laughing Verna and Warren, arm in arm, dancing lightly across the open area ringed by applauding soldiers.

"When they're done," Kahlan asked, "and after you've given your first to Adie, would you dance with me, sir? Stand in for him? I'm sure he would want that."

Kahlan couldn't bring herself to say his name at that moment, or the spell of the joyful celebration would have been broken.

Zedd lifted an eyebrow with playful delight. "What makes you think I can dance?"

Kahlan laughed. "Because there isn't anything you can't do."

"I be able to name a number of things this skinny old man can't do," Adie said with a smile as she shuffled up behind him.

When the dance was done, and others began joining in as the newly married couple began the second, Zedd and Adie went out in the ring to have a dance and show the young people how it was done. Kahlan stood at the edge of the circle with Cara close at her side. General Meiffert, laughing and shaking men's hands, slapping others on the back, made his way over.

"Mother Confessor!" He was pushed up close by the press of the crowd. "Mother Confessor, this is a wonderful day, isn't it? Have you ever seen the likes of it?"

Kahlan couldn't help but to smile at his delight. "No, General Meiffert, I don't think I have."

He glanced briefly at Cara. He stood awkwardly a moment, then turned to watch the dancing. Despite how well the men had come to know her, Kahlan was still a Confessor—a woman people feared to be near, much less touch. No one was likely to ask a Confessor to dance.

Or a Mord-Sith.

"General?" Kahlan asked, tapping him on the back of his shoulder. "General, could you do me a great personal favor?"

"Well, of course, Mother Confessor," he stammered. "Anything. What is it I can do?"

Kahlan gestured out at the dance area and the soldiers and Sisters ringing it. "Would you please dance? I know we're supposed to be on guard for any mischief, but I think it would let the men see the true festive nature of this party, were their general to go out there and dance."

"Dance?"

"Yes. Please?"

"But, I—that is, I don't know who . . ."

"Oh, do please stop trying to get out of it." Kahlan turned, as if suddenly struck with a thought. "Cara. Would you go out there with him and dance so his men will see that it's all right to join in?"

Cara's blue eyes shifted between Kahlan and the general. "Well, I don't see how—"

"Do it for me? Please, Cara?" Kahlan turned back to the general. "I believe I heard someone mention that your given name is Benjamin?"

He scratched his temple. "That's right, Mother Confessor."

Kahlan turned back to Cara. "Cara, Benjamin, here, needs a partner for a dance. How about you? Please? Do it for me?"

Cara cleared her throat. "Well, all right. For you, then, Mother Confessor."

"And don't break his ribs, or anything. We have need of his talents."

Cara scowled back over her shoulder as a smiling Benjamin led her away.

Kahlan folded her arms and grinned as she watched the man take Cara in his arms. It was just about a perfect day. Just about.

Kahlan was watching Benjamin gracefully swirl Cara around, and other soldiers pulling suddenly shy Sisters out of the line at the edge of the dance area, when Captain Ryan stumbled up.

He straightened before her. "Mother Confessor . . . uh, well, we've been through a lot together and, if I'm not being too forward, could I ask you to . . . you know, dance?"

Kahlan blinked in surprise at the tall, young, broad Galean.

"Why, yes, Bradley, I would love to dance with you. I would love it. But only if you promise not to hold me like I'm made of glass. I don't want to look foolish out there."

He grinned and nodded. "All right."

She placed one hand in his, and laid the other over his shoulder. He put his big hand to the side of her waist, under her open fur mantle, and twirled her out amid the merrymakers. Kahlan smiled and laughed as she endured it. She thought of *Spirit*, and willed herself to remember that kind of strength, and she was able to relax, and take the party for what it was, and not think about what was missing as another man held her in his arms, if timidly.

"Bradley, you're a wonderful dancer."

Pride shined in his eyes. She felt him loosen up, and let the music flow more smoothly through his movements. Kahlan caught sight of Cara and Benjamin, not far away, doing their best to dance and not look at each other. When he whirled her around him, his arm securely holding her waist, Cara's long blond braid sailed out behind her. Then Kahlan actually saw Cara look up into Benjamin's blue eyes and smile.

Kahlan was relieved when the song ended and Captain Ryan was replaced for the next dance by Zedd. She held him close as she moved to a slower tune with him.

"I'm proud of you, Mother Confessor. You gave a wonderful thing to these men."

"And what is that?"

"Your heart." He tilted his head. "See them watching you? You've given them courage. You've given them a reason to believe in what they're doing."

Kahlan lifted an eyebrow. "You trickster, you. You may fool others, but not me. It is you who has given me heart."

Zedd only smiled. "You know, not since the very first Confessor has a man ever again figured out how to love such a woman without her power destroying him. I'm glad it was my grandson who accomplished such an exploit, and that it was for his love of you. I love you as a granddaughter, Kahlan, and look forward to the day when you are back with my grandson."

Kahlan held Zedd close, resting her head against his shoulder, as they both danced on with their memories.

As the dancing went on, the golden setting sun was finally replaced by torches and warm fires. Sisters changed partners after each dance, and still there were jovial men lined up out of sight waiting a turn, and not just with the younger, more attractive Sisters. Cooks' helpers set out simple fare on food tables, sampling some and joking with the soldiers as they went about their task. Between dances, Warren and Verna tried the variety of food from different tables.

Kahlan danced once more with Captain Ryan, and once more with Zedd, but then busied herself speaking to officers and soldiers alike so she wouldn't have to dance with anyone, should anyone feel awkward about asking her, yet work up the nerve. She was more able to enjoy the festivities without having to dance.

As she was greeting a line of young officers, and they were telling her how much they appreciated the party, someone tapped Kahlan on the shoulder. She turned to a smiling Warren.

"Mother Confessor, I would be honored were you to have a dance with me."

Kahlan noticed Verna dancing with Zedd. This was one dance that would be different. "Warren, I would love to dance with the handsome groom."

333

He moved smoothly with her, not at all haltingly as she had expected. He seemed to be blissfully at peace, and not nervous about the crush of people or the men constantly clapping him on the back, or the joking remarks from some of the Sisters.

"Mother Confessor, I just wanted to thank you for making this the best day I've ever had."

Kahlan smiled up into his young face, his ageless eyes. "Warren, thank you for agreeing to this big party. I know it's not the sort of thing that fits you—"

"Oh, but it is. That's just it. People used to call me the mole."

"They did? Why?"

"Because I used to stay down in the vaults all the time studying the prophecies. It wasn't just that I liked to study the books—I was afraid to come out."

"But you finally did."

He turned her in time with the sweep of music. "Richard brought me out."

"He did? I never knew that."

"In a way, you've helped add to what he started." Warren smiled distantly. "I just wanted to thank you. I know how much I miss him, and how much Verna misses him. I know the men miss their Lord Rahl."

Kahlan was only able to nod.

"And I know how much you miss your husband. That's why I wanted to thank you—for giving us this, and the gift of your grace, despite your heartache. Everyone here feels it with you. Please know that while you miss him, you are not alone, and are among those who love him too."

Kahlan smiled, and managed to get out a "Thank you."

As they danced across the open area, laughing at the merry tune and the awkward steps of some of the soldiers, the music abruptly trailed off.

It was then that she heard the horns.

Alarm swept through the assembled soldiers, as men ran for their weapons, until one of the sentries sprinted in, waving his arm, calling out for everyone to stand down, that it was friendly forces.

Puzzled, Kahlan stretched her neck along with everyone else, trying to see. They had no forces out. She had let them all be present to enjoy the wedding party.

The crowd parted as horses trotted through the throng. Kahlan's eyebrows went up, and her jaw dropped. The distinguished General Baldwin, commander of all Keltish forces, was at the fore, riding a handsome chestnut gelding. He brought the horse to a smart halt. He ran his first finger along the length of his white-flecked dark mustache as he took in the crowd gathered in around him. His graying black hair grew down over his ears, and his pate shone through on top. He was a striking figure in his serge cape fastened on one shoulder with two buttons, allowing it to show the rich green silk lining. His tan surcoat was decorated with a heraldic emblem slashed through with a diagonal black line dividing a yellow and blue shield. The man's high boots were rolled down below his knees. Long black gauntlets, their flared cuffs lying over the front, were tucked behind a wide belt set with an ornate buckle.

The press of men made way for Kahlan to step through. "General!"

He lifted a hand in his noble manner, a smile spreading wide. "Mother Confessor, how good to see you."

Kahlan started to speak, but horses charged through, the crowd falling back for them. They stormed into the dance area like a wind-borne fire—a dozen Mord-Sith in red leather. One of the women leaped from her horse.

"Rikka!" Cara called out.

The woman's bold glare swept over the gathered people. She finally settled her gaze, taking in Cara. Cara moved out of General Meiffert's arms.

"Cara," she said as way of greeting. She glanced around. "Where is Hania?"

Cara stepped closer. "Hania? She's not here."

The woman pressed her lips together in bitter disappointment. "I thought as much. When I never received word back, I feared we had lost her. Still, I was hoping . . ."

Kahlan stepped forward, a little miffed that the woman saw fit to step in front of General Baldwin. "Rikka, is it?"

"Ah," Rikka said, a knowing smile stealing onto her face, "You could be none other than Lord Rahl's wife—the Mother Confessor. I recognize the description." The woman saluted casually with a fist to her heart. "Yes, I am Rikka."

"I'm glad to have you here, and your sisters of the Agiel."

"I came from Aydindril as soon as Berdine received your letter. It explained a lot. She and I discussed it, and decided I should come with some of my sisters to help in our effort. I left six sister Mord-Sith with Berdine to watch over Aydindril and the Wizard's Keep. I also brought twenty thousand troops." She lifted a thumb, pointing with it behind her. "We met up with the general, here, a week back."

"We can certainly use your help. That was wise of Berdine—I know how eager she was to come herself, but she knows the city and the Keep. I'm glad she followed *my* instructions." Kahlan settled her most unsettling Mother-Confessor-gaze on Rikka. "Now, if you don't mind, you interrupted General Baldwin."

Cara shoved Rikka, pushing her back out of the way. "We need to talk, Rikka, before you're up to the task of serving Lord Rahl and his wife, who just happens to be a sister of the Agiel."

Rikka lifted and eyebrow in surprise. "Really? How could—"

"Later," Cara said with a smile before Rikka could get herself into any more trouble, moving the woman and her sister Mord-Sith back. Zedd, Adie, and Verna eased closer to Kahlan.

General Baldwin, now off his horse, stepped forward at last and went to a knee in a bow. "My queen, Mother Confessor."

"Rise, my child," Kahlan said in formal answer as the camp looked on with the same rapt attention they had devoted to the wedding. This had important bearing on them, too.

The general rose to his feet. "I came as soon as I received your letter, Mother Confessor."

"How many men did you bring?"

He looked surprised by the question. "Why . . . all of them. One hundred seventy thousand men. When my queen asks for an army, I bring her one."

Whispers spread through the men as they passed word back.

Kahlan was stunned. She no longer even felt the cold. "That's wonderful, General. They are sorely needed. We have a real fight on our hands, as I explained in my letter. The Imperial Order is getting reinforcements all the time. We need to cut those lines."

"I understand. With the D'Harans from Aydindril come with us, we can just about triple the size of your force down here."

"And we can still bring more in from D'Hara," General Meiffert said.

Kahlan felt the hot spark of faith in their chances swelling within her breast. "By spring, for sure, we will need them." She cocked her head at General Baldwin. "What about Lieutenant Leiden?"

"Who? Oh, you must mean Sergeant Leiden. He only has a scout patrol, now. When a man deserts his queen, he's lucky to keep his head, but he acted to protect her people, so I sent him to guard some remote pass. I hope the man dresses warmly."

Kahlan wanted to throw her arms around the dashing General Baldwin. Instead, she touched her fingers to his arm in a gesture of her gratitude. "Thank you, General. We surely need the men."

"Well, they're up country a little ways, half a day back. Couldn't fit them all in here with your army."

"That's fine." Kahlan waggled her fingers, calling the Mord-Sith forward. "I'm very glad to see you, too, Rikka. With Mord-Sith, we can better handle the enemy gifted. We may even be able to turn the tide. Cara, here, has helped eliminate some of the gifted already, but I'm afraid that Lord Rahl has her under orders to protect me. She will continue in that capacity. But you will be free to go after their gifted."

Rikka bowed. "Love to." She came up and smiled. "Berdine warned me about her," she said under her breath to Cara.

"You should listen to Berdine," Cara said, clapping her on the back. "Come, I'll help you find some quarters—"

"No," Kahlan said, stopping them in their tracks. "This is a party. The general, Rikka, and her sisters are invited. In fact, I insist."

"Well," Rikka said, brightening, "as long as we're protecting Lord Rahl's wife, we would be only to happy to stay."

Kahlan took Rikka's arm and pulled her close. "Rikka, we have a lot of men here, and few women. This is a dance. Get out there and dance."

"What! Are you out of your—"

Kahlan shoved her out into the dance area. She snapped her fingers at the musicians. "Shall we resume?" She turned to General Baldwin. "General, you have come at a wonderful time, a time of celebration. Please, would you dance with me?"

"Mother Confessor?"

"I am your queen, also. Generals dance with queens, do they not?"

He smiled and offered his arm. "Of course they do, my queen."

Long after it was dark, the wedding procession made its way through the makeshift streets, greeting all the men. Thousands of soldiers congratulated Warren and Verna on their marriage, offered jesting advice, a gentle slap on the back, or just a merry wave.

Kahlan recalled a time when the Midlands feared these men. Under Darken Rahl, they were a formidable invader, inspiring dread and terror. She was amazed at how civil these men could be, how human, when given a chance. It was Richard, really, who had given them that chance. She knew that many of them understood that, and appreciated it.

When finally they reached the end of the long winding walk through the sprawling camp, they came at last to the tent Verna and Warren thought was to be theirs. Those following along bid the couple a good night and wandered back to the party, leaving the three of them alone.

Rather than let Verna and Warren slow, Kahlan stepped between them, took each under an arm, and guided them onto the path among the towering trees. Moonlight through the boughs cast wavering patterns on the snow. Not knowing what she was up to, neither Verna nor Warren protested as Kahlan kept them moving.

Finally, Kahlan spotted the lodge off through the trees. She stopped a little distance away to let them see the candlelight coming from behind the lace-like curtain. The juxtaposition against life in an army camp made it looked all the more romantic.

"This is a long and difficult struggle," Kahlan told them. "Starting a marriage under these conditions is a harsh burden. I can't tell you how happy I am that you two chose to go forward with it at a time like this. It means a great deal to all of us. We're all very happy for you. More than anything, I would like to thank you both for choosing life in all its glory.

"We will one day have to move on, as surely the Order will move again when spring comes, if not before. But for now, I want this place to be yours. I can give you at least this much, this little piece of a normal life together."

Verna unexpectedly burst into tears and buried her face in Kahlan's shoulder. Kahlan patted the Prelate's heaving back, chuckling at how out of character it was for Verna to show such emotion.

"Not a good idea, Verna, to let your new husband see you cry just as he's about to take you to his bed."

That did it, and Verna laughed, too. She gripped Kahlan's shoulders as she searched her eyes.

"I don't know what to say."

Kahlan kissed her cheek. "Love each another, be good to each other, and treasure being together—that's what I would like more than anything."

Warren hugged her, whispering his thanks in her ear. Kahlan watched as he led Verna the remaining distance to the lodge. At the door, both turned and waved. At the last moment, Warren swept Verna off her feet. Her lilting laugh drifted among the trees as he carried her through the doorway.

Alone, Kahlan turned back to the camp.

The door opened a crack. One bloodshot eye peered out into the dingy hall.

"You have a room? My wife and I are looking for a room." Before the man could close the door, Richard quickly added, "We were told you had one."

"What of it?"

Despite it being self-evident, Richard answered politely. "We've no place to stay."

"Why bring your problems to me?"

Richard could hear angry words going back and forth between a man and woman upstairs. Behind several of the doors in the hall, babies wailed without pause. The heavy odor of rancid oil hung in the dank air. Out the door at the back standing open to the narrow alley, young children, being chased by older children, squealed as they ran through the cold rain.

Richard spoke without expectation into the narrow slit. "We need a room."

A dog not far up the alleyway barked with monotonous persistence.

"Lots of people need a room. I only have one. I can't give it to you."

Nicci eased Richard aside and put her face close to the crack.

"We have the money for the first week." She shoved her hand against the door when he started to shut it. "It's a public room. Your duty is to help the public get rooms."

The man shouldered his weight into the door, shutting it in her face.

Richard turned away as Nicci began knocking. "Forget it," he said. "Let's go get a loaf of bread."

Nicci usually followed his lead without admonishment, challenge, or even comment, but this time, instead of minding him, she rapped persistently on the door. Layers of peeling paint, every color from blue to yellow to red, fell from under her knuckles.

"It's your duty," Nicci called to the closed door. "You've no right to turn us away." No answer came. "We're going to report you."

The door opened a crack again. The eye glared out with menace.

"Has he a job?"

"No, but—"

"You go away. The both of you—or I'll report you!"

"For what, might I ask?"

"Look, lady, I got a room, but I got to keep it for people at the top of the list."

"How do you know we're not at the top of the list?"

"Because if you were you would have said so first off and showed me the approval you got with a seal on it. People at the head of the list have been waiting a long time for a place. You're no better than a thief, trying to take the place of a good citizen who's followed the law. Now, go away, or I will take down your names for the lodging inspector."

The door slammed shut again. The threat of having their names taken down appeared to take some of the fight out of Nicci. She huffed a sigh as they walked away, the bowed floor creaking and groaning underfoot. At least they had been able to get in out of the rain for a brief time.

"We will have to keep looking," she told him. "If you had a job, first, it would probably help. Maybe tomorrow you can look for a job while I keep looking for a room."

Out in the cold rain once more, they crossed the muddy street to the cobbled walkway on the other side. There were yet more places to check, though Richard didn't hold out any hope of getting a room. They'd had doors shut in their faces more times than he could count. Nicci wanted a room, though, so they kept looking.

The weather was unusually cold for this far south in the Old World, Nicci had told him. People said the cold spell and rain would soon pass. A few days before it had been muggy and warm, so Richard had no reason to doubt their judgment. It was disorienting for him to see woods and fields of lush green vegetation in the dead of winter. There were some trees with limbs bare for the season, but most were in full leaf.

As far south as they were in the Old World, it never got cold enough for water to freeze. People only blinked dumbly when he spoke of snow. When Richard explained snow as flakes of frozen white water that fell from the sky and covered the ground with a cottony blanket, some people turned huffy, thinking he was making a joke at their expense.

He knew that back home winter would be raging. Despite the turmoil around him, Richard felt an inner tranquillity knowing that Kahlan was most likely to be warm and snug in the house he had built; in that light, nothing in his new life was of enough importance to distress him. She had food to eat, firewood to keep her warm, and Cara for company. For now, she was safe. Winter was wearing on and in spring she would be able to leave, but, for now, Richard was confident that she was safe. That, and his thoughts and memories of her, were his only solace.

People without rooms huddled in the alleyways, using whatever scrap of solid material they could find to prop up over themselves for a roof. Walls were fashioned from sodden blankets. He supposed that he and Nicci could continue to do the same, but he feared Nicci falling ill in the cold and wet—feared that then Kahlan, too, would fall ill.

Nicci checked the paper she carried. "These places on this register they gave us are all supposed to be available for people newly arrived—not just for people on a list. They need workers; they should be more diligent in seeing to it that places are available. Do you see, Richard? Do you see how hard it is for ordinary people to get along in life?"

Richard, hands shoved in his pockets, shoulders hunched against the wind and rain, asked, "So, how do we get on a list?"

"We will have to go to a lodging office and request a room. They can put us on a housing list."

It sounded simple, but matters were proving far more complex than they sounded.

"If there aren't enough rooms, how will being on a list get us a place to stay?"

"People die all the time."

"There's work here, that's why we came—that's why everyone else has come.

I'll work hard and then we can afford to pay more. We still have a little money. We just need to find a place that wants to rent a room for the right price—without all this list foolishness."

"Really, Richard, are you that inhumane? How would those less fortunate ever get rooms, then? The Order sets the prices to stop profiteers. They make sure there is no favoritism. That makes it fair for all. We just need to get on a list for a room, and then everything will be fine."

Watching the glistening cobbles before him as he walked, Richard wondered how long they would be without a place until their name worked its way to the top of a list. It looked to him as if a lot of people would need to die before his and Nicci's names came up for a room—with more yet waiting in turn for them to die.

He stepped first to one side and then the other to avoid bumping into the river of people swirling past, making their way in the opposite direction while trying to stay out of the mud of the street. He considered again staying outside the city—a lot of people did that. But there were outlaws and desperate people aplenty who preyed on those who were forced to stay out in the open where there were no city guards. Were Nicci not opposed to the idea, Richard would have found a place farther out and built a shelter, perhaps with some other people so that they could together discourage trouble.

Nicci wasn't interested in the idea. Nicci wanted to be in the city. Multitudes came to the city looking for a better life. There were lists to get on, and lines to wait in to see official people. You had a better chance of doing those things if you had a room in the city, she said.

It was getting late in the day. The line at the bakery was out the door and partway down the block.

"Why are all these people in line?" Richard whispered to Nicci. It was the same every day when they went to buy bread.

She shrugged. "I guess there aren't enough bakeries."

"Seems like with all the customers, more people would want to open bakeries."

Nicci leaned close, a scolding scowl darkening her brow. "The world isn't as simple as you would like it to be, Richard. It used to be that way in the Old World. Man's evil nature was allowed to flourish. People set their own prices for goods— with greed being their only interest, not the good of their fellow man. Only the well-to-do could afford to buy bread. Now, the Order sees to it that everyone gets needed goods for a fair price. The Order cares about everyone, not just those with unfair advantages."

She always seemed so impassioned when she spoke about the evil nature of people. Richard wondered why a Sister of the Dark would care about evil, but he didn't bother to ask.

The line wasn't moving very fast. The woman in front of him, suspicious of their whispering, scowled back over her shoulder.

Richard met her glare with a broad smile.

"Good afternoon, ma'am." Her somber scowl faltered in the light of his beaming grin. "We're new in town"—he gestured behind—"my wife and I. I'm looking for work. We need a room, though. Would you know how a young couple, strangers to the city, could go about getting a room?"

She half turned, holding her canvas bag in both hands, letting it pull her arms straight as she leaned her shoulders against the wall. Her bag held only a yellow wedge of cheese. Richard's smile and his friendly conversational tone—artificial though they were—were apparently so out of the ordinary that she seemed unable to maintain her gruff demeanor.

"You have to have a job if you hope to get a room. There aren't enough rooms in the city, what with all the new workers come for the abundance provided by the wisdom of the Order. If you're able-bodied, you need to have work, then they'll put your name on the list."

Richard scratched his head and kept smiling as the line slowly shuffled along. "I'm eager to work."

"Easier to get a room if you can't work," the woman confided.

"But, I thought you just said you had to have a job if you were to have any hope of getting a room."

"That's true, if you're able, like you look to be. Those folks with a greater need, because they can't do for themselves, are rightly entitled to benevolence and to be put higher on the list—like my husband, the poor man. He's afflicted terrible like with consumption."

"I'm so sorry," Richard said.

She nodded with the weight of her burden. "It's mankind's wretched lot to suffer. Nothing can be done about it, so there's no use trying. Only in the next life will we get our reward. In this life, it's the duty of every person with ability to help those unfortunate souls with needs. In that way the able earn their reward in the next life."

Richard didn't argue. She shook a finger at him.

"Those who can work owe it to those who can't to do their best for the good of all."

"I can work," Richard assured her. "We're from . . . a little place. We're simple folks—from farming stock. We don't know much about how to go about things like getting work in the city."

"The Order has brought the people a great abundance of work," a man behind Nicci said, drawing Richard's attention. The man's oiled canvas coat was buttoned tight at his throat. His big brown eyes blinked slowly, like a cow as it chewed its cud. The way his jaw wobbled sideways as he spoke only added to the impression. "The Order welcomes all workers to our struggle, but you must be mindful of the needs of others—as the Creator Himself wishes—and go about getting work in the proper fashion."

Richard, his stomach grumbling with hunger, listened as the man explained. "You first need to belong to a citizen workers' group; they protect the rights of citizens of the Order. You'll have to go before a review assembly for approval to join the workers' group, and a fitness panel to hear from a spokesman from the workers' citizen group who can vouch for you. You must do this before you can go for a job."

"Why can't I just go to a place and show myself? Why can't they hire me, if I fit their needs?"

"Just because you're from the country, that doesn't mean you shouldn't be mindful of contributing toward the greater good of the Order."

"Of course not," Richard said. "I've always worked for myself, though—farming to bring food to my fellow man, as is our duty. I don't know how businesses do things."

The big brown eyes paused their blinking. The man peered suspiciously for a moment, then his eyes finally went moony again. His jaw resumed its wobbling as he chewed his words.

341

"It's the primary responsibility of business to be sensitive to the needs of the people, to contribute to the public welfare, to be equitable. The review board helps see to this. There is much more involved than the narrow goals of businesses."

"I see," Richard said. "Well, I'd be grateful if you could tell me how to go about it properly." He glanced briefly at Nicci. "I want to be a good citizen and do things right."

By the man's pride in the explanation, and the way his big eyes blinked faster as he laid it all out, Richard expected that the man was somehow involved in the labyrinthine process. Richard didn't ask how you got a spokesman from the citizen workers' group to vouch for you. The line inched forward as the man explained the finer details of different sorts of work, what each required, and how it was all for the benefit of those living within the Order and under the grace of the Creator.

As he droned on, delivering his information with smug satisfaction, Nicci watched Richard discreetly, and without comment, as he listened to the procedures. She looked as if she was expecting him to suddenly turn from polite to deadly. Richard knew there could be no point to a battle with this man, so he remained polite.

It turned out that the man, named Mr. Gudgeons, seemed to know the most about the quarry workers. Since Richard knew little about quarries, he passed the time as they stood in line by asking a few questions that pleased Mr. Gudgeons to answer—at great length.

The store ran out of bread and closed before they got any. The line of people dissolved into the downpour, mumbling to one another as they went about their woeful lot in life. Richard thanked the woman and Mr. Gudgeons before he and Nicci moved on.

Richard paused at a cross street while Nicci studied her paper with the list of rooms. All around, the blocky shapes of buildings rose out of the gloom. Red paint on the side of one brick building was so faded that it left the figure painted there looking like a blushing ghost. The faded whitewash of words beneath the vanishing man were no longer legible.

Passing men gazed at Nicci in her wet clinging clothes, never seeing her face. Her hair was plastered to her skull, her jaw quivered, and her hands trembled, yet she didn't complain about the cold, as did everyone else. They had been told that they couldn't get another list, with any new rooms that might have recently become available, until the next day, so Nicci was trying to keep this one whole, but in the rain it was a losing battle.

Mangy horses slogged through the mud, some of the wagons they pulled squeaking and groaning under the weight of a load. Only the main thoroughfares, like the one they were on, were wide enough to allow teams of horses and full-size wagons to easily pass in both directions. Some streets were only wide enough for wagons to go in one direction. Some of those, with no room to pull aside, were choked off by broken-down wagons. Richard saw a dead horse in one narrow street, the rotting animal, attended by a cloud of flies, still hitched to its wagon as it awaited someone to come haul it away. The blocked streets only added to the congestion of the others. Some streets were wide enough only for handcarts. In many of the narrower passageways only foot traffic could fit.

The smell of garbage and the stench of streets that also functioned as open sewers had been enough to gag Richard for the first week until he'd become numb to it.

The alleyways where he and Nicci had slept were the worst. The rain only served to flush the filth out of every hole and carry it out into the open, but at least as long as he was standing it washed off some of the dirt.

All the cities Richard had seen after they'd entered the Old World and traveled south from Tanimura were similar to this one, all suffering under grinding poverty and inhuman conditions. Everything seemed caught in a timeless trap, a morass of rot, as if the cities had once been vibrant with life and people striving to fulfill dreams, had once been places of hope and ambition, but somewhere the dreams had disintegrated into a gray pall of stagnation and decay. No one seemed to much care. Everyone seemed in a daze, biding their time, waiting for their lot in life to improve without even having a concept of the shape of that better life or how it might come to be. They existed on disembodied faith, confident only that the afterlife would be perfect.

The cities Richard had seen were startlingly similar to what Richard envisioned the future held for the New World under the yoke of the Order.

This place, though, was the single largest city Richard had ever seen. He would never have believed the size of it had he not seen it himself. Dilapidated buildings entangled by streets teeming with people sprawled over a sweep of low hills, across a broad bottomland, for miles along the convergence of two rivers. Squat ramshackle huts built haphazardly of wattle and daub, scraps of wood, or salvaged mud and straw bricks beset the city's core to a great distance out into the surrounding land, like fetid scum surrounding a rotting log in a stagnant pond.

It was the city of Altur'Rang—the namesake of the land which was now the heart of the Old World and the Imperial Order—the home city of Emperor Jagang.

When they had first entered the Old World on their way south toward Altur'Rang, Richard and Nicci had stopped at the northernmost large city in the Old World, Tanimura, where the Palace of the Prophets had once stood. Tanimura, one of the last places in the Old World to fall under the rule of the Imperial Order, was a grand place, with wide boulevards lined with trees and ornate buildings soaring several stories high, faced with columns and arches and windows that let in the light. Tanimura, as large as it was, turned out to be but an outpost of the Old World, far enough away that the rot was only now reaching it.

For a span of a little over a month, Richard had found work in Tanimura as a mason's tender, one of a dozen, hauling stone and mixing mortar for a squat, unattractive building. The masons had simple huts the workers and their families lived in, so Nicci had shelter. The master came to trust Richard to keep up with his masons. When one of the stonecutters fell sick, Richard was asked to stand in at squaring the blocks of granite for the masons.

He found holding a chisel and mallet in his hands, cutting stone—shaping it to his will—a revelation. In some ways, it was like carving wood . . . but somehow much more.

From time to time, the master stood with fists on his hips, watching Richard chisel square edges into the hard granite. Occasionally, in a gruff voice, he would make minor corrections to Richard's method. After a time, as the master saw that Richard took to the job and could cut a block square and true, he no longer bothered watching. Before long Richard's blocks were chosen first by the masons as cornerstones.

Other stonecutters arrived to do more demanding work—the adornments. When they had first shown up, Richard had been eager to see their work. They cut into the face of blocks, meant to surround the entrance, a large flame representing the Light of the Creator. Below that, they carved a crowd of cowering people.

Richard had seen a number of stone carvings in the various places he had been, from the Confessors' Palace in Aydindril to the People's Palace in D'Hara, but he had never seen anything like the figures he saw being cut on that building in Tanimura. They were not graceful, or grand, or inspiring, but just the opposite. They were distorted, thick-limbed, cringing figures recoiling below the Light. Richard was told by one of the artisans that this was the only proper representation of mankind—profane, hideous, sinful. Richard kept his mind on cutting square stones.

When the stonework to the Order's headquarters building was finished, the job ended. The carpenters didn't need any more help. The artisans said they could use some assistance carving the anguish of mankind and offered Richard the work. He declined, telling them that he had no ability for carving.

Besides, Nicci had been eager to move on; Tanimura had only been a place to earn some money to buy provisions for the long journey ahead of them. Richard was glad to be away from the depressing sight of the carving going on.

Along the way southeast to Altur'Rang, in the cities they passed through, Richard saw many carvings on buildings, and many more freestanding in public squares, or in front of entrances. They depicted horrors: people being whipped by a grinning Keeper of the underworld; people stabbing out their own eyes; suffering people twisted, deformed, and crippled; people like packs of dogs, running on all fours, attacking women and children; people reduced to walking skeletons or covered in sores; woeful people throwing themselves into graves. In most such scenes the pitiful people were watched over by the Light of the all-perfect Creator represented by the flame.

The Old World was a celebration of misery.

Along the way south, they had stopped in a number of cities when Richard could find menial work temporary enough not to require waiting on lists. He and Nicci went for stretches eating cabbage soup that was mostly water. Sometimes they had rice or lentils or buckwheat mush, and, on occasion, the luxury of salt pork. Sometimes, Richard was able to catch fish, birds, or the odd hare. Living off the land in the Old World, though, was difficult. A lot of other people had the same idea. They both had gotten thinner on their long march. Richard began to understand the carvings of the skeletal people.

Nicci had set their destination, but dictated little else, leaving most decisions to him, complying without complaint. Week in and week out, they walked, occasionally paying a few copper pennies to ride in wagons headed their way. They crossed rivers straddled by cities large enough to have numbers of stone bridges, and went through town after town. There were vast fields of wheat, millet, sunflower, and any number of other crops, though much of the land lay fallow. They saw flocks of sheep and herds of cattle.

Farmers sold the travelers goat cheese and milk. Ever since the gift had awakened in him, Richard was able to eat meat only when not doing any fighting. He thought it might be part of the requirement to balance his need to sometimes take life. Since he wasn't doing any fighting, he could eat meat without it making him sick. Unfortunately, they could rarely afford meat. Cheese, which he had once loved, he could hardly stomach since his gift had come to life in him. Unfortunately, it was often eat cheese, or starve.

But it was the size of the Old World, and in particular its population, that most unsettled him. Richard had naively thought that the New and the Old Worlds must be somewhat alike. They were not. The New World was but a flea on the back of the Old.

From time to time on their journey south, vast columns of men at arms moved past them on their way north to the Midlands. Several times, it had taken days for all the soldiers to march past. Whenever he saw the rank upon rank of troops, he felt a wave of relief that Kahlan was trapped in their mountain home. He would hate to think of her fighting in an army facing as many men as he saw going to the war.

By spring, when she could finally get out of the mountain home, and all those Imperial Order troops could truly begin their siege of the New World, whatever resistance the D'Haran Empire put up would be crushed. Richard hoped General Reibisch chose not to go up against the Order. He hated to think of all those brave men being slaughtered under the weight of the coming onslaught.

At one small city, Nicci had gone to a stream to wash their clothes while Richard worked the day mucking out stalls at a large stable. A number of officials had come to town and there were more horses than the stablemaster could handle. Richard had been at the right place at the right time to get the job. Not long after the officials arrived and took all the rooms at the inns, a large unit of the Imperial Order troops marched in behind them and set up camp at the city limits.

Fortunately, Nicci was on the other side of the city doing their washing. Unfortunately, a squad of men passing through the city, and doing some drinking, decided to accept volunteers. Richard kept his head down as he carried water to the horses, but the sergeant saw him. At the wrong place at the wrong time, Richard was "volunteered" into the Imperial Order. The new volunteers were quartered in the center of the immense encampment.

That night, after it was dark and most of the men were asleep, Richard unvolunteered himself. It took him until three hours before sunrise to extract himself from his service to the Imperial Order. Nicci had gone to the stable and found out what had happened to him. Richard found her at their camp, pacing in the darkness. They quickly collected their things and marched south for the rest of the night. They went cross country, since the moon was out, rather than on the roads, in case a patrol came looking for him. From then on, whenever Richard saw soldiers he did his best to become invisible.

In general, though, it wasn't a serious concern. Hordes of youths, lusting after the promise of plunder, were only too eager to join the army. They often had to wait weeks or months to be accepted into training, so many were the numbers joining. Richard had seen crowds of them in the cities, playing games, gambling, drinking, fighting—young men dreaming of the glory of killing the evil foes of the great empire of the Order. They enjoyed the adoration of the populace when they joined the army to go off and fight the frightful wickedness and sin that was said to infect the New World.

Richard was horrified to see the numbers of people living in the Old World, because it meant that the Order's army already in the New World was hardly a drain on the populace—and only the beginning. He had thought that perhaps the Order might lose their enthusiasm for a war conducted so far from their homeland, or that the people of the Old World would tire of the hardship necessary to conduct such a war. He now knew that thought had been but a feeble daydream.

It didn't take a wizard, or a prophet, to know that the armies the New World could raise, even given wildly optimistic conditions, had no hope whatsoever of prevailing against the millions upon millions of soldiers Richard had seen pouring north, to say nothing of the ones he hadn't seen who would be taking other routes. The Midlands was doomed.

Ever since the people of Anderith chose the Order over freedom, he had known in his heart that the New World was going to fall to the Order. He felt no satisfaction in realizing how right he had been. Seeing the size of the enemy, he realized that freedom was lost, and resisting the Order was but suicide.

The course of events seemed irrevocable, the world lost to the Order. The future for him and Kahlan seemed no less hopeless.

By far the strangest place he and Nicci had visited in their journey southeast, a place she never spoke of afterward, had been less than a week south of Tanimura. Richard had still been in a dismal mood thinking about the carvings he had seen, when Nicci took an old, seldom-used track off the main road. It led back toward the hills, to a rather small city beside a quiet river.

Most of the businesses had been abandoned. The wind, at will, carried dust through the broken windows of warehouses. Many of the homes had fallen to ruin, their roofs caved in, weeds and vines doing their best to bring down crooked walls. Only the homes on the outskirts were still occupied, mostly by people raising animals and farming the surrounding land.

On the northern side of the city, one small store remained to sell staples to surrounding farmers. There was also a leather shop, a fortune-teller, and a lonely inn. In the center of town stood the bones of buildings, long since picked clean by scavengers. Several of the buildings still stood, but most had long ago collapsed. Richard and Nicci walked through the center of town watched only by a fitful wind.

At the southern edge, they arrived at the remains of what had once been a large brick building. Without a word, Nicci turned off the road and marched deliberately into the forlorn site. The wood beams and roof had been consumed by fire. A thick mat of weeds and brush were devouring the wood floor. The brick walls were all that was left, really, and they were mostly fallen to rubble, with only a portion of the east wall still tall enough to contain a lone window frame.

The wind ruffled Nicci's sunlit hair as she looked down the length of the skeletal remains of the building. Her arms languid at her sides, her back not quite as straight as it usually was, she stood vulnerable where once a roof would have sheltered her.

For nearly an hour, she was lost among the ghosts.

Richard stood off to the side, leaning a hip against the charred remains of part of a workbench, one of the only things left inside the brick frame.

"Do you know this place?" he finally asked her.

She blinked at his question. She stared into his eyes for a long time, as if he, too, were a ghost. She stepped close to him then, her blue eyes finally looking away to let her fingers reminisce as they glided lightly over the remains of the workbench.

"I grew up in this town," she answered in a distant voice.

"Oh." Richard gestured around them. "And this place?"

"They made armor here," she whispered.

He couldn't imagine why she would want to see such a place. "Armor?"

"The best armor in all the land. Double-proofed standard. Kings and noblemen came here to buy armor."

Richard gazed around at the ruins of the place, wondering what more there must be to the story.

"Did you know the man who made the armor?"

Her blue eyes seeing ghosts again, she shook her head.

"No," she whispered. "I'm so sorry, but I never knew him."

A tear ran down her cheek to drip off her smooth jaw. She seemed very much a child at that moment, alone in the world, and frightened.

Had he not known what he knew about her, Richard would have put his arms around this forlorn frail child and comforted her.

Nicci was tired, cold, and impatient. She wanted a room.

Her purpose in guiding Richard to the center of the empire in Altur'Rang was to bring him face-to-face with the righteous cause of the Order. She knew Richard to be a man of profound moral integrity, and she wanted to see how he would react when confronted by the undeniable virtue of his enemy's intentions.

She wanted Richard to learn how difficult it was for ordinary people to live, to get along in the world. She was curious as to how he would fare in the same circumstances—she wanted to throw him into the fire and see how he reacted to the heat, as it were. She had expected him to be agitated and frustrated by now. He remained cool and unruffled.

She thought he would be furious at learning what he had to do to get a job. He was not. He had listened to that Mr. Gudgeons fellow explaining the near impossible task that faced anyone wanting work. Nicci had expected him to punch the pompous official; instead, Richard had cheerfully thanked him. It was as if the things he so naively stood for, so selfishly defended when she had known him before, no longer mattered to him.

At the Palace of the Prophets when she had been his teacher, every time she thought she knew how he would react, he did something she would never have anticipated. He did that now, too, but in a subtly different way. What before had been, in a manner of speaking, unorganized youthful rebellion had turned to the dangerous scrutiny of a predator. Only the chains around his heart kept him from turning his claws on her.

When Nicci had first captured Richard, she had briefly seen, standing in the window of his house, a carving of a proud woman. Nicci had known, as sure as she knew night followed day, that Richard had carved it; it betrayed his unique vision, which she recognized. The statue was tangible evidence of a hidden side to his gift; it was a form of balance to his ability for war, yet she detected no magic in it.

Knowing that Richard had carved it, Nicci expected that he would have been interested in the carving job offered him back in Tanimura. He turned it down. He became moody and hardly spoke for several days afterward.

Whenever they went through a new city, she saw him taking in the statues and relief carvings. Since he, too, carved, she expected him to find such creations fascinating. He did not. She couldn't understand it. None were as finely executed as what he had carved, to be sure, but still, they were carvings and she thought he would be at least interested in them. She was baffled by his grim mood whenever he saw them.

One time, she had taken the two of them out of their way for no reason but to show him a famous city square and the heroic work of art proudly displayed there. It was her thought to bring him a bit of cheer at seeing such a widely heralded work. He was not cheered. Surprised, she had asked him why he appeared to so dislike the sculpture, called *Tormented Vision*.

"It's death," he had said with distant revulsion as he turned away from the widely worshiped work.

It was a grand scene of a group of men, some gouging out their eyes after having seen the perfect Light of the Creator. Other of the men at the base of the statue, who'd not blinded themselves, were being mauled by underworld beasts. The Keeper's minions shrank from the blinded men wailing at what they had seen before taking their own sight.

"No," Nicci said, trying not to laugh and thereby humiliate him for his unenlightened view. She sought instead to gently rectify his perception of the famous work by explaining it to him.

"It's a portrayal of the unworthy nature of mankind. It shows men who have just witnessed His perfect Light, and in so doing have thus been able to see the hopeless nature of man's depravity. That they would cut out their own eyes shows how perfect the Creator is that they could no longer bear to look upon themselves.

"These men in the statue are heroes for showing us that we must not arrogantly endeavor to rise above our corrupt essence, for that would be sinfully comparing ourselves to the Creator. It shows that we are but faceless, insignificant parts of a greater whole of mankind, which He created, and thus no single life can hold any importance. This work teaches us that only the society as a whole can be worthwhile. Those at the bottom, here, who failed to join in with their fellow man and blind themselves, are suffering their grim eternal fate at the Keeper's hands.

"Do you see, now? It honors mankind as the flawed creature he is, in order that we may see that each of us must devote ourselves to the betterment of our fellow man because that is our only means of doing good and honoring the Creator's creation—us. So, you see, it's not about death at all, but about the true nature of life."

Nicci had been taught that the statue was uplifting for the people, since it confirmed everything they knew to be true.

In the whole of her life, no one had ever given her a look that made her feel smaller than the look Richard gave her.

Nicci swallowed in horror at that look in his eyes—it was the complete opposite of that elusive thing she sought from him. Without saying a word, he had made her want nothing so much at that moment as to crawl under a rock and die.

She couldn't fathom how, but he made her feel unworthy to live. In some bewildering way, that look made her feel as blind as the men in the statue. He hadn't said one word, but it was days before she could bring herself to look him in the eye again.

Sometimes, Richard seemed meek when she expected fierceness, and intense when she expected indifference. She was beginning to wonder if she had been mistaken in thinking there was something special about him.

Once, she had even given in to despair of there really being anything in him worth discovering. Watching him sleep, dejected that she had dared hope to uncover some meaning to life beyond what her mother had taught her, she had sadly resolved that the next day, after visiting the place she had grown up, she would end the whole senseless undertaking and return to Jagang.

After they went to her father's business, though, she had seen again that quality in his gray eyes, and knew beyond doubt that she had not been mistaken.

This dance had only begun.

As they marched down the dim hallway of a rooming house, she gestured for Richard to stand aside. Nicci wanted this room. She wanted to lie down where it was dry and go to sleep. She resolutely rapped her knuckles on a door that looked as if it might come apart if she wasn't careful.

She peered down at the register she had and then stuffed it in her pack as she waited for the door to be answered. The lodging house, like all the others they had been to, was supposed to let rooms to those new to the city. The emperor needed workers.

In her mind, she imagined that this would be the place. She stared at the stain on the sickly green plaster. She imagined seeing the tea-colored stain, in the shape of a horse's rump with its tail flicked up, every day as she went about her life. She imagined Richard walking past the stain every day when he went to a job, and every night when he came home. Just like everyone else had to do.

Richard was watching the stairway beyond the door where Nicci again knocked. The stairs faced away. She couldn't understand why he watched all the things he watched, but she didn't discount his instincts. By the look on his face, he wasn't pleased about the shadowed stairway. Being a Sister of the Dark, she was hardly frightened by the simple things that frightened other people. She knocked again.

A voice inside told them to go away.

"We need a room," Nicci declared to the door in a tone that said she meant to have it. She knocked harder. "You're on the register. We want the room."

"It's a mistake," came the muffled voice from inside. "No room."

"Now look here," Nicci called out heatedly, "it's getting late—"

Three youths she hadn't seen sitting on the stairs swaggered around the newel post. The three were without shirts, showing off their muscles as young men were wont to do. All three had knives.

"Well, well," one of the youths said with a cocky grin as his eyes took her in with lewd intent. "What have we here? Two little drowned rats?"

"I like the fancy tail on the little blond rat," a second chortled.

Richard seized her arm and without a word shepherded her out the front door, back out into the rain. Nicci dragged her heels, protesting in a whisper the whole way. She couldn't believe that Lord Rahl himself, the Seeker of Truth, and the bringer of death would be intimidated by three men—boys, really.

As they descended the rickety front stoop, Richard lifted an eyebrow at her while tipping his head close. "You have no power, remember? We don't want this kind of trouble. I'd not like to get knifed over a room. This fight isn't worth it. Knowing when not to fight is just as important as knowing how."

Nicci wanted the room, but she finally conceded that Richard was probably right. The three sneering youths slouched at the door and watched, laughing, calling Richard names. So far, they weren't interested in going out in the rain. She had seen young men like them before. This latest crop was no different from any of the others—arrogant, aggressive, and often dangerous. At least they made good soldiers for Jagang's army.

Richard hurried her along the street. He cut through some of the narrow passageways, taking several turns at random just to be sure they wouldn't be followed.

The city of Altur'Rang seemed endless. In the overcast and rain, visibility was limited. The haphazard streets and byways were a confusing maze. It had been many years since she had been here last. With all the Order's efforts, the place still had fallen on hard times. She feared to think of what it would have been like had the Order not been here to help.

When they emerged on a wider street, they found shelter under a small overhanging roof along with a small group of others trying to stay out of the rain. Nicci hugged herself against the cold. Richard, along with the others huddled under the roof, watched the occasional wagon making its way past on the muddy street. She didn't know how Richard could keep warm in such weather. She appreciated his warmth, though, when the small crowd pressed her up against him. Richard glanced down at her, seeing her shiver, but he couldn't bring himself to put an arm around her to help keep her warm. She didn't ask.

Nicci sighed; the Old World didn't stay cold for long. In another day or two it would again be warm and muggy.

When she had been at the crumbled remains of her father's business, just before they left, Richard had looked as if he almost wanted to put his arms around her and comfort her. As much as he hated her, as much as he wanted to get away from her, he had been moved to sympathy.

Standing in the ruins, Nicci had let the memories wash through her, and had reveled in the exquisite anguish.

Richard's eyes were fixed on something. She followed his gaze and saw that a wagon not far down the street was moving with an odd wiggle. Almost as soon as she noticed it, the wheel broke with a loud crack.

With the strain imposed by the wagon slipping and being twisted in the ruts, the spokes had snapped under the heavy load. The side of the wagon bed dropped with a splash. People on the walkway were splattered with mud. They cursed the two men in the wagon. The four-horse team struggled to a halt as the uneven load broke the axle, causing the good rear wheel to snap its spokes, too. The whole rear of the wagon collapsed into the mud.

The two men climbed down to assess the damage. The rawboned driver cursed and kicked at the broken wheel lying at a lopsided angle. The other man, shorter and stoutly built, calmly checked the rest of the wagon and its load.

With a frown of curiosity, Richard nudged Nicci ahead of him as he moved down the street toward the wagon. She went reluctantly, unhappy to be out from under the roof.

"We have to," the husky man said with calm resolve. "It's only a short distance."

The other cursed again. "It's not my job, Ishaq, and you know it. I'll not do it!"

Then Ishaq threw up his hands in a helpless gesture as his headstrong partner went to the front of the wagon and urged the team on, managing to drag the wagon to the side of the road and out of the way of the other wagons that were beginning to back up down the street. Once he had the wagon to the side, he started unhitching the team.

The man at the back of the wagon turned and peered around at the people watching.

"I need some help," Ishaq called to the sparse crowd.

"Doing what?" a nearby man asked.

"I've got to get this load of iron to the warehouse." He stretched his thick neck and pointed. "Just there—in the brick building with the faded red paint on the side."

"How much will you pay?" the bystander asked.

Ishaq was getting frustrated as he glanced over his shoulder and saw his partner leading the horses away. "I'm not authorized to pay anything, not without approval, but I'm sure that if you came round tomorrow—"

The people watching laughed with knowing disgust and went on their way. The man stood in the downpour, ankle deep in mud, alone. He sighed and turned to his wagon, pulling back the tarp to reveal iron bar stock.

Richard stepped out into the street. Nicci wanted to check some more rooms on the list before it got dark. She snatched at his sleeve, but he only gave her a scolding look. She huffed her displeasure but followed anyway as he made his way through the mud to the man struggling to pull a long bar from the wagon bed.

"Ishaq, is it?" Richard asked.

The man turned and gave Richard a nod. "That's right."

"If I help you, Ishaq," Richard asked, "will I really get paid tomorrow? The truth, now."

Ishaq, a stocky fellow with a curious red hat with a narrow brim all around, finally shook his head in resignation.

"Well," Richard said, "if I help you get this load into your warehouse, then would you allow me and my wife to sleep in there where we could get out of the rain for the night?"

The man scratched his neck. "I'm not allowed to let anyone in there. What if something happened? What if things came up missing? I'd be out of work"—he snapped his fingers—"quick as that."

"Just until tomorrow. I only want to get her out of the rain before she comes down sick. I have no use for iron. Besides, I don't rob people."

The man scratched his neck again as he gazed back at the wagon over his shoulder. He glanced at Nicci. She was shivering and it was not an act. He peered at Richard.

"Sleeping in the warehouse for one night is not a fair price for lugging all this in there. It will take hours."

"If you agree to it, and I agree to it," Richard said over the sound of the rain, "then it's a fair price. I asked for no more, and I'm willing to do it for that price."

The man stared at Richard as if he might be crazy. He pulled off his red hat and scratched his head of dark hair. He swept his wet hair back and replaced the hat.

"You would have to clear out when I come first thing in the morning with a new wagon. I could get in trouble—"

"I'll not let you get in trouble over me. If I should get caught, I'll say I broke in."

The man thought about it for a moment, looking surprised at the last term Richard had thrown in an effort to close the deal. The man took another look over his shoulder at the load, then nodded his consent.

Ishaq hoisted a long bar of steel and put his shoulder under it. Richard lifted two and extended his arm forward to steady it, resting the heavy steel on the bunched muscles of his shoulder.

"Come on," he said to Nicci. "Let's get you inside where you can start to dry out and get warm."

She tried to lift a steel bar to help, but it was beyond her strength. There were times when Nicci missed her power. She could at least feel it through the link to the Mother Confessor. It took more effort, but even at this great of a distance she was still able to maintain the link. She walked beside Richard as they followed the man to the dry room Richard had just won for her.

The next day dawned clear. Rainwater still dripped from the eaves, though. The night before, as Richard helped Ishaq lug the load into the warehouse, Nicci had used a light rope Richard had in his pack, stringing it between racks so she could hang up their wet things. By morning, most of their clothes were reasonably dry.

They'd slept on wooden pallets, the only other choice being the dirt. Everything smelled of iron dust, and was covered with a fine black film. There was nothing in the warehouse to keep them warm, other than a single lantern Ishaq had left them, over which Nicci could at least warm her hands. They slept as best they could in their wet clothes. By morning, those, too, were reasonably dry.

Much of the night, Nicci hadn't slept, but, by the light of that lantern warming her hands, had watched Richard sleep as she thought about his gray eyes. It had been a shock to see those eyes in her father's business. It brought back a flood of memories.

Richard opened the warehouse door just enough to squeeze through and carried their things out into the breaking dawn. The sky over the city looked as if it were rusting. He left her to watch their things while he went back in to lock the door from inside. She could hear him climbing the racks in the warehouse to get up to a window. He had to jump to the ground.

When Ishaq finally came up the street with the fresh wagon, Richard and Nicci were sitting on a short wall on the entrance road to the warehouse doors. When the wagon rolled past them into the yard outside the building and came to a halt before the double doors, Nicci saw that the driver who had abandoned Ishaq the night before was at the reins.

The lanky driver set the brake as he eyed them suspiciously.

"What's this?" he asked Richard.

"I'm sorry to bother you," Richard said, "but I just wanted to get here before you opened up so I could inquire if there might be any work available."

Ishaq glanced at Nicci, seeing that she was dried out. He eyed the locked door and realized Richard had kept his word, and kept him from the possibility of getting in trouble for letting someone sleep in the warehouse.

"We can't hire people," the driver said. "You have to go to the office and put your name on the list."

Richard sighed. "I see. Well, thank you, gentlemen. I'll give it a try. A good day to you both."

Nicci had learned to recognize in Richard's voice when he was up to something. He gazed up the street, and then down the street, as if he were lost. He was up to something, now. He seemed to be giving Ishaq an opportunity to offer more than he had paid for the help. Ishaq had let Richard carry twice as much of the load the night before. Richard had done so without a word of protest.

Ishaq cleared his throat. "Hold on there." He climbed down from the wagon to unlock the door, but paused before Richard. "I'm the load master. We need another man. You look to have a strong back." Using the toe of his boot, he drew a little map in the mud. "You go to the office"—he lifted his thumb over his shoulder—"down this street, here, to the third turn, then right, past six more streets." He made an X in the mud. "There's the office. You get your name on the list."

Richard smiled and bowed his head. "I'll do that, sir."

Nicci knew that Richard remembered Ishaq's name, but he was playing like he didn't for the sake of the driver, whom Richard didn't trust, after the man had abandoned his fellow the night before. What Richard didn't understand was that the driver had only done what he was supposed to do. It was not permitted for one man to take the work that belonged to others. That was stealing. The load was the responsibility of the load man, not the driver.

"You go enlist first in the load workers' group," Ishaq told Richard. "Pay your dues. They have an office in the same building. Then you go put your name on the list for the job. I'm in the citizen workers' group that goes before the review assembly to consider new applicants. You just sit tight and wait outside. When we meet, later on, I'll vouch for you."

The driver leaned out and spat over the far side of the wagon. "Why you want to go and do that, Ishaq? You don't even know this fellow."

Ishaq scowled up at the driver. "Did you see anyone at the hall who was as big as this fellow? We need another loader for the warehouse. We just lost a man and need a replacement. You want me to get stuck with some skinny old man so as I'll have to do all the work?"

The driver chuckled. "Suppose not."

Ishaq gestured toward Nicci. "Besides, look at his young wife. She needs some meat on her bones, don't you think? Looks like a nice young couple."

The driver spat over the side of the wagon again. "I suppose."

Ishaq casually flicked a hand at Richard on his way to unlock the door to the warehouse. "You be there."

"I'll be there."

Ishaq paused and turned back. "Almost forgot—what's your name?"

"Richard Cypher."

Ishaq gave him a nod and turned back to the door. "I'm Ishaq. See you tonight, Richard Cypher. Don't you let me down—you hear? You turn out to be lazy and let me down, and I'll throw your sorry hide in the river with an iron bar tied around your neck."

"I won't let you down, Ishaq." Richard smiled. "I'm a good swimmer, but not that good."

As they trudged though the muddy streets on their way to find some food before they went to the offices to get on the list for work, Richard asked, "What's wrong?"

Nicci shook her head in disgust. "Ordinary people don't have your luck, Richard. Ordinary people suffer and struggle while your luck gets you into a job."

"If it was luck," Richard asked, "then how come my back hurts from lugging that load of iron bars into the warehouse?"

When Richard had finished unloading the last wagon of iron, he leaned forward and placed his hands on the pile, hanging his head as he panted. The muscles in his arms and shoulders throbbed. It was always easier having two men to handle the bars, one in the wagon, and one on the ground, but the man who was supposed to help with the load had quit several days back, saying he hadn't been treated properly. Richard didn't really miss him all that much; even when the man got up off his backside, his assistance was more trouble than it was worth.

The light coming in the high windows was fading, leaving the sky in the west a deep purple. Sweat ran down his neck, making trails through the black iron dust. He wished he could jump in a cool mountain lake. That thought, in and of itself, was refreshing. He let his mind go there as he caught his breath.

Ishaq came down the aisle with the lantern. "You work too hard, Richard."

"I thought I was hired to work."

Ishaq peered at Richard for a moment, one eye catching the harsh yellow light of the lantern he was holding. "Take my advice. You work too hard, it's only going to get you into trouble."

Richard had been working at the warehouse for three weeks, unloading wagons and loading others. He'd come to know a number of the other men. He had a good idea of what Ishaq meant.

"But I'm still worried about trying to swim with an iron bar wrapped around my neck."

Ishaq gave up on his scowl and grunted a laugh. "I was just spouting for Jori's sake, that day."

Jori was the driver who had refused to help unload the wagon when it broke down. Richard yawned. "I know, Ishaq."

"This isn't no farm, like where you came from. This is different, living under the ways of the Order. You got to take the needs of others in mind if you hope to get along. It's just the way the world is."

Richard caught the thread of caution in Ishaq's voice, and the meaning of the gentle warning.

"You're right, Ishaq. Thanks. I'll try to remember."

Ishaq gestured with his lantern toward the door. "Workers' group meeting tonight. Best be on your way."

Richard groaned. "I don't know. It's late and I'm tired. I'd really rather—"

"You don't want your name to start going around. You don't want people to start talking that you're not civic-minded."

Richard smirked. "I thought the meetings were voluntary."

Ishaq barked a laugh again. Richard collected his pack from a shelf in the back corner and then ran to the door so Ishaq could lock it.

Outside, in the gathering darkness, Richard could just make out Nicci's curvaceous form sitting on the wall at the warehouse entrance. Her curves often put him in mind of nothing so much as a snake. They had no room, yet, so she often came by the warehouse after she'd spent much of the day waiting in lines to buy bread and other necessities. They would walk together back to their shelter in a quiet alley about a mile away. Richard had paid a small price to some of the boys there to guard their place and make sure no one else took it. The boys were young enough to be thankful for the small price and old enough to be diligent about their job.

"Get any bread?" Richard asked as he approached.

Nicci hopped down off the wall. "No bread today—they were out. But I got us some cabbage. I'll make us a soup."

Richard's stomach was growling. He'd been hoping for bread so he could eat a piece right then. Soup would take time.

"Where's your pack? And if you bought cabbage, where is it?"

She smiled and produced something small. She held it out before them as they walked so as to silhouette it against the deep violet of dusk. It was a key.

"A room? We got a place?"

"I checked the lodging office this afternoon. Our name finally came up. They assigned a room to us. Mr. and Mrs. Cypher. We can sleep inside tonight. Good thing, too; it looks like it will rain tonight. I already put my things in our room."

Richard rubbed his sore shoulders. He felt a wave of revulsion at the sham she was putting him through . . . putting Kahlan through. There were times when he felt a hint of something profoundly important about her and what she was doing, but most of the time he was merely overwhelmed by the lunacy of it all.

"Where is this room?" He was hoping it wasn't clear over on the other side of the city.

"It's one we were at before—not too far from here. The one with the stain on the wall just inside the door."

"Nicci, they all had stains on the walls."

"The stain that looked like a horse's rear end with its tail flicked up. You'll see it soon."

Richard was starving. "I have to go to a workers' group meeting again tonight."

"Oh," Nicci said. "Workers' group meetings are important. They help keep a person's mind on what's proper and on everyone's duty to his fellow man."

The meetings were torture. Nothing worthwhile ever came about at the meetings. They sometimes lasted hours. There were people, though, who lived for the meetings so they could stand up in front of others and talk about the glory of the Order. It was their shining hour, their time to be somebody, to be important.

Those who didn't show up for the meetings were used as examples of people who weren't properly committed to the cause of the Order. If the absent person didn't mend his ways, it was possible he could end up being suspected of subversion. The lack of truth to the suspicion was irrelevant. Stating the charge made some people feel more important in a land where equality was held as the highest ideal.

Subversion seemed to be a dark cloud hovering constantly over the Old World. It wasn't at all unusual to see the city guard taking people into custody on suspicion of subversion. Torture produced confessions, which proved the veracity of the accuser. The people who spoke at length at the meetings had, by this logic, accurately pointed a finger at a number of insurrectionists, as evidenced by their confessions.

The undercurrent of tension in Altur'Rang left many worried over the constant scourge of insurrection—coming from the New World, it was said. Officials of the Order wasted no time in stamping it out whenever it was discovered. Other people were so consumed with fear that the finger would turn toward them that the speakers at the workers' group meetings were assured of having a large number of zealous supporters.

In many a public square, as a constant reminder of what would happen should you fall into the wrong company, the bodies of subversives were left to hang from high poles until the birds picked their bones clean. The running joke, if an incautious person said anything that sounded at all out of line, was "You looking to be buried in the sky?"

Richard yawned again as they turned down the street toward the meeting hall. "I don't remember the stain that looks like a horse's rear end."

Rocks crunched beneath their boots as they walked down the side of the dark street. Off ahead of them, in the distance, he could see Ishaq's lantern swinging as the man hurried to the meeting.

"You were paying attention to something else at the time. It's the room where those three live."

"Three what?"

A number of other people, some he knew, most he didn't, hastened along the street on their way to the meeting.

Richard remembered then. He stopped.

"You mean the place where those three bullies live—the three with the knives?"

He could just barely see her nod in the dim light. "That's the place."

"Great." Richard wiped a hand across his face as they started out again. "Did you ask if we could have a different room?"

"New people in the city are fortunate to get rooms. Rooms are assigned as your name comes up. If you turn it down, you go back to the bottom of the list."

"Did you have to give the landlord any money, yet?"

She shrugged. "Just what I had."

Richard ground his teeth as he walked. "That's all we have for the rest of the week."

"I can stretch the soup."

Richard didn't trust her. She probably somehow saw to it that they got that particular room. He suspected that she wanted to see what he would do about the three young men, now that he was forced into the situation. She was always doing little things, asking odd questions, making bold statements, just to see what his reaction would be, how he would handle matters. He couldn't imagine what it was she wanted from him.

He began to worry about the three. He remembered quite clearly how Cara's Agiel had caused Kahlan to suffer the same pain as Nicci. If those three abused Nicci, Kahlan would suffer it, too. That thought made him go cold and sweaty with worry.

At the workers' group meeting, Richard and Nicci sat on benches at the rear of a smoky room while people up front spoke about the glory of the Order, and how it helped all people to live a moral life. Richard's mind drifted to the brook behind the house he had built, to the sunlit summer afternoons watching Kahlan dangle her feet in the water. He ached with longing as his mind's eye traced the curve of her legs. There were speeches about every worker's duty to their fellow man. Many of the discourses were given in a droning monotone, having been repeated so often that it was clear that the words were meaningless, and that only the act of saying them mattered. Richard recalled Kahlan laughing as he caught the fish he'd put in jars for her. Many of the people, the group leaders, or citizen spokesmen, delivered with passion and fire their praise for the ways of the Order. A few people stood up and talked about those who weren't there, giving their names, saying what poor attitudes they had toward the welfare of their fellow workers. Whispers passed among the crowd.

After the speeches were given, some of the workers' wives stood up and explained that they had extra need of late because they had just had new children, or their husbands were laid up, or the relatives they cared for were ill. After each spoke, there was a show of hands. If you agreed to do the right thing and have the group help them, then you raised your hand.

The names of these who didn't raise their hand were noted. Ishaq had explained to Richard that you were allowed not to raise your hand, if you didn't agree, but if you did it very often, you were put on a watch list. Richard didn't know what a watch list was, but it was easy enough to surmise, and Ishaq had told Richard that he didn't want to be on one, and to see to it that he raised his hand more often than not.

Richard raised it every time. He didn't really care what happened. He had no interest in taking part, no interest in trying to make things better, and no interest in how well or poorly people's lives went. Most seemed to want the comfort of the Order running their lives, relieving them of the burden of thinking on their own. Just like Anderith. Nicci seemed surprised, and occasionally even disappointed, to see his hand go up every time, but didn't object or question.

He was hardly even aware of his hand going up. He was smiling inwardly as he recalled the wonder in Kahlan's expression, the astonishment in her green eyes, when she saw *Spirit* for the first time. Richard would have carved a mountain for her, just to see her tearful joy in seeing something she admired, something she cherished, something she valued.

Another man spoke, complaining about the conditions, how unfair they were, and how he had been forced to quit rather than subject himself to such abuse by the transport company. He was the man who had quit and left Richard to handle the loads by himself. Richard raised his hand along with all the others to grant the man full wages for six months in recompense.

After the show of hands, and some whispering and scratching on paper as all the obligations were figured up, the healthy working members were assessed their just share to help those in need. Those who were able, Richard had been told, had a duty to produce with all their effort in order to help those who couldn't.

When men's names were called, they stood to hear the share to be taken from their wages the next week. Because he was new, Richard's name was called last. He stood, staring off across the dimly lit room at the people in moth-eaten coats sitting behind the long table made of two old doors. Ishaq sat at one end, going along with the others in everything. Several of the women still had their heads together. When they finished, they whispered to the chairman and he nodded.

"Richard Cypher, being as you are new, you still have some catching up to do on your duty to your workers' group. Your next weeks wages are assessed as due in aid."

Richard stood dumbly for a moment. "How am I to eat—to pay my rent?"

People in the room turned to frown at him. The chairman slapped his hand on the table, calling for silence.

"You should thank the Creator to be blessed with good health so as you can work, young man. Right now, there are those who are not as fortunate in life as you, those with greater need than you. Suffering and need comes before selfish personal enrichment."

Richard sighed. What did it really matter? After all, he was lucky in life.

"Yes, sir. I see what you mean. I'm happy to volunteer my share toward those with needs."

He wished Nicci hadn't given away all their money.

"Well," he said to Nicci as they shuffled out into the night, "I guess we can ask the landlord for the rent money back. We can stay on where we were staying before, until I can work some more and save up some money."

"They don't give rent money back," she said. "The landlord will understand our need and let our debt build until we can start paying on it. Next meeting, you just have to go up before the review board and explain your hardship. If you present it properly, they will give you a hardship charity to pay your rent."

Richard was exhausted. He felt like he were having some kind of silly dream.

"Charity? It's my wages—for the work I do."

"That's a selfish way of looking at it, Richard. The job is at the grace of the workers' group, the company, and the Order."

He was too tired to argue. Besides, he didn't expect any justice in anything done in the name of the Order. He just wanted to go to their new room and get some sleep.

When they opened the door, one of the three youths was pawing through Nicci's pack. Holding some of her underthings in one hand, he aimed a smirk back over his shoulder at them.

"Well, well," he said as he stood. He still wore no shirt. "Looks like the two drowned rats have found a hole to live in." His leering gaze slid to Nicci. He wasn't looking at her face.

Nicci snatched the pack away first, then her things from his other hand. She stuffed her personal clothes back in the pack while he watched, grinning the whole time. Richard feared she might abandon the link to Kahlan in order to use her power, but she only glared at the youth.

The room reeked of mold. The low ceiling made Richard feel uncomfortably hemmed in. The ceiling had once been whitewashed, but was now dark with soot from candles and lamps, making the room feel cavelike. A candle sitting on a rusted bracket by the door provided the only light. A wardrobe stood crookedly in the corner in front of dirty walls spotted with flyblows. The wardrobe was missing a door. Two wooden chairs at a table under one small window on the far wall were the only place to sit, other than the warped and gouged pine floor. The small squares of window glass were opaque under a variety of different-colored layers of paint.

Through a small triangle in the corner where the glass was broken out, Richard could see the gray wall of the next building.

"How did you get in here?" Nicci snapped.

"Master key." He waved it like a king's pass. "See, my father's the landlord. I was just checking your things for subversive writings."

"You can read?" Nicci sniped. "I would have to see that to believe it."

The defiant grin never left his face. "We'd not like to find we have subversives living under our roof. Could endanger everyone else. My father has a duty to report any suspicious activity."

Richard stepped aside to let the young man by as he headed for the door, but then caught his arm as the youth picked up the candle.

"That's our candle," Richard said.

"Yeah? What makes you think so?"

Richard tightened his grip on the bare, lean, muscular arm. Looking him in the eye, he gestured with his other hand.

"Our initials are scratched in the bottom, there."

Before he thought, the young man instinctively turned the candle to have a look. The hot wax spilled over his hand. He dropped the candle with a yelp.

"Oh my, I am sorry," Richard said. He stooped and picked up the candle. "You're all right, I hope. You didn't get any of that burning wax in your eyes, did you? Hot wax in your eyes hurts something fierce."

"Yeah?" He swiped his straight dark hair back from his eyes. "How would you know that?"

"Back where I came from, I saw it happen to some poor fellow."

Richard leaned partway out into the hall, into the light of another candle on a shelf. With his thumbnail, he made a show of carving an R and a C in the bottom of the candle. "See, here? My initials."

The youth didn't bother to look. "Uh-huh."

He swaggered out the door. Richard went with him and lit the candle from the flame of the one in the hall. Before walking away, the young man turned back with a haughty look.

"How did that fellow manage to be stupid enough to get hot wax in his eyes? Was he a big dumb ox like you?"

"No," Richard said offhandedly. "No, not at all. He was a cocky young man who foolishly put his hands on another man's wife. He got the hot wax dripped in his eyes by the husband."

"Yeah? Well why didn't the dumb jackass just shut his eyes?"

Richard gave the lad a deadly smile for the first time.

"Because his eyelids had been cut off, first, so he couldn't close them. You see, where I come from, anyone touching a woman against her wishes isn't treated indulgently."

"Yeah?"

"Yeah. The young man's eyelids weren't the only thing that got cut off."

The young man swiped his black hair back again. "You threatening me, ox?"

"No. There would be nothing I could do to you that would harm you more than what you're already doing to harm yourself."

"What's that supposed to mean?"

"You are never going to amount to anything. You will always be the worthless muck people scrape from their shoes. You only get one life and you are wasting

360

yours. That's a terrible shame. I doubt you will ever know what it is to be truly happy, to achieve anything of worth, to have genuine pride in yourself. You bring it all on yourself, and I could do no worse to you."

"I can't help what life deals me."

"Yes, you can. You create your own life."

"Yeah? How do you figure?"

Richard gestured around himself. "Look at the pigsty you live in. Your father is the landlord. Why don't you show some pride and fix up the place?"

"He's the landlord, not the owner. The man who owned it was a greedy bastard, charging more rent than many could afford. The Order took the place over. For his crimes against the people they tortured the owner to death. My father was given the job of landlord. We just run the place to help out fools like you who don't have a place; we've no money to go around fixing up the building."

"Money?" Richard pointed. "It takes money to pick up that garbage left there in the hall?"

"I didn't put it there."

"And these walls—it doesn't take money to wash the walls. Look at the ceiling in this room. It hasn't been washed in a decade, at least."

"Hey, I'm no scrub woman."

"And the front stoop? Someone is going to break their neck on it. Could be you, or your father. Why don't you do something worthwhile for a change and fix it?"

"I told you, we've no money to fix things."

"It doesn't take money. You just need to take it apart, clean the joints, and put in some new wedges. You can cut them from any little scrap of wood lying around."

The young man wiped his palms on his pants. "If you're so smart, then why don't you fix the stairs?"

"Good idea. I will."

"Yeah?" His sneer returned. "I don't believe you."

"Tomorrow, after I get home from work, I will fix the stairs. If you show up, I'll teach you how it's done."

"I might show up just to see some dupe going to the work of fixing something that isn't even his, and for nothing besides."

"It isn't for nothing. It's because I use the front steps, too, and for the pleasure in the place where I live. I care if my wife falls and breaks her leg. But if you want to come and learn how to fix the steps, you will wear a shirt out of respect for the women in your building."

"And if I show up and watch you, and I don't wear a stupid shirt like some old geezer?"

"Then I wouldn't have enough respect for you to bother teaching you how to fix the stairs. You will learn nothing, then."

"What if I don't want to learn something?"

"Then you will have taught me something, about you, instead."

He rolled his dark eyes. "Why should I care about learning to fix some dumb stairs?"

"You shouldn't necessarily care about fixing some stairs, but if you care about yourself, you should care about learning—even learning simple things. You come to have pride in yourself only by accomplishing things, even from fixing some old stairs."

"Yeah? I got pride in myself."

"You intimidate people and then mistake that for respect. Others can't grant you self-respect, even others who care about you. You have to earn self-respect yourself. All you know right now is how to stand around and look stupid."

He folded his arms. "Who you calling—"

Richard jabbed a finger against the young man's smooth chest, forcing him back a pace. "You only get one life. Is that all you want out of it—standing around calling names, scaring people with your gang? Is that all you want your one life to mean to you?

"Anyone who wants more out of life, who wants their life to mean something, would care about learning things. Tomorrow I'm going to fix those stairs. Tomorrow we'll see what sort you are."

The youth folded his arms again in a defiant stance. "Yeah? Well, maybe I'd rather spend time with my friends."

Richard shrugged. "That's why your lot in life isn't fate. I don't have any say in much of my life, but I make whatever choices I can make in my own rational best interest. It's my choice to fix those stairs and make the place I live a little better— instead of whining and waiting and hoping for someone else to do something for me. I have pride that I know how to do that for myself.

"Fixing stairs isn't going to make you a man, but it's going to make you a little more confident in yourself. If you want, bring your friends, and I'll teach you all how to use those knives of yours for something more than just waving in people's faces."

"We might come to laugh at you working, Ox."

"Fine. But if you and your pals want to learn anything of worth, then you'd better start out by showing me you mean to learn by showing respect and showing up with shirts. That's the first choice you have. If you make it wrong, then your choices as you go along are only going to become more limited. And my name is Richard."

"Like I said, you might be good for a laugh." He made a face. "Richard."

"Laugh all you want. I know my own worth and don't need to prove it to someone who doesn't know theirs. If you want to learn, you know what you must do. If you ever wave a knife at me again, though—or, worse, my wife—then you will be making the last of your many mistakes in life."

He chose to ignore the threat with more bravado. "What am I ever going to be? Some dupe, like you, working your tail off for that greedy Ishaq and his transport company?"

"What's your name?"

"Kamil."

"Well, Kamil, I work in exchange for wages so I can support myself and my wife. I have have something of value—myself. Someone values my worth enough to pay me for my time and ability. Right now, choosing to work at loading wagons is one of the few choices I have to make in my life. I chose to fix the steps because it improves my life." Richard narrowed his eyes. "And what does Ishaq have to do with it, anyway?"

"Ishaq? He's the one who owns the transport company."

"Ishaq is just the load master."

"Ishaq used to live here, back before the Order took over the building. My father knew him. Matter of fact, you'll be sleeping in his parlor. Back then, it was his transport company. He chose the path of enlightenment over greed, though, when it was offered him. He let the citizen workers' group help him to learn to be a better citizen of the Order, learn his place under the Creator. Now he knows he's no better than any of the rest of us—even me."

Richard glanced at Nicci, who was standing in the middle of their room, watching the conversation. He'd forgotten all about her. He didn't feel like talking anymore.

"I'll see you tomorrow evening, whether you come to laugh or to learn. It's your life, Kamil, and your choice."

The sun was just coming up. Dusty shafts of light angled into the warehouse through the high windows. When he saw Ishaq coming down the aisle to give him the list of iron to be loaded for various wagons, Richard hopped down off the rack where he'd been waiting.

Richard hadn't seen the load master for a week. "Ishaq. Are you all right? Where have you been?"

The burly load master hurried up the aisle. "Hello to you, too."

"I'm sorry—hello. I was worried. Where have you been?"

He made a face. "Meetings. Always meetings. Wait in this office, wait in that office. No work, just meetings for this and for that. I had to go see people to try to arrange for loads people need. Sometimes I think no one really wants any goods to move in this city. It would be easier for them if everyone got paid, but had to do no work—then they would not have to sign their name on a piece of paper and worry if maybe someday they will be called to account for having done it."

"Ishaq, is it true that this transport company used to be yours?"

The man paused to catch his breath. "Who tells you these things?"

"What about it? Did the transport company used to be yours?"

Ishaq shrugged. "Still is, I guess."

"What happened?"

"What happened? Nothing happened, except maybe I got smart and figured out it was more work than I needed."

"What did they threaten you with?"

Ishaq peered at Richard for a time. "Where are you from? You don't seem like any farmboy I ever met."

Richard smiled. "You didn't answer my question, Ishaq."

The man gestured irritably. "What for you want to know about past history? Past is past. A man has to look at the way things are and do the best he can from what life presents him. A choice was put to me, and I made it. Things are they way they are. Wishing don't put food before my children."

Richard's inquisitive frown suddenly felt cruel on his face. He let it go. "I understand, Ishaq. I really do. I'm sorry."

The man shrugged again. "Now I work here just like everyone else. Much easier. I must follow the same rules, or I could lose my job, just like everyone else. Everyone is equal, now."

"Praise be to the Order." Ishaq smiled at Richard's gibe. Richard held out his hand. "Let's have the list."

The load master handed over the paper. It only had the names of two places on it, with some directions for grade, length, and amounts.

"What's this?" Richard asked.

"We need a loader to go with a wagon to pick up some iron and see it delivered."

"So, I'm working on the wagons, now? Why? I thought you needed me in the warehouse."

Ishaq took off his red hat and scratched his head of dark, thinning hair. "We had some . . . complaints."

"About me? What did I do? You know I've worked hard."

"Too hard." Ishaq readjusted his hat on his head. "Men in the warehouse say you are petty and spiteful. Their words, not mine. They say you make them feel bad by flaunting how young and strong you are. They say you are laughing behind their backs."

Many of the men were younger than Richard, and strong enough.

"Ishaq, I never—"

"I know, I know. But they feel that you do. Don't make trouble for yourself, now. Their feelings are what matter, not what is."

Richard let out a frustrated sigh. "But I was told by the workers' group that I have the ability to work whereas others don't, and that I was supposed to contribute my full effort in order to help relieve the strain on those less able—those who don't have my ability. They said that I would lose the job if I didn't do my full effort."

"It's a fine line to walk."

"And I stepped over the line."

"They want you dismissed."

Richard sighed. "So, I'm through, here?"

Ishaq waggled his hand. "Yes, and no. You are dismissed from the warehouse for having a bad attitude. I convinced the committee to give you another chance and let you be moved to the wagons. The wagons aren't as much work, because you can only load it, and then when you get to where it's going, you unload it. Can't get in much trouble, that way."

Richard nodded. "Thanks, Ishaq."

Ishaq's gaze sought refuge among the racks of iron and the bins of charcoal and long rows of ore that needed delivery. He scratched his temple.

"The pay is less."

Richard brushed the iron and ore dust from his hands and rear of his pants. "What's the difference? They just take it from me anyway and give it out. I'm not really losing any pay, other people are losing my pay."

Ishaq chuckled and clapped Richard on the shoulder. "You are the only one around here I can count on, Richard. You are different than the others—I feel I can talk to you and it won't drift to other ears."

"I wouldn't do that to you."

"I know. That's why I tell you what I don't tell the others. I am expected to be equal, and to work like anyone else, but I am also expected to provide jobs. They took my business, but they still expect me to run it for them. Crazy world."

"You don't know the half of it, Ishaq. So what about this wagon-loading job? What is it you need done?"

"The blacksmith out at the site is dealing me a fit."

"Why?"

"He has orders for tools, but he has no iron. Lots of people are waiting on things." He swept a hand out at the rack of iron. "Most of this is what was ordered last autumn. Last autumn! It's nearly spring and it's only now come in. It's all been promised to those who ordered it before."

"So, why did it take so long for it to get here?"

Ishaq slapped his forehead. "Maybe you are an ignorant farmboy, after all. Where you been? Under rocks? You can't just get things because you want them. You got to wait your turn. Your order must pass before the review board."

"Why?"

"Why, why, why. Is that all you know?"

Ishaq sighed and said something under his breath about the Creator testing his patience. He slapped the back of his fingers to the palm of his other hand as he explained it to Richard.

"Because you've got to think of others, that's why. You got to take other people's needs into consideration. You have to consider the good of everyone. If I get all the runs picking up and delivering the iron, then what chance have others who want to do the same? If I have all the business, that's unfair. It would put people out of work. What's available has to be divided up. The board of supervision must make sure everything is equal to all. Some people can't handle the orders so fast as I can, or they have trouble, or they can't get workers, or their workers have troubles, so I got to wait until they can catch up."

"It's your business, why can't—"

"Why, why, why. Here, take this order. I don't need to have that blacksmith come all the way down here again and yell at me. He's in trouble with his orders and he needs the iron."

"Why is he in trouble? I thought everyone had to wait their turn."

Ishaq lifted an eyebrow and lowered his voice. "His customer is the Retreat."

"The Retreat? What's that?"

"The Retreat." Ishaq spread his arms, indicating something big. "That's the name of the place being built for the emperor."

Richard hadn't known the name. The emperor's new palace was the reason for all the workers coming to Altur'Rang. He supposed it was the reason Nicci had insisted they come to the city, too. She had some interest in having him be part of the grand project. He assumed it was her grotesque sense of irony.

"The new palace is going to be huge," Ishaq said, waving his arms again. "A lot of work for a lot of people. It will be work for years building the Retreat."

"So, when the goods are for the Order, then you had better deliver, I take it."

Ishaq smiled and dipped a deep nod. "Now, you are starting to understand, Mr. Richard why, why, why. The blacksmith is working directly from the orders of the builders of the palace, who report to the highest people. The builders need tools and things made. They don't want to hear excuses from a lowly blacksmith. The blacksmith doesn't want to hear excuses from me, but I have to go by what the review board says—he doesn't, he goes by what the palace says. I'm in the middle."

Ishaq paused when one of the other loaders came down the aisle with a piece of paper. Ishaq read the paper the man gave him, while the man gave a sidelong look at Richard. Ishaq sighed and gave brief directions to the man. After he was gone, Ishaq turned back to Richard.

"I can only transport what the review board allows me to move. That paper, just now—it was instructions from the board for me to hold a shipment of timbers to the mines because the load was going to go to a company that needs the work. You see? I can't put other people out of business by being unfair and delivering more than they do, or else I have trouble, and I get replaced by someone who will not be so unfair to his competitors. Ah, it's not like the old days, when I was young and foolish."

Richard folded his arms. "You mean to say that if you do a good job, you get in trouble—just like I did."

"Good job. Who's to say what is a good job. Everybody's got to work together for the good of everybody. That is a good job—if you help your fellow man."

Richard watched a couple of men off in the distance loading a wagon with charcoal. "You don't really believe that mouthful of mush, do you, Ishaq?"

Ishaq sighed in a long suffering manner. "Richard, please, load the wagon when you get to the foundry and then go with the wagon out to the Retreat and unload it at the blacksmith's shop. Please. Don't get sick on me, or get a bad back, or have infirm children in the middle of the run? I don't need to see the blacksmith again, or I will have to go swimming with an iron bar around my neck."

Richard grunted a laugh. "My back is feeling fine."

"Good. I'll get a driver over here to drive the wagon." Ishaq waggled a cautionary finger. "And don't ask the driver to help load or unload. We don't need that kind of grievance brought up at the next meeting. I had to beg Jori not to lodge a complaint after I asked him to help me unload the wagon that day in the rain, when the wheels broke—the day you helped me get the load to the warehouse. Remember?"

"I remember."

"Please, don't give Jori any trouble. Don't touch the reins—that's his job. Be a good fellow, then? Get the iron loaded and unloaded so that blacksmith doesn't come to see me again?"

"Sure, Ishaq. I won't make any trouble for you. You can trust me."

"There's a good fellow." Ishaq started away, but turned back. "Was not so much trouble on a farm—am I right?"

"No, it wasn't. I wish I was back there, now."

Before he got far, Ishaq turned back once more. "You be sure to bow and scrape if you see any of those priests. You hear?"

"Priests? What priests? How will I know them?"

"Brown robes and creased caps—oh, you'll know them. You can't miss them. If you see any, you be on your best manners. If a priest suspects you of having an improper attitude toward the Creator or such, he can have you tortured. The priests are Brother Narev's disciples."

"Brother Narev?"

"The high priest of the Fellowship of Order—" Ishaq waved his arms impatiently. "I have to get Jori to come with the wagon. Please, Richard, do as I ask. That blacksmith will feed me to his forge if I don't have that iron out there today. Please, Richard, get that load out there. Please?"

Richard gave Ishaq a smile in order to put his mind at ease.

"You have my word, Ishaq. The blacksmith will have the iron."

Ishaq heaved a sigh and hurried off to find his driver.

I t was late in the muggy afternoon by the time they made it to the site of the Retreat. Sitting in the wagon beside Jori as they cleared the top of the final hill, Richard was awestruck by the sight. It was beyond huge. He couldn't imagine how many square miles had been cleared. Gangs of thousands of men, looking like ants spread out below, worked in lines with shovels and baskets reshaping the contour of the land.

Jori was disinterested in the construction, and only spat over the side, offering the occasional "I suppose" to some of Richard's questions.

The foundation was still being laid in deep trenches, enabling Richard, looking down from the road, to see on the ground the outline of the future structure. It was hard to fathom how enormous the building was going to be. Seeing the specks moving slowly beside it, it was hard to keep in mind that they were men.

For sheer size, the structure would rival anything Richard had ever seen. There were miles of grounds and gardens going in. Fountains and other towering structures along entrance roads were beginning to be erected. Sweeping stretches of mazes were being constructed with hedges. Hillsides were dotted with trees that had been planted according to a grand plan.

The Retreat faced a lake in what was to be that majestic park. The short side of the main building was to run a quarter mile along the river. Stone pilings marched partway out into the river, with a series of connecting arches just starting to be constructed. Apparently, part of the palace was to extend out over the water, with docks for the emperor's pleasure craft.

Across the river lay more of the city. On the palace side of the river, too, the city spread all around, though at a great distance from the Retreat. Richard couldn't imagine how many buildings and people had been displaced for the construction. This was to be no distant and remote emperor's palace, but rather it was set right in the center of Altur'Rang. Roads were being paved with millions of cobbles, giving the multitudes of citizens of the Order access to come and see the grand structure. There were already crowds of people standing behind rope barricades, watching the construction.

Despite the poverty of the Old World, it would appear that this grand palace was to be a crown jewel of unsurpassed splendor.

Stone of various kinds lay in great piles. In the distance, Richard could see men working at cutting it into the required shapes. The heavy afternoon air rang with the faraway knells of hundreds of hammers and chisels. There were stockpiles of granite and marble in a variety of colors, and massive quantities of limestone blocks. Special quarry wagons waited in serpentine columns to deliver yet more. The long blocks of stone, called lifts, were slung under heavy beams that bridged the front and rear axles. Huts and great open shelters had been built for the stone workers so they could work no matter the weather. Timber was stickered in row upon row of huge stacks covered with purpose-built roofs. The overflow was covered in canvas. Small mountains of materials for mortar were scattered around the foundation, looking like anthills, the illusion aided by all the dark specks of men moving about.

Away from the site itself, on a road that snaked its way along the side of a hill, among a small city of new work buildings overlooking the site, lay the blacksmith's shop. It was quite large, compared with such places Richard had seen before. Of course, Richard had never seen anything on this scale being built. He had seen grand places that already existed. To see one just beginning was a revelation. The sheer scale of everything was disorienting.

Jori expertly backed his team, putting the rear of the wagon right at double doors standing open into blackness.

"There you be," Jori said. It was a long speech for the lanky driver. He pulled out a loaf of bread and a waterskin filled with ale and climbed down from the wagon to find a place farther down the hill, where he could sit and watch the building while Richard worked at unloading the iron.

The blacksmith's shop was dark and stifling hot, even in the outer, cluttered, stockroom. Like all blacksmith's shops, the walls in the workroom were covered in soot. Windows were kept to a minimum, mostly located overhead and covered with shutters, so as to keep it dark in order to more easily judge the nature of the glowing metal.

Despite being recently built for the work at the palace, the blacksmith's shop already looked a hundred years old. Nearly every spot held some tool or other in a dizzying array and variety. There were rows of tools, piles of them. The rafters were hung with tongs and fire pots and crucibles and squares and dividers and contraptions like huge insects which looked to be used for clamping pieces together. Low benches seemingly cobbled together in haste were hung all round with long-handled dies of every sort. Some benches held smaller grindstones. Slots around some tables held hundreds of files and rasps. Some of the low tables were covered in a jumble of hammers in such variety as Richard had never imagined, their handles all sticking out, making the tabletops look like huge pincushions.

The floor was choked with clutter: boxes overflowing with parts, bars, rivets; wedges; lengths of iron stock; clippings; pry bars; pole hooks; dented pots; wooden jigs; tin snips; lengths of chain; pulleys; and a variety of special anvil attachments. Everything was covered with soot or dust or metal filings.

Broad short barrels full of liquids sat around the anvils where men hammered on glowing iron held in tongs, flattening, stretching, cutting, squaring, clipping. Glowing metal hissed and smoked in protest as it was quenched in the liquid. Other men used the horns of their anvils to bend metal that looked like bits of sunset held captive in tongs. They held up those fascinating bits and matched them to patterns, hammered on the metal some more, and checked it again.

Richard could hardly think in all the noise.

In the darkness, a man worked a big bellows, putting all his weight on the downstroke. The blast of air made the fire roar. Charcoal overflowed from baskets sitting wherever there had been room to put them. Cubbyholes held pipe and odd scraps of metal. Metal hoops leaned against benches and planks. Some of the hoops were for barrels, bigger ones were for wagon wheels. Tongs and hammers lay here and there on the floor where men had dropped them in the haste of battle with the hot iron.

The whole place was as agreeable a clutter as he had ever seen.

A man in a leather apron stood not far away at a door to another workroom. He held out a chalkboard covered with a maze of lines as he studied a large contraption of metal bars on the floor in the room beyond. Richard waited, not wanting to interrupt the man's concentration. The sharply defined muscles of his sooty arms glistened with sweat. The man tapped the chalk against his lip as he puzzled, then swiped a line clean on the board and drew it again, moving its connecting points.

Richard frowned at the drawing. It looked familiar, somehow, even though it was no recognizable object.

"Would you be the master blacksmith?" Richard asked when the man paused and looked over his shoulder.

The man's brow seemed enduringly fixed in an intimidating scowl. His hair was cropped close to his skull—a good practice around so much fire and white-hot metal—adding to his menacing demeanor. He was of average height and sinewy, but it was his countenance that made him look big enough for any trouble that might come along. By the way the other men moved, and glanced at this man, they feared him.

Taken by inexplicable compulsion, Richard pointed at the line the man had just drawn. "That's wrong. What you just did is wrong. You have the top end right, but the bottom should go here, not where you put it."

He didn't so much as blink. "Do you even know what this is?"

"Well, not exactly, but I—"

"Then how can you presume to tell me where to put this support?"

The man looked like he wanted to stuff Richard in the forge and melt him down.

"Offhand, I don't know, exactly. Something just tells me that—"

"You had better be the man with the iron."

"I am," Richard said, glad to change the subject and wishing he had kept his mouth shut in the first place. He had only been trying to help. "Where would—"

"Where have you been all day? I was told it would be here first thing this morning. What did you do? Sleep till noon?"

"Ah, no, sir. We went right to the foundry first thing. Ishaq sent me right there at dawn. But the man at the foundry was having problems because—"

"I'm not interested. You said you had the iron. It's already late enough. Get it unloaded."

Richard looked around. Every spot seemed occupied.

"Where would you like it?"

The master blacksmith glared around at the crammed room as if he expected some of the piles to get up and move for him. They didn't.

"If you'd have been here when you were supposed to be here, you could have put it out there, just inside the door in the outer supply room. Now they brought that big rock sled that needs welding, so you will have to put the iron in the back. Next time, get out of bed earlier."

Richard was trying to be polite, but he was losing his patience with being castigated because the blacksmith was having a troubled day.

"Ishaq made it quite clear that you were to get iron today, and he sent me to see to it. I have your iron. I don't see anyone else able to deliver on such short notice."

The hand with the chalkboard lowered. The full attention of the man's glower focused on Richard for the first time. Men who had heard Richard's words scurried off to attend to important work farther away.

"How much iron did you bring?"

"Fifty bars, eight feet."

The man let out an angry breath. "I ordered a hundred. I don't know why they sent an idiot with a wagon when—"

"Do you want to hear the way it is, or do you want to yell at someone? If you just want to spout off to no point and no useful end, then go right ahead as I'm not much injured by ranting, but when you finally want to hear the truth of the way things are, just let me know and I'll give it."

The blacksmith peered silently for a moment, a bull bewildered by a bumblebee. "What's your name?"

"Richard Cypher."

"So, what's the truth of the way things are, Richard Cypher?"

"The foundry wanted to fill the order. They have bar stock stacked to the rafters. They can't get it delivered. They wanted to let me have the whole order, but a transport inspector stationed there wouldn't let us have the whole hundred bars because the other transport companies are supposed to get their equal loads, but their wagons are broken down."

"So Ishaq's wagons aren't allowed to take more than their fair share, and fifty was their allotment."

"That's right," Richard said. "At least until the other companies can move some more goods."

The blacksmith nodded. "The foundry is dying to sell me all the iron I can use, but I can't get it here. I'm not allowed to transport it—to put transport workers, like you, out of work."

"Were it up to me," Richard said. "I'd go back for another load today, but they told me they couldn't give me any more until next week at the earliest. I'd suggest you get every transport company you can find to deliver you a wagonload. That way, you'll have a better chance to get what you need."

The blacksmith smiled for the first time. It was amusement at the foolishness of Richard's idea. "Don't you suppose I already thought of that? I've got orders in with them all. Ishaq is the only one with equipment at the moment. The rest are all having wagon problems, horse problems, or worker problems."

"At least I have fifty bars for you."

"That will only keep me going the rest of the day and for the morning." The blacksmith turned. "This way. I'll show you where you can stack it."

He led Richard through the congested workshop, among the confusion of work and material. They went through a door and down a short connecting hall. The noise fell away behind. They entered a quiet building in back, attached, but set off on its own. The blacksmith unhooked a line attached at a cleat and let down a trapdoor covering a window in the roof.

Light cascaded down into the center of the large room, where stood a huge block of marble. Richard stood staring at the stunning stone heart of a mountain.

It seemed completely out of place in a blacksmith's workshop. There were tall doors at the far end, where the monolith had been brought in on skids. The rest of the room had space left open all around the towering stone. Chisels of every sort and various-size mallets stuck up from slots along the pitch black walls.

"You can put the bars here, on the side. Be careful when you bring them in."

Richard blinked. He had almost forgotten the man was there with him. Still he stared at the lustrous quality of the stone before him. "I'll be careful," he said without looking at the blacksmith. "I won't bang it into the stone."

As the man started to leave, Richard asked, "I told you my name. What's yours?"

"Cascella."

"Is there more to it?"

"Yes. Mister. See that you use it all."

Richard smiled as he followed the man out. "Yes, sir, Mr. Cascella. Ah, mind if I ask what this is?"

The blacksmith slowed to a stop and turned back. He gazed at the marble standing in the light as if it were a woman he loved.

"This is none of your business, that's what it is."

Richard nodded. "I only asked because it's a beautiful piece of stone. I've never seen marble before it was a statue or made into something."

Mr. Cascella watched Richard watching the stone. "There's marble all over this site. Thousands of tons of it. This is just one small piece. Now, get my shorted order of iron unloaded."

By the time Richard was done, he was soaked in sweat, and filthy, not only from the iron bars, but from the soot of the blacksmith's shop. He asked if he could use some of the water in a rain barrel that the men were using to wash in as they were getting ready to leave for the day. They told him to go ahead.

When he finished, Richard found Mr. Cascella back at the chalkboard, alone in the suddenly silent shop, making corrections to the drawing and writing numbers down the side.

"Mr. Cascella, I'm finished. I kept the bars well off to the side, away from the marble."

"Thank you," he mumbled.

"Mind if I ask what you will have to pay for that fifty bars of iron?"

The glare was back. "What's it to you?"

"From what I heard at the foundry, the man there had been hoping to fill the whole order so he could get three point five gold marks, so, since you got half your order, I believe you will be paying one point seven five gold marks for the fifty bars of iron. Am I correct?"

The glare darkened. "Like I said, what's it to you?"

Richard put his hands in his back pockets. "Well, I was wondering if you would be willing to buy another fifty bars for one point five gold marks."

"So, you're a thief, too."

"No, Mr. Cascella, I'm not a thief."

"Then how are you going to sell me iron for a quarter mark less than the foundry is selling it for? You smelting a little iron ore in your room at night, Mr. Richard Cypher?"

"Do you want to hear what I have to say, or not?"

His mouth twisted in annoyance. "Talk."

"The foundry man was furious because he wasn't allowed to transport your whole order. He has more iron than he can sell because he isn't allowed to transport it, and the transport companies are all jammed up so they aren't showing up. He said he would be willing to sell it to me for less."

"Why?"

"He needs the money. He showed me his cold blast furnaces. He owes wages and needs charcoal and ore and quicksilver, among other things, but hasn't enough money to buy it all. The only thing he has plenty of is smelted metal. His business is strangling because he can't move his product. I asked what price he would be willing to sell me iron for, if he didn't have to transport it—if I picked it up myself. He told me that if I came after dark, he would sell me fifty bars for one point two five gold marks. If you're willing to buy it from me for one point five, I'll have you another fifty bars by morning, when you said you need it."

The man gaped as if Richard was a bar of iron that had just come to life before his eyes and started talking.

"You know I'm willing to pay one and three-quarters, why would you offer to sell it to me for one and a half?"

"Because," Richard explained, "I want to sell it for less than you'd have to pay through a transport company so that you'll buy it from me, instead, and, because I need you to loan me the one and a quarter gold marks, first, so I can buy the bars in the first place and bring them to you. The foundry will only sell them to me if I pay when I come to take them."

"What's to keep you from disappearing with my one and a quarter gold marks?"

"My word."

The man barked a laugh. "Your word? I don't know you."

"I told you, my name is Richard Cypher. Ishaq is scared to death of you, and he trusted me to get you the iron so you won't come wring his neck."

Mr. Cascella smiled again. "I'd not wring Ishaq's neck. I like the fellow. He's stuck in a tight spot. —But don't you tell him I said that. I'd like to keep him on his toes."

Richard shrugged. "If you don't want me to, I won't tell him you know how to smile. I know, though, that you're in a tighter spot than Ishaq. You have to deliver goods for the Order, but you're at the mercy of their methods."

He smiled again. "So, Richard Cypher, what time will you be here with your wagon?"

"I don't have a wagon. But, if you agree, I'll have your fifty iron bars right there"—Richard pointed at a spot out the double doors beside where Jori had parked the wagon—"in a pile, by dawn."

Mr. Cascella frowned. "If you don't have a wagon, how you going to get the bars here? Walk?"

"That's right."

"Are you out of your mind?"

"I don't have a wagon, and I want to earn the money. It's not all that far. I figure I can carry five at a time. That only makes ten trips. I can do that by dawn. I'm used to walking."

"Tell me the rest of it—why you want to do this. The truth, now."

"My wife isn't getting enough to eat. The workers' group assesses most of my wages, since I'm able to produce, and gives it to those who don't work. Because I can work, I've become a slave to those who can't, or who don't wish to. Their methods encourage people to find an excuse to let others take care of them. I intensely dislike being a slave. I figure I can entice you to go along with the deal by offering you a better price. We each gain a benefit. Value for value."

"If I were to go along, what do you plan to do with all that money—go live off it for a while? Drink it away?"

"I need the money to buy a wagon and a team of horses."

The frown knotted tighter. "What do you need with a wagon?"

"I need the wagon to deliver you all the iron you're going to buy from me because I can get it for you cheaper, and because I can deliver it when you need it."

"You looking to get buried in the sky?"

Richard smiled. "No. I just happen to think that the emperor wants his palace built. From what I've heard, they have a lot of slave labor down there—people they've captured. But they don't have enough slave labor to do it all for them. They need people like you, and the foundries.

"If the officials of the Order want to have the work progress—and not have to explain to Emperor Jagang why it isn't—they will be inclined to look the other way. In that narrow crack of need, there is opportunity. I expect I'll have to bribe a few officials to get them to be busy elsewhere when I come to pick up loads, but I've already figured that cost into it. I'll be acting on behalf of myself, not an established transport company, so they will be more inclined to see this as a way of accomplishing what they need without suspending their morass of restrictions.

"You will be getting iron for less than you pay now, and I can deliver. You can't even get what you need at the higher price. You will make more, too. We both benefit."

The blacksmith stared for a moment as he tried to find a flaw in Richard's plan.

"You're either the stupidest crook I ever saw, or the . . . I don't even know what. But I have Brother Narev breathing down my neck, and that isn't pleasant. Not pleasant at all. I probably shouldn't tell you this, but you know how Ishaq sweats over me? I sweat ten times that much when Brother Narev comes to ask why the tools aren't ready. The brothers don't want to hear my troubles, they just want what they want."

"I understand, Mr. Cascella."

He let out a sigh. "All right, Richard Cypher, one and a half gold marks for fifty bars delivered by dawn tomorrow—but I'll only give you the one and a quarter now. You get the other quarter mark in the morning, when my iron is here."

"Agreed. Who is this Brother Narev, anyway?"

"Brother Narev? He's the high priest—"

"Did I hear someone mention my name?" The voice was deep enough to nearly rattle the tools off the walls.

Richard and the blacksmith turned to see a man approaching from around the corner of the shop. Here and there, his heavy robes betrayed his large bony frame. His face seemed to pull the gathering darkness into the deep creases of his face. Dark eyes gleamed out from under a hooded brow overspread with a tangle of graying hairs. Wiry hair above his ears curled up from under the edges of a dark, creased cap. The cap sat halfway down his forehead. He looked like a shadow come to life to stalk the world.

Mr. Cascella bowed. Richard followed his lead.

"We were just discussing the problem of getting enough iron, Brother Narev."

"Where are all my new chisels, blacksmith?"

"I have yet to—"

"I have stone sitting down there with no chisels to cut it. I have stonecutters who need more tools. You are holding up my palace."

The blacksmith lifted a hand toward Richard. "This is Richard Cypher, Brother Narev. He was just telling me how he thought he might be able get me the iron I need and—"

The high priest held up his hand for silence.

"You can get the blacksmith what he needs?" Brother Narev snapped at Richard.

"It can be done."

"Then do it."

Richard bowed his head. "By your command, Brother Narev."

The shadowed figure turned to the shop. "Show me, blacksmith."

The blacksmith seemed to know what the high priest wanted and followed behind him, gesturing for Richard to come along. Richard understood; he couldn't get the money to buy the iron until the blacksmith first took care of the important man who had just vanished into the shadows of the shop.

When the blacksmith snapped his fingers and pointed at a lamp on his way by, Richard snatched it up. He lit a long splinter in the glowing coals of the forge and then lit the lamp. He held it up behind the two men as they stood just inside the doorway to the room with the complex contraption of metal bars sitting on the floor beyond.

Mr. Cascella held the chalkboard up in the light. Brother Narev looked at the drawing on the chalkboard, then to the maze of iron lines on the floor, comparing them.

Richard felt an icy tingle at the base of his scalp when he suddenly realized what the thing on the floor was.

Brother Narev pointed to the drawing, to the line Richard had said was wrong.

"This line is wrong," Brother Narev growled.

The blacksmith wagged his finger over the chalk drawing. "But I have to stabilize this mass over here."

"I told you to add braces, I didn't invite you to ruin the main scheme. You can leave the top of the support where you have it, but the bottom should be attached . . . here."

Brother Narev pointed to where Richard had said it should go.

Mr. Cascella scratched his head of short hair as he stole a glance over his shoulder just long enough to scowl at Richard.

"That would work," the blacksmith conceded. "It won't be as easy, but it will work."

"I'm not concerned with how easy it is," Brother Narev said with menace. "I don't want anything attached to this area, here."

"No, sir."

"It must be seamless, so none of the joining work shows through when it is covered in gold. Get me those tools made, first."

"Yes, Brother Narev."

The high priest turned an uncomfortable scrutiny on Richard. "There's something about you. . . . Do I know you?"

"No, Brother Narev. I've never before met you. I would remember. Meeting a great man such as yourself, I mean. I would remember such a thing."

He glared askance at Richard. "Yes, I suppose you would. You get the blacksmith his iron."

"I said I would."

The Brother grunted irritably. "So you did."

As the tall shadow of a man stared into Richard's eyes, Richard absently reached to lift his sword a little to make sure it was clear in its scabbard. The sword wasn't there.

Brother Narev opened his mouth to say something, but his attention was caught by two young men entering the shop. They wore robes like the high priest, but without caps. They had simple hoods pulled up over their heads, instead.

"Brother Narev," one called.

"What is it, Neal?"

"The book you sent for has arrived. You asked that we come for you at once."

Brother Narev nodded to the young disciple, then directed a sour look at Mr. Cascella and Richard.

"Get it done," he said to both.

Both Richard and the blacksmith bowed their heads as the high priest swept out of the shop.

It felt as if a thundercloud had just departed over the horizon.

"Come on," Mr. Cascella said. "I'll get you the gold."

Richard followed him into a little room where the master blacksmith pulled out a strongbox attached with massive chain to a huge pin in the floor under the plank serving as his desk. He unlocked the strongbox and handed Richard a gold mark.

"Victor."

Richard looked up from the gold mark and frowned. "What?"

"Victor. You asked what more there was to my name." He set silver to make up the quarter mark on top of the gold mark resting in Richard's palm. "Victor."

After leaving Ishaq's place and before going to get the iron for Victor, Richard rushed back to his room. It wasn't dinner he wanted, but to let Nicci know that he had to go back to work. She had in the past made it clear that they were husband and wife, and that she would take a dim view of him vanishing. He was to remain in Altur'Rang and work, just like any other normal man.

Kamil and one of his friends were waiting for him. Both were wearing shirts.

Richard stood at the foot of the stairs, looking up at the two. "I'm sorry, Kamil, but I have to go back to work—"

"Then you're a bigger dupe than I thought—taking work at night, too. You should just stop trying. It's no use trying in life. You just have to take what life gives you. I knew you would have an excuse not to do what you said you would do. You almost had me thinking that you might be different than—"

"I was going to say that I have to go back to work, so we have to do this right away."

Kamil twisted his mouth, as was his habit to express his displeasure with those older and stupider than he.

"This is Nabbi. He wants to watch your foolish labor, too."

Richard nodded, not showing any irritation at Kamil's arrogant attitude. "Glad to meet you, Nabbi." The third young man glared from the shadows back by the stairs in the hall. He was the biggest. He wasn't wearing a shirt.

To pry the steps apart, Richard used his knife and a rusty metal bar Kamil found for him. It wasn't difficult—they were ready to fall apart on their own. As the two youths watched, Richard cleaned the grooves in the stringers. Since they were chewed up from being loose, he deepened their bottoms, showing the two what he was doing and explaining how he would bevel the ends of the treads to lock into the deepened channel. Richard watched Kamil and Nabbi as they whittled wedges to match the one he made as a pattern for them. They were only too delighted to show him their knife work; Richard was delighted that it helped get the job done sooner.

Once they had them back together, Kamil and Nabbi both ran up and down the repaired steps, apparently surprised that they really were now sturdy underfoot, and pleased that they were partly responsible for the repair.

"You both did a good job," Richard told them, because they had. They didn't make any smart remarks. They actually smiled.

Richard's dinner was watery millet eaten by the light of a burning wick floating in linseed oil. The smell from the simple light went poorly with dinner, which was more water than millet. Nicci said she'd already eaten, and didn't want any more. She encouraged him to finish it.

He didn't give Nicci the details of his second job. She was insistent only that he work; the work itself was irrelevant to her. She tended to her household chores and expected him to earn them a living.

She seemed satisfied that he was learning how ordinary people had to work themselves sick just to make enough to get along in life. The promise of money to buy them more food seemed to spark a longing in her eyes that her lips did not express. He noticed that the black material covering her once full bosom was now slack and half empty. Her elbows and hands had become bony.

As he took another spoonful of millet, Nicci casually mentioned that the landlord, Kamil's father, had come by.

Richard looked up from his soup. "What did he say?"

"He said that since you have a job, the area citizens' building committee had assessed us extra rent in order to help pay the rent of those in the local buildings who can't work. You see, Richard, how life under the ways of the Order cultivates caring in people, so that we all work together for the benefit of all?"

Nearly all of what was not taken by the workers' group was taken by the area building committee, or some other committee, and all for the same purpose: for the betterment of the people of the Order. Richard and Nicci had next to nothing left for food. Richard's clothes were getting looser all the time, but not as loose as Nicci's dresses were getting.

She seemed smug about the fact that their rent was past due. Foodstuffs, at least, were relatively inexpensive—when they were available. People said that it was only by the grace of the Creator and the wisdom of the Order that they could afford any food at all. Richard had heard talk at Ishaq's place that more plentiful and varied food could be had, for a price. Richard didn't have the price.

On his wagon ride with Jori to the foundry and the blacksmith, Richard had spotted distant houses that looked to be quite grand. Well-dressed people walked those streets. Occasionally, he saw them in carriages. They were people who neither dirtied their hands or soiled their morals with business. They were men of principle. They were officials of the Order who saw to it that those with the ability sacrificed for the cause of the Order.

"Self-sacrifice is the moral duty of all people," she said in challenge to his clenched teeth.

Richard could not hold his tongue. "Self-sacrifice is the obscene and senseless suicide of slaves."

Nicci gaped at him. It was as if he had just said that a mother's milk was poison to her newborn.

"Richard, I do believe that that's the cruelest thing I've ever heard you say."

"It's cruel to say that I would not happily sacrifice myself for that thug, Gadi? Or for some other thug I don't know? It's cruel not to willingly sacrifice what's mine to any greedy wretch who lusts to possess plundered goods, the unearned, even at the cost of their victim's blood?

"Self-sacrifice for a value held dear, for a life held dear, for freedom and the freedom of those you respect—self-sacrifice such as mine for Kahlan's life—is the only rationally valid sacrifice. To be selfless means you are a slave who must surrender your most priceless possession—your life—to any smirking thief who demands it.

"The suicide of self-sacrifice is but a requirement imposed by masters on slaves. Since there is a knife to my throat, it is not to my good that I am stripped of what I earn by my own hand and mind. It is only to the good of the one with the knife, and those who by weight of numbers but not reason dictate what is the good of all—those cheering him on so they might lap up any drop of blood their masters miss.

"Life is precious. That's why sacrifice for freedom is rational: it is for life itself and your ability to live it that you act, since life without freedom is the slow, sure death of self-sacrifice to the 'good' of mankind—who is always someone else. Mankind is just a collection of individuals. Why should everyone's life be more important, more precious, more valuable than yours? Mindless mandatory self-sacrifice is insane."

She stared, not at him, but at the flame dancing on the pool of linseed oil. "You don't really mean that, Richard. You're just tired and angry that you have to work at night, too, just to get by. You should realize that all those others you help are there to help society, including you, should you be the one in desperate need."

Richard didn't bother to argue with her, and said only, "I feel sorry for you, Nicci. You don't even know the value of your own life. Sacrifice could mean nothing to you."

"That's not true, Richard," she whispered, "I sacrifice for you. . . . I saved what millet we had for you, that you might have strength."

"The strength to stand upright when I throw my life away? Why did you sacrifice your dinner, Nicci?"

"Because it was the right thing to do—it was for the good of others."

He nodded as he peered at her in the dim light. "You would endanger your life to starvation for others—for any others." He pointed a thumb back over his shoulder. "How about that thug, Gadi? Would you starve to death so he might eat? It might mean something, Nicci, if it was a sacrifice for someone you value, but it isn't; it's a sacrifice to some mindless gray ideal of the Order."

When she didn't answer, Richard pushed the rest of his dinner before her. "I don't want your meaningless sacrifice."

She stared at the bowl of millet for an eternity.

Richard felt sorry for her, for what she couldn't understand as she stared at the bowl. He thought about what would happen to Kahlan if Nicci were to fall sick from not getting enough to eat.

"Eat, Nicci," he said softly.

She finally picked up her spoon and did as he said.

When she had finished, she looked up with those blue eyes that seemed so eager for the sight of something he could not make her see. She slid the empty bowl to the center of the table.

"Thank you, Richard, for the meal."

"Why thank me? I am a selfless slave, expected to sacrifice for any worthless person who presents their need to me."

He strode to the door. With his hand on the loose knob, he turned back. "I have to go, or I will lose my work."

Her big blue eyes were brimming with tears as she nodded.

Richard made the first trip from the foundry through the dark streets to Victor's shop carrying five bars. From windows along the way, a few people blinked out at the man lugging a load past. They blinked without comprehension at the meaning of what he was doing. He was working for nothing but his own benefit.

Bent under the weight, Richard kept telling himself that carrying five bars each time would make it only ten trips, and the less trips, the better. He carried five the second trip, and the third. By the fourth time he returned to the foundry, he decided that he would have to make an extra trip in order to give himself a break and only carry four bars for a few of the trips. He lost track of how many times he went back and forth throughout the empty night. The next to last time, he struggled to lift but two bars. That left three. He forced himself to carry all three the last time, trading the extra effort for the lesser distance.

He got the last three bars to Victor's place before dawn. His shoulders were bruised and painful. He had to walk all the way to his job at Ishaq's place, so he couldn't wait for Victor to arrive to complete his payment of the last quarter gold mark.

The day of work was a break from the night of exhausting lugging of iron bars. Jori didn't talk unless spoken to, so Richard lay in the wagon bed with a load of charcoal and snatched a few minutes of sleep here and there as the wagon bounced along. He only felt relieved that he had done as he had promised.

As he returned home after an interminable day, Richard looked up and saw Kamil and Nabbi standing at the head of the stairs. They both had on shirts.

"We've been waiting for you to come home and finish the job," Kamil said.

Richard swayed on his feet. "What job?"

"The stairs."

"We did that last night."

"You did only the stairs in the front. You said you intended to fix the stairs. The front is only part of the stairs. The back stairs are twice as long and in worse shape than the front were. You don't want your wife and the other women of the building to fall and break their necks when they go out back to the cooking hearth or the privy, do you?"

This was their idea of a little test. Richard knew he would lose an opportunity if he put them off. He was so tired he couldn't think straight.

Nicci stuck her head out the front door. "I thought I heard your voice. Come in to dinner. I have soup waiting on you."

"Got any tea?"

Nicci cast a sidelong glance at the two in shirts. "I can make tea. Come on, and I'll get it while you have your soup."

"Please bring it out to the back," Richard said. "I promised to fix the stairs."

"Now?"

"There are still a couple hours of light. I can eat while we're working."

Kamil and Nabbi asked more questions than the evening before. The third youth, Gadi, passed by occasionally as Richard and the other two worked. Gadi, without his shirt, made a point of looking Nicci up and down when she brought Richard his soup and tea.

When Richard had finally finished, he went to the room that had once been Ishaq's parlor, and was now his and Nicci's home. He took off his shirt and splashed water on his face from the washbasin. His head was throbbing.

"Wash your hair," Nicci said. "You're filthy. I don't want lice in here."

Rather than argue that he had no lice, Richard dipped his face in the water and scrubbed his head with the cake of coarse soap. It was easier than talking her out of it so he could go to sleep. Nicci hated lice.

He was thankful, he supposed, that she was at least a clean wife in their fraudulent arrangement. She kept the room, bedding, and his clothes clean, despite the difficulty of hauling water from the well down the street. She never objected to any work necessary to simulate the lives of normal people. She seemed to want something so badly that she often lost herself in the role to the extent that while he never forgot she was a Sister of the Dark and his captor, she occasionally did. He dunked his head again, swishing his hair, rinsing out the soap.

As a stream of water ran off his chin and back into the basin, he asked, "Who is Brother Narev?"

Nicci, sitting on her pallet sewing, paused and looked up. Her sewing suddenly looked out of place, as if her parody of domestic life lost its aura for her.

"Why do you ask?"

"I met him yesterday, out at the blacksmith's."

"Out at the site of the project?"

Richard nodded. "I had to deliver iron out there."

She bent back to her needlework. Richard watched in the light of the linseed-oil lamp sitting beside her as she took a few more stitches in the patch to the knees of a pair of his pants. She finally paused and let her arms, one sheathed in his pant leg, sink to her lap.

"Brother Narev is the high priest of the Fellowship of Order—an ancient sect devoted to doing the Creator's will in this world. He is the heart and soul of the Order—their moral guide—so to speak. He and his disciples lead the righteous people of the Order in the ways of the everlasting Light of the Creator. He is an advisor to Emperor Jagang."

Richard was taken aback. He hadn't expected her to be so versed on the subject. His caution, along with the hair at the back of his neck, lifted.

"What sort of advisor?"

She took another stitch, pulling the long thread through. "Brother Narev was Jagang's pedagogue—his teacher, advisor, and mentor. Brother Narev put the fire in Jagang's belly."

"He's a wizard, isn't he." It was more statement than question.

She looked up from her sewing. He could see in her blue eyes that she was weighing whether or not to tell him, or perhaps how much she wanted to tell him. His steady gaze told her that he was expecting the whole truth.

"In the language of the street, you could describe him as such."

"What does that mean?"

"Common people, those who understand little about magic, would describe him as a wizard. Strictly speaking, though, he is not a wizard."

"Then what is he? Strictly speaking."

"Actually, he is a sorcerer."

Richard could only stare at her. He had always assumed that a wizard and a sorcerer were the same thing. When he thought about it, he realized that people who knew about magic spoke exclusively of a male with the gift as a wizard. He had never heard any of those people mention a sorcerer.

"You mean he's like you, like a sorceress, only male?"

The question stymied her for a moment. "I suppose you could think of it that way, but that's not really right. If you want to compare it, then you would have to say he has more in common with a wizard, since both are male. The concept of sorceress introduces irrelevant issues."

Richard swiped water from his face. "Please, Nicci, I've been up all last night working, and I'm dead on my feet. Don't go all abstract and complex on me? Just tell me what it means?"

She set her sewing aside and gestured to his pallet for him to sit near her, in the light. Richard pulled his shirt back on. He yawned as he crossed his legs under himself on his pallet.

"Brother Narev is a sorcerer," she began. "I'm sorry, but the distinction is just not something simply explained. It's a very complex matter. I will try to make it as clear as I can, but you must understand that I can't boil it down too much or it will lose any real flavor of the truth.

"Sorcerers are much the same as wizards, but different—in much the way that water and oil are both liquids, you might say. Both pour and can dissolve things, but they don't mix and they dissolve different things. Neither do the magic of a wizard and a sorcerer mix, nor do they work on the same things.

"Anything he did against a wizard's gift, or anything a wizard did against his, would not work. While both are the gift, they are different aspects—they don't mix. The magic of each nullifies the other, making it just sort of . . . fizzle."

"You mean like Additive and Subtractive are opposites?"

"No. While on the surface, that would seem a good way to understand it, it's entirely the wrong way to think of it." She lifted her hands as if to begin again, but then let them drop back into her lap. "It's very hard to explain the difference to one such as you who has little understanding of how his own gift works; you have no basis in which to ground anything I could tell you. There are no words which are both accurate and which you would understand; this is beyond your understanding."

"Well . . . do you mean that, much like a wolf and a cougar are both predators, they are not the same sort of creature?"

"That's a little closer to it."

"How common are these sorcerers?"

"About as common as dream walkers . . ." she said as she gave him a meaningful look, "or war wizards."

Even though he couldn't understand it and she couldn't explain it, Richard, for some reason, found that bit of news troubling.

"What is it, though, that he does differently?"

Nicci let out a sigh. "I'm no expert, and I'm not entirely sure, but I believe he does the same basic sort of things a wizard would do, but just does them with a sorcerer's unique quality of magic—liquor and ale both get you drunk, but they are different kinds of drink made from different things."

"One of those is stronger."

"Not so with wizards and sorcerers. Do you see why words and these kinds of comparisons are so inadequate? The strength of a wizard and sorcerer's gift is dependent on the individual, it is not influenced by the fundamental nature of his magic."

Richard scratched his stubble as he considered her words. In view of the fact that both could do magic, he couldn't come up with any distinction that seemed of any practical importance.

"Is there anything that he can do that a wizard can't?" He waited. She didn't look like she was thinking about his question, but more like she was considering whether she wanted to answer it at all. "Nicci, you told me when you first captured me that you would tell me the truth about things. You said you had no reason to deceive me."

She watched his eyes, but finally looked away as she pulled her blond hair back from her face. The gesture unexpectedly, painfully, reminded him of Kahlan.

"Perhaps. I believe he may have learned how to replicate the spell that surrounded the Palace of the Prophets. It took wizards, thousands of years ago, with both sides of the gift to create that particular spell. I believe that one of the ways sorcerers are different is that their power is not divisible into its constituent elements, as it is in wizards. So, while his magic works differently, he may have learned enough of how the wizards—who at that time possessed both sides of the gift, as do you—were able to create the spell around the Palace of the Prophets to be able to replicate it in his own fashion."

"You mean the spell that slowed aging? You think he can cast such a web?"

"Yes. Jagang intimated as much to me. I knew Brother Narev when I was young. He was a grown man then, a visionary, preaching the doctrine of the Order. He spoke pensively about wishing to live long enough to see his vision of the Order come to fruition. When I was taken to live at the palace in Tanimura, I believe that may have given him the idea as he not long after went there, too.

"The Sisters knew nothing of him. They thought him no more than a humble worker. Since his gift is different than that of a wizard, they didn't detect his ability. I now believe that he went there for the express purpose of studying the spell around the Palace of the Prophets so that he could re-create such a spell for his own benefit."

"Why didn't he storm the palace—take it over—and then he could have the spell for his purpose?"

"It's possible that in the beginning he thought he might one day take over the palace for his cause—in fact, Emperor Jagang had that exact plan—but it's also possible that he was from the beginning studying the spell because he wanted not simply to re-create it, but to enhance it."

Richard rubbed his brow, trying to comfort his aching head. "You mean that now maybe he thinks he can create the spell over the Retreat—the emperor's new palace—like that one at the Palace of the Prophets, but better, so that aging will be slowed even more, so that he and his chosen will live even longer?"

"Yes. Don't forget, age is relative. To one who lives to a thousand years, living less than one century would seem all too brief. To a person who lives many thousands of years, though, a lifetime that lasts but a mere one millennium would seem fleeting.

"I suspect that Brother Narev has learned to slow aging to such an extent that it would make him the next best thing to immortal. Jagang had planned on capturing the Palace of the Prophets. It might have been that once they secured the palace, Brother Narev intended to augment its spell to suit his purposes."

"But I spoiled that plan."

Nicci nodded. "As are all of us who were once at the palace, Brother Narev now grows older just like everyone else. Once away from the spell, it feels like a headlong rush toward the grave. What youth Brother Narev has left, he is no doubt eager to preserve. Remaining relatively young forever has much to be said for it. Remaining old forever would be less attractive. Because you destroyed the Palace of the Prophets, where he could have had ample time to bring his plan to bear, he has been forced to act sooner, rather than later."

Richard flopped back on his mat. He laid the back of a wrist over his forehead. "He has the blacksmith making a spell-form in iron. The blacksmith has no idea what it is he's creating. The spell-form is to be covered with gold, eventually."

"For purity. It's likely that is merely part of the process. It could even be that the gold-covered spell-form is nothing more than a pattern, from which the true spell-form will be cast in pure gold."

Richard squinted in thought. "If it is a pattern for casting, that would make it more likely that Narev intends to cast a number of these spell-forms—that they will work together."

Nicci looked up and frowned. "Yes, that is a possibility."

"Will making such a thing harm the blacksmith?"

"No. It is propitious conjuring. Disregarding for the moment the purpose for which it is desired, such a spell is meant to be beneficial; it is to slow aging in order to lengthen life."

"What about Brother Narev's disciples?"

"Young wizards from the Palace of the Prophets."

Alarmed, Richard sat up. "I was at the Palace of the Prophets. They will recognize me."

"No. They were young wizards in training there, but they left to follow Brother Narev before you arrived. If they see you, they will not know you."

"If they're wizards, won't they recognize that I have magic?"

A smile of contempt colored her features. "They are not that talented. They are but bugs to what you are."

Richard found no comfort in the compliment. "Won't Brother Narev, or his disciples, recognize you?"

Her face turned serious. "Oh, they would know me."

"It sounds as if Brother Narev must be strong in his gift. Won't he be able to recognize that I have the gift? He was looking at me strangely. He asked if he knew me. He sensed something."

"Why did you think him a wizard?"

Richard picked at the straw stuffing coming out of the pad over his pallet as he considered the question.

"There was nothing that gave it away for a fact, but I strongly suspected it from a lot of little things: the way he carried himself; the way he looked at people; the way he spoke—everything about him. Only after I surmised that Narev was a wizard did I realize that the thing the blacksmith was making for him looked like some sort of spell-form."

"He would suspect you of being gifted in much the same way. Can you tell the gifted?"

"Yes. I've learned to recognize an ageless look in their eyes. I can in some way see the aura of the gift around those in whom it is powerful—you, for instance. At times, the air crackles around you."

She stared in fascination. "I've never heard of such a thing. It must have something do to with you having both sides."

"You have both sides. Don't you see it?"

"No, but I acquired the Subtractive side in a different manner."

She had given her soul to the Keeper of the underworld.

"But you see nothing of the sort in Brother Narev, do you?" When Richard shook his head, she went on with her explanation. "That is because, as I explained, you have different aspects of the gift. Other than with your faculty of reason, you have no wizardly ability to recognize the gift in him; he has no sorcerous ability to recognize the gift in you. Your magic won't work on one another. Only your faculty of reason betrayed his gift to you."

Richard realized that, without saying it, she was telling him that if he didn't want Narev to learn that he had the gift, then he had better be careful around the man.

There were times when he thought he had her game figured out.

There were times, like now, when it seemed his entire perception of her purpose shifted. At times, it almost seemed to him as if she threw her beliefs in his face, not because she believed them, but because she was desperately hoping for a reason not to, hoping he would find her in some lost, dark world and show her the way out. Richard sighed inwardly; he had given her his arguments as to why her beliefs were wrong, but, rather than sway her, it only angered her, at best, or worse, further entrenched her in her convictions.

As tired as he was, he lay in his bed, his eyes but narrow slits, watching Nicci lit by the light of a single wick, bent in concentration over her sewing—one of the most powerful women ever to walk the world, and she appeared perfectly content to sew a patch in the knee of his pants.

She accidentally stuck herself with the needle. As she shook her hand and winced with the pain, Richard had the sudden cold recollection of the link between her and Kahlan; his beloved would feel that prick.

Richard took the snow-white slice when Victor held it out.

"What's this?"

"Try it," Victor said as he waved an insistent hand. "Eat. Tell me what you think. It's from my homeland. Here, a red onion goes well with it."

The white slice was smooth, dense, and rich with salt and herbs. Richard let out a rapturous moan. He rolled his eyes.

"Victor, this is the best thing I've ever had. What is it?"

"Lardo."

They sat on the threshold of the double doors out of the room with the marble monolith, watching dawn break over the site, where the walls of the Retreat had begun to rise. Only a few people stirred below. Before long, laborers would arrive in great numbers to begin again their work on the Retreat. It went on every day without pause, rain or shine. Now that spring was wearing on, the weather was pleasant nearly every day, with afternoon rains every few days, but nothing dreary or oppressive—just enough to wash you clean and make you feel refreshed.

If not for the ever-present ache of missing Kahlan, his worry over the war far to the north, his loathing of being held prisoner, the slave labor at the site, the abuse of people, the people who disappeared or those who confessed under torture, and the grindingly repressive nature of life in Altur'Rang, he might have found the spring quite enjoyable.

Day by day, too, his worry grew that Kahlan would soon be able to leave their mountain home. He dreaded her getting caught up in such a war as would be soon be roaring into full flame.

After he had eaten some of the mild onion, Richard went back to the delightful lardo. He moaned again.

"Victor, I've never tasted anything like this. What's lardo?"

Victor held out another thin slice. Richard gladly accepted. After a long night of work, the dense delicacy was really hitting the spot.

Victor gestured with his knife to the tin beside him holding the pure white block. "Lardo is paunch fat from the boar."

"And this tin of it is from your homeland?"

"No, no—I make it myself. I come from far to the south of here, far away—near the sea. That is where we make lardo. When I come here, I make it here.

"I put the paunch fat in tubs I carved myself out of marble as white as the lardo." Victor gestured with his hands as he spoke, working the air as vigorously as he worked iron. "The fat is put in the tubs with coarse salt and rosemary and other spices. From time to time I turn it in the brine. It must rest a year in the stone to cure, to became lardo."

"A year!"

Victor nodded emphatically. "This we are eating, I made last spring. My father taught me to make lardo. Lardo is something only men make. My father was a quarry worker. Lardo gives quarry workers the stamina they need to work long hours sawing blocks of our marble, or swinging a pickaxe. For blacksmiths, too, lardo gives you power to lift a hammer all day."

"So, there are quarries where you lived?"

He waved his thick hand at the towering block behind them. "This. This is Cavatura marble—from my homeland." He pointed out at several of the stock areas below. "That, there, and there, is marble from Cavatura, too."

"That's where you're from? Cavatura?"

Victor grinned like a wolf as he nodded. "The place where all that beautiful marble came from. Our city gets its name from the marble quarries. My family are all carvers, or quarry workers. Me? I end up a blacksmith making tools for them."

"Blacksmiths are sculptors."

He grunted a laugh. "And you? Where are you from?"

"Me? Far away. They had no marble there. Only granite." Richard changed the subject, lest he have to start inventing lies. Besides, it was getting light. "So, Victor, when do you need more of that special steel?"

"Tomorrow. Are you up to it?"

The steel Victor needed was from farther away, at a foundry out near the charcoal makers. They needed a lot of charcoal to cook with the iron to make high-grade steel. Ore came in by barge, from not far away. It would take most of the night for Richard to get there and back.

"Sure. I will be sick today and get some sleep."

He had become sick quite a lot over the last several months. It fit right in with the way most of the others worked. Work some, be sick, tell the workers' group that you were ailing. Some people limped in with a story. It wasn't necessary; the workers' group never questioned.

The only thing he rarely missed were the meetings where those with bad attitudes were named. People at the meetings were often named, but you were more likely to bring attention if you missed the meetings. Those named were often subsequently arrested and given an opportunity to confess. More than once, a person named at a meeting as having an unsatisfactory attitude killed themselves.

"One of Brother Narev's disciples, Neal, came around last evening with some new orders." Victor's voice had taken on a tense edge. "What you just brought will last me the day, but I need that steel by tomorrow."

"You will have it."

"Are you sure?"

"Have I ever let you down, Victor?"

Victor's hard face melted into a helpless smile. He passed Richard another slice of lardo. "No, Richard, you never have. Not once. I had given up hope of ever meeting another man who kept his word."

"Well, I'd best be off and take care of my horses. They've had a hard night, and I'll need them rested for tonight. How much steel do you need?"

"Two hundred. Half square, and half round."

Richard performed a pained moan. "You're going to make me strong, or kill me, Victor."

Victor smiled his approval. "You want the gold?"

"No. You can pay me when I deliver."

Richard no longer needed the money in advance. He had a heavy wagon, now, and a strong team of horses. He paid Ishaq to care for them along with the transport company's teams in the company stables. Ishaq helped Richard with any number of the special arrangements that he'd had to make. Ishaq knew which officials lived in the nice homes. They couldn't afford those homes with just their pay as officials of the Order.

"You be careful of Neal," Richard said.

"Why's that?"

"For some reason, he believes I'm in need of lecturing. He truly believes that the Order is mankind's savior. He puts the good of the fellowship of Order above the good of mankind."

Victor sighed as he stood and tied on his leather apron. "My thoughts about him, too."

As they passed into the building, the sun was just lighting the marble standing there. Richard lingered and put a hand to the cold stone, as he always did whenever he passed it. It almost felt alive to him. Alive with potential.

"Victor, I asked you once what this was. Mind telling me, now?"

The blacksmith paused beside Richard and gazed up at the pure stone before him. He reached out and touched it lightly, letting his fingertips glide over the surface, testing, caressing.

"This is my statue."

"What statue?"

"The one I want to carve, someday. Many in my family are carvers. As far back as I can remember, I always wanted to carve, too. I wanted to be a great sculptor. I wanted to create great works.

"Instead, I had to work for the master blacksmith at the quarry. My family needed to eat. I was the oldest living son. My father and the blacksmith were friends. My father asked the blacksmith to take me on. . . . He didn't want another son lost to the stone. It's a hard and dangerous life, cutting stone from a mountain."

"Did you carve other things? I mean, like wood, or something."

Victor, still staring at his stone, shook his head. "I only wanted to carve stone. I bought this block with my savings. I own it. Few men can say they own a part of a mountain. A part as pure and beautiful as this."

Richard could understand the sentiments. "So, Victor, what will you carve out of it?"

He squinted, as if trying to peer beyond the surface. "I don't know. They say that the stone will speak to you and tell you what it should be."

"Do you believe that?"

Victor laughed his deep laugh. "No—not really. But the thing is, this is a beautiful piece of stone. There is none finer for statues than Cavatura marble, and few blocks of Cavatura marble with as fine a grain as this piece. I couldn't bear to see it carved up into something ugly, like what they carve nowadays.

"It used to be, long ago, that only beauty was carved from beauty such as this. No more," he whispered in distant bitterness. "Now, man must be carved with a twisted nature—as an object of shame."

Richard had delivered tools down to the site for Victor, down to where the carving was taking place, and had had the opportunity to get a closer look at the work being done. The outside of the stone walls was to be covered with expansive scenes on a scale that was staggering. The walls that would enclose the palace went on for miles. The carvings being produced for the Retreat were the same as those Richard had seen everywhere in the Old World, but would have no equal in sheer, overpowering quantity. The entire palace was to be an epic portrayal of the Order's view of the nature of life, and of redemption in the afterlife of the underworld.

The figures being carved were stilted, with limbs that could not possibly function. Those carved in relief were forever bound to the stone from which they only haltingly emerged. The poses reflected a view of man as ineffective, shallow, unsubstantial.

The elements of the hated anatomy of man, his muscle, bone, and flesh, were melted together into lifeless limbs, their proportions distorted to strip the figures of their humanity. Expressions were either impassive, if the statue was supposed to portray virtue, or filled with terror, agony, torment, if intended to illustrate the fate of evildoers. Proper men and women, bent under the weight of labor, were always made to look out at the world through the vacant stupor of resignation.

Most often, it was difficult to tell male from female; their worldly bodies, an everlasting source of shame, were hidden by bulky garments like those the priests of the Order wore. Further reflecting the Order's teachings, only the sinful were shown naked, so that all could see their detestable cankerous bodies.

The carvings represented man as helpless, doomed by the inadequacy of his intellect to suffer every blow of existence.

Most of the sculptors, Richard suspected, feared to be questioned, or even tortured, and so repeated the view that man was to be carved accepting his vile nature, thus earning his reward only through death. The carvings were meant to assure the masses that this was the only proper goal for which man could hope. Richard knew that a few of the carvers vehemently believed such teachings. He was always careful of what he said around them.

"Ah, Richard, I wish you could see beautiful statues, instead of today's scourge."

"I have seen statues of great beauty," Richard softly assured the man.

"Have you? I'm so glad. People should see those things, not this, this"—he waved a hand toward the rising walls of the Retreat—"this evil in the guise of goodness."

"So you will one day carve such beauty?"

"I don't know, Richard," he finally admitted. "The Order takes everything. They say that the individual is of no importance except inasmuch as he can contribute to the good of others. They take what art can be, the lifeblood of the soul, and turn it to poison, turn it to death."

Victor smiled wistfully. "This way, as it is, I can enjoy the beautiful statue inside the stone."

"I understand, Victor—I really do. The way you describe it, I can see it, too."

"We will both enjoy my statue the way it is, then." Victor took his hand from the stone and pointed to the base. "Besides, you see there? There is an imperfection in the stone. It runs all the way through. That is why I could afford this piece of marble—because it has this flaw. Were most anyone to carve this, it would endanger the stone. If not done just right, and with the flaw taken in mind, the entire piece could easily shatter. I have never been able to think of how to carve this stone to take advantage of its beauty, but to also avoid the flaw."

"Perhaps, someday, it will come to you how to carve the stone, to create a thing of nobility."

"Nobility. Ah, but wouldn't that be something—the most sublime form of beauty." He shook his head. "But I will not do it. Not unless the revolt comes."

"Revolt?"

Victor's careful gaze swept the hillside through the open door. "The revolt. It will come. The Order cannot stand—evil cannot stand, not forever, anyway. In my homeland, when I was young, there used to be beauty, and there used to be freedom. They were shamed into giving up their lives, their freedom, bit by bit, to the cause of fairness to all men. People didn't know what they had, and let freedom slip away for nothing but the hollow promise of a better world, a world without effort, without struggle to achieve, without productive work. It was always someone else who would do these things, who would provide, who would make their lives easy.

"We used to be a land of abundance. Now, what food is grown, rots, while it awaits committees to decide who should have it, who should move it, and what it should cost. Meanwhile, people starve.

"Insurgents, those disloyal to the Order, are blamed for all the starvation and strife that slowly destroys us, and so ever more people are arrested and put to death. We are a land of death. The Order continually proclaims its feelings for mankind, but their ways can but cultivate death. On my way here, I have seen corpses by the thousands go uncounted and unburied. The New World is blamed for every ill, every failure, and young men, eager to smite their oppressors, march off to war.

"Many people, though, have come to see the truth. They, and the children of these people—me, and others like me—hunger for freedom to live our own lives, rather than be slaves to the Order and their reign of death. There is unrest in my homeland, as there is here. A revolt is coming."

"Unrest? Here? I've seen no unrest."

Victor smiled a sly smile. "Those with revolt in their hearts do not show their true feelings. The Order, always fearful of insurrection, tortures confessions from those they wrongly arrest. Every day more are put to death. Those who want things to change know better than to make themselves targets before the time has come. Someday, Richard, revolt will come."

Richard shook his head. "I don't know, Victor. Revolt takes resolve. I don't think such real resolve exists."

"You have seen people who are unhappy with the way things are. Ishaq, those at the foundries, my men and me. All those you deal with, other than the officials you bribe, hunger for change." Victor lifted an eyebrow at Richard. "Not one of them complains to any board or committee about what you do. You may want nothing to do with it, as I believe is your right, but there are those who listen to the whispers of the freedom to the north."

Richard tensed. "Freedom to the north?"

Victor nodded solemnly. "They speak of a savior: Richard Rahl. He leads them in the fight for freedom. They say that this Richard Rahl will bring us our revolt."

Had it not all been so overwhelmingly tragic, Richard would have burst out laughing.

"How do you know this Rahl character is worth following?"

Victor fixed Richard with a look that Richard remembered from the first time he met the blacksmith.

"You can judge a man by his enemies. Richard Rahl is hated by the emperor, and by Brother Narev, and by his disciples, as no other man is hated. He is the one. He bears the torch of revolution."

Richard could muster only a desolate smile. "He is but a man, my friend. Don't worship a man. Worship his cause, but not him."

Victor's glare, so full of his emotion, his burning hunger for freedom, turned back to his wolfish grin.

"Ah, but that is what Richard Rahl would say. That is why he is the one."

Richard thought it would be best to change the subject. He saw that it was getting light.

"Well, I have to get going. I'm sure you'll figure out what to do with the stone, Victor. It will come to you when the time is right."

The blacksmith feigned a scowl, but it was a poor spoof of the very real one that had just departed. "That is always what I thought, too."

Richard scratched his head. "Have you ever carved anything Victor?"

"No, nothing."

"Are you sure you are able to carve? That you have the ability?"

Victor tapped his temple, as if to dissuade a skeptic. "In here I have ability. In here I have beauty. That is all that matters to me. If I never touch steel to this stone, then I will always have the beauty of what it could be, and that, the Order can never take away from me."

Nicci wiped the sweat off her brow as she went down the line, checking to see if her clothes were dry. Summer was only around the corner, and it was already hot. Her back hurt from her earlier work at the washtub and various other chores. The other women were chatting in the warm sunshine. They occasionally giggled over some quirk that one of them, after a round of amiable urging, would divulge about her husband. Everyone in the building, it seemed, had begun coming alive along with the new spring growth.

Nicci knew that spring had nothing to do with it.

That knowledge drew frustration up from her darkest recesses. She couldn't figure out how Richard did it. No matter how hard she tried, she just couldn't unravel the knot he seemed to tie around everything. She was beginning to believe that if she took him down into the deepest cave she could find, the sunlight would make its way into the darkest recesses to shine on him. She would think it was some kind of magical luck, except she knew beyond doubt that he had not used any magic whatsoever.

The backyard, such an overgrown tangled place, so filthy, with piles of scrap and garbage, was now a garden. The men who lived in the building, after they came home from work, had rid the yard of the refuse. Even several of the ones who didn't work had come out of their rooms to help cart away an item or two. After it was cleared out, the women of the building had turned the soil and planted a garden. They were going to have vegetables. Vegetables! There was talk of getting a few chickens.

The single latrine off in the back corner, so overused and so foul, was now two privies in good repair. Now, there was rarely a wait to use a privy and there were no more urgent pleas or frayed tempers. Kamil and Nabbi had helped Richard build them—partly out of scraps of lumber salvaged from the refuse piles in the yard, before they were hauled away, and some they collected from other rubbish heaps.

Nicci had hardly believed her eyes when she had seen Kamil and Nabbi—in shirts—digging the holes for the new privies. Everyone thanked them profusely. The two toughs beamed with pride.

The outdoor cooking hearth had been repaired, so the women could set more pots in it and cook at the same time, requiring less wood to be hauled. Richard and some of the other men of the building built stands for the washtubs, so the wives wouldn't have to bend so far or chafe their knees raw. The men made a simple roof of canvas salvaged from the refuse so that the women could cook and wash without getting wet when it rained.

The people in the buildings to either side, at first surly and suspicious of the activity, began asking curt questions. Richard, Kamil, and Nabbi went over and explained what they had done, and how they could put their place in shape, too, and even helped them get started. Nicci had yelled at Richard for spending his time at other people's places. He said that she was the one who had told him that it was his duty to help others. Nicci had no answer—at least, none that made any sense so as she could say it aloud and not sound a fool.

When Richard showed people how to improve their homes, he didn't lecture, or teach, but rather, somehow—Nicci couldn't understand how—managed to infect them with his enthusiasm. He hadn't told them what to do, but rather he'd made them want to figure out for themselves how they could make things better for themselves. Everybody took a liking to Richard. It made her growl under her breath.

Nicci collected her washing in the woven basket Richard had shown the women of the building how to make from thin strips of wood. Nicci had to admit that the basket was easy enough to make, and a better way to lug clothes.

She climbed the sturdy stairs—stairs that she'd once thought would be the end of her. The hallway inside was spotless. The floors had been washed. Somewhere, Richard had come up with ingredients for paint, and the men had a grand time of mixing it up and painting over the stains on the walls. One of the men in the building knew about roofs, so he fixed the roof so it wouldn't leak and stain the walls again.

As Nicci walked down the hall, she saw Gadi, without his shirt, sitting up the stairway, in the shadows. He was using his big knife to whittle at a piece of wood and in so doing make clear his dangerous nature. Later, the women living in the building would tsk and clean it up. Gadi, not happy about people nagging at him of late, leered down at her. She now had something for him to leer at, now that she had gained her weight back.

Richard's second job at night enabled him to be able to afford more food. He brought home things she had missed for months—chicken, oil, spices, bacon, cheese, and eggs. She could never find such things in the city stores. Nicci had thought they sold the same food everywhere in the city shops, but Richard's travels while delivering things, he said, took him to places where they sold a wider variety of food.

Kamil and Nabbi, sitting on the front steps, saw her through the open door. They stood and bowed politely as she came down the hall.

"Good evening, Mrs. Cypher," Kamil said.

"Could we help you carry that?" Nabbi asked.

She found it all the more irritating because she knew for a fact that they were sincere; they liked her because she was Richard's wife.

"Thank you, no. I'm there, now."

They held the door for her and closed it behind her when she had passed into her room.

She thought of them as Richard's soldiers. He seemed to have a private army of people who broke into grins when they saw him coming. Most people seemed only too pleased to do whatever they thought Richard might like done. Kamil and Nabbi would have washed diapers, if he asked it, for the chance to ride with him at night in the wagon as he picked up and delivered things around Altur'Rang. He only rarely took them with him, saying that he could get in trouble with the workers' group. The youths didn't want Richard to get in trouble and lose his job, so they patiently waited for the rare times when he tilted his head for them to come along.

Their room had been transformed. The ceiling had been cleaned and white-washed. The flyblown walls had been scrubbed and painted a salmon color—a color she had picked, thinking that Richard would not possibly be able to come up with the rare ingredients needed for the color. The walls were now mockingly salmon.

One day a man had shown up with an armload of tools. Kamil said that Richard had sent him over to fix their room. The man spoke a language Nicci didn't understand. He waved his arms a lot and chattered and laughed good-naturedly, as if she must understand at least a little of what he told her. He pointed around at walls and asked questions. She hadn't the foggiest notion of what he was there to do.

She suspected he had come to fix the wobbly table. She rapped the top with the flat of her hand and then showed him how it wobbled. He nodded and grinned and chattered. She finally left him to his work while she went to the city store to wait in line to buy bread. She was there the entire morning. In the afternoon, she waited in line for millet.

When Nicci finally returned home, the man was gone. The old window, broken and not only long painted over but also painted shut, had new glass, and it was raised. And, they had a new window in the other wall. Both windows were open. A cool cross-breeze let fresh air into the stuffy room.

Nicci stood in the center of the room, stunned to be looking through the window to the building next door. She gaped out the window in the wall where there had been no window before. She was able to see the street. Mrs. Sha'Rim, from next door, had smiled and waved as she'd walked past.

Nicci set down the wash basket and opened the window at the side, to get some air into the stifling room. She pushed the curtains back. With windows you could see though, she had decided that curtains were in order. Richard somehow got her fabric. When she was finished, he told her she had done a wonderful job. Nicci found herself grinning just as everyone else grinned when Richard told them they had done well.

She had brought Richard to the worst place in the Old World, to the worst building she could find, and he somehow ended up making everything better—just as she had insisted was his duty.

But she had never meant it to be like this.

She didn't know what she'd meant.

She only knew that she lived for the times Richard was with her. Even though she knew he hated her, and wanted nothing more than to be away from her and back with his Kahlan, Nicci could not help feeling her heart rise into her throat when he came home. Through the link to Kahlan, she thought that at times she could feel the woman's longing for him. Every inch of her ached with understanding of Kahlan's longing.

The room grew darker as she waited. Life didn't start until Richard came home. As the daylight faded, the lamplight took its place. They had a real lamp, now, not just a wick through a wooden button floating in linseed oil.

The door opened. Richard put one foot inside. He was speaking to Kamil as the young man was going off to his family's place upstairs. It was getting late. Finally, still smiling, Richard came in and shut the door. The smile faded, as it always did.

He held out a burlap sack. "I came across some onions, carrots, and some pork. I thought you might like to make a stew."

Nicci lifted a hand weekly toward the millet she had spent the afternoon in line to buy. It had bugs in it. It was moldy.

"I bought millet. I thought I would make you a soup."

Richard shrugged. "If you prefer. Your millet soup saw us through some pretty lean times."

Nicci felt that flash of pride that he had acknowledged what she had done as valuable.

She shut the windows. It was dark out. With her back to the windows as she watched him, she closed the curtains tight.

Richard stood in the center of the room, watching her, a puzzled frown creasing his brow between his eyes. Nicci closed the distance to him. She was aware of the exposed flesh of her bosom rising and falling above the top of her black dress. Gadi had just been staring at her bosom. She wanted Richard to stare at her like that. Richard watched only her eyes.

Her fingers tightened around his muscled arms.

"Make love to me," she whispered.

His brow drew down. "What?"

"Richard, I want you to make love to me. Now."

He appraised her eyes for an eternity. Her heart thundered in her ears. Every fiber of her being screamed out for him to take her. She teetered on the edge, waiting, her life suspended in the exquisite anguish of expectation.

His voice came, not at all harsh. If anything, it was tender, but it was also resolute. "No."

Nicci felt as if a thousand needles of ice were dancing up her arms. His refusal stunned her. No man had ever refused her.

It hurt to her core—worse than anything Jagang or any other man had ever done. She had thought . . .

Blood rushed to her face, melting the ice in a flash of heat. Nicci flung open the door. "Come out into the hall and wait," she commanded in a shaky voice.

He was standing in the center of their room, looking into her eyes. The lamp on the table cast harsh shadows across his face. His shoulders looked so broad, tapering down to his waist, a waist she ached to encircle with her arms. She wanted to scream. Instead she spoke softly, but with authority he could not mistake.

"You will come out into the hall and wait, or . . ."

Nicci made a snipping gesture with two fingers.

By the look in his eyes, he knew that she was not bluffing. Kahlan's life now hung by a thread, and if he didn't do as she ordered, she would not hesitate to cut that thread.

With his gray eyes on her the whole time, Richard stepped out into the hall. She put a finger to the center of his chest and pushed until his back was against the wall beside their door.

"You are to wait right there, on that spot, until I tell you that you may move from it." She gritted her teeth. "Or Kahlan will die. Do you understand?"

"Nicci, you're better than this. Think about what you're—"

"Or Kahlan will die. Do you understand?"

He let out a breath. "Yes."

Nicci marched to the stairwell. Gadi stood halfway up the stairs, his dark eyes watching. He arrogantly descended toward her, until he was at the bottom with her. He had a fine form, she supposed, displayed as it was without a shirt. He was close enough to feel the heat of him.

Nicci looked him in the eye. He was the same height as she.

"I want you to have sex with me."

"What?"

"My husband does not adequately take care of my needs. I wish you to."

A smirk spread on his face as his gaze slid to Richard. He looked back at her bosom, at what was within his power to possess.

Gadi was young and bold and stupid enough to believe himself irresistible to her, to believe his puerile primping had swept away her inhibitions to the point of helpless lust for what he had to offer.

One arm pulled her to him. With his other hand, he swept her hair out of the way. His thin lips kissed her neck. When his teeth raked her flesh, she moaned to encourage him to be rough. The last thing in the world she wanted was tenderness. There could be no retribution in tenderness. Tenderness would not cleave Richard's soul with anguish. Tenderness would not hurt him.

Gadi's hands squeezed her bottom, pulling her hard against his groin. He moved against her in a lewd fashion. She panted in his ear to encourage his confidence in his dominion over her body.

"Tell me why."

"I'm sick of his gentle nature, his kind touch, his caring ways. That's not what a real woman needs. I want him to know what a real man can do—I want what he can't give me."

She nearly cried out in pain when he twisted her nipple.

"Yeah?"

"Yes. I want what a real man like you can do for a woman."

His rough hands squeezed her breast. She performed another moan. He smiled.

"My pleasure."

His smirk sickened her. "No, mine," she whispered in breathy submission.

He cast one more hateful glare at Richard, then bent to slip a hand up the front of her dress to see if she really meant it, if she would really let him have his way with her. His hand slid up the inside of her bare thigh, commanding surrender. She obediently parted her legs for him.

Nicci held on to his shoulders as he groped her. His upper lip curled in a haughty grin. His fingers worked without mercy. Her eyes watered. She trembled and bit the inside of her cheek to hold back her cry. Mistaking agony for lust, he was inflamed by her whimpers.

Jagang and his friend Kadar Kardeef, to name but a few, took her without her consent. None of it had ever approached the sense of violation she felt at that moment as she stood there in the hall letting that smirking little thug do to her as he would.

She forced her hand down between them and seized him.

"Gadi, are you afraid of Richard? Are are you man enough to take me while he is outside the room, listening to us, knowing you are his better with me?"

"Afraid? Of him?" His voice came in a husky growl. "Just tell me when."

"Right now. I need it from you now, Gadi."

"I thought so."

Nicci smiled inwardly at his solemn look of lust.

"Say 'please,' first, you little whore."

"Please." She ached only to crush his worthless skull. "Please, Gadi."

With his arm around her waist, Gadi gave Richard a taunting sneer as he swaggered past. Nicci's fingers on Gadi's back urged him to go on into their room and wait. He smiled over his shoulder and did as she wanted. Nicci paused to glare into Richard's eyes.

"We are linked. What happens to me, happens to her. I hope you are not foolish enough to think I wouldn't make you sorry for the rest of your days if you don't stay right there. I swear to you, she will die this night if you don't stay there."

"Nicci, please don't do this. You're only hurting yourself."

His voice was so tender, so compassionate. She almost threw her arms around him to beg him to stop her . . . but the flame of his refusal still burned shamefully in her heart.

Nicci turned back from the doorway and gave Richard a vicious grin. "I hope your Kahlan enjoys this as much as I'm going to enjoy it. After tonight, she will never believe in you again."

Kahlan gasped. Her eyes opened. She could only make out obscure shapes in the swirling darkness. She gasped again.

A feeling she couldn't define, couldn't interpret, couldn't put a nature to, welled up in her. It was something totally foreign, yet at the same time bewitchingly familiar. Something inappropriate, yet longed for. It filled her with a kind of passionate terror that undulated seductively to indecent pleasure, pushing before it a sense of shapeless dread.

She felt the weight of a shadow over her.

Feelings and sensations she could not grasp or control inundated her even as she fought them. Nothing seemed real. She gasped again at the crude sensation. It confused her. It hurt, and at the same time she felt a kind of wild hunger awakening.

It was as if Richard were there, in bed with her. It felt so good again. She was panting. Her mouth was dry as dust.

In Richard's intimate embrace she had always felt a kind of expectant delight that their shameless lust could never be completely sated—that there was always a spark of something left to explore, to reach toward, to define. She had always exalted in the idea of that endless quest for the unattainable.

She drew a sharp breath. She felt herself in that headlong rush, now.

But this was something she had never imagined. Her fists clutched at the sheets, her mouth opened in a silent scream against the ripping thrust of pain.

This was not human. It made no sense. She gasped again in panic as the most awful feelings burgeoned through her. She moaned at the horror of it, at the hint of pleasure in it, and at the confusion of nearly enjoying the sensation.

The realization came to her. She knew what this meant.

Tears stung her eyes. She rolled onto her side, torn between the joy of feeling Richard, and the pain of knowing that Nicci was feeling him in this way, too. She was slammed onto her back.

She gasped again, her eyes going wide, her whole body rigid.

She cried out at the pain. She twisted and struggled, covering her breasts with her arms. Her eyes watered at agony she couldn't explain or completely identify.

She missed Richard so much. She wanted him so badly it hurt.

She gave in to him, even in this, she surrendered herself to him. A low wail escaped her throat.

Her muscles knotted as tight as oak roots. She was racked with wave after wave of startling pain mixed with an unsatisfied longing that had turned to revulsion. She couldn't get her breath.

She burst into tears as it ceased, her body finally able to move again, but too exhausted to do so. She had hated every violent appalling brutal second of it, and grieved that it had ended because she had at least felt him.

397

She felt joy that she had so unexpectedly sensed him, and blind rage at what it meant. She clutched the sheets in her fists as she wept inconsolably.

"Mother Confessor?" A dark form slipped into the tent. "Mother Confessor?"

It was Cara's whisper. Cara set a candle on the table. The light seemed blindingly bright as Cara looked down. "Mother Confessor, are you all right?"

Kahlan pulled a ragged breath. She was lying on her back in her bed, tangled in her blanket. It was twisted around between her legs.

Maybe it was just a dream. She wished it was. She knew it wasn't.

Kahlan ran her fingers back into her hair as she sat up. "Cara—" It came out as a choking sob.

Cara knelt on the ground beside her and gripped Kahlan's shoulders. "What is it?"

Kahlan struggled to get her breath.

"What's wrong? What can I do? Are you hurt? Are you sick?"

"Oh, Cara . . . he's been with Nicci."

Cara held her at arms length, her face a picture of concern.

"What are you talking about? Who's been—"

Her words cut off when she realized what Kahlan meant.

Kahlan struggled against Cara's grip. "How could he—"

"She no doubt made him," Cara insisted. "He must have done it to save your life. She would have had to threaten him."

Kahlan was shaking her head. "No, no. He was enjoying it too much. He was like an animal. He never took me like that. He never acted . . . Oh, Cara, he's fallen for her. He couldn't resist her any longer. He's—"

Cara shook her until Kahlan thought her teeth would come loose.

"Wake up! Open your eyes. Mother Confessor, wake up. You're half asleep. You're still half dreaming."

Kahlan blinked as she looked around. She was panting, still getting her breath. She had stopped crying.

Cara was right. It had happened, there was no doubt in Kahlan's mind, but it had happened when she was sleeping, and in her sleep, it had taken her unaware. She hadn't reacted rationally.

"You're right," Kahlan said in a voice hoarse from crying. Her nose was stuffed up so that she could only breath through her mouth.

"Now," Cara said in a calm voice, "tell me what happened."

When she felt her face go red, Kahlan wished for the darkness. How could she tell anyone what had happened? She wished Cara hadn't heard her.

"Well, through the link"—Kahlan swallowed—"I could sense that, that, well, that Richard made love to Nicci."

Cara looked skeptical. "Did it feel like when, well, I mean, are you sure? Could you tell it was him?"

Kahlan felt her face go a darker shade of red. "Not exactly, I guess. I don't know." She covered her breasts. "I could feel his . . . his teeth on me. He was biting . . ."

Cara scratched her head, averting her gaze, unsure how to frame her question. Kahlan answered it for her.

"Richard never hurt me like that."

"Oh. Well then, it wasn't Richard."

"What do you mean it wasn't Richard? It had to be Richard."

"Did it? Would Richard want to make love to Nicci?"

"Cara—she could make him. Threaten him."

"Do you think Nicci is an honorable person?"

Kahlan frowned. "Nicci? Are you out of your mind?"

"There you go, then. Why must it be Richard? Nicci may have simply found some man she had to have—some handsome farmboy. It could be nothing more than that."

"Really? You think so?"

"You said it didn't seem like Richard. I mean, you were half asleep, and in . . . shock. You said he never . . . ."

Kahlan looked away. "No, I suppose not." She looked back at the Mord-Sith in the dim light. "I'm sorry, Cara. Thank you for being here with me. I'd not have liked it if it had been Zedd, or someone else. Thank you."

Cara smiled. "I think we'd best keep this between the two of us."

Kahlan nodded gratefully. "If Zedd ever started in asking all his detailed questions about this, well, I'd die of embarrassment."

Kahlan realized then that Cara was wrapped in a blanket that was open in the front enough to reveal that she was naked underneath. There was a dark mark on the upper half of her breast. There were a few more, but faint. Kahlan had seen Cara naked, and didn't recall there being any such mark on her. In fact, except for her scars, her body was exasperatingly perfect.

Frowning, Kahlan gestured. "Cara, what's that there?"

Cara glanced down and then threw the blanket closed.

"It's, I mean, well, it's . . . just a bruise."

A love bruise—from a man's mouth.

"Is Benjamin over there in your tent with you?"

Cara got to her bare feet. "Mother Confessor, you are still half asleep and having dreams. Go back to sleep."

Kahlan smiled as she watched Cara leave. The smile faded as she lay back in her bed. In the quiet loneliness, her doubts crept back.

She cupped her breasts. Her nipples throbbed and ached. As she moved on the bed a little, she winced as she only then began to realize how much she hurt, and where.

She couldn't believe that, even in her sleep, a part of it had been . . . She felt her face reddening again. She felt an overwhelming sense of shame at what she had done.

No. She had done nothing. She was only sensing something through her link to Nicci. It wasn't real. She hadn't really experienced it—Nicci had. But Kahlan suffered the same injuries.

As she had at various times, Kahlan still felt that connection to Nicci through the link, and an aching sort of caring about the woman. What had happened left Kahlan feeling saddened. She felt that Nicci had so desperately wanted . . . something.

Kahlan slipped her hand down between her legs. She flinched in pain as she touched herself. She brought her fingers up to the candlelight. They glistened with blood. There was a lot of blood.

Despite the burning pain of being torn inside, the confused embarrassment, and the shadow of shame, she most of all felt a sense of relief.

She knew without doubt: Cara was right, it had not been Richard.

Ann peered among the stand of birch trees crowded in the deep shadows of cliffs for which the place was named. The dense wood was thick with the trees, their peeling white bark covered with dark blotches making it disorienting and difficult to make sense of anything. To become disoriented, here, and wander into the wrong place, uninvited, was the last mistake you would ever make.

It had been in her youth that she'd last come here, to the Healers of Redcliff. She'd promised herself she would never return. She'd promised the healers as much, too. In the nearly thousand years since, she hoped they had forgotten.

Few people knew of the place, and even fewer ever came here—with good reason.

The term "healers" was an odd and highly misleading designation for such a dangerous lot, yet it wasn't entirely without merit. The Healers of Redcliff weren't concerned with human ailments, but with the well-being of things that mattered to them. And very odd things indeed mattered to them. To tell the truth of it, after all this time, she would be surprised to find them still in existence.

As much as she hoped their talents could help, and as desperately as she needed help, she hoped to find that the healers no longer stalked the Redcliff Wood.

"Visitooor . . ." hissed a teasing voice from the dim shadows in the crags of the cliff off behind the trees.

Ann stood still. Cold sweat dotted her brow. Among the confusion of lines and spots made by the trees, she could not make out what it was she saw move. She didn't really need to see them. She had heard the voice. There were no others like theirs. She swallowed, and tried to sound composed.

"Yes, I am a visitor. I'm glad to find you well."

"Only us few left," the voice said, echoing among the rock walls. "The chiiiimes took most."

That was what Ann had feared . . . what she had hoped.

"I'm sorry," she lied.

"Tried," the voice said, moving through the trees. "Could not heal the chiiiimes away."

She wondered if they could still heal at all, and how long they would last.

"Comes sheeee for a healings?" teased a voice from the depths of the jagged clefts to the other side.

"Come to let you look," she said, letting them know she had terms, too. It would not be all their way.

"Costsssss, you know."

Ann nodded. "Yes, I know."

She had tried everything else. Nothing had worked. She had no other choice, at least none she could think of. She was no longer sure if it mattered to her what happened, if it mattered if she ever came out of the Redcliff Wood.

She was no longer sure if she had ever done any real good in her entire life.

"Well?" she asked into the shadowy silence.

Something flashed back behind the trees, back in the shade under low rock ledges, as if inviting her further along the path, deeper into the twisting cleft in the mountains. Rubbing her knuckles, which still ached from the burns long healed, she followed the path, and the rustle of brush. Shortly, she came to a small gap in the trees. Back through that gap, she could see the craggy opening of a cave.

Eyes watched from that dark maw.

"Comes sheeee in," the voice hissed.

In resignation, Ann let out a sigh as she stepped off the trail, and into a place she had never forgotten, despite how much she had tried.

Kahlan's hair whipped around, lashing at her face. She gathered it in a fist over the front of her armored shoulder as she made her way through the hectic camp. Thunderstorms collided violently with the mountains at the east side of the valley, throwing off lightning, thunder, and intermittent sheets of rain. Sporadic gusts bent the trees, and their leaves shimmered as if trembling in fright before the onslaught.

Usually, the camp was relatively quiet so as not to give any unwanted information to the enemy. Now, the noise of camp breaking up was jarring by contrast. The noise alone was enough to make her pulse race. If only that were all.

As Kahlan hurried through what to the untrained eye would look like mass confusion, Cara, in her red leather, shoved men out of the way to break a clear path for the Mother Confessor. Kahlan knew better than to try to get the Mord-Sith not to do it. At least it caused no harm. Most of the men, when they saw Kahlan in her leather armor with a D'Haran sword at her hip and the hilt of the Sword of Truth sticking up over her shoulder, moved out of her way without Cara's help.

Horses nearby reared as they were being harnessed to a wagon. Men shouted and cursed as they struggled to get the team under control. The horses bellowed in protest. Other men ran through camp, leaping over fires and gear as they rushed to deliver messages. Men sprang out of the way as wagons sped along, splashing mud and water. A long column of lancers five men wide was already marching off into the threatening gloom. Their supporting archers were scrambling to fall in with them.

The path to the lodge was set with stones so people heading for it would not have to walk in the mud, though one still had to run the gauntlet of mosquitoes. Rain swept in just as Kahlan and Cara made the door. Zedd was there, with Adie, General Meiffert and several of his officers, Verna, and Warren. They were all loosely gathered around the table pulled to the center of the room. Half a dozen maps lay atop one another on the table.

The mood in the room was tense.

"How long ago?" Kahlan asked without any greetings.

"Just now," General Meiffert said. "They're taking their time striking camp. They're not organizing for an attack. They're simply forming up to move out."

Kahlan rubbed her fingertips against her brow. "Any word on the direction?"

The general shifted his posture, betraying his frustration. "The scouts say that by all indications they're going north, but nothing more specific than that, yet."

"They aren't coming after us?"

"They could always change course, or send an army over here, but right now, it appears they aren't interested in coming in here after us."

"Jagang doesn't need to come after us," Warren said. Kahlan thought he looked a little pale. Small wonder. She imagined they were all a little pale. "Jagang has to know we are going to come at him. He's not going to bother coming in here after us."

Kahlan couldn't dispute his logic. "If he goes north, he has to know we're not going to sit here and wave good-bye."

The emperor had changed his tactics—again. Kahlan had never seen a commander like him. Most military men had their preferred methods. If they had once won a battle in a certain way, they would suffer a dozen losses with the same tactics, thinking it had to work because it once had. Some were limited by their intellect. Those were easy enough to read; they usually waged an artless campaign, content to throw men into a meat grinder, hoping to clog it with sheer numbers. Some leaders were clever, inventing tactics as they went. Those often thought too much of themselves and ended up on the point of a simple pike. Others slavishly went about using textbook tactics, thinking of war as a kind of game, and that each side should oblige the other by following rules.

Jagang was different. He learned to read his enemy. He held to no favored method. After Kahlan had hit him with quick limited attacks driven into the center of his camp, he learned the tactic and, instead of relying on his overpowering numbers, sent the same kind of attack back at the D'Haran army to good effect. Some men could be driven to making foolish mistakes by shaming them. Jagang didn't make the same mistake twice. He reined in his pride and changed his tactics again, not obliging Kahlan with foolhardy counterattacks.

The D'Harans had still managed to carve him up. They had taken out Imperial Order troops in unprecedented numbers. Their own losses, while painful, were remarkably low considering what they had accomplished.

Winter, though, had killed far more of the enemy than anything Kahlan and her men could conceive. The Imperial Order, being from far to the south, was unfamiliar with and ill prepared for winter in the New World. Well over half a million men had frozen to death. Several hundred thousand more had succumbed to fevers and sickness from the harsh life in the field.

The winter alone had cost Jagang nearly three-quarters of a million men. It was almost beyond comprehension.

Kahlan now commanded roughly three hundred thousand troops in the southern reaches of the Midlands. Under ordinary circumstances, that would be a force capable of crushing any enemy.

The men streaming up from the Old World had replaced the enemy losses several times over. Jagang's army was now well over two and a half million men. It grew by the day.

Jagang had been content to sit tight for the winter. Fighting in such conditions was, for the most part, impossible. He had wisely waited out the weather. When spring had come, he still sat. Apparently, he was smart enough to know that warfare in spring mud was a deadly undertaking. In the muddy season, you could lose your supply wagons if they got strung out. Streams became impassable floods. Losing wagons was a slow death by starvation. Cavalry were next to useless in the mud. Losses to falls in a cavalry charge cost valuable mounts, to say nothing of the men. Soldiers could make an attack, of course, but without supporting services, it was likely to be a bloodbath for no real gain.

Jagang had sat out the spring mud. His minions had used the time to spread the word about "Jagang the Just." Kahlan was infuriated when she got reports, weeks after the fact, about "envoys of peace" who had shown up in various cities throughout the Midlands, giving speeches about bringing the world together for the good of all mankind. They promised piece and prosperity, if they were welcomed into cities.

Now, with summer finally upon them, Jagang was beginning his campaign anew. He planned his troops to now visit those cities his envoys had been to.

The door burst open. It was not the wind, but Rikka. The Mord-Sith looked like she hadn't slept in days.

Cara went to her side, to be ready to offer assistance if requested, but didn't directly lend a hand for support. A Mord-Sith did not look favorably upon help in front of others.

Rikka stepped up to the table, opposite Kahlan, and tossed two Agiel down atop the map.

Kahlan closed her eyes for a moment, then looked up into Rikka's fierce blue eyes. "What happened?"

"I don't know, Mother Confessor. I found their heads impaled on pikes. Their Agiel were tied to the pikes."

Kahlan held her anger in check. "Are you satisfied, now, Rikka?"

"Galina and Solvig died as Mord-Sith would want to die."

"Galina and Solvig died for nothing, Rikka. After the first four, we knew it wouldn't work. With the dream walker in their minds, the gifted are not vulnerable to Mord-Sith in the way that would otherwise be the case."

"It could have been something else. If we can catch their gifted where the Mord-Sith can get at them, then we might be able to take them out. It's worth the risk. Their gifted can cut down thousands of soldiers with a sweep of their hand."

"I understand the wish, Rikka. Wishing, however, does not make it possible. We have six dead Mord-Sith to show us the reality of what is. We will not throw away the lives of any more because we refuse to recognize the truth of it."

"I still think—"

"Those of us here have important things to decide; I don't have time for this." Kahlan put her fists on the table and leaned toward the woman. "I am the Mother Confessor, and the wife to Lord Rahl. You will do as I say or you will leave. Do you understand?"

Rikka's blue eyes shifted to Cara. Cara stood as expressive as a stone. Rikka looked back at Kahlan and let out a long sigh.

"I wish to remain with our forces and do my duty."

"Fine. Now, go get yourself something to eat while you still have a chance. We need you to be strong."

For a Mord-Sith, Rikka's little nod was about as close to a salute as it came. After she was gone, Kahlan swatted at the plague of mosquitoes and returned her attention to the map.

"So," she said, removing the two Agiel from the map, "who has any suggestions?"

"I'd say we have to keep at their edges," Zedd offered. "Obviously, we can't be throwing ourselves in front of them. We can do nothing but to continue to fight them as we have been doing."

"I agree," Verna said.

General Meiffert rubbed his chin as he stared down at the map spread out before them on the table. "What we have to worry about is his size."

"Well, of course we have to worry about the size of the Order," Kahlan said. "They have enough men to split up and still be too huge to handle. That's what I'm talking about—what we're going to do when he splits. If I were him, that's what I'd do. He knows how it would complicate our lives."

There was an urgent knock. Warren, over by the window, not bothering to look at the map with the rest of them, opened the door.

Captain Zimmer stepped in, giving a quick salute of his fist to his heart. Panting as he entered, he brought with him a swirling rush of warm air that smelled like a horse. Ignoring the rest of them, Warren returned to his brooding at the window.

"He's splitting his force," Captain Zimmer announced, as if their fear had given birth to the reality.

Most in the room sighed unhappily with the news.

"Any direction, yet?" Kahlan asked.

Captain Zimmer nodded. "From the looks of it, he's sending maybe a third, possibly a little more, up the Callisidrin Valley toward Galea. The main force is heading to the northeast, probably to enter and go north up the Kern Valley."

They all knew the eventual goal.

Zedd made a fist. "There's no joy in being right, but that's just what Kahlan and I talked about. That was our guess."

General Meiffert was still rubbing his chin as he studied the map. "It's an obvious move, but with the size of his force the obvious is not a liability."

No one wanted to broach the issue, so Kahlan settled the matter. "Galea is on its own. We're not sending any troops to help them."

Captain Zimmer finally waggled a finger at the map. "We need to put our forces in front of their main force to slow them down. If we stay on their heels instead, we will only be cleaning up the mess they make."

"I'd have to agree." The general shifted his weight to his other foot. "We have no choice but to try to slow them. We'll have to keep giving ground, but at least we can slow them. Otherwise, they are going to move up through the center of the Midlands with the speed and power of a spring flood."

Zedd was watching the young wizard off by himself at the window. "Warren, what do you think?"

Warren looked up at the sound of his name, as if he hadn't been paying attention. Something about him didn't look well. He took a breath and straightened, his face brightening, making Kahlan think she had been mistaken. Hands clasped behind his back, Warren strode to the table.

He peered at the map from over Verna's shoulder. "Forget Galea—it's a lost cause. We cannot help them. They will suffer the sentence imposed upon them by the Mother Confessor—not because she spoke the words, but because her words were simple truth. Any troops we sent to help would be forfeit."

Zedd cast a sidelong glance at his fellow wizard. "What else?"

Warren finally moved closer to the table, wedging himself between Verna and the general. With authority, he firmly planted his finger on the map, far to the north—almost three-quarters of the way to Aydindril from where they were camped.

"You have to go there."

General Meiffert frowned. "Up there? Why?"

"Because," Warren said, "you can't stop Jagang's army—his main force. You can only hope to slow them as they move north, up into the Kern Valley. This is where you must make a stand, if you hope to delay them next winter. Once they move through you, they will be upon Aydindril."

"Move through us?" General Meiffert asked in an surly manner.

Warren looked up at him. "Well, do you suppose you are going to be able to stop them? It wouldn't surprise me if by then they have three and a half to four million men."

The general let out an ill-tempered breath. "Then why do you think we should be at that spot—right in their way?"

"You can't stop them, but if you harry them sufficiently as they move north, you can keep them from reaching Aydindril this year. At this spot, they will be running out of time before the weather closes in. With a bit of stiff resistance, you can grind them to a halt for the winter, buying Aydindril one more season of freedom."

Warren looked up into Kahlan's eyes. "The following summer, a year from now, Aydindril will fall. Prepare them for it in whatever way you are able, but make no mistake: the city will fall to the Order."

Kahlan's blood ran cold. To hear him say the words aloud staggered her. She wanted to slap him.

To contemplate the Imperial Order taking their attack into the heart of the Midlands was horrifying. To accept, as foreordained, the Imperial Order seizing the heart of the New World was unthinkable. Kahlan's mental image of Jagang and his bloodthirsty thugs strolling the halls of the Confessors' Palace sickened her.

Warren leaned around the general to look at Zedd. "The Wizard's Keep must be protected—you know that better than I. It would be the end of all hope if their gifted were to gain the Keep and the dangerous things of magic stored there. I think the time has come to keep that above all else in our thinking. Holding the Keep is vital."

Zedd smoothed back his unruly white hair. "I could hold the Keep by myself, if I had to."

Warren looked away from Zedd's hazel eyes. "You may have to," he said in a quiet voice. "When we get to this place"—he tapped the map again—"then you can do no more with the army, Zedd, and you must go to safeguard the Wizard's Keep and the things of magic kept there."

Kahlan could feel the blood heating her face. "You're talking about this as if it's all settled—as if it has been decided by fate and there is nothing we can do about it. We can't win if we hold such a defeatist attitude."

Warren smiled, his shy manner suddenly surfacing. "I'm sorry, Mother Confessor. I didn't mean to give you that impression. I am only offering my analysis of the facts of the situation. We aren't going to be able to stop them—there's no use deluding ourselves about that. They grow larger by the day. We must also take into account that there are going to be lands, such as Anderith and Galea, which fear the Order and will join them rather than suffer the brutal fate of those who refuse to surrender.

"I lived in the Old World as it fell, bit by bit, to the Imperial Order. I've studied Jagang's methods. I know the man's patience. He methodically conquered the entire Old World when such a feat seemed inconceivable. He spent years building roads just to be able to accomplish his plans. He never wavers from his goal. There are times when you can anger or humiliate him into a rash action, but he quickly comes to his senses.

"He quickly comes to his senses because he has a cause that is paramount to him.

"You must understand something important about Jagang. It's the most important thing I can tell you about the man: he believes with all his heart that what he is doing is right. He revels in the glory of conquest and victory, to be sure, but his deepest pleasure is being the one who has brought what he sees as righteousness to those he views as heathens. He believes that mankind can only advance, ethically, if they are all brought under the moral authority of the Order."

"That's just nonsense," Kahlan said.

"You may think so, but he truly believes he is serving the cause of the greater good for mankind. He believes piously in this. It is a sacred moral truth to him and his ilk."

"He believes that murder, rape, and enslavement are just?" General Meiffert asked. "He would have to be out of his mind."

"He was raised at the feet of priests of the Fellowship of Order." Warren lifted a finger to make sure they all noted his point. "He believes that all those things and more are justified. He believes that only the next world matters, because then we will be in the eternal Light of the Creator. The Order believes that you earn that reward in the next world by sacrificing for your fellow man in this world. All those who refuse to see this—that would be us—must either be brought to follow the Order's ways, or die."

"So," General Meiffert said, "it's his sacred duty to crush us. It's not plunder he seeks, primarily, but his bizarre version of the salvation of mankind."

"Exactly."

"All right," Kahlan said with a sigh. "So, what do you think this holy man of justice will do?"

"He basically has two choices, I believe. If he is to conquer the New World and bring all of mankind under the authority of the Order, he must take two important places, or he has not really succeeded: Aydindril, because it is the seat of power in the Midlands, and the People's Palace in D'Hara, because it reigns over the D'Haran people. If those two fall, everything else will crumble. He could have gone for either. Emperor Jagang has now made his choice of which falls first.

"The Imperial Order is going for Aydindril in order to split the Midlands. Why else would they go north? What better way to defeat an enemy than to cleave them in two? After they have Aydindril, they will turn their swords to an isolated D'Hara. What better way to demoralize an enemy than to first go for their heart?

"I am not saying that it is preordained, but merely telling you the way the Order goes about its grisly work. This is the same thing Richard has already figured out. Given that we can't realistically expect to stop them, I think it only wise to face the reality of what is, don't you?"

Kahlan's gaze sank to the map. "I believe that in the darkest hours we must believe in ourselves. I do not intend to surrender the D'Haran Empire to the Imperial Order. We need to wage the best war we can until we can turn it around."

"The Mother Confessor is right," Zedd insisted with quiet authority. "The last great war I fought, in my youth, seemed just as hopeless for a time. We prevailed, and drove the invaders back to the place from where they had come."

None of the D'Haran officers said anything. It was D'Hara that was that invader.

"But things are different, now. That was a war pressed by an evil leader." Zedd met the gaze of General Meiffert, Captain Zimmer, and the other D'Haran officers. "Every side in a war has good people, just as they all have the bad. Richard, as the new Lord Rahl, has given those good people a chance to flourish.

"We must prevail in this. As difficult as it may now be to believe, there are good people in the Old World, too, who would not wish to be under the boot heel of the Order, or to press a war for the Order's reasons. Nonetheless, we must stop them."

"So," Kahlan said, gesturing at the map before Warren, "how do you think Jagang will press the war?"

Warren tapped the map again, to the south of Aydindril. "Knowing Jagang and the way he conquers his opponents, I think he will stick to his grand plan. He has a goal and will doggedly continue to move toward it. There is nothing we have shown him that he has not seen from other opponents for his whole life. With that experience, I'm sure he finds this war unexceptional. I don't mean to discount our efforts—all war has its surprises, and we've given him some nasty ones. I would say, though, that it is going largely as he expected.

"It will take them the summer to advance to this place I've shown you, given his usual pace and the fact that you will be harrying them. Jagang, in general, has always moved slowly, but with unstoppable force. He will simply pour in enough men to crush the opposition. He feels that if he takes time to get to his enemy, it only gives them more time to tremble in fear of him. When he finally arrives, his enemies are often ready to crumble from the agony of the wait.

"If you put your force there, where I showed you, you will be able to protect Aydindril next winter, as Jagang will be content to bide his time. He has learned what a hardship the winters are in the New World. He will not needlessly press a winter campaign. But in the summer, when they move again, like they do now, then Aydindril will fall—whether or not you stand against the weight of their main force. When they move on Aydindril, we must hold the Wizard's Keep. That is all we can do."

The room was silent. The fire was cold, now. Warren and Verna had already packed their things and were ready to go, as was most of the rest of the army. Warren and Verna were losing their home. Kahlan glanced to the side, letting her gaze linger on the curtains she had long ago made for them. Their wedding seemed but a dim memory.

Her own wedding seemed but a distant dream. Every time she woke, Richard seemed almost a ghost to her. Mind-numbing, relentless, never-ending war seemed the only reality. There were occasional fleeting moments when she thought that she might have only dreamed him, that he couldn't possibly have really existed, that their long-ago happy summer home in the mountains never happened. Those moments of doubt terrified her more than Jagang's army.

"Warren," Kahlan asked in a soft voice, "what then? What do you think will happen the following summer, after they have taken Aydindril?"

Warren shrugged. "I don't know. Maybe Jagang will be content to digest Aydindril for a while, to establish firm control over the Midlands. He believes it his duty to his Creator to bring all of mankind under the Order. Sooner or later, he will move on D'Hara."

Kahlan finally directed her attention to Captain Zimmer.

"Captain, get your men ready. While we're getting all our supplies and such on

407

the way, you might as well go and remind Jagang that we have kept our blades sharp."

The captain grinned and clapped his fist to his heart.

Kahlan swept her gaze across everyone in the room.

"I intend to make the Order shed blood for every inch they take. If that is all I can do, then I will do it until I breathe my last breath."

The dead-still air was sweltering and reeked of stagnant sewage. Richard wiped sweat from his brow. At least as long as his sturdy wagon was rolling through the streets he could enjoy a little breeze.

Distracted out of his concern over knowing Kahlan and Cara had to have long since left the safety of their mountain home, he noticed an unusual amount of activity for the middle of the night. Shadowy figures hurried down the dark streets to dart into dim buildings. Slashes of light briefly fell to the street until doors could be pulled shut. The moon was out, and in the darker alleys he thought he saw people watching him, waiting until he passed before they went on their way. Over the rumble of his wagon's wheels he couldn't hear anything they might be saying.

As he turned onto the road that would take him out to the charcoal maker, he had to pull his team up short as men with long pole weapons stepped out and blocked his way. A guard seized the horses' bits. Other of the city guard swept out of the side street to point lances up at him.

"What are you doing out here?" one of the voices asked from the side of the wagon.

Richard calmly yanked up on the lever to set the brake.

"I have a special pass to move goods at night. It's for the emperor's palace."

The words "emperor's palace" were usually enough to have him on his way.

The guard waggled his fingers. "If you have a special pass, then let's see it."

This night, the guards wanted more. Richard pulled a folded piece of paper from a protective leather sleeve inside his shirt and held it down to the guard. Metal squeaked as the guard slid open a tiny door on his shielded lantern, letting a narrow slit of light fall across the paper. Several heads bent in to read the words and inspect the official seals. They were all genuine. They should be—they had cost Richard a small fortune.

"Here you go." The guard handed the paper back to Richard. "Have you seen anything unusual as you have gone through the city?"

"Unusual? What do you mean?"

The guard grunted. "If you had seen anything, you wouldn't have to ask." He waved his hand. "On your way."

Richard made no effort to leave. "Should I be worried?" He made a show of looking around. "Are there highwaymen about? Am I in danger? Is it safe for a citizen to be out? I'll take the wagon back if it's dangerous."

The man chuckled derisively. "You've got nothing to be afraid of. It's just some foolish people making trouble because they've nothing better to do."

"That's all it is? Are you sure?"

"You have work to do for the palace. Get to it."

"Yes, sir." Richard clicked his tongue and flicked the reins. The heavy wagon lurched ahead.

He didn't know what was going on, but suspected the guards were out to catch some more insurgents for questioning. They probably wanted to get back to their post, so anyone they got their hands on was likely to end up being an insurgent. A man from Ishaq's place had been arrested several days before. He had been drunk on homemade liquor and left a meeting early. He never made it home. A few days later, Ishaq had received word that the man had confessed to crimes against the Order. The man's wife and daughter were arrested. The wife was released after receiving a specified number of lashes for confessing to speaking ill of the Order and having hateful thoughts about her neighbors. The daughter had not yet been released. No one even knew where she was being held.

Eventually he reached the edge of the city where it gave way to open fields. Richard took a deep breath of the agreeable aroma of freshly turned earth. Lights from occasional farms glimmered like lonely stars. In the moonlight Richard could finally see the rough skyline of forest. As he rolled into the charcoal maker's place, the charcoal maker, a nervous man named Faval, scurried up to the side of the wagon.

"Richard Cypher! There you are. I was worried about you coming."

"Why?"

The man let out a high-pitched titter. Faval frequently giggled at things that weren't funny. Richard understood that it was just his way. He was a jumpy fellow and his laugh was not meant as disrespect, but was rather something he couldn't help. A lot of people, though, avoided Faval because of his strange laugh, fearing he might be crazy—a punishment, they believed, imposed on sinners by the Creator. Others got angry at him because they thought he was laughing at them. That only made Faval more nervous, which made him laugh all the more. Faval was missing his front teeth and his nose was crooked from being broken a number of times. Richard knew the man couldn't really help it, and so never gave him trouble about it. Faval had taken a liking to him.

"I don't know, I just thought you might not come."

Faval's big eyes blinked in the moonlight. Richard's face wrinkled in a puzzlement.

"Faval, I said I was coming. Why would you think I might not?"

Faval's fingers worried at his earlobe. "No reason."

Richard climbed down. "The city guards stopped me—"

"No!" Faval's titter rippled out through the darkness. "What did they want? Did they ask you anything?"

"They wanted to know if I'd seen anything unusual."

"But you didn't." He giggled. "They let you go. You saw nothing."

"Well," Richard drawled, "I did see that fellow with the two heads."

Crickets chirped in the silence. Faval blinked in astonishment. In the moonlight, Richard could see his mouth hanging open.

"You saw a man with two heads?"

This time, it was Richard who laughed. "No, Faval, I didn't. It was just a joke."

"It was? But it wasn't funny."

Richard sighed. "I suppose not. Have you got the load of charcoal ready? I've got a long night ahead of me. Victor needs a load of steel, and Priska needs charcoal or he said he would have to close down. He said you didn't send your last order."

Faval giggled. "I couldn't! I wanted to, Richard Cypher. I need the money. I owe the loggers for the trees I made into this charcoal. They told me they were going to quit bringing me wood if I didn't pay them."

Faval lived at the edge of a forest, so his source of wood was handy, but he wasn't allowed to cut the wood. All resources belonged to the Order. Trees were cut when the loggers, who had permits, needed work, not when someone needed wood. Most of the wood lay on the ground and rotted. Anyone caught picking up wood was liable to be arrested for stealing from the Order.

Faval held his hands up as if to implore Richard's understanding. "I tried to get the charcoal transported to Priska, but the committee denied me permission to transport it. They said I don't need the money. Don't need the money! Can you imagine?" He laughed painfully. "They told me that I was a rich man, because I had a business, and that I had to wait while they saw to the needs of the common people, first. I am only trying to live."

"I know, Faval. I told Priska that it wasn't your fault. He understands—he has troubles like that of his own. He's just desperate because he needs the charcoal. You know Priska; he gets hot at those who have nothing to do with the problem. I told him I would bring a load of charcoal tonight, and another two tomorrow night. Can I count on you for two more loads tomorrow?"

Richard held out the silver coins for the load of charcoal.

Faval clapped his hands together prayerfully. "Oh, thank you, Richard Cypher. You are a savior. Those loggers are a nasty lot. Yes, yes, and two tomorrow. I have them cooling now. You are as good as a son to me, Richard Cypher." He motioned off into the darkness as he tittered. "They are there, cooking. You will have them."

Richard could see the dozens and dozens of mounds, like little haystacks, that were the earthen ovens. Small pieces of split wood were tightly stacked around in a circle, with tinder stuffed in the center, building them up into a rounded pile which was then covered over with fern leaves and broom and then plastered over with firm earth. Fire was put in at the bottom, then that opening was closed over. Moisture and smoke escaped from small vents in the top for six to eight days. When the smoke ceased, the vents were sealed to kill the fire. After it cooled, the earthen ovens could be opened and the charcoal removed. It was a labor-intensive occupation, but rather simple work.

"Let me help you load your wagon," Faval said.

Richard caught the man's shirt at his shoulder as he started away. "Faval, what's going on?"

Faval put a finger to his lower lip as he laughed. It almost sounded like it was painful for him to laugh. He hesitated, but finally whispered his answer.

"The revolt. It has started."

Richard had suspected as much. "What do you know about it, Faval?"

"Nothing! I know nothing!"

"Faval, it's me, Richard. I'm not going to turn you in."

Faval laughed. This time it sounded more like relief. "Of course not. Of course not. Forgive me, Richard Cypher. I get so nervous, I wasn't thinking."

"So, what about this revolt?"

Faval turned up his hands in a helpless gesture. "The Order, they strangle people. We can't live. If not for you, Richard Cypher, I would be . . . well, I don't want to think about it. But others, they are not so fortunate. They starve. The Order takes

411

the food they grow. People have loved ones who have been arrested. They confess to things they did not do.

"Did you know that, Richard Cypher? That they confess to things they did not do? I never believed it myself. I thought that if they confessed, then they were guilty. Why confess if you are innocent?" He giggled. "Why? I thought they were terrible people wanting to hurt the Order. I thought it served them right, and I was glad they were arrested and punished."

"So what changed your mind?"

"My brother." Faval's chuckles suddenly were sobs. "He helped me make charcoal. We made it together. We supported our families making charcoal. We worked from sunup until sundown. We slept in the same house, there. That one there. One room. We were together all the time.

"Last year, at a meeting where we all had to stand up and tell how the Order made our lives better, as we were leaving, they arrested him. Someone gave his name as maybe an insurgent. I was not worried. My brother was not guilty of anything. He makes charcoal."

Richard waited in the darkness, sweat trickling down his neck, as Faval stared off into the dark visions.

"For a week, I went every day to the barracks to tell them that he would not do anything against the Order. We loved the Order. The Order wishes all people to be fed and cared for.

"The guards said my brother finally confessed. High crimes, they called it— plotting to overthrow the Order. They said he confessed it to them.

"The next day, I was going to go to see more people, the officials at the barracks—I was so angry—to tell them that they were cruel animals. My wife, she cried and begged me not to go back to the barracks yet again, for fear they would arrest me, too. For her sake, and the children, I did not go. It would do no good, anyway. They had my brother's confession. No one who confesses is innocent. Everyone knows that.

"They put my brother to death. His wife and children live with us, still. We can hardly . . ." Faval giggled as he bit down on his knuckle.

Richard put a hand on the man's shoulder. "I understand, Faval. There was nothing you could have done."

Faval wiped at his eyes. "Now I am guilty of thinking hateful thoughts. That is a crime, you know. I am guilty of it. I think about life without the Order. I dream of having a cart of my own—just a cart—and my sons and nephew could deliver the charcoal we make. Wouldn't that be wonderful, Richard Cypher? I could buy . . ." His voice trailed off.

He looked up in confusion. "But the Order says such thoughts are a crime because I am putting my wants before the needs of others. Why are their needs more important than mine? Why?

"I went to ask for a permit to buy a cart. They say I cannot have one because it would put the cart drivers out of work. They said I was greedy for wanting to put people out of work. They called me selfish for having such thoughts."

"That's wrong," Richard said in quiet assurance. "Your thoughts are not a crime, nor are they evil. It's your life, Faval—you should be able to live it as you see fit. You should be able to buy your cart and work hard and make the best of your life for you and your family."

Faval chortled. "You sound like a revolutionary, Richard Cypher."

Richard sighed, thinking about how useless the whole thing was. "No, Faval."

Faval appraised him in the moonlight for a time. "It has already started, Richard Cypher. The revolt. It has begun."

"I have charcoal to deliver." Richard went around the back of the wagon and hoisted a basket up onto the wagon bed.

Faval helped with the next basket. "You should join them, Richard Cypher. You are a smart man. They could use your help."

"Why?" Richard wondered if he dared get his hopes up. "What do they have planned? What are they going to do with this revolt?"

Faval giggled. "Why, they are marching in the streets, tomorrow. They are going to demand changes."

"What changes?"

"Well, I think they want to be able to work. They are going to demand they be allowed to do what they want." He giggled. "Maybe, I can get a cart? Do you think, Richard Cypher? Do you think that when they have this revolt I can get a cart and deliver my charcoal? I could make more charcoal, then."

"But what do they plan to do? How are they going to change anything if the Order says no?—Which they will."

"Do? Why, I think they will be very angry if the Order tells them no. They may not go back to their jobs. Some say they will break into the stores and take the bread."

Richard's hopes faded back into the shadows.

The man clutched at Richard's sleeve. "What should I do, Richard Cypher? Should I join the revolt? Tell me."

"Faval, you should not ask anyone else what you should do about something like this. How can you endanger your life, the lives of your family, on what a man with a wagon says?"

"But you are a smart man, Richard Cypher. I am not so smart as you."

Richard tapped his finger against the man's forehead. "Faval, in here, in your head, you are smart enough to know what you must do. You have already told me why the Order can never help people have better lives by telling them how they must live. You figured that out all on your own. You, Faval the charcoal maker, are smarter than the Order."

Faval beamed. "You think so, Richard Cypher? No one ever told me before that I was smart."

"You're smart enough to decide for yourself how much it means to you and what you want to do about it."

"I fear for my wife, and my brother's wife, and all our children. I don't want the Order, but I'm afraid for them if I am arrested. How would they live?"

Richard heaved another basket into the wagon. "Faval, listen to me. Revolt is the kind of thing you must be sure of. It's dangerous business. If you are going to join a revolt, you have to be sure enough of what you want to do to be ready to lay down your life for your freedom."

"Really? You think so, Richard Cypher?"

The spark of hope was gone.

"Faval, you stay here and make charcoal. Priska needs charcoal. The Order will arrest those people, and then that will be the end of it. You're a good man. I don't want to see you arrested."

Faval grinned. "All right, Richard Cypher. If you say so, I will stay here and make charcoal."

413

"Good. I'll be back tomorrow night. But Faval, if there is still trouble, I may not make it tomorrow night. If there is still marching going on and the streets and roads are blocked, I may not be able to make it out here."

"I understand. You will be back as soon as you can. I trust you, Richard Cypher. You never let me down."

Richard smiled. "Look, if they are having a revolt tomorrow, and I can't make it out here right away, here's the money for the next load." He handed the man another silver mark. "I don't want those loggers to stop getting wood for you. The foundries need charcoal."

Faval giggled in genuine delight. He kissed the silver mark and slipped it down his boot. "The charcoal will be ready. Now, let me help you load your wagon."

Faval was only one of the charcoal makers with whom Richard dealt. He had a whole string of them he kept going so the foundries could have charcoal. They were all humble people just trying to get along in life. They did the best they could under the yoke of the Order.

Richard made a little profit selling the charcoal to the foundries, but he made more selling iron and steel he bought from them. Charcoal was just a small sideline to help fill his nights, as long as he was out with his wagon. What he made from the charcoal covered the bribes, mostly. He made a good bit more hauling the odd load of ore, clay, lead, quicksilver, antimony, salt, molding powders, and a variety of other things the foundries needed but couldn't get permits for or get transported when they needed them. There was as much of that business as Richard could want. It paid for the care of his team with some profit left over. The iron and steel was pure profit.

By the time he made it to the foundry with the load of charcoal, Priska, the hulking foundry master, was pacing. His powerful hands grabbed the side of the wagon. He peered in.

"About time."

"I had to wait for an hour after I came from Faval's while the city guards inspected the load."

Priska waved his beefy arms. "Those bastards!"

"It's all right—calm down. They didn't take any. I have it all."

The man sighed. "I tell you, Richard, it's a wonder I've kept my furnaces going."

Richard ventured a dangerous question. "You're not involved with the . . . trouble, in the city, are you?"

In the light coming from his office window—really no more than a hut—Priska appraised Richard for a time. "Richard, change is coming. Change for the better."

"What change?"

"A revolt has begun."

Richard felt the spark of hope grow anew, but stronger this time—not so much for himself, his chains held him too tenaciously, but for the people who yearned to be free. Faval was a kind man, a hardworking man, but he was not the clever man, the resourceful man, that Priska was. Priska was a man who knew more than it would seem possible for him to know. Priska had given Richard the names of all the officials who could be bribed for papers, and advised him how much to offer.

"A revolt?" Richard asked "A revolt for what?"

"For us—for the people who want to be able to live our lives as we wish. The new beginning is starting. Tonight. In fact, it has already begun." He turned to his

414

building and pulled open the doors. "When you get to Victor's, you must wait for him, Richard. He must speak with you."

"About what?"

Priska waved dismissively. "Come, give me my charcoal and then load your steel. Victor will bite my head off if I keep you."

Richard pulled the first basket out of the wagon and carried it to the side, where Priska added another.

"What have these people who starting the revolt done? What are their plans?"

Priska leaned close as Richard dragged another basket to the rear of the wagon. "They have captured a number of officials of the Order. High officials."

"Have they killed them, yet?"

"Killed them! Are you crazy? They aren't going to harm them. They will be held until they agree to loosen the rules, satisfy the demands of the people."

Richard gaped at the man. "Loosen the rules? What are they demanding?"

"Things must change. People want to be allowed more say in their businesses, their lives, their work." He lifted a basket of charcoal. "Less meetings. They are demanding to have their needs taken more into consideration."

This time, the spark of Richard's hopes didn't dim, rather, it plunged into icy waters.

He didn't much pay attention to Priska as they unloaded the wagon and then loaded the steel. He didn't really want to listen to the plans for the revolt. He couldn't help getting the gist of it, anyway.

The revolutionaries had it all figured out. They wanted public trials for those people the Order arrested. They wanted to be allowed to see prisoners. They wanted to have the Order give them a list of what had happened to a number of people who had been arrested, but never heard from. There were other details and demands but Richard's mind wandered to other things.

As Richard was climbing up into his wagon to leave, Priska seized his arm in a iron grip. "The time has come, Richard, for men who care to join the revolt."

The two of them shared a long look. "Victor is waiting."

Priska released Richard's arm and grinned. "So he is. I'll see you later, Richard. Perhaps the next trip you make here will be after the Order meets the demands, and you will be able to come in the day, without papers."

"That would be grand, Priska."

By the time he arrived at Victor's, Richard had a headache. He felt sick over what he'd heard, and what he feared yet to hear.

Victor was there, waiting for him. It was a little early, yet, for the man to be there; usually, he didn't arrive until closer to dawn. The blacksmith threw open the doors to his outer stockroom. He set a lantern on a shelf so Richard could see to back his wagon close.

Victor was wearing a wolfish grin as Richard climbed down.

"Come, Richard, unload your wagon, then we will have some lardo, and talk."

Richard went methodically about his task, not really wanting to talk. He had a good idea what Victor wanted to talk about. Victor, as was his way, left Richard to unload. He was the man buying the steel, and enjoyed the service of having it delivered where he wanted it. It was a service he could rarely get from a transport company, despite the higher price.

Richard didn't mind being left alone. Summer this far south in the Old World was miserable. The humidity was oppressive, with the nights rarely better than the days.

As he worked, he thought about the sparkling bright days spent with Kahlan beside the brook at their mountain home. It seemed a lifetime ago. His hopes of ever seeing her again were difficult to keep alive, but his worry for her, now that summer was here, never ceased. Sometimes, it hurt so much to think about her, to miss her, to worry, that he had to put her from his mind. At other times, thoughts of her were all that kept him going.

By the time he had finished, the sky was turning lighter. He found Victor in the far room, the doors open wide so that dawn's light lit Victor's marble monolith. The blacksmith was gazing at the beauty in his stone, at the statue still inside that only he saw.

It was a long moment before he noticed Richard standing not far away.

"Richard, come have lardo with me."

They sat on the threshold looking out over the site of the Retreat, watching the miles of stone walls turn pink in the hazy dawn. Even from the distance, Richard could see along the top of one wall the vile figures representing the evil of mankind.

Victor handed Richard a pure white slice of lardo. "Richard, the revolt I told you about has started. But you probably already know that."

"No it hasn't," Richard said.

Victor stared, dumbfounded. "But it has."

"A lot of trouble has started. It is not the revolt you and I spoke of."

"It will be. You will see. Many men will be marching today." Victor gestured expansively. "Richard, we want you to lead us."

Richard had been expecting the question. "No."

"I know, I know, you think the men don't know you, and they won't follow you, but you are wrong, Richard. Many do know you. More than you think. I have told many of them about you. Priska and others have spoken of you. You can do it, Richard."

Richard stared out at the walls, at the carvings of cowering men.

"No."

Victor was taken aback, this time. "But why not?"

"Because a lot of men are going to die."

Victor chuckled. "No, Richard, no. You misunderstand. This will not be that kind of revolt. This will be a revolt of men of goodwill. This is a revolt for the betterment of mankind. That is what the Order always preaches. We are the people. They say they are for the people, and now, when we put the demands of the people to them, they will have to listen and give in."

Richard shook his head sadly to himself.

"You want me to lead you?"

"Yes."

"Then I want you to do something for me, Victor."

"Of course, Richard. Name it."

"You stay far away from anything to do with this uprising. Those are my orders to you as your leader. You stay here and work today. You stay out of it."

Victor looked as if he thought Richard might be making a joke. After a moment, he saw that Richard was not joking.

"But why? Don't you want things to get better? Do you wish to live like this all your life? Don't you want things to improve?"

"Are you willing to kill those men of the Order that have been captured?"

"Kill them? Richard, why do you want to talk about killing? This is about life. About things being better."

"Victor, listen to me. These men you go up against are not going to play by your rules."

"But they will want—"

"You stay here and work, or you will die along with a lot of other men. The Order will crush this uprising within a day or two, and then they will go after everyone they even suspect had a hand in it. A lot of people are going to die."

"But if you were to lead us, you could present our demands. That is why we want you to lead us—to prevent that kind of trouble. You know how to convince people. You know how to get things done—just look at how you help all the people in Altur'Rang: Faval, Priska, me, and all the others. We need you, Richard. We need you to give people a reason to follow the revolt."

"If they don't know what they stand for and what they want, then no one can give them a reason. They will only succeed when they burn for freedom, and are not only willing to kill for it, but to die for it." Richard stood and brushed the dirt from his pants. "Stay out of it, Victor, or you will die with them."

Victor followed him to his wagon. In the distance, men were arriving to work on the emperor's palace. The blacksmith picked at the wood on the wagon's side, apparently wanting to say more.

"Richard, I know how you feel. I really do. I, too, think these men are not burning with the kind of hunger for freedom that I have, but they are not from Cavatura, as I am, so perhaps they do not know what true freedom is, but for now, this is all we can do. Won't you give it a try, Richard?

"Richard Rahl, of the D'Haran Empire to the north, understands our passion for freedom, and would try."

Richard climbed up into his wagon seat. He wondered where people heard such things, and marveled at how the spark of such ideas could travel so far. After he took up the reins and whip, Richard shared a long look with the sober blacksmith, a man intoxicated with the whiff of freedom in the air.

"Victor, would you try to hammer cold steel into a tool?"

"Of course not. The steel must be white-hot before it can become something."

"So must men, Victor. These men are cold steel. Spare your hammer. I'm sure this Richard Rahl would tell you the same thing."

The uprising lasted a day. Richard stayed home. He asked Nicci to stay home, too. He told her that he'd heard rumors of possible trouble and said he didn't want her to get hurt.

The purge of the insurrectionists by the Order, on the other hand, lasted a week. Men who had participated in the marching had been slaughtered in the streets, or captured by the city guard. Those who were captured were questioned until they eventually confessed the names of others. People questioned by the Order always confessed.

The ripples of arrest, confession, and further arrest spread through the city and went on for days. Hundreds of men were buried in the sky. Eventually, the fires of unrest were snuffed out. The ash of regret covered every tongue as people wanted to forget the whole thing. The marches were rarely even mentioned, as if it had never happened.

Richard finally went back to work at the transport company, rather than risk having his wagon out at night. Jori had nothing to say as they rolled through the city, past the poles holding up rotting corpses buried in the sky.

Jori and Richard made trips out to the mines to pick up ore for the foundries. They made one trip to a sandstone quarry a little ways to the east of the city. That took the whole day there and back. The next day they delivered the stone to the west side of Retreat, where it was needed for a buttress. There were a number of poles, maybe fifty or sixty, on the other side of the walls, over near the carving area. Apparently, some of the workers had been purged, too.

On the way out, they went up the road past the blacksmith's shop. Richard jumped down off the wagon and told Jori that he would go up the hill and join him after the wagon made its way around the twists in the road. He said he had to report to the blacksmith about their next delivery.

Inside the dark workshop, Victor was hammering a long piece of steel, bending the red-hot metal over the horn of an anvil. He looked up and, when he saw it was Richard, thrust the hot metal in the liquid beside this anvil, where it bubbled and hissed.

"Richard! I'm glad to see you."

Richard noticed several of Victor's men were missing. "Sick?"

Victor grimly shook his head.

Richard acknowledged the news with a single nod. "I'm glad to see you well, Victor. I just wanted to stop and make sure you were all right."

"Richard, I'm fine." He hung his head. "Thanks to your advice. I could be buried in the sky, now." He gestured toward the Retreat. "Did you see? Many of the carvers . . . all hanging from the poles down there."

Richard had seen the bodies, but hadn't realized it was many of the stone carvers. He knew how some had felt about the things they carved—how they hated to create scenes of death.

"Priska?"

Victor gave a desolate shake of his head, too choked up to say it.

"Faval?"

"Saw him yesterday." Victor took a purging breath. "He said you told him to stay home and make charcoal. I think he is going to rename one of his children after you."

"If Priska . . . What about your special steel?"

Victor gestured with the bar he held in tongs. "His head man is going to carry on. Can you make a run for iron? I haven't had a supply since before the trouble. Brother Narev is in a foul mood; he wants some iron supports for the piers. He suggested that a blacksmith loyal to the Order and the Creator would get them made."

Richard nodded. "I think it's calmed down enough. When?"

"I could really use it now, but I can make do until the day after tomorrow. I have some of these fussy chisels to make, for the detail work, and I'm short men, so it can wait that long."

"Day after tomorrow, then. It should be safe enough by then."

The sun had set as Richard was walking up the street to his room with Nicci, but the twilight let him see his way well enough. He was thinking about Victor when half a dozen men stepped out from behind a building.

"Richard Cypher?"

They weren't dressed like regular city guards, but that didn't mean a whole lot, lately. There were a number of special men, not in uniform, who, it was said, hunted down troublemakers.

"That's right. What is it you wish?"

He saw the men each had swords under their light capes. They each had a hand on a long knife at their belts.

"As sworn officers of the Imperial Order, it is our duty to place you under arrest for suspicion of insurrection."

When Nicci woke, Richard still wasn't home. She growled unhappily. She rolled onto her back and saw that light was coming in through the curtains. By the angle of the sunlight, it looked like it must be shortly past dawn.

She yawned and stretched in her bed, letting her arms drop back as she stared at the ceiling, the clean, whitewashed ceiling. She felt her anger building. It was upsetting when he wasn't there at night, but it made her feel a fraud if she berated him for working so hard. Her intent had been to make him see how hard ordinary people had to work to get along in life, to make him see how the Order was the only hope of improving the lives of the common people.

She had warned him not to become involved in the recent uprising. She was pleased he didn't try to argue with her about it. If anything, he seemed opposed to them. It surprised her that he had even stayed home from work while the marches took place. He warned Kamil and Nabbi, in the strongest terms, to keep away from the insurrection.

Now that the rebellion had been crushed, and the authorities had arrested many of the troublemakers, it was safe again, so Richard had finally been able to return to work. The rebellion had been a shock. The Order needed to do more to make people understand their duty to help make the lives of those less fortunate more tolerable. Then there wouldn't be any trouble in the streets. To that end, many of the officials had been purged for not doing enough to further the cause of the Order. At least there was that much good out of it.

Nicci splashed water on her face from the basin Richard had brought home one day. The flowers around the edges matched the salmon-colored walls, and the rug he had been able to purchase from savings. He was certainly industrious, managing to save from his meager wage.

She pulled off her sweaty nightshirt and bathed herself as best she could with a wet washcloth. It felt refreshing. She hated to look sweaty and dirty in front of Richard.

She saw that the bowl of stew she'd made for his dinner the night before was still sitting on the table. He hadn't told her that he had to work at night, but sometimes he didn't have time to come home for dinner first. When he worked at night, he usually came home shortly after dawn, so she expected to see him at any moment.

He would likely be hungry. Maybe she would make him eggs. Richard liked eggs. She realized she was smiling. She had been angry when she first woke, and now, thinking about what Richard liked, she was smiling. She combed her fingers through her hair, already eagerly looking forward to seeing him walk in, to asking if he would like her to make him eggs. He would say yes, and she would have the pleasure of doing something she knew he wanted.

She loathed doing things she knew he didn't like.

It had been several months since that awful night with Gadi. That had been a mistake. She knew that afterward. At first, she had enjoyed it, not because she wanted to have sex with that repulsive thug, but because she had been so humiliated by Richard refusing to make love to her that she wanted to get back at him. She had in the beginning of it reveled in what Gadi did to her, reveled in how he hurt her, because it was hurting Kahlan, too. Nicci enjoyed it only in the sense that it was punishment for what he had done to her. Nothing hurt Richard like hurting Kahlan.

Gadi hated Richard. Having Nicci, he thought, got back at Richard and made Gadi a king again. As much as he wanted her, he wanted to get back at Richard more. Richard had taken Gadi's kingdom and made it his own. Nicci was only too happy to let the little bully be king again. Every sincere cry, she knew, Richard heard, and would know that Kahlan felt the same pain.

But as Gadi went at her with wild abandon, doing his best to degrade Richard by what he did to her, Richard's words—"Nicci, please don't do this. You're only hurting yourself"—began to haunt her.

As Gadi took her, she tried to make believe it was Richard, tried to have Richard if even by proxy. But she couldn't make herself believe it, not even for the pleasure of such a fantasy. Richard, she knew, would never humiliate and hurt a woman in that way. She couldn't even pretend for a second that it was Richard.

More, though, Nicci began to comprehend that Richard's words were not a plea to spare Kahlan pain, but to spare Nicci the pain. As much as he must hate her, Richard had expressed concern for her. As much as he must hate her, he didn't want to see her hurt.

Nothing else Richard could have said would have cut deeper into her heart. That kindness was the cruelest thing he could have done to her.

The pain afterward was her punishment. Nicci was so ashamed of what she had done that she pretended to Richard that she hadn't suffered in the incident. She wanted to spare him the distress of knowing what Kahlan was suffering along with her. The next morning, she told Richard that she had made a mistake. She didn't expect his forgiveness; she wanted him to know she knew she had been wrong, and that she was sorry.

Richard said nothing; he only watched her with those gray eyes of his as he listened before leaving for work.

She bled for three days.

Gadi had bragged to his friends about having her. To her further humiliation, he revealed all the details. To Gadi's surprise, Kamil and Nabbi had been furious at him. They were intent on dripping hot wax in his eyes and doing some other things—what, Nicci wasn't sure, but could imagine. The threat was so deadly serious that Gadi had gone off and joined the Imperial Order army that very same day. He had joined just in time to leave with a new troop on their way north to the war. Gadi had sneered to Kamil and Nabbi that day, telling them that he was going off to be a hero.

Nicci heard footsteps coming down the hall. She smiled and pulled three eggs out of the cupboard. Instead of Richard opening the door, as she was expecting, someone knocked.

Nicci stepped to the middle of the room. "Who is it?"

"Nicci, it's me, Kamil."

The urgency in his voice made the fine hairs on her arms stand on end.

"I'm decent. Come in."

The young man burst in, panting. His face was white, as were his knuckles around the doorknob. Tears stained his cheeks.

"They've arrested Richard. Last night. They have him."

Nicci was only dimly aware of the eggs hitting the floor.

With Kamil at her side, Nicci ascended the dozen stone steps up into the city guard barracks. It was a huge fortress, its high walls stretching off down the entire block. Nicci hadn't asked Kamil to go with her. She doubted that anything short of death would have stopped him. She couldn't really decipher precisely how Richard managed to inspire such reactions in people.

As they had left, Nicci was in a state of frantic shock, but she had noticed that the entire building of people seemed tense and alert. Faces peered from windows as she and Kamil had rushed out the building and down the road. People had come out of other buildings to watch her go. They all wore grim expressions.

What was it that made people care so much about this one man?

What was it that made her care?

The inside of the filthy barracks was crowded with people. Hollow-cheeked, unshaven, old men stood as if in a daze, staring off at nothing. Plump-cheeked women with scarves covering their heads wept as wailing children clung to their skirts. Other women stood around without expression, as if they were expecting to buy bread or millet. One small child, with only a shirt and nothing from the waist down, stood forlorn, his tiny fists at his mouth as he bawled.

The room felt like a death watch.

City guards, mostly large young men with indifferent expressions, pushed through the throng as they passed on into dark halls guarded by their fellows. A short, roughly constructed wooden wall held back all the people, confining the pandemonium to half the room. Beyond the short wall, more of the guards casually talked among themselves. Others brought reports to men at a simple table, joked, or picked up orders on their way through.

Nicci cut right through the crowd, forcing her way to the short wall where cowering women pressed close, hoping to be called, hoping for word, hoping for the miracle of intercession by the Creator Himself. Pressing up against the rough boards, they received splinters, instead.

Nicci seized the sleeve of a passing guard. He halted in midstride. His glare rose from her hand to her eyes. She reminded herself that she was without her power and released his sleeve.

"May I ask, please, who is in charge?"

He looked her up and down, a woman he appeared to judge was about to be without a husband and available. His face slid into an affected smile. He gestured.

"There. At the table. People's Protector Muksin."

The older man sat ensconced behind his sovereign stacks of papers. Beneath a chin that sank down toward his chest, his spreading body looked as if it were melting in the summer heat. His loose white shirt bore big dark rings of sweat, adding its bit of stink to the stench of the sultry room.

Guards leaned down to speak into his ear while his dull gaze roamed, never settling. Others behind the table to either side of him were busily engaged in work at stacks of their own papers, or speaking among themselves, or dealing with the other stream of officials and guards that was ebbing and flowing through the room.

Protector Muksin, the shiny top of his head concealed about as well as an aged turtle napping beneath a few blades of grass, watched the room. His dark eyes never stopped moving, gliding past the guards, the officials, the milling crowd. When they glided over Nicci's face, they registered no more interest than in any of the other people. All were citizens of the Order, equal pieces, each unimportant in and of itself.

"Could I see him?" Nicci asked. "It's important."

The guard's smile turned to mockery. "I'm sure it is." He waved a finger at the clump of people to the side. "End of the line. Wait your turn."

Nicci and Kamil had no choice but to wait. Nicci knew enough about such petty officials to know better than to make a scene. They lived for the times when someone made a scene. She leaned her shoulder against the plastered wall dark with oily stains of countless other shoulders. Kamil took up station behind her.

The line wasn't moving because the officials weren't seeing anyone. Nicci didn't know if they only saw citizens at certain times. There was no choice but to keep their place in the line. The morning dragged on without the line in front of her changing. It grew more crowded in back.

"Kamil," she said in a low voice after several hours, "you don't need to wait with me. You can go home."

His eyes were red and swollen. "I wish to wait." He sounded surprisingly distrustful. "I care about Richard," he added in a tone that sounded like an accusation.

"I care about him, too. Why do you think I'm here?"

"I only came to get you because I was so afraid for Richard, and I didn't know what else to do. Everyone else was off to work, or to buy bread." Kamil turned and leaned his back against the wall. "I don't believe that you care for him, but I didn't know what else to do."

Nicci swiped a sweaty strand of hair off her forehead. "You don't like me, do you?"

Still he didn't look at her. "No."

"Might I ask why?"

Kamil's gaze snuck a glance around to see if anyone was listening. They were all concerned with their own problems.

"You are Richard's wife, yet you betrayed him. You took Gadi to your room. You are a whore."

Nicci blinked in surprise at his words. Kamil glanced around again before he went on.

"We don't know why a man like Richard would be with you. Every woman without a husband in the house, and the other houses nearby, told me she would be his wife and never lie with another man as long as she lived. They all say they don't understand why you would do that to Richard. Everyone was sad for him, but he would not listen to us tell him."

Nicci turned away. Suddenly, she couldn't bear the shame of looking at a young man who had just called her a vile name, and had been right.

"You don't understand the situation," she whispered.

From the corner of her eye, she saw Kamil shrug. "You are right. I don't understand. I don't understand how anyone could do such a hurtful thing to a husband like Richard, who works hard and takes such good care of you. To do such a thing, you must be a bad person who does not care about your husband."

She felt tears join the sweat on her face. "I care about Richard more than you could ever know."

He didn't answer. She turned to look at him. He was bouncing his shoulders gently against the wall. He was too ashamed of her, or angry at her, to look her in the eye.

"Kamil, do you remember when we first came to live in the room in your building?"

He nodded, still not looking at her.

"Do you remember how cruel you and Nabbi treated Richard, all the mean things you said to him? All the hurtful names you called him? How you threatened him with your knives?"

"I made a mistake," he said, and sounded as if he meant it.

"Kamil, I made a mistake, too." She didn't bother trying to hide her tears—half the women in the room were weeping. "I can't explain it to you, but Richard and I were having an argument. I was angry with him. I wanted to hurt him. I was wrong. It was a foolish thing for me to do. I made a terrible mistake."

She sniffled and dabbed her nose on a small handkerchief. Kamil watched her from the corner of his eye.

"I admit it's not the same kind of mistake that you and Nabbi made when you were acting tough when you first met Richard, but it was a mistake. I was acting tough, too."

"You don't desire Gadi?"

"Gadi turns my stomach. I only used him because I was angry with Richard."

"And you are sorry?"

Nicci's chin trembled. "Of course I'm sorry."

"You are not going to get angry and do it again? With some other man?"

"No. I told Richard I made a mistake, I was sorry, and I would never do such a thing to him again. I meant what I said."

Kamil thought it over as he watched a woman shake a child by the arm. The child wouldn't stop crying, because it wanted to be picked up. She said something under her breath and the child leaned against her leg and pouted, but didn't cry anymore.

"If Richard can forgive you, then I should not be angry at you. He is your husband. It is for the two of you to settle, not for me." He touched her arm. "You made a foolish mistake. It is over. Don't cry for that anymore? There are more important things, now."

Nicci smiled through her tears and nodded.

He smiled a little bit. "Nabbi and I told Gadi we were going to cut off—we told him we would cut him for what he had done to Richard. Gadi showed us his knife, so we would let him pass. Gadi loves his knife. He has cut men with it, before. Cut them bad. He told us to let him pass to go to join the army, that he was going to use his knife to slice the guts out of the enemy, to be a war hero, and to have many women better than Richard's wife."

"I'm sure I will not be the only woman to be sorry they ever met Gadi."

In the late afternoon, People's Protector Muksin began seeing people. Nicci's

424

back ached, but it was nothing to compare to her fear for Richard. The people were taken one at a time by a pair of guards to stand before Protector Muksin.

The line moved fairly rapidly because the Protector tolerated no long conversations. At most, he would riffle through some of his papers before telling the supplicant something. What with all the wailing and weeping in the room, Nicci couldn't hear any of it.

When it was her turn, one of the guards shoved Kamil back. "Only one citizen may speak with the Protector."

Nicci tilted her head to signal Kamil to stand back and not make a scene. The guards each grabbed an arm and fairly carried her to the spot in front of the Protector. Nicci was indignant at being treated so roughly—like some common . . . citizen.

She had always enjoyed a kind of authority, sometimes spoken, sometimes unspoken, and had never really given it much thought. She wanted to have Richard see what it was like to live as the common working people. Richard seemed to flourish.

The two guards stood close at her shoulders, in case she caused any trouble. They must have seen it enough. She felt her face flushing at her treatment.

"Protector Muksin, my husband was—"

"Name." His dark-eyed gaze was skipping over the people remaining in line, no doubt measuring how far off dinner was.

"Richard."

He looked up sharply. "Full name."

"His name is Richard Cypher. He was taken in last evening."

Nicci didn't want to say the word "arrested," fearing to lend weight to a serious charge.

He shuffled through papers, not at all seeming to be interested in looking at her. Nicci found it slightly confounding when the man didn't look at her in that calculating way men had of measuring her dimensions in their mind, imagining what they couldn't see, as if she didn't know what they were doing. The two guards, though, were looking down the front of her dress.

"Ah." Protector Muksin waved a paper. "You are lucky."

"He has been released, then?"

He looked up as if she were daft. "We have him. His name is on this paper. There are many places people are taken. The Protectors of the people can't be expected to know where they all are."

"Thank you," Nicci said without knowing what she was thanking him for. "Why is he being held? What are the charges?"

The man frowned. "How would we know the charges. He has not yet confessed."

Nicci felt dizzy. A number of the other women fainted when they spoke to the Protector. The guard's hands on her arms tightened. The Protector's hand started to lift to signal them to remove her. Before he could, Nicci spoke in as calm a voice as she could muster.

"Please, Protector Muksin, my husband is no troublemaker. He never does anything but work. He never speaks ill of anyone. He is a good man. He always does as he is told."

For one fraction of a second, as she watched sweat roll down the man's cheeks, he seemed to be considering something.

"Has he a skill?"

"He is a good laborer for the Order. He loads wagons."

She knew the answer was a mistake before she had completed it. The hand lifted, flicked, dismissing her like a gnat. With a mighty jerk, the guards lifted her from her feet and whisked her from the important man's presence.

"But my husband is a good man! Please, Protector Muksin! Richard did not cause any of the trouble! He was home!"

Her words were sincere, and much the same as those spoken by the women before her. She was furious that she could not convince him that she was different—that Richard was different. The others, she knew now, had all tried to do the same.

Kamil ran behind as the guards carried her down a short, dark hall to a side door out of the stone fortress. Evening light stole in when they opened the door. They shoved her. Nicci stumbled down the steps. Kamil was shoved out right behind her. He fell facedown in the dirt. Nicci knelt to help him up.

From her knees, she looked up to the doorway. "What about my husband?" she pressed.

"You can come back another day," one guard said. "When he confesses, the Protector can tell you the charges."

Nicci knew he would never confess. He would die, first.

That was not a problem, as far as these men were concerned.

"Can I see him?" Nicci folded her hands prayerfully as she knelt beside Kamil. "Please, can I at least see him?"

One of the guards whispered to the other.

"Have you any money?" he asked her.

"No," she said in a mournful cry.

They started to go back in.

"Wait!" Kamil cried out.

When they paused, he ran up the steps. He lifted his pant leg and pulled off a boot. Upending it, a coin fell into his palm. Without reservation, he handed the silver coin to the guard.

The man made a sour face when he looked at the coin. "This isn't enough for a visit."

Kamil seized the big man's wrist as he started to turn. "I have another at home. Please, let me go get it. I can run. I can be back in an hour."

The man shook his head. "Not tonight. Visits for those who can pay the fee are the day after tomorrow, at sunset. But only one visitor is allowed."

Kamil waved his hand at Nicci. "His wife. She will visit him."

The guard swept an appraising look over Nicci, smirking, as if to consider what more she might have to give to see her husband.

"Just be sure to bring the fee."

The door slammed shut.

Kamil raced down the steps and seized her arm, his big eyes brimming with tears. "What are we going to do? That's two more days they will have him. Two more days!"

He was starting to choke on his panic. He hadn't said it, but she knew what he meant. That was two more days to torture a confession out of him. Then they would bury Richard in the sky.

Nicci took a firm grip on the boy's arm and walked him away. "Kamil, listen to me. Richard is strong. He will be all right. He's been through a lot before. He's strong. You know he's strong?"

Kamil was nodding as he bit his lower lip and wept, reduced to a child by his fear for his friend.

Nicci stared at the ceiling the entire night. The next day, she went to stand in line for bread. She realized, as she stood with the other women, that she must have the same hollow look as they. She was in a daze. She didn't know what to do. Everything seemed to be disintegrating.

That night, she slept only a few hours. She was in a state of restless anxiety, counting the minutes until the sun would come up. When it did, she sat at the table, clutching the loaf of bread she would take to Richard, waiting the eternity it took for the day to drag by. The neighbor lady, Mrs. Sha'Rim, brought Nicci a bowl of cabbage soup. She stood over Nicci, smiling sympathetically, while she waited to make sure Nicci ate the soup. Nicci thanked Mrs. Sha'Rim, and said the soup was delicious. She had no idea what the soup tasted like.

In the early afternoon, Nicci decided to go wait at the stronghold until she was allowed in. She didn't want to be late. Kamil was sitting on the steps, waiting for her. A small crowd of people milled about.

Kamil shot to his feet. "I have the silver mark."

Nicci wanted to tell him that he didn't have to pay it, that she would, but she didn't have a silver mark. She had only a few silver pennies.

"Thank you, Kamil. I will find the money to pay you back."

"I don't want it back. It is for Richard. It is what I choose to do for Richard. It is worth it to me."

Nicci nodded. She knew she would rot before anyone came up with a penny for her, yet she had devoted her entire life to helping others. Her mother told her once that it was wrong to expect thanks, that she owed help to those people because she was able to give it.

As Nicci walked down the steps, people came up and offered their best wishes. They asked her to tell Richard to be strong, and not to give in. They asked her to tell them if there was anything they could do, or if she needed money.

They'd had Richard for days. Nicci didn't even know if he was still alive. The silent walk to the prison stronghold was terror. She feared to find he had been put to death, or to see him, and know he would die a lingering, suffering agony from his questioning. Nicci knew very well how the Order questioned people.

At the side door, a half-dozen other women along with a few older men stood in the sweltering sun. All the women had sacks of food. None of the people spoke. They were all bent under the weight of the same dread.

Nicci stared at the door as the sun slowly sank. In the gathering dusk, Kamil hung his waterskin on Nicci's shoulder.

"Richard will probably want something to drink with his bread and chicken."

"Thank you," she whispered.

The ironbound door squeaked open. Everyone looked up at the guard standing in the door, signaling for everyone to approach. He glanced down at a piece of paper. As the first woman raced up the stairs, he stopped her and asked her name. When she told him, he checked it against his list, then let her pass. The second woman he turned away. She cried out, saying she had paid for the visit. He told her that her husband had confessed to crimes of treason and was allowed no visitors.

She wailed as she fell to the ground. Everyone else watched in horror, fearing the same fate. Another woman gave her name and was sent in. Another went in, then the next was told that her husband had died.

Nicci, in a daze, started up the stairs. Kamil grabbed her arm. He put a coin in her hand.

"Thank you, Kamil."

He nodded. "Tell Richard I said . . . Just tell him to come home."

"Richard Cypher," she answered the guard, her heart hammering.

He looked at the paper briefly, then waved her in. "That man will take you to him."

Relief flooded through her. He was still alive.

Inside the dark hall, another soldier waited. He tilted his head in command. "Follow me." He moved into the darkness, a lamp swinging from each hand. She stayed close behind as he descended two long flights of narrow stairs into the damp dark underground.

In a small room with a hissing torch, People's Protector Muksin sat on a bench, sweating, as he talked to two men—minor officials, judging by their deferential treatment of the rotund Protector.

The Protector stood after briefly inspecting the paper the guard handed him. "You have the fee?"

"Yes, Protector Muksin." Nicci handed over the coin.

He glanced at it before pocketing the silver. "Fines for civil violations are steep," he said cryptically as his dark eyes halted to measure her reaction.

Nicci licked her lips, her hopes suddenly buoyant. She had passed the first test by paying the fee. The greedy bastard was now demanding money for Richard's life.

Nicci spoke cautiously, fearing to make a mistake. "If I knew the fine, Protector, I believe I could raise the money."

The Protector peered at her with an intensity that made sweat break out across her brow. "A man needs to prove his repentance. A fine that cuts to the bone is a sure way to show remorse for a civil infraction. Less, and we will know the penance insincere. Day after tomorrow, at this time, those who have confessed to such infractions and have someone who can pay the price of the fine, are brought before me for disposition."

He had named the price: everything. He had told her what Richard had to do. She wanted to tear out the man's fat throat.

"Thank you for your kind understanding of my husband's civil indiscretion. If I could see him, I will see that he hurts to the bone in remorse."

He smiled a thin sweaty smile. "See that you do, young lady. Men left too long down here with their guilt end up confessing to the most terrible things."

Nicci swallowed. "I understand, Protector Muksin."

The torture would not stop until the man had the price.

The guard seized her arm abruptly and yanked her off down a pitch-black corridor, holding his two lanterns in his other hand. They went down another flight of stairs, down to the very bottom of the stronghold. The narrow passageway burrowed its crooked way through the stone of the foundation, past rooms purpose-built to hold criminals. Being not far from the river, water seeped into the place, leaving it forever slimy, wet, and reeking of rot. She saw things skitter away into the blackness.

The sound of their feet splashing through ankle-deep water echoed back from the distance. Decomposing carcasses of huge rats bobbed on the waves caused by their passing footsteps. The place reminded Nicci of her childhood nightmares of the underworld, a fate her mother had promised awaited all those who failed in their duty to their fellow man.

The short doors to the sides each had a small opening about the size of a hand—so that the guards could look in, she supposed. There was no light at all but what the guards brought, so there was nothing for those inside to look out at. In several of those doors, fingers gripped the edge of the opening. As the lamplight passed, Nicci saw wide eyes peering out from the black holes. From many of the openings came weeping of anguish, or agony.

The guard stopped. "Here it is."

Her heart beating wildly, Nicci waited. Instead of opening the door, the guard turned to her and grabbed her breasts. She stood motionless, fearing to move. He fondled her, as if he were testing melons in the market. She was too afraid to say anything, lest he not let her see Richard. He pressed closer to her and pushed his meaty hand down inside the top of her dress, fingering her nipples.

Nicci knew that men like this were necessary if the Order was to bring their teachings to all. You had to accept that the nature of mankind was perverted. There had to be sacrifices. Brutes were necessary to enforce morality on the masses. She stifled a yelp as he pinched her tender flesh.

The guard chuckled, pleased with his grope, and turned to the door. After some difficulty with the rusty lock, he finally got the key to turn. He grasped the door through the opening and gave a mighty tug. The door slowly grated open just enough to get by. The guard hung a lantern just inside on the wall.

"After I've seen to some other matters, I'll be back and your visit will be over." He chortled again. "Don't waste any time getting your skirts up for him—if he's in any condition for it."

He shoved her in the room. "Here you go, Cypher. I got her nice and randy for you." The door shut with a clang that echoed up and down the crooked passageway. Nicci heard the key turn and the guard's sloshing footsteps as he departed.

The square room was so tiny she could have stretched her arms and touched the walls to each side at the same time. The ceiling brushed the top of her head. She was overwhelmed by the terrifying closeness of it. She wanted out.

She feared the body crumpled at her feet was dead.

"Richard?"

She heard a little groan. His arms were behind his back, locked in some kind of wooden binders. She feared he might drown.

Tears stung her eyes. She sank to her knees. The slimy water that had sloshed into her boots now soaked up through her dress.

"Richard?"

She pulled at his shoulder to turn him over. He cried out and shrank away from her hand.

When she saw him, she covered her mouth with both hands to stifle her scream. She felt the tears flooding down her face as she gasped to get her breath.

"Oh, Richard."

Nicci stood and tore off a strip of her shift from under her dress. Kneeling once more, she used the cloth to gently wipe the blood from his face.

"Richard, can you hear me? It's Nicci."

He nodded. "Nicci."

One eye was swollen shut. His hair was matted with mud and slime from the water he lay in. His clothes were torn open. In the harsh light from the small lamp, she could see puffy red wounds crisscrossing his flesh.

He saw her staring at his wounds. "I'm afraid you'll never be able to patch this shirt."

She offered a feeble smile at his grim humor. Her fingers trembled as she wiped his face. She didn't know why she would react this way. She had seen worse than this.

Richard pulled his head back away from her ministrations.

"Am I hurting you?"

"Yes."

"Sorry. I have some water."

He nodded eagerly. Nicci poured water into his mouth from the waterskin. He drank greedily.

While he caught his breath, she said, "Kamil came up with the money for the fee to get me in to see you."

Richard only smiled.

"Kamil wants you out of here."

"I want me out of here." He didn't sound like himself. His voice was hoarse and almost gone.

"Richard, the Protector—"

"Who?"

"The official in charge of this, this prison. He told me that there is a way to get you out. He said you must plead guilty to a civil infraction, and pay a fine."

Richard was nodding. "I figured as much. He asked if I had money. I told him I did."

"You do? You've saved money?"

He nodded. "I have money."

Nicci's fingers desperately gathered his collar into her fist. "Richard, I can't pay the fine to get you out for two more days. Can you hold on? Please, can you hold on until then?"

He smiled in the dim lamplight. "I'm not going anywhere."

Nicci remembered then, and pulled the bread out of the sack. "I brought food. Bread, and some roasted chicken."

"Chicken. Bread won't sustain me long. They don't feed me."

She tore at the chicken with her fingers. She held a piece up to his mouth for him. She couldn't stand to see Richard helpless. It angered her. It made her sick.

"Eat, Richard," she urged when his head sank forward. He shook his head, as if to banish sleep. "Here, have some more."

She watched him chew. "Can you sleep in this water?"

"They don't let you sleep. They—"

She pushed a long chunk of chicken in his mouth. She knew too many of the details of the Order's methods. She didn't want to know which technique they had chosen for him.

"I'll get you out, Richard. Don't give up. I'll get you out."

He shrugged as if to say it didn't matter.

"Why? Covetous of your prisoner? Jealous to see others abuse me in your place? Fear they might destroy me before you can?"

"Richard, that's not—"

"I am just a man. Only the greater good matters. That I'm innocent is immaterial,

430

because no one man's life has value. If I must suffer and die this way to help drive others to the ways of your Creator and your Order, who are you to deny them that virtuous end? What do your wishes matter? How can you put your life, or mine, above the good of others?"

How many times had she lectured him with that same moral doctrine? How contemptuous, how venomous, how treacherous it sounded from his lips.

She hated herself at that moment. He somehow put the lie to everything the Order stood for, to everything she had devoted her life to. He somehow made doing good seem . . . evil. That was why he was so dangerous. That he even existed threatened everything for which they stood.

She was so close. So close to knowing what she needed to understand. The very fact that there were tears running down her face told her that there really was something that made the whole ordeal worthwhile—made it essential. The indefinable spark she had seen in his eyes from the first instant was real.

If she could just reach that little bit more, then she could finally do what was best. It would be better for him. What kind of life could he ever have? How much suffering could he endure? She hated that she was condemned to serving the Creator in such a way.

"Look around, Nicci. You wanted to show me the better way of the Order. Look around. Isn't it glorious?"

She hated to see one of his beautiful eyes swollen shut.

"Richard, I need the money you saved. If I'm to get you out of here, I'll need it all. The official told me it had to be all of what you had."

A hoarse whisper was all he had left. "It's in our room."

"Our room? Where? Tell me where."

He shook his head. "You could never get it out. You have to know the trick to open it. Go to Ishaq."

"Ishaq? At the transport company? Why?"

"It was his parlor, once. There's a hidden compartment in the floor. Tell him why you need the money. He will open it for you."

She held more chicken up to his mouth. "All right. I'll go to Ishaq." She hesitated while she watched him chew. "I'm sorry that you have to give up what you've managed to save. I know how hard you work. It's not right for them to take it."

He shrugged again. "Just money. I'd rather live."

Nicci smiled and wiped the tears from her cheeks. That was the best thing she could have hoped to hear.

The door opened. "Pull your skirt down, woman. Time's up."

As he dragged her out by her arm, she stuffed the last of the chicken in Richard's mouth.

"Civil infraction!" she called to him. "Don't forget!"

He had to confess to a civil infraction that could be paid with a fine. Then they would release him. Any other crime was death.

"I won't forget."

She reached back toward him as she was pulled from the tiny cell. "I'll be back for you, Richard! I swear!"

Nicci paced as Ishaq bent over the trapdoor in the corner of the room. He had been at it a long time. He had pushed the wardrobe aside to get at the secret place in the floor. Occasionally he muttered under his breath, cursing himself for having made it so difficult to get into.

"At last!" Ishaq scrambled to his feet.

Nicci hoped that the meager money Richard could have managed to save would be enough to satisfy Protector Muksin. In her head, she was going through a list of people who had offered money to help Richard.

Ishaq scurried close. "Here it is."

He hurriedly placed the leather purse in her hand. The weight shocked her. The purse filled her palm. It didn't make sense. She realized Richard must have put some metal items in with his savings—that would account for the weight. She pulled open the top and dumped the contents in her palm.

Nicci gasped. There were close to two dozen gold marks. There wasn't any silver. It was all gold.

"Dear Creator . . ." she whispered, her eyes wide. "Where would Richard get all this money?"

It was more money than most wealthy men saw in their lifetime. She looked up into Ishaq's eyes.

"Where would Richard get all this money?"

He swept his red hat off his head. He waved impatiently at all the gold lying in her palm. "Richard earned it."

She felt her frown darkening. "Earned it? How? No one man could earn this much money—not honestly, anyway." She felt her anger building. "Richard stole this gold, didn't he?"

"Don't be silly." Ishaq gestured irritably. "Richard earned it. He bought and sold goods."

She gritted her teeth. "How did he get this money?"

The man flung up his hands. "I'm telling you. He earned it himself—all by himself. He bought things, and sold them to people who needed them."

"Things? What kind of things? Contraband?"

"No! Things like iron and steel—"

"Nonsense. How would he move it? Carry it on his back?"

"At first. But then he bought a wagon to—"

"A wagon!"

"Yes. And horses. He bought charcoal and ore and sold them to the foundries. Mostly, he bought metal from the foundry, and sold it to the blacksmith. The blacksmith uses a great deal of metal. He bought it from Richard. That was how he earned the money."

Nicci seized the man's collar at his throat. "Take me to this blacksmith."

Nicci was furious. All this time, she had thought Richard an honest hardworking man, and now she had discovered that he was imprisoned properly. He was guilty of swindling honest working people out of their money. He was profiteering.

At that moment, she was not sorry at all for what they were doing to him in the prison. He deserved it all, and more. He was a criminal, cheating honest hardworking people out of gold. She burned with humiliation, knowing she had been deceived by him.

Nicci had seen the site of the palace before, but at a distance as she went about her business in the city. She had never been this close. It was going to be everything Jagang said it would be. It filled her with awe. All the inspiring words of Brother Narev from her youth were like a sacred choir singing from the depths of her memories as she looked upon the sweep of scenes being erected.

The walls were already up over the openings for the windows on the first floor. In some sections, beams were being laid, spanning the interior walls, to support the next story.

But it was the outside which took her breath. The stone walls were banded with carvings on a scale she had never imagined. Just as Brother Narev would have directed, the carvings were inspirational, and convincing. Nicci saw people gazing upon the scenes, weeping at the events recounted in stone, weeping at the depiction of the miserable creature that was man, and the unattainable glory that was the perfection of the Creator. With such moving visions, there could be no doubt that the Order was mankind's only hope of salvation. Just as Jagang had said, this would be a palace to stir the people with overpowering emotion.

"Why are those poles there?" she asked Ishaq as they marched along the wide cobbled path where people stood and watched the construction, while others knelt and prayed at various horrific scenes depicted on the walls.

"Carvers." Ishaq removed his red hat as he looked at the sight. "It was said they took part in the revolt."

Nicci's gaze passed among the rotting corpses hanging at the tops of the poles. "Why would the carvers take part in the revolt? They have work." More than that, they were working on the scenes of the glory of the Order. They, of all people, should have known how their only hope of reward in the next world required suffering in this.

"I did not say they took part. I said that it was said that they took part."

Nicci didn't correct the man. All men were corrupt. There wasn't a man who could not be put to death without it being justified. That included Richard.

Many of the stones under protective roofs where men had worked now sat idle. Ramps were constructed, along with scaffolding, for the masons to work on the palace walls. As they placed their stone, other men, slave labor, worked at hauling huge blocks up the ramps to them, carried baskets of mortar or dirt and rock, or worked in trenches building the underground cells where the Order would purge the world of the worst sinners and where criminals would confess their crimes.

It was a terrible business, but you couldn't have a garden unless you got your hands dirty first.

The blacksmith's shop, up on the side of a hill overlooking the colossal undertaking, was the largest she had ever seen. With a project of this scale, it was understandable. She stood outside while Ishaq hurried in to fetch the blacksmith for her.

The sounds of hammers ringing on steel, the smells of the forge, the smoke, the oils, the acid, the brine, all brought back a flood of memories of her father's shop. For a brief moment, Nicci's heart beat faster—she was a girl again. She almost expected to see her father come out and smile at her with that wondrous energy of his showing in his blue eyes.

Instead, a brawny man stepped out of the shadows into the daylight. He wore no smile, but a menacing glare. At first, she thought he was bald. Then she saw that his full head of hair was simply cropped close to his scalp. Some of her father's men who worked with hot iron did the same. His scowl would have set any other woman back three paces.

He wiped his hands on a rag as he walked through the milky sunlight toward her, appraising her eyes more carefully than most men—other than Richard. His thick leather apron was speckled with hundreds of tiny burn marks.

"Mrs. Cypher?"

Ishaq backed away, contenting himself to be a shadow.

"That's right. I'm Richard's wife."

"Funny, Richard never really spoke of you. I guess I just assumed he had a wife, but he never said—"

"Richard has been taken into custody."

The scowl changed in an instant to wide-eyed concern. "Richard's been arrested? For what?"

"Apparently, for the most base of crimes: cheating people."

"Cheating people? Richard? They're out of their minds."

"I'm afraid not. He is guilty. I have the evidence."

"What evidence?"

Ishaq swooped in close, unable to contain himself any longer. "Richard's money. The money he made."

"Made!" Nicci's shout drove Ishaq back a step. "You mean the money he stole."

The blacksmith's scowl had returned. "Stole? Who do you think he stole this money from? Who are his accusers? Where are his victims?"

"Well, you are one."

"Me?"

"Yes, I'm afraid you were one of his victims. I'm here to return your money. I can't use stolen money to rescue a criminal from his just punishment. Richard will have to pay the price for his crime. The Order will see that he does."

The blacksmith tossed his towel aside and planted his fists on his hips. "Richard never stole one silver penny from anyone—least of all, me! He earned his money."

"He cheated you."

"He sold me iron and steel. I need iron and steel to make things for the Retreat. Brother Narev comes in here and growls at me to get things made, but he doesn't deliver me the iron from which I must make them. Richard does. Until Richard came along, I nearly got buried in the sky myself, because Ishaq, here, couldn't get me enough iron and steel."

"I couldn't! The committee only gives me permission to bring what I bring. I would be buried in the sky myself if I bring more than I have permission to bring. Everybody at the transport company watches me. They report me to the workers' group if I spit wrong."

"So," Nicci said, folding her arms, "Richard has you over your own brine barrel. He brings you iron at night and you have no choice but to pay him his price, and he knows it. He makes all this gold by gouging you. That's how he got rich—by overcharging you. That's the worst kind of thievery."

The blacksmith frowned at her as if she were daft.

"Richard sells me iron and steel for a lot less than I can buy it through the regular transport companies—like from Ishaq."

"I charge what the committee on fair pricing tells me! I have no say!"

"That's just crazy," Nicci said to the blacksmith, ignoring Ishaq.

"No, it's smart. You see, the foundries produce more than they can sell, because they can't get it moved. Their furnaces have to be heated whether they make one ton or ten. They need to make enough iron to make the heat worth it, to pay their workers, and to keep their furnaces going. If they don't buy enough ore, the mines close and then the foundry can't get any ore at all. They can't exist if they can't get raw materials. But the Order won't let Ishaq, and those like him, move as much as the foundries need moved. The Order takes weeks to decide on the simplest request. They consider every imaginable person who they fancy might conceivably be hurt if Ishaq were to move the load. The foundries were desperate. They offered to sell their extra to Richard at less money—"

"So they are cheated in Richard's scheme, too!"

"No, because Richard takes it, they sell more, so it costs them less to make. They make more money than they would have otherwise. Richard sells it to me for less than I have to pay from the regular transport companies, because he buys it for less."

Nicci threw her hands up in disgust. "And to top it off, he is putting working men out of jobs. He's the worst sort of criminal—making his profit off the backs of the poor, the needy, and the workers!"

"What?" Ishaq protested. "I can't get enough people to work, and I can't get enough permits to haul the goods people need. Richard puts no one out of work—he helps create more business for everybody. The foundries he hauls for have each hired more men since they are able to sell through Richard."

"That's right," the blacksmith said.

"But, you just don't see it," Nicci insisted as she raked back her hair. "He's pulled the wool over your eyes. He's cheating you—milking you dry. You're getting poor because Richard—"

"Don't you get it, Mrs. Cypher? Richard has made half a dozen foundries money. They are working now only because of Richard. He moves their goods when they need them moved, not when they can finally get some asinine permit with seals all over it. Richard has, by himself, enabled a whole string of charcoal makers to earn a living supplying those foundries, along with a number of miners and any number of other people. And me? Richard has made me more money than I ever thought I'd make.

"Richard has made us all rich by doing something that is desperately needed, and doing it better than others can do it. He has kept us all working. Not the Order and their committees, boards, and groups—Richard.

"I've been able to keep men on because of Richard. He never says it can't be done; he figures a way to do it. In the process, he has earned the trust of every man he deals with. His word is as good as that gold.

"Why, even Brother Narev told Richard to do what needed doing to get me the iron I needed. Richard told him he would. The palace wouldn't be this far along if not for Richard keeping everyone going with what he gets for us, when we need it.

"The Order owes Richard a debt of gratitude, not torture and punishment. He has helped the Order by doing what they need done. Those piers standing out there would not be built yet, if Richard hadn't found me the iron to make the bracing ties. Those carvings on the palace walls down there would not be done if he hadn't gotten me the steel I needed to make the tools to carve them. The goods down there are only moved in by wheels turning on iron bands I make to repair them because Richard got me the steel. Richard has done more to raise that palace up out of the ground than any other single man. Besides that, he's made friends doing it."

Nicci couldn't make it work in her head. It had to be true; she remembered that Richard had met Brother Narev. How could someone make so much money, help the Order, and have the people he deals with still trust him?

"But he has made all this profit . . ."

The blacksmith shook his head as if she were a snake among them. " 'Profit' is a dirty word only to the leeches of the world. They want it seen as evil, so they can more easily snatch what they did not earn."

The frown returned as the blacksmith leaned toward her. His voice became as hot as the iron he worked.

"What I want to know, Mrs. Cypher, is why Richard is in some stinking prison being tortured to give a confession, while his wife is standing here acting a fool over him earning money and making us all happy and rich in the process?"

Nicci felt a lump rising in her throat. "I can't pay the fine until tomorrow night."

"Until I met you, I never thought Richard ever made a mistake." The man pulled his leather apron off over his head and heaved it at the wall of his shop. "With that kind of money, we can bargain him out sooner. I hope it's soon enough. Ishaq, are you with me?"

"Of course. They know me. I'm trusted. I go, too."

"Give me the money," the blacksmith commanded.

Nicci dropped it into his upturned palm without even thinking about it. Richard wasn't really a thief. It was a wonder. She didn't know how, but these people were all happy with him. He made them all rich. It didn't make any sense to her.

"Please, if you can help, I'd be indebted to you."

"I'm not doing it for you, Mrs. Cypher; I'm helping a friend I value who is worth helping."

"Nicci. My name is Nicci."

"I'm Mr. Cascella," he growled as he started away.

Mr. Cascella tossed four gold coins on the table in front of People's Protector Muksin. He had told Nicci and Ishaq that he wanted to hold something in reserve so they could "pump the bellows" if they "needed more heat."

The blacksmith towered over the man behind the table. Several officers put their noses to their work. The guards around the room all watched.

"Richard Cypher. You have him. We're here to pay the fine."

Protector Muksin blinked at the coins like a fat carp that was too full to eat a worm.

"We don't assess fines until tomorrow night. Come back then, and if this man, Cypher, has not confessed to involvement in anything more serious, you can pay then."

"I work out at the new palace," Mr. Cascella said. "Brother Narev keeps me busy. I'm here now, so couldn't we just take care of this matter while we're all here? It would make Brother Narev happy if his head blacksmith didn't have to come all the way over here again tomorrow, when I'm here now."

Protector Muksin's dark eyes turned from side to side, traversing the crowded room of wailing people. His chair chattered as he scooted it closer to the table. He folded his stubby fingers atop a pile of tattered papers.

"I would not wish to inconvenience Brother Narev."

The blacksmith smiled. "I thought not."

"However, Brother Narev would not want me to overlook my duty to the people."

"Of course not!" Ishaq put it. He swiped his red hat off his head when the dark eyes turned his way. "Such was not implied, of course. We are trusting in you to do your duty."

"Who are you?" the Protector asked Nicci.

"I am the wife of Richard Cypher, Protector Muksin. I was here before. I paid a fee to see him. You explained the fine to me."

He nodded. "I see so many."

"Look," Mr. Cascella said, "we have a lot of money for the fine. If we could pay it now and get Richard Cypher out today, that is. Some of it is money other people might not be willing to contribute tomorrow."

The blacksmith slid four more gold marks across the table. The Protector's dark eyes looked unimpressed.

"The money all belongs to the people. There is great need."

Nicci suspected that the great need was in his pocket, and that he was holding out for more. As if to answer the charge, Protector Muksin slid the eight gold coins—a fortune by any standard of measure—back across the table.

"The money would not be paid here. We have no use for it. We are humble servants of the Order. The amount of the fine would be noted in the ledger, but you would have to deliver it to a citizen committee for distribution to those in need."

Nicci was surprised that she had been wrong about the man. He was indeed an honest official. This changed the nature of the whole business. Her hopes brightened. Perhaps it wouldn't be so difficult to get Richard released, after all.

Behind her, on the other side of the short wall, women were wailing, children were crying, and people were praying. Nicci could hardly breathe in the stinking sweltering room. She hoped that the official would be moved to hurry the case so he could get to attending the matter of the small crowd of guards who waited off in the side halls for papers and orders.

"But you make a mistake," the Protector added, "if you think money can buy this man's release. The Order is not concerned with the life of one man, for no man's life is of any real importance. I'm inclined to tell you to keep your money—until we can look into why anyone would have such a large sum. I think this man must be disruptive to civil order if he stirs up this much support. No one man is any better than another. That he can bring so much money to bribe him out of his just punishment proves my suspicion that he has something to confess."

His chair creaked as he leaned back to peer up at them. "It appears you three would think otherwise—think that he is better than any other man."

"No," the blacksmith said in an offhanded manner, "it's just that he is our friend."

"The Order is your friend. Those in need are your concern. You have no business caring for one man over another. Such unseemly behaviour is blasphemy."

The three of them before the desk stood mute. Behind them, the weeping, the wailing, the panicked praying for those in the darkness far below, went on without pause. Everything they said only seemed to turn the man more against them.

"If he had a skill, then it might be different. There is great need for contributions to the Order by those with ability. There are many who hold back when they should be doing their best to contribute. It is the duty of those with ability to—"

It all came clear to Nicci in one blinding instant.

"But he does have a skill," she blurted out.

"What skill?" the Protector asked, not pleased at being interrupted.

Nicci stepped closer. "He is the greatest—"

"Greatness is a delusion of the wicked. All men are the same. All men are evil by nature. All men must struggle to overcome their baser nature by devoting their lives selflessly to the cause of helping their fellow man. Only selfless acts will enable a man to gain his reward in the afterlife."

Mr. Cascella's fists tightened. He started to lean in. If he argued, now, it would render the matter irredeemable. Nicci gave him a stealthy kick with the side of her foot, hoping to convince him to be quiet and let her do the talking before it was too late. Nicci bowed her head as she retreated a step, forcing the blacksmith aside without making it look obvious.

"You are wise, Protector Muksin. We could all learn valuable lessons from you. Please forgive the inept words of a poor wife. I am a simple woman, humbled and discomposed in the presence of such a wise representative of the Fellowship of Order."

Startled, the Protector said nothing. Nicci had traded in such words for over a hundred years, and knew their value. She had given the man, but a petty official, a standing in the core of the Order—in the fellowship itself—that he could never attain. This sort of man would aspire to wear the mantle of social merit. To a man like this, to be thought to hold such intellectual status was as good as earning it; perception was reality to such men. The perception was what counted, not the actual accomplishment.

"What is this man's skill?"

Nicci bowed her head again. "Richard Cypher is an undistinguished stone carver, Protector Muksin."

The men to either side of her stared in disbelief.

"A stone carver?" the Protector asked, lingering in thought over the words.

"A faceless artisan, his only hope in life that he could one day work in stone to show man's wickedness, so that he might help others see the need to sacrifice to their fellow man and the Order and in this way hope to earn his reward in the afterlife."

The blacksmith quickly recovered and added to her words. "As you may know, many of the carvers at the Retreat were traitors—thank the Creator they were discovered—and so there is much carving to be done for the glory of the Order. Brother Narev can confirm this for you, Protector Muksin."

The Protector's dark eyes shifted among the three. "How much money do you have?"

"Twenty-two gold marks," Nicci said.

He scowled his condemnation as he pulled a ledger book close and dipped his pen in a chipped ink bottle. The Protector bent forward and wrote the fine in his book. He next wrote an order on a piece of paper and handed it up to the blacksmith.

"Take this to the workers' hall at the docks"—he gestured with his pen off behind them—"down that street. I will release the prisoner after you bring me a workers' group seal to prove that the fine was paid to the men who deserve it most—those in need. Richard Cypher must be stripped of his ill-gotten gains."

Richard deserved it most, Nicci thought bitterly. He had earned it, not those other men. Nicci thought about all the nights he'd worked without sleep, without food. She remembered him wincing as he lay down to sleep, his back aching from his labor. Richard had earned that money—she knew that, now. Those men who would get it had done nothing for it but to desire it, thus proclaiming their right to it.

"Yes, Protector Muksin," Nicci said as she bowed. "Thank you for your wise justice."

Mr. Cascella let out a quiet sigh. Nicci leaned confidentially toward the Protector.

"We will carry out your equitable instructions immediately." She smiled deferentially. "Since you have treated us so fairly in this matter, might I ask one further consideration?" It was a lot of gold that would be credited to his effort on behalf of the Order; she knew he would likely be in a generous mood at that moment. "It's more a matter of curiosity, really."

He wheezed an annoyed sigh. "What is it you want?"

Nicci leaned closer, close enough to smell the man's stale sweat. "The name of the person who reported my husband. The one who rightly brought Richard Cypher to justice."

Nicci knew that he was thinking that men were more likely to be welcomed into the fellowship when they helped collect great sums for those in need. The matter of the name would only be a gnat bothering his pleasant thoughts. He pulled some papers close and scanned through them, flipping them aside as he searched.

"Here it is," Protector Muksin said at last. "Richard Cypher's name was reported by a young soldier volunteering in the Imperial Order army. His name is Gadi. The report is months old. It took some time to see justice done, but the Order always sees justice done in the end. That is why they call our great emperor 'Jagang the Just.' "

Nicci straightened. "Thank you, Protector Muksin."

Her calm face concealed her inner fury that the little thug was out of her reach. Gadi deserved to suffer.

The Protector wrote out his sentence for a civil crime as he spoke. "Take the order of fine I gave you to the workers' group at the docks and return here when you have seals to prove that his fine of twenty-two gold marks was paid in full.

"Richard Cypher is further ordered to report to the carver's committee for work assignment." He handed her the paper with the orders. "Richard Cypher is now a stone carver for the Order."

The sun was setting by the time they returned with all the papers and seals. The blacksmith was impressed with the way she had handled the official when the offer of gold failed to work. Ishaq thanked her a hundred times. It only mattered to her that Richard would be freed.

She was relieved to know that she had been wrong, that Richard wasn't a cheat and a thief after all. It had been such an ugly feeling, thinking ill of Richard. It had for a time tainted her whole world. She had never been so happy to be wrong.

Better yet, they had done it; she was to have him back.

At the side door to the stronghold, Mr. Cascella, Ishaq, and Nicci waited. The shadows grew darker. Finally, the door opened. Two guards held Richard between them as they came out onto the landing. When they saw Richard, his condition, Mr. Cascella cursed under his breath. Ishaq whispered a prayer.

The guards released Richard with a shove. He stumbled forward. The blacksmith and Ishaq raced to the steps to help him.

Richard caught himself and straightened, a dark form upright in the last of the light, defiant of the long shadows around him. He held a hand out, commanding the two men to stay where they were. Both stopped with a foot on the bottom step, ready to run up to him should he need them. Nicci couldn't imagine what pain it had to cost Richard to walk so steadily, proudly, smoothly down the stairs without help, as if he were a free man.

He did not yet know what she had done to him.

Nicci knew there could be no worse plight for Richard. The torture down in the depths of the stronghold was not as bad as what she had just condemned him to.

Nicci was sure that this was the one thing, at last, that would force out the answer she sought, if there really was an answer to be found.

440

Brother Narev paused behind Richard's shoulder, a shadow come to visit. He often lurked nearby, making sure the carvings were progressing as directed. This was the first time the great man himself had stopped to watch Richard work.

"Don't I know you?" The voice was like stone grating on stone.

Richard let his arm holding the hammer drop to his side as he looked up. He wiped the dusty sweat from his brow with the back of his left hand, still holding the clawed stone chisel.

"Yes, Brother Narev. I was a laborer hauling iron, at the time. I was bringing a load to the blacksmith one day when I was honored to meet you."

Brother Narev frowned suspiciously. Richard allowed no crack in his façade of innocent calm.

"A laborer, and now a carver?"

"I have ability which I am joyful to contribute to my fellow man. I am grateful for the opportunity the Order has given me to earn my reward in the next life by sacrificing in this."

"Joyful." Neal, the shadow of the shadow, stepped forward. "You are joyful to carve, are you?"

"Yes, Brother Neal."

Richard was joyful that Kahlan was alive. He didn't think about the rest of it. He was a prisoner, and what he had to do to keep Kahlan alive, he would do; that was all there was to it. What was, was.

Brother Neal smirked his superiority at Richard's obeisance. The man had come often to lecture the carvers, and Richard had come to know him all too well. The carvers' work, being the influential face the palace would show to the people, was critically important to the Fellowship of Order. Richard was frequently the object of Neal's harangues. Neal, a wizard, not a sorcerer like Brother Narev, always seemed to feel the need to prove his moral authority around Richard. Richard gave him no rough edge to grip, yet Neal still persisted in clawing for one.

Brother Narev believed his own words with grim conviction: mankind was evil; only through selfless sacrifice to your fellow man had you any hope to redeem yourself in the afterlife. There was no joy in his faith, simply a ruthless duty to it.

Neal, on the other hand, bubbled over with his feelings. He believed in the Order's doctrine with an impassioned, incandescent, arrogant pride, gleefully convinced the world needed iron-fisted direction which only enlightened intellectuals, such as himself, could provide—with grudging deference to Brother Narev, of course.

Richard had more than once overheard Neal proclaim with conviction that if he had to order the tongues cut out of a million innocent men, it would be better than to allow one man to blaspheme against the self-evident, righteous nature of the Order's ways.

Brother Neal, a fresh-faced young man—no doubt deceptively young, considering that Nicci said he had once lived at the Palace of the Prophets—frequently accompanied Brother Narev, basking in his mentor's approval. Neal was Brother Narev's chief lieutenant. His face might have been fresh, but his ideas were not; tyranny was ancient, even if Neal deluded himself in believing it the bright new salvation of mankind when applied by him and his fellows. His ideas were a paramour he embraced with a lover's boundless, blind passion—a truth discovered with a lover's lust.

Nothing stirred him to anger quicker than the whiff of argument or contradiction, no matter how reasoned. In the heat of his passion, Neal was perfectly willing to destroy any dissension, torture any opposition, kill any number, who failed to bow before the pedestal upon which stood his irrefutably noble ideals.

No misery, no failure, no amount of wailing and anguish and death, could dim his glowing conviction that the ways of the Order were the only correct course for mankind.

The other disciples, all, like Neal, wearing hooded brown robes, were an incongruous collection of the cruel, the pompously idealistic, the bitterly greedy, the resentful, the spiteful, the timid, and, most of all, the dangerously deluded. All shared an underlying, caustic, inner loathing for mankind which manifested itself in a conviction that anything pleasurable for the people could only be evil and accordingly only sacrifice could be good.

All, with the exception of Neal, were blind followers and completely under the spell of Brother Narev. They believed Brother Narev far closer to the Creator than to man. They hung on his every word, believing each to be divinely inspired. Were he to tell them they must kill themselves for the cause, Richard was sure they would break their necks rushing for the nearest knife.

Neal was alone in that he believed in the divinity of his own words, in addition to Brother Narev's. Every leader had to have a successor. Richard was pretty sure Neal had already decided who would best serve as the next incarnation of the Order.

"A peculiar choice of words, joyful." Brother Narev circled a knobby finger toward the cowering, deformed, frightened figures Richard was working on. "This makes you . . . joyful?"

Richard gestured to the Light he had carved so as to shine down on the wretched men. "This, Brother Narev, is what makes me joyful—being able to show men cowering before the perfection of the Creator's Light. It makes me joyful to show mankind's wickedness for all to see, for in this way they will know their duty to the Order above all else."

Brother Narev made a suspicious sound deep in his throat. The sunlight hooded his dark eyes more than usual and seemed to deepen the creases around his mouth as he regarded Richard with a look sharing mistrust and loathing, laced with apprehension. Only the apprehension was any different than the look he gave everyone. Richard fed him a vacant stare. The brother's mouth finally twisted with the dismissal of his private thoughts.

"I approve . . . I forgot your name. But then, names are not important. Men are not important. Individually, each man is but a meaningless cog in the great wheel of mankind. How that wheel turns is all that matters, not the cogs."

"Richard Cypher."

One brow, flocked in tangled white and black hair, lifted.

"Yes . . . Richard Cypher. Well, I approve of your carving, Richard Cypher. You seem to understand better than most how man is properly depicted."

Richard bowed. "It is not my hand, but the Creator guiding it to help the Order show the way."

The suspicious look was back, but Richard's expression made Brother Narev finally believe the words. Brother Narev, his hands clasped behind his back, glided away to see to other matters. Neal, like a child sticking close to his mother's skirts, scurried to stay close to Brother Narev's robes. He cast a scowl back over his shoulder. Richard almost expected to see Neal stick out his tongue.

As best as Richard could figure, there were about fifty of the brown-robed disciples. He saw them often enough to come to know their nature. Victor had mentioned to Richard that one of the foundries had cast in pure gold, from the master that the blacksmith had made, somewhere near the same numbers of the spell-forms. Victor thought them only decorations. Richard had seen several of the gold spell-forms being installed onto the tops of huge, ornate stone pillars set out around the grounds of the Retreat. The pillars, in polished marble, were designed and placed to look like grand decorations for a grand place. Richard suspected they were more.

Richard went back to chiseling a thick, unbending limb. At least, now, his own limbs worked again. It had been a while, but he was healed. This, though, seemed no less a torture.

People gathered every day to view the low relief carvings already up on the walls. Some people knelt on the cobblestone walks before the scenes, praying, till their knees bled. Some brought rags to put beneath their knees as they prayed. Many simply stared with forsaken looks at the nature of mankind depicted in stone.

Richard could see in the faces of many who came that they had come with some kind of vague, undefinable hope, hungering for some essential answer to a question they could not formulate. The emptiness in their eyes as they left was heartbreaking. They were people being drained of life no less than those bled to death in the dungeons of the Order.

Some of those people gathered to watch the carvers work. In the two months Richard had worked at carving for the Retreat, the crowds grew larger to watch him than any of the other men. The people sometimes wept at what they saw emerge from beneath Richard's chisels.

In the two months Richard had worked at carving for the Retreat, he had come to understand the nuance of carving in stone. What he carved was dispiriting, but the act of carving itself helped to make up for it. Richard reveled in the technical aspects of applying steel to stone, guided by intent.

As much as he hated the things he had to carve, he came to love working stone with a chisel. The marble seemed almost alive under his touch. He would often carve some tiny part with reverence for the subject—a finger gracefully lifted, a eye with knowing vision, a chest holding a heart of reason.

After he accomplished such grace, he would deface it to suit the Order. More often than not, that was when people wept.

Richard invented impossibly stiff, stilted, contorted people bent under the weight of guilt and shame. If this was the way to preserve Kahlan's life, then he would make everyone who saw the carvings weep their hearts out. In a way, they were doing the weeping for him, suffering over the carvings for him, being destroyed by what they saw, for him.

In this way, he was able to endure the torture.

When the shadows lengthened to dusk and the day was finished, the carvers started putting away their tools into simple wooden boxes before going home for the night. They all would return not long after first light. The master builder provided them with orders for areas and shapes to be covered with carving so they could shape the stones to the correct size. Brother Narev's disciples came by to provide the details of the stories to be told in stone.

The stone Richard carved was for the grand entrance to the Retreat. Marble steps swept around in a half circle, leading up to the huge, round plaza. A colonnade of pillars in a half circle, mirroring the steps, surrounded the back half of the plaza. Richard's job was carving the sweep of scenes that were placed above those columns.

It was to be an entrance which set the tone for the entire palace. In the center of the plaza Brother Neal had told Richard that Brother Narev's vision was that there would be the statue dominating the entrance to the palace, and it was to be a work which would strike down any observer with an overpowering sense of their own guilt and shame at mankind's evil nature. The statue, in its horror, was a call to selfless sacrifice, and was to be built into the form of a sundial, showing people cowering under the Light of their Creator.

Neal had described it with such delight that the image it created in Richard's mind sickened him.

Richard was the last to leave the site. As he often did, he headed up the hill, along the winding road, to the workshops. Victor was in his shop, banking his coals for the night. With autumn upon them, the days weren't insufferably hot, so the forge wasn't the miserable place it had been in high summer. Winter this far south in the Old World was never harsh, but the forge in winter would be a good place to banish the chill that would come on cold rainy days.

"Richard! So good to see you." The blacksmith knew why Richard was there. "Go on back. Maybe I will come sit with you when I'm finished, here?"

Richard gave his friend a smile and said, "I'd like that."

Richard opened the double doors at the rear, letting the last of the light fill the room where stood the marble. He came often to see the monolith. Sometimes, after a day of carving ugliness, he had to come and look at the stone and imagine the beauty inside. That balance sometimes seemed as if it was all that sustained him.

Richard's fingers, dusty from his work carving stone, reached out to feel the white Cavatura marble. It was slightly different from the stone he carved down at the site. He had the experience, now, to discern the subtle difference. The grain was finer in Victor's stone, harder; it would better take and hold detail.

Under Richard's fingers, the stone was as cool as moonlight, and just as chaste.

When he looked up, Victor was standing nearby, smiling wistfully, watching Richard and the stone.

"After carving such ugliness, it is good to look upon the beauty of my statue?"

Richard chuckled in answer.

Victor strode across the room, gesturing. "Come, sit with me and have some lardo."

In the failing light, they sat on the threshold, eating thin slices of the heavy delicacy, savoring the cool air coming up the hill.

"You know, you don't need to come here to look at my beautiful statue," Victor said. "You have a beautiful wife to look at."

Richard didn't say anything.

"I never recalled you mentioning your wife. I never knew about her, until she came to me that day. For some reason, I always believed you had a good woman. . . ."

Victor frowned off at the shell of the Retreat. "Why didn't you ever mention her?"

Richard shrugged.

"I hope you don't think me a terrible person, Richard, but she just doesn't fit my idea of the woman I thought would be with you."

"I don't think you're a terrible person, Victor. Everybody should have the right to think for themselves."

"Do you mind if I ask you about her?"

Richard sighed. "Victor, I'm tired. I'd really rather not talk about my wife. Besides, there's nothing to say. She's my wife. What is, is."

Victor grunted as he chewed a big bite of red onion. After he swallowed, he waved the half of onion he had left. "It's not good for a man to carve such things in the day, and then at night have to go home to—What am I saying! What has gotten into me? Forgive me, Richard. Nicci is a beautiful woman."

"Yes, I suppose so."

"And she cares for you."

Richard didn't say anything.

"Ishaq and I tried to get you out of that place by bargaining for you with your gold. It wasn't enough. The man was a pompous official. Nicci knew how to wiggleworm him. She used her words to turn the key on your prison door. Without Nicci, you would be buried in the sky."

"So, she told them that I could carve—to save my life."

"That's right. It is she who got you the job of carver."

Victor waited for more, and finally sighed in resignation when it wasn't forthcoming.

"How are those chisels I sent down?"

"Good. They work well. I could use a clawed chisel with finer teeth, though."

Victor handed Richard another small slice of lardo. "You will have it."

"What about the steel?"

Victor waved his onion. "Not to worry. Ishaq is doing well in your place. Not as good as you, but he is doing well. He gets me what I need. Everyone likes Ishaq, and is happy he decided to fill in the need. The Order is so desperate for progress to continue that they turn a blind eye to his work. Faval the charcoal maker asked about you. He likes Ishaq, but misses you."

Richard smiled at the memory of the nervous fellow. "I'm glad Ishaq is buying his charcoal."

There were a lot of good people in the Old World. Richard had always envisioned them as the enemy, and now he was friends with a number of them. It had happened to him so often and in the same way; people were basically the same everywhere, once you got to know them.

There were those who loved liberty, who cried out to live their own lives, to strive, to rise above, to achieve, and those bent on the mindless equality of stagnation brought about through the enforcement of an artificial, arbitrary, gray uniformity—those who wanted to transcend through their own effort, and those who wanted others to think for them and were willing to pay the ultimate price for it.

Kamil and Nabbi both stood and grinned when Richard climbed the steps.

"Nabbi and I worked on our carving, Richard. Will you come and see?"

Richard smiled and put an arm around Kamil's shoulders. "Sure. Let's see what you've done today."

Richard followed them down the clean hallway and out to the back, where Kamil and Nabbi had carved faces in an old log. The carvings were terrible.

"Well, Kamil, it looks pretty good. Yours, too, Nabbi."

The carvings of the faces wore smiles, and to Richard that alone was priceless. Despite how poorly done, they had more life to them than what Richard saw executed day in and day out in precious marble by master carvers.

"Really, Richard?" Nabbi asked. "You think Kamil and I could be carvers?"

"Someday, maybe. You need more practice—you still have much to learn—but all carvers have to practice to become adept. Here, look at this, right here, for example. What do you think of this? What's wrong with it?"

Kamil folded his arms as he frowned in concentration at the face he'd carved. "I don't know."

"Nabbi?"

Ill at ease, Nabbi shrugged. "It doesn't look like a real face. But I can't tell why."

"Look at my face, at my eyes. What's different?"

"Well, I think your eyes are a different shape," Kamil said.

"And they are closer together—not out at the side of the head," Nabbi added.

"Very good." Richard smoothed some of the dirt where the carrots had been pulled up, and then molded the moist dirt into a mound. He used his finger and thumb to shape a simple face. "See here? By putting the eyes closer, like this, it looks more like a real person."

Both young men nodded as they studied what he had done.

"I see," Kamil said. "I'll start a new one, and do it better."

Richard clapped him on the back. "Good man."

"Maybe one day we can be carvers, too," Nabbi said.

"Maybe" was all Richard said.

Nicci had dinner on the table, waiting for him. A bowl of soup sat next to the glowing lamp. The rest of the room was left to the evening gloom. Nicci, too, sat at the table waiting.

"How was the carving today?" she asked as Richard went to the basin to wash the dirt from his hands.

He splashed the soapy water on his face, rinsing off the stone dust.

"Carving is carving."

Nicci rubbed her thumb on the base of the lamp.

"Are you able to stand it?"

Richard wiped his hands. "What choice have I? I can either stand it, or I can end it all. What choice is that? Are you asking me if I am ready to commit suicide, yet?"

She looked up. "That isn't what I meant."

He tossed the towel down beside the basin. "Besides, how can I not be grateful for a job you got for me?"

Nicci's blue eyes turned back to the table. "Victor told you?"

"It wasn't all that hard to figure out. Victor said only that you were beautiful, and you saved my life."

"I had no choice, Richard. They would only release you if you had a skill. I had to tell them."

More than most days, he felt the essence of the engagement with her, the dance. She felt secure behind her shield of "had to tell them." Yet it allowed her to watch him, to see how he would react.

All the effort of the day, moving heavy stone blocks, lifting the hammer countless times, had sapped his strength. His hands tingled with the effect of all those ringing blows. Now, he had begun yet again the battle with Nicci. He sat down on his pallet as exhaustion took him.

Fatigue was part of any battle. As much as he ever felt it when he held the blade, he felt it now, that life-or-death dance. This was no less a battle than any Richard had ever fought. Nicci stood in opposition to freedom, to life.

This was a dance with death.

The dance with death was really the definition of life itself, since all people eventually must die.

"I want to know something, Nicci."

She gazed expectantly at him. "What is it?"

"Can you tell if Kahlan is alive?"

"Of course. I can feel the link to her at all times."

"And is she still alive, then?"

Nicci smiled in that assuring manner of hers. "Richard, Kahlan is fine. Don't let that weigh on your mind."

Richard stared at Nicci for a time. Finally, he withdrew his gaze and lay down in his prison bed. He rolled away from Nicci's gaze, from the dance.

"Richard . . . I made you soup. Come eat."

"I'm not hungry."

He shut her from his mind and tried to remember Kahlan's green eyes as weariness engulfed him.

Richard could feel Neal's breath on the back of his neck. The young disciple watched over Richard's shoulder as he tap-tap-tapped the back of the chisel, carving the gaping mouth of a sinner crying out in agony as his body was being torn apart by the Keeper of the Underworld.

"Quite good," Neal murmured, overcome with delight in what he was seeing.

Richard rested the wrist of his chisel hand against the stone to help push himself upright. "Thank you, Brother Neal."

Neal's brown eyes, the same color as his drab robes, stared with arrogant challenge. Richard did nothing to meet that challenge.

"You know, Richard, I don't like you."

"No man is worth liking, Brother Neal."

"You always have an answer, don't you, Richard?" The young wizard smiled then as he reached under his hood and scratched his closely cropped brown hair. "Do you know why you have this job?"

"Because the Order gave me a chance to help—"

"No, no," Neal interrupted as he suddenly grew impatient. "I mean do you know why the position was open? Do you know why we needed carvers, enabling you to gain this great opportunity at employment?"

Richard knew very well why they had needed carvers.

"No, Brother Neal. I was a laborer, at the time."

"Many of them were put to death."

"Then they must have been traitors to our cause. I'm happy the Order caught them."

Neal's sly smile returned as he shrugged. "Maybe. I could tell that they had a bad attitude. They thought too much of themselves, of what they selfishly considered their . . . talent. A very old-fashioned notion, don't you think, Richard?"

"I wouldn't know, Brother Neal. I only know I am able to carve, and I am grateful for the opportunity to do my duty to help my fellow man by contributing my efforts."

Neal backed away, giving Richard an appraising look, as if to measure whether or not the words had been mocking. Richard hadn't given Neal the opening he wanted, so Neal simply spilled out his point.

"I thought some among them might be deriding the Order with their work. I thought they might be using their carving to mock and ridicule our noble cause."

"Really, Brother Neal? I never suspected."

"That is why you are nobody, and never will be anybody. You are a nothing. Just like all those carvers."

"I realize I am nobody important, Brother Neal. It would be wrong to think I was of any value other than in what I can contribute. I aspire only to work hard in service to the Creator so I might earn my reward in the next life."

The smile was gone, replaced by a fiery scowl. "I ordered them put to death—after I had confessions tortured out of each one of them."

Richard's fist tightened on the chisel. Through a calm expression, he contemplated driving his chisel through Neal's skull. He knew he could do it before the man could react. But what would it gain? Nothing.

"I am grateful, Brother Neal, that you uncovered the traitors in our midst."

Neal squinted in suspicion for a moment. He finally dismissed it with a twist of his mouth before suddenly swirling amid a flourish of his robes.

"Come with me," the brother commanded in a grave tone as he marched away.

Richard followed him across the field churned to mud by all the workers going back and forth, by all the supplies being dragged, carried, or rolled to the construction site. They strode past what seemed the endless face of the palace. The stone walls were getting ever higher, with row upon row of window openings. Their trim was beginning to take form. Many of the beams for the second floor had been placed in sockets in the walls. A maze of inner walls was going up, too, defining the interior rooms and hallways. There would be miles of corridors in the palace. Dozens of stairwells stood in various stages of construction.

It wouldn't be long before oak floors were laid over some of the rooms below, enclosing them. The roof had to be completed over those sections, first, though, lest rain ruin the flooring. Some of the outer rooms were to have roofs lower than the main section, which was to rise up to a towering height. Richard expected to see those lower rooms capped with slate and lead roofs before the winter rains.

He stayed close behind Brother Neal as they marched toward the main opening into the palace. There, the walls were higher and more complete, with many of the ornate decorations in place. Neal charged two at a time up the semicircle of marble steps leading up to the entry plaza. The white marble pillars stood in an impressive sweep, and over the top of them many of the stone carvings had been installed. With all the tortured people frozen in stone, it was an intimidating sight, as it was meant to be.

The floor of the plaza was gray-veined white Cavatura marble. The sun on the marble made the plaza, half encircled by the soaring columns, glow with glorious light. The decrepit people in the stone ringing the plaza seemed to be screaming in pain at that light—which was just the effect Brother Narev had wanted.

Neal made a sweeping gesture with an arm. "Here will be the great statue—the statue to crown the entry to the emperor's Retreat." He turned a complete revolution while holding the arm aloft. "This will be the place where people enter the great palace. This is where people will come while on their way to see the officials of the Order. This is where they will come closer to the Creator."

Richard said nothing. Neal watched him for a moment, then stood in the center and threw his arms up toward the sunlight.

"Here!—will be the statue to the glory of the Creator, using His Light in a sundial. The Light will reveal the loathsome creatures of the statues—mankind. This will be a monument to man's evil nature, doomed to the misery of his existence in this world, wicked of character, cowering in humiliation as His Light reveals man's hateful body and soul for what it is—perverted beyond hope."

Richard thought that if madness had a champion, it was the Order, and people who thought like them.

Neal's arms swept back down, a conductor concluding a triumphant performance.

"You, Richard Cypher, are to carve this statue."

Richard was acutely aware of the hammer in his straining fist. "Yes, Brother Neal."

Neal waggled a finger held close to his nose as he grinned with fiendish delight. "I don't think you understand, Richard." He thrust up a commanding hand. "Wait. Wait right there."

He strode off, his brown robes swirling behind like muddy waters in a flood. Neal collected something from behind the marble pillars and returned holding it in one hand.

It was a small statue. He set it down, where the radiating lines of the marble floor converged at a point in the middle of the plaza. It was a plaster statue of what Brother Neal had just revealed to Richard. If anything, it was even more gruesome than Neal had described it. Richard ached to smash it with his hammer, right on the spot. It would almost be worth dying to destroy such a vile thing.

Almost.

"This is it," Neal said. "Brother Narev had a master carver do up the model of the sundial to his instructions. Brother Narev's vision is truly remarkable. It's perfect, don't you think?"

"It is just as horrifying as you said it was, Brother Neal."

"And you are to carve it. Just scale this model up into a great statue in white marble."

Feeling numb, Richard nodded. "Yes, Brother Neal."

The finger waggled again with great delight. "No, no, you don't yet really understand, Richard." He was grinning like a washwoman standing at a fence with basket full of dirty gossip. "You see, I did some checking on you. Brother Narev and I never trusted you, Richard Cypher. No, we never did. Now, we know all about you. I found out your secret."

Richard's flesh went cold. His muscles tightened as hard as stone. He prepared to throw himself into battle. There appeared to be no choice but to fight, now. Neal was about to die.

"You see, I talked to People's Protector Muksin."

Richard was taken aback. "Who?"

Neal displayed a triumphant grin. "The man who sentenced you to work as a carver. He knew your name. He showed me the disposition of the case. You confessed to a civil infraction. He showed me the fine—twenty-two gold marks. Quite a sum." Neal waggled the finger again. "That was a miscarriage of justice, Richard, and you know it. No man can get a fortune like that through a mere civil infraction. Such a gain can only be ill-gotten."

Richard relaxed a bit. His fingers ached from how hard he had been gripping the hammer.

"No," Neal said, "you had to have done something much more serious to have collected a fortune of twenty-two gold marks. You are obviously guilty of a very serious crime."

Neal spread his hands like the Creator before one of his children. "I am going to show you mercy, Richard."

"Does Brother Narev approve of your showing mercy?"

"Oh, yes. You see, the statue is to be your penance to the Order—your way to atone for your evil deed. You will create this statue when you are not doing your other carving for the palace. You will receive no pay for it. You are commanded not to steal any marble from that which the Order has purchased for the emperor's Retreat, but to procure the marble with your own money. If you have to work for a decade to earn such a sum, all the better."

"You mean, I am to carve, here, in the day, at my job, and I am to carve this statue for you on my own time, at night?"

"Your own time? What a corrupt concept."

"When am I to sleep?"

"Sleep is not the concern of the Order—justice is."

Richard took a calming breath. He pointed with his hammer at the thing on the ground.

"And this is what I am to carve?"

"That's right. The stone will be purchased by you, and your labor will be contributed by you to the benefit of your fellow man. It will be your gift to the people of the Order in penance for your evil deeds. Men like you, with the ability, must happily contribute their all to help the Order."

Brother Neal swept his arm out. "There is to be a dedication of the palace, this winter. The people need to see tangible evidence that the Order can bring such a great project as this magnificent palace to reality. They desperately need the lessons this palace will teach them.

"Brother Narev is eager to dedicate the palace. He wishes to hold a great ceremony, this winter, which will be attended by many dignitaries of the Order. The war is progressing; the people need to see that their palace is, too. They need to see results for their sacrifices.

"You, Richard Cypher, are to carve the great statue for the entrance to the emperor's Retreat."

"I am honored, Brother Neal."

Neal smirked. "You should be."

"What if I'm not . . . up to the task?"

Neal's smirk widened into a grin. "Then you will go back into custody, and Protector Muksin's questioners will have you until you confess. After you finally confess, you will be hung on a pole. The birds will feast on your flesh."

Brother Neal pointed down at the grotesque model.

"Pick it up. This is what you shall devote your life to."

Nicci looked up when she heard Richard's voice. He was talking to Kamil and Nabbi. She heard him say that he was tired and couldn't look at their carving, that he would look tomorrow. Nicci knew they would be disappointed. That was unlike Richard.

She spooned buckwheat mush and peas from a dented pot into a bowl. She placed the bowl and a wooden spoon on the table. There was no bread.

She wished she could make something better for him, but after their voluntary contributions were taken out, they had no money. If not for the garden the women of the building had taken to planting in the back of the house, they would be in desperate straits. Nicci had learned how to grow things so she could have food for him.

451

His shoulders were stooped, his eyes distant. He was carrying something in one hand.

"I have your dinner. Come and eat."

Richard set the thing on the table, beside the oil lamp. It was a small, intricately carved statue of figures cowering in terror. They were partially surrounded by a section of a ring. A tall lightning bolt, a common symbol of retribution by the Creator, came down in the center, piercing a number of obviously evil men and women, pinning them to the ground. It was a staggering representation of the evil nature of mankind, and the Creator's anger at their wanton ways.

"What's this?" she asked.

Richard slumped down into a chair. His face sank into his hands, his fingers stabbed back into his hair. After a time, he looked up.

"What you wanted," he said quietly.

"What I wanted?"

"My punishment."

"Punishment?"

Richard nodded. "Brother Narev found out about the fine of twenty-two gold marks. He said I must have done something criminal to get that much money, and he sentenced me to make a statue for the grand entrance to the emperor's palace."

Nicci glanced down at the small thing on the table. "What is it?"

"A sundial. This is the ring with the times etched on it. The lightning bolt casts a shadow of the Creator's Light on the ring to tell the time of day."

"I still don't understand. Why is it a sentence? You are a carver. That is your job."

Richard shook his head. "I am to buy the stone out of my own money, and I am to carve this at night, on my own time, as my gift to the Order."

"And why do you see this as what I wanted?"

Richard ran a finger down the lightning bolt, his eyes studying the statue. "You brought me here, to the Old World, because you wanted me to learn the errors of my ways. I have. I should have confessed to a crime and let them end it."

Without thinking, Nicci reached across the table and put her hand over his. "No, Richard, that's not what I wanted."

He pulled his hand away.

Nicci pushed his bowl closer to him. "Eat, Richard. You need your strength."

Without complaint, he did as she told him. A prisoner, doing as ordered. She hated to see him like this.

The spark was gone from his eyes, just as it had left her father's eyes.

When he looked at the statue sitting in the center of their table, his eyes were dead. It was as if the life, the energy, the hope, was gone from him. When he was finished with his meal, he went without a word to his bed and lay down, facing away from her.

Nicci sat at the table, listening to the sputter of the lamp's flame, watching Richard's even breathing as he went to sleep.

It seemed his spirit was crushed. She had believed for so long that she would learn something valuable when he was pushed to such extremes. It appeared she had been wrong, that he had finally given up. She could learn nothing from him, now.

There was little left for her to do. Little reason to continue the whole thing. For a moment, she felt the crushing weight of her disappointment; then even that was gone.

Empty and unfeeling, Nicci collected the bowl and spoon and carried them to the wash bucket. She worked quietly, to let him sleep, as she resigned herself to returning to Jagang.

It wasn't Richard's fault he could teach her nothing; there was nothing more to life to learn. This was all there was. Her mother had been right.

Nicci took out the butcher knife and set it quietly on the table.

Richard had suffered enough.

It would be for the best.

Nicci sat at the table, the knife under her fingers, forever. She watched his back. His chest slowly expanded with his breath of life, and sank again. There was time enough to slip the knife into his back, between his ribs, to pierce his heart.

There was time enough yet before dawn.

Death was so final. She wanted to watch him for a while. Nicci never tired of watching Richard.

After she did it, she wouldn't be able to watch him anymore. He would be gone forever. With the damage the chimes had done to the worlds and their interconnection, she didn't even know if a person's soul could still go to the spirit world. She didn't even know if the underworld still existed and if Richard's spirit would go there, or if he would simply be . . . gone forever—if he and that which was his soul would simply cease to exist.

In her numb state, she had lost track of time.

When she glanced out the window that Richard had had installed with the money he had earned, she noticed that the sky had taken on a the color of a week-old bruise.

Linked as she was to Kahlan, Nicci couldn't accomplish the deed with her magic. As much as she abhorred the idea of it, and knowing how gruesome it would be, she had to use the sharp blade.

Nicci curled her fingers around the wooden handle of the stout knife. She wanted it to be quick. She couldn't bear to think of him suffering. He had suffered enough in life, she didn't want him to suffer in death, too.

He would struggle briefly, but then it would be over.

Richard abruptly rolled onto his back and then sat up. Nicci froze, still sitting in her chair. He rubbed the sleep from his eyes. Could she kill him when he was awake? Could she look into those eyes of his as she plunged the knife into his chest?

She would have to.

It was for the best.

Richard yawned and stretched. He sprang to his feet.

"Nicci. What are you doing? Haven't you gone to bed?"

"I . . . I guess I fell asleep in the chair."

"Oh, well, I—there it is. I need that."

He snatched the knife out of her hand. "Mind if I borrow this? I need to use it. I'm afraid I'll have to sharpen it for you later. I won't have time before I have to leave. Can you make me something to eat? I'm in a hurry. I have to go see Victor before I start to work."

Nicci was dumbfounded. He was suddenly revived. In the lamplight, and the faint dawn coming in the windows, he had that look in his eyes. He looked . . . resolute, determined.

"Yes, all right," she said.

"Thanks," he called over his shoulder while hurrying out the door.

"Where are you—?"

But he was gone. She decided he must be going out back to get some vegetables. But why would he need the big knife for that? She was confused, but she was revived, too. Richard seemed himself again.

Nicci pulled from the pantry some eggs she had been saving, along with an iron skillet, and hurried out back to the cooking hearth. The coals were still glowing from the cook fires of the evening before, providing a little light. She carefully fed in some small twigs and kindling, then stacked a bed of finger-thick branches on top. She simply set the iron skillet atop the wood as it caught, rather than set up the rack—eggs were quick.

As she waited for the skillet to get hot, she heard an odd scraping noise. In the flickering light of the fire, she didn't see Richard in the garden. She couldn't imagine where he had gone, or what he was up to. She broke the eggs into the hot skillet and tossed the shells in the compost bucket at the side of the hearth. With a wooden spoon she scrambled the eggs around as they cooked.

As Nicci stood, using her skirt to hold the hot handle of the skillet, she was surprised to see Richard coming out from behind the broad cooking hearth.

"Richard, what are you doing?"

"There are some loose bricks back here. I was just seeing to it before I went to work. I cleaned out the joints. I'll bring some mortar home and fix it later."

He pulled a handful of thick-bladed grass and used it as a potholder to take the skillet from her. With his other hand, he flipped the knife into the air, caught it by the point, and held the handle out to her. Nicci took the heavy knife, now scratched and dulled from scraping the bricks clean. He ate standing, using the wooden spoon.

"Are you all right?" she asked.

"Fine," he said around a hot mouthful of eggs. "Why?"

Nicci gestured toward the house. "Well, last night . . . you seemed so . . . defeated."

He frowned at her. "So, I've no right to feel sorry for myself now and again?"

"Well, yes, I suppose. But now . . . ?"

"Now I've thought it over."

"And . . . ?"

"It's to be my gift to the people, is it? I shall give the people a gift they need."

"What are you talking about?"

Richard waved the wooden spoon. "Brothers Narev and Neal said this will be my gift to the people, and so it shall be." He shoveled more eggs into his mouth.

"So you are going to carve the statue they want?"

He was already running up the stairs before she had finished the question.

"I have to get the model of the statue and be off to work."

Nicci raced after him up the stairs. He was still eating the eggs as he went. He stood in their room, peering down at the small statue on the table as he finished the eggs. She couldn't make sense of it—he was smiling.

He set the skillet on the table and scooped up the model. "I'll probably be home late. I have to get started on my penance for the Order, if I can. I may have to work all night."

In astonishment, she watched him hurry off to work.

455

She could hardly believe that he had once again somehow evaded death. Nicci couldn't recall ever being so grateful about anything. She couldn't understand it.

Richard reached the blacksmith's shop shortly after Victor had opened up for the day's work. His men had not yet arrived. Victor wasn't surprised to see him; Richard sometimes came early and the two of them would sit and watch the sun come up over the site.

"Richard! I'm glad to see you."

"And I you, Victor. I need to talk to you."

He let out a gruff grunt. "The statue?"

"That's right," Richard said, a little taken aback. "The statue. You know?"

With Richard following behind, Victor made his way through the dark shop, weaving among the clutter of benches, work, and tools. "Oh, yes, I heard." Along the way, he stooped to pick up a hammer here, a bar of iron there, and set them on a table, or shoved them in a bin, as if one could tidy a mountain by arranging a few pebbles and picking up a fallen limb.

"What did you hear?"

"Brother Narev paid me a visit last evening. He said there is to be a dedication of the Retreat, to show our respect to the Creator for all he provides for us." He glanced back over his shoulder as he strode past his huge block of Cavatura marble. "He told me you are to carve a statue for the entrance plaza—a big statue. He said it is to be done for the dedication.

"From what I hear from people, from Ishaq and others, the Order credits the uprising to the drain of building such a monumental project as the Retreat in addition to waging the war. They have armies of men working for the construction—not just here, but from quarries far and wide, to mines for the gold and silver, to forests where they cut the wood. Even slaves must be fed. The purge of officials, leaders, and skilled workers after the uprising was expensive. With a dedication, I think Brother Narev wants to show people the progress, to inspire them, to involve outlying lands in the celebration, believing this will head off further troubles."

In the blackness of the room, only the skylight in the high ceiling above let light cascade down over the stone. The marble took the light deep into its fine crystalline structure, and gave it back as a loving gift.

Victor opened the double doors that looked out over the Retreat. "Brother Narev told me that your statue is also to be a sundial, with the Creator's Light shining down on mankind's torment. He told me I am to oversee the making of the gnomon and dial plane for its shadow to fall upon. He said something about a lightning bolt . . ."

Victor turned around, his eyes following as Richard set the model of the statue on a narrow tool shelf that ran the length of the room.

"Dear spirits . . ." Victor whispered. "That is grotesque."

"They want me to carve this. They want it to be a statue with the power to dominate the grand entrance."

Victor nodded. "Brother Narev said as much. He told me how big would be the metal for the dial plane. He wants bronze."

"Can you cast the bronze?"

"No." With the backs of his fingers, Victor tapped Richard's arm. "Here is the

456

good part: few people can cast such a piece. Brother Narev ordered Priska released to do the casting."

Richard blinked in astonishment. "Priska is alive?"

Victor nodded. "High people must have not wanted him buried in the sky in case they needed his skills. They had him locked away in a dungeon. The Order knows they need people with ability; they released him to get this done. If he wants to remain alive, and out of the dungeon, he is to cast the bronze, at his own expense, as a gift to the people. They say it is his penance. I am to give him the specifications and see to its assembly and placement on the statue."

"Victor, I want to buy your stone."

The blacksmith's brow slid into an unfriendly frown.

"No."

"Narev and Neal found out about my civil fine. They think I got off too lightly. They ordered that I carve their statue—much like Priska is to provide the casting—as my penance. I must buy the stone myself, and I must carve it after my work at the site is finished for the day. They want it for this winter's dedication of the Retreat."

Victor's eyes turned toward the model on the shelf, as if it was some monster come to visit ruin on him. "Richard, you know what this stone means to me. I won't—"

"Victor, listen to me."

"No." He held his palm up toward Richard. "Don't ask this of me. I don't want this stone to become ugly, like all the Order touches. I won't allow it."

"Neither will I."

Victor gestured angrily at the model. "That is what you are to carve. How can you even think of that ugliness visiting my pure marble?"

"I can't."

Richard set the plaster model on the floor. He picked up a large hammer, its handle leaning against the wall, and with a mighty blow shattered the abomination into a thousand pieces. He stood as the white dust slowly billowed over the threshold, out the door, and down the hill toward the Retreat like some ghost of evil returning to the underworld.

"Victor, sell me your stone. Let me liberate the beauty inside."

Victor squinted his distrust. "The stone has a flaw. It can't be carved."

"I've thought about it. I have a way. I know I can do it."

Victor put his hand to his stone, almost as if he were comforting a loved one in distress.

"Victor, you know me. Have I ever done anything to betray you? To harm you?"

His voice came softly. "No, Richard, you have not."

"Victor, I need this stone. It is the best piece of marble—the way it can take in light and send it back. It has grain that can hold detail. I need the best for this statue. I swear, Victor, if you trust me with it, I will be true to your vision. I won't betray your love of this stone, I swear."

The blacksmith gently ran his beefy, callused hand up the side of the white marble that towered to nearly twice his height.

"What if you were to refuse to carve them their statue?"

"Neal said that then they will take me back to the prison until they get a confession out of me, or until I die from the questioning. I will be buried in the sky in return for nothing."

457

"And if you do as you want, instead"—Victor gestured to the fragments of the model—"and don't carve them what they want?"

"Maybe I would like to see beauty again before I die."

"Bah. What would you carve? What would you see before you die? What could be worth your life?"

"Man's nobility—the most sublime form of beauty."

The man's hand paused on the stone, his eyes searching Richard's, but he said nothing.

"Victor, I need you to help me. I'm not asking you to give me anything. I'm willing to pay your price. Name it."

Victor returned his loving gaze to his stone.

"Ten gold marks," he said with bold confidence, knowing Richard had no money.

Richard reached into his pocket and then counted out ten gold marks. He held the fortune out to Victor. The blacksmith frowned.

"Where did you get such money?"

"I worked and I saved it. I earned it helping the Order build their palace. Remember?"

"But they took all your money. Nicci told them how much you had, and they took it all."

Richard cocked his head. "You didn't think I'd be foolish enough to put all my money in one place, did you? I have gold stashed all over. If this isn't enough, I will pay you whatever you ask."

Richard knew that the stone was valuable, although not worth ten gold marks, but it was to Victor, so Richard would not argue the price. He would pay whatever the man asked.

"I can't take your money, Richard." He waved a hand in resignation. "I don't know how to carve. It was but a dream. As long as I never carved it, I could dream of the beauty in the stone. This is from my homeland, where once there was freedom." His fingers blindly found the wall of marble. "This is noble stone. I would like to see nobility in this Cavatura marble. You may have the stone, my friend."

"No, Victor. I don't want to take your dream. I want to, in a way, fulfill it. I cannot accept it as a gift. I want to buy it."

"But, why?"

"Because I will have to give it to the Order. I don't want you giving this to the Order; I will have to do that. More than that, though, they will no doubt want it destroyed. It must be mine when they do that. I want it to be paid for."

Victor held out his hand. "Ten marks, then."

Richard counted out the ten gold marks and then closed the man's big fingers around them.

"Thank you, Victor," Richard whispered.

Victor grinned. "Where do you wish me to deliver it?"

Richard held out another gold mark. "May I rent this room? I would like to carve it here. From here, when I'm done, it can be sledged down to the entrance plaza."

Victor shrugged. "Done."

Richard handed over a twelfth gold mark. "And I want you to make me the tools with which I will carve this stone—the finest tools you have ever made. The kind of tools used to carve beauty in your homeland. This marble demands the best. Make the tools out of the best steel."

"Points, toothed chisels, and chisels for fine work—I can make them for you. There are hammers aplenty about you may use."

"I also need rasps, in a variety of shapes. And files, too. Straight, curved—a wide selection—the finest smoothing files. I need you to get me pumice stones, the fine white close-grained pumice—ground to the same shapes to match the rasps and files, and a good supply of powdered pumice, too."

Victor's eyes had gone wide. The blacksmith had come from a place where they had once done such carving. He knew full well what it was Richard meant to do.

"You intend to do flesh in stone?"

"I do."

"You know how?"

Richard knew from statues he had seen in D'Hara and in Aydindril, and from what some of the other carvers told him, and from his own tests in his work for the Order's palace, that if carved properly, then smoothed and polished to a high luster, quality marble could take in the light and give it back in a way that seemed to liberate the stone from its hardness, softening it, so that it assumed the look of flesh. If done properly, the marble could seem to almost come alive.

"I've seen it done before, Victor. I've carved before. I've learned how to do it. I've thought about it for months. Ever since I started carving for them, this purpose has kept my mind alive. I've used my work for the Order to practice what I've seen, what I've learned, and what I've thought of on my own. Even before, when they questioned me . . . I thought about this stone, about the statue I know is in it, to keep my mind from what they did to me."

"You mean it helped you to endure their torture?"

Richard nodded. "I can do it, Victor." He lifted a fist in firm conviction. "Flesh in stone. I only need the proper tools."

Victor rattled the gold in his fist. "Done. I can make the proper tools for what you want to do. This is what I know. I don't know how to carve, but this will be my part—what I can do to bring the beauty out."

Richard clasped forearms with Victor to seal their agreement.

"I have one thing I would ask you—as a favor."

Victor laughed his deep belly laugh. "I must feed you lardo so you may have the strength to carve this noble stone?"

Richard smiled. "I wouldn't ever turn down lardo."

"What is it then?" Victor asked. "What is the favor?"

Richard's fingers tenderly touched the stone. His stone.

"No one is to see it until it is done. That includes you. I would like to have a canvas tarp, so I can cover it. I would ask that you not look at it until it is done."

"Why?"

"Because I need it to be mine alone while I carve it. I need solitude with it as I shape it. When I'm finished, then the world can have it, but when I work on it, it is to be my vision and mine alone. I wish no one to see it before it is finished.

"But most of all, I don't want you to see it because if anything goes wrong, I don't want you involved in this. I don't want you to know what I do. If you don't see it, you can't be buried in the sky for not telling them."

Victor shrugged. "If that is your wish, then it shall be so. I will tell the men that the back room is rented, and it is off-limits. I will put a lock on the inner door. I will put a chain on the outer double doors, here, and give you the key."

"Thank you. You don't know what that means to me."

"When do you need the chisels?"

"I need the heavy point to rough it out, first. Can you have it done by tonight? I need to get started. There isn't much time."

Victor dismissed Richard's concern with a flourish of his hand. "The heavy point is easy. I can make that in short order. It will be done when you come from your work down there—your work with the ugliness. Long before you need the other chisels, they will be ready for you to carve beauty."

"Thank you, Victor."

"What is this 'thank you' talk? This is business. You have paid me in advance— value for value between honest men. I can't tell you how good it is to have a customer other than the Order."

Victor scratched his head and turned more serious. "Richard, they will want to see your work, won't they? They will want to see how you are doing on their statue."

"I don't think so. They trust my work. They gave me the model they want scaled up. They have already approved it. They've told me my life depends on this. Neal delighted in telling me how he ordered those other carvers tortured and put to death. He wanted to frighten me. I doubt they will give it a second thought."

"But what if a Brother does come, wanting to see it?"

"Then I will have to bend an iron bar around his neck and let him pickle in the brine barrel."

Richard touched the length of the point chisel to his forehead, as he had so often touched the Sword of Truth there in much the same way. This was no less a battle. This was life and death.

"Blade, be true this day," he whispered.

The chisel had eight sides, so as to provide grip in a sweaty hand. Victor had given it a proper heavy blunt point. He had also put his initials—V C—in small letters on one of the facets, proclaiming the pride of its maker.

Such a heavy chisel would shatter stone and remove a great excess material in short order. It was a weapon that would do a lot of damage, fracturing the structure of the marble down the width of three fingers. A point used carelessly on unnoticed flaws could shatter the entire piece.

Finer points would cause shallower fractures, but remove less material. Even with the finest point punches, Richard knew that he could only approach to within the last half finger of the final layer. The network of spidery cracks left by a point were fractures in the crystalline structure of the marble itself. So damaged, the stone lost its translucence and its ability to take a high polish.

To do flesh in stone, the final layers had to be approached with care, and be left undamaged by any tool.

After the heavy point removed much of the waste, then finer-point chisels would allow Richard to get closer, refining the shape. Once he was within as close as a half finger of the final layer, he would turn to the clawed chisels, simply chisels with notches in their edge, to shear away the stone without fracturing the underlying structure of the marble. The coarse claws took off the most stone, leaving rough gouges. He would use chisels with a series of finer and finer teeth to refine the work. Finally, he would use smooth-bladed chisels, some only half as wide as his little finger.

Down at the site, where he carved scenes for the frieze, that was as far as the carvers went. It left an ugly surface, ungainly and coarse, rendering flesh as wooden, leaving no definition or refinement to muscle and bone. It robbed the people in the carvings of their humanity.

On this statue, Richard would really only begin where the carvings for the Order ended. He would use rasps to define bone, muscle, even veins in the arms. Fine files would remove the marks left by the rasps and refine the most subtle contours. The pumice stones would remove the filing marks, leaving the surface ready to polish with pumice paste held in leather, cloth, and finally straw.

If he did it right, he would have his vision in stone. Flesh in stone. Nobility.

Holding the heavy point chisel to his palm with his thumb, Richard put his hand to the stone, feeling its cool surface. He knew what was inside—inside not only the stone, but inside himself.

There were no doubts, only the heart-pounding passion of expectation.

As he so often did, Richard thought of Kahlan. It had been nearly a year since he had looked into her green eyes, touched her cheek, held her in his arms. She would have long ago left the safety of their home for dangers he could vividly imagine. For a moment, he was overwhelmed with the weight of despair, choked by the sadness of how much he missed her, humbled at how much he loved her. Now he knew he must dismiss her from his mind so that he could devote himself entirely to the task he had to do.

As he so often did, Richard said his silent good-night to Kahlan.

Then he set the point at ninety degrees to the face of the stone, and took a powerful swing with the steel club. Stone chips exploded away.

His breaths came deeper and faster. It was begun.

With great violence, Richard attacked the stone.

By the light of lamps Victor left for him after the work day was done, Richard lost himself in the work, raining down blow upon blow. Sharp stone chips rattled off the wooden walls, and stung when they hit his arms or chest. With a clear vision of what he wanted to do, he broke away the waste stone.

His ears rang with the sound of steel on steel and steel on stone. It was music. Jagged chips and chunks fell away. They were the fallen enemy. The air boiled with the white dust of battle.

Richard knew precisely what we wanted to accomplish. He knew what needed to be done, and how to do it. He was filled with a clarity of purpose, a course to follow. Now that it had begun, he was lost in the work.

Dust billowed up around him until his dark clothes were white, as if the stone were absorbing him, as he was transforming with it, until they were one. Sharp shards nicked him as they shot away. His bare arms, white as the marble itself, were soon streaked here and there with blood from the battle.

From time to time, he opened the doors to shovel out the ankle-deep scree. The white scrap avalanched down the hill, tinkling with a sound like a thousand tiny bells. The white dust covering him was cut through with dark rivulets of sweat, and red scratches. The cool air felt refreshing against his sweat-soaked skin. But then he once again shut out the night, shut out the world to be alone.

For the first time in nearly a year, Richard felt free. In this, he was in complete control. No one watched him. No one told him what he must do.

This work was his singular purpose, in which he strove for perfection. There were no chains, no limitations, no desires of others to which he must bow. In this struggle to accomplish his best, he was utterly free.

What he intended would stand in unyielding opposition to everything the Order represented. He intended to show them life.

Richard knew that when the Brothers saw the statue, they would sentence him to death.

Stone chips burst forth with each blow, taking him closer to his goal. He had to stand on a work stool to reach the top of the marble, moving it around the monolith to work all sides, narrowing it down to what would be.

Richard swung the steel club with the fury of battle. His chisel hand stung with the ringing blows. As violent as the attack was, though, it was controlled. A trimming hammer, called a pitcher, could be used for such rough work. It removed waste with greater speed than a heavy point to shape the block, but it was used with a full swing, and Richard feared, because of the flaw, to unleash that much power against the stone. In the beginning, the block had strength in its sheer mass, but even so, he considered such a trimming hammer too dangerous for this particular stone.

Richard would have Victor make him a set of drill bits for a bow drill. With a bow's cord run around the shaft of the drill, it could be twisted and driven through the marble. Richard had thought long and hard about the problem of the flaw. He had resolved to cut out most of it. First, to stop any further cracks from running through more of the stone, he would drill holes through the crack to relieve the stress. With another series of closely spaced holes, he would weaken the stone in a waste area around the flaw and simply remove most of it.

There would be two figures: a man, and a woman. When finished, the space between them would be where Richard had removed the worst of the flaw. With the weakest stone removed, the sound stone that remained would be strong enough to take the stress of the work. Since the defect started at the base, he couldn't eliminate it all, but he could reduce the problem it presented to a manageable level. That was the secret to this piece of stone: eliminating its weakness, then working in its strength.

Richard considered it a fortunate flaw, first of all because it had reduced the value of the stone, enabling Victor to purchase it in the first place. To Richard's mind, though, the flaw had been valuable because it had caused him to think about the stone, and how to carve it. That thought had brought him to his design. Without the flaw, he might not have come to the same design.

As he worked, he was filled with the energy of the fight, driven onward by the heat of the attack. Stone stood between him and what he wanted to carve, and he craved to eliminate that excess so he could get to the essence of the figures. A huge corner of waste broke loose, slipping away, slowly at first, then crashing down. Chips and shards rained down as he worked, burying the fallen foe.

Several more times he had to open the doors and shovel out the scrap. It was invigorating to see what was once an irregular shaped block, becoming a rough shape. The figures were still completely encased, their arms far from being free, their legs not separate, yet, but they were beginning to emerge. He would have to be careful, drilling holes in the open areas to prevent breaking off the arms.

Richard was surprised to see light streaming through the window overhead. He had worked the entire night without realizing it.

He stood back and appraised the statue that was now more or less roughly a cone shape. Now, there were only lumps where the arms would extend out from the bodies. He wanted the arms to be free, the bodies to convey grace and movement. Life. What he carved for the Order was never free, always tightly bound to the stone, forever stiff, unable to move, like cadavers.

Half of what had been there the night before was now gone. Richard ached to stay and work on, but he knew he couldn't. From the corner, he excavated the canvas tarp Victor had left for him, and flung it over the statue.

When he threw open the door, the white dust billowed out. Victor was sitting among the rubble of his stone monolith.

The blacksmith blinked. "Richard, you have been here the whole night!"

"I guess I have."

He gestured as a grin split his face. "You look like a good spirit. How goes the battle with the stone?"

Richard could think of nothing to say. He could only beam with the joy of it.

Victor laughed his belly laugh. "Your face says it all. You must be tired and hungry. Come, sit and rest—have some lardo."

Nicci heard Kamil and Nabbi shout a greeting as Richard came down the street, and then their footsteps as they ran down the front stairs. She glanced out the front window and, in the failing light of dusk, saw them meet up with Richard as he came down the street. She, too, was happy to see him coming home this early.

Nicci had seen precious little of Richard in the weeks since he took on the duty of carving the statue for Brother Narev. She couldn't imagine how Richard could endure carving a statue she knew had to be agony for him—not so much because of its size, but because of its nature.

If anything, though, Richard seemed invigorated. Often, after working all day carving the moral lessons for the façade of the palace, he would then work late into the night on the grand statue for the entrance plaza. As tired as he had to be when he came home, he would sometimes pace. There were nights when he would only sleep for a couple of hours, rise, and go to work on the statue for hours before his workday at the site began. Several times he had worked the entire night.

Richard seemed driven. Nicci didn't know how he could do it. He sometimes came home to eat and to take a nap for an hour, and then he would go back. She would urge him to stay and sleep, but he would say that the penance had to be paid or they would put him back in prison. Nicci feared that possibility, so she didn't insist that he stay home to sleep. Losing sleep was preferable to him losing his life.

He had always been muscular and strong, but his muscles had become even more lean and defined since he came to the Old World. All that labor of loading iron and now moving rock and swinging a hammer had built him up even more. When he went out back to the washtubs and removed his shirt to rinse off the stone dust, the sight of him made her knees weak.

Nicci heard footsteps passing down the hallway, and the excited voices of Kamil and Nabbi asking questions. She couldn't understand Richard's words, but she easily recognized the timbre of his voice calmly giving the two the answers to their questions.

As tired as he was, as much as he was away at his work, he still took time to talk to Kamil and Nabbi, and to the people of the building. He was no doubt now on his way out back to give pointers to the two young men on their carving. During the day, they worked around the building, cleaning and caring for the place. They turned over the dirt in the garden, mixing in compost when it was ready. The women appreciated having the heavy spade work done for them. The two washed, painted, and repaired, hoping Richard would approve and then show them how to do new things. Kamil and Nabbi always offered to help Nicci with anything she might need—she was, after all, Richard's wife.

Richard came in the door as Nicci stood at the table cutting up carrots and onions into a pot. He slumped down into the chair across the table. He looked spent from his day of work—after having been up hours earlier working on the statue.

"I came home to get something to eat. I have to go back and work on the statue."

"This is for tomorrow's stew. I have some millet cooked."

"Is there anything more in it?"

She shook her head. "I only had enough money for the millet today."

He nodded without complaint.

Despite how exhausted he looked, there was some remarkable quality in his eyes, some inner passion, that made her pulse race faster. Whatever it was that she had seen in him from the first moment seemed to have only gotten stronger since that night she had almost put the knife through his heart.

"Tomorrow, we'll have this stew." she said. His gray eyes were staring off into his private visions. "From the garden."

She retrieved the cook pot after setting a wooden bowl on the table before him and spooned millet into his bowl until it was full. There was little left, but he needed it more than she. She had spent the morning waiting in line for the millet, and then had spent the afternoon picking all the worms out of it. Some of the women just cooked it until you couldn't tell. Nicci didn't like to feed that to Richard.

Standing close to the table, cutting up carrots, she could finally stand it no more. "Richard, I want to come to the site with you and see this statue that you're carving for the Order."

He was silent for a moment as he chewed and then swallowed. When he finally did speak, it was with a quiet quality that matched that inexplicable look in his eyes.

"I want you to see the statue, Nicci—I want everyone to see it. But not until I'm finished."

"Why?"

He stirred his spoon around in his bowl. "Please, Nicci, will you grant me this? Let me finish it, then you will see it."

Her heart pounded against her ribs. This was important to him.

"You aren't carving what they told you to carve, are you?"

Richard's face turned up until his gaze met hers.

"No, I'm not. I'm carving what I need to carve, what people need to see."

Nicci swallowed. She knew: this was what she had been waiting for. He had been ready to give up, then he wanted to live, and now he was willing to die for this.

Nicci nodded, having to look away from those gray eyes of his. "I'll wait until it's ready."

Now she knew why he seemed so driven, lately. That quality hinted at in her father's eyes, and blazing in Richard's, she felt was somehow tied to this. The very idea was intoxicating.

In more ways than one, this was a matter of life and death.

"Are you sure about this, Richard?"

"I am."

She nodded again. "All right, I will honor your request."

The next day, Nicci got an early start to buy bread. She wanted Richard to have bread with the stew she was cooking. Kamil offered to go for her, but she wanted to get out of the house. She asked him to keep an eye on Richard's stew as it simmered on the banked coals.

It was an overcast day, and cool—a hint of the rapidly approaching winter. The streets were crowded with people out looking for work, with carts hauling everything from manure to bolts of coarse dark cloth, and with wagons, mostly carrying building materials for the palace. She had to step carefully to avoid the dung in the road and squeeze between all the people moving as slowly as the sludge of the open sewers as she made her way through the city.

There were crowds of needy people in the street, many come to Altur'Rang for work, no doubt, although there were few people at the workers' group hall. The lines at the bakeries were long. At least the Order saw to it that people got bread, even if it was gray, tough bread. You had to go early, though, before they ran out. With more people all the time, the shops ran out earlier every week.

Someday, it was rumored, they were going to be able to provide more than one kind of bread. She hoped that this day, at least, they might have some butter, too. Sometimes, they sold butter. The bread, and the butter, were inexpensive, so she knew she could afford to buy a little for Richard—if they had any. They almost never had any butter.

Nicci had spent a hundred and eighty years trying to help people, and people seemed no better off now than they ever were. Those in the New World were prosperous enough, though. Someday, when the Order ruled the world, and those with the means were made to contribute their fair share to their fellow man, then everything would finally fall into place and all of mankind could at last live with the dignity they deserved. The Order would see to it.

The bread shop stood at an intersection of two roads, so the line turned around the corner onto another street. Nicci was around that corner, leaning a shoulder against the wall, watching the passing throngs, when a face in the crowd caught her attention.

Her eyes went wide as she straightened. She could hardly believe what she was seeing. What was *she* doing in Altur'Rang?

Nicci didn't really want to find out—not now, when it seemed she was getting close to finding her answers. Matters seemed to be at a critical state with Richard. She felt sure that it would soon come to resolution.

Nicci flipped her dark shawl up over her head of blond hair and tied it snug under her chin. She sank back behind a wide woman and hugged the wall as she peeked out between the people in line.

Nicci watched Sister Alessandra, her nose held high as her calculating gaze swept the faces of all the people on the street. She looked like a mountain lion on the prowl.

Nicci knew who Alessandra was hunting.

Ordinarily, Nicci would have been only too happy to cross paths with the woman, but not now.

Nicci sank back against the rough clapboards, staying low behind the people ahead of her, until Sister Alessandra had vanished into the vast sea of people crowding the street.

$\mathbf{A}$s Kahlan rode out of her home city of Aydindril for the last time, she pulled her wolf-fur mantle up over her shoulders for protection against the bitter wind. She recalled that the last time the weather had been about to close in for the winter was the last time she had seen Richard. With the world in such constant turmoil and the battle burning hot, her thoughts, by necessity, always seemed to be on urgent matters. The unexpected memory of Richard was a welcome, if bittersweet, respite from the worries of war.

She took a last look before cresting the hill, to see the splendor of the Confessors' Palace on the distant rise. It made her ache with the sense of home whenever she saw the soaring white marble columns and rows of tall windows. Other people were stricken with awe or fear at the sight of the palace, but Kahlan's heart was always warmed by it. She had grown up there, and it was a place of many happy memories for her.

"It won't be forever, Kahlan."

Kahlan glanced over at Verna. "No, it won't."

She wished she could believe that.

"Besides," Verna said, offering a smile, "we will be denying the Imperial Order the people, and that is what they are really after. The rest is just stone and wood. What matters stone and wood, if the people are safe?"

Kahlan, despite her desolate tears, was overcome with a smile. "You're right, Verna. That really is all that matters. Thank you for reminding me."

"Don't worry, Mother Confessor," Cara said, "Berdine and the rest of the Mord-Sith, along with the troops, will watch over the people and see them safely to D'Hara."

Kahlan's smile widened. "I wish I could see Jagang's face when he finally gets here next spring to be greeted by ghosts."

The season of war was drawing to an end. If the summer with Richard in their mountain home had been a wonderful dream, then the summer of endless warfare had been a nightmare.

The fighting had been desperate, intense, and bloody. There were times when Kahlan thought she and the army could not go on, that they were finished. Each of those times, they had managed to pull through. There were occasions when she almost welcomed death, just to have the nightmare end, just to stop seeing people in agony and pain, to stop seeing all the precious lives in ruins.

Against the seemingly indomitable millions of the Imperial Order, the forces of the D'Haran Empire had managed to slow the enemy enough to keep them from taking Aydindril this year. With thousands of lives lost in the fighting, they had bought the hundreds of thousands of people of Aydindril and other cities that lay along the path of the Order the time they needed to escape.

As autumn had turned bitter, the immense force of the Imperial Order had reached a broad valley at a convergence of the Kern River and a large tributary, where the lay of the land provided space to accommodate their entire force. With winter closing in, Jagang knew better than to be caught unprepared. They had dug in while they had the opportunity. The D'Haran forces had set up their defensive lines to the north, bulwarking the way to Aydindril.

Just as Warren had forecast, Aydindril was more than Jagang's army could take in this season of war. Jagang, once again, had proven his prudent patience; he had chosen to preserve the viability of his army so he would be able to press on successfully when conditions allowed. In the short run, it gave Kahlan and her forces breathing room, but in the long run, it would spell their doom.

Kahlan felt sweet relief that Warren's prediction, of Aydindril falling the following year, at least would not be at the cost of a slaughter of the city's citizens. She didn't know what hardships the people would have to endure escaping to D'Hara, but it was better than the certain slavery and widespread death of remaining behind in Aydindril.

Some people, she knew, would refuse to leave. In cities along the Order's march up the Midlands, some people put their faith in "Jagang the Just." Some people believed that the good spirits, or the Creator, would watch over them no matter what. Kahlan knew they couldn't save everyone from themselves. Those who wished to live, and were willing to see reason, stood a chance. Those who saw only what they wished to see, would, at the least, fall under the pall of the Order's domination.

Kahlan reached back and touched the hilt of the Sword of Truth sticking up behind her shoulder. It was comforting, sometimes, to touch it. The Confessors' Palace was no longer her home. Home was wherever Richard and she were together.

The fighting was often so intense, the fear so palpable, that there were times— days at a stretch—when she never thought of him. Sometimes, she had to devote all her physical and mental effort to just staying alive one more day.

Some men, feeling the war was hopeless, had deserted. Kahlan could understand the way they felt. All they ever did, it seemed, was to fight for their lives against overwhelming odds as they backed their way up through the Midlands.

Galea had fallen. That there was no word from any city in Galea probably said it all.

They had lost Kelton, too. Many of the Keltans in Winstead, Penverro, and other cities had fled, first. Most of Kelton's army were still with them, though some had rushed home in desperation.

Kahlan tried not to think too long on everything that had gone wrong, lest she give up. They had saved a good many people—gotten them out of the way of the Order. At least for the time being. It was the best they could do.

Along the long retreat north, tens of thousands of their joint forces had lost their lives in the fierce battles. The Order had lost many times that number. In the high summer heat, the Order had lost a quarter million men to fever alone. It made little difference; they continued to grow and to roll onward.

Kahlan recalled the things Richard had told her, that they could not win, that the New World was going to fall to the Order, and if they resisted, it would only cause greater bloodshed. She was reluctantly coming to understand that hopeless outlook.

She feared she was only getting people killed to no good end. Yet giving up still was out of the question for her.

Kahlan looked over her shoulder, past the long column of men escorting her, past the trees and up the mountain, to the great dark mass of the Wizard's Keep looming up on the mountain overlooking Aydindril.

Zedd would have to go there; they could not stop the Imperial Order from having Aydindril, but they dared not let them have the Keep.

It was dusk, ten days later, when Kahlan and her company rode back into the D'Haran camp. It was obvious from the first instant that something was wrong. Men were running through camp, swords drawn. Others were rushing pole weapons to the barricades. Men were donning leather and chain mail as they ran to their posts. It was a tense scene, but one Kahlan had seen repeated so often that it seemed almost routine.

"I wonder what this is all about," Verna said with a scowl. "I'll not like it if Jagang spoils my dinner."

Kahlan, not wearing her leather armor, suddenly felt naked. It was uncomfortable to wear on long rides, so, going through friendly territory, she had tied it to her saddle. Cara moved close as they dismounted. They handed the reins to soldiers as men closed in protectively.

Kahlan couldn't remember what color cloth would be used to mark the command tents. She had lost track of the exact number of days she had been gone. It had been somewhat over a month. She took the arm of an officer among the men who had swept in around her.

"Where are the commanders?"

He pointed with his sword. "Down that way, Mother Confessor."

"Do you know what's going on?"

"No, Mother Confessor. The alarm sounded. As a Sister rushed past, I heard her say it was genuine."

"Do you know where my Sisters, or Warren, are?" Verna asked the officer.

"I've seen Sisters running around everywhere, Prelate. I've not seen Wizard Warren."

Darkness was settling in, leaving only the fires to guide them through camp. Most of the fires, though, had been doused at the alarm, so the camp was becoming a black maze.

Horses with D'Haran riders flashed past, headed out on patrol. Foot soldiers raced out of camp to scout. No one seemed to know what the threat was, but that wasn't unusual. Besides being frequent and varied, attacks were usually confusing, in addition to being frightening.

It was over an hour before Kahlan, Cara, Verna, and their heavy ring of guards made it through the sprawling camp that was the size of a city, to the officers' tents. None of the officers were there.

"This is a foolish way to go about it," Kahlan muttered. She found her tent, with *Spirit* standing on the little table, and tossed her saddlebags inside, along with her armor. "Let's just wait here so people can find us."

"I agree," Verna said.

Kahlan gestured to include a number of the group of men who had set up a defensive guard around her. "Spread out and find the officers. Tell them that the Mother Confessor and the Prelate are at the command tents. We'll wait here for reports."

"Tell any Sisters you see," Verna added. "And if you see Warren or Zedd, tell them, too, that we've returned."

The men raced off into the night to carry out their instructions.

"I don't like this," Cara muttered.

"I don't, either," Kahlan said as she stepped into her tent.

Cara stood guard, along with a small army of men, as Kahlan took off her fur mantle and slipped on her leather armor. It had saved her from taking wounds often enough that she was not shy about wearing it. All it would take was one man to slip up close and thrust a sword into her, and that might well be the end. If she got lucky, and they ran it through a leg, or even her belly, she had a chance of being healed by a Sister, but if it was in some other place—heart, head, some major artery so that the loss of blood was too fast—then even the gifted wouldn't be able to heal her.

The leather was extremely tough, and while not impervious to blades, spears, or arrows, it afforded a good degree of protection while allowing enough freedom of movement to enable her to fight. A blow with a blade had to be landed just right, or it would glance harmlessly off the leather. Many of the men wore chain mail, which afforded better protection, but it was too heavy for Kahlan to be practical for her to wear. In combat, speed and maneuverability were life.

Kahlan knew better than to risk her life needlessly. She was more valuable to their cause in her capacity as a leader than as a combatant. Still, while she rarely went directly into combat, the fighting had often enough come to her.

A sergeant finally arrived to give her a report.

"Assassins" was all he said.

That one chilling word was enough. It was what she had figured, and explained the state of the camp.

"How many casualties?" Kahlan asked.

"I only know for sure that one attacked Captain Zimmer. He was eating at a campfire with his men. The captain managed to miss a killing blow, but took a nasty wound in the leg. He's lost a lot of blood. The surgeons are seeing to him right now."

"What about the assassin?" Verna asked.

The sergeant looked surprised at the question. "Commander Zimmer killed the assassin." He screwed up his face with the distaste of the rest of what he had to say. "The assassin was dressed in a D'Haran uniform. He walked through the camp without notice until he found a target—Captain Zimmer—and attacked."

Verna let out a worried breath. "A Sister might be able help the captain."

Kahlan dismissed him with a nod. The sergeant saluted with a fist to his heart before rushing off to his duties.

It was then that Kahlan spotted Zedd approaching. The front of his robes was wet and dark—undoubtedly with blood. Tears ran down his face. Gooseflesh tingled up Kahlan's arms and legs.

Verna gasped when Zedd suddenly saw her and for an instant faltered before rushing toward them. Verna clutched Kahlan's arm.

Zedd seized Verna's hand. "Hurry" was all he said.

It was all he needed to say; they all understood.

Verna let out a mournful cry as she was pulled along after the old wizard. Kahlan and Cara ran behind as Zedd led them on a winding charge through the confusion of shouting men, galloping horses, squads in formation dashing in every direction, and unit officers taking roll call.

The roll call was needed because the assassins were in D'Haran uniforms so they could sneak up close to their quarry. It was necessary to account for every man in order to single out those who didn't belong. It was tedious and difficult, but essential.

They rushed into the swirl of turmoil around the tents where wounded men were being treated. Men shouted orders as others brought in men crying out in pain, or men with their limp arms dragging the ground. Each tent could hold up to ten or twelve men.

Verna's composure was frayed with panic. Zedd stopped her, holding her by her arms. His voice was choked with his emotion.

"A man stabbed Holly. Warren was nearby and tried to protect the girl. Verna, I swear to you on my dead wife's soul . . . I did everything I could do. Dear spirits forgive me, but I must be the one to tell you . . . he is beyond my power to help him. He asked for you and Kahlan."

Kahlan stood in a stupor, her heart in her throat. Zedd's hand on her back urged her to move quickly. She followed Verna, ducking into the tent.

Half a dozen dead men lay at the far end of the tent, covered with blankets. Here and there a bloody hand stuck out from under a cover. One man was missing a boot. Kahlan stared, unable to make her mind work, unable to understand how the soldier had lost a boot. It seemed so silly—dying and losing a boot. Tragedy and comedy together under a shroud.

Warren lay on his back on a pallet on the ground. Sister Philippa was on the far side of him, her tall frame bent over the youthful wizard, holding his hand. Sister Phoebe was on the near side, holding his other hand. Both women turned tear-stained faces up to see Verna above them.

"Warren," Sister Philippa said, "it's Verna. She's here. And Kahlan, too."

The two Sisters quickly moved out of the way for Verna and Kahlan to take their places. They covered their mouths to hold in their cries as they fled the tent.

Warren was as white as the stacks of clean bandages lying nearby. His eyes were open wide as he stared up . . . as if he could no longer see. His curly blond hair was matted in sweat. His robes were soaked in blood.

"Warren," Verna moaned. "Oh, Warren."

"Verna? Kahlan?" he asked in a breathy whisper.

"Yes, my love." Verna kissed his hand a dozen times.

Kahlan squeezed his other limp hand. "I'm here, too, Warren."

"I had to hold on. Till you both came back. To tell you both."

"Tell us what, Warren?" Verna asked through her tears.

"Kahlan . . ." he whispered.

She leaned in. "I'm here, Warren. Don't try to talk, just—"

"Listen to me."

Kahlan pressed his hand to her cheek. "I'm listening, Warren."

"Richard is right. His vision. I had to tell you."

Kahlan didn't know what to say.

A smile came to his ashen face. "Verna . . ."

"What is it, my love?"

"I love you. Always have."

Verna could hardly get her words past her choking tears. "Warren, don't die. Don't die. Please don't die."

"Give me a kiss," Warren whispered, "while I still live. And don't mourn what ends, but what a good life we've had. Kiss me, my love."

Verna bent over him and met his lips with hers, giving him a gentle, loving kiss as her tears dripped onto his face.

Unable to bear the scene, Kahlan staggered out of the tent, finding Zedd's protective arms waiting. She hid her weeping against his shoulder.

"What are we doing?" she cried. "What's it all for? What good is any of it? We're losing everything."

Zedd had no answer for her tears at the futility of it all.

The minutes dragged on. Kahlan forced herself to be strong, to be the Mother Confessor. She couldn't let the men see her giving up.

Silent men stood nearby, not wanting to look in the direction of the tent where Warren lay dying.

When General Meiffert materialized out of the darkness, the relief on Cara's face was evident. He rushed up close to Cara, but didn't touch her.

"I'm glad to see you safely returned," he said to Kahlan. "How is Warren?"

Kahlan couldn't speak.

Zedd shook his head. "I didn't think he would live this long. I think he held on so he could see his wife."

The general nodded sorrowfully. "We caught the man who did it."

Kahlan came to full attention. "Bring him to me," she growled.

Without hesitation the general hurried off to retrieve the assassin. When Kahlan gestured, Cara went with him.

"What did he say to you?" Zedd asked in a quiet voice so that others wouldn't hear. "He wanted to tell you something."

Kahlan took a purging breath. "He said, 'Richard is right.' "

Zedd looked away in forlorn misery. Warren was his friend. Kahlan never knew Zedd to take a liking to anyone the way he had taken to Warren. They shared things she knew she could never understand. Despite his young appearance, Warren was over a hundred and fifty years old, close to the same age as Verna. To Zedd, who was always looked up to as the wise old wizard, it must have been a particular comfort to share wizardly matters with one who understood such things, instead of constantly needing explanation and direction.

"He said the same to me," Zedd whispered tearfully.

"Why didn't Warren use his gift?" Kahlan asked.

Zedd wiped a finger across his cheek. "He was walking past, just as the man seized and stabbed Holly. Perhaps the assassin couldn't find his target, or maybe he became lost and confused, or he could have just panicked and decided to stab someone and Holly was handy at that moment."

Kahlan wiped her hands back across her cheeks. "Maybe he had been told to look for a wizard in such robes, and when he saw Warren, he stabbed Holly to cause a commotion so he could get at Warren."

"That could be. Warren doesn't really know. It all happened in an instant. Warren was right there, and just reacted. I asked, but he didn't know why he didn't use his power. Perhaps in that terrible flash of the knife, he feared to kill Holly in the process, since the man had her and was stabbing her. His instinct to save her just caused him to snatch for the knife. It was a fatal mistake."

"Maybe Warren simply hesitated before using his power."

Zedd shrugged painfully. "A split-second hesitation has been the end of a lot of wizards."

"If I hadn't hesitated," Kahlan said as she stared off into bitter memories, "Nicci wouldn't have had me. She wouldn't have Richard, now."

"Don't try to fix the past, dear one—it can't be done."

"What about the future?"

Zedd's gaze sought hers. "Meaning?"

"Remember at the end of last winter, when we left camp—when the Order began moving?" When Zedd nodded, she went on. "Warren pointed at this place on the map. He said we had to be here to stop the Order."

"Are you suggesting he knew he would die here?"

"You tell me."

"I'm a wizard, not a prophet."

"But Warren is." When he said nothing, Kahlan asked in a whisper, "What about Holly?"

"I don't know. I was just arriving to talk to Warren. It had just happened. Soldiers were jumping the man. Warren yelled orders for them not to kill him. I guess he was thinking the assassin might have valuable information. I saw Holly, bleeding from her wounds, in shock. I immediately had Warren brought in here and started to work on him. Sisters rushed in and took Holly to another tent."

Zedd's heartsick gaze sank to the cold ground. "I did everything I know to do. It wasn't enough."

Kahlan enclosed his shoulders protectively in her arm. "It was out of your hands from the first, Zedd."

It was disorienting to see her source of strength in a state of such painful weakness. It was irrational to expect him to be unemotional and strong in such circumstances, but it was still disconcerting. In that moment, Kahlan was overcome with a sense of all the loss Zedd had suffered in his life; it was all there in his wet hazel eyes.

Men made way for the returning General Meiffert and Cara. Behind them, two burly soldiers had a wiry young man—little more than a boy, really. He was muscular, but no match for the men who had him. His hair tumbled down across a forehead above dark contemptuous eyes. He wore a proud sneer.

"So," the lad said, trying to sound tough, "I guess that in my service to the Order I knifed someone important. That makes me a hero of the Order."

"Make him kneel before the Mother Confessor," General Meiffert said with quiet command.

The two soldiers kicked the back of the young man's knees to take him down. He snickered as he knelt before her.

"So, you're the big important whore I've heard so much about. Too bad you weren't around—I'd have loved to have cut you. I guess I showed some people I'm pretty good with a knife."

"So in my absence," Kahlan said, "you cut a child, instead."

"Just for practice. I'd have cut a lot more people if these big dumb oxen wouldn't have lucked into jumping me. But I still did my duty to the Order and the Creator."

It was the bravado of someone who knew he was about to pay the ultimate price for his actions. He was trying to convince himself that he had fulfilled a valuable service. He wanted to die a hero, and then go straight to the Creator for his reward in the afterlife.

Verna emerged from the tent. There was no hurry in her movements. Her face was ashen and drawn. Kahlan took hold of her arm, ready to help if Verna should need it.

Verna stopped when she saw the young man on his knees.

"This is him?" she asked.

Kahlan put her other hand tenderly to Verna's back, silently offering support.

"This is him," Kahlan confirmed.

"That's right." The lad sneered up at Verna. "I'm the one who knifed the enemy wizard. I'm a hero. The Order will bring relief and justice to the people, and I helped do it. Your kind is always trying to keep us down."

"Keep you down," Verna repeated in a dead tone.

"Those who are born with all the luck and advantages—they never want to share. I waited, but no one ever gave me a chance in life until the Order did. I'm a hero of downtrodden people everywhere. I've struck a blow against the oppressors of mankind. I've helped bring justice to those who are never given a chance. I killed an evil man. I'm a hero!"

The silence of everyone nearby was all the more grim with the backdrop of activity going on as men searched the camp for other assassins. Officers called out names, getting quick replies. Troops searching for invaders trotted through the night, their chain mail and weapons jingling like thousands of tiny bells.

The man on his knees grinned at Verna. "The Creator will give me my reward in the next life. I'm not afraid to die. I've earned eternity in his everlasting Light."

Verna passed her gaze among the eyes of all those gathered.

"I don't care what you do to him," she said, "but I want to hear his screams the entire night. I want this camp to hear his screams the entire night. I want the Order's scouts to hear his screams. That will be my tribute to Warren."

The young man licked his lips, realizing things weren't going as he had expected.

"That isn't fair!" the young assassin shouted in protest.

Panic began to tremble through his body. He had been prepared for a martyr's death, a quick end. This was something unforeseen.

"He died quick. I should have the same consideration! This isn't fair!"

"Fair? What isn't fair," Verna said with terrible calmness, "is that your mother ever opened her legs for your father. We shall now belatedly correct her mistake. What isn't fair is that a good and kind man died at the hands of a sniveling little coward so lacking in sense that he is incapable of recognizing the lies he now spews out at us.

"You wish to trade your life for the one you have taken? You wish to die in a cause you foolishly believe to be noble? You shall have your wish, young man. But before you die, you shall fully understand what it is you have surrendered, how precious is your life, and how utterly wasted. You shall come to regret your mother's act of creation as much as do we."

Verna swept a look of finality over the group watching. "This is my wish. Please see to its execution."

Cara took a step forward. "Let me do it, then." Her grim face held no hint of relish. "I would be best at carrying out your wish as you intend it, Verna."

The lad laughed hysterically. "A woman? You all think you're going to have some big blond bitch try to teach me a lesson? You're all as crazy as I've heard."

Verna nodded. "I will be indebted to you, Cara." She started to leave, but paused. "Don't let him die before morning, when I will come to witness it. I wish to look into his eyes and see if this young man has come to understand the nature of reality, and its lack of fairness, before he forfeits his life for nothing of worth and for his part in a great evil."

"I promise you," Cara said softly to Verna, "that even though this night will seem forever to you in your grief, it will be infinitely longer for him."

Verna simply touched Cara's shoulder in appreciation on her way past.

After Verna had walked off into the darkness, Cara turned to Kahlan. "I would ask to use a tent. No one should have to see what I do to him. His screams will be knowledge enough."

"As you wish."

"Mother Confessor!" The young man struggled frantically, but the soldiers had him in a firm grip. "If you're so good as you claim, then show me mercy!"

Drool ran from the corner of the boy's mouth and hung swinging in rhythm with his panting.

"But I have," Kahlan said. "I am allowing you to suffer the sentence Verna has named, and not the one I would impose."

Cara snapped her fingers and pointed at the young man as she marched off. The soldiers dragged the shrieking boy after her.

"The others we captured?" the general asked Kahlan.

Kahlan started for her tent. "Cut their throats."

Kahlan sat up when she realized that she didn't hear the distant screams any longer. It was still hours till dawn. Maybe his heart had stopped unexpectedly.

No, Cara was Mord-Sith, and was well trained in what Mord-Sith did.

As she had lain fully dressed in her bed, listening to the bloodcurdling screams, aching for Verna, missing Warren, sweat had occasionally beaded her brow whenever she thought about how Richard had once been the one under a Mord-Sith's Agiel.

To banish the uninvited, ghastly images invading her thoughts, she looked up at *Spirit*. The lamp hanging from the ridgepole cast a warm light on the carving, stressing the graceful lines of her flowing robes, her fisted hands, her head thrown back. No matter how many times Kahlan looked at the statue, she never tired of it. Every time, it was a thrill.

Richard had chosen this view of life over the terrible bitterness he could have fallen into. Clinging to such bitterness would only have robbed him of his ability to experience happiness.

Kahlan heard a commotion outside. Just as she sprang to her feet, Cara poked her head in through the flap Kahlan had left open. The Mord-Sith's blue eyes were in a lethal rage. She stepped into the tent, pulling the lad behind by a fistful of his hair. He shook as he blinked frantically, blinded by the blood in his eyes.

Gritting her teeth, Cara shoved him. He fell to the dirt at Kahlan's feet.

"What's this about?" Kahlan asked.

The look in Cara's eyes revealed a woman at the edge of a feral fury, at the edge of control, at the far-distant reaches of what it was to even be human. She was treading the soil of another world: madness.

Cara dropped to her knees and seized the young man by the hair. She yanked him back up and held him against her red-leather-clad body as she pressed her Agiel to his throat. He choked and coughed. Blood frothed from his mouth.

"Tell her," Cara growled.

He held his hands out to the sides in surrender. "I know him! I know him!"

Kahlan frowned down at the terrified young man. "You know who?"

"Richard Cypher! I know Richard Cypher!—And his wife, Nicci."

Kahlan felt as if the world crashed down around her. The weight of that world sank her to her knees before Cara's charge.

"What is your name?"

"Gadi! I'm Gadi!"

Cara pressed her Agiel into his back, causing him to let loose a wild scream. She slammed his face to the ground.

Kahlan held a hand out. "Cara, wait . . . we need to talk to him."

"I know. I'm just making sure he wants to talk to us."

Kahlan had never seen Cara quite like this, unleashed this way. This was more than doing as Verna asked. This was personal to Cara. Warren had been someone she liked, but worse for Gadi, Richard was Cara's life.

The Mord-Sith pulled him upright again. Red bubbles grew around his broken nose. When the light caught Cara just right, Kahlan could see blood glistening on the red leather.

"Now, I want you to tell the Mother Confessor everything."

He was nodding as he wept and before Cara had even completed the command.

"I lived there—where they came to live. I lived where Richard and his wife—"

"Nicci," Kahlan corrected.

"Yes, Nicci." He didn't understand what she meant. "They came to live in a room in our house. My friends and I didn't like him. Then, Kamil and Nabbi started talking to him. They started liking Richard. I was angry—"

He fell to such blubbering that he couldn't finish. Kahlan seized his jaw, slick with blood, and shook his face.

"Talk! Or I'll have Cara start in again!"

"I don't know what to say, what you want," he sobbed.

"Everything you know about him and Nicci. Everything!" Kahlan yelled inches from his face.

"Tell her the rest of it," Cara said in his ear as she pulled him to his feet.

Kahlan followed him up, fearing to miss a precious word.

"Richard started to get people to fix up the place. He works for Ishaq, at the transport company. When he came home at night, he would fix things. He showed Kamil and Nabbi how to fix things.

"I hated him."

"You hated him because he made things better?"

"He made Kamil and Nabbi and others think they could do things for themselves, when they can't—people can't do for themselves. That's a cruel deception. People have to be helped by those with the ability. It's their duty. Richard should have made things better, because he could—he shouldn't have made Kamil and Nabbi and the others think they could change their lives for themselves. No one can do that. The people need help, not such heartless and unfeeling expectations.

"I found out Richard was working at night. He was hauling extra loads for greedy people. He was making money he shouldn't be allowed to make.

"Then, one night, I was sitting on the steps, and I heard Nicci get mad at Richard. She came out to me on the steps and asked me to have sex with her. Women always want me. She was a whore—no better than the rest—despite all her airs. She told me that Richard wasn't man enough to take care of her, and she wanted me to have her because he wouldn't.

"I gave it to her good—just the way she wanted it. I gave it to the whore good. I hurt her good, just like she deserved—"

With all her strength, Kahlan rammed her knee into his groin. Gadi doubled over, unable to draw his breath. His eyes rolled up in his head and he went down hard.

Cara smiled. "I thought you might like to hear that part."

Kahlan wiped the tears from her cheeks. "It wasn't Richard. I knew it wasn't Richard. It was this pig."

Kahlan kicked him in the ribs as he started coming around. He let out a cry. She wagged her fingers impatiently. Cara seized him by the hair and yanked him to his feet.

"Finish your story," Kahlan said with icy rage.

He coughed and gagged and drooled. Cara had to steady him on his feet. She held his arms behind his back so he couldn't comfort his groin. The pain was clearly evident in his contorted face.

"Talk, or I'll do it again!"

"Please! I was telling you when you stopped me."

"Get on with it!"

He nodded frantically. "When I was done with the whor—when I left Nicci, Kamil and Nabbi were crazy."

Kahlan lifted her chin. "What do you mean, they were crazy?"

"They were crazy angry because I was with Richard's wife. They like Richard, so they were crazy angry with me. They were going to do things to me. Hurt me. So, I decided to go into the army to fight for the Order against the heathens, and . . ."

Kahlan waited. She glanced up at Cara. The Mord-Sith did something behind Gadi's back that made him gasp in a cry.

"And then I turned in Richard's name!"

"You did what?"

"I turned in his name before I left. I told the city guards at Protector Muksin's office that Richard was doing criminal things, that he was stealing work from working people—that he was making more than his fair share."

Kahlan frowned. "What does that mean? What happens when you turn in a name?"

Gadi was trembling in terror. He clearly didn't want to answer. Cara pressed her Agiel against his side. Blood oozed down his sweat-soaked shirt. He tried, but couldn't draw a breath. His ashen face began to turn purple.

"Tell her," Cara said in cold command.

Gadi gasped in a breath when she released the pressure. "They will arrest him. They will . . . make him . . . confess."

"Confess?" Kahlan asked, fearing the answer.

Gadi nodded reluctantly. "They will torture a confession out of him, most likely. They might even hang his body from a pole and let the birds pick his bones if he confesses to something bad."

Kahlan swayed on her feet. She thought she might throw up. The world had disintegrated into madness.

She kicked over the map basket and pawed through the maps until she found the one she wanted. She pulled a pen and an ink bottle out of their box, set the statue of *Spirit* on the ground, and spread the small map across the table.

"Come here," Kahlan ordered, snapping her fingers and pointing to the ground before the table. She put the pen in his trembling fingers after he had shuffled close.

Kahlan pointed at the map. "We are here. Show me where you traveled with the Order."

He pointed. "This river. I came up from the Old World with reinforcement troops, after some training. We joined the emperor's force and we advanced up this river basin over the summer."

Kahlan pointed to the Old World. "Now, I want you to mark the place where you lived."

"Altur'Rang. That's it, there."

She watched him dip the pen and circle the dot and the name Altur'Rang, far to the south—the heart of the Old World.

"Now," she said, "mark the roads you came up in the Old World—including any cities or towns you went through."

Cara and Kahlan both watched Gadi mark roads and circle a number of cities and towns. Warren and the Sisters were from the Old World; they knew a great deal about the lay of the land, enabling them to provide detailed maps.

When he'd finished, Gadi looked up.

Kahlan turned over the map. "Draw the city of Altur'Rang. I want to see the major roads—anything you know of it."

Gadi immediately set to drawing the map for her. When he was finished, he looked up again.

"Now, show me where this room is where Richard lives."

Gadi marked the map to indicate the place. "But I don't know if he will be there. Lots of people turn in the names of people suspected of wrongdoing against their fellow man. If they take the name and they arrest him . . . the Brothers may order penance, or they could even question him and then order him put to death."

"Brothers?" Kahlan asked.

Gadi nodded. "Brother Narev and his disciples. They are the head of the Fellowship of Order. Brother Narev is our spiritual guide. He and the brothers are the heart of the Order."

"What do they look like?" Kahlan asked, her mind already racing ahead.

"The brothers wear dark brown robes, with hoods. They are simple men who have given up the luxuries of life to serve the wishes of the Creator and the needs of mankind. Brother Narev is closer to the Creator than any man alive. He is mankind's savior."

Gadi was clearly awed by the man. Kahlan listened while Gadi told her everything he knew about the Fellowship of Order, about the brothers, and about Brother Narev.

Gadi shook in the silence after he had finished. Kahlan wasn't watching him, but staring off.

"What did Richard look like," she asked in a distant voice. "Was he well? Did he look all right?"

"Yes. He's big and strong. Foolish people like him."

Kahlan spun around, landing the heel of her hand against Gadi's face hard enough to knock him from his feet.

"Get him out of here," she told Cara.

"But you must show me mercy, now! I told you what you want to know!" He broke down in tears. "You must show me mercy!"

"You have a job to finish," Kahlan said to Cara.

Kahlan pulled the tent flap back and peeked in. Sister Dulcinia was snoring softly. Holly looked up.

Tears filled the girl's eyes as she stretched out her arms pleadingly. Kahlan knelt beside the girl and bent over to hug her. Holly started crying.

Sister Dulcinia woke with a snort. "Mother Confessor."

Kahlan put a hand on the Sister's arm. "It's late. Why don't you go get some sleep, Sister."

Sister Dulcinia smiled her agreement and then grunted with the effort of struggling to her feet in the low tent. In the distance, on the far side of the camp, Kahlan could hear Gadi's bloodcurdling screams.

Kahlan smoothed the downy hair from Holly's brow and kissed her there. "How are you, sweetheart? Are you all right?"

"Oh, Mother Confessor, it was awful. Wizard Warren got hurt. I saw it."

Kahlan hugged her as she started weeping again. "I know. I know."

"Is it all right? Is he healed like they healed me?"

Kahlan cupped the little cheek and wiped a tear away with her thumb. "I'm sorry, Holly, but Warren died."

Her brow bunched up with her misery. "He shouldn't have tried to save me. It's my fault he's dead."

"No," Kahlan soothed. "That's not the way it is. Warren gave his life to save us all. He did what he did out of his love of life. He didn't want to let evil be free among those he loved."

"Do you really think so?"

"Of course I do. Remember him for how he loved life, and how he wanted to see those he loved free to live their own lives."

"He danced with me at his wedding. I thought he was the most handsome groom ever."

"He was indeed a handsome groom," Kahlan said with a smile at the memory. "He was one of the best men I've ever known, and he gave his life to help keep us free. We honor his sacrifice by living the best lives we can live."

Kahlan started to rise, but Holly hugged her all the tighter, so Kahlan lay down beside her. She stroked Holly's brow, and kissed her cheek.

"Will you stay with me, Mother Confessor? Please?"

"For a while, sweetheart."

Holly fell asleep cuddled up to Kahlan. Kahlan wept frustrated bitter tears over the sleeping girl, a girl who should have the right to live her life. Others, though, lusted to steal that right at the point of a blade.

After she had finally decided what she must do, Kahlan slipped silently out of the tent to go pack her things.

It was just turning light when Kahlan emerged from her tent carrying her bedroll, saddlebags, D'Haran sword, the Sword of Truth, leather armor, and pack with the rest of her things. *Spirit* was safely rolled up in her bedroll.

A light snow was just beginning to fall, announcing to the muted camp that winter had arrived in the northern Midlands.

Everything seemed as if it was ending. It wasn't just Warren's death that convinced her, but rather the futility it symbolized. She could no longer delude herself. The truth was the truth. Richard was right.

The Order would have it all. Sooner or later, they would have her and kill her, along with those who fought with her. It was only a matter of time until they enslaved all of the New World. They already had much of the Midlands. Some lands

480

had fallen willingly. There was no way to resist a force of their overwhelming size, the terror of their threats, or the seduction of their promises.

Warren had attested it as part of his dying words: Richard was right.

She had thought she could make a difference. She had thought she could drive back the advancing horde—by the sheer weight of her will, if need be. It was arrogance on her part. The forces of freedom were lost.

Many of the people in those fallen lands had put their faith in the Order at the cost of their liberty.

What was left to her? Running. Retreat. Terror. Death.

She had nothing to lose anymore, really. Nearly everything was already lost, or soon would be. While she at least still had her life, she was going to use it.

She was going to go to the heart of the Order.

"What are you doing?"

Kahlan spun around to see Cara frowning at her.

"Cara, I . . . I'm leaving."

Cara gave a single nod. "Good. I, too, think it is time. I won't be long getting my things together. You get the horses, and I'll meet—"

"No. I'm going alone. You will stay here."

Cara stroked her long blond braid laying over the front of her shoulder. "Why are you going?"

"There's nothing left here for me to do—nothing I can do. I'm going to go drive my sword into the heart of the Order: Brother Narev and his disciples. It's the only thing I can do to strike back at them."

Cara smiled. "And you think I want to stay here?"

"You will stay here, where you should be . . . with Benjamin."

"I'm sorry, Mother Confessor," Cara said tenderly, "but I can't follow such orders. I am Mord-Sith. My life is sworn to protecting Lord Rahl. I promised Lord Rahl I would protect you, not stay and kiss Benjamin."

"Cara, I want you to stay here—"

"It's my life. If this is the end, all there is to be, then I will do with the rest of my life as I wish. It's my life to live, not yours to live for me. I'm going, and that is final."

Kahlan saw in Cara's eyes that it was. Kahlan didn't think she had ever heard Cara express such a sentiment about her own wishes. It was indeed her life. Besides, Cara knew where Kahlan was going. If Kahlan left without Cara, Cara would simply follow. Getting Mord-Sith to obey orders was often more difficult than herding ants.

"You're right, Cara; it is your life. But when we get down into the Old World, you're going to have to wear something to disguise who you are. Red leather in the Old World will be the end of us."

"I will do what I must to protect you and Lord Rahl."

Kahlan smiled at last. "I believe you would, Cara."

Cara wasn't smiling. Kahlan's smile faded.

"I'm sorry I tried to leave without you, Cara. I shouldn't have done it that way. You're a sister of the Agiel. I should have talked it over with you. That's the proper way to treat someone you respect."

Cara smiled at last. "Now you are making sense."

"We might not ever come back from this."

Cara shrugged. "And you think we will live the high life if we stay? I think only certain death awaits us if we stay."

Kahlan nodded. "That's what I think, too. That's why I must go."

"I'm not quarreling."

Kahlan gazed out at the falling snow. The last time winter had come, she and Cara had just managed to escape in time.

Kahlan steeled herself and asked, "Cara, do you really believe Richard is still alive?"

"Of course Lord Rahl is alive." Cara held up her Agiel, rolling it in her fingers. "Remember?"

And then she did: the Agiel would only work if the Lord Rahl to whom she was sworn was alive.

Kahlan handed Cara some of her load. "Gadi?"

"He died as Verna wished it. She showed him no pity."

"Good. Pity for the guilty is treason to the innocent."

It was not long after dawn when Kahlan made it to Zedd's tent. Cara had gone to get horses and supplies. When Kahlan called, Zedd asked her to enter. He rose from the bench beside Adie, the old sorceress.

"Kahlan. What is it?"

"I've come to bid you good-bye."

Zedd's eyes showed no surprise. "Why don't you stay and get some rest? Leave tomorrow."

"There are no tomorrows left. Winter is upon us again. If I am going to do as I must, I don't have a day to waste."

Zedd gently gripped her shoulders. "Kahlan, Warren wanted to see you. He felt he had to tell you that Richard was right. It meant a great deal to him that you know that. Richard told us that you must not attack the heart of the Order before the people prove themselves to him, or all will be lost. Such a thing is even less likely to happen today than the day he said it."

"And maybe Warren meant that Richard was right—that we are going to lose the New World to the Order, so what is there to stay for? Maybe it was Warren's way of trying to tell me to go to Richard before I'm dead, or he's dead, and then it's too late to even try."

"And Nicci?"

"I'll find out when I get there."

"But, you can't hope to—"

"Zedd, what else is there for me? To watch the Midlands fall? To aspire at most to live out my life running, to live as a recluse, hiding every day from the clutches of the Order?

"Even if Warren hadn't said it, I've come to realize—no matter how much I wish it was otherwise—that Richard is right. The Order will only be pinned down for the winter while we help the people escape Aydindril. In the spring, the enemy will flood into my city. Then they will turn to D'Hara. There will be nowhere to run. Though they escape for the moment, the Order will subjugate those people.

"There is no future for me. Richard was right. The least I can do is spend the last of my life living for myself, and for Richard. There is nothing else left for me, Zedd."

Tears brimmed in his eyes. "I will miss you so. You've brought back good memories of my own daughter and given me so many good times."

Kahlan threw her arms around him. "Oh, Zedd, I love you."

She couldn't hold back her own tears, then. She was all he had left, and he was losing her, too.

No—that wasn't true. Kahlan pulled back.

"Zedd, the time has come for you to leave, too. You must go to the Keep and protect it."

He nodded with great reluctance, great sadness. "I know."

Kahlan knelt before the sorceress and took up her hand. "Adie, will you go with him and keep him company?"

A beautiful smile came to the woman's weathered face. "Well, I . . ." She looked up. "Zedd?"

Zedd scowled. "Bags, now you've ruined the surprise of the invite."

Kahlan smacked his leg. "Stop cursing in front of ladies—and stop being so sour. I'd like to know you're not going to be lonely up there."

A smile stole across his face. "Of course Adie is going to the Keep with me."

Adie scowled in turn. "How do you know that, old man? You never asked my approval. Why, I have a mind—"

"Please stop it," Kahlan said. "Both of you. This is too important to be fussing over."

"I can fuss if I want to," Zedd protested.

"That be right." Adie shook a thin finger. "We are old enough to fuss if we wish."

Kahlan smiled through her tears. "Of course you can. It's just that, after Warren . . . it reminds me of how much I hate to see people waste their lives on things that don't matter."

Zedd truly did scowl, now. "You've a thing or two to learn, dear one, if you don't know how important fussing is."

"That be right," Adie said. "Fussing keeps you sharp. When you get old, you need to stay sharp."

"Adie is entirely right," Zedd said. "Why, I think—"

Kahlan silenced him with a hug that Adie joined.

"Are you sure about this, dear one?" Zedd asked after they parted.

"I am. I'm going to take my sword into the belly of the Order."

Zedd nodded as he hooked his bony fingers around the back of her neck. He pulled her head close and kissed her brow.

"If you're to go, then ride hard and strike harder."

"My thought, exactly," Cara said as she stepped into the tent.

Kahlan thought Cara's blue eyes looked a little more liquid than usual. "Are you all right, Cara?"

Cara frowned. "What's that supposed to mean?"

"Nothing," Kahlan said.

"General Meiffert got us the six fastest horses he could find." Cara smiled her pleasure at the prospect. "We'll have fresh mounts with us and be able to cover a lot of ground fast. I have all our supplies loaded up.

"If we leave now, we should be able to escape winter's grip. We have the map, so we can stay away from the routes the Order's troops use, and the heaviest population centers. There are good roads, and open country down there. Riding hard, I think that we can make it in a few weeks. A month at most."

Zedd's face contorted with concern. "But the Order controls much of the southern Midlands. It's dangerous country, now."

"I have a better way." Cara flashed a sly smile. "We'll go where I know the country—D'Hara. We will go east from here and cross over the mountains, then go south down through D'Hara—through mostly wide-open country were we can make good time—down through the Azrith Plains, to eventually join the Kern River far to the south. After the river valley clears the mountains, we will cut southeast into the heart of the Old World."

Zedd nodded his approval of the plan. Kahlan curled her fingers lovingly around the old wizard's thin arm.

"When will you go to the Keep?"

"Adie and I will leave in the morning. I think it best not to dally here any longer. Today we'll settle matters of the army with the officers and the Sisters. I think that as soon as the people are out of Aydindril, and when the snow quickly deepens to insure the Order won't be going anywhere until spring, then our men should begin slipping out of this place to make their way over the mountains to the safety of D'Hara. It will be slow going in winter, but without having to fight as they travel, it won't be as difficult as it otherwise would be."

"That would be best," Kahlan agreed. "It will get our men out of harm's way for now."

"They won't have me to be the magic against magic for them, but they will have Verna and her Sisters. They know enough by now to carry on protecting the army from magic."

At least for a while. The words hung in the air, unspoken.

"I want to go see Verna before I leave," Kahlan said. "I think it will be good for her to have other people to worry about. Then I want to see General Meiffert; and then we'd best start riding. We have a long way to go, and I want to be south before the snow hobbles us."

Kahlan embraced Zedd fiercely one last time.

"When you see him," Zedd whispered in her ear, "tell the boy I love him dearly, and I miss him something awful."

Kahlan nodded against his shoulder, and told him a bold lie.

"You'll see us both again, Zedd. I promise you."

Kahlan stepped out into the early light of winter's first breath. Everything was dusted with snow, making it look as if the world were carved from white marble.

In one long fluid motion, with his fingertips adeptly guiding the far end of the file, Richard glided the steel tool down the fold of cloth held forever crisp in white marble. Concentrating on applying steady pressure to cut a precise, fine layer, he was lost in the work.

The file held hundreds of ridges, row upon row of tiny blades of hardened steel, which did the work of cutting away and shaping the noble stone. These were blades he wielded with the same commitment with which he wielded any blade. He blindly reached back and set the file down on the wooden bench, careful to put it on the wood and not to let it clang against other steel, lest he dull it prematurely. He exchanged the file for another, with even finer teeth, and took out the roughness left by the correction accomplished with the one before.

With fingers as dusty-white as those of a baker laboring with flour, Richard examined the surface of the man's arm, testing it for flaws. Until polished, the minor flaws and facets were often easier to see with the fingers than the eye. Where he found them, he used a smaller file in one hand, while his other hand followed behind, riding the swell of muscle, feeling the subtle difference in what the tool had done to the stone. He was removing only paper-thin layers of material, now.

It had taken him several months to arrive at this final layer. It was exhilarating to be so close to the flesh. The days had passed, one upon another, in an endless procession of work, carving death in the day down at the site, and life in the night. Carving for the Order was balanced by carving for himself—slavery and freedom in opposition.

Whenever one of the brothers inquired about the statue, Richard was careful to hide his satisfaction with what he was creating. He did it by recalling the model he had been commanded to carve. He always bowed his head respectfully and reported his progress on his penance, assuring them that his work was on schedule and would be done on time to install in the palace plaza for the dedication.

Stressing the word "penance" helped to direct their thoughts to that issue and away from the statue itself. The brothers were invariably much more satisfied with his weariness from his toil at his work of contrition that they were interested in yet another dreary stone carving. There were carvings everywhere; this was but one more manifestation of the irredeemable inadequacy of mankind. Just as no one man in their cosmos was important, no one work mattered. It was the sheer number of carvings which was to be the Order's overpowering argument for man's impotence. The carvings were merely background props for the stage upon which the brothers moralized on sacrifice and salvation.

Richard always humbly reported his nights with little food and little sleep as he worked on his penance after his carving work during the day. Selfless sacrifice being the proper cure for wickedness, the brothers went away pleased.

Richard switched to a smaller file, one bent in a decreasing radius curve, and worked the muscle where it narrowed into sinew, showing the tension in the arm which revealed the underlying structure. During the day he observed other men as they worked, in order to study the complex shapes of muscle as it moved with life. At night, he referred to his own arms held up to the lamplight so that he might accurately depict veins and tendons standing proud on the surface. He referred to a small mirror at times. The surface of the skin he carved was a rich landscape stretched over bone and muscle, creased in corners, drawn smooth as it swept over curves.

For the woman's body, his memory of Kahlan was vivid enough to require little other reference.

He wanted this work to show the capacity for movement, for intent, for accomplishment. The posture of the figures displayed awareness. The expression of the faces, especially the eyes, would show that most sublime human characteristic: thought.

If the statues he had seen in the Old World were a celebration of misery and death, this was a celebration of life.

He wanted this to show the raw power of volition.

The man and woman he carved were his refuge against his despair over his captivity. They embodied freedom of spirit. They embodied reason rising up to triumph.

To his great annoyance, Richard noticed that light was coming in the window above the statue, taking over from the lamps that had burned all night. All night; he had done it again.

It was not the quality of the light, which he actually very much favored, which vexed him, but that it signified the end of his time with his statue; he now had to go carve ugliness down at the site. Fortunately, that work required no thought or careful effort.

As he draw-filed the curve of the man's shoulder muscle, there was a knock at the door. "Richard?"

It was Victor. Richard sighed; he had to stop.

Richard pulled the red cloth tied around his neck down away from his nose and mouth, where it kept him from breathing all the marble dust. It was a little trick Victor had told him about, used by the marble carvers from his homeland of Cavatura.

"Be right there."

Richard stepped down off the ledge made by the base, where he had carved out the legs at midcalf. He stretched his back, realizing how much it hurt from hunching over, and from lack of sleep. He retrieved the canvas tarp and shook the dust from it.

Just before he flung the cover over the statue, he got the full view of the figures. The floor, shelves, and tools were covered in a fine layer of marble dust. But against the black walls, the marble stood out in the glory of light from above.

Richard threw the tarp over the incomplete figures and then opened the door.

"You look a ghost," Victor announced with a lopsided grin.

Richard brushed himself off. "I forgot the time."

"Did you see in the shop last night?"

"The shop? No, what?"

Victor's grin returned, wider this time. "Priska had the bronze dial delivered yesterday. Ishaq brought it. Come see."

Around the other side of the blacksmith's shop, in the stock room, the bronze sat in a number of pieces. It was too big for Priska to cast as one piece, so he had made several that Victor would join and mount. The pedestal for the partial ring that would be the dial plane was massive. Knowing it was for a statue Richard was carving, Priska had done a job to be proud of.

"It's beautiful," Richard said.

"Isn't it, though? I've seen him do fine work before, but this time Priska has outdone himself."

Victor squatted and ran his fingers over the strange symbols filled in with black. "Priska said that at one time, long ago, his home city of Altur'Rang had freedom, but, like so many others, lost it. As a tribute to that time, he cast it with symbols in his native tongue. Brother Neal saw it, and was pleased because he thought it a tribute to the emperor, who is also from Altur'Rang."

Richard sighed. "Priska has a tongue as smooth as his castings."

"Would you have some lardo with me?" Victor asked as he stood.

The sun was already well up. Richard stretched his neck and peered down at the site.

"I'd best not. I need to get to work." Richard squatted down and lifted one end of the pedestal. "First, though, let me show you where this goes."

Victor grabbed the other end and together they lugged the bronze casting around the shop. When Richard opened the double doors, Victor saw the statue for the first time, even if it was covered in a tarp that revealed only the round bulges that were the two heads. Even so, Victor's eyes feasted. It was apparent in those eyes how his vivid imagination was filling in some of it with his fondest hopes.

"Your statue is going well?" Victor nudged Richard with an elbow. "Beauty?"

Richard was overcome with a blissful smile. "Ah, Victor, you will see for yourself soon enough. The dedication is only a couple weeks off. I will be ready. It will be something to bring a song to our hearts . . . before they kill me, anyway."

Victor dismissed such talk with a flourish of his hand. "I am hoping that when they see such beauty again, and at their palace, they will approve."

Richard held out no such illusion. He remembered then, and reached into a pocket to pull out a piece of paper. He handed it to the blacksmith.

"I didn't want Priska to cast words on the back of the dial because I didn't want the wrong people to see them. I would ask you to engrave these words on the back surface—about the same height as the symbols on the front."

Victor took the paper and unfolded it. His grin melted away. He looked up at Richard with an open look of surprise.

"This is treason."

Richard shrugged. "They can only kill me once."

"They can torture you a long time before they kill you. They have very unpleasant ways to kill people, too, Richard. Have you ever seen a man buried in the sky while he was still alive, bleeding from a thousand cuts, his arms bound, so that the vultures could feast on his living flesh?"

"The Order binds my arms, now, Victor. As I work down there, as I see the death around me, I am bleeding from a thousand cuts. The vultures of the Order are already feasting on my flesh." With grim resolve, Richard held Victor's gaze. "Will you do it?"

Victor glanced down at the paper again. He took a deep breath and then let it slowly out as he studied the paper in his hand. "Treason though these words be, I like them. I will do it."

Richard clapped him on the side of the shoulder and gave him a confident smile. "Good man. Now, look here, where the pedestal is to be attached."

Richard lifted the tarp enough to uncover the base. "I've carved you a flat face tilted at the proper angle. I didn't know where the holes in the casting would be, so I left it for you to drill the holes and fill them with lead for the pins. Once you attach the pedestal, then I can calculate the angle of the hole I'll need to drill for the gnomon."

Victor nodded. "The gnomon pole will be ready soon. I will make you a drill bit the proper size for it."

"Good. And a round rasp to do final fitting in the hole?"

"You will have it," Victor said as they both stood. He waved his hand toward the covered statue. "You trust me not to peek while you are off carving your ugly work?"

Richard chuckled. "Victor, I know you want more than anything to see the nobility of this statue when it is finally finished. You would not spoil that experience for yourself for anything."

Victor let out his rolling belly laugh. "I guess you are right. Come after your work, and we will have lardo and talk of beauty in stone and the way the world once was."

Richard hardly heard Victor. He was staring at what he knew so well. Even though it was covered from his eyes, it was not hidden from his soul.

He was ready to begin the process of polishing. To make flesh in stone.

Her head bent, her scarf protecting her from the chill winter wind, Nicci hurried down the narrow alleyway. A man coming the other way bumped against her shoulder, not because he was rushing, but because he simply didn't seem to care where he was going. Nicci threw a fiery scowl at his empty eyes. Her fierce look fell away down a bottomless well of indifference.

She clutched her sack of sunflower seeds closer to her stomach as she moved on through the muddy alleyway. She stayed close to the rough wooden walls of the buildings so she wouldn't be jostled by the people going the other way. People bundled against the current cold snap moved through the alleyway toward the street beyond, looking for rooms, for food, for clothes, for jobs. She could see men beyond the alley sitting on the ground, leaning against buildings on the far side of the street, watching without seeing as wagons rumbled down the roads, taking supplies out to the site of the emperor's palace.

Nicci wanted to get to the bread shop. She had been told they might have butter today. She wanted to get butter for Richard's bread. He would be home for dinner— he had promised. She wanted to make him a good meal. He needed to eat. He had lost some weight, though it only added distracting definition to his muscular build. He was like a statue in the flesh—like the statues she used to see, long ago.

She remembered how when she was little her mother's servants made cakes out of sunflower meal. She had been able to buy enough to make him some sunflower cakes, and maybe she would have butter to put on them.

Nicci was growing increasingly anxious. The dedication was to take place in a few days. Richard said his statue would be ready. He seemed too calm about it, as if he had come to some inner peace.

He seemed almost like a man who had accepted his imminent execution.

Whenever Richard spoke to her, despite the conversation, his mind seemed elsewhere, and his eyes held that quality which she so valued. In the wasteland that was life, the misery that was existence, this was the only hope left to her. All around her, people looked forward only to death. Only in her father's eyes when she was younger, and more so now in Richard's, did she see any evidence that there was something to make it all worthwhile, some reason for existence.

Nicci was slowed to a halt by the clink-clink-clink of pebbles rattling in a cup. The sound was the unmistakable rattle of her chains. She had been a servant to need her whole life, and as much as she tried, there it was, the cup of some poor beggar, still rattling for her help.

She could not deny it.

Tears filled her eyes. She had so wanted to serve Richard butter with his bread. But she had only one silver penny, and this beggar had nothing. She at least had some bread and some sunflower seeds. How could she want butter for Richard's bread and cakes, when this man had nothing?

She was evil, she knew, for wanting to keep her silver penny, the penny Richard had earned with his own sweat and effort. She was evil for wanting to buy butter for Richard with it. Who was Richard, to have butter? He was strong. He was able. Why should he have more, while others had none?

Nicci could almost see her mother slowly shaking her head in bitter disappointment that the penny was still in Nicci's fist, and not helping the man in need.

How was it that she could never seem to live up to her mother's example of morality? How was it she could never overcome her evil nature?

Nicci turned slowly and dropped her silver penny in the beggar's cup.

People gave the beggar a wide berth. Without seeing him, they avoided coming near him. They were deaf to the rattle of his cup. How could people not yet have learned the Order's teachings? How could they not help those in need? It was always left to her.

She looked at him, then, and recoiled at the sight of the hideous man swathed in filthy rags. She pulled back more when she saw lice hopping through his thatch of greasy hair. He peered out at her through a slit in the rags draped around his face.

But it was what she saw through that slit that caught her breath in her throat. The scars were gruesome, to be sure, as if he had been melted by the Keeper's own fires, yet it was the eyes that gripped her as the man slowly rose to his feet.

The man's grimy fingers, like a claw, curled around her arm. "Nicci," he hissed in startled triumph, drawing her close.

Caught in the grip of his powerful fingers, and his burning glare, she was unable to move. She was so close she could see his lice hopping at her.

"Kadar Kardeef."

"So, you recognize me? Even like this?"

She said nothing else, but her eyes must have said that she thought he was dead, for he answered her unspoken question.

"Remember that little girl? The one you seemed to care so much about? She urged the town's people to save me. She refused to allow me to die there on the fire, where you had put me. She hated you so much she was determined to save me. She selflessly devoted herself to caring for me, to helping her fellow man, as you had ordered the town's people to do.

"Oh, I wanted to die. I never knew a person could have that much pain and still live. As much as I wanted to die, I lived, because I want you to die even more. You did this to me. I want the Keeper to sink his fangs into your soul."

Nicci looked deliberately at his grotesque scars. "And so, for this, you have come seeking your revenge."

"No, not for that. For making me beg, where my men could hear it. For allowing other people to hear me beg for my life. It was for that reason they saved me—and their hatred of you. It is for that that I seek revenge—for not allowing me to die, for condemning me to this life of a freak where passing women toss pennies in my cup."

Nicci gave him a smooth smile. "Why, Kadar, if you want to die, I can certainly oblige you."

He released her arm as if it had burned his fingers. His imagination gave her powers she didn't have.

He spat at her.

"Kill me, then, you filthy witch. Strike me dead."

Nicci flicked her wrist and brought her dacra to hand. The dacra was a knifelike weapon carried by Sisters. Once the sharpened rod was stuck into a victim, no matter where, releasing her power into the dacra killed them instantly. Kadar Kardeef didn't know she had no power. But even without her power behind it, the dacra was still a dangerous weapon that could be driven into a heart, or through a skull.

He wisely backed away. He wanted to die, yet he feared it.

"Why didn't you go to Jagang. He would not have let you become a beggar. Jagang was your friend. He would have taken care of you. You would not have to beg."

Kadar Kardeef laughed. "You'd have liked that, wouldn't you? To see me living off the scraps of Jagang's table? You would love to sit at his side, the Slave Queen, and have him see me fallen to this, to watch as you two tossed me your crumbs."

"Fallen to what? To see you wounded? You've both been wounded before."

He snatched her wrist again. "I died a hero to Jagang. I would not want him to know I begged like any of the weak fools we have crushed beneath our boots."

Nicci pressed her dacra against his belly, backing him off.

"Kill me, then, Nicci." He opened his arms. "Finish it, like you should have. You never left a job incomplete before. Strike me dead, like I should have been long ago."

Nicci smiled again. "Death is no punishment. Every day you live is a thousand deaths. But you know that, don't you, Kadar?"

"Was I that repulsive to you, Nicci? Was I that cruel to you?"

How could she tell him that he was, and how much she hated him having her as chattel for his amusement? It was for the good of all that the Order used men like Kadar Kardeef. How could she put herself, her own interests, above the good of mankind?

Nicci turned and rushed off down the alleyway.

"Thank you for the penny!" he called mockingly after her. "You should have granted my request! You should have, Nicci!"

Nicci wanted only to go home and scrub the lice out of her hair. She could feel them burrowing into her scalp.

Richard pulled away the fistful of straw. He brushed the fragments of grasses from his leather apron. His arms ached from the labor of rubbing the straw, lightly loaded with fine abrasive clays, against the stone.

Yet, when he saw the luster of the stone, the character of the high polish, the way the marble glowed, taking light deep into the stone and returning it, he felt only exhilaration.

The figures emerged from a sparkling stone base of rough marble. The grooved lines of the toothed chisels used in opposing directions to shear off thin layers of stone were still evident on the lower calves, where the legs emerged—he wanted the statue to bear testimony to the hand of man and the figures' origin in stone.

They rose up to nearly twice his height. The statue was in part a representation of his love for Kahlan—he could not keep Kahlan out of the work, because Kahlan was his ideal of a woman—yet the woman in the statue was not Kahlan. It was a man of virtue with a woman of virtue joined in purpose. They complemented each other, the two universal parts of what it was to be human.

The curved section of the sundial had been placed by Victor and his men several days before, when Richard had been working down at his job at the site of the emperor's palace. They had left the tarp over the statue as they worked. After the ring had been set, Richard had placed the pole that served as the gnomon, and finished the hand holding it. The base of the pole was fixed with a gold ball.

Victor had yet to see the statue. He was beside himself with eager anticipation.

As Richard stared at the figures, only the light from the window above entered the darkened room. He had been given the day from work down at the site in order to prepare the statue to be moved to the plaza that evening. In the rooms beyond the shop door, the hammers of the blacksmiths rang ceaselessly as Victor's men worked on orders for the palace.

Richard stood in the near darkness, listening to the sounds of the blacksmith shop, as he stared up at the power of what he had created. It was exactly as he had intended.

The figures of the man and woman seemed as if they might draw a breath at any moment and step out of the stone base. They had bone and muscle, sinew and flesh.

Flesh in stone.

There was only one thing missing—one thing left to do.

Richard picked up his mallet and a sharp chisel.

When he looked up at the finished statues, there were moments when he could almost believe, as Kahlan insisted, that he used magic to carve, yet he knew better. This was a conscious act of human intellect, and nothing more.

Standing there, chisel and mallet in hand, gazing at the statue that was his vision in stone, was a moment when Richard could savor the supreme achievement of having his creation exist exactly as he had originally conceived it.

For this singular moment in time, it was complete, and it was his alone.

It was, for this moment, pure in its existence, untainted by what others thought. For this moment it was his accomplishment, and he knew its value in his own heart and mind.

Richard went to one knee before the figures. He laid the cold steel of the chisel to his forehead and closed his eyes as he concentrated on what he had left to do.

"Blade, be true this day."

He pulled the red cloth tied at his throat up over his nose so not to have to breathe the stone dust, then set the chisel to the marks in the flat place he had already prepared just above the heart of the flaw. Richard brought the mallet down, and began to carve the title of the statue in the base for all to see.

Nicci, standing behind the corner of a building around a curve in the road, watched farther down the hill as Richard left the shop where he had carved his statue. He was probably going to see about getting the team to move the stone. He closed the door, but he didn't put the chain on it. No doubt, he didn't intend to be gone for long.

Men were working all over the hillside at a variety of shops. Tradesmen from leather workers to goldsmiths contributed to a constant din of saws, grinding, and hammering. The ceaseless uproar of the labor was nerve-racking. While many of the men coming and going gave Nicci a good look-see, her glare warned them off.

Once she saw Richard disappear beyond the blacksmith's shop, she started down the road. She had told him she would wait until he was done before she came to see it. She had kept her word.

Still, she felt uneasy. She didn't know why, but she felt almost as if she would be invading a sacred site. Richard hadn't invited her to see his statue. He had asked her to wait until it was done. Since it was done, she would wait no longer.

Nicci didn't want to see it up on the plaza of the palace along with everyone else. She wanted to be alone with it. She didn't care about the Order and their interest in the statue. She didn't want to be standing with everyone else, with people who would not recognize it as something of significance. This was personal to her, and she wanted to see it in private.

She reached the door without anyone accosting her, or even paying her any mind. She looked around in the bright, hazy midafternoon light, but saw only men attending to their work. She opened the door and slipped inside.

The room was dark, its walls black, but the statue inside was well lit by light coming down from a window in the high roof. Nicci didn't look directly at the statue, but kept her eyes to the floor as she hurried around the huge stone so she could see it for the first time from the front.

Once in place, her pulse pounding, she turned.

Nicci's gaze rose up the legs, the robes, the arms, the bodies of the two people, up to their faces. She felt as if a giant fist squeezed her heart to a stop.

This was what was in Richard's eyes, brought into existence in glowing white marble. To see it fully realized was like being struck by lightning.

In that instant, her entire life, everything that had ever happened to her, everything she had ever seen, heard, or done, seemed to come together in one flash of emotional violence. Nicci cried out in pain at the beauty of it, and more so at the beauty of what it represented.

Her eyes fell on the name carved in the stone base.

LIFE

Nicci collapsed to the floor in tears, in abject shame, in horror, in revulsion, in sudden blinding comprehension.

. . . In pure joy.

After Richard had returned with the fine white linen he had bought to cover the statue until the ceremony the following day, he helped Ishaq and a number of the men he knew from down at the site begin the slow process of sledging the heavy stone down to the plaza. Fortunately, it hadn't rained in a while, and the ground was firm.

Ishaq, knowing such business well, had brought along greased wooden runners, which were placed before the hefty wooden rails supporting the wooden platform under the statue so that the teams of horses could more easily pull the heavy load across the ground. After the statue was dragged onto the second set of greased runners, the men brought the ones left behind to the front, leapfrogging the statue as it was moved along.

The hillside was white with the scree of waste stone, so the statue weighed considerably less than it once had. Victor had originally hired special stone-hauling wagons to move the block. They couldn't use them now because the finished piece couldn't be turned on its side or handled in such a rough manner.

Ishaq waved his red hat in his fist, yelling orders, warnings, and prayers as they had moved along. Richard knew that his statue could be in no better hands. The men who helped seemed to pick up Ishaq's nervous tension. They sensed this was something important, and, though the work was difficult, they seemed more pleased to be a part of it than they were about their everyday labor at the site. It took until late afternoon to move the statue the distance from the shop to the foot of the steps leading up to the plaza.

Men shoveled dirt at the bottom of the stairs and packed it tight in order to ease the transition in grade. A team of ten horses was taken around the other side of the columns. Long lengths of rope were passed through the vacant doorways and windows, and then secured around the stone base in order to draw the sledge up the steps. The extra runners were laid on the leading edge of the dirt ramp, later to be moved up onto the steps as the statue progressed upward. Near to two hundred men swooped in at Ishaq's frantic screaming to help pull on the ropes along with the horses. Inch by inch, the statue ascended the steps.

Richard could hardly stand to watch. If anything went wrong, all his work would tumble back and shatter. The flaw would destroy it all. He smiled to himself, realizing how silly it was to worry that the evidence of his crime against the Order might be ruined.

When the stone had finally arrived safely up on the plaza, sand was packed underneath the platform to support its weight. With the sand holding the wooden platform secure, the heavy runners were removed. With the runners off, the platform was slid off its hill of sand. From there, it was a relatively simple task to coax the statue off the wooden base and onto the plaza itself. At last, marble sat on marble. Gangs of men with ropes around the stone base tugged the freed statue into its final resting place at the center point of the plaza.

Ishaq stood beside Richard when it was over, mopping his brow with his red hat. The entire statue and sundial was shrouded in its white linen cover, with line securing it, so Ishaq couldn't see what it was. Still, he sensed something of importance stood before him.

"When?" was all Ishaq asked.

Richard knew what he meant. "I guess I'm not sure. Brother Narev is to dedicate the palace to the Creator tomorrow, before all the officials who have traveled to see how the money they've looted from the people is being spent. I guess that tomorrow the officials, along with everyone who comes to the ceremony, are to see the statue along with the rest of the palace. It's just another display of the Order's view of man's place—I don't think they intend any unveiling or anything like that."

From what Richard had learned, the ceremony was a matter of great concern to the brothers. The drain of the expense of the palace on top of the expense of the war required justification to the people who were paying that price not only with their sweat, but with their blood. The Fellowship of Order ruled, through the Imperial Order, with the necessary collaboration of brutes to whom they gave moral sanction. While the brutes had easily crushed the bodies of those who had revolted, the brothers wanted to crush the ideas such revolt represented, before they could spread, because it was such ideas that were the greatest threat to them.

To that end, it was also important to inspire the officials: the minions of the Order's tyranny. Richard imagined that with scenes of man's depravity carved into thousands of feet of stone wall, the flock of far-flung officials of the Order were going to be given guided tours, by the brothers, of all mankind's failings, and thus coerced into their duty of turning over money they had already confiscated at the point of a blade—a blade they wielded under the moral sanction of the brothers through the Fellowship of Order. Such petty officials were allowed a slice for their service to the Order, but the brothers no doubt wanted to forcefully dissuade them from any grander notions.

Under the direction of the brothers, the collective of the Order, like any autocratic ruler, ultimately ruled only by the acquiesce of the people, who were controlled either by moral intimidation, or by physical threat, or by both. Tyranny required constant tending, lest the illusion of righteous authority evaporate in the light of its grim toll, and the brutes be overpowered by the people who greatly outnumbered them.

That was why Richard had known he couldn't lead: he could not bludgeon people into understanding that bludgeoning was wrong because their lives were of great value, whereas the Order could have them bludgeoned into obedience by first making people believe that their lives were of no value. Free people were not ruled. Freedom had first to be valued before its existence could be demanded.

"From what I'm told, it is to be a big event," Ishaq said. "People from all over are coming to the dedication of the emperor's palace. The city is full of people from far and near."

Richard looked around at the site as the workers trudged back to their regular jobs.

"I'm surprised none of the officials have come to have a look at the palace in advance."

Ishaq waved his hat dismissively. "They are all at the gathering of the Fellowship of Order. In the center of Altur'Rang. Big doings. Food, drink, speeches by the brothers. You know how the Order likes meetings. Very boring, I imagine. From what I know of such events, the officials will be kept busy hearing of the needs of the Order and their duty to get people to sacrifice to that need. The brothers will keep them all under tight rein."

That meant the brothers would all be busy—too busy to come out to the site for the trivial task of checking a statue one of their slaves had carved. In the scheme of things, Richard's statue was insignificant. It was only the starting point of the stately tour of the miles of walls displaying extensive scenes depicting the grand cause of the Order, as dictated by the brothers, under Narev's leadership.

If the officials and the brothers were too busy to come today, the people of the city were not. Most would probably attend the events of the next day, but they wanted to get a sense of the place for themselves, first, without the boring speeches that would drag out the ceremony. Richard watched many of those people go from one scene on the walls to another, their faces stricken with the desolate emotion of what they were seeing.

Guards kept people at a respectful distance, and out of the labyrinth of rooms and hallways inside, now enclosed by upper floors, and in some places, roofs. Now that the statue was set in place, those guards moved in to clear the plaza entrance.

Richard had only gotten a few hours of sleep in the last week. Now that the statue was in place, exhaustion overwhelmed him. With all the work on top of so little sleep, and little to eat, he was almost ready to drop where he stood.

Victor appeared out of the long shadows. Some workers were leaving, but others would still be at it for several more hours. Richard hadn't even realized that it had taken the better part of the day to move the statue. With the heat of the work over, his sweat-soaked shirt felt like ice against his flesh.

"Here," Victor said, handing Richard a slice of lardo. "Eat. In celebration that you are done."

Richard thanked his friend before devouring the lardo. His head was pounding. He had done all he could do to show people what they needed to see. With the work done, though, Richard felt suddenly lost. He realized only then how much he hated having finished, to be without the noble work. It had been his reason to go on.

"Ishaq, I'm dead on my feet. Do you think you could give me a ride in your wagon partway to my house?"

Ishaq clapped Richard on the back. "Come, you can ride in the back. I'm sure Jori would not mind. At least he can save you part of your walk. I must stay here and see to the teams and wagons."

Richard thanked the smiling Victor. "In the morning, my friends, in the full light, we will remove the cover and see beauty one last time. After that . . . well, who knows."

"Tomorrow, then," Victor said with his sly laugh. "I don't think I will sleep tonight," he called after Richard.

The months of effort seemed to all come down upon him at once. He climbed into the back of Ishaq's wagon and bid the man a good night. As Ishaq left, Richard curled up under a tarp to shut out the light and was asleep before Jori returned. He was dead to the world as the wagon rolled away.

Nicci watched as Richard departed with Ishaq. She wanted to do this on her own. She wanted it to be her part. She wanted to contribute something of value.

Only then could she face him.

She knew precisely how the Order would react to the statue. They would view it as a threat. They would not allow other people to see it. The Order would destroy it. It would be gone. No one would ever know about it.

Twining her fingers together, she wondered how to proceed—what should be first. Then it came to her. She had gone to him before. He had helped Richard. He was Richard's friend. Nicci rushed across the sprawling site of the palace and up the hill.

She was winded by the time she reached the blacksmith's shop. The grim black-smith was putting away tools. He had already banked the fire in his forge. The smells, the sights, even the layer of iron dust and soot gave Nicci a joyful flash of her father's shop. She understood, now, the look that had been in her father's eyes. She doubted he had fully understood it himself, but she did, now. The blacksmith looked up without smiling as she rushed into his shop.

"Mr. Cascella! I need you."

His frown grew. "What's that matter? Why are you crying? Is it Richard? Have they—"

"No. Nothing like that." She grabbed his meaty hand and tugged at him. It was like tugging on a boulder. "Please. Come with me. It's important."

He gestured with his other hand around at his shop. "But I have to clean up for the night."

She yanked again on his hand. She felt tears stinging her eyes. "Please! This is important!"

He wiped his free hand down his face. "Lead the way, then."

Nicci felt a little foolish pulling the burly blacksmith along by the hand as she raced down the hill. He asked where they were going, but she didn't answer. She wanted to get down there before the light was gone.

When they reached the plaza, guards were patrolling up at the top of the steps, keeping everyone off the plaza. Nicci saw Ishaq nearby, loading long planks in a wagon. She called to him, and, seeing the blacksmith with her, he ran over.

"Nicci! What is it? You look a frightful—"

"I have to show you both the statue. Now."

Victor's scowl grew. "It will be unveiled tomorrow when Richard—"

"No! You must see it now."

They both fell silent. Ishaq leaned close as he gestured covertly.

"We can't go up there. It's guarded."

"I can." Nicci angrily wiped the tears from her cheeks. Her voice regained the quality of grave authority she had wielded so often, that dark intonation that had passed judgment on countless lives, and sent people to their death. "Wait here."

Both men pulled back at the menace in her eyes.

Nicci straightened her back. She lifted her chin. She was a Sister of the Dark.

She ascended the steps in a measured pace, as if the palace were hers. It was. She was the Slave Queen. These men were hers to command.

She was Death's Mistress.

The guards approached her warily, sensing that the woman in black was a threat. Before they could speak, she spoke first.

"What are you doing here?" she hissed.

"What are we doing here?" one asked. "We're guarding the emperor's palace, that's what we're doing—"

"How dare you talk back to me. Do you know who I am?"

"Well . . . I don't think I—"

"Death's Mistress. Perhaps you have heard of me?"

All dozen men straightened. She saw their eyes take in the black dress again, then her long blond hair, her blue eyes. By their reaction to what they saw, it was obvious to Nicci that her reputation preceded her. Before they could say another word, she spoke again.

"And what do you suppose Emperor Jagang's consort is doing here? Do you suppose I came without my master? Of course not, you idiots!"

"The emperor . . ." several mumbled together in shock.

"That's right, the emperor is arriving for the dedication tomorrow. I have come to make my own examination, first, and what do I find? Idiots! Here you stand, with your thumbs in your ears, while you should be standing to greet His Excellency as he arrives into the city mere hours from now."

The guards' eyes widened. "But . . . no one told us. Where is he coming in? We haven't been informed—"

"And do you suppose a man as important as Jagang wishes his whereabouts to be known for any assassin in the neighborhood to find him? And if there are assassins about, here you fools stand!"

All the men bowed urgently.

"Where?" the sergeant asked. "Where is His Excellency arriving?"

"He's arriving from the north."

The man licked his lips. "But, but, which road from the north? There are any number of routes—"

Nicci planted her fists on her hips. "Do you suppose His Excellency is going to announce his route beforehand? And to the likes of you? If only one road was guarded, then any assassin would know where to expect the emperor, now wouldn't they? All the roads are to be guarded! And here you stand, instead!"

The men bobbed and bowed nervously, wanting to leave to do their duty, but not knowing where to go.

Nicci gritted her teeth and leaned toward the sergeant. "Get your men out to one of the north roads. Now. That is you duty. All the roads are to be guarded. Pick one!"

The men bowed repeatedly as they sidestepped away. After scurrying only a few feet, they broke into a dead run. She watched them collect other guards as they went.

As they vanished out of the plaza, Nicci turned to the two startled men. They climbed the stairs, now unhindered by guards. Some of the people treading the cobblestone paths, come to look at the carvings on the walls, had heard yelling and turned to watch what she was doing. Women on their knees, praying up at the carvings in stone of the Light shining down on depraved people, looked over their shoulders.

As Victor and Ishaq reached the top of the plaza, Nicci untied the line, grabbed the linen in her fists, and ripped the shroud off the statue.

Both men stopped in their tracks.

In a half circle around the plaza, the walls were covered with the story of man's inadequacy. All around them, man was shown small, depraved, deformed, impotent, terrified, cruel, mindless, wicked, greedy, corrupt, and sinful. He was depicted forever torn between otherworldly forces controlling every aspect of his miserable existence, an existence incomprehensible in its caldron of churning evil, with death his only escape into salvation.

Those who had found virtue in this world, under the protection of the Creator's Light, looked lifeless, their faces without emotion, without awareness, their bodies as unbending as cadavers. They stared out at the world through a vacant, mindless stupor, while all around them danced rats, through their legs wriggled snakes, and over their heads flew vultures.

In the vortex of this torrent of tortured life, this cataclysm of corruption, this depravity and debauchery, rose up Richard's statue in bold, glowing opposition.

It was a devastating indictment of all around it.

The mass and weight of the ugliness surrounding Richard's statue seemed to shrink back into insignificance. The evil of the wall carvings seemed now to be crying out at their own dishonesty in the face of incorruptible beauty and truth.

The two figures in the center posed in a state of harmonious balance. The man's body displayed a proud masculinity. Though the woman was clothed, there was no doubt as to her femininity. They both reflected a love of the human form as sensuous, noble, and pure. The evil all around seemed as if it was recoiling in terror of that noble purity.

More than that, though, Richard's statue existed without conflict; the figures showed awareness, rationality, and purpose. This was a manifestation of human power, ability, intent. This was life lived for its own sake. This was mankind standing proudly of his own free will.

This was exactly what the single word at the bottom named it:

LIFE

That it existed was proof of the validity of the concept.

This was life as it should be lived—proud, reasoned, and a slave to no other man. This was the rightful exaltation of the individual, the nobility of the human spirit.

Everything on the walls all around offered death as its answer.

This offered life.

Victor and Ishaq were on their knees, weeping.

The blacksmith lifted his arms up toward the statue before him, laughing as tears ran down his face.

"He did it. He has done as he said he would. Flesh in stone. Nobility. Beauty."

People who had come to see the other carvings, now began gathering to see what stood in the center of the plaza. They stared with wide eyes, many seeing for the first time the concept of man as virtuous in his own right. The statement was so powerful that it alone invalidated everything up on the walls. That it had been carved by man underscored its veracity.

Many of them saw it with the same understanding Nicci had.

The carvers wandered away from their work to come see what stood in the plaza. The masons came down from the scaffolding. The tenders set down their mortar buckets. The carpenters climbed down from their work at setting beams. The tilers laid aside their chisels. The drivers picketed their horses. Men digging and planting the surrounding grounds set down their shovels. They came from all directions toward the statue in the plaza.

People flowed up the steps in ever expanding ranks. They flooded around the statue, gazing in awe. Many fell to their knees weeping, not in misery as they had before, but with joy. Many, like the blacksmith, laughed, as tears of delight ran down their happy faces. A few covered their eyes in fear.

As people took it in, they began to run off to get others. Soon, men were coming down from the shops on the hill to see what stood in the plaza. Men and women who had come to watch the construction now ran off home to get loved ones, to bring them to see what stood at the emperor's palace.

It was something the like of which most of these people had never in their lives seen.

It was vision to the blind.

It was water to the thirsty.

It was life to the dying.

Kahlan pulled her map out and took a quick look. It was hard to tell for sure. She glanced up and down the road and noted that the other buildings were not quite as well kept.

"What do you think?" Cara asked in a low voice.

Kahlan slipped the map back inside her mantle. She snugged the fur up over her shoulders a little, making sure it covered the hilt of Richard's sword she wore strapped behind her shoulder. Her own sword was hidden under her cloak. At least the sun had just gone down.

"I don't know. We don't have much light left. I guess there's only one way to be sure."

Cara eyed the people who looked their way. For the most part, everyone in the city seemed remarkably incurious. With their horses stabled outside of the city, there would not be any swift escape if they needed to get away. The general indifference of people, though, somewhat eased Kahlan's concern.

They had decided to simply be as aloof and casual as possible. She had thought they looked pretty simple in their traveling clothes, but in a place as drab as Altur'Rang, the two of them had a hard time being inconspicuous. In retrospect, she wished they would have had the time to find something shabby to wear. Kahlan felt they were about as inconspicuous as a pair of painted whores at a country farm fair.

She climbed the stairs to the place as if she knew where she was going and belonged there. Inside, the hallway was clean. It had the smell of freshly scrubbed wood floors. With Cara close at her heels, Kahlan moved down to the first door on the right. She could see the stairway farther down the hall. If this was the correct building, this would be the proper door.

Looking both ways, Kahlan gently rapped on the door. No answer came. She knocked again, a little louder. She tried the knob, but it was locked. After checking the hall again, she pulled a knife from her belt and worked it under the molding, springing it out until the door popped open. She grabbed Cara's sleeve and pulled the woman in with her.

Inside, they both struck a pose prepared to fight. There was no one in the room. In the light coming in from two windows, Kahlan saw first that there were two sleeping pallets. What she saw next was Richard's pack.

Kneeling on the floor in the far corner, she flipped back the flap and saw his things inside—his war wizard's clothes were in the bottom. Near tears, she clutched the pack to her chest.

It had been over a year since she had seen him. For almost half the time she had known him, he had been gone from her. It seemed she could not endure another moment.

Kahlan heard a sudden noise. Cara seized the wrist of a young man as he charged in brandishing a knife. In one fluid motion she had his arm twisted behind his back.

Kahlan thrust her hand into the air. "Cara! No."

Cara made a sour face as she lowered her Agiel from the young man's throat. His eyes were wide with both fear, and indignation.

"Thieves! You're thieves! That's not yours! Put it back!"

Kahlan rushed to the youth, motioning for him to keep his voice down.

"Is your name Kamil, or Nabbi?"

The young man blinked in surprise. He licked his lips as he glanced over his shoulder at the woman towering above him.

"I'm Kamil. Who are you? How do you know my name?"

"I'm a friend. Gadi told me—"

"Then you're no friend!"

Before he could scream for help, Cara clamped a hand over his mouth.

Kahlan shushed him. "Gadi murdered a friend of ours. After we captured him, Gadi told me your name."

When she saw that he was taken aback by the news, Kahlan signaled for Cara to lower her hand.

"Gadi killed someone?"

"That's right," Cara said.

He stole a quick glance over his shoulder. "What did you do to him? To Gadi?"

"We put him to death," Kahlan said, not revealing the full extent of the deed.

The young man smiled. "Then you really are friends. Gadi is a bad person. He hurt my friend. I hope he suffered."

"It took him a long time to die," Cara said.

The young man swallowed when he saw her grin from over his shoulder. Kahlan gestured and Cara released him.

"So, who are you two?" he asked.

"My name is Kahlan, and this is Cara."

"So, what are you doing here?"

"That's a little complicated, but we're looking for Richard."

His suspicion returned. "Yeah?"

Kahlan smiled. He was indeed Richard's friend. She put her hand to the side of his shoulder as she held his gaze.

"I'm his wife. His real wife."

Kamil blinked dumbly. "But, but—"

Kahlan's voice hardened. "Nicci isn't his wife."

His eyes brimmed with tears as a grin overcame him. "I knew it. I knew he didn't love her. I could never understand how Richard could have married her."

Kamil suddenly threw his arms around Kahlan, hugging her with fierce happiness for Richard. Kahlan laughed softly as she smoothed the young man's hair. Cara seized his collar and pulled him back, but at least did it gently.

"And you?" Kamil asked Cara.

"I am Mord—"

"Cara is Richard's good friend."

Kamil unexpectedly hugged Cara, then. Kahlan feared the Mord-Sith might crush his skull, but she endured it politely, even if she was ill at ease. Kahlan thought Cara might even have started to smile.

Kamil turned back to Kahlan. "But what is Richard doing with Nicci, then?"

502

Kahlan took a deep breath. "It's a long story."

"Tell me."

Kahlan appraised his dark eyes for a moment. She liked what she saw there. Still, she thought it best to keep it simple.

"Nicci is a sorceress. She used magic to force Richard to go with her."

"Magic? What magic?" he pressed without pause.

Kahlan took another breath. "She could have used her magic to hurt me, kill me, if Richard didn't agree to go with her."

Kamil gazed skyward as he thought it over. He finally nodded. "That makes sense. That's the kind of man Richard is—he would do anything to save the woman he loved. I knew he didn't love Nicci."

"And how did you know that?"

Kamil gestured at the two pallets. "He didn't sleep with her. I bet he slept with you, when you were together."

Kahlan could feel her face flushing at his boldness. "How do you know that?"

"I don't know." He scratched his head. "You just look like you belong with him. When you say his name I can see how you care for him."

Kahlan couldn't help but smile through her weariness. They had been riding at a breakneck pace for weeks. They had lost a few horses along the way, and had to acquire others. They had gone with little sleep for the last week. She had trouble even thinking straight.

"So, do you know where Richard is, now?" Kahlan asked.

"At work, I'm sure. He usually comes home about now—unless he has to work at night, too."

Kahlan briefly scanned the room. "What about Nicci?"

"I don't know. She may have gone to buy bread or something. It's a little funny—she's usually home long before now. She almost always has dinner ready for Richard."

Kahlan's gaze drifted through the darkening room, from table, to basin, to cupboard. She would hate to leave, only to have him show up a minute after she left. Kamil thought it was odd that Nicci wasn't home. That they were both gone was troubling.

"Where does he work?" Kahlan asked.

"At the site."

"Site? What site?"

Kamil gestured into the distance. "Out at the emperor's new palace they're building. Tomorrow's the big dedication."

"The new palace is done?"

"Oh, no. It's years and years from being done. It's only started, really. But they are going to dedicate it to the Creator, now. A lot of people have come to Altur'Rang for the ceremony."

"Richard is a laborer helping build the palace?"

Kamil nodded. "He's a carver. At least, he is now. He used to work at Ishaq's transport company, but then he got arrested—"

Kahlan seized him by the shirt. "He was arrested? They . . . tortured him?"

Kamil's eyes turned away from her frantic expression.

"I gave Nicci my money so she could get in to see him. She and Ishaq and Victor the blacksmith got him out. He was hurt bad. When he got better, the officials made him take a job carving."

Kamil's words spun through her head. The ones that floated above all the rest were that Richard had recovered.

"He carves statues, now?"

Kamil nodded again. "He carves people in stone to decorate the walls of the palace. He helps me with my own carvings. I can show you, out back."

Wonder of wonders. Richard carving. But all the carvings they had seen in the Old World were grotesque. Richard would not like to carve such ugliness. Obviously, he had no choice.

"Maybe later." Kahlan rubbed her fingers across her brow as she considered what to do. "Can you take me there, now? To the site where Richard works?"

"Yes, if you'd like. But don't you want to wait to see if he comes home, first? He may be home soon."

"You said he works at night, sometimes."

"For the last few months, he worked at night a lot. He's carving some special statue for them." Kamil's face brightened. "He told me to go tomorrow to see it. With the dedication tomorrow, it may be he's still finishing it. I've never seen where he works, but Victor, the blacksmith, may know."

"We should go see this blacksmith, then."

Kamil scratched his head again as his expression turned to disappointment. "But the blacksmith will be gone for the night."

"Is there anyone else out there, now?"

"There may be a lot of people there. Crowds go out there to see the place—I've gone out there myself—and tonight there may be more than usual, because of tomorrow's ceremony."

That might be just what they needed. They wouldn't look so out of place searching the area for Richard if there were crowds out there. It would give them an excuse to look around.

"We'll give him an hour," Kahlan said. "If he doesn't return by then, then it's most likely because he's working. If he doesn't come back, we'll have to go out there and look for him."

"What if Nicci shows up?" Cara asked.

Kamil waved his hand to dismiss their concern. "I'll go out on the front steps and watch for Nicci. You two can wait in here, where no one will see you. I'll come warn you if I see Nicci coming up the street. I can always take you out the back way if I see her returning home."

Kahlan laid a hand over his shoulder and gave it a squeeze.

"That sounds good to me, Kamil. We'll wait in here."

Kamil hurried out to his guard post. Kahlan glanced around the tidy room.

"Why don't you get some sleep," Cara said. "I'll stand guard. You stood guard last."

Kahlan was exhausted. She glanced down at the sleeping pallet closest to Richard's things, then nodded. She lay down on his bed. The room was getting dark. Just being where he slept was a comfort. Being so close, but so far, she couldn't fall asleep.

Nicci's heart sank when she saw that Richard wasn't in their room. Kamil was nowhere to be found. She had felt so good out at the site, watching all the people come to see Richard's statue. Throngs of people had come to see it and had been uplifted.

Some had been angered by it. She, of all people, understood that. Still, Nicci could hardly believe the hateful reaction of some people to such beauty. Some people hated life. She understood that, too. There were those who refused to see—who didn't want to see.

Other people, though, had a reaction much like hers.

It had all come clear for her. For the first time in her life, life made sense. Richard had tried to tell her, but she hadn't listened. She had heard the truth before, too, but others—her mother, Brother Narev, the Order—had shouted it down, and shamed her out of listening.

Her mother had trained her well, and from the first day she had seen Brother Narev, Nicci had been a soldier in the Order's army.

When she saw the statue, she saw at last the truth she had always refused to see, suddenly and clearly standing before her. This was the valid vision of life for which she had hungered, yet which she had evaded, her entire life.

She understood, now, why life had seemed so empty, so pointless: she herself had rendered it so in refusing to think. Nicci had been a slave to everyone of need. She had given her masters their only real weapon against her; she had surrendered to their twisted lies by putting the crippling chains of guilt around her own neck for them, giving herself freely into slavery to the whims and wishes of others instead of living her life as she should have—for herself. She had never asked why it was right for her to be a slave to another's desires, but not evil for them to enslave her. She was not contributing to the betterment of mankind, but was merely a servant to countless puling little tyrants. Evil was not one large entity, but a ceaseless torrent of small wrongs left unchallenged, until they festered into monsters.

She had lived her whole life on shifting quicksand, where reason and the intellect were not to be trusted, where only faith was valid, and blind faith was sacred. She, herself, had enforced mindless conformity to that empty evil.

She had helped bring everyone together, so they might have one collective neck around which the worst among men, in the name of good, could put their leash.

Richard had answered their tower of empty lies in one righteously beautiful statement for all to see, and had punctuated it with the simple words on the back of the bronze sundial.

Her life was hers to live by right. She belonged to no one.

Freedom exists first and foremost in the mind of the rational, thinking individual—that was what Richard's statue had shown her. That he had carved it, proved it. A captive of her and the Order, his ideals had risen above both.

Nicci realized only now that she had always known her father held this same value—she had seen it in his eyes—even though he could never rationalize it. His values were expressed through the integrity of his work; that was why, from a young age, she had wanted to be an armorer like him. It was his vision of life she had always loved and admired, but suppressed, because of Mother and her ilk. It was that same look in Richard's eyes, that same value for life held dear, that had drawn Nicci to him.

Nicci knew now that she had worn black ever since her mother's death in an endless, shapeless longing to bury not just her mother's hold over her, but, more important, her mother's evil ideals.

She was so sorry Richard wasn't home. She wanted to tell him that he had given her the answer she had sought. She could never ask his forgiveness, though. What she had done to him was beyond forgiveness. She saw that now. The only thing she could do now was to reverse the wrong she had done.

As soon as she found him, they would leave. They would go back to the New World. They would find Kahlan. Then, Nicci would set things right. She had to be close to Kahlan, at least within sight, in order to undo the spell. Then Kahlan would be free. Then Richard would be free.

As much as Nicci loved Richard, she understood, now, that he should be with Kahlan, the woman he loved. Her desire for him gave her no right to do as she had done. She had no right to another's life, as they had no right to hers.

Nicci lay down in her bed and wept at the thought of the outrage she had done to them both. She was overcome with shame. She had been so blind for so long.

She could not believe how she had thrown her entire life away fighting for evil just because it claimed to be good. She truly had been a Sister of the Dark.

She at least could work to correct the harm she had caused.

Kahlan could hardly believe the size of the crowd. By the light of the moon brightening the thin layer of hazy clouds, and by torches here and there throughout the valley, it looked like the open area as far as she could see was packed with people. The numbers had to be in the hundreds of thousands.

Thunderstruck, Kamil threw up his arms. "It's the middle of the night. I've never seen so many people out here. What are they all doing here?"

"How would we know?" Cara sniped. She was in a foul mood, unhappy that they hadn't found Richard, yet.

The city had been crowded with people, too. With the city guards prowling the streets, uneasy about all the late-night activity, it had been necessary to restrain their eagerness in favor of caution. It had taken them hours to get out to the site by way of back streets, dark roads, and Kamil's guided tour of alleyways.

The lad pointed. "It's up there."

They followed him up a road lined with workshops, most closed up and dark. A few had men inside, still working at benches by the light of lamps or candles.

Kahlan reached under her cloak and curled her fingers around the hilt of her sword when she saw a man running in their direction. He saw them and skidded to a halt.

"Have you seen it?"

"Seen what?" Kahlan asked.

He pointed excitedly. "Down at the palace. In the plaza." He started running again. He called behind as he went. "I have to go get my wife and sons. They have to see it."

Kahlan and Cara shared a look in the near darkness.

Kamil ran over to a shop and tugged on a door, but it was shut up tight. "Victor isn't here." His voice couldn't conceal his disappointment. "It's too late."

"Do you know what's down in the plaza?" Kahlan asked him.

He thought a moment. "The plaza? I know the place, but . . . wait, that's where Richard told me to go. The plaza. He said to go to the plaza tomorrow."

"Let's go down there now and have a look," Kahlan said.

Kamil waved a hand, pointing. "This is the shortest way, down the hill behind the blacksmith shop."

So jammed was the place with people, that it took them over an hour just to make it down the hill and across the expanse of grounds around the palace. Even though it was the middle of the night, more people kept arriving all the time.

Once they reached the palace, Kahlan discovered that they couldn't get to the plaza. There was a huge mob of people stretching back forever along the front wall, waiting to go up to the plaza. When Kahlan, Cara, and Kamil tried to go around and get up there to see what was going on, it nearly started a riot. People had been waiting a long time to reach the plaza, and they didn't like having others try to push ahead. Kahlan saw several men try to get ahead by going around the waiting crowd. They were set upon by the mob.

Cara pulled her hand out from under her cloak and casually showed Kahlan her Agiel.

Kahlan shook her head. "Long odds with Jagang's army are one thing, but the three of us against a few hundred thousand does not sound good to me."

"Really?" Cara asked. "I thought it roughly even."

Kahlan only smiled. Even Cara knew better than to go against a mob. Kamil frowned in puzzlement at Cara's humor. When they found the back of the line, they melted in.

It wasn't long before the line behind them grew so large that they could no longer see the back end winding out into the grounds. The people all around seemed filled with a strange kind of nervous expectancy.

A round woman in front, bundled up in little more than rags, turned a plump grin on them. She held out what looked like a loaf of bread.

"Would you like some?" she asked.

"Thank you, no," Kahlan said. "But that's very kind of you to offer."

"I've never made such an offer, before." The woman giggled. "Seems the right thing to do, now, doesn't it?"

Kahlan had no idea what the woman was talking about, but said, "Yes, it does."

Throughout the night, the line inched along. Kahlan's back ached painfully. She even saw Cara grimace as she stretched.

"I still think we just ought to draw weapons and get up there," Cara finally complained.

Kahlan leaned in close. "What difference does it make? Where have we to go before morning? When morning comes, we can go up to the blacksmith's place or to the carving areas over there and hopefully find Richard, but we can do nothing tonight."

"Maybe he will be at his room, now."

"You want to run into Nicci again? You know what she's capable of. The next time we may not be so lucky to escape. We haven't come all this way to battle her—I just want to see Richard. Even if Richard goes back there—and we don't know that he will—we do know he's got to return here in the morning."

"I suppose," Cara grouched.

The sky was taking on a faint reddish glow by the time they made it to the foot of the marble steps. They could hear moaning and wailing up ahead. Kahlan couldn't see the cause, but people up on the plaza were weeping freely. Oddly enough, some people could be heard to laugh joyfully. A few others cursed, as if they had been robbed of their life savings at the point of a knife.

As they slowly made their way up the steps, Kahlan and Cara tried to stay low behind the people surrounding them so as not to draw attention to themselves. The plaza above was lit by dozens of torches, their flickering light giving an indication of the vastness of the crowds. The smell of the burning pitch mixed sourly with the stale sweat of the packed multitude.

Through a momentary gap between people in front of her, Kahlan snatched a quick glance ahead. She blinked at what she saw, but it was gone almost as fast as she saw it, screened by the throng. The people ahead wept—some, it sounded, with joy.

Kahlan began to make out the polite voices of men asking the crowd to keep moving, imploring them to give others a chance. The ragtag collection of people steadily advanced up onto the white marble of the plaza, like beggars at a coronation. The torchlight was finally being replaced by radiant daylight as the sun cleared the horizon. Golden rays washed the face of the palace.

The scenes carved in the stone up on the walls were disturbing. If they were any different from the others she had seen in the Old World, it was only in that they were more gruesome, more horrifying, more desolately hopeless, and more plentiful.

Kahlan's mind played over the lines of her statue of *Spirit*. The idea of Richard having to carve such things as she saw up on the walls sickened her.

She felt a sense of gloom overcoming her. This was the Order: pain, suffering, death. This was what was in store for the New World at the hands of these monsters. She couldn't take her eyes from the scenes on the walls, from the fate that awaited the people of her homeland—the fate so many blindly embraced.

Then, all of a sudden, as the people shuffled around and past, Kahlan beheld the white marble figures rising up before her. The sight took her breath in a gasp. The rays of dawn lit them as if the sun itself had risen just to caress the lustrous forms in all their glory.

Cara gripped Kahlan's arm, her fingers digging in painfully as she, too, was taken by the sight. The statue of the man and woman seized Kahlan's imagination with their nobility of spirit.

She felt tears run down her cheeks, and then she was weeping openly, like the people around her, at the majesty, the dignity, the beauty, of what stood before her. It was everything the carvings on the walls all around were not. It offered freely everything they denied.

LIFE, it said at the base.

Kahlan had to gasp through her tears to draw breath. She clutched at Cara's arm, and Cara clutched at hers, the two of them holding on to each other for support as the crowd swept them along in a current of shared emotion. The man in the statue was not Richard, but there was much of Richard in it. The woman was not Kahlan, but there was enough of her form in it that Kahlan felt her face flushing at others seeing it.

"Please look and move along so that others may view it too," the men at the sides kept calling. They weren't wearing uniforms; they were as tattered-looking as everyone else. They appeared to be ordinary citizens who had just stepped in to help.

The woman who had offered the bread fell to her knees in wailing. Arms respectfully lifted her and helped her to move on. The woman, living in the Old World, had probably never seen a thing of such beauty.

As Kahlan shuffled around the statue, unable to take her eyes from it, she reached out to touch it, as did everyone else. As she was carried past, her fingers met the smooth flesh in stone, knowing it was also where Richard's fingers had been. She wept all the harder.

As she moved past, Kahlan saw then that the curve of the sundial had words on the back:

"Your life is yours alone. Rise up and live it."

The words were visible on the lips of many who saw them.

The crowd kept coming up the steps, forcing the people around the statue to move on. Men at the rear guided people between the columns, out through the rear of the partially built palace, and out of the way so that others could come up to view the statue.

"I wish Benjamin could see this," Cara said, her blue eyes brimming with tears.

Kahlan was overcome with a burble of laughter. "I was going to say, 'I wish Richard could see it.' "

Cara laughed with her as they were swept away by the river of people.

Kamil grabbed Kahlan's hand. She saw him take Cara's, too.

"Yeah," he said with authority, "Richard carved it."

"Where to?" Kahlan asked him. "Where do you think we can find him?"

"I guess we should make our way back up to the blacksmith's place. Hopefully, Richard will show up there. If not, maybe Victor will know where he is."

Kamil's words, "Richard carved it," rang joyfully through her mind.

Richard climbed through the high window and dropped to the ground, his boots hitting with a thud. He could hardly believe he had slept the whole night under a tarp in the back of a wagon. He could hardly believe that Jori didn't wake him so he could go home when they were close. The man probably didn't think it was his job, and so he wouldn't do it. Richard sighed. Maybe Jori hadn't known he was in the back.

Richard brushed himself off. He stood outside the transport company building where he used to work when he had first come to Altur'Rang, and where he had been locked in all night. Of course, he had been asleep, so he didn't know Jori had locked him inside.

Richard didn't know where to go—home, or to the Retreat. The sky glowed orange and violet in the bright sunrise. He supposed there was no point in going home; that would only make him late to work. He decided he had better get to work.

Work. What work? This was the day of the celebration, the dedication. When Brother Narev saw the statue, Richard was not going to have to worry about work anymore.

He knew that if he ran, tried to escape, it would only trigger Nicci's anger, and then Kahlan's life would be forfeit. Richard had spent over a year with Nicci—as long a time as he had spent with Kahlan—and Nicci repeatedly had made clear his choices. Kahlan's life was always the price in the balance.

Richard had no real choice. At least he would get to see Victor's face when he saw the statue. Richard smiled at that thought. It was the only pleasant prospect the day held.

The day was most likely to end in the wet dark hole where he had been before. He missed a step at that thought. He didn't want to go back into that place. It was so small. Richard didn't like being trapped—especially in small places. He didn't like either of those concepts; together, they were terrifying.

As fearful as the prospect of such a fate was, he had carved the statue with conscious intent and with forethought, knowing the probability of the eventual price. What he had accomplished was worth that price. Slavery was not life. Nicci had once promised him that if he died, or chose death, that would in itself be her answer, and she would not harm Kahlan. Now, Richard could only put his faith in that promise.

The statue existed. That was what mattered. *Life* existed. People needed to see that. So many people in the Old World needed to see that life existed, and was to be lived.

For so early in the morning, there was an unusual amount of activity on the streets of Altur'Rang. Now and again, squads of heavily armed city guards rushed down the streets. There were a lot of people come to the city for the dedication celebration. He supposed that was why there were so many people out on the streets.

The guards paid him no attention. He knew they soon would.

When he arrived at the Retreat, Richard was shocked by what he saw. The open miles of grounds were covered with people. They crowded in around the palace walls like ants around spilled honey. He couldn't even begin to estimate how many people blanketed the surrounding hills. It was disorienting to see the panoply of color where before he had seen only brown dirt and green winter rye. He had no idea that this many people had wanted to come to the dedication. But then, he had been working day and night for months—how would he hear what people planned?

Richard skirted the worst of the throngs and made his way up the road toward the blacksmith's shop. He wanted to get Victor and go down with him to the site to see the statue before the Order came out to begin the dedication. Victor would no doubt be eagerly waiting.

The road was crowded with people. They seemed excited, happy, and expectant. It was a far cry from the way most people in the Old World usually appeared or behaved. Maybe a celebration, even one such as this, was better than the rest of their dreary days.

A half mile from Victor's place, a wild-looking Brother Neal leaped into the road and thrust an arm in Richard's direction.

"There he is! Grab him!"

Guards combing throughout the surrounding crowds drew weapons at Neal's command. As they swept in around him, Richard's first instinct was to fight. In an instant, he had assessed the enemy and calculated his attack. He had only to grab one sword from a clumsy guard and he would have them all. In his own mind, the grisly deed was already done. He had only to bring it to reality.

The guards came at him in a dead run. People scattered out of the way, some screaming in fright.

There was the matter of Neal, though. Neal was a wizard. But Richard could deal with that threat, too—need powered his ability. Need, and anger. He certainly had enough anger for the task. That part of him that the Sword of Truth used, that rage of dark violence, already thundered through him.

Except that Nicci had told him that if he used his magic, Kahlan would die. Would she know?

Sooner or later, she would.

Richard stood submissively still as the guards roughly seized him by his arms to subdue him. Others snatched his shirt from behind.

What did it really matter? If he resisted, it would only hurt Kahlan. If they executed him, Nicci would let Kahlan live her life.

But he didn't want to go back into that dark hole.

Neal raced up, shaking a finger in Richard's face. "What is the meaning of this, Cypher! What did you think you were going to accomplish!"

"May I ask what are you talking about, Brother Neal?"

Neal's face was crimson. "The statue!"

"What, you don't like it?"

With all his might, Neal slammed his fist into Richard's middle. The guards holding him laughed. Richard had seen it coming and had tightened his muscles, but it still drove the wind from him. He finally managed to draw his breath.

Neal found that he enjoyed administering punishment, and did it again.

"Oh, you're going to pay for your blasphemy, Cypher. You're going to pay the price, this time. You'll confess to it all, before we're done. But first, you'll watch your wicked perversion destroyed." Neal, his face twisted with superior, self-righteous indignation, gestured to the burly guards. "Let's get him down there. And don't be shy about making way through the crowd."

By midmorning, Kahlan's hopes of the blacksmith showing up had all but vanished.

"I'm sorry," Kamil said, looking glum as he watched her pace. "I don't know why Victor isn't here. I thought he would be, I really did."

Kahlan finally halted and gave the worried lad a pat on the shoulder. "I know you did, Kamil. With the celebration today, and with what's going on down there with the statue, this is hardly a normal day around here, I'm sure."

"Look," Cara said. Kahlan saw she was peering down toward the palace. "Guards with spears are moving the crowd off the plaza."

Kahlan squinted off down at the hill. "Your eyes are better than mine. I can't tell." She cast a frustrated glare at the closed blacksmith's shop. "But it's doing us no good waiting up here. Let's see if we can make it down there and get a better look." Kahlan put a restraining hand on Cara's arm. "But let's not start a war with this crowd?"

Cara's mouth twisted in exasperation. Kahlan turned to the young man kicking a toe at the dirt, looking shamed by his failed plan to help them find Richard.

"Kamil, will you do something for me?"

"Sure. What?"

"Will you wait up here, in case Richard comes here, or even the blacksmith? If the blacksmith comes to his shop, he might know something."

Kamil stretched his neck and gazed down at the palace. "Well, all right. If Richard does come here, I wouldn't want him to miss you. What shall I tell him, if I see him?"

Kahlan smiled. *That I love him,* she thought, but said instead, "Tell him I'm here, with Cara, and we've gone down there looking for him. If he does show up, I don't want to miss him. Have him wait here—we'll come back."

Kahlan thought they could make it down to the plaza to have a look, but everyone else seemed to have the same idea. It took forever just to make it down the hill to the grounds. The closer they got, the tighter the people were jammed together. Kahlan's progress ground to a halt. It was a struggle just to keep contact with Cara. Everyone in the crowd seemed intent on squeezing forward toward the plaza. More people crushed in all the time.

Kahlan soon realized that she and Cara were trapped in the press of people.

The conversation on everyone's lips was about only one thing: the statue.

It was late in the day by the time Nicci had worked herself partway toward the plaza. Every inch gained had been a struggle. She was close enough to see the people up around the statue, but she could get no closer. Try as she might, she could not make any more headway. Just like her, everyone else wanted to get closer, too. They were pressed up against her, pinning her arms. It was at times a frightening, helpless

512

feeling. She managed to pull one arm free so she could help herself maintain her balance. It came to her that to fall in such circumstances could be fatal.

If only she had her power.

Her own arrogance had driven her to trading it away. What she had gotten in return, though, was life. But it had cost Richard and Kahlan their freedom. Nicci couldn't simply withdraw her power from the link, in order to have use of her gift again, or Kahlan would die. Nicci didn't want her life at the cost of another's—that was what she had come to understand was true evil.

Nicci had searched for Richard. She hadn't found him. She hadn't been able to find the blacksmith, Mr. Cascella, or Ishaq, either. As soon as she could find Richard, she could tell him that she had been wrong, and then they could leave Altur'Rang. She wanted so much to see his face when she told him she was taking him back to Kahlan and that she was going to reverse the spell. Of all people, they were the last who should have to suffer for what Nicci had learned.

The only place left that she could think to look for him was at the statue. He might be there. Try as she might, though, she couldn't get any closer. Now, she realized that she probably couldn't even extract herself from the crush of hundreds of thousands of people around her. There had to be well over a half million people in the huge throng around the palace.

And then, Nicci saw Brother Narev and his disciples appear up on the plaza, all in their dark brown robes, Brother Narev in his creased cap, the rest with their faces hidden in deeply cowled hoods. Crowding the rear of the plaza were a few hundred officials of the Order who had traveled in to attend the palace dedication—important men, all.

If only she had her power, she could have killed them where they stood.

It was then that she caught a fleeting glimpse of Richard behind the officials, with guards surrounding him. The whole central area around the plaza was thick with the surly guards.

Brother Narev stepped out to the edge of the plaza, all angles under dark robes. Beneath his creased cap, beneath his hooded brow, his dark gaze swept the assembly. The people were in a noisy, emotional state. Brother Narev did not look pleased, but then, Brother Narev never looked pleased. Pleasure, he would say, was wicked. He raised his arms, commanding silence.

When the crowd quieted, he began in that terrible grating voice of his, a voice that had haunted her from that day in her house when she was little, that voice that she had allowed to rule her mind, that voice that, along with her mother's, had done her thinking for her.

"Fellow citizens of the Order. We have a special event planned for you today. Today, we bring you the spectacle of temptation . . . and more."

His arm glided back toward the statue. His long thin fingers opened. His voice rumbled with revulsion. "Evil, itself."

The crowd murmured uneasily. Brother Narev smiled, the thin slash of his mouth pleating back his hollow cheeks as he grinned like death's own skull. His eyes were as dark as his robes. The setting sun was fleeing the scene, taking clarity, leaving behind the tremors of flickering light from the dozens of torches to cast their flickering orange light across the massive columns towering behind the plaza, and the weak light of the moon to wash the faces of the grim officials. The air, so cloying with the heavy scents of the crowd, had turned chill.

"Fellow citizens of the Order," Brother Narev said in a voice that Nicci thought might crack the stone walls, "today you will see what happens to evil, when confronted by the virtue of the Order."

He hooked a skeletal finger, signaling behind the heads of the officials. Guards muscled Richard forward. Nicci cried out, but her voice was lost in the clamor of tens of thousands of other voices.

Brother Neal swaggered forward, then, lugging with him a sledgehammer.

Nicci checked to the sides and saw that there were several thousand armed guards at hand. More screened the plaza off from the people. Brother Narev had taken no chances. Neal, with a polite smile and a deferential bow, handed the sledgehammer to Brother Narev.

Brother Narev lifted the sledgehammer above his head as if it were a sword held high in triumph.

"Evil, wherever it is found, must be destroyed." He aimed the weaving head of the sledgehammer toward the statue. "This is a thing of evil, created by an extremist who hates his fellow man, to victimize the weak. He contributes nothing to the advancement of his fellow man, nothing to the succor of his fellow man, nothing to the education or support of his fellow man. He offers only lewd and profane images to prey on the susceptible and feebleminded among us."

The crowd was silent in their bewildered disappointment. From what Nicci could tell as she had walked among them throughout the day, they had come to believe that this statue was some new offering by the Order to the people—some grand thing for them to see at the emperor's palace, some bright shining hope. They were confused and stunned by what they were hearing.

Brother Narev lifted the sledgehammer. "Before this criminal's corpse is hung from a pole for his crimes against the Order, he is to see his vile work destroyed to the cheers of virtuous people!"

As the sun's last ray fled below the horizon, Brother Narev lifted the heavy sledgehammer high in the flickering light of smoking torches. The sledgehammer wobbled momentarily at the apex of its arc before descending in a heavy swing. The crowd sent up a collective gasp as the steel head rang out when it struck the male statue's leg. A few small chips fell away. It had done surprisingly little damage.

In the absolute silence, Richard laughed derisively at Brother Narev's impotent swing.

Even from the distance, Nicci could see Brother Narev's face turning crimson as Richard stood watching and chuckling. The crowd murmured, hardly able to believe any man would laugh at a brother of the Order—at Brother Narev himself.

Brother Narev could hardly believe it.

The dozens of guards who had their spears leveled at Richard could hardly believe it.

In the tense silence, Richard's laugh echoed off the semicircle of stone walls and soaring columns behind them. Death's grin returned. Brother Narev lifted the sledgehammer by the head, its weight awkward in his bony hand, and held the handle out to Richard.

"You will destroy your depraved work yourself."

The words "or you will die on the spot" were not spoken, but everyone heard them implied.

Richard accepted the handle of the sledgehammer. He could have looked no more noble doing so if he had been taking a jewel-encrusted sword.

Richard's raptor gaze left Brother Narev and swept out over the crowd as he took several strides toward the steps. Brother Narev lifted a finger, signaling the guards to hold their spears. By the smirk on the faces of Brothers Narev and Neal, they didn't think the crowd would care to hear anything a sinner had to say.

"You are ruled," Richard said in a voice that rang out over the multitude, "by mean little men."

The people gasped as one. To speak against a brother was treason, most likely, and heresy for sure.

"My crime?" Richard asked aloud. "I have given you something beautiful to see, daring to hold the conviction that you have a right to see it if you wish. Worse . . . I have said that your lives are your own to live."

A rolling murmur swept out through the multitude. Richard's voice rose in power, demanding in its clarity to be heard above the whispering.

"Evil is not one large entity, but a collection of countless, small depravities brought up from the muck by petty men. Living under the Order, you have traded the enrichment of vision for a gray fog of mediocrity—the fertile inspiration of striving and growth, for mindless stagnation and slow decay—the brave new ground of the attempt, for the timid quagmire of apathy."

With gazes riveted and lips still, the crowd listened. Richard gestured out over their heads with his sledgehammer, wielded with the effortless grace of a royal sword.

"You have traded freedom not even for a bowl of soup, but worse, for the spoken empty feelings of others who say that you deserve to have a full bowl of soup provided by someone else.

"Happiness, joy, accomplishment, achievement . . . are not finite commodities, to be divided up. Is a child's laughter to be divided up and allotted? No! Simply make more laughter!"

Laughter, pleased laughter, rippled through the crowd.

Brother Narev's scowl grew. "We've heard enough of your extremist rambling! Destroy your profane statue. Now."

Richard cocked his head. "Oh? The collective assembly of the Order, and of brothers, fears to hear what one insignificant man could say? You fear mere words that much, Brother Narev?"

Dark eyes stole a quick glance at the crowd as they leaned forward, eager to hear his answer.

"We fear no words. Virtue is on our side, and will prevail. Speak your blasphemy, so all may understand why moral people will side against you."

Richard smiled out at the people, but he spoke with brutal honesty.

"Every person's life is theirs by right. An individual's life can and must belong only to himself, not to any society or community, or he is then but a slave. No one can deny another person their right to their life, nor seize by force what is produced by someone else, because that is stealing their means to sustain their life. It is treason against mankind to hold a knife to a man's throat and dictate how he must live his life. No society can be more important than the individuals who compose it, or else you ascribe supreme importance, not to man, but to any notion that strikes the fancy of that society, at a never-ending cost of lives. Reason and reality are the only means to just laws; mindless wishes, if given sovereignty, become deadly masters.

"Surrendering reason to faith in these men sanctions their use of force to enslave you—to murder you. You have the power to decide how you will live your life.

These mean little men up here are but cockroaches, if you say they are. They have no power to control you but that which you grant them!"

Richard pointed with the sledgehammer back at the statue. "This is life. Your life. To live as you choose." He swept the head of the sledgehammer in an arc, pointing out the carvings up on the walls. "This is what the Order offers you: death."

"We've heard enough of your blasphemy!" Brother Narev shrieked. "Destroy your evil creation now, or die!"

The spears rose.

Richard calmly swept a fearless glance around at the guards, then stepped to his statue. Nicci's heart was pounding against her ribs. She didn't want it destroyed. It was too good to destroy. This couldn't be happening. They couldn't take this away.

Richard rested the sledgehammer across his shoulder. He lifted his other hand up to the statue as he addressed the crowd one last time.

"This is what the Order is taking from you—your humanity, your individuality, your freedom to live your own life."

Richard briefly touched the sledgehammer to his forehead.

With a mighty swing, the steel head arced around. Nicci could hear the air whistle. The entire statue seemed to shudder as the sledgehammer struck the base with a thunderous boom.

In a moment of brittle silence, she heard the faintest sound, the ripping popping crackling whisper of the stone itself.

Then, the entire statue crashed down in a roar of fragments and billowing white dust.

The officials at the back of the plaza cheered. The guards hooted and hollered as they waved their weapons in the air.

They were the only ones. The crowd was dead silent as dust rolled out across the plaza. All their hope, embodied in the statue, had just been destroyed.

Nicci stared in a daze. Her throat constricted with the agony of it. Her eyes watered. They all watched, as if having just witnessed a tragic, pointless death.

The guards moved toward Richard with their spears leveled, prodding him back to other guards waiting with heavy shackles.

Down closer to the steps, a clear voice rang out from the stunned crowd. "No! We'll not stand for it!"

In the gathering darkness, Nicci saw the man who had yelled. He was up close to the front, furiously trying to fight his way through the press of people to get to the plaza.

It was the blacksmith, Mr. Cascella.

"We'll not stand for it!" he roared. "I'll not let you enslave me any longer! Do you hear? I'm a free man! A free man!"

The entire mass of people before the palace erupted in a deafening roar.

And then, as one, they lunged forward.

Fists in the air, voices raised in cries of rage, the mass of humanity avalanched toward the plaza. Ranks of heavily armed men marched down the steps to meet the advance. They vanished beneath the onslaught.

Nicci screamed with all her might, trying to get Richard's attention, but her voice was lost in the hurricane.

Richard didn't know what stunned him more: to see his statue in rubble, or to see the crowd charging up the steps after Victor had declared himself a free man.

The mob rolled without pause over armed guards descending the steps to meet them. A number of people fell wounded or killed. The bodies were trampled beneath the surge of people. Those in front couldn't stop if they wanted to—the weight of tens of thousands behind them propelled them onward. But they didn't want to stop. The roar was deafening.

The brothers panicked. The officials in the rear panicked. The few thousand armed guards panicked. In that instant, the nature of the world transformed from the omnipotent power of the Order assembled on the plaza, to every man for himself.

Richard wanted Brother Narev. He saw, instead, armed men rushing in at him. Richard swung and buried the head of the sledgehammer in the chest of a man who came at him with sword raised high. As the man flew past, the handle of the sledgehammer sticking from the crater in his chest, Richard snatched the sword from his fist, and then, blade in hand, he unleashed himself.

A small group of guards saw fit to protect the brothers. Richard charged into them, cutting with every stroke. Every slash or thrust took a man down.

But guards were not what Richard was mainly interested in. If he was to lose everything, he wanted Narev's head in the bargain. As he fought his way through the chaos of people crushing into the plaza, he couldn't find Brother Narev anywhere.

Victor appeared out of the melee gripping a brother by the hair. Other men had joined Victor—and each had a hand on the brother. The burly blacksmith wore a scowl that would bend iron. The brother's eyes were rolling around as if he'd been hit on the head, and couldn't gather his senses.

"Richard!" Victor called out.

The men, some still grasping the brother's brown robes, rushed in around Richard. They stood in a sweep around him, ten or fifteen deep.

"What should we do with him?" one man asked.

Richard glanced around at all the people. He saw men he knew from the site. Priska was among them, and Ishaq, too.

"Why ask me? It's your revolt." He met the eyes of the men with challenge. "What do you think you should do with him?"

"You tell us, Richard," one of the carvers said.

Richard shook his head. "No. You tell me what you intend to do with him. But you should know, this man is a wizard. When he comes around, he's going to start killing people. This is a matter of life and death, and he knows it. Do you? This is about your lives. It is for you to decide what to do, not me."

"We want you with us this time, Richard," Priska called out. "But if you still won't join us, then we're having our lives back, having this revolt, without you. That's the way it's going to be!"

The men all shook their fists as they yelled their agreement.

Victor hugged the groggy brother to his chest and wrenched his head until his neck broke. The limp body slipped to the floor.

"And that's what we intend to do with him," Victor said.

Richard held out his hand as he smiled. "Always glad to meet a free man." They clasped forearms. Richard looked into Victor's eyes. "I'm Richard Rahl."

Victor blinked; then his belly laugh rolled out. With his free hand, he clapped Richard on the side of his shoulder.

"Sure you are. We all are! You had me going for a second, there, Richard. You really did."

The press of the crowd drove them back to the columns. Richard reached down and snatched the dead brother's robes, pulling the body along with him. The mass of towering stone walls and marble columns afforded some protection from the raging river of people.

The ground shuddered. A blast from the inside blew a hole out through the wall. The darkness ignited with light. Stone fragments whistled through the air. Dozens of bloodied people were thrown back.

"What was that!" Victor called out through the din of screaming, yelling, and the roar of the explosion.

Ignoring the danger, the crowd continued to advance on the men who had enslaved them. Throngs swarmed over the spot where the statue had stood, scooping up shards of marble. They kissed their fingers and, as they swept past, planted those kisses on the words on the back of the fallen bronze ring. They were choosing life.

Hordes of people had captured a number of the brothers and officials, and were beating them to death with chunks of white marble from the rubble of the statue.

"Brother Narev is a sorcerer," Richard said. "Victor, you have to organize some of these men—get control of this mob. Narev can use powerful magic. I commend people's desire to be free, but we're going to have a great many killed and injured if we don't get this under control."

"I understand," Victor said as he fought to keep from being swept away.

A number of men who had been crowded around Richard, protecting him, heard what he said and nodded their agreement. The commands to organize started to spread through the crowd. These people wanted to succeed. They were willing to work toward their goal, and saw reason in the orders beginning to be called out. Many of these men were used to handling large groups of workers. They knew the business of organizing men.

Richard started pulling off the dead brother's robes. "You men have to keep these people out of the palace. Narev is in there. Anyone who goes in could easily be killed. You have to keep people out. It will be a death trap in there with the brothers."

"I understand," Victor said.

"We'll keep them back," men called to Richard.

Richard threw the dead brother's brown robes up over his head. Victor snatched him by the arm. "What are you doing?"

Richard popped his head up through the neck opening. "I'm going in there. In the darkness, Narev will think I'm a brother, and I'll be able to get close to him." He poked his confiscated sword through the robes to hide the blade. He covered the hilt with his wrist. "Keep people out—Narev commands dangerous magic. I have to stop him."

"You watch yourself," Victor said.

The men who had assumed command began fanning out, urging people to follow their orders. Some people did, and as they did, yet more followed. With all the officials who they'd captured now dead, the mob was slowly being brought to task, and not a moment too soon. The crushing weight of people flooding up onto the plaza was a danger to everyone.

Passing people wept as they picked up pieces of marble from the statue, holding the tokens of freedom and beauty to their breast as they moved on to allow others to do the same. These were people who had been offered life, and had taken it. They had proven themselves.

Victor saw what everyone was doing. "Richard . . . I'm so sorry—"

A fiery blast exploded through the plaza, cutting down well over a hundred people. Bodies were ripped apart in the violence of it. A huge stone column toppled, crushing people who couldn't get out of the way because of the press of the throng.

"Later!" Richard yelled over the pandemonium. "I've got to stop Narev! Keep these people out—they'll only die in there!"

Victor nodded before he rushed off with the other men he knew to try to gain control of the situation.

Richard put the tumult and confusion behind him, and stepped through a gaping doorway between the columns . . . into the darkness.

There were miles of unfinished corridors, some clogged with bodies. In the first crush, as the people swept up onto the plaza, they had chased brothers and officials into the labyrinth of the palace. Many of those people had been unfortunate enough to find Brother Narev. The stench of burned flesh filled Richard's nostrils as he moved silently through the darkness.

Richard had been a woods guide long before he became the Seeker, long before he became Lord Rahl. Darkness was his element. In his mind, he gathered that cloak of darkness around himself.

Within the massive stone walls, under the heavy beams, partial wooden floors, and slate roofs overhead, the riot of the crowd was a distant, echoing rumble. Through the gaping openings of undressed doorways stood rooms without roofs or floors above, allowing in a flood of moonlight. It all created a tangled mesh of shadows and faint light that suggested every form of danger.

Richard came across an older woman lying bleeding in the hall, whimpering in agony. He bent to one knee, putting a hand gently to her shoulder as he kept his eyes on the dark hall ahead and its sockets of blackness to each side.

He could feel the woman trembling beneath his fingers. "Where are you hurt?" he whispered. He pushed the hood of the robe back so that in the moonlight coming between the unfinished beams above she could see his face. "I'm Richard."

A smile of recognition overcame her. "Leg," she said.

She pulled her dress up. In faint light, he saw a dark wound just above the knee. With his sword, he sliced off the hem of her dress to use as a bandage to close the wound.

"I want to live. I wanted to help." She took the strip of cloth and pushed his hands away. "Thank you for cutting me the cloth. I can do it, now." She clutched his robe, pulling him closer. "You've showed us life with your statue. Thank you."

Richard smiled as he squeezed her shoulder.

"I was trying to get that cockroach. Will you do it?"

Richard kissed his finger and pressed the kiss to her forehead. "I will. Bandage up your leg and lie still until we have the situation under control; then we'll send people in to help."

Richard started moving again. From the distance came screams of rage, and pain. Guards who had escaped into the maze of the unfinished palace were battling people who had gone in after them.

Richard spotted a brother trembling behind a corner. It wasn't Narev—there was a hood, not a cap. Playing the part of a brother, Richard pulled his hood up again and strode to the man. The brother looked relieved to see a comrade.

"Who are you?" he whispered toward Richard, lifting his hand to use his magic to light a small flame above his palm.

"Justice," Richard said to the wide eyes as he drove his sword through the man's heart.

Richard pulled his sword free and concealed it once more under his robes.

Nicci would no doubt take her revenge. There seemed nothing he could do about it. Nicci had often enough made Richard's choices clear. He was bound and determined to at least lay waste to the Order. If only there were a way to get Nicci to see reason, to get her to help him. At times, the look in her blue eyes seemed so tantalizingly close to comprehension. He knew Nicci had feelings for him. He wished he could use those feelings to get her to see reason, to help him, to cast off her chains, but he didn't know how.

Richard stepped back into the blackness of a room as he heard guards running his way. As they turned into the hallway, Richard again drew his sword. When they were close, he burst out of the doorway and took off the first guard's head. The second swung his sword, missed, and lifted it for another strike. Richard ran his sword through the man's belly. The wounded guard pulled back, off the blade. Before Richard could finish him, more men burst into the hall. The man with the gut wound wasn't going to be a problem anymore; it would take him hours of agony to die.

Richard retreated through the dark doorway, tempting men in after him. He stood still in the dark, and as they rushed in, panting, crunching debris beneath the balls of their feet as they turned, Richard located them by sound alone and cut them down. Half a dozen men died in the pitch black room before the rest ran.

Richard raced onward toward the sounds of explosions. Every time gouts of flame flashed through the morass of hallways, he hid his eyes with a hand in order to preserve his night vision. When the blinding flashes ceased, he quickly continued in the direction from which they had come.

There were mile upon mile of halls in the palace. Some opened out into grounds where nothing had yet been built. Others went along between walls open overhead. Still others tunneled through the darkness, enclosed by upper floors or roofs. Richard descended stairs into blackness, into the palace underground, following the roar of conjured flames.

Down below the main floor were networks of interconnected rooms, made up of a confusing snarl of chambers and narrow halls. As he plunged through a labyrinth of shadowy rooms, going through holes in unfinished walls and empty doorways, he came suddenly upon a cloaked man with a sword. He knew none of the people were armed.

The man spun around, his sword leading, but since Richard was disguised in robes, he knew the man might not be a true foe.

In a flash of moonlight, Richard was stunned to see the Sword of Truth over the shoulder of the person. It was Kahlan.

He froze in shock.

She saw only a figure in brown robes—a brother—standing in a shaft of moonlight. The hood shadowed his face.

In the same instant, before he could call her name, he saw, over Kahlan's shoulder, someone running their way. Nicci.

In one terrible blinding instant, Richard knew what he had to do. It was his only chance—Kahlan's only chance—to be free.

In that crystal clear instant of understanding, terror flashed through him. He didn't know if he could do it.

He had to.

Richard drew his sword and blocked Kahlan's thrust.

And then he attacked her.

He drove into her with controlled violence, careful not to hurt her. He knew how she fought. He knew because he had taught her. He played the role of a clumsy, but lucky, opponent.

Nicci was getting closer.

Richard couldn't drag it out. It had to be timed just right. He waited until Kahlan was slightly off balance and then with a powerful clash, caught her sword near the cross guard. She cried out with the shock as her sword flew from her hand and the blow spun her around, just as he had intended.

She didn't hesitate for an instant. Without pause, still spinning, her hand reached up and pulled free the Sword of Truth. The air rang with the unique sound of steel he knew so well.

Kahlan whirled around, the blade leading. He saw for a split second the terrible violent rage in her eyes. It hurt him to see that in Kahlan's beautiful eyes. He knew what it did to a person.

Richard entered a numb world all his own. He knew what he had to do. He felt no emotion. He blocked high, controlling her attack and where he wanted her to go with the blade. He had to get her to put it where he intended, if there was to be any chance.

Teeth gritted, Kahlan drove her sword for the opening he deliberately left her.

Kahlan was in the realm of uncontrollable rage. The instant she seized the hilt, the Sword of Truth had inundated her with pounding fury. Nothing in the world felt better than knowing she was going to kill with it. The weapon, too, demanded blood.

These people had Richard. These brothers had twisted their lives. These men had sent murderers to her homeland. These men had sent assassins to slaughter Warren.

Now, she had one of them.

She screamed as she spun, screamed with the rage, screamed with the demand for blood. It was glorious to have the object of such perfect rage within reach.

He made a mistake—leaving an opening. Without hesitation, she went for it with cold fury, the blade leading.

He was hers.

Richard felt the blade hit him. It was shocking. It felt unlike what he expected. It felt something like he imagined the mighty blow of the sledgehammer on the statue might feel.

His mouth opened. Now was the time; he had to stop her—keep her from doing any more. He had to do it now. If she wrenched the blade through him, ripped him open any more, Nicci would never be able to heal him. Her power could only heal so much.

Nicci would have to free Kahlan from the spell in order to regain the use of her sorceress's magic—in order to heal him.

He reasoned that she cared enough for him to do that.

Richard's mouth was open as he felt the blade still driving through him. It was a sickening shock. Even expecting it, as he had, it still seemed unreal. It still surprised him.

He needed to tell her it was him. To stop.

He needed at least to call out her name so she would stop without doing too much damage.

His mouth was still open.

He had no breath.

He couldn't make himself say her name.

As she searched frantically for Richard, Nicci saw the two people battling. One was a brother. The other she didn't recognize, yet there was something deeply unsettling about it all. Nicci felt a strange stirring. The feeling was oddly familiar, but in all the confusion of emotion, she just didn't recognize it.

They were a good distance away.

The man in the cape lost his sword. It looked as if the brother had him. Nicci wanted to help—but how? She had to find Richard. Someone said they saw him go into the palace. She had to find him.

She ran toward the pair. The man pulled free another sword strapped over his shoulder. The strange feeling welled up in Nicci. Something was terribly wrong, but she didn't know what.

And then she saw the brother make a mistake. Nicci halted.

With a cry of lethal fury, the man in the cape drove his sword through the brother.

When the force of the blow drove the brother back a step, a shaft of moonlight fell across his face under in the cowl of the hood.

And then the feeling slammed into her with full recognition.

Nicci's eyes went wide. She screamed.

"Kahlan. Stop."

Kahlan's eyes twitched up in shock. She saw his face in the moonlight. In that same instant, he heard Nicci scream.

Kahlan recoiled, her hand flying from the hilt of the Sword of Truth as if she had been struck by lightning.

She fell back with a horrified shriek.

Richard seized the blade of the sword, his sword, to keep the weight from twisting it in him. She had driven it through him almost up to the cross guard. Warm blood ran down the blade onto his fingers.

"Richard!" Kahlan cried. "Nooo! Nooo!"

Richard felt his knees hit the stone floor. He was surprised it didn't hurt more to have a sword through him. It was the shock of it, mostly, that had scrambled his mind. It was hard to think. He struggled not to fall forward, fall on the blade and wrench it through his insides. The room seemed to be moving.

"Pull it out," he whispered.

He wanted it out. As if that would help. He wanted the awful thing out. He could feel the razor sharp edges all the way through him. He could feel it sticking out his back.

Kahlan, nearly hysterical, scrambled to do as he asked. Richard saw Cara limping up out of the darkness. She seized his shoulders as Kahlan drew out the blade in one swift, panicked yank, as if she hoped the action would somehow undo what she had done.

"What happened?" Cara cried. "What did you do?"

The world seemed to tip and whirl. Richard could feel the sickeningly wet warmth of his blood soaking down him. He could feel his weight against Cara. Kahlan hovered close.

"Richard! Oh, dear spirits, no. This can't be happening. It can't." Panicked tears streamed down her beautiful face. He couldn't understand what she was doing here. Why was she in the Old World? What was she doing in the emperor's palace?

He couldn't help smiling at seeing her.

He wondered if she had seen his statue before he destroyed it.

He wondered if he had made a terrible mistake.

No, it was Kahlan's only chance at freedom. His only chance to break Nicci's spell.

Nicci was still running toward them.

"Help me, Nicci," Richard called. It came out as little more than a whisper. "I need you to save me, Nicci. Please."

Even if it was no more than a whisper, Nicci heard his plea.

Nicci had never run so fast. Terror had her in its fierce grip. Kahlan had stabbed her sword through him. It was a terrible mistake. It was all such a terrible mistake. Nicci had brought such pain to them both. It was her fault.

Even in her shock, Nicci knew with clarity what she must do.

She could heal him. Kahlan was there. Nicci couldn't begin to imagine why, or how, but she was. With Kahlan there, Nicci could break the spell. Once the spell was broken, Nicci could use her gift. She could heal Richard. It was all right. She could save him. It would be all right. She could fix it. She could.

She could do something right and help—really help—for once. She could help them both.

An arm swept out of the darkness and hooked her by the neck, taking her from her feet. She cried out as she was yanked into the blackness. She could feel the bulge of hard muscles as she clawed at the arm. The man stank. She could feel his lice ticking against her face as they sprang at her.

Terror seized her. Such sudden and intense terror was an unfamiliar sensation, smothering her mind.

She dug her heels into the stone as he drew her back into the black labyrinth. She kicked furiously at him. She tried to draw her dacra from her sleeve, but he seized her arm and twisted it behind her back.

His forearm crushed against her exposed throat, choking off her air as he lifted her from her feet.

Nicci couldn't breathe. He chortled with glee as he dragged her into the darker recesses of the rooms beneath Jagang's palace.

Their eyes met just when she had been abruptly and violently snatched into the darkness. Richard saw in those eyes something important, saw that Nicci intended to help him. But she was gone.

Cara desperately clutched his shoulders as he lay back against her. He was cold. She was warm.

Kahlan fell back, writhing in the darkness. She clawed at her throat. He could hear her choking.

"Mother Confessor! Mother Confessor! What's wrong?"

Richard reached up and seized Cara behind her head. He pulled her face close.

"Someone has Nicci. They're choking her. Cara—you have to go save Nicci, or Kahlan will die. And Nicci is the only one who can heal me. Go. Hurry."

He felt Cara nodding before he released her head.

"I understand" was all she said as she gently, but swiftly, laid him back on the cold stone.

And then she was gone.

It was wet. He didn't know if it was blood, or water. They were underground, in the nether reaches of the Retreat. Through open beams where the flooring above hadn't been laid, moonlight flooded down to light Kahlan struggling not far away. He could see, then, as she fought an invisible foe, that it was water. That's what it was. Not blood. Water. The palace was next to the river. It was wet in the little rooms and halls down in the bottom.

"Kahlan," he murmured. She didn't respond. "Hold on . . ."

Gripping his abdomen, holding the wound closed lest his insides burst out, he inched his way through the water, across the cold stone. The pain had finally and firmly arrived. He could feel the terrible damage inside. He tried to blink away the tears of hot agony. He had to hold on. Icy sweat drenched his face. Kahlan had to hold on.

His hand, covered in blood, reached out to her. His fingers found hers. She hardly responded, but at least her fingers moved. He was thankful beyond words that her fingers moved.

It had been a good plan. He was sure it was. It would have worked, if only someone hadn't snatched Nicci. Would have worked.

It seemed a stupid way to die, really. He thought it should be somehow more . . . grand.

Not in a dark, cold, wet palace underground.

He wished he could tell Kahlan that he loved her, and that she hadn't killed him but that he had done it. It was his doing, not hers. He'd just used her in his plan. It would have worked.

"Kahlan," he whispered, not knowing if in her stillness she could hear him any longer. "I love you. No one else. Just you. I'm glad we had our time together. I wouldn't trade it for anything."

Richard opened his eyes and groaned in agony. He wanted it to end. It hurt too much. Now, he just wanted it to end. It hadn't worked. He would have to pay the price. But he wanted the sickening, ripping, terrifying pain to end.

He didn't know how much time had passed. He looked and saw Kahlan sprawled on the wet floor. She wasn't moving.

A shadow fell across him.

"Well, well. Richard Cypher." Neal chuckled. "Imagine that." He chuckled again as he glanced at Kahlan. "Who's the woman?"

Richard could sense the Sword of Truth, sense its magic. It wasn't far from his fingers.

"Don't know. She's killed me. Must be one of yours."

Richard's fingers found the sword. They curled around the wire-wound hilt.

Neal stepped on the blade. "Can't have any of that. You've caused enough trouble."

A glow ignited around Neal's fingers. He was conjuring magic. Lethal magic. Richard, in his barely conscious condition, despite his need, could not focus his mind, could not call forth his own ability to do anything to stop Neal. At least, the pain would end. At least, Kahlan wouldn't think it was she who had killed him.

Richard heard a sudden, terrible, bone-snapping crack. Neal dropped heavily to his knees.

Richard, his hand already around the hilt, pulled the sword from underneath the man's legs and in one mighty lunge, ran it through Neal's heart.

Neal looked up in surprise, his eyes glassy. Richard saw then that the man was as good as dead before the blade had run him through. Neal's eyes rolled back in his head and he slumped to the side as Richard yanked the sword free.

Standing behind Neal was the woman Richard had helped. She had bandaged her leg. In both hands, she held the marble hand of the woman Richard had carved. She had crushed Neal's skull with her keepsake of the statue.

Richard heard footfalls splashing toward him down the wet hallway. The woman had gone to find help. Maybe she had found it.

In the rooms and hallways in the distance, Richard could hear occasional screams as blasts of magic exploded through the night, as people were injured and killed.

A woman appeared in the moonlight. "Richard? Richard?"

Richard squinted in the darkness. "Who are you?" he managed to whisper.

She rushed to his side and fell to her knees. She gasped at seeing Kahlan sprawled on the floor close to him.

"What happened to the Mother Confessor?"

Richard frowned. She knew Kahlan.

"Who are you?"

She looked back at him. "I'm a Sister. Sister Alessandra. I've been in the city for a while, looking for Nicci, and—never mind. A woman found me—just down the hall—and said you were hurt. The man who carved the statue. I was trying desperately to get to you earlier, but I couldn't get near—there I go again. Tell me where you're hurt. I can try to heal you."

"I was run through with a sword."

She was still and silent for a moment.

"Under my hands."

She looked then, and spoke a prayer under her breath. "I think I can help. I feared—"

"I need Nicci to do it."

Sister Alessandra glanced about. "Nicci? Where is she, then? I've been searching for her. Ann sent me to find her."

Richard's eyes fell on the still form of Kahlan. "Can you help her?"

He could see the woman's eyes look away from his. "No, I can't. She's linked by magic to Nicci. I met her before, and she told me about it. I can do nothing through the shield of Nicci's link."

"Is she . . . is she still . . ."

The woman looked and then leaned back over him. "She's alive, Richard."

He closed his eyes in relief, and in pain.

"Lie still," she said.

"But I need Nicci to—"

"You're bleeding. This is bad, Richard. In a short time more, you will have lost too much blood. If I wait, no one will be able to heal you. You will have slipped too far beyond this world for any gift to help you. I can't wait.

"Besides, I came to try to stop Nicci. I know her better than anyone. You can't put your life in her hands. You can't put your faith in her."

"It's not faith. I know—"

"She's a Sister of the Dark. I'm the one who led her down that dark road. I came to try to lead her back. Until and unless that time comes, you can't trust her. Now, you've not much time. Do you want to live, or not?"

It had all gone for nothing. He felt a tear run from the corner of his eye and across his cheek.

"I choose life," he said.

"I know," she whispered with a smile. "I saw the statue. Now, move your hands for me. I need to have mine there."

Richard let his hands slip to his sides as hers covered his wound. He felt helpless. He could focus on nothing but the searing pain.

He felt magic tingle into him, following the damage down deep inside him. He clenched his teeth as he held in a cry.

"Hold on," she whispered. "This is bad. It will hurt, but then in a while it will be all right."

"I understand," he said. He gasped sharply. "Do it, then."

The pain of her magic seared into him like white-hot coals thrown on bare flesh. He almost cried out, but then the pain abruptly ceased. Richard lay with his eyes closed, panting, waiting for it to start again. He felt her hands slip from him.

Richard opened his eyes and saw that Sister Alessandra's eyes were opened wide. For an instant, he wondered why.

And then he saw a foot of steel jutting from her chest. Her fingers went to her throat as blood gushed from her open mouth. A silent scream formed on her lips.

A bony hand shoved her aside.

She had been impaled on the sword Richard had used to fight Kahlan. His hand blindly went for the hilt he knew was there, but a foot kicked the Sword of Truth aside.

Death's own skull grinned down at him.

"You are a troublesome man, Richard Cypher," came the grating voice from the darkness above. "But at last, that trouble is ended."

The tall angular figure in robes and a creased cap towered above him as he lay helpless on the cold wet floor.

"This little rebellion of yours will be crushed, I can promise you that much, before you die. Their foolish little tantrum will be brought to an end. The people will soon come to their senses. Your kind appeals only to the extremist fringe. Most people see their duty to their fellow man. Your efforts have been for nothing."

Brother Narev swept his arm around, as if in introduction.

"An appropriate place for you to die, don't you think, Richard? These rooms are the future questioning chambers. You eluded the chambers once, but not this time. You will die in one as you should have died in one before.

"I, on the other hand, will live here a long, long time, and see the Order bring morality to the world. Down here, in these chambers, radicals like you will confess their wickedness. I just wanted you to know, before you are embraced in the Keeper's cold arms for all eternity."

Brother Narev's skeletal hands clawed as he called forth his magic. Richard saw white-hot light blossom around the high priest's hands and expand downward. Richard squeezed Kahlan's hand as he watched the white light of death come for him.

The bloom of light turned a honey color. As if the air had thickened, the light slumped off to the sides.

A howl of fury grew in Narev's throat. His shook his fists in rage.

"You have the gift of a wizard! Who are you?"

"I am your worst nightmare. I am a thinking man who can't be deluded by your lies, any more than I can be burned by your foul magic."

Brother Narev tried to smash his foot down on Richard's face, but Richard was able to deflect the blow. He seized Narev's ankle. The man caught his balance and pulled madly to get free. The effort of holding on felt as if it ripped the wound through Richard's insides. He tried to hold on, but his fingers slipped from the wet leather.

Once free, and out of Richard's reach, Narev bent and seized the hilt of the sword lodged in the Sister's back. He tugged but it didn't come completely out. He growled in fury, his boots slipping on the slimy floor, as he yanked on the sword.

Richard knew that, once armed, Narev would be a swift executioner.

With all his strength, Richard lunged at the man's legs. Brother Narev toppled back onto the wet floor. Richard, his middle wrenched in torture, threw himself atop Narev's legs to hold him down. Bony fingers clawed at Richard's face, trying to gouge his eyes. Richard turned his head away. With fierce effort, he clutched at the heavy robes, dragging himself up the man's body, ignoring the blows to his face as he did so.

He seized Brother Narev by the throat. Brother Narev's bony fingers closed savagely around Richard's throat. Both men growled with the effort of trying to strangle each other to death. Richard twisted his head, trying to prevent Narev from getting a death grip, while at the same time trying to get his own thumbs over Narev's windpipe so he could choke off his air.

Narev tried to roll, to throw Richard off. Richard spread his legs to make it harder for Narev to flip him over, and held tight as the man twisted and fought. He could feel his insides tearing.

Richard had wielded a chisel and hammer for the Order for months. He was stronger, but he was also losing a lot of blood, and that strength was fading. He squeezed with all his might. The fingers at his throat loosened a little.

The man's eyes bulged as Richard finally managed to start to choke the life out of him. Bony hands thumped at Richard's shoulders.

The hands suddenly and fiercely seized Richard by his hair.

Narev freed a leg and brought his knee up into Richard's wound.

The world went white with pain.

Nicci woke, dazed, to the sound of a low, wicked laugh. She knew the voice. She knew the smell. Kadar Kardeef.

She heard a snapping, popping, hissing sound. A torch, she realized. He whipped it around in front of her face, so close she could feel the terrible heat against her flesh. Burning pitch dripped off, falling on her leg.

Nicci screamed in pain as the pitch burned into the flesh of her thigh.

"What goes around, comes around," Kadar said in her ear.

"I don't care what you do to me," Nicci cried in rage. "I'm glad I burned you. I'm glad you've had to beg."

"Oh you'll be begging, too, before long. You may not think so, but you'll be surprised what fire makes a person do. You will yet know what it was like. You will yet beg."

With all her might, Nicci struggled against him. She could undo the spell, if only Kahlan were closer. So near, but so far.

The fire before her eyes sent terror scorching through her. She had only to snip the cord linking her to Kahlan. She could break the link. She didn't have to undo it in order to have her power back. Nicci could escape, then. It would cost Kahlan her life, but Nicci would have her power, and she could escape the flames.

But she would have to kill Kahlan to do it.

"Shall I burn your face, first, Nicci? Your lovely face? Or maybe I should start with your legs. Which shall it be? You pick."

Nicci panted as she struggled, trying to back away from the heat on her flesh. The hissing torch waved in front of her face. She knew she deserved such a fate, but she was driven to wild panic by the fear of it.

She didn't want to snip the link, to kill Kahlan, but she didn't want to die this way. She didn't want her flesh to burn.

"I say we start at the bottom, so we can hear your screams."

Kadar brought the torch down and touched it to the hem of her dress. Nicci screamed as the black cloth caught flame. Such fear was a new sensation for her; for the first time since she was very small, she had something she cared about, and didn't want to lose: life.

In a moment of stark terror, Nicci knew that no matter how much it was to hurt, no matter how frightening it was to be, she would not take Kahlan's life. Richard had given her the answer she had sought. She had taken too much already. In return for that lesson, she could not now violate it.

Even though Kahlan, linked to Nicci, was to suffer the same fate, would die the same agonizing death, Nicci would not be the one who inflicted it. She would not take Kahlan's life from her. Kadar would be bringing their death, but Nicci would not. She would not kill Kahlan to save herself.

Kadar Kardeef laughed as he watched her dress ignite. He held her in a firm grip Nicci could not escape.

Just then, a dark shape flew at her from midair, crashing into them both. They tumbled back, the air all around filled with fire. As Nicci rolled, it put the flaming dress out in the water.

The one who had crashed into them was just getting up, shaking her head as if to clear it. Nicci recognized her. It was the Mord-Sith, Cara.

Kadar sat up, saw the woman, and lunged at her with the torch.

Nicci threw herself at Kadar, grabbing the torch in both hands as she pushed it into the big man's face. The pitch splashed against his mask of rags. The cloth on his chest and around his head ignited with a loud *whoosh*.

Kadar screamed as the flames burned into his already melted flesh. Nicci had heard that heat to previously burned flesh was worse than the first burning. By the sound of his screams, it appeared to be true.

Nicci snatched Cara's hand as the woman was regaining her feet. "Hurry! I must get to Richard!"

Outside the room where Kadar's shrieks fell to strangled whimpers as the flames suffocated him, Cara seized Nicci by the hair and held her Agiel inches from her face.

"Give me one reason why I should trust you with Lord Rahl's life."

Nicci gazed into Cara's eyes. "Because I saw his statue, and I understand, now, how wrong I've been. Have you ever been wrong, Cara? Really wrong? Can you ever understand what it's like to realize you've been unthinkingly serving evil, and hurting good people? Can you understand that Richard has shown me there is something to live for?"

Nicci found Richard lying on his back, unconscious, or at least close to it. His head was pillowed on a marble hand. Kahlan lay beside him, clinging to him, weeping as his life bled away.

Nicci was shocked to see the bodies strewn on the floor around them. Sister Alessandra, Brother Neal, Brother Narev. She knew by the way Richard looked that there was precious little time—if it was not already too late.

Nicci knelt beside Kahlan. The woman was in abject misery, hanging by the last threads of desperate hope over the black brink of despair. She had come all this way, wanting to be with him, willing to suffer any end to do so. And here he lay, the lifeblood draining out of the one she loved most in life, knowing it was by her hand.

Nicci took Kahlan by her shoulders and gently pulled her back. Kahlan looked up in confusion, hatred, and hope.

"Kahlan, I need to remove the spell from you if I'm to help him. There's not much time."

"I don't trust you. Why would you help?"

"Because I owe it to him—to both of you."

"You have brought nothing but suffering and—"

Cara took Kahlan's arm. "Mother Confessor, you don't have to trust her. Trust me. I'm telling you that Nicci might be able to save him. I believe she will do her best. Please, let her do it."

"Why should I trust her with his last few minutes of his life?"

"Please, let Nicci have the chance Lord Rahl once gave me."

Kahlan searched Cara's eyes for a moment, then turned to Nicci.

"I know what it's like to be where he is now. I've been there. I chose life. Now, he must. What do I need to do?"

"You and Richard have already done enough." Nicci took Kahlan's tearstained face in her hands. "Just be still, and let me do this."

The woman was shivering in misery. Her long hair was matted and dripping wet. She was covered in Richard's blood. She could do no more for him, and she knew it.

Nicci had to.

As Kahlan gazed into her eyes, Nicci re-ignited the connecting cord of magic, hoping that she had enough time.

Kahlan went rigid with the shock of pain it caused. Nicci knew exactly how it felt, because she felt the same pain.

Milky light connected both women, heart to heart. Its wavering glow grew to blinding brightness, taking the pain to a new level in intensity.

Kahlan's mouth opened in a silent cry. Her green eyes widened with the torment flooding through them both—as the root of magic embedded in every fiber of their two beings vibrated in response to the call of the light.

Nicci placed her hands over her heart, in that incandescent shaft of light, and began to withdraw her power.

Richard pulled a shuddering breath as he opened his eyes. Somehow, he was lying in a position that didn't hurt. He feared to move, lest the crushing pain return.

How could that be? He'd been run through with a sword.

The darkness around him was still and quiet. In the distance, he could hear the sounds of battle raging on. The ground beneath him shuddered with some great impact.

There were people around him. Bodies lay on the wet floor. He realized he was on a board, keeping him up out of the water. He was covered in a warm cloak. He could see the dark hunched shapes of people huddled around in the little room.

Under his fingers lay the hilt of the Sword of Truth. Because the storm of magic was calmed, he knew the sword was in its scabbard.

He looked up, and through the openings between beams, through broken stone and splintered wood, and could see the rosy blush of dawn.

"Kahlan?" he whispered.

Three figures in the room sprang up, as if stone had suddenly come to life.

The closest leaned in. "I'm here." She took up his hand.

With his other hand, he reluctantly probed for his wound. He couldn't find it. He felt no pain, only a lingering ache.

Another figure leaned in. "Lord Rahl? Are you awake?"

"What happened?"

"Oh, Richard, I'm so sorry. I'm so sorry. I stabbed you. It was all my fault. I should have taken an instant to be sure before I did it. I'm so sorry."

Richard frowned. "Kahlan, I let you win."

Silence greeted him.

"Richard," Kahlan finally said, "you don't have to try to ease my guilt. I know it's my fault. I ran you through with the sword."

"No," Richard insisted, "I let you win."

Cara patted his shoulder. "Of course you did, Lord Rahl. Of course you did."

"No, really."

When the third figure turned to him, Richard's fingers tightened around the hilt of his sword.

"How do you feel?" Nicci asked in that silken voice he knew so well.

"Did you remove the link to Kahlan?"

Nicci raised her hand and made a scissors motion with two fingers. "Gone for good."

Richard let out a breath. "Then I feel fine." He tried to sit up, but Nicci's hand restrained him.

"Richard, I can never ask your forgiveness because I can never return what I stole from you, but I want you to know that I now understand how wrong I've been. My whole life, I have been blind. I'm not making an excuse. It's just that I want you to know that you have restored my vision. In giving me the answer I sought, you gave me my life. You gave me a reason to want to live."

"And what did you see, Nicci?"

"Life. You sculpted it so big that even someone who had so blindly served evil, as I had done, could see it. You must no longer prove yourself to me. Now, it is for me, and those here you have inspired, to prove ourselves to you."

"You and they have already begun, or I would not be alive."

"So . . . you are a Sister of the Light again?" Kahlan asked.

Nicci shook her head. "No. I am Nicci. My ability as a sorceress is mine; it is who I am. My ability does not enslave me to others because they want it. It's my life. It does not belong to anyone—except maybe to you two.

"You both have shown me the value of life, the rationale of freedom. If I am to serve beside anyone, now, it will be beside others who hold dear the same values."

Richard placed his hand over Nicci's. "Thank you for saving my life. For a while there, I thought I'd made a mistake when I let Kahlan run me through."

"Richard," Kahlan objected, "you don't have to try to assuage my guilt by saying that."

Nicci was gazing into his eyes, even as she addressed Kahlan. "He's not. He's telling you the truth. I saw him do it. He was forcing me to make a choice to save him, so that I would have to break the spell holding you. I'm sorry you had to endure such a thing, Richard; I'd already made the choice—the moment I saw your statue."

Richard tried to sit up again. Nicci restrained him again.

"It is going to take time for you to recover fully. You are still suffering the lingering effects of the injury. Just because you are alive, that doesn't mean it won't take some time before you are completely recovered. You have gone through a formidable ordeal. You lost a lot of blood. You will need to rebuild your strength. You could yet die if you don't go easy."

"All right," Richard conceded. He sat up carefully with Kahlan's help. "I'll keep your words in mind, but I still have to get up there." He turned to Kahlan. "By the way, what are you doing all the way down here? How did you know where I was? What's happening to the north, in the New World?"

"We'll talk about all that later," she said. "I had to be with you. I decided that it was my life, and I wanted to be with you. You were right about the war in the New World. It took me a long time to come to understand that. I finally did. I came to be with you because that was all that was left for me."

He looked to Cara. "And you?"

"I always wanted to see the world."

Richard smirked as he rose with the help of Kahlan and Cara, both. He felt light-headed, but was joyful to trade that for the way he had been before. Kahlan handed him his sword. He slipped the baldric over his head, laying the leather across his shoulder and the scabbard at his hip. Knowing the weapon a little more intimately, now, he had a new respect for it.

"I can't tell you how happy I am to return it to you," Kahlan said. She smiled sheepishly. "Like this, I mean."

Farther down the hall Kamil was anxiously waiting in the darkness pierced by only a couple of candles. There were a number of people with him. Richard didn't know any of the people, except Kamil. He put a hand to the grinning young man's shoulder.

"Kamil. Good to see you."

"Richard, I saw it. I saw the statue." His smile faded. "I'm sorry it was destroyed."

"It was only a piece of stone. It was the ideas it represented that were its true beauty."

People in the dim hallway nodded. Richard saw, then, the woman with the wounded leg. He smiled at her. She returned a kiss, on the end of her fingers, to his forehead.

"Bless you for your bravery in carving that statue," she said. "We are all joyful to know you survived the night, Richard."

He thanked them all for their concern.

The ground shook again.

"What *is* that?" Richard asked.

"The walls," one of the men said. "The people are pulling down the walls with those carvings of death on them."

Even as some people were pulling down the walls, others were still engaged in pitched battle. Richard could see in the faint light of dawn the fighting on the distant hillsides. It appeared that many people were not happy about the ideas Richard's statue had represented. There were those who feared freedom, and preferred the numb existence of not having to think for themselves.

The palace grounds, though, were in secure hands. The fires of liberty were spreading outward, igniting a conflagration of change.

In the plaza, the semicircle of walls and all the columns but one still stood. It felt somehow different here. This was the place where people had seen the statue and had chosen life. They weren't destroying this part of the palace.

Richard dragged his boot through the marble dust. In the center of the plaza, the layer of white dust was all that remained. Every precious fragment had been saved as a reminder.

From out on the grounds where several men were gathered, Victor spotted Richard, Kamil, and Nicci, whom he knew. He called out as he and Ishaq came running.

"Richard!" Victor raced up the steps. "Richard!"

Richard had Cara under one arm and Kamil under the other, supporting him. He didn't have the strength to shout, so he simply waited until the two men were close, both panting from their run.

"Richard, we're winning!" Victor said as he pointed at the hills. "All those officials, gone, and we—"

The blacksmith went silent as his eyes fell on Kahlan. Ishaq, too, stared at her, then swept his red hat off his head.

Victor's mouth labored a moment before words finally worked their way out. His hand, usually so expressive, simply pointed at her as if she could not be real flesh.

"You . . ." he said to Kahlan. "You are Richard's love."

Kahlan smiled. "How do you know that?"

"I saw the statue."

In the dawn light, Richard could see her face go red.

"It didn't look exactly like me," she protested, graciously.

"Not the way it looked, but the . . . character. You have that quality."

Kahlan smiled, pleased by his words.

"Victor, Ishaq, this is Kahlan. My wife."

Both men blinked dumbly and looked as one to Nicci.

"As you know," Nicci said, "I am not a very good person. I am a sorceress. I used my power to force Richard to come here with me. Richard has shown me, along with many other people, the nobility of life."

"Then you're the one who saved his life?" Victor asked.

"Kamil told us you were hurt, Richard," Ishaq said, "and that a sorceress was healing you."

"Nicci healed me," Richard confirmed.

Victor gestured expansively—at last. "Well, I guess that has to count for something, saving Richard Cypher."

"Richard Rahl," Richard said.

Victor's rolling laugh rumbled up from deep inside. "Right. This day, we are all Richard Rahl."

Nicci leaned in. "It really is Richard Rahl, Mr. Cascella."

"Richard Rahl," Kahlan said, adding her nod.

"Lord Rahl," Cara said in ill humor. "Show the proper respect to the Seeker of Truth, the master of the D'Haran Empire, war wizard, and the husband to the Mother Confessor herself." Cara lifted her hand in graceful, regal introduction. "Lord Rahl."

Richard shrugged. He lifted the gleaming, silver-wound hilt of his sword, showing them the word TRUTH in gold, and then let it drop back into its scabbard.

"What a beauty!" Kamil shouted.

Victor and Ishaq both blinked again, and then dropped to a knee. They bowed their heads deeply.

Richard rolled his eyes. "Will you two stop it." He shot Cara a scowl.

Victor peered up cautiously. "But we never knew. I'm sorry. You're not angry I made fun of you?"

"Victor, it's me, Richard. How many times have we eaten your lardo together?"

"Lardo?" Kahlan asked. "You know how to make lardo, Victor?"

Victor rose up, a grin growing across his face as he peered at her. "You know of lardo?"

"Of course. The men who used to come to work on the white marble at the Confessors' Palace used to eat lardo they made themselves in big marble tubs. I used to sit and eat it with them when I was little. They used to say I would grow up to wear the white dress of the Mother Confessor one day because I ate their lardo and would grow strong from it."

Victor thumped his chest with a big thumb. "I make lardo in marble tubs, too."

"Do you let it age for a year?" Kahlan asked. "You have to let proper lardo age for a year."

"Of course, a year! I make only proper lardo."

Kahlan gave him her most beautiful, green-eyed smile. "I would love to taste it sometime."

Victor draped his massive arm around Kahlan's shoulders. "Come, Richard's wife, I will give you a taste of my lardo."

Cara, a dark look on her face, put a hand to the blacksmith's chest to stop him. She lifted his arm from Kahlan's shoulders.

"No one but Lord Rahl touches the Mother Confessor."

Victor gave Cara a quizzical look. "Have you ever had lardo?"

"No."

Victor slapped Cara on the back as he laughed. "Come, then, and I will give you lardo, too. Then you will see—anyone who eats lardo with me is my friend for life."

Kahlan took Kamil's place under one of Richard's arms, Victor under the other, and they made their way across newly free ground up to the blacksmith's shop, to have some lardo.

Verna pulled the candle close. She warmed her hands over it a moment, then laid the journey book on the table. The sounds of the army camp outside her small tent were by now so familiar she almost didn't hear them.

It was a cold D'Haran winter night, but at least they and all the people they had helped were safely over the mountains. Verna understood their quiet anxiety: it was a new and mysterious place, D'Hara, a land once only a source of nightmares. At least they were safe for the time being. In the distance the wolves' long plaintive howls echoed through the frigid mountains, off the moonlit snow blanketing the seemingly endless, desolate, colossal slopes.

It was the proper phase of the moon, even if it was the moon in a new land, a strange and unknown land. Verna had checked for months, but there was never a message. She didn't really expect one, since Kahlan had thrown Ann's twinned journey book in the fire. But still, it was a journey book, an ancient thing of magic, and Ann was a resourceful woman. It didn't hurt to look.

Verna opened the little book with no real hope.

There, on the first page, was a message.

All it said, was, *Verna, I am waiting, if you are there.*

Verna drew the stylus from the spine and immediately began writing. *Prelate! You have been able to fix the damaged journey book? That's wonderful. Where are you? Are you well? Have you found Nathan?*

Verna waited. Shortly, the reply began to appear.

Verna, I am well. I was able to restore the journey book with the help of some . . . people. Strange people. But the important part is that it is restored—for the most part. I am still searching for the prophet. I have some good clues on Nathan's whereabouts, and I am looking into them. But how are you, Verna? How goes the war? Warren? Kahlan? Is Zedd giving you much trouble? That man can try the patience of stone. Have you had word of Richard?

Verna stared at words on the page. A tear fell near Warren's name. She picked up the stylus once more, and slowly began her reply.

Oh, Prelate, some terrible things have happened.

I am sorry, Verna, came the reply. *Verna, I am here. I am going nowhere for the night. Take all the time you need. Tell me what happened. Tell me how you are, first. I worry so for you. Verna, I love you like a daughter. You know I do.*

Verna nodded to the book. She did know it.

And I love you, too, Prelate, Verna began. *I fear my heart is broken.*

536

Kahlan stood silently beside him in the warm midday breeze as Richard looked out over the river, at the city beyond. The city was peaceful, now. Battle had raged for weeks, various factions struggling for power, lusting to be the new local incarnation of the Order, each faction swearing that they had the best interest of the people at heart, each promising that they would be compassionate in their rule, each pledging that life would be easier under their mandate because they would see to it that everyone of means contributed to the common good.

After decades of such altruistic tyranny, decay and death had been the only product of the business of the common good. Despite graveyards full of evidence and a people left impoverished, these aspirants to power offered only more of the same, and yet many still believed them simply because they uttered such good intentions.

While a great number of brothers and officials had been killed, some had escaped. Some of those, who had not fled, thought to take advantage of the confusion and establish control, thinking they could rein in the hunger for freedom, the ideas loosed, and put things back to the way they were.

The free people of Altur'Rang, their numbers growing daily, eradicated each of these factions as they emerged from under their rocks. Nicci had been no small aid in the bloody battles. She knew the methods of such people, where they went to ground, and pounced on them like a wolf on vermin.

The forces lusting to oversee the welfare and betterment of mankind came to greatly fear that which they had in fact created: Death's Mistress.

There was no telling, yet, if freedom's flame, now ignited, would spread through the Old World. It was still a very small flame in a vast and dark place, but Richard knew that such a flame burned brightly.

To the north, matters were not nearly so auspicious. With Nicci's magic withdrawn, Richard supposed that the D'Harans would know where he was, and send him messages. Cara was immensely relieved to be able to sense his location again through her bond.

He had listened quietly as Kahlan and Cara had told him all the details of the war, and how they had sent the people of Aydindril on a long and difficult journey to D'Hara before Jagang could march into the city in the spring. It would give them heart to know that Lord Rahl had struck a mighty blow against the Old World, to know that the Mother Confessor was with him, and that they were well. A number of men had requested the job of carrying that invaluable news north.

Soon, the D'Haran Empire and the people they were protecting who had fled their homes would know of the victory to the south. The messengers would actually be carrying a more precious commodity than that news: they would in reality be carrying hope.

Richard had also sent his grandfather the same word.

Richard could hardly believe that Warren, his friend, was gone. The terrible anguish, he knew, would be slow to fade.

Richard had sent one other thing north.

Nicci had told him of Brother Narev's importance to Emperor Jagang, of their long history together, and of their shared vision of the future of mankind. In the spring when Jagang finally, triumphantly, rode in to seize the Confessors' Palace, waiting for him there, before his empty victory, would be his mentor's head on a pike, topped by his creased brown cap.

Nicci had woven a spell around it, to preserve it, to keep scavengers away. Richard wanted to be sure that when Jagang finally saw it, he would not mistake who it was.

In the teeming city of Altur'Rang, peace had returned, along with freedom. Life had returned. People had begun to open new businesses. In a matter of weeks, there was already a variety of bread available. New enterprises were starting every day. Ishaq was making a fortune hauling goods, but already had competitors vying for the business. Nabbi had gone to work for him. Ishaq had begged Richard to come work for him when he was strong enough. Richard had only laughed.

Faval, the charcoal maker, had beseeched Ishaq to ask Richard to come to visit and have dinner with him and his family. Faval had bought a cart, and his sons now delivered charcoal.

Richard leaned with his forearms on the railing at the edge of the pier and gazed down over the edge, to the swirling water below, as if trying to divine what the future held.

The piers out into the river and the walkway atop them, along with the plaza, were about all that remained of the palace. Richard had seen to it that the spell-forms were removed from the tops of the columns around the grounds, and had Priska melt them down.

Richard had regained most of his strength. Kahlan was strong, and as beautiful as he remembered her. She had changed, though. Her face had grown more mature in the year they had been apart. When he gazed at her, he hungered for a piece of marble and his chisels so he could carve her face in stone.

Flesh in stone.

He turned and looked back along the pier, toward the plaza, with its semicircle of columns behind it. The fallen column had been restored. The plaza had been renamed "Liberty Square," Victor's idea. Richard asked if it shouldn't be called "Liberty Circle," since it was round, and not square. Victor thought it sounded better as Liberty Square, so Richard called it Liberty Square. After all, the first man to declare himself free, there, had been Victor.

Kahlan gazed with him back toward the plaza.

"What do you think?" Richard asked her.

She shook her head, looking at best a little uneasy. "I don't know, Richard. It just seems so strange to see it so . . . big. So . . . white."

"You don't like it?"

She quickly put a hand on his arm to dispel the notion. "No, it isn't that, it's just that it's so . . ."—her uncertain gaze returned down the pier—"big."

The center of the plaza, where the statue Richard had carved had briefly stood, now held a towering marble statue being worked on by a number of stone carvers who used to work at the site carving misery and death. Kamil was down there, learning the craft of stone carving from masters. His education started with a broom.

Richard had hired the carvers. With the fortune he had made helping the Order build its palace, he could easily afford it. The carvers were glad for such work—to exchange value for value.

The expert carvers were working on scaling up the small statue of *Spirit*, which Richard had carved for Kahlan, way back in their mountain home when she needed to witness vitality, courage, and indomitable spirit. It emerged anew in the best white Cavatura marble.

The bronze ring of the sundial had survived intact, and was being added to the piece. The statue rising in the center would cast its shadow on the curved dial plane. The words so many had touched that day would be there for all to see, now.

Kahlan had been enthusiastic about the concept, but had spent so many months with the carving Richard had done, that it was disorienting for her to see it on such a massive scale. She was eager for the day when the carvers were finished scaling it up and she could have her own statue of *Spirit* back.

"I hope you don't mind sharing it with the world," he said.

Kahlan smiled wistfully. "No, not at all."

"Everyone loves it," he assured her.

Her wonderful lilting laugh drifted out across the warm afternoon air. "I'll just have to get used to you showing people my body and soul."

Together, they watched as the carvers working on the flowing robes checked their work with calipers against the statue Richard had carved and the reference points from wooden braces used to scale up the work.

Kahlan rubbed his lower back. "How are you feeling?"

"I'm fine. Now that you're with me, I couldn't feel better."

Kahlan laughed, then. "As long as I don't run you through?"

Richard's laugh fell in easily with hers. "You know, when we tell our children how their mother ran their father through with a sword, it's going to look pretty bad for you."

"Are we going to have children, Richard?"

"Yes, we are."

"Then I'll risk the tale."

As the warm breeze ruffled her hair, he kissed her brow.

Glancing along the line of trees, their leaves shimmering in the sunlight, Richard watched birds cavort above the riverbank, sweep into a group, and then soar together up over the semicircle of white marble columns standing in the expanse of green grass.

Kahlan leaned contentedly against his shoulder as they watched men, filled with pride, smiling while they worked on the statue standing before those columns.

In Altur'Rang, there was a new spirit.

In the former heart of the Order beat freedom.